The Forget-Me-Not Summer

Katie Flynn has lived for many years in the north-west. A compulsive writer, she started with short stories and articles and many of her early stories were broadcast on Radio Merseyside. She decided to writer her Liverpool series after hearing the reminiscences of family members about life in the city in the early years of the twentieth century. For many years she has had to cope with ME, but has continued to write. She also writes as Judith Saxton.

Also available by Katie Flynn

A Liverpool Lass
The Girl from Penny Lane
Liverpool Taffy
Te Mersey Girls
Strawberry Fields
Rainbow's End
Rose of Tralee
No Silver Spoon
Polly's Angel
The Girl from Seaforth Sands
The Liverpool Rose
Poor Little Rich Girl
The Bad Penny
Down Daisy Street
A Kiss and a Promise
Two Penn'orth of Sky
A Long and Lonely Road
The Cuckoo Child
Darkest Before Dawn
Orphans of the Storm
Little Girl Lost
Beyond the Blue Hills
Forgotten Dreams
Sunshine and Shadows
Such Sweet Sorrow
A Mother's Hope
In Time for Christmas
Heading Home
A Mistletoe Kiss
The Lost Days of Summer
Christmas Wishes
The Runaway
A Sixpenny Christmas

Available by Katie Flynn writing as Judith Saxton

You Are My Sunshine
First Love, Last Love
Someone Special

Katie Flynn

The Forget-Me-Not Summer

arrow books

Published by Arrow Books 2013

4 6 8 10 9 7 5 3

First published in Great Britain in 2013 by Century

Arrow Books
The Random House Group Limited
20 Vauxhall Bridge Road, London, SW1V 2SA

www.randomhousebooks.co.uk

Addresses for companies within The Random House Group Limited can be found at:
www.randomhouse.co.uk/offices.htm

The Random House Group Limited Reg. No. 954009

A CIP catalogue record for this book
is available from the British Library

ISBN 9780099574651

The Random House Group Limited supports the Forest Stewardship Council® (FSC®), the leading international forest-certification organisation. Our books carrying the FSC label are printed on FSC®-certified paper. FSC is the only forest-certification scheme supported by the leading environmental organisations, including Greenpeace. Our paper procurement policy can be found at:
www.randomhouse.co.uk/environment

Typeset in 11/13.5pt Palatino by Palimpsest Book Production Limited,
Falkirk, Stirlingshire
Printed and bound by CPI Group (UK) Ltd, Croydon, CR0 4YY

For Barbara Turnbull who has been a good friend and has run the Clwyd Support for M.E. Group so enthusiastically for so long.

My thanks go to my niece, Heather Cross (nee Hague), for drawing my attention to Liverpool's connection to the slave trade. Thank you, Heather.

Note to the reader

Dear Reader,

Long ago, when my niece, Heather Hague, was about twelve, she was taken by her school to an exhibition regarding the slave trade in Liverpool during the eighteenth century. After visiting the exhibition, their teacher took them to the Goree Piazza to see the bucket fountain, which intrigued Heather so much that she told me about both visits in great detail.

For some reason I had not, until then, heard of the Liverpool connection with the 'black birders', as slave traders were called, but when I myself visited the Goree Piazza, I was tremendously impressed by the sculpture which was there then; a most dramatic and intriguing memorial to those men and women, stolen from their own lands, who were brought to this country, auctioned like animals, and worked out the rest of their lives in miserable slavery.

And when I began to think about the plot of *The Forget-Me-Not Summer*, I remembered what Heather had told me and found it the perfect solution for a problem which had haunted me. The mystery of Arabella is never quite solved, but that long ago connection between what goes on in any port and a missing woman began to take shape in my mind. In the thirties, white slave traders were feared in all the English ports and *The Forget-Me-Not Summer* takes place in the thirties and forties, so the story seemed credible and, whilst my heroine, Miranda, searched for her mother, I hoped devoutly that I should find out what had happened to her before the story ended, for, as is so often the case, my characters tell me what is going to happen rather than vice versa.

You cannot see the exhibition of slavery now, and neither can you see the magnificent sculpture of slaves in the Goree Piazza, bearing buckets which tilt as they fill so that the water runs constantly down, progressing from bucket to bucket, in a fascinating and indeed beautiful way, because some councillor or official decided that the splash of water into buckets reminded him of toilets flushing (how odd!!), so he had the sculpture removed, which is sad.

But I still remember the bucket sculpture and my niece's contribution to this particular story with gratitude. Have I got you hooked??

All best wishes,

Katie Flynn

Chapter One

1937

Miranda Lovage was dragged up from fathoms deep in sleep by some unexpected sound. Groggily she sat up on her elbow and peered about the room, suddenly aware that her heart was fluttering. An only child, she shared her room with no one, had it all to herself, but night noises had never previously worried her. Indeed, she seldom heard them, for she usually went to bed late, at the same time as her mother, and slept as soon as her head touched the pillow, continuing to do so until roused by her mother's call up the stairs, or even a hand on her shoulder.

But then Miranda remembered the row which had raged between herself and Arabella – she always called her mother Arabella – earlier that evening. Now that she thought about it, she realised that it had started because she had been telling Arabella that her teachers thought she stood a good chance of getting her School Certificate, perhaps even going to university. She had come home from the Rankin Academy both excited and delighted, and had been horrified when Arabella had said, flatly, that university was out of the question. 'I've done my best to get you a decent education, living in a good neighbourhood and seeing that you were always nicely turned out, with everything the other girls have, even though I've been on my own ever since your father died,' she had said. 'Well, Miranda, I've been meaning to tell you that I've reached the end of my tether. I simply can't afford to go on paying your school fees indefinitely, so I'm afraid that next term you'll have to start at an ordinary council school.' She had wagged a reproving finger when Miranda began to protest. 'Don't try to bully me, Miranda. Just remember you are still a child and have to do as I tell you. Next year you will be at the same school as your cousin Beth . . .'

She would have gone on to explain more fully but Miranda had not been listening. She had been too busy trying to shout her mother down, saying that she had no intention of changing schools, that Arabella must jolly well find the money for the fees from somewhere; she had even suggested that her mother might do 'a real job' instead of hanging round the theatre taking every tuppenny-ha'penny part she was offered.

Arabella had waited until Miranda had run out of breath and had then replied, with a cold finality which had frightened her daughter. 'Miranda, in case you have not noticed, we are in the middle of a depression. I admit my wages from the Madison Players are small, but I'm sure that one day I'll get the sort of parts I deserve and then money will not be so tight. As it is, the only means I have of continuing our present way of life is by what I think of as clipping both our wings. You will go to a council school until you are old enough to work on your own account, and we'll move into a house in one of the courts and take a lodger – two, if necessary – because the rent of this house is crippling me, honest to God, queen. The only alternative is to marry Mr Gervase, that fellow who haunts the stage door . . .'

'A stage-door Johnny?' Miranda had been both scornful and incredulous. 'But you laugh at them, say they've never got two pennies to rub together . . . isn't Mr Gervase that little weaselly one with a bush of grey hair? You scoffed at him, you know you did! You said he ought to be a monk because he had a built-in tonsure. You can't mean to marry him!'

'He's rich,' Arabella had said simply. 'During the week he lives in a service flat. Oh, Miranda, it's the height of luxury. He gets his breakfasts and the most wonderful dinners as part of his rent, and the flat is kept clean as well. And then he's got a mansion in the Lake District – I've always loved the Lakes – and he says that if I marry him, we'll live there whenever I haven't got an important part at the theatre.'

'But you told me ages ago that if you got an important part at the theatre we'd be in clover . . .' Miranda had begun, only to be immediately interrupted.

'Don't rub it in. It was sheer prejudice which got Maria the part of Lady Macbeth instead of me,' Arabella had said hotly. 'So now you jolly well choose, Miranda Lovage: a pauper's existence on our own or a life of pampered luxury with Gervase. And since it would be me who had to put up with him day *and* night, I don't see why you should even be asked which you would prefer.' She had looked sideways at her daughter through her thick, curling, blonde lashes. 'I've told him that *if* I agree to marry him it will be what you might call a marriage of convenience. I shall have my own room, and though we shall share a name I will be like a – a sister to him. Or a housekeeper. Do you understand, Miranda? He is offering me a way out of my difficulties and expecting nothing in return, save for the duties a house-keeper would perform. Of course he hopes I will become truly fond of him as time goes by, but . . .'

But Miranda had heard enough. 'Just because you aren't a good enough actress to earn a decent salary, that doesn't mean I have to suffer,' she had shouted, but even as she did so she realised her own helplessness. Until she was old enough to earn her own living, she really had no choice. Her father had died some years previously, and she knew of no living relative save for her Aunt Vi, her mother's half-sister, and Aunt Vi's daughter Beth, both of whom disliked Arabella and her offspring and would, Miranda knew, be more likely to gloat over the Lovages' misfortune than to offer help.

So when Arabella had said: 'Oh, darling, if I'd got Lady Macbeth . . . or if you'd agreed to my joining that repertory company last year, when I was offered a place – only you didn't want to move up to Scarborough – then we would have managed somehow, but as it is . . .'

She had held out her arms as she spoke and Miranda had hesitated, then heaved a sigh and gone stiffly into her mother's embrace, saying: 'But do try to think of a way out, Arabella. Surely there must be something you could do so I wouldn't have to change schools and houses and everything. I'll think as well, and perhaps between us . . .'

'My dearest little Miranda, do you not realise that I've been racking my brains for a solution ever since the Madison Players gave Lady Macbeth to Maria? Things have got to change. The rent for this house has gone up again; your school fees are downright ridiculous – even the uniform . . . but it's no good talking. It's either marry

Mr Gervase or change our whole way of life, and I do think Mr G's offer is extremely generous. However, we'll both sleep on it and tomorrow we'll talk about it again.'

So now Miranda, finding herself abruptly awake, remembered the quarrel and thought it was a miracle that she had ever managed to get to sleep at all. Indeed, it had taken her quite a while to drop off, but having done so she had slept so deeply that for a moment she wondered what on earth could have woken her, apart from a trumpet call, or a brigade of guards marching through the bedroom and exhorting her to get up at once. But judging by the dim light coming from between the curtains, it was still the middle of the night. So what had woken her? Miranda lay down again, but sleep would not come. Suppose her mother had been so upset by the quarrel that she had failed to lock the door, and burglars had entered the house? The Lovages lived in Sycamore Avenue, near Prince's Park, for Arabella Lovage believed appearances were important, and if a thief did ransack their home it would be a major expense. Worse, even, than the increase in the rent and school fees, to say nothing of the smart uniform.

Miranda took a deep breath, slid out of bed and crossed to the window. They were having a hot summer so the casement was up and the night air, warm and scented, came pleasantly into the room. She peered up and down the street, examining their neat little garden and those of the neighbours on either side, but saw no sign of any living soul except for a cat which appeared on the pavement opposite and made its way down the hill, no doubt on some nefarious business of its own.

Miranda squatted on the comfortable bench beneath

the open window trying to guess what had disturbed her. Suddenly it came to her. It must have been the front door closing; she guessed that Arabella, to calm her nerves and forget their quarrel, had decided to take a walk before coming up to bed. Miranda knew she sometimes did this and was reassured by the thought. But perhaps she really ought to go downstairs and make sure that Arabella was all right, and had locked the door against night-time intruders.

But the annoyance she had felt over her mother's arbitrary decision to take her away from her school or present her with Gervase as a stepfather still rankled. Arabella had no right to change their whole way of life without consulting her. Well, all right, she had consulted her, but it wasn't much of a consultation! Live in penury or accept that ugly old man as a stepfather. Drowsily, she decided that there was no need to investigate. If her mother needed a period for quiet reflection and had chosen to go walking in the middle of the night, that was her affair. Miranda got off the bench and returned to her bed, suddenly conscious of chilled feet and the flimsiness of her white cotton nightie. She cuddled down, pulling the sheet up round her ears, and this time, as her body warmed into a delicious glow, she slept.

Afterwards, she could never decide at what moment her life had truly changed. Had it been when she heard the sound which had woken her from her deep and peaceful sleep? Or had it been next morning, when nobody woke her, and she was left to wash in the tiny bathroom on her own and to struggle into her clothes whilst her heart beat a wild tattoo, for when she had put her head round her mother's door there was no one there and Arabella did not answer Miranda's shout. Galloping down the stairs, she had burst into the kitchen expecting to see her mother turn from the stove with a smile and apologise for not waking her even as she spooned creamy porridge into two small earthenware bowls, before exhorting her daughter to eat her breakfast whilst it was hot.

But the kitchen was empty, nobody stood by the table, the curtains were still drawn across the windows and when Miranda ran to the back door, to check that her mother was not in the garden, it was unlocked.

Miranda stood in the cold kitchen and big tears welled up in her eyes. Arabella must have gone for a walk, and something must have happened to her! Suppose she had fallen, or been attacked by some wicked person intent upon stealing her fine gold chain with the locket, or her thin little wedding ring, who had then left her unconscious in the gutter? Suddenly, their quarrel seemed of no significance; what mattered now was the whereabouts of her beautiful, talented mother. That she was beautiful had never been in question and now Miranda told herself, loyally, that only jealousy and spite had prevented Arabella's talent from carrying her to the very top of her profession.

Miranda burst out of the house and looked wildly up and down the street. What should she do? She must go to the neighbours, get help, contact the police. She knew she should do one or all of these things, but she was, after all, only thirteen, and had never had to take a decision without consulting an adult in her life. So she returned to the kitchen and simply sat down at the table, put her head on her folded arms and began to weep in earnest.

When someone knocked on the back door she flew across to it, wrenching it open and almost falling into the arms of the girl standing there. 'Miranda! What on earth's the matter? You don't look as though you're ready for school; aren't you well?'

Miranda stared at her friend, who often called for her so that they might walk to school together. 'Oh, Louise, it's you. I thought it was my mother . . . oh, Lou, I heard something in the night which woke me up, and when I came down for breakfast this morning, Arabella had gone.'

'I 'spect she ran out of milk or bread or something and has gone down to the shops to buy some more,' Louise said cheerfully. 'Why are you in such a taking? But for God's sake make your own breakfast or we'll be late for school.'

'But there's no note; if my mother means to go anywhere she always leaves me a note,' Miranda said, but she was insensibly cheered by the other girl's easy acceptance of the situation. Perhaps Louise was right and her mother had simply slipped out to buy milk; there was a delivery every morning but sometimes it came too late for breakfast. Hastily, Miranda went to the pantry, and her hopeful heart dropped into her neat button shoes once more; there was a good three quarters of a loaf and a whole pint of milk left, besides all the usual things: porridge oats, butter, jam and a couple of the little milk rolls she always took to school for elevenses.

Turning, she saw that her practical friend had filled the kettle, put it on the stove and lit the gas, and was looking at her expectantly. Then Louise seized the loaf from its place on the shelf and cut two rather chunky slices, buttered them briskly, and pushed them and the jam pot across to her friend. 'Come along, Miranda,' she said impatiently, 'we've not got all day. Your mam will be back in time to get your tea. Did she take the key with her? We don't want to lock her out.' Miranda crossed the room and checked the hiding place: no key. She returned to the kitchen, went across to where her school blazer hung on its peg, and checked again. Her key was in the pocket. She said as much to Louise who nodded with satisfaction. 'There you are then!' she said triumphantly. 'Your mam realised she needed something from the shops, unlocked the back door, tucked the key in her jacket pocket, and went off. That means that when we leave – do eat up, Miranda, or we'll be late for class – we can lock the back door and know we're not shutting her out.'

Miranda stared doubtfully at her friend's bright, self-confident face. Louise was almost a year older than she and far more worldly wise. She must be right; her own abrupt awakening in the night must have had an innocent cause. Miranda finished her breakfast and tidied round quickly so that her mother would not have to do so on her return, for during the quarrel the previous evening Arabella had claimed, with justice, that her daughter never helped in the house, made her own bed or offered to do the messages. When she sees the nice tidy kitchen she'll know she misjudged me, Miranda told herself defiantly. And I'll make our tea just as soon as I get home from school; that'll show her!

'Come on, slowcoach,' Louise said, helping herself to a round of bread and butter and shoving it into her mouth rather less than delicately. 'Here's your blazer.'

'Thanks,' Miranda said, shrugging it on and locking the back door carefully behind them. 'What's our first subject, Lou? Oh, *not* French! I didn't learn that poem last night – Mum and I had a bit of a disagreement – but if you'll hear me when we're on the tram I'll get it lodged in my brain somehow, before Mamselle asks awkward questions.'

When Miranda returned home from school later that day, however, it was to find a deputation from the theatre awaiting her outside the house in Sycamore Avenue. The manager, Tom Fox, Miss Briggs the wardrobe mistress, Lynette Rich, who was a member of the chorus, and Alex Gordon, the theatre's leading man, had all come along. They wanted to know if Arabella was ill because there had been a matinée performance that day and she had neither arrived at the theatre nor sent a message to say she was unwell. Miranda nearly fainted, but fortunately Louise was with her and between the two of them they explained the little they knew.

Arabella's colleagues gazed at one another before saying that the police must be informed and ordering Miranda to unlock the door so that they could search the house to see if there were any clues as to why on earth their bit-part player and assistant stage manager should suddenly disappear. Only the wardrobe mistress seemed to realise that this was a body blow for Arabella's daughter. 'You can't stay here tonight, chuck,' she said kindly. 'Not all by yourself, at any rate. Got any aunties, have you? You could move in with 'em for a few days, just till your mam turns up again, which she's bound to do.'

'I dunno,' Miranda said doubtfully. 'I've got an aunt and a cousin that live up Old Swan, but I don't know them very well. Couldn't I – couldn't I stay here, if Lou's mum will let her stay with me? My mother can't have gone far. Oh, I wonder . . . does anyone know where Mr Gervase lives? She – she was talking about marrying him, though I can't believe she'd really do it. But she might have gone to his house to talk things over, I suppose.'

'She could have gone anywhere, lighting out without a word to a soul,' Alex Gordon said irritably, and Miranda saw the wardrobe mistress give him an angry look and flap a hand to shut him up. Alex, however, was clearly more annoyed than worried. 'Typical of a bloody woman to bugger off without a word to anyone. Arabella's got a contract, the same as the rest of us, but if she's prepared to let us down in mid-run . . .' He turned angrily to Miranda. 'Do you mean that stage-door Johnny? He's got a service flat in the city centre. I went there once, so I'll nip round and hear what he has to say. If she really means to marry him, though . . . to let us down without a word . . .'

Now it was the manager's turn to scowl at Alex. 'She's never let us down before, and I see no reason why you should think the worst,' he said angrily. 'Just you mind your tongue, Alex Gordon, or it'll be you searching for a company prepared to take you on, because you can say goodbye to the Madison Players.'

The man muttered something like 'That'll be your loss' but said no more, and Lynette Rich cut in before more acid comments could be exchanged. 'I'll go to the flat, find out what Mr Gervase knows,' she said. 'If Arabella's not there and he can't help us, I suppose I'd better take

Miranda up to her aunt's house, since she can't possibly stay here alone, though I'm sure Arabella will be home before dark. I'll pack a bag with the kid's night things and that and leave a note for Arabella, explaining what we've done.' She turned to Miranda and gave her a reassuring smile. 'Your mam will be home tomorrow, sure as check,' she said. 'I'm rare fond of Arabella, 'cos I've known her these past six years, and to my knowledge she's never done a mean thing or let anyone down before.' She glared at Alex, then held out a hand to Miranda. 'Come and help me pack a bag with a few bits and pieces to last you till your mam gets home.' She turned to the rest of the players. 'You'll do the necessary? I'm sure Arabella will be back tomorrow, but just in case, the scuffers ought to be told, and the neighbours . . .' She glanced uneasily at Miranda. 'Now don't you worry, chuck, it's just a precaution, like.'

So saying, she led the way into the house and let Miranda take her up to her bedroom where the two of them packed a bag with rather more clothing than Miranda thought necessary, but, as her new friend pointed out, you could never tell what you might need until you needed it. As they crossed the room, Miranda took one last look around her and suddenly realised that she was saying farewell to her own little room, for a while at least. She would have to share not only her cousin's bedroom, but maybe her bed as well, and she knew that her aunt despised her half-sister's feckless ways. But then Beth and Aunt Vi were not beautiful or talented, Miranda reassured herself; they were just ordinary, as she was. Nevertheless she lingered in the bedroom doorway and, on impulse, ran back into the room and snatched the beautiful old-fashioned looking-glass, with its gilt cherubs and swags of gilded fruit, from its hook on the wall. She loved that little mirror and told herself that it would be safer with her than in an empty house. She tucked it into the top of the bag she and Lynette had packed and set off, leaving the only home she had ever known behind her.

Though she did not know it, she would never again sleep in that cosy little bed, or bask in the solitude of her lovely room. In fact, her life would never be the same again.

For the first few weeks of her sojourn in Jamaica Close, Miranda was so unhappy and so bewildered that nothing seemed real. Arabella neither returned nor got in touch, and Mr Gervase had been as puzzled – and upset – as Miranda herself. She felt as though she were enclosed in a glass case, through which she could see people and movement, but could make no sense of what was said. She had terrifying dreams in which she saw Arabella's body floating in the dock, or cast up by the roadside after a fatal accident. She began to see her mother – or someone very like her – in the street and would run in pursuit, sometimes even following a woman on to a tram or a train, only to realise, with sickening disappointment, that this was yet another stranger whose resemblance to Arabella was so slight that she wondered how she could possibly have made such a mistake.

Things simply grew worse when Mr Gervase, saying ruefully that he had always known Arabella was too good for him, left the city, whilst the police stopped being comforting and simply said that she must remain with her aunt in the little house in Jamaica Close until such time as her mother chose to return. To her horror, the contents of the house in Sycamore Avenue had to be sold, as Arabella had owed a month's rent, and now Miranda was dependent on Aunt Vi if she needed so much as a tram fare.

But she continued her search. Desperate, she asked everyone in the Avenue if they had seen Arabella that fateful night, and very soon it was commonly accepted, as Mr Gervase had clearly believed, that she had gone off with some man. This cruel slander was backed up when word got around that a handsome young acrobat, working at a larger and more prestigious theatre in the city, had disappeared on the same day as Arabella. Perhaps it was this that persuaded the police, and the Madison Players, to say that they had done all they could, although they advised Miranda to keep on asking around. However, it was soon clear to her that Arabella's disappearance was something of a nine-day wonder, and the nine days were up.

Because she was living in a nightmare, the attitudes of her aunt and cousin did not bother her at first, but gradually it was borne in upon her that her mother's half-sister had cared nothing for the younger woman. She began to realise that Aunt Vi and Beth actually resented her, hard though she tried to be useful, and her unhappiness was so intense that she would have run away, save that she had nowhere to run. She would simply have to endure until she was old enough to leave Jamaica Close. Then she would concentrate on searching for her mother, because she was sure she had a better chance of finding Arabella once she was able to leave her aunt's malignant influence. She knew Aunt Vi did not believe her half-sister would ever return.

Perhaps because Aunt Vi was much older than Arabella, the two women had not really known one another very well. Arabella had taken Miranda to see her aunt and her cousin Beth in Jamaica Close perhaps twice a year, once at Christmas and once in summer, but had never attempted any sort of friendship. She had explained to Miranda that their mother had been a gentle soul, but that her first husband had been totally different from her second. Vi's father had been a warehouseman and a bully, and Arabella had confided in her daughter that when he was killed in an industrial accident her gran must have heaved a sigh of relief. 'She couldn't stand up to him; she wasn't that sort of person,' she had said. 'But despite the life he had led her, your gran – my mum – was still a very pretty woman. Then John Saunders fell in love with her and they got wed; I was their only child and your aunt thought I was spoiled rotten.' She had sighed. 'Compared to the way Vi had been brought up, I guess I was. The thing is, though, it didn't make for a happy relationship between her and myself, so I wasn't sorry when she got married and moved away.'

The young Miranda had nodded her comprehension. She had seen the spiteful glances cast at her mother when they met her aunt, had heard the muttered comments, indicating that Vi thought Arabella was what she called toffee-nosed, too big for her boots, and considered herself above ordinary folk.

And so she might, because she *was* better than other folks, the young Miranda had thought rebelliously.

Arabella was not just pretty, she was very beautiful. She had a great mass of curly white-gold hair, skin like cream and the most enormous pair of blue eyes, the very colour of the forget-me-not flowers she loved. And those eyes were framed by curling blonde lashes whilst her eyebrows, two slender arcs, were blonde as well.

Aunt Vi, on the other hand, was short and squat, with sandy hair and a round, harsh face, for she took after her father, whereas Arabella's looks seemed to have come from their mother. Miranda would have loved to look like that too, but in fact she did not. To be sure, Arabella often congratulated her on her colouring; her hair was what her mother called Plantagenet gold, but kids in the street called carrot, or ginger. 'When you're older, it will darken to a beautiful deep auburn,' Arabella had been fond of saying. 'You're going to be a real little beauty one of these days; you'll knock me into a cocked hat, so you will.'

But Miranda had no desire to knock anyone into anything. She had no urge to be an actress, though she admired her mother tremendously, and was proud of her. However, it was one thing to be proud of someone, and quite another to wish to emulate them. Miranda's own ambitions were far less exotic. She wanted to be a writer of books and had already hidden away in her bedroom cupboard a number of wonderfully imaginative fairy stories. To be sure, these stories were often connected with the theatre – perhaps one day she would turn them into plays – but wherever her writing ended up, it was her secret hope for the future.

Now, though, nothing was important but to find Arabella and escape from the horrors of life in Jamaica

Close, for after the first few days, during which Aunt Vi and Beth had pretended anxiety for her mother and affection for herself, they began to show their true colours. They had disliked Arabella and now they disliked her daughter, besides resenting her presence in the dirty, neglected little house. She was forced to sleep in a creaking and smelly brass bedstead with her cousin Beth, who was a year older than she, though they were now in the same class at the council school, for Beth was slow-witted and Miranda was bright. The pair of them did not have the bed to themselves, however; fat Aunt Vi took up more than her fair share of the thin horsehair mattress – she kept promising to buy another bed, since she had sold Miranda's beloved mirror, but so far had failed to do so – and grumbled every night that her bleedin' sister might have taken her horrible brat with her when she ran off. Miranda tried to ignore such jibes, but when she had nightmares she soon learned to slip out of bed and go down to the kitchen, for if her cries woke her aunt she would speedily find herself being soundly slapped, whilst her aunt shouted that she was a selfish little bitch to disturb folk who had been good enough to take her in.

Another threat was that she would be sent to an orphanage, but Miranda thought that as long as she was useful she need not fear such a fate. Beth was lazy and spoilt, encouraged by her mother never to do her share around the house, and very soon Miranda got all the nastiest jobs. So when her aunt pretended her young half-sister had dumped her child and gone off just to annoy them, Miranda said nothing, deciding that the remark was too stupid to even merit a reply.

The members of the cast at the theatre had done their best to persuade the police, and anyone else who was interested, that Arabella Lovage was not the sort of woman to simply walk out on her colleagues and friends and particularly not on her daughter. But unfortunately the police had felt it incumbent upon them to visit Aunt Vi and had gained a very different picture of the missing woman there.

'She'll ha' gone orf with that young feller she's been seein', the acrobat, you mark my words,' her aunt had assured everyone. 'Oh aye, a right lightskirt, our Arabella.'

For a few moments anger had driven Miranda out of her glass case, and she had shouted at her aunt that this was a wicked falsehood. The Players had agreed that they were sure their fellow actor had had nothing to do with any young man, save Gervase, who could scarcely be described as young. It was he who had discovered that the rival company's acrobat had also gone missing, leaving his lodgings and the variety show on the very day that Arabella had disappeared.

Furious, Miranda had assured anyone who would listen that her mother would never have left her to go off with a man, but though she knew, with utter certainty, that her mother would never have willingly deserted her, she stopped repeating her conviction. She felt life was stacked against her, that the harder she tried, the less convincing she became. So she retreated into her glass case and simply waited.

After the first month of bewildered misery, Miranda had stopped expecting the door to open and her mother to reappear. She had forced herself to face up to the fact that something had happened to keep Arabella from her, and when spiteful remarks were made by Aunt Vi, indicating that Arabella had deliberately landed her with her unwanted daughter, she simply folded her lips tightly and said nothing. What, after all, was the point? She and the cast at the theatre had tried hard enough, heaven knew, to make the authorities take Arabella Lovage's case seriously, but with little success. The police had gone over the house with a fine-tooth comb, searching for any clue as to Arabella's disappearance or evidence of foul play; there had been none. They had asked Miranda if any clothing was missing, but she could not say. Arabella's wardrobe bulged with garments; for all her daughter knew, she might have taken away a dozen outfits without Miranda's being any the wiser. In fact, she could not even remember what her mother had been wearing that last evening.

Only one small indication, several weeks after Arabella's disappearance, caused people to raise their brows and become a little less certain that she had gone of her own free will. One dark night, Miranda was woken from a deep slumber by someone shaking her shoulder and speaking to her in a rough, kindly voice.

'What's up, me love? Good thing it's a fine night, but if you asks me them clouds up there mean business.' The hand on her shoulder gave a little squeeze. 'Lost your way to the privy, queen? My goodness, I know it's not as cold as last night, but you've got bare feet and the road's awful rough, and there was you walkin' down the middle of the carriageway as though you'd never heard of cars, trams or buses . . .'

Miranda, completely bewildered, opened sleep-drugged eyes and stared about her. In the bright moonlight everything looked very different; the shadows black as pitch, the moonlight dazzlingly white. She looked down at her feet and saw that they were indeed bare, as well as very dusty and dirty. Then her eyes travelled up her white cotton nightie and across to the man bending over her. He was a policeman, quite young, and his expression was puzzled. 'Where's you come from, chuck? I don't know as I reckernise you. How did you get here?'

Miranda's brows knitted; how had she come here? Where was here, anyhow? She shook her head. 'I dunno,' she mumbled. 'Where am I? It doesn't look much like Jamaica Close to me.'

The policeman hissed in his breath. 'Jamaica Close?' he said incredulously. 'Is that where you come from, queen?' He stood back and Miranda looked up into his face properly for the first time. It was a young face, and pleasant; a trustworthy face, she decided. But he was giving her shoulder another gentle shake and repeating his question: 'Have you come from Jamaica Close?'

Miranda looked wildly about her, but could recognise nothing. Reluctantly, she nodded. 'I suppose I must have walked from there to wherever we are now,' she said slowly, 'only I must have done it in my sleep because I don't remember anything. I guess I was searching for my mother; she's disappeared. Only I know she's still alive somewhere and needing me.'

The policeman stared, then nodded slowly. 'Oh aye, you'll be Arabella Lovage's daughter. Well, you won't find her here, my love, so I guess I'd best take you back home again. You live up the Avenue, don't you?'

Miranda heaved a sigh, realising suddenly that she

was terribly tired and wanted nothing more than her bed. Even a miserable little four inches of mattress, which was all she managed to get at Aunt Vi's house, would be preferable to standing in the cold moonlight whilst she tried to explain to a total stranger why she no longer lived up the Avenue.

But explain she must, of course, and managed to do so in a few quick words. The scuffer pulled a doubtful face. 'That's well off my beat, chuck, so perhaps the best thing will be for the pair of us to walk back to the station. The sarge is a good bloke; he'll get you a cup of tea and see that someone – probably me – takes you home. I reckon there'll be a fine ol' to-do in Jamaica Close when they find you're missing.'

They carried out the policeman's suggestion, and as he had assumed he was told to accompany Miranda back to her aunt's house. First, though, because of the chill of the night, he wrapped her in a blanket and sat her on the saddle of his bicycle so that she was pushed home in some style, and for the first time in many weeks she felt that somebody cared what became of her.

They reached the house to find the back door standing open, but it soon became clear that she had not been missed. The policeman, who told her his name was Harry, was rather shocked and wanted to wake the household, but Miranda begged him not to do so and he complied, though only after she had promised to come to the station the next day to discuss what had happened. 'For we can't have young ladies wanderin' barefoot in the streets, clad only in a nightgown,' he told her. 'I'm on duty tomorrow from three in the afternoon so you'd best come to the station around four o'clock; I'll see you there.'

Miranda slipped into the house, closed the door behind her and went up to bed. Beth moaned that her feet were cold, but then fell immediately asleep once more and made no comment when the family awoke the following day.

Miranda, usually the most eager of pupils, sagged off school and went straight to the theatre, because she wanted at least one member of the cast to hear about her weird experience, a desire that was fully justified by the excitement her story engendered.

'If you walks in your sleep, ducks, then it's quite likely your mam did as well,' Miss Briggs informed her. 'Runs in families that does, sleepwalkin' I mean. In times of stress some folk can go miles; I've heard of women catchin' trams or buses – trains, even – when they's sound asleep and should be in their beds. If your mam was loose on the streets, someone could ha' took advantage.' She gave Miranda a jubilant hug. 'Mebbe we're gettin' somewhere at last. Wharra lucky thing it were a scuffer what found you. He'll know full well you didn't make nothin' up and mebbe they'll start searchin' for Arabella all over again. Oh, if your mam's e'er to be found we'll find her, don't you fret.'

But the days turned into weeks, and the weeks into months, and both dreams and nightmares grew rarer. The picture of Arabella which Miranda kept inside her head never faded, but Miranda's pretty clothes grew jaded and dirty whilst hope gradually receded, though it never disappeared altogether.

Harry, the policeman, became a friend and Miranda knew it was he who was responsible for notices which appeared around the city asking for information as to the whereabouts of Arabella Lovage, the beautiful actress who had charmed the citizens of Liverpool whenever she appeared on the stage. The cast, too, clubbed together to pay for notices in the papers, begging anyone with information as to Arabella's whereabouts to come forward. They might have enquired also for the young acrobat, but since it seemed he had left the theatre under a slight cloud, and Miranda objected vociferously to any linking of her mother's name with his, they did not. Gradually, Miranda began to accept the terrible change in her circumstances until it was almost as though she had had two lives. The first one, a life of pleasure and luxury, was gone for ever; the second one, of penury and neglect, had come to stay, at least until she could claw her way out of the hateful pit into which she had been dragged.

There had been many advantages to the life she had lived in Sycamore Avenue, and very few indeed to the one she now endured. Her cousin Beth occasionally showed signs of humanity, appearing to want if not friendship at least mutual tolerance, but Miranda ignored such overtures as were offered. She became, almost without knowing it, a sort of Cinderella, a general dogsbody, belonging to no one and therefore ordered about by everyone. She was not even sure that she cared particularly; why should she? She had a strong will, however, and beneath all her outward meekness there gradually blossomed a determination to succeed. She felt she was just marking time, waiting for something wonderful to happen. So she continued to work conscientiously at school, made no objection when her clothes grew shabbier, the food on her plate shrank to the leftovers no one else wanted, and her share of the housework grew heavier and heavier. Once or twice Beth, who wasn't such a bad creature after all, gave her a hand, or put in a word for her; sometimes even stole food for her, but by and large, had she but realised it, Miranda was playing a waiting game. Arabella Lovage, she reminded herself half a dozen times a day, had disliked her half-sister, and would have moved heaven and earth rather than have her daughter live in the dirty, dilapidated house in Jamaica Close. If Arabella could see her daughter now, pale, dirty, always hungry and bitterly overworked, she would tell her miserable half-sister what she thought of her and whisk Miranda off back to the Avenue and the life they had both enjoyed.

But that time had not yet come, and the weeks continued to turn into months until at last it was a whole year, and the hope which had brightened the eyes of the Madison Players grew dim. Then the acrobat returned. He told anyone who was interested that he had got a job with the circus for the remainder of the summer season and then gone on to act in panto – a scene in the giant's kitchen, his ex-colleagues guessed – and had met and married one of the chorus to their mutual pleasure, though this romantic narrative was slightly tempered by the fact that the chorus girl had just announced she would be having a baby before Christmas.

Folk who had been convinced that Arabella had fled with the acrobat had to eat their words, but by now few people thought twice about it. Miranda, who had never believed it anyway, was shocked by her own lack of surprise; why should she be surprised, indeed? But perhaps it was then that little by little Miranda's confidence in her mother's return began to trickle slowly away. She thought afterwards that it bled away, as if from a horrible wound which would not heal, and the worst thing was there was nothing she could do about it. She knew she should fight against the way her aunt treated her, she knew she should tell somebody – Harry, or one of her teachers, or some other responsible adult – but she was too weary. Money was short as the Depression bit deeper and deeper. If you argued about the price of a simple apple in the market the stallholder would throw the Depression in your face. If you chopped kindling, ran messages, or carted heavy buckets of water, where once a few coppers would be pressed into your hand now you were lucky to be given a ha'penny, or maybe a cut off a homemade loaf with a smear of margarine. Yes, times were hard, and if it hadn't been for Steve . . .

Chapter Two

'Lovage! Drat the girl, where's she got to?'

Miranda, who was awaiting her turn to jump into the skipping rope being expertly twirled by two of the older girls who lived in the small cul-de-sac, stood up and headed for the steps of Number Six, upon the top one of which her Aunt Vi stood. She hung back a little, however, for her aunt's expression was vengeful, and even from halfway across the paving Miranda could see her hand preparing for a slap.

'Yes, Aunt?' she said, knowing that it would annoy Aunt Vi if she spoke nicely; her aunt would have preferred impudence so she could strike out with a clear conscience. Not that she would hesitate to hit her niece if the fancy took her, as Miranda knew all too well. Aunt Vi waited for her to get closer, and when she failed to move began to swell with indignation, even her pale sandy hair seeming to stand on end.

'Come *here*, I say,' she shouted, her voice thin with spite. 'Why can't you ever do as you're told, you lazy little madam? There's your poor cousin sick as a cat, smothered in perishin' spots, and instead of givin' me a hand to nurse her, you're off a-pleasurin'. Considerin' it was you give my poor girl the measles . . .'

'She might have caught them off anyone.'

'No; it were bloody well you what passed them on,'

her aunt said aggressively. 'Why, you were still a-scrawpin' and a-scratchin' at the spots when my poor Beth began to feel ill. And now she's been and gone and thrown up all over her bed and the floor, so since it's your bleedin' fault you can just git up them stairs and clean up.' She grinned spitefully as her niece approached the front door, then scowled as the girl looked pointedly at her right hand.

'If you so much as raise your arm you can clear up the mess yourself,' Miranda said bluntly. 'When I was sick and ill you never even brought me a cup of water, but you expect me to wait on Beth. Well, I won't do it if you so much as touch me, and if you try anything else I'll tell the scuffers.'

It would be idle to pretend that the spiteful look left her aunt's face, but she moved to one side and made no attempt to interfere as Miranda squiggled past. Miranda had lately discovered that Vi did not want anything to do with the police, and though mention of Harry's name might not save her from all her aunt's wrath it certainly made Vi think twice before hitting her without reason.

But right now she had work to do and if her aunt had bothered to use her brain she might have realised that Miranda was perfectly willing to clear up the mess. Not only because she shared Beth's bed, but also because she and Beth were getting on slightly better. Whilst Miranda herself had had the measles Beth had brought food up to her occasionally, and had insisted that her cousin should have a share of anything soft that was going. Thanks to Beth, Miranda had kept body and soul together with bread and milk. Now Miranda was actually quite happy to do as much for her cousin, so she went into the kitchen, poured water from the kettle into a bucket, added a scrubbing brush and a bar of strong yellow soap and hurried upstairs. And it was nowhere near as bad as she had feared; the bed seemed to have escaped altogether, and though Beth, lying back on her pillows, was clearly still feeling far from well, it was the work of a moment for Miranda to clean the floor and to grin cheerfully at her cousin. 'Awful, isn't it?' she said. 'The first three days are the worst, but then you begin to realise you ain't goin' to die after all.' She stood the bucket down by the door and sat on the sagging brass bedstead. 'Poor ol' Beth! But at least you'll get all sorts of nice things once you feel a bit better; I had to exist on bread and milk. No wonder I were weak as a kitten and could scarcely climb the stairs.'

Beth sniffed. 'You were lucky to get bread and milk,' she said sullenly. 'Mam wanted to give you bread and water; said milk were too rich . . . well, conny onny was, at any rate. So if it weren't for me sneakin' a spoonful on to your bread and water you'd likely still be in bed and covered in spots.' She pulled a face. 'And aren't you the lucky one? When you had measles it was term time so you missed school, but me, I got 'em on the very first day of the summer holidays.' She glared at her cousin. 'I tell you, you're lucky you even had pobs.'

'You're probably right and I'm real grateful to you,' Miranda said. 'But if you don't mind me sayin' so, Beth, your mam isn't very sensible, is she? When I were ill and couldn't clean or cook or scrub, she had to do all my work whilst you got the messages and prepared the meals. You'd have thought she'd be keen to get me back on me feet, and that would have happened a good deal quicker if I'd had some decent grub now and then.' She sighed. 'Sometimes the smell of scouse comin' up the stairs tempted me to go down and ask for a share – like Oliver Twist, you know – but I guessed I'd only get a clack round the ear and I could do without that.'

She waited, half expecting her cousin to react angrily, for though Beth must know how badly her cousin was treated neither of them ever referred to it aloud. Now, however, Beth gave Miranda a malicious smile. 'Your mam spoiled you when you lived in the Avenue, made sure you got the best of everything going,' she said. 'And my mam gives me the best what's on offer; you can't blame her for that.' Her eyes had been half closed, but now they opened fully and fixed themselves on Miranda's face. 'You're an extra mouth to feed; Mam's always saying so, and neither you nor your perishin' missin' mother contributes a brass farthing to this house. You don't pay any of the rent, nor a penny towards the messages, so don't you grumble about my mam, because you're just a burden, you!'

This was said with such spite that Miranda's eyes rounded. She had always supposed that Beth was jealous of her because she was encouraged to be so by her mother. Aunt Vi knew that Miranda was a good deal cleverer than Beth and found this alone difficult to forgive. But now Beth had made it plain that she resented her cousin on her own account, so to speak. Or perhaps it was just the measles talking? Miranda hoped so, but got off the bed and headed for the door, telling herself that she did not have to stop and listen to her cousin's outpourings. It was true that she did not contribute to the rent of Number Six, but she thought indignantly that on all other counts her cousin was way out. She washed and scrubbed, dusted and tidied, peeled potatoes and prepared vegetables, and sometimes even cooked them, though usually under her aunt's supervision. When she earned a penny or two by running messages or chopping kindling, she was usually forced to hand over the small amount of money she had managed to acquire, whereas Beth got sixpence pocket money each week, and quite often extra pennies so that she might attend the Saturday rush at the Derby cinema, or buy herself a bag of homemade toffee from Kettle's Emporium on the Scotland Road. With her hand on the doorknob, Miranda was about to leave the room when a feeble voice from the bed stopped her for a moment. 'I'm thirsty,' Beth whined. 'I want a drink. Mam went up to the Terrace to get advice on how to look after me and Nurse said I were to have plenty of cool drinks; things like raspberry cordial, or lemonade. Get me both, then I'll choose which to drink.'

The words 'Get 'em yourself' popped into Miranda's head and were hastily stifled; no point in giving her cousin ammunition which she might well hand on to her mother, who would see that Miranda suffered for her sharp tongue. Instead, she pretended she had not heard and went quietly out of the room, shutting the door on Beth's peevish demand that she bring the drinks at once . . . at once, did she hear?

When Miranda entered the kitchen she found her aunt sitting at the table with last night's *Echo* spread out before her and a mug of tea to hand. Miranda contemplated saying nothing about raspberry cordial or lemonade – after all, her aunt had said that she herself intended to be her daughter's principal nurse – but realised that it would be unwise to irritate the older woman any further. Whilst Vi's sudden protective interest in Beth lasted, which would not be for very long, Miranda guessed, she would take offence at any tiny thing, and when Aunt Vi took offence Miranda headed for the hills. She went outside and emptied her bucket down the drain, then walked down to the pump and rinsed it out before returning to the kitchen. 'Beth wants a drink, either raspberry cordial or lemonade,' she said briefly. 'Did you buy 'em when you were out earlier, Aunt Vi? If so, I'll pour some into a jug and take it upstairs . . . unless you would rather do it yourself?'

She had not meant to sound sarcastic, but realised she had done so when her aunt's hard red cheeks began to take on a purplish tinge. Hastily, she went into the pantry and scanned the shelves until she spotted a bottle of raspberry cordial. Pouring some into a jug, she mixed it with water and, making sure first that her aunt's back was turned, took a cautious sip. It was delicious. The nicest thing she had tasted over the past twelve months, she told herself dreamily, heading for the stairs. Lucky, lucky Beth! When I had the measles all I got was water to drink and old copies of the *Echo* to read. Earlier she had seen a big pile of comics beside the bed – *Chicks' Own*, *The Dandy*, *The Beano* and *The Girl's Own Paper* – and had offered to read them to her cousin. Beth, however, clearly thought this a ruse on Miranda's part to get at the comics and had refused loftily. 'You can't read pictures,' she had said. 'And comics is all about pictures, not words. Go off and buy yourself comics if you're so keen on 'em, 'cos you ain't havin' mine.'

Upstairs, balancing jug and glass with some difficulty,

Miranda got the bedroom door open and glanced cautiously across to the bed. Beth was a pretty girl, dark-haired and dark-lashed with large toffee brown eyes and a neat little nose, but today, flopped against her pillows, she looked like nothing so much as a stranded fish. Her skin was so mottled with spots that she could have been an alien from outer space; her curly dark hair, wet with sweat, lay limply on the pillow, and when she opened her eyes to see what her cousin had brought, the lids were so swollen that she could scarcely see from between them. Miranda, having only just recovered from the measles herself, could not help a pang of real pity arrowing through her. Poor Beth! When she felt better she would be given in abundance all the things that Miranda had longed for when she herself was recovering, but right now no one knew better than she how Beth was suffering. Accordingly she set the glass down on the lopsided little bedside table and poured out some of the delicious raspberry cordial. Beth heaved herself up in the bed and picked up the glass. She took a sip, then another, then stood the glass down again. 'Thanks, Miranda,' she whispered. 'It's the nicest drink in the world, but I can't drink it! Oh, how I wish I were well again.' She looked fretfully up at her young cousin. 'Why does it taste so sticky and sweet? I so want to drink it, but if I do . . . if I do . . .'

'Poor old Beth. I felt just the same,' Miranda assured her cousin. 'Just you cuddle down, and try to sleep. When you wake up you'll feel better, honest to God you will. Why, tomorrow morning you'll be eating your breakfast porridge and drinking cups of tea and telling Aunt Vi that you fancy scouse for your dinner.' She smiled with real affection at the other girl. 'You'll be all right; I told you it's only bad for the first three days.'

Beth obeyed, snuggling down into the bed and giving Miranda a sleepy smile. 'You're all right, Miranda Lovage,' she said drowsily. 'I'm sorry I was horrid to you, but I've never felt this ill before. When you come up to bed I'll try some lemonade; perhaps that'll go down easier.'

Miranda did not point out that she would not be coming up to bed for a good many hours, since it was only just eleven o'clock in the morning. In fact, seeing how her cousin tossed and turned, she had already decided to sleep on one of the kitchen chairs that night. After all, she had done so throughout her own attack of the measles, since Aunt Vi had turned her out of the brass bedstead at ten every night and told her not to return to it until breakfast time the next morning. She seemed to think that this might prevent herself and her daughter from catching the infection, but of course time had proved her wrong.

Miranda trod softly downstairs and entered the kitchen, saw that her aunt was snoozing, and let herself out of the front door and back into the sunshine of Jamaica Close. The girls were still twirling the rope and the game was going on just as usual, so Miranda wondered whether to go over and ask to be put in, but decided against it. The measles, and her enforced diet of bread and milk, had made her lethargic, unwilling to exert herself. She had been aware of a great lassitude when she had climbed the stairs the second time, balancing the jug of raspberry cordial and the glass.

Now she decided that since no one else cared what

became of her she would have to start looking after herself, so she strolled slowly along the length of the Close and for the first time it occurred to her that it was a very odd little street indeed. On her left were half a dozen terraced houses, each boasting three steps and a tiny garden plot. Most householders ignored the latter, but some had planted a solitary rose, a handful of marigolds, or a flowering shrub. However, the houses on her right were not terraced but semi-detached; bigger, more substantial. Rumour had it that whilst the even numbers two to ten had to use the common pump against the end wall of the Close, the odd numbers one to nine had piped water, though all the houses had outdoor privies in their back yards. Miranda frowned. She had never seriously considered the Close before, but now it seemed to her that it was downright odd to have such different sorts of houses in one very short street. And perhaps the oddest thing of all was the wall at the very end of Jamaica Close. It must be twenty or twenty-five feet high and blackened by soot, but what was it doing there? Why had they chosen to block off the Close with what looked like the back view of an enormous warehouse or factory? Yet Miranda knew that it could be neither; had there been a building in which people worked so near to Jamaica Close, then surely she would have heard sounds of movement, or people talking when they took their breaks. And the wall was so high! Because of it, the inhabitants of Jamaica Close could not see the setting sun, though its rays poured down on the rest of the area. For the first time, a spark of curiosity raised itself in Miranda's mind. What was the wall there for? Why did no one ever mention what was on the far side of the great mass of bricks which chopped Jamaica Close off short? Had it once been all houses, or all factories for that matter? She could not say, but the imp of curiosity had been roused and would not go away. Useless to ask her aunt, who never answered her questions anyway. But there must be someone who could explain the presence of that enormous wall.

She was standing, hands on hips, gazing up with watering eyes at the topmost line of bricks and wondering what it hid – and, for that matter, why the road should be called Jamaica Close. 'Jamaica's miles and miles away, and all the other roads which run parallel with this one have nice Irish names – Connemara, Dublin, Tallaght, St Patrick's and so on. So why Jamaica? As far as I know it's a tropical island and nothing whatsoever to do with Liverpool.'

'You don't know nothing, gairl.' The voice, cutting across her thoughts, made Miranda jump several inches. She had not realised she had spoken her thoughts aloud, or that anyone was close enough to hear, and, consequently, felt both annoyed and extremely foolish. This, not unnaturally, caused her to turn sharply on the speaker, a boy a year or two older than she, with light brown tufty hair, a great many freckles and, at this moment, a taunting grin.

'Shurrup, you!' she said crossly. 'Trust a feller to stick his bloomin' nose in!'

The boy sniggered. 'If you don't want nobody to answer, then you shouldn't ask questions,' he said. 'What you doin', gal? Ain't you never see'd a wall before? You're the kid what lives at Number Six, ain't you?' He guffawed rudely. 'First time I ever see you without a bag or a basket or without that perishin' Beth Smythe a-grabbin' of your arm and a-tellin' you what to do.' He guffawed again. 'Slipped your leash, have you? Managed to undo your bleedin' collar?'

Miranda glared at him. She knew him by sight, knew he and his parents lived two doors down from her aunt. He was one of a large family of rough, uncouth boys, ranging in age from eighteen or nineteen down to a baby of two or three. Many folk did not approve of the Mickleborough family and this particular sprig, Miranda knew, was reckoned by her aunt – and indeed by Beth – to be a troublemaker of no mean order. On the other hand she knew that she herself was often accused by Aunt Vi of all sorts of crimes which she had most certainly never committed. Could it be the same for this boy? Miranda scowled, chewing her finger. She had not managed to make any friends amongst the children in Jamaica Close, for several reasons. One was that despite the fact that everyone disliked her aunt, despised her meanness, her spite, and her reluctance to help others, they believed her when she told lies about her niece. It seemed strange, but Miranda supposed that grown-ups, even if they didn't like each other, tended to take another adult's word against that of a child.

Then there was Beth. She wasn't all bad, as Miranda acknowledged, but she was an awful whiner, bursting into tears the moment she failed to get her own way and telling the most dreadful fibs to get herself out of trouble and somebody else into it. This naturally made her extremely unpopular.

A sharp poke in the ribs brought Miranda back to the present, and she turned to the boy by her side, eyebrows climbing. 'What business is it of yours if I stare at the wall? And who are you, anyway? I know you're one of the Mickleborough boys – my aunt says you're all horrid – but I don't know which one you are.'

The boy grinned, a flash of white teeth in an exceedingly dirty face. 'I'm Steve, the one me mam calls the turnover. I 'spect you've heard bad things about me, but that's because we used to have a rather mean dad. But now we've gorra nice one – a huge feller what could give you a clout hard enough to send you into next week. Not that he has – clouted me, I mean – but I wouldn't take no chances wi' a feller as big as the church tower. So I'm a reformed character, like.'

Miranda stared at him, eyes rounding. 'I'm like that . . . well, my mam was anyway. She and Aunt Vi had different dads; Aunt Vi's was a right pig, so when he died and Gran married again she chose a gentle, loving feller – John Saunders, that was, who was my mother's father. I never knew my grandparents because they died before I was born, but Aunt Vi blamed my mother for her own hard upbringing. She said my mam was spoiled rotten, never had to raise a finger or contribute anything towards the household expenses, and that's why she blames me for every perishin' thing which goes wrong,' she said, rather breathlessly.

'Well I'm blowed!' Steve remarked. 'It's like my family, too, except that there're more than two of us. I'm the last of the bad 'uns; me little brother Kenny is me step-dad's kid.'

The pair had fallen into step and were strolling along the Close, heading for the main road. 'Wish I had a little brother or sister,' Miranda said sadly. 'Not that I wanted one when Mum and I lived on the Avenue; we had each other and that was all that mattered.'

'Aye, I heard you and your mam were close,' Steve acknowledged. He peered down into her face. 'Things is a bit different now, ain't they? I see'd you runnin' errands, humpin' water, goin' up to the wash house with everyone's dirty clothes . . . and you've got a lot thinner than you were when you first arrived. Reckon they only feed you on odds and ends.'

Miranda thought of the plate which would be put down in front of her at dinner time: a spoonful of gravy, a couple of small spuds, a bit of cabbage if she was lucky, and that would be all the food she'd get until tomorrow's breakfast, unless of course she helped herself and risked being called a thief.

But the boy was looking at her enquiringly, his look half curious, half sympathetic. Miranda gave a rueful smile. 'You're right there; I get what the rest won't eat,' she admitted. She raised her eyebrows, returning look for look. 'You aren't exactly Mr Universe yourself. What did you say your name was?'

'Steve,' her companion said. 'I might be skinny, but I get me fair share of whatever's going; our mam sees to that. And fellers can always pick up fades from the market, or earn a few pennies sellin' chips to housewives.' He looked at her, his own eyebrows rising. 'What's your moniker? I know your cousin's Beth.'

'I'm Miranda Lovage,' Miranda said shortly. By now they had reached the end of Jamaica Close and had emerged on to the pavement, which was thronging with people. Women were shopping, children too. Folk were waiting for trams or buses, whilst others sauntered along peering into shop windows and enjoying the warm sunshine. Miranda would have turned right, chiefly because she expected Steve to turn left, heading for the city centre, but instead he jerked her to a halt.

'What say we pal up a bit, go round together?' he suggested. 'Your cousin's got measles, I've heard, so she won't be out and about for two or three weeks, which means you'll be all on your lonesome unless you join forces wi' me.' He grinned at her and suddenly Miranda realised how lonely she had been, and how much more fun the summer holidays would be if she did as this strange boy suggested.

She turned to face him. They were about the same height – perhaps he was an inch or two the taller – and now she was looking directly into his face she saw that beneath the dirt it wasn't a bad face at all. His hair was mousy brown, his skin only one shade lighter, and he met her regard steadily from a pair of hazel eyes set beneath straight dark brows. But there was something about his eyes . . . Miranda stared harder, then smiled to herself. His eyes tilted up at the corners, giving him a mischievous look; she rather liked it. But her new friend was jerking her arm, expecting a reply to his last remark, so she grinned at him, nodding so vigorously that her bush of long straight carroty hair swung forward like a curtain, momentarily hiding her face. 'That's a grand idea, Steve. We could do all sorts if we could earn a bit of gelt, and two of us ought to be able to earn more than one. The feller who sells carpets from a market stall will always give a kid a few pence to carry a carpet back to a customer's house. I'm not strong enough to do it alone, and Beth wouldn't lower herself, but if you and I offered our services . . .'

Steve grinned delightedly. 'You've got the right idea, pal,' he said exuberantly. 'We'll make a killing while your cousin's laid up . . . but what will happen when she's fit again, eh? I don't fancy being dropped like a hot potato.'

Miranda chuckled. 'Don't worry; at the mere mention of earning a few pence by working for it Beth will come down with a headache, or find some other excuse to let me get on with it alone,' she assured him. 'So what'll we do now?'

'Ever been to Seaforth Sands? It's grand up there on a fine day like this. If we could earn ourselves a few coppers we could stay out there all day. Can you swim?'

'Course not; girls don't,' Miranda said scornfully. 'Besides, where would I learn? I know there's a public baths on Vauxhall Road but they charge you at least sixpence – maybe a shilling – and anyway, you need a bathing costume to swim there.'

'I could learn you. And what's wrong with the Scaldy, anyhow?'

Miranda opened her mouth to make some blighting remark, then changed her mind. Steve was offering friendship, with no strings; the least she could do was to be honest with him. 'I've never heard of the Scaldy, whatever that is,' she admitted. 'I've heard of Seaforth Sands, of course, but I wouldn't have a clue how to get there. You see, when I lived with my mother in the Avenue we hardly ever came into the city, except for shopping and that. Why, I couldn't even find my way to the Pier Head! I've heard other kids talking about playing on the chains of the floating bridge, but I don't even know what that means. You might as well realise, Steve, that all this is strange to me. I know Prince's Park – the boating lake, and the café where they sell you a lemonade and a sticky bun for sixpence – and of course I know the theatre where my mother worked, and most of the Madison Players. But apart from that, I'm a stranger here. Go on, tell me what the Scaldy is.'

Thus challenged, Steve began to explain, then gave up. 'When does your aunt expect you home?' he asked. 'Can you get away for a whole day? If so we'll do the grand tour and I'll show you everything as we go. It'll be easier if you can see what I'm talking about with your own eyes.'

Miranda sniggered. 'I shouldn't be able to see with anybody else's eyes,' she pointed out, and dodged as Steve gave her a friendly punch. 'I can't say when Aunt Vi expects me home but she won't worry, even if I disappear like my mother did. So come on, let's have the grand tour.'

By the end of that momentous day, Miranda felt she was now as familiar with the delights of the city as Steve himself. They had visited the Scaldy, just past Burlington Bridge, so called because that was where the Tate and Lyle sugar manufactory belched out the hot water it no longer needed into the canal. They had watched enviously as boys small and large ran along the towpath and plunged into the steaming water. Miranda had wanted to follow, clad in knickers and vest, but Steve, though he applauded her pluck, had thought it unwise. 'Girls don't swim here,' he had assured her, 'but now you've seen it we'll skip a lecky out to Seaforth Sands. There'll be a deal of folk there, but if you tuck your skirt into your knickers you'll be able to paddle. After that we'll go up to the barracks – sometimes the soldiers will chuck a kid a penny or two to buy tobacco for 'em – and after that . . .'

After that they had a marvellous day. They went down to the floating road, slipped under the chains, and played at mudlarks. They begged a wooden orange box from a friendly greengrocer and took it back to Steve's crowded back yard, where they chopped it into kindling. Miranda divided the pieces into bundles which they sold up and down Scotland Road for threepence each, and with the money earned Steve bought a bag of sticky buns. Miranda had been diffident about following Steve into his mother's kitchen, partly because she was shy and feared a rebuff, and partly because she was frightened of Steve's older brothers, who Aunt Vi was always declaring were dangerously wild and best avoided, but this proved to be yet another of her aunt's spiteful and untruthful comments. Ted, Reg and Joe were easy-going young men, accepting Miranda as their brother's friend, whilst little Kenny, who was just three, clamoured for her to play with him.

Miranda was just thinking how delightfully different Steve's home life was from her own when the back door opened and Mr Mickleborough came in. He was an enormous man, well over six foot tall, with huge hands and feet. Steve had told her that his stepfather was an engine driver and Miranda would have liked to ask him about his work, but Mrs Mickleborough began to lay the table and the older boys disappeared, though Kenny, the baby, rushed to his father, winding soft little arms about Mr Mickleborough's knees and begging for a shoulder ride.

Miranda, all too used to knowing when she was not

wanted, thanked Mrs Mickleborough for her hospitality and headed for the back door. She almost cut Steve in two by trying to shut it just as he was following her outside.

Out in the jigger which ran along the backs of the houses the two stared at one another. 'Isn't he big?' Miranda said rather breathlessly. 'He makes your brothers look quite small. Gosh, I wouldn't like to get a clack from him!'

Steve puffed out his cheeks and whistled. 'You're right there. He's got hands like clam shovels. But he's real good to little Kenny, and Mam says he's gentle as a lamb. Still an' all, I tries to keep me 'ead down, never gives back answers, stays out of the way as much as possible, and do what he says right smartly.' He sighed ruefully. 'He's strict, but he's fair, and much better to our mam than my real dad was, so I reckon I should count me blessings.'

Miranda was looking thoughtful. 'If he's only your step-dad, why do you have the same name?' she asked. 'I thought boys always kept their fathers' names?'

'Oh, me real dad were a right mean old bugger, used to knock Mam about as well as us kids, so when he were killed and Mam married me stepfather she asked us if we'd mind being called Mickleborough too, since she wanted to forget everything to do with our dad. I don't think Reg and Ted were too happy, or even Joe, but I were only a nipper meself and couldn't see as it made any difference, so I said yes at once and the others came round in the end. So now we're the Mickleborough boys – isn't that what your aunt called us?'

By this time the two of them had emerged into Jamaica

Close, and Miranda looked towards Number Six, half expecting her aunt to appear in the doorway shouting for her, but the doorstep was deserted, as indeed was the Close itself. Most families would be either preparing or eating their evening meal, so if she wanted to be fed she would have to go indoors at once and think up some good reason why she had been away all day. She said as much to Steve, who shook his head. 'You've already said they don't care where you go or what you do, unless they need you, and since you also said your aunt was staying at home to look after Beth you don't even have to invent an excuse. All you have to do is look astonished and say if they needed you why didn't they call.'

Miranda sighed. 'It's been the nicest day I've had since Mum disappeared,' she said wistfully. She fished in her pocket, produced her share of the money they had earned, and thrust the pennies into Steve's hand. 'You take care of it; my aunt will only nick it if I take it into Number Six. She'll say I have to pay something towards the rent, or she needs some coal . . . any excuse to take it off me.'

Steve accepted the money and shoved it into the pocket of his ragged kecks. 'Tomorrer, if you get up real early, I'll show you where I cache my gelt,' he said, 'then you can put yours there too and know it'll be safe.' He hesitated, then jerked a thumb at the great wall at the end of the Close. 'Remember we were talking about the wall earlier? Well, now we knows each other pretty well I'll take you round t'other side of that wall tomorrer and tell you something I've not told another soul.'

'Tell me now,' Miranda said eagerly. 'Go on. You've told me so much I might as well know the rest. I was sure there was some mystery about that wall as soon as I began to notice it. Go on, Steve, tell me!'

But though Steve laughed indulgently, he also shook his head. 'No chance,' he said. 'It's like what I told you earlier about the Scaldy; better to see it for yourself than me have to drive myself half crazy trying to explain. Tomorrer is quite soon enough.'

'Oh, but suppose I can't get away?' Miranda wailed. 'Suppose my aunt needs me? She'll only interest herself in Beth for a bit, then she'll expect me to dance attendance twenty-four hours out of the twenty-four. And then you'll be sorry you were so mean.'

But Steve only laughed. 'Maybe I will and maybe I won't,' he said infuriatingly. He seized her shoulders and ran her up the three steps to the front door of Number Six. 'Off you go.' He lowered his voice. 'Don't forget; meet me here tomorrow at six in the morning.'

'Well, I will if I can,' Miranda said. 'My aunt never gets up before eight o'clock, so maybe I'll be lucky.'

She left him, turning to give a little wave as she shut the dirty paint-blistered front door behind her. Then she went down the short hallway and into the kitchen. Her aunt was sitting by the table eating cake, having clearly had her fill of the scouse, potatoes and cabbage Miranda had helped to prepare earlier in the day. She swung her chair round so that she could stare at her niece. 'Where've you been?' she said belligerently. 'I come back after me shopping trip and you was nowhere to be seen. Poor Beth had shouted herself hoarse, but did you appear? Did you hell! All you thought of was your perishin' self.'

Aunt Vi continued to upbraid her as though she had done something really wicked, instead of merely being out of hearing when her aunt had called. As soon as she could make herself heard above the barrage of complaints, accusations and name calling, Miranda took a deep breath and reminded Aunt Vi that it was *she* who was supposed to be looking after her daughter. 'You said *you* were going to nurse Beth; don't you remember?' Staring into her aunt's furious face, she saw recollection dawn there and saw, too, how dangerous it was to be right, especially if it made Aunt Vi wrong. She knew she should have reminded herself that a soft answer turneth away wrath, but it was too late for that now: she had erred and must pay the price.

'Well, since you weren't around when I were dishin' up you can go supperless to bed,' Aunt Vi said, her little eyes gleaming malevolently. 'Now just you go upstairs and see if there's anything Beth wants. If there's nothing you can fetch her, then you can read her the serial story out of *The Girl's Own Paper*.'

Miranda hesitated. She had had a large slice of bread and jam at the Mickleborough house and she and Steve had shared some fades from St John's market and a paper of chips from the chippy in Homer Street, which meant of course that she was not really hungry at all. However, her day with Steve had put fresh courage into her veins and she decided to be bold for once. She pointed to the blackened pan on the stove. 'I prepared that before I went out this morning, and I've had nothing to eat all day,' she said firmly, though untruthfully. 'I've had measles myself, you know, and it's left me quite weak. I'm not running up and down stairs at Beth's beck and call until I've had some supper. And a nice hot cup of tea,' she added defiantly.

Auntie Vi surged to her feet, crossed to the stove and heaved the pan well back. 'You ain't havin' none of this, norrif I have to chuck it out for the perishin' birds,' she said nastily. 'Bread and water's good enough for you; you can help yourself to that if you like.'

Miranda looked at her. She realised that this was the first time she had ever confronted her aunt and that Vi must be wondering what had got into her, but having made a stand she must not back down unless she wanted to live on bread and water. For a moment she contemplated cutting herself a large slice of the cake which her aunt had been devouring when she had entered the kitchen, then changed her mind. She had prepared the scouse, and had looked forward to having at least a helping of the stuff, so she went to the sideboard, took down a tin plate and held it out wordlessly, almost beneath Aunt Vi's nose. Her aunt began to gobble that she should not get a shred of the delicious stew, but Miranda continued to hold the plate and, to her secret astonishment, when their eyes met it was Aunt Vi who lowered hers first. To be sure, she did not ladle any stew on to the tin plate, but turned away, muttering. Miranda heard words like 'forbid' and 'don't you dare' and 'defyin' me in me own house' as her aunt stomped back to her chair, picked up the teapot and poured herself another cup of tea, though her hand trembled so much that tea sprayed out of the spout and puddled on the wooden table.

Miranda could not believe her luck. Never, in her wildest dreams, had she expected it to be Aunt Vi who backed down, but it had happened. She seized the ladle and helped herself to a generous portion, then sat down at the table and began to eat. Halfway through the meal she reached over and cut herself a wedge of bread from the loaf to sop up the last of the gravy, and when she had finished she went across to the sink and put her dirty plate with the others, while Aunt Vi continued to munch cake and stare at her as though she could not believe her eyes.

Miranda gave her aunt a big bright smile and headed for the stairs. 'I don't suppose Beth wants anything now, or she would have shouted,' she said cheerfully. 'However, a bargain is a bargain; I said I wouldn't wait on Beth until I'd had something to eat. Well, now I've had a meal, and a good one, so I think I'm strong enough to get up the stairs and see if there's anything I can do for my cousin.' As she left the kitchen Miranda glanced back at her aunt and had real difficulty in preventing herself from giving a great roar of laughter. Aunt Vi had her hand across her mouth as she shovelled cake into it, and just for a moment she could have modelled for the monkey in the well-known portrayal of *Speak no Evil*. But she managed to contain her mirth until she was well out of hearing.

Upstairs, her cousin was already looking a little less unhappy, though her skin was still scarlet with spots. She had drunk at least one full glass of the raspberry cordial, but the scouse beside it had scarcely been touched. She looked up as her cousin entered the room and indicated the plate of stew with a weary hand. 'Want it?' she asked in a hoarse whisper. 'I can't eat the flamin' stuff; food makes me feel sick.' She sat up on one elbow, peering at Miranda through swollen lids. 'Where's you bin all day? Mam can't make the stairs more'n twice in twenty-four hours, she says, and anyway I wanted *you*. She bought the latest copy of *The Girl's Own Paper* so's you could read me the serial story, but you weren't here.'

Miranda sat down on the bed and pulled the magazine towards her. 'I offered to read to you this morning but you told me comics were pictures and to go and buy me own.'

'So I did,' Beth said feebly. 'But I didn't mean it, you know that, Miranda. And anyway, me mam can't read as well as you. She says her glasses steam up so she misses words out and has hard work to read her shopping list, lerralone a magazine story.' She gave a gusty sigh. 'I telled Ma to send you up as soon as you come home.'

'And I told your ma that I needed some food before tackling the stairs again,' Miranda said. 'She let me have a plate of scouse and some bread; I must say it were prime. As for what I've been doing all day, you wouldn't be interested; it was just – just messing around. You know the Mickleborough boys? I know your mum doesn't like them, but they're all right really. One of them – he's called Steve – said he'd take me on a grand tour of the area and he showed me all sorts. Do you know, Beth, there's a huge art gallery quite near the London Road and a marvellous library as well as a museum . . . oh, there's all sorts of things I never dreamed of. While you're laid up I mean to get to know the city as well as he does. Then, when you're better . . .' But Beth's interest in her cousin's doings was already fading.

'Never mind that. Just you do what my mam says and read me my serial story,' Beth commanded. 'If you want to go around with some perishin' rough boy, that's up to you. Oh, and I could do with another drink. Me throat's that sore, even talking hurts.'

Miranda stood up, took the almost empty jug and returned to the kitchen. Presently she was back in the bedroom and sitting down on the bed with the magazine spread out on her knees. 'Ready?' she said brightly. 'Well, Louisa Nettlebed is hot on the trail of the mysterious letter, though it is to be hoped that Phyllis, the heroine, will get to it first. I'll read on from there.'

Miranda enjoyed reading aloud, but was rather chagrined to discover, when she reached the end of the episode, that her cousin had fallen asleep. That meant re-reading the story the next day and she particularly wanted to go off early with Steve. Still, when Aunt Vi came up to bed she told Miranda to sleep in the kitchen, which was all to the good. The clock above the mantel has a very loud tick, and if I pull the curtains back so the early light can come in I'll be ready for the off at six, she told herself.

It was a pearly summer morning when Miranda let herself quietly out of the house. As arranged, Steve was hanging around outside, and he greeted her with a broad grin. 'Ain't it a grand day?' he said. 'I reckon it's too good to waste poundin' the streets and showin' you where I stash me gelt, so I've took some bread and cheese – Mam won't mind – and we can catch the number twenty-two tram out to Fazakerley and then walk to Simonswood, where we can have us dinners and muck about . . .'

'Where's that?' Miranda interrupted. She could feel excitement flooding through her at the thought of another wonderful day with this new – and knowing – friend, though excitement warred with disappointment. Steve had roused her curiosity about the other side of the wall and she longed to see it. However, the prospect of a day in the country was almost enough to cause her to forget what she now thought of as 'the mystery of the wall'. After all, the wall would be there probably for the rest of her life, whereas a day out with Steve could be ruined if rain fell heavily, or her aunt discovered her intention and forbade her to leave the house.

But Steve was staring at her; he looked annoyed. 'What do you mean, where's that?' he said rather truculently. 'Didn't I just tell you? Simonswood's real countryside; there's streams with tiddlers in, ponds for the ducks and geese, orchards full of apples and pears and that . . . oh, everything to make the day real special. But if you don't want to come, of course . . .'

Hastily, Miranda hid her curiosity about the wall and assured him that he was mistaken; she wanted to go to Simonswood very much indeed. As they trotted along to the tram stop, however, she admitted that if she was out for a whole day again there would undoubtedly be reprisals. 'But I don't care,' she added defiantly. 'Mostly I'm in trouble for doing nothing, so it'll be quite a change for my aunt to have a real reason to knock me about.'

'Knock you about? But you're not her kid, and you're a girl . . .' Steve was beginning, but Miranda was saved the necessity of answering as a number twenty-two tram drew up beside them. 'Tell you what,' he said as they settled themselves on one of the slatted seats, 'if your aunt treats you bad, suppose we take back something she'll really like – a sort of bribe, you could say. I know a little old tree what has real early apples; someone telled me they're called Beauty of Bath. Suppose we fill our pockets with 'em? You can give your share to your aunt if you think that'll sweeten her.'

Miranda thought this an excellent idea, and when they got off the tram she chatted to Steve quite happily as they strolled along country lanes whose verges were thick with sweet-smelling spires of creamy coloured flowers, and in marshy places with the delicate pale mauve blossoms which Steve told her were called lady's smock.

Once again Miranda had a wonderful time. She accompanied Steve to a farmhouse where they bought a drink of milk, and were told they were welcome to take as many apples as they liked from the little tree down by the gate. After they had eaten their bread and cheese, Miranda was all set to dam a tiny stream so that she might paddle in the pool she meant to create, when Steve astonished her by saying that he felt like a nap.

'You don't,' Miranda said scornfully. 'Naps are for old people. Just you come and help me dam this stream.'

'I'm too tired,' Steve said obstinately. 'I dunno why, but if I don't get some sleep I'll not have the strength to walk back to the tram stop. Ain't you tired, Miranda?' As he spoke he had been taking off his ragged pullover and folding it into a pillow, but even as he lay down upon it and composed himself for sleep, Miranda jerked his faded shirt up and stared at the back thus revealed.

'Oh, Steve, you've been and gone and got the flippin' measles,' she said, her voice vibrant with dismay. 'I thought you'd have been bound to have had them . . . but you've got them now at any rate. No wonder you're so perishin' tired; I reckon I slept for near on three days when I first had them, and Beth's the same. She couldn't even stay awake to listen to me reading her serial story.'

Steve sat up, heaved his shirt up and surveyed his spotty skin with a groan of dismay. 'Oh, hell and damnation, wharra thing to happen right at the start of the summer holidays,' he said. 'I'll try to keep it a secret from me mam, but I doubt it's possible. I say, Miranda, I'm real sorry, but until the spots go I'll be lucky to escape from the house for ten minutes, lerralone ten hours.'

'Well, I suppose we ought to be counting our blessings because we've had two great days,' Miranda said. 'And once you begin to feel better, surely your mam will let you play out? She's an awfully nice woman and I don't suppose she'll want you under her feet for the whole three weeks.'

'We'll see. Mebbe she'll let you come in, 'cos you've already had 'em, and read to me, or just chat,' Steve said, but he didn't sound too hopeful. He grinned up at her and Miranda saw that already spots were beginning to appear amongst the freckles on his cheeks. Soon he would be smothered in the bloomin' things, which meant that he would be unable to fool anyone; one look and he would be driven back to his own home, though Miranda thought this was yet another example of the stupidity of grown-ups. When a measles epidemic struck, the sensible thing would be to let all the kids catch it. Then the next time it happened they would be safe, since she was pretty sure you couldn't catch the measles twice. So Miranda continued her work of damming the stream and paddled contentedly whilst Steve slumbered, though they had to make their way back to the tram stop in good time. Steve pulled his cap well down over his spotty brow and to

Miranda's relief no one tried to stop them getting aboard, though once they were back in Jamaica Close Steve got some funny looks from the kids playing on the paving stones.

As she had expected, Miranda was met by a tirade of abuse from Aunt Vi, and a storm of reproaches from Beth, since the first resented having to look after her daughter and the second wanted amusing, and was fed up with her mother's constant complaints. As Steve had predicted, the large bag of apples went some way to placating her aunt, but later in the evening, when Miranda went round to Steve's house, she was told politely but firmly that he was feverish, could see no one and most certainly was not allowed out.

Oh well, I've had two wonderful days and three weeks isn't such a very long time after all, Miranda comforted herself as she pushed two chairs together to form a bed after her aunt had gone upstairs. The maddening thing is that Steve had promised to tell me about the high wall at the end of Jamaica Close, only we both forgot about it when we realised he had got the measles. I wonder when he'll be able to explain just what's mysterious about that wall.

Chapter Three

Despite Miranda's hopes, the three weeks of Steve's incarceration felt more like three months. Beth got better and even more demanding than usual, and though Miranda's show of spirit had confounded her aunt for a little while, Aunt Vi soon began to slip into her old ways. If Miranda tried to defy her, a sly clack round the head would be handed out when she least expected it, making her feel dizzy, and though she persisted in saying she would not work unless she got at least a share of the food on offer this tactic was only partially successful. Sometimes her share seemed to consist of gravy, half a potato and some cabbage, though Beth, when warned that her cousin would not wait upon her unless she was decently fed, saw that Miranda got bread and cheese or a conny-onny sandwich in return for reading anything Beth wanted to hear.

She did manage to see Steve from time to time; once she sneaked into his yard when she had seen him making his way to the privy and the two of them exchanged news. Steve, much to his surprise, found that his mother would not allow his stepfather to so much as enter the little room he shared with Kenny, since the older man had never had the measles. She also bought her son special food, and this was probably as well since Steve got them very badly, and was feverish for a whole week.

To be sure, once that week had passed he made rapid progress and was soon eating hearty meals, playing quiet games with Kenny and occasionally sneaking downstairs to meet Miranda in the cobbled yard at the back of the house, but he was careful to keep these activities undemanding since he had no wish to make himself even more sickly.

When Miranda and Steve met, as they began to do regularly, in the little cobbled courtyard of Number Two, he was eager for any news of Jamaica Close and their various neighbours. Miranda had taken advantage of his absence to spend a good deal of time each day with the Madison Players, who were always good for a bit of gossip, but Steve had never been to the theatre and Miranda soon realised that he was not much interested in her mother's friends.

'When you're better – well, when all the spots have gone – I'll take you with me when I go down after the matinée performance and introduce you to everyone,' Miranda told him. 'You'll like them, honest to God you will, Steve. And then you can hear what they've been doing to try and find my mother; you'd like that, wouldn't you?'

But though Steve agreed that this would be a grand idea, Miranda had the uneasy feeling that he was not much interested either in the theatre or in the disappearance of her mother and she supposed, ruefully, that she could scarcely blame him. A whole year was a long time in anyone's book and even the Madison Players no longer talked as though Arabella would turn up with some believable explanation of where she had been during the past year. Even the sleepwalking incident had been long ago. Several times since then Miranda had woken to find herself halfway down the stairs, tiptoeing barefoot across the cobbled yard or actually in the roadway, but she had never again gone out of sight of Jamaica Close. She had mentioned these episodes to no one but Harry, the policeman who had found her on her very first sleepwalk, and though interested he had not thought it particularly important. 'I've talked about it to me mates, and they say that most folk grow out of it; I reckon you're doing that right now.'

It was unfortunate that as Beth's health improved her temper worsened and she became demanding, fractious and quite spiteful. She had always told tales but now she twisted her remarks to put her cousin in an even worse light, until Miranda was forced to bargain with her. She would refuse to read to Beth or help her with a jigsaw or play draughts unless her cousin would agree to her playing out for at least an hour each day. Beth was well enough to play out herself had she wanted to do so, but on this point at least the cousins were totally different. Miranda thought she would die cooped up in the house, Beth thought she would die if she were forced to breathe fresh air, so arguments were frequent and tempers frayed and grew shorter than ever.

The day came at last, however, when the nurse from Brougham Terrace pronounced Steve free from infection and the next morning the two met outside the front door of Number Six, to gloat over their newly won freedom. 'Mam's give me a few coppers so we won't have to skip a lecky; we can ride like Christians and go all the way out to Seaforth Sands, like we did before I caught the perishin' plague,' Steve said. 'Gawd, I hope I never get the measles again, I'm tellin' you. I scratched, of course – who wouldn't – and when Mam saw me at it, what did she do but trot down to the chemist shop on Great Homer and buy a bottle of pink yuck what the pharmacist telled her was good for spots . . .'

Miranda giggled. 'Calamine lotion,' she supplied. 'It's awful, isn't it? When I was six and lived in the Avenue I got chickenpox and my mother dabbed the stuff all over me. It was all right while it was wet – quite cooling, in fact – but when it dried it was awful. Aunt Vi sent me to the chemist to buy a bottle for Beth but I told her how it would be, so we emptied it down the sink and put a tiddy bit of plate powder in the bottle with water and shook it up. Then Beth pretended we'd used it and said it wasn't any good, and when Aunt Vi got a plug of cotton wool and tried to dab it on the spots Beth grabbed the bottle and threw it out of the window. Good thing it was open, because she threw it pretty damn hard, I'm telling you.'

Steve laughed. His skin seemed oddly pale after being shut up indoors for three weeks but otherwise, Miranda considered, he was beginning to look like himself once more. But she vetoed his suggestion that they should go to Seaforth Sands. 'No, I don't want to do that,' she said firmly. 'Before you were taken ill you promised you'd show me the place where you hide your gelt, so I could add mine to it. And you sort of hinted that I'd be surprised when I saw the other side of that great wall at the end of Jamaica Close. I've waited three weeks and never nagged you, but I'm going to nag you now. I want to see the other side of that wall and I want to know where you hide your gelt and where I shall hide mine in future. Why, Steve, if you were to be run over tomorrow I wouldn't be able to inherit your wealth, because I don't know where you keep it.'

Steve laughed. 'I don't mean to get run over tomorrow, nor the next day neither,' he said cheerfully. 'But I know what you mean and I reckon you're right. We'll save Seaforth Sands for another day, and as soon as you've had your breakfast we'll set off for the other side of the wall.'

They agreed to meet outside Number Two in half an hour, and Miranda trotted down the jigger, crossed the courtyard of Number Six and entered the kitchen, where she found Aunt Vi eating porridge whilst Beth sat on a low stool, clutching a fork upon whose prongs was spiked a round of bread. She looked up as Miranda entered the room, and frowned. 'I don't fancy porridge, norreven with brown sugar or golden syrup,' she said crossly. 'I'm havin' toast wi' raspberry jam. What'll you have?'

Miranda knew that this was a rhetorical question. The raspberry jam, her cousin's favourite, was most certainly not on offer so far as she herself was concerned. Not that she minded; porridge with just a sprinkling of brown sugar was her favourite breakfast, and if she helped herself to a full dish it would not matter if she did not come in for the midday meal.

However, when she examined the saucepan there were only about two spoonfuls of porridge left in it, so her hopes of a good filling breakfast were dashed. She put it into her dish, however, then cut herself a round of bread, keeping one hand on it so that no one should filch it whilst she ate her porridge.

A rich smell of burning caused Beth to give a squeak

of dismay and throw the cindered slice down on the table, then reach for the slice of bread beneath her cousin's palm. 'Gimme!' she commanded. 'You can have the burned bit.'

'Beth Smythe, you are the most selfish . . .'

Aunt Vi's hand clipped Miranda so hard across the ear that she nearly fell off her chair, making Beth give a muffled snort of laughter. 'Serve you right,' she said tauntingly. 'What's to stop you cutting yourself another slice, if you don't like a bit of burn?' But Aunt Vi was already scuttling pantry wards with the remains of the loaf clutched in her hot and greedy hands, so Miranda jammed the piece of bread into her skirt pocket, ignored her aunt's shout that she was to bleedin' well wash up before she took one step out of the door, and crossed the kitchen.

'No time; I'm meeting a friend,' she called over her shoulder. 'See you later, Beth.' Miranda was sure her aunt would think nothing of pursuing her down the Close, so she decided that loitering outside Number Two was not a good idea and turned right into the main road. Because the summer holidays were now in full swing there were a great many children about, one or two of whom Miranda knew. She stopped and spoke to Jane and Elizabeth Meredith, twins who were in her class at school, and they told her that they had just returned from a wonderful week down on the coast; at Rhyl, in fact. 'Oh, girls, how lucky you are!' Miranda breathed. 'My mother was always promising to take me down to the coast, but somehow she never got round to it.'

She had heard much of the delights of seaside resorts in summer and remembered her mother's description of golden sands, gentle blue seas and the enthusiastic audiences who had attended the shows on the pier. One day, Arabella had assured her daughter, they would go to Rhyl, or Llandudno, or even further afield, but at present she was content to stay with the theatre over the summer, helping with scenery painting, costume repair and other such tasks which were best done when the theatre was empty.

Lizzie was a sweet-tempered girl, but it was her sharp-tongued twin who responded. 'Your mam, your mam!' Jane said contemptuously. 'That were when you were in that posh private school, I suppose? I bet they never knew your mam was on the stage, 'cos that's common that is . . . bein' on the stage, I mean. If she took you to the seaside at all you'd have had your face blacked up and a black curly wig on your horrible head, so's you could earn a few pennies in the black and white minstrel show . . .'

Miranda was interrupted just as she was contemplating handing out a punch on the nose. Someone caught her arm and a voice spoke warningly in her ear. 'Hello-ello-ello? Hangin' round waitin' for me, was you? Gorrany grub? That bleedin' aunt o' yours might hand over a bit of cake or a chunk of bread and cheese. Still, I've got some of each so we shan't starve.'

It was Steve, of course, and as he spoke he had been drawing her away from the twins, giving her arm a warning pinch as he did so. Miranda, who had taken a deep breath, preparing to shout abuse at Jane even as she threw the punch, subsided, though she shook Steve's hand off her arm as they moved away. 'It's all right; it's just that when somebody says something nasty about my mother, I lose my temper,' she said ruefully. She turned to her friend. '*Are* we going to see the other side of the wall, Steve? It's not fair to keep talking about some mystery or other and then making excuses not to go round there.'

They had been walking quite briskly along the pavement, but at this Steve stopped short. 'Look, I told you I've not said a word to anyone else, about either where I stash me gelt or what goes on on t'other side of that there wall. I'm still not sure if I'm doin' the right thing . . .' He heaved a sigh. 'But a promise is a promise, so we turn right here and keep goin' for a bit. Despite what you might think, it's a long way round to reach the other side of that wall and it's no use you askin' me a lot of silly questions 'cos I shan't answer 'em. Chatter away all you like, tell me stories about your mam, but don't ask me no questions about where we're goin' or what we'll do when we get there, gorrit?'

'Yes, all right, if that's the way you want it,' Miranda said rather sulkily. 'But I think you're being awful silly; how can a wall which is so ordinary on the back be mysterious and different on the front? That's what I want to know.'

As Steve had said, it was a long walk to reach the other side of the wall, but when they did so it was just as mysterious and extraordinary as Steve had hinted. The wall which truncated Jamaica Close hid what appeared to be a huge, crumbling mansion of a house; it was only visible over the top of another large wall, and the roof was half missing, telling Miranda that it was now a ruin, though it must have been magnificent years ago. She could see the tops of trees and the staring glassless eyes of windows, but could see no way in. She turned and stared at Steve. 'Are you sure that Jamaica Close is on the other side of that crumbling great house?' she asked uneasily. How did one tell from the only sort of view they could get that Jamaica Close was really so near? For all she knew Steve might have led her for miles, through dozens of tiny streets – well, he had done so – before stopping in front of the only building of sufficient height to own that wall. Miranda looked at the neighbouring buildings, but none of them were houses. There were small and large factories with busy yards full of bicycles in racks, the occasional car, and men strolling to and fro, smoking cigarettes or eating food from greaseproof wrappers, for by now, Miranda guessed, it must be dinner time. Clearly, the reason that no one was interested in the old walled house was because people came here to work and not to live; this was not a family neighbourhood. Whereas in Jamaica Close there were always children playing, mothers shouting to their offspring to run messages or go indoors for a meal, here, Miranda guessed, when the siren sounded for the end of the shift, workers were merely intent upon getting back to their homes and had little or no interest in their surroundings.

She said as much to Steve, who grunted assent. 'The strange thing is that when I'm in Jamaica Close I hardly hear any noise from over here, apart from the hooter which marks the end of the shift; I suppose it's because the wall's so high. And then, of course, grown-ups' voices don't carry in the way ours do. But now that you know what's on this side of the wall, you'll maybe notice sounds which you wouldn't have noticed before.'

Miranda agreed to this, though with reservations. But

then Steve gave her a friendly poke in the ribs. 'What are you thinking?' he asked. 'Don't tell me . . .' he pointed to the slated roof of the mansion so far above their heads, 'you don't believe that Jamaica Close is a stone's throw away. Tell you what, how about if we prove it? No use doing anything now, in broad daylight, but tonight when we're back in the Close and there's no one about I'll get something real brightly coloured and shy it as high as I can, right over the wall and the house as well, if I'm lucky. Then tomorrow we'll come round again, and the proof will be there.'

Miranda sniffed, but gave Steve a reluctant grin. 'All right, all right, I'm sure you've worked it all out and Jamaica Close is just over the wall. And now, how the devil do we get to the house?'

'I suppose you think it's impossible, don't you?' he asked mockingly. 'Like most people, you see what you expect to see, not what is really there. Walk very slowly around this bleedin' great wall and mebbe you'll see a way in and mebbe you won't. I aren't goin' to help you, 'cos this is a sort of test. Go on, start lookin'.'

Forewarned, Miranda began to walk very slowly along the wall. She kept her eyes on the ground, half expecting to find that some animal had dug a tunnel beneath it, but saw nothing. Then she began to examine the brick-work and in a remarkably short space of time, or so her gratified pal assured her, she had found the way in. Perhaps a dozen feet from where she had started looking a mass of ivy hid the uneven brickwork, and had it not been for the sudden tension of the figure beside her Miranda might have passed it by without a second glance, assuming that, in the way of ivy, it had rooted and clung to every crevice in the great wall. But the slight stiffening of Steve's body was enough to make Miranda not only look, but also to put a hand to the gleaming ivy. She prepared to tug, then realised that the ivy was rooted on the far side of the wall and what she beheld was simply a curtain, which, as soon as she moved it away, revealed a tiny scratched, scarred door.

'Well done you!' Steve said in a low voice. 'Better make sure no one's watching . . .' He glanced quickly round, then reached down and pulled open the door. To Miranda's surprise it opened easily, without a squeak or a protesting creak, and though she turned towards Steve to remark on it, he pushed her through and shut the door behind the pair of them before turning to her and blowing out his cheeks in a parody of relief. 'Phew!' he said. 'Now I'll show you where I hide my gelt.' He turned towards the house, but Miranda put a detaining hand on his arm.

'Hold on a minute!' she whispered. 'This is a perishin' garden. Oh, I don't deny it's been let run wild, but it really is a garden, Steve. I didn't know there were gardens anywhere near Jamaica Close. Why, there's fully grown trees – flowers an' all. Someone could live here. I wonder who owns it? Oh, look, roses, really beautiful ones! Gosh, don't they smell sweet? And there's masses of black-berries, only they're still red berries now – and look at the rhubarb! The stems are as thick as my wrist; I bet they'd be really tough if you tried to put 'em in a pie.'

Steve followed her glance. 'Is that rhubarb?' he said, sounding surprised. 'I've never seen them big leaves on top of it when it's for sale in St John's market. But there's gooseberries, two or three different sorts, and I reckon there were strawberries once, only they've all gone tiny.

But the blackcurrant bushes, though the fruit is getting thinner, are still just about alive.'

Miranda drew in a deep ecstatic breath and expelled it in a low whistle. 'Oh, Steve, this place is just about perfect! We could come here every day and bring it back to what it was years ago. We could root out the weeds, harvest the fruit – I've already seen two apple trees, a Victoria plum and a greengage – and then we could sell the fruit and buy seed with the money. The first thing we ought to do is get rid of the weeds and dig over all the beds. I remember my mum saying you should always plant potatoes in ground that's new to cultivation, and before the crash came she was a farmer's daughter and knew what she was talking about. Oh, Steve, do let's.'

She looked at her pal and saw that he was laughing. 'Honest to God, Miranda, you're mad as meself,' he said approvingly. 'I had the same thought when I first found me way in, but it ain't possible, of course. Someone must own both the house and the garden, and I'll take a bet that if we started to interfere somebody would fetch the scuffers.' He pointed to the wall. 'See that loose brick? It's the one with the splash of white paint on it, which I put there so's to identify it. Pull it out.'

Miranda did as she was told and found that the brick had been hollowed out and contained an interesting number of coins and one beautiful, if dirty, ten shilling note. Hastily, she plunged a hand into her skirt pocket and produced almost a shilling in pennies and ha'pennies, which she slid into the hollow of the brick. She watched as Steve replaced it in the wall, then jerked her thumb towards it. 'Isn't it time we took a look at the house itself? You were kidding when you said someone would get the scuffers if we dug the beds over, weren't you?' she asked hopefully. 'No one's been here for years – ten, or twenty, or even more! The garden's a wonderful tangle, but we shan't be able to play in it until we've cut the weeds and brambles down. Goodness, Steve, there's a bed of nettles up agin that old door that's almost as tall as I am, and though the brambles are covered in berries, they're covered in prickles as well. We can't do much out here until we've armed ourselves with a scythe, a couple of spades and some garden shears. As it is, we'll have to be right careful, because the path's disappeared and if we aren't really clever we'll arrive at the house just about covered in stings and scratches. You'd better go first, because my legs are bare and you've got kecks. Look, that's where the path was once; it goes straight to the door, and . . .'

Steve gave a snort. 'If you think I'm goin' to walk, bold as brass, up to that door you're bleedin' well wrong,' he said roundly. 'I've not told you, because I didn't imagine you'd be daft enough to risk goin' into a tottering old house, but since you are I'll tell you why I won't go with you. It's haunted, that's why!'

Miranda stared at him, scarcely able to believe her ears. This was one of the rough Mickleborough boys, and everyone knew boys feared nothing, so why should he pretend that the house was haunted, unless he was simply saying it to frighten her? Well, he wouldn't succeed. She pulled a face at him, then tried to push him along the almost obliterated path. 'Don't be so stupid. If you'd said it might fall down and crush the pair of us to a jelly then I would have believed you, but haunted? Ha, ha, ha! You'll tell me next that it's the ghost of your great-uncle who lived in the house when he was a boy and got trapped in an old oak chest, like the woman in the story.'

She looked at Steve, waiting for him to begin to laugh, and to say that he was only kidding, but he did nothing of the sort. 'If you go in there, you go alone,' he said firmly. 'I've only ever been in once, and that was enough for me. Honest to God, Miranda, I never believed in ghosts until I discovered this place. I liked it so much that I fought my way through the nettles and brambles and went in through that door, the one you can see there. I crossed the kitchen – I think it was the kitchen – and went into the next room. It were pretty dark because the windows have been boarded up, though of course the wall goes all the way round the whole building so there ain't a lot of light anyhow. There's furniture in there; I reckon it were a dining room once, but no sooner had I took a look round than I heard someone singing. At first I thought it were coming from outside, but then I realised it were in the next room along. I'm tellin' you, Miranda, for two pins I would have cut and run . . .' he grinned unhappily, 'but I didn't have a pin on me, so I fumbled my way along a short corridor, which smelled horrible, until I found the doorknob of the next room, and . . . oh, Miranda, even remembering makes me go cold all over . . . and before I could turn the handle I felt it turn in my fingers. I swear to God I hadn't moved it, so I knew there was someone on the other side of the door. I can tell you I snatched my hand back as though the doorknob were red hot, but the door swung open and after a moment I peered inside. The singing had stopped, but I couldn't see no one; the room was empty and dark.

Then . . . someone started to laugh. It was a horrible laugh, the sort madmen give, you know? I took one last look round the room – it was empty all right – and then I ran like a rabbit and didn't stop until I had me hand on the outside door. Then I collapsed on to the grass and telled myself that I'd imagined the whole thing. Only I'm not the imaginative kind.' He straightened his shoulders and grinned perkily at Miranda. 'So if you go into the house, you go alone,' he repeated firmly. 'And now let's have the bread and cheese me mam gave me. I wish I'd thought to bring a bottle of cold tea – even telling you about the ghost has dried me mouth.'

Miranda stared at him; he was the most down to earth person she could imagine, which meant that if he said he had heard mysterious laughter coming from an empty room then she simply had to believe him. He had said he thought the house was haunted, but Miranda thought this most unlikely. She knew sound travels in peculiar ways and decided it was quite possible that a tramp had moved into the old house, but did not want anyone to know the place was occupied. Being a child of the theatre she knew very well that it was possible for someone to 'throw their voice', so that the sound appeared to come from somewhere quite different. Therefore, she patted Steve's arm in a motherly fashion and sat him down beside her on a low wall. 'I know what I'm going to tell you sounds odd, but we have had variety acts in the theatre from time to time. All sorts of different ones – conjurers, tight rope walkers and mystery acts – and one of the latter is a chap called Cheeky Charlie, who can throw his voice. It's really odd; he can stand stage left, smiling at the audience, but his voice will come from stage right, and because he's also what they call a ventriloquist you won't see his lips move, not even a little bit.'

Steve snorted. 'Do you expect me to believe that a feller with a gift like that is wasting his time frightenin' kids so's they don't investigate a tumble-down old house?' he enquired, his voice vibrant with disbelief. 'Pull the other one, Miranda Lovage, it's got bells on! Tell you what, if you go in, and can find a logical reason for that awful laughter, then I'll give you a bag of Mrs Kettle's gobstoppers and not even ask for a suck.'

Miranda giggled. It was a good offer, and one she should have seized immediately, yet to her own surprise she did not do so. Instead, she got up and, skirting the worst of the nettles and brambles, made her way towards the house. Even as she did so, she found herself hoping that something would occur to save her from having to put her theory to the test. She looked back hopefully at Steve. 'If you come with me you'll be able to see that it's all moonshine and there's no ghoulies or ghosties or long-leggedy beasties waiting to jump out and shout boo,' she said. 'If you won't come in, how can I prove that I've even crossed the threshold?'

Steve chuckled. 'I'll see you go in, and I can guarantee that if you get into the room I told you about you'll come out of there like a rocket, and that'll be proof enough for me.'

That was scarcely reassuring, but Miranda took a deep breath, squared her shoulders and began to push her way through the waist-high leaves, having to stop every now and again to detach the clinging brambles as she approached the old house. As she got closer, two things occurred to her. One was that the door which she took to lead into the kitchen was sturdy and strong-looking; the other was that it looked quite modern, not at all in poor repair like the rest of the house. Insensibly, Miranda found this cheering. Indeed, she found herself hoping that the door would be firmly locked against her, which would be a cast iron excuse for going no further. When she reached it, however, her secret and unworthy hopes were proved false. The door swung open easily beneath her touch, with no eldritch shriek of old and unused hinges. Indeed it swung wide, letting in light which penetrated the room for several feet.

Behind her, Miranda heard a peculiarly nasty chuckle which made her blood run cold, until she realised that it was only Steve trying to frighten her. Then she walked steadily into the room, which was indeed the kitchen. It was, as Steve had said, very dark inside, because every window was covered by shutters, firmly closed.

She crossed the kitchen on silent feet, beginning to be aware of a rather unpleasant sensation. She felt that she was being watched, though there was no one in the room beside herself – she could tell that even in the semi-darkness – but she wasn't afraid, only annoyed with Steve, who had refused to back her up and search through the building with her. She glanced back at the open door and through it she saw Steve sitting on one of the low walls eating an apple, staring through the aperture at her. Miranda gave a little wave and was disproportionately glad when Steve waved back. She wished she had an apple, and for a moment contemplated returning to the garden and insisting that Steve share his ill-gotten gains, but then, with a resigned sigh, she decided to get her exploration over. She left the kitchen, mouse quiet, and entered the passageway of which her pal had spoken. Because there was no light at all, not even a crack from a badly shuttered window, the corridor was pitchy black, and though Miranda told herself over and over that she did not believe in ghosts, she still felt a frisson of something very close to fear when she stretched out her hand and laid it on the doorknob of the room which Steve had said was haunted. She moved her fingers very carefully, half believing that the door knob would be wrenched out of her hand by sepulchral fingers, but greatly to her relief it was only she who gently twisted the knob, opened the door silently and peered inside.

Blackness met her eyes, total blackness without one speck of daylight. Miranda took one faltering step into the room and even as she did so she thought she heard a low chuckle begin. It was, as Steve had said, an inhuman noise; it sounded as though it came from hell itself and all Miranda's courage and determination fled. She shot out of the door backwards, clouting her elbow so hard on the unseen door jamb that she emitted a startled shriek, and as she ran at top speed along the corridor, crossed the dimly lit kitchen at a gallop and burst into the warm and sunny garden she was only too willing to admit that there was something very odd indeed hidden away in the crumbling mansion.

Steve was laughing. 'Told you so,' he said mockingly. 'Did you hear that awful laugh? I've been sitting out here telling myself it was some sort of trick, like what you told me about the man who could throw his voice. Well, I dare say it is, but it's put me off and I bet it's put you off too.'

He had remained sitting on the low wall and Miranda

sat down beside him. She was still breathless, both from her fast run up the garden, heedless of nettles and brambles, and her fear over what had befallen her in the house, but she was beginning to calm down and to examine what had happened with a critical eye. 'What is really odd is that I still like the house, and the garden too. The garden's beautiful, somewhere I wouldn't mind spending a great deal of time. And I think, if we came back here with an electric torch each and threw open all the shutters in the house, and got to work cleaning it, then it would be a grand place to play. We could have it for our own, because no one else seems to want it. In fact we could kit it out – the kitchen at any rate – and stay here overnight, if we had a mind.'

Steve stared at her, and she read awe in his glance. 'You're a girl and a half, you are!' he exclaimed. 'Ain't you afraid of nothin', Miranda Lovage? I wouldn't stay in that bleedin' evil mansion, norrif they paid me a hundred quid a night. And as for likin' it – you must be mad! Don't tell me you wasn't scared, because I shan't believe you.'

Miranda snorted. 'I was frightened all right, when I heard that laugh,' she admitted. 'But I'll tell you something really weird, Steve. I know it sounds daft – quite mad, really – but when I was in the kitchen I kept having the oddest feeling that the house had something to do with my mother and her disappearance. The police stopped being interested ever so soon after she went, and though some of her friends, especially the Madison Players, tried their best to contact her, even their interest faded away after a few months. But I still believe somebody stole my mother away and if I hunt really hard I'll find her.' She looked hopefully at her companion. 'Will you help me, Steve? You've never met my mother, but she's ever so beautiful and the nicest person in the world. If we find her, she'll take me away from my aunt and reward you somehow, though I don't know how. What do you say to that, eh?'

Steve was sitting, elbows on knees, hands supporting his chin, but now he stood up, nodding slowly. 'I'd like to get you away from your perishin' aunt. That woman has some nerve, to knock you about when you aren't even her own child,' he said, and Miranda had to turn her head away to hide the smile. She thought it funny that Steve believed mums and dads had a perfect right to scalp you alive, but other relatives should keep their distance; still, no point in raising the matter now. Instead she got up and headed for the door in the garden wall.

'Let's be getting home so we can earn some money. Torches are expensive, but candles are pretty cheap. Suppose we come over here tomorrow with a few candle ends and explore the house that way? If we wait until we've saved enough for electric torches, we'll still be waiting come Christmas.'

'Shurrup,' Steve said briskly. 'I agree with you that the garden's prime, but I won't go into the house again, not if you were to pay me a hundred smackeroos. Not by torchlight, nor candlelight, not even by bleedin' searchlight. Hear me?'

'Where have you been, Miranda Lovage?' Beth's voice was shrill with annoyance. 'You're supposed to be a friend of mine, as well as me cousin, but you bobby off without me whenever you've a mind, leavin' me to do

Mam's messages while you play with that nasty, dirty Mickleborough kid from Number Two.' She glared spitefully at the younger girl. 'Mam were goin' to take the pair of us to New Brighton tomorrow because she's got a load of starched tablecloths for one of the big hotels on the front, and she said if we'd carry half a dozen each then once they were delivered – and paid for, o'course – she'd let us play on the sand and paddle and have tea and doughnuts before we come home again. But when I tell her how you've been off wi' that scruffy Steve Mickleborough, that'll be you out.'

Once, Miranda would have jumped at the thought of such a delightful day out, but now she shook her head in pretended sorrow. 'Sorry Beth, I've got other plans,' she said briefly, and then, seeing the spiteful look deepen on her cousin's face, she broke into hurried speech. 'I'd come with you and give you a hand if I could, honest to God I would, but it just isn't on. I promised Mrs Mickleborough that I'd tidy round after they left, and then lock up. I told you, they're having a whole week at the seaside to make up for them all having the measles. They're renting two rooms down by the funfair; all she wants to do now is cook enough grub for the first three or four days of the holiday. I'm going to help her, I promised, and she's going to give me a sixpence if I agree to check the house every few days to make sure all's well.'

'You're a liar,' Beth said at once. 'Mrs Mickleborough's quite capable of doin' her own cookin'; she won't want you hangin' about. And if you told her you were needed to help with the tablecloths she'd probably say to leave the cleanin' till they're due back.' Her tone abruptly descended from demanding to coaxing. 'Aw, come on, Miranda, be a sport. You'll enjoy New Brighton, you know you will, and it'll be no fun for me if I have to go with Mam alone, 'cos she hates the seaside. If you've got any pennies we might have a go on the funfair – I'm rare fond of the swing boats – so why not be a pal and come with us?'

The two cousins were sitting on the steps outside Number Six, in Beth's case simply watching the other girls as they jumped in and out of the rope, chanting 'Salt, mustard, vinegar, pepper' as they played. Miranda, on the other hand, was waiting her turn to join in the skipping, so only had half her attention upon her cousin. She understood why Beth was so keen to have her company and was tempted to agree to go along, for though she and Steve had been saving up every penny they could they still had not got enough money to buy really strong torches. Miranda had finally persuaded Steve to relent, but though each had acquired a pocketful of candle ends and a box of Swan Vestas, they had only essayed one attempt to look round the house by candlelight and they both remembered, with a jolt of sickening horror, how the moment they had opened the door the invisible laugher had reached out an invisible hand and snuffed their candles, to the accompaniment of mad giggling.

Naturally enough, their retreat had been fast and terrified; Steve almost trampling Miranda underfoot as they had both fought to escape back into the garden, whilst the mad giggle behind them had gradually faded into silence. Later, without telling anyone why he was interested, Steve had made some casual enquiries about the place and learned that a man who had made himself a huge fortune by dealing in slaves had lived here. That man had profited by the misery and degradation of the people whose lives he had ruined. And now, Miranda had thought dramatically when Steve told her the story, his restless soul was not allowed to enter heaven, but was tied for ever to the place where he had lived in uncaring luxury for so long.

'Miranda? What is it you and that feller get up to?' Beth whined. 'You never used to go off without me. Sometimes you used to hang around the Close, sometimes you went wanderin' off up towards the centre where the big shops are, sometimes I believe you even went home to the Avenue, though there's strangers livin' in your house now. Oh, and you went to the theatre of course, hoping they'd tell you somethin' about your mam, only they never did, 'cos they don't know nothin'. But after we'd all had the measles, you changed. You and that Steve went off just about every day, I dunno where. And now, when the Mickleboroughs are off to the seaside for a whole week, you might at least do things wi' me until they get back.'

Miranda sighed, and was about to agree to go to the seaside with Beth – it was better than hanging around the Close, after all – when something suddenly occurred to her. Steve was nice all right, probably the only real friend she had, but after that one ill-fated expedition he had refused point-blank to explore the slave trader's mansion again. Miranda herself had learned a good deal about the house lately. She had gone to what the school children called the museum of slavery and seen for herself the leg irons and manacles, the instruments of punishment, and talked to old folk who still remembered hearing how the slaves had been lined up in one of the city squares and auctioned to the highest bidder in those far off days. Miranda's soft heart had wept for the misery the slaves had suffered. Husbands, wives and children had been torn apart and Miranda, robbed of her own mother, thought she knew how they must have felt, the depths of their suffering.

One old man had told her many stories of how brutal and sadistic were the men who ran the sugar cane plantations on the island of Jamaica, where many of the slaves were destined to go. She had heard stories of dead or dying slaves being thrown overboard from the clipper ships, so many that sharks would follow in the ships' wake, eager for the 'food' thrown out by such uncaring hands.

Though the stories had horrified her, Miranda had been tempted to pass them on to Steve, but in the end had decided against it. She guessed he would show a ghoulish interest in them, but she also guessed that it would probably make him even less keen to enter the house. And now, with the summer holidays looming to a close and even the sheltered trees in the walled garden beginning to take on the tints of autumn, their free time would soon become severely restricted. Opportunities to visit their playground would be limited to weekends, and once the really bad weather set in she imagined that Steve's enthusiasm, always somewhat lukewarm even for the garden, would probably disappear altogether.

Before her conversation with old Mr Harvey, Miranda had told herself that since she most certainly did not believe in ghosts it was some trick of sound, perhaps from an underground stream, or even an echo, which had frightened her so. But now, with her new knowledge of the terrible past of the old house, she shared a good deal of Steve's apprehension, along with a growing feeling that, if there were a ghost, the ghost of some poor tormented slave who had suffered at the hands of the mansion's owner, it might recognise in her a kindred spirit.

For although it was perhaps unfair to compare living with her aunt to slavery, she was undoubtedly bullied and derided. Aunt Vi treated her like dirt, took pleasure in piling work on her weary shoulders, and the only emotion she showed her was dislike; never a hint of gratitude. Mr Harvey had called her 'Cinderella', though only in jest, but to Miranda the nickname was no joke; it was too close to the truth. Furthermore, she too had known the pain of loss when her dearly beloved mother had been torn from her arms. It occurred to her now that if she went into the house alone, and there really was a ghost living there, then she would be able to identify with the poor creature, which was more than Steve could do.

'*Miranda!*' Beth's whining voice jerked Miranda abruptly back into the present. In her mind's eye she had been seeing the tall white clipper ships and their miserable cargo as they sailed ever further from the country of their birth, and now here she was back in Jamaica Close with the girls playing jump the rope on the dirty paving stones and her cousin jerking at her arm. 'Miranda, *will* you answer me! If that horrible boy is off to the seaside then why can't you come to New Brighton with Mam and me?'

'I've *told* you . . . I promised to help . . .'

But Beth cut ruthlessly across her sentence. 'I don't care what you promised, and nor will me mam,' she said angrily. 'We can't manage all them bloody tablecloths without someone to give us a hand, so you can just make up your mind to it that you're coming to New Brighton with us; savvy?'

Miranda reflected with an inward smile that Beth was just like her mother. She never considered the feelings of others but simply went straight for whatever she wanted, either bullying or whining, depending which she thought would be more successful. Today, however, Miranda told herself, she was doomed to disappointment. She turned to her cousin, giving her a falsely sweet smile. 'Sorry, Beth, you and your mum are on a loser. Unless you intend to drag me to the ferry in chains, you're going to have to carry those tablecloths yourselves.' She got briskly to her feet, dusting down her skirt, but moving judiciously out of her cousin's reach before she did so. 'I can't even promise to help as far as the ferry because I shall be too busy. See you later, queen!'

'One, two, three spells out! You goin' to jump in, Miranda?'

Elsie Fletcher, one of the older girls, grinned encouragingly at Miranda and indicated that they would slow the rope if she wanted to jump in. Miranda ran forward and saw Elsie and the other girls grin as Beth began to sob. 'You're supposed to be me pal . . .' she was wailing, but when no one took the slightest notice she got heavily to her feet and went slowly through the front door of Number Six, still calling Miranda every bad name she could think of.

'That there cousin of yours is a right nasty piece of work,' Elsie said as the rope began to revolve smoothly once more. 'Dunno how you stand her meself.'

'She can be all right at times, and anyway she's not nearly as horrible as my aunt,' Miranda confessed ruefully. 'They want me to go with them to help carry a load of starched tablecloths back to one of the big hotels in New Brighton . . .' she grinned at Elsie, 'but I've other fish to fry, and won't my aunt be mad when Beth tells on me!'

Elsie returned her grin. 'I might have guessed she were a tale-clat as well,' she said. 'Still, a day in New Brighton ain't to be sneezed at. You might even get an ice cream cornet out of the old witch; mebbe even a dinner, or at least a paddle in the briny.'

Miranda snorted. 'If she bought me an ice cream she'd charge me for it, and the same goes for a dinner,' she said gloomily. 'Aunt Vi doesn't give anything away for nothing. But I've got business of my own to attend to, so I'll bypass New Brighton, just this once.'

Elsie nodded understandingly. 'Don't blame you; I only met your mam a couple of times, but Gawd above knows how she managed to have such a 'orrible sister as Vi,' she said. 'If I were you I'd sag off, find meself somewhere else to live . . . ever thought of it?'

'Heaps of times,' Miranda admitted. She and Elsie, being in different classes, had never had much to do with each other in the past but now Miranda realised she had an ally in the older girl. 'But I'm always hoping my mother will turn up again; she'd never leave me on purpose, honest to God she wouldn't.'

The other girl grinned. 'Course she wouldn't,' she said

firmly. 'Well, kid, if you ever need help in gettin' away from that aunt of yours, just let me know. I'd be tickled pink to put a spoke in her wheel, especially if it helped you. And one of these days your mam will return; I'm as sure of it as I am that you'll escape from the witch. Did you know we called her that – the witch, I mean?'

Miranda shook her head. Not only had she found a friend, but she was now aware of how much her aunt was disliked. She thought the nickname suited Vi admirably and could not wait to tell Steve. She must go round to Number Two straight away, and help her pal's mother – who so generously fed her on bread and cheese when Aunt Vi let her go hungry – to get ready for their longed-for holiday.

Chapter Four

Two mornings later, having made up her mind to take advantage of Steve's absence to visit the old house, Miranda slid out of bed as soon as the first grey light of dawn could be glimpsed between the thin bedroom curtains. She had had an uncomfortable night, with Aunt Vi taking up three quarters of the bed and Beth occupying the remaining quarter, so that Miranda was forced to cling on to the edge of the mattress and hope she would not be pushed out by either of the other two occupants. She had managed to sleep for the first few hours, too exhausted to remain awake, for her aunt, furious over her refusal to accompany them to New Brighton, had brought back a large quantity of dirty linen which, despite the heat of the day, she had taken straight to the wash house. After tea, she had refused to allow Miranda to leave the kitchen; had actually locked the door so that escape was impossible. Then she had built the fire up, stood a row of irons in the hearth and made her niece iron every single one of the huge white tablecloths. Miranda's arms, shoulders and back had ached agonisingly by the time she tackled the last one, and though she had done her best and worked as hard as she possibly could she had somehow managed to scorch the hem, causing Aunt Vi to slap her head resoundingly and say that, had it not been so late, she would have sent her niece back to the wash house to scrub away at the scorch mark and then made her iron the tablecloth again, wet though it would have been.

But the discomfort of her position had woken her long before the others were stirring, so she was able to slip out of bed without either of them appearing to notice that she had gone. She dressed quickly, not wanting to wash since the splashing might awaken one of them, and made her way down to the kitchen. There, the gingham curtains were still drawn across and the banked down fire showed red gleams where it was beginning to come to life. Miranda looked round the room; she could make herself some breakfast, but it would be best if she did not start to cook; just the smell of porridge might bring her relatives sleepily down the stairs. If so, they might start nagging again, or say she should stay at home to do the chores, or run messages; whichever it was, escape might become impossible, so Miranda cut a chunk off the loaf and spread it thinly with margarine, then generously with jam. She peeped into the pantry and saw a bottle of her cousin's favourite raspberry cordial standing on the slate slab beneath the window to keep cool. It was three quarters full. Miranda picked up an empty bottle, poured some cordial into it, went to the sink and added a judicious amount of water, capped the bottle and was about to investigate the contents of the large cake tin when she heard a slight noise from upstairs. It was probably only her cousin, or her aunt, turning over in their sleep, but Miranda was taking no chances. She glided across the kitchen and slipped out into the freshness of the morning. Closing the door behind her with infinite caution, she padded across the yard and let herself out into the jigger; then she headed for the old house.

It was the first time Miranda had ever been out alone this early; on the only other occasion when she had abandoned her bed at such an early hour she had been meeting Steve, but now she was on her own and able to appreciate the coolness and quietness of the streets. To be sure there were one or two people about, mostly making their way down to the docks, and she saw several cats, going about their mysterious business without so much as a glance in her direction. She saw a dog as well; a miserable skinny stray with sores on its back and a look in its eyes which caused Miranda to stop her onward rush. She knew that look too well, knew that her own eyes often reflected the desperation she could see in the mild gaze of the little brown and white cur. She held out a hand to it and it came slowly, clearly more used to kicks than caresses, but when she produced her jam sandwich and broke off a generous piece, hunger obviously overcame fear and it slunk closer, taking the food from her fingers with such careful gentleness that she could have wept. Instead, however, she squatted down on the pavement and fed the little creature a good half of the sandwich before tucking the food back into the pocket of her skirt. 'Tell you what, dog,' she said to it as she straightened up once more, 'if you're still around when I'm headin' for home later today – if the ghost hasn't killed me, that is – then I'll try to make do with a few apples, so you can have the rest of my bread and jam.'

It sounded like a generous offer but Miranda knew, guiltily, that she was unlikely to have to make it good.

Stray dogs don't hang around in one vicinity, they are for ever moving on, and she was sure this dog would be no exception. However, she was rather touched to realise, after half a mile, that the dog was still following her. She told herself firmly that it was not she the dog followed but the bread and jam, yet in her heart she did not believe it. The dog had recognised a fellow sufferer and wanted her company even more than he wanted food.

But he'll never stand the pace, Miranda told herself. I've simply got to hurry because I must be in the garden before the shift change, and I don't know when that is. Come to that I don't know if the factory works twenty-four hours because Steve and I only ever come here during the day, and then of course we avoid the times when we hear the hooter and know there will be folk about. I think Steve said he thought the chaps on the factory floor worked from 8 a.m. to 4 p.m., but for the office workers it's 9 to 6. Oh gosh, I wonder what the time is now? I really am an idiot; it's all very well coming early but I wouldn't want to be on the wrong side of the wall when there are crowds about. Someone would be bound to spot me and start asking questions, questions which I wouldn't want to answer, even if I could.

She told herself that there was no point in lingering, however, and she and the dog continued to twist and turn through the many little streets which separated them from the mansion. Presently her doubts were resolved when the breeze brought them the sound of a clock striking six times. Miranda smiled to herself, then glanced back at the little dog, trudging wearily along behind her, with what looked like a foot of pink tongue dangling from between its small jaws. Miranda slowed, then stopped, and addressed her companion. 'Am I going too fast for you, feller? Tell you what, when we reach the garden I'll get you a drink of water; I can see you could do with one.'

The dog glanced up at her, seeming to smile, definitely indicating that a drink of water would be extremely welcome, Miranda thought. And the dog wasn't the only one; as the heat of the day increased she grew thirstier herself and began to think longingly of the apples and greengages which still hung from the trees in the garden. She wondered if the dog's thirst could be slaked by fruit, but doubted it. Time, however, would tell, and if the little dog took to fruit then she would have no need to go into the kitchen in order to find him a drink.

Judging by the chimes of the clock she had heard, Miranda thought she must have left Jamaica Close well before six and it was still early – only around seven o'clock – when she and the dog slid quietly along the rosy brick wall and approached the garden door. No one was about, and Miranda paused to listen. She was relieved to realise that there was no sound at all coming from the big ugly factory next door, which during the daytime buzzed with every sort of noise: talk, laughter, the clattering and clash of machinery and many other sounds. It was pretty plain that whatever the factory made – Steve had told her he thought it was munitions, though why such things should be manufactured when the country was at peace she had no idea – they did not work twenty-four hours, which meant that if they were careful their presence need never be discovered. However, habit made Miranda open the garden door as softly as possible and take a quick look round the walled garden, which she thought should more accurately be called the wilderness, before closing the door behind her. When she glanced back she saw the little dog standing uneasily in the aperture, wearing the expression of one who has too often been rudely rejected to take acceptance for granted.

Miranda patted her knee. 'Come along in, little feller,' she said encouragingly. 'This here is our place – yours and mine, and Steve's too of course – so don't you hesitate, just come straight in.'

The dog did hesitate but then he trotted through the doorway and moved as close as he could to Miranda without actually touching. She could see he was shivering and put a protective hand on the top of his smooth brown and white speckled head. 'I told you it was all right for both of us to come in, and so it is,' she whispered. 'And now we're going to get you that drink of water. I wonder if there's a well anywhere in the garden which we've not noticed? If so, we could get the water from there.'

But even as she said the words she knew she was kidding herself, knew she was still none too keen on entering the house itself. That was why she had nagged Steve so relentlessly, begging him to accompany her. She, Miranda Lovage, was frightened of sounds which she did not understand. How ashamed her mother would be if she knew that her daughter was hesitating before giving a poor little dog a drink, just because of a noise which, after all, she had only heard once – she did not count the time she and Steve thought they had heard giggling in the kitchen because they had bolted out so quickly that it had probably been their imagination. She produced her bottle of raspberry cordial and took a quick swallow, and watched with guilty dismay as the little dog's eyes followed the movement of bottle to mouth with obvious wistfulness. Thinking back, Miranda realised that it had been at least a month and possibly more since it had rained. Puddles had dried up, gutters had run dry; a stray dog would have a long walk before finding even the tiniest puddle.

Miranda had come here determined to investigate the house. One pocket in her skirt contained half the jam sandwich and the raspberry cordial. The other was full of candle ends and a box of matches. Yet having arrived at her destination, she found she was still reluctant to actually walk into the house. If only it wasn't so dark! There were shutters at most of the windows, and the ones without shutters had been boarded up.

Miranda stood for a moment with her hand on the knob of the kitchen door. She wondered what Steve was doing, imagined him wading through the shallows with the hot sun on his back, then plunging into deeper water, whilst Kenny jumped up and down at the water's edge, shouting to his brother to give him a piggy back so that he too might get wet all over.

How Miranda envied them! How she wished that she too was on a beautiful sunny beach with the sea creaming against her bare feet and the whole happy day in front of her. But it was no use wishing; she had promised the dog a drink and a drink he would jolly well have even though it did mean entering the old house and fumbling her way across to the low stone sink. She had never been anywhere near it, had only glimpsed it as she had crossed the kitchen, heading for the corridor which led to the rest of the house, but now, she told herself firmly, she was going to stop acting like a superstitious idiot and get the dog some water. Resolutely she turned the knob and pushed the door open wide, letting in the dappled sunlight, making the place seem almost ordinary. Standing in the doorway, still hesitating before actually entering the room, she glanced cautiously around her. She saw the huge Welsh dresser which she had glimpsed on her first visit and a long trestle table; also the low stone sink with a pump handle over it. There was another door to her right which she imagined must once have opened on to the pantry, and a door to her left which she knew led to the passageway, and now that her eyes were growing a little more accustomed to the gloom she could make out piles of pans, dishes, and other such paraphernalia spread out upon the shelves which ran from one end of the room to the other. Good! She would fill a bowl or dish with water for the dog and then, if her courage held, use one of her candle ends to investigate the rest of the house.

She was halfway across to the sink, her hand extended to the pump handle, when once more she began to suspect that she was being watched. Uneasily, she glanced around her, then down at the dog, and she knew that had he shown any sign of wanting to bolt she would have been close behind him. But the little animal's attention was fixed on the pump and the enamelled bowl she held. Sighing, she seized the pump handle and began to ply it, and immediately two things happened: a trickle of water emerged from the big brass tap and something scurried across the sink, making for Miranda.

She gave a shriek so loud that she frightened herself.

The dog backed away, whining, and then ran forward, put his front paws on the side of the sink and began to lap at the narrow stream of water emerging from the tap, whilst Miranda, clutching the bodice of her dress against her thumping heart, backed away from the enormous spider which had been driven into activity by the action of the pump.

'Oh, oh, oh! You hateful horrible creepy-crawly!' she shrieked, unable to stop herself. 'Don't you come near me or I'll stamp on you and squash you flat.' She turned reproachfully to the little dog. 'Why don't you defend me?' She peered into the sink but could see no movement and, keeping well back, held the enamelled bowl beneath the trickle of water until it contained a reasonable amount. She looked all round her, but it was much too dark to see where the spider had disappeared, so she placed the dish on the floor with extreme caution, clutching her ragged skirts close to her knees as though she feared that the dreaded enemy would presently creep out of cover and climb up her bare legs. She stood very still, trying to convince herself that the spider was probably long gone, having spotted the open door and galloped into the sunlight. She wanted to pick up the bowl of water and carry it outside, but the little dog was still drinking and it seemed a mean thing to do, to interrupt him when he had had so many disappointments already in his short life. And anyway, Miranda was growing used to the kitchen. To be sure, she had felt she was being watched, but she now concluded that it must have been the spider and wondered why it had never occurred to her to open the shutters. There was light coming through the back door – sunlight, what was more

– but if anything it tended to make the rest of the room seem even darker in comparison, whereas if she were to open all the shutters . . .

She had actually stretched out a hand to the nearest pair when she realised that by opening up she might be letting in more than sunlight. Safely hidden away in the slats there might be whole colonies of spiders similar to the one which had apparently been living in the sink. Miranda decided that opening the shutters would have to wait until Steve returned from the seaside. Boys, she knew, were not afraid of creepy-crawlies. No, she would not touch the shutters, but as soon as the dog had finished drinking she would light one of her candle ends, protect it as far as she could with a hand around it, and investigate at least a part of the house. She had never seen the stairs, but today for the first time she'd noticed that the window of one of the attic rooms gaped black and open, neither shuttered nor boarded up. If she could find that room she might be able to see why it had not been blacked out like most of the other windows.

The dog finished lapping and glanced up at her, apparently to give her an encouraging grin; he actually wagged his disgraceful little tail, which had formerly been clipped so firmly between his back legs that Miranda had thought it had been docked, before giving one last sniff at the enamelled basin. Miranda took a deep breath and set off across the kitchen, and just as she entered the shaft of sunlight coming through the back door she discovered where the spider had gone. It was crouching in that very shaft of sunlight, its hateful legs forming a sort of cage around what looked like a sizeable moth. Poor Miranda gave an even louder shriek than the one which had heralded the spider's first appearance, and even as the echoes of her scream died away a soft voice spoke, seeming to do so almost in her ear. 'I no like spiders either,' the voice said sympathetically. 'I shriek like the factory hooter if I see one near my bed.'

Miranda nearly fainted and her heart, which had speeded up with the spider's reappearance, doubled its pace. She looked wildly round but could see no one, though she noticed that the door leading into the corridor, which had been firmly closed, now swung open.

There was no doubt that, had she been able to do so, Miranda would have cut and run, but fear nailed her to the spot. Once more her gaze raked the room, including the open doorway into the corridor, but she could see nothing, only darkness. 'Where are you?' she quavered. 'I – I hear your voice but I can't see you.'

The chuckle which greeted this remark no longer seemed threatening, but merely amused. 'I here, in the doorway,' the voice said. 'Can't you see me? Where your eyes gone?' The voice suddenly changed from mere curiosity to fear. 'I done nothin' wrong. Why you come here, take my water and eat my apples and plums?'

'I didn't know they were yours – the apples and plums, I mean – and if they are I'm very sorry,' Miranda said, trying hard to keep her voice steady.

There was a short silence, then the voice said: 'Why you come here secretly, instead of knocking on door like Christian?'

'Because we didn't know anybody lived here,' Miranda said, speaking each word separately and with great care. 'For that matter, why are you hiding? I can hear your voice plain as plain but I can see neither hide nor hair of you.' She hesitated, then decided to put the question uppermost in her mind. 'Are you a – a ghost?'

This time the pause was very much longer and the voice, when it spoke again, sounded extremely puzzled. 'Ghost? Why you think I ghost?'

Miranda shrugged helplessly. 'If you're invisible, and I think you are, then you must be a ghost.'

This time the pause was shorter. 'Can ghost own house? I told you this my house; you not believe me?' Miranda was growing accustomed to the voice now. Sometimes it sounded puzzled, sometimes unsure, but at other times impatience with her foolishness seemed uppermost. She shifted her position slightly, almost certain now that the speaker was standing in the corridor, but when she drew her candle out of her pocket and fumbled for the matches, the voice spoke sternly. 'This is old house and catch fire quick. Didn't your mammy tell you not to play wi' matches? Go away now and take candles with you; I'm best in dark. But come back another day and we talk more . . .'

Miranda thought she heard a soft sort of shuffling sound and then she became convinced that she was alone once more, save for the little dog. The ghost had gone without leaving any clue as to his or her identity. Indeed, did a ghost have an identity? Miranda was not sure; the only thing she was sure of was that the woman – thinking back she was positive that it had been a woman's voice – meant no one any harm. Perhaps she was a ghost, or perhaps she was just a very shy person who now owned the place. Miranda was about to return to the garden when her attention was drawn to the little dog. It was staring at the doorway which led to the rest of the house and wagging its poor little scrap of a tail, its shabby ears pricked and its tongue lolling out once more.

The Mickleborough family arrived home quite late on the Saturday, but as soon as day dawned on Sunday Steve was down in the kitchen helping his mother to prepare breakfast, since he was all on fire to get round to Number Six and see what Miranda had been doing in his absence. He had been surprised by how much he had missed her. She wasn't particularly pretty, or particularly clever, but she was grand company, and, despite her miserable home circumstances, game for anything.

Of course, he and his brothers had had a glorious time at the seaside. Little Kenny had watched with envy as the older boys splashed in and out of the sea and became totally at ease in the water. Then there were the wonderful fish and chip suppers, and perhaps best of all the new understanding between himself and his stepfather. Steve was not sure exactly why he and Albert Mickleborough had begun not merely to tolerate but to like one another. He thought it might be the fact that he had begun to call his stepfather 'Dad', whereas previously he had simply avoided calling him anything at all. And then he had greeted the news that his mother was expecting another baby with real enthusiasm; Steve liked small children and had no objection at all to looking after Kenny, whereas his other brothers, particularly Joe, had no interest in their mother's second family. When Albert expressed his hope that the baby would be a girl this time, Steve entered into the discussion with zest, suggesting names, and promising to take the new baby off his mother's hands whenever she and her husband fancied a night out.

All this had made the holiday one of the happiest Steve had ever known, and though normally he would have regretted it when they packed up and made for home, this time, though he knew he would miss the freedom the holiday had given him, his eagerness to tell Miranda all about it was a real compensation for the loss of the seaside he had so enjoyed.

'Wake up, Steve! Aren't you the one for dreaming. Got any plans for today? You've been such a good lad, lookin' after young Kenny so's your dad and I could have time to ourselves, that it's only fair to let you have time off to go around with your pals. If so, I'll pack you up a carry-out, enough for you and that poor little scrawny scrap of a girl what's livin' at Number Six.'

'Oh, Mam, that'd be grand,' her son said with real gratitude. 'But I'll help meself if it's all the same to you. Jam sandwiches, and your oatcakes and cheese, will be fine. I bet she's had a miserable time while we were away so I'll call for her and mebbe we can take a tram out into the country. Simonswood is her favourite place; we were dammin' a stream there to make ourselves a pool deep enough to swim in. She wants me to learn her how. I'd take her up to the Scaldy, but that's a place for fellers really, not girls.'

His mother smiled, and Steve reflected that she was still a pretty woman even though she was old; Steve considered anyone past forty to be over the hill. But now he returned her smile gratefully as he began to lay the table. 'I'll go and get Kenny up if you like, and give him his breakfast,' he volunteered, but Moira Mickleborough shook her head.

'It's all right, lad. You deserve some time to yourself.

And while I'm about it, I'd just like you to know that though I've said nothing, that don't mean I've not appreciated the way you've behaved towards my Albert. Life will be easier for all of us, particularly now that Joe's followed your lead and started calling him Dad too. I'm real grateful to you, 'cos sometimes I've felt like a bone between two dogs, and that ain't a comfortable way to feel.'

Steve chuckled. 'I know what you mean; I've felt the same meself now and then. I won't wait for breakfast. I'll cut myself a carry-out now, with enough spare for Miranda.'

Ten minutes later Steve left the house with the food in his old school satchel and a bottle of water sticking out of the top. He approached Number Six rather cautiously, and was glad he had done so when the front door shot open and fat Vi Smythe appeared on the top step, with Beth hovering close behind her. She was in the middle of shouting for Miranda to come in at once and give a hand with the chores when she spotted Steve, and immediately switched her attention to him. 'You're that blamed iggorant Mickleborough boy, what used to keep company with me niece,' she boomed. 'Aye, you're a nasty piece of work as I remember. So where's Miranda got herself to this time? Not that you'll know, 'cos we've scarce seen either of you for the past week. But now you're back from wherever your mam's fancy feller took you, you might as well be useful. Tell me niece she's to come back here immediate, no messin', else I'll see she gets the thumpin' she deserves.'

Steve did not even answer, though he smiled to himself. If Miranda had not been around Jamaica Close, then he could hazard a pretty good guess where she had been. Not that he intended to give her Aunt Vi any clue. He simply shrugged his shoulders and strolled past Number Six as though he had not even heard the fat woman's shout. However, he paused outside Number Eight when he heard his name hissed in a low voice. Turning his head he saw Jackie Jones gesturing to him. 'I dunno if it's any help, but I seen Miranda goin' off around six o'clock, or even earlier, most mornin's,' the boy said. 'I'm helpin' Evans the Milk to deliver – he pays me a bob an hour – and Miranda goes off real quiet, slippin' out of the front door and closin' it softly behind her. She gives me and Evans a wave, then puts her finger to her lips so we knows as she means we've not seen her, like. Any clues?'

Steve grinned. Jackie was only a kid, but like everyone else in the Close he hated Aunt Vi and pitied Miranda. 'Thanks, Jackie; I guess I know where she's gone,' he said, and set off towards the main road, reaching it just as a nearby clock struck eight. Steve sighed. It would have been more fun had he and Miranda met at six o'clock so that he could have told her all about his wonderful week at the seaside. He felt a trifle peeved, since he had impressed upon Miranda the fact that the family would be returning to Liverpool on Saturday, and had hoped she might have called for him if she wanted to go to the garden. Still, he supposed it was asking too much to expect her to linger anywhere near Number Six and risk being nabbed, either by her aunt or even by Beth, who was not only a year older than her cousin, but taller and a good deal stronger as well.

'Boo!'

Steve jumped quite six inches in the air and turned wrathfully to give whoever had scared him a thump, only to find Miranda, grinning from ear to ear and looking so happy that he nearly gave her a hug. However, he did not do so, merely punching her shoulder lightly and saying: 'Well, well, well! So you *did* wait for me. It was nice of you to hang about when you might have been grabbed by your 'orrible aunt; and there was me thinkin' you'd forgot all about me!'

Miranda's whole face was lit up by an enormous happy smile and Steve saw that she, too, had a shabby satchel on her shoulder, which he guessed must contain food. As he fell into step beside her, he pointed to it. 'Don't say you nicked some grub off of that fat old cow! But won't she take it out on you tonight, when you go home?'

Miranda giggled. 'Who says I do go home?' she asked mockingly. 'Well, sometimes I do, but I make sure it's so late that my aunt's abed, and I leave so early that her snores are still lifting the roof tiles. At first I was afraid she'd twig that food left the house at the same time as I did, but since I only ever take bread and jam and a tiddy bit of lemon water or raspberry cordial, I suppose she thinks it's cheaper than having to feed me a hot meal each evening. And of course there's fruit in the garden; the raspberry canes are awfully overgrown but I pick a good cupful each day, and aren't they the most delicious thing you ever tasted? And there's strawberries, too, and apples, and plums . . . oh, all sorts.'

'Yes,' Steve said, 'but bread and jam and raspberries won't keep you goin' for ever. You ought to have hot meals now and then, you know.'

'I do; once or twice I've stayed in and told my aunt

I'd do her messages, help with the chores and so on, but only in return for a good meal.' She chuckled suddenly. 'You should have seen her face! She was that furious I was quite frightened to go back into the house; but to be fair to Beth, she backed me up. Why, she even helped me with the cooking, though she mainly fetched and carried; didn't want to get flour and fat on her nice clean hands! I'm getting to know her better, and she's all right, underneath. In fact if she ignored her mum we might even be pals. Anyway, working around the house helped the week to pass quicker, which was a good thing, 'cos I don't mind telling you, Steve, that time didn't half drag while you were away.'

'That's nice,' Steve said absently. 'But I guessed you'd been goin' to the garden each day . . . well, you must have been, 'cos where else would you get raspberries?' He hesitated, then asked the question uppermost in his mind. 'Have you been in the house while I was away? Have you – have you seen the ghost?'

'No-oo, but I've heard it,' Miranda said cautiously. 'In fact I wonder if there are secret passages in the house because I don't believe it is a ghost; well, ghosts don't eat, do they? The day before yesterday I put a slice of bread and cheese on the draining board in the kitchen, and yesterday when I went back the bread and cheese was gone. There wasn't so much as a crumb left, so if the ghost didn't take it, who did?'

'Rats,' Steve said succinctly. 'Or mice, I suppose.' He glanced over his shoulder. 'I don't know if you've noticed, but there's a most peculiar-looking little dog following us.' He chuckled. 'Half dog, half rabbit, half rat, at a guess. Shall I shoo it away?'

Miranda stopped short, broke off a piece of whatever it was in her satchel and held it out. The extraordinary little dog came timidly forward, glancing cautiously at Steve as it did so, then reared up on its hind legs and took the proffered titbit so gently that Steve thought it must have been trained to do so. Miranda turned to her pal. 'This here little dog is mine; I call him Timmy. He's bright as a button and knowing as a human. I don't know where he goes at nights, he must have found himself a quiet spot somewhere, but the minute I reach the main road he comes trotting out and joins me. He stays with me all day, wherever I go, but when we get back to Jamaica Close he disappears.' She glared defiantly at Steve. 'I know he's an odd-looking dog but I'm rare fond of him and he's rare fond of me. And he's extraordinarily polite; he waited to be invited before he would come into the garden. Why, if he hadn't been with me I don't believe I'd ever have gone into the kitchen and got to know the Voice . . .'

'The Voice?' Steve interrupted. 'Do you mean the giggler?'

Miranda sighed. 'I'll begin at the beginning and go right up to this morning, when I popped out and said boo,' she told him. 'Timmy attached himself to me the day after you went away, pretty well as soon as I left Jamaica Close, but I'm afraid I walked rather fast and because he's a stray and had been living on any scraps he could pick up he got terribly tired and terribly hot. His tongue hung out a yard and when I had a swig from my bottle of raspberry cordial I could see how thirsty he was. As you know, there's no pond or water tap in the garden, but there's a pump over the sink in the kitchen . . .'

She told her story well, even imitating the strange accent in which she had been addressed, and telling Steve she was sure the voice was a woman's, which made it hard for Steve to believe that she had imagined the whole thing. His own Uncle George, who was in the merchant navy, had once visited Jamaica, and when he came home had often imitated the accent of the Jamaicans he had met on his trip. Hearing that same accent on his pal's lips added authenticity to her story, and when she finished Steve whistled softly beneath his breath. 'You aren't half brave,' he said admiringly. 'You wouldn't have seen me getting into conversation with a perishin' ghost. I say, Miranda, has it occurred to you that there must be some connection between the Voice and the house itself? Why else should a Jamaican be living in Jamaica House?'

Miranda stared at him, her eyes rounding. 'How do you know it's called Jamaica House?' she whispered. 'I suppose you aren't a ghost yourself, come back to haunt the old place and me?'

Steve laughed. 'I see'd a picture in an old book – that were the name carved over the main entrance door, before they built the wall which divides the house from Jamaica Close. I didn't take much notice at the time because I didn't know about the slaves then, but now it all fits, wouldn't you say?'

Miranda nodded slowly. 'Yes, I suppose you're right. Tell you what, we'll ask the Voice. Sometimes questions make her either angry or sad, and when that happens she just goes away and won't come back, no matter how often you say how sorry you are. But I don't see why she should mind talking about the name of the house.' By now they were approaching the little door in the wall and as they went through it, with Timmy close behind them, Miranda said enticingly: 'But now you're here, Steve, you can hear her for yourself. In fact we might be able to trick her into showing herself with two of us. If I engage her in conversation and you sort of go behind where you think she is . . .'

Steve gave a strong shudder. He would do a lot for Miranda, but he did not mean to become part of a ghost hunt. He told himself it was not cowardly to be afraid of ghosts. If she had been a flesh and blood woman, as Miranda had seemed to imply, then that was one thing, but a ghost was different. He knew from his reading of such authors as Edgar Allan Poe, Charles Dickens and even Oscar Wilde that ghosts could do unexpectedly horrible things. Walking through walls, clanking chains and whisking a human being through time and space were but three of their accomplishments, and Steve had no wish to find himself mixed up in such goings-on. But Miranda was looking at him hopefully, so he decided to disillusion her at once. 'I won't go ghost hunting with you, or anyone else for that matter,' he said doggedly. 'I said I'd never go into that perishin' house again, and I meant every word. I've brung a bottle of water to drink and if you and that horrible little dog wants anything out of the kitchen you can get it yourselves; so there!'

Miranda moaned. 'Oh, please, please, please, Steve, help me to find out whether the Voice is a real person or a ghost,' she said urgently. 'I'm not afraid of going into the house any more because Timmy always runs ahead of me now, with his tail wagging. I'm sure she's a real person, and I'm sure it's she who ate the bread and cheese. If only you'll give it a try . . .'

'Just you shut up and listen to me for a moment,' Steve said crossly. 'Suppose it was a real person who took the bread and cheese? If that's so, then how has she been living for the past goodness knows how many weeks on just one piece of bread and cheese? I don't believe she's ever picked any fruit in the garden since we've been coming here – or at least not enough to notice. So go on, tell me. How is she keeping alive?'

Miranda stared at him for a moment while a pink flush crept up her cheeks, then she stamped her foot, took the satchel off her shoulder and slung it down on the grass. Steve noticed that the garden looked a good deal tidier than it had done when he had first entered it, many weeks ago. He asked Miranda if it was her doing, which made her smile. 'Are you saying we're like Mary and Dickon in *The Secret Garden*? If so, you're wrong. Oh, I've done a bit of tidying, rooting out the weeds and clearing a path through the nettles so that I can reach the door without being stung to bits.' She looked around her thoughtfully. 'Do you know, I've not noticed, but you're absolutely right. Someone *has* been tidying up the garden. Well, I'm sure it's not someone from outside, so it must be the Voice. And if you've ever heard of a ghost who did gardening on the side, it's more than I have. Doesn't that convince you that the Voice is real?'

Steve shrugged, then grinned. 'You've got a point,' he admitted. 'And I'll come into the kitchen with you – maybe even further. But if someone starts giggling or walking through walls, or interfering with me in any way whatsoever, I'm off. Is that understood? Oh, and the dog has to go first, because dogs can sense things and if there was a ghost I reckon he'd bolt out of the kitchen howling like a banshee with his tail between his legs.'

Miranda beamed at him. 'And then, when we've both heard the Voice, we'll come out into the garden again and have our carry-out whilst you tell me all about your holiday,' she said. 'Oh, I meant to tell you. If you go into the big trees right up against the wall there's a swing. It's quite safe, I've tried it, and because it's beneath the shade of the trees you get a lovely cool breeze when you swing.'

Steve stared at her, then followed the direction of her pointing finger. It wasn't a proper swing, just a length of very thick rope with a couple of knots around a somewhat dilapidated piece of plank. But it was a swing all right, and Steve was pretty sure that it had not been there on his previous visits. He opened his mouth to say as much, then shut it again and caught hold of Miranda's hand. 'Come on then,' he said cheerfully, pulling her up the path towards the door. He would not have admitted it to Miranda for the world, but the sight of the swing, such a very mundane object, had reassured him as to the nature of the Voice. A ghost would not – could not – erect a swing, but a real person would only do so in order to encourage young people such as himself and Miranda to continue visiting the garden. What was more, Miranda had said it was not she who had attacked the weeds, and in his experience she was a truthful girl and unlikely to tell an unnecessary fib.

She was smiling at him, clearly delighted by his change of heart. 'I'm so glad you're going to come into the house with me; I'm sure you won't regret it,' she said eagerly. 'I've got a good feeling about today; today I think we shall find out why the Voice hides away in the old building and disappears whenever I ask a question which she doesn't want to answer.'

By this time they had reached the door and Miranda pushed it open, whereupon Timmy the dog trotted fearlessly into the darkened kitchen, then looked over his shoulder as if to ask why they were so slow. The three of them walked into the middle of the room and waited for a moment. It was pretty clear that Miranda, and Timmy the dog, expected something to happen, but nothing did, so Miranda crossed the floor and pulled open the door which led to the pitch black hallway, which was the only way to reach all the other rooms in the house. Despite himself, Steve felt a pang which, if not of fear, was definitely of discomfort. Miranda, however, seemed completely at ease. She put her head back and called softly. 'Coo-ee, where are you, Voice?' There was a soft chuckle and despite himself Steve felt the short hairs on the back of his neck bristle like a dog's hackles, but then, as his eyes began to get used to the dark, he thought he saw a slight movement.

'So you have come to visit the lady of the house; I real pleased to welcome you,' the Voice said, and Steve clung even tighter to Miranda's small delicate hand. 'But let us introduce us. I know dog is Timmy, and my friend is Miranda, but who you, boy?'

'I'm Steve Mickleborough,' Steve said awkwardly, and to his complete astonishment he suddenly saw hovering in front of him what looked like a half-moon of white in the darkness. It was so startling, so unexpected, that he gave a squawk of fright and jumped backwards, but Miranda, who had also gasped, suddenly broke into delighted laughter.

'You aren't a ghost, nor just a voice, you're a Cheshire Cat grin,' she said triumphantly. 'Open the shutters so we can see each other properly; you've had your fun, Voice, but it's time you came clean.'

The grin disappeared, if it was a grin, and for a moment Steve thought that the Voice had left the room, possibly annoyed by the fact that she was no longer a mystery to her two guests. But then one of the shutters creaked back a couple of inches and in the sunlight which poured through the gap Steve saw that the mystery woman was black as coal, and dressed entirely in black as well. Liverpool being a port, Steve was well used to the sight of black seamen roaming the streets. They were friendly and much addicted to the markets, where they spent lavishly on all sorts of strange objects. But by and large these visitors were men, whereas the person smiling uncertainly at them in the shaft of sunlight was most definitely a woman. She was tiny, even smaller than Miranda, and very skinny, which Steve thought not surprising considering that she must have been existing on any scraps she could find, plus a bit of fruit from the garden. Her face was wrinkled, her nose hooked, but her eyes twinkled at them and Steve was sure she was enjoying their surprise, and was even more sure of it when she grinned again. Her thin black hair was pulled into a tight little bun at the nape of her neck but Steve could not guess her age, though he thought she must be very old, fifty or sixty at least.

As soon as the light had entered the room, Miranda had bounded forward and seized the woman's hands in both of hers. 'So *that's* why we couldn't see you, and thought you were just a voice; we never thought you might be black,' she said. 'Do let's go into the garden to talk, though, because the house is awfully musty and I'm afraid if we start to open the shutters . . .'

'No,' the woman said quickly, shutting the one she had opened and plunging them into darkness once more. 'People come lookin'; mebbe he come again . . . at night-times I bolt doors and shutters. He not know I here, but if he did . . .'

She stopped speaking, looking anxiously from one face to the other, and Miranda spoke quickly, keen to calm any fears which the older woman might feel. 'It's all right, Voice, we won't touch the shutters. But who are you afraid of? No one comes here, do they? Well, not in daylight anyhow. So let's go outside, shall we? Oh, by the way, you know our names, but what's yours?'

As she spoke Miranda had been leading the way out of the dining room, through the kitchen and into the bright sunlight, to the place where she and Steve usually ate any food they had managed to bring with them. It was a long stone seat, set in a curved alcove in the great brick wall, and was a delightful spot. One could sit in the full sun on the right-hand side of the seat, or take advantage of the shade cast by an ancient cherry tree on the left-hand side. The three of them sat down and Miranda and Steve looked hopefully at their companion. 'Go on, what's your name?' Miranda repeated eagerly. 'It's not a secret, is it?'

The woman shook her head, flashing them a small, rather embarrassed smile. 'I Melissa. My family call me Missie, but men on ship call me Ebony.' She pulled a face. 'They meant to insult, but why should I care? In my own head I call them ruder names. Cap'n Hogg, I called Pig . . .' she chuckled, 'but you can call me Missie, as my children did.'

Miranda turned to Steve. 'Get out the grub and we'll divide it three ways; I'm sure there's plenty. And while we're eating, Missie can tell us her story.'

'And we'll tell her ours,' Steve said rather reproachfully. He was older than Miranda and had been the one to introduce her to Jamaica House, so he thought it should be he who took the lead, and decided to start with the question which fascinated him most of all. He produced the pile of jam sandwiches, oatcakes and cheese from his satchel and handed them round. Then he addressed Missie directly for the first time.

'If you don't mind me askin', what have you been livin' on all this while? You've been here ages to my knowledge, so what have you had to eat? Oh, I know there's fruit in the garden, but that hadn't even begun to ripen when I first found the place, and you were here then. I went into the kitchen and heard you giggling . . .'

Their new friend laughed. 'I saw you run like rabbit,' she said cheerfully. 'At first I scared you was Cap'n Pig, but when I saw you were stranger, I pleased and gave little laugh.' She repeated the giggle which had so frightened Steve the first time he had heard it. 'When you ran off, I thought I do it again if bad men come.'

Steve nodded wisely. 'Yes, I quite see that your giggle would put most people off exploring any further. But you still haven't said how you've been keeping body and soul together.' He saw her puzzled look, and rephrased the question. 'What've you been eatin'? Where did your food come from? You can't have existed on fresh air, nor on the odds and ends the factories chuck out.'

Missie glanced uneasily from one to the other, and Miranda gave Steve a scowl, before saying: 'You needn't tell us if you don't want to, Missie, only it seems so strange . . .'

'In summer, big factory leave window open just tiny bit. When it really dark and no one about, I get in to room where food is. I never take much, just a little.'

'What about winter? Or when someone notices and closes the window?' Steve asked. 'What do you do then?'

'I used to go down to docks and take from ships, or from boxes waiting collection,' their new friend said promptly. 'But better tell you my story from start.' She smiled at them both. 'I been here for many months, have seen seasons come and go, yet you first to come here in all that time.'

She looked enquiringly at them, but Steve shook his head. 'Go on,' he said firmly. 'Right from the very beginning, so that we truly understand.'

Melissa finished off the oatcake she had been eating, drew a deep breath and began. 'I come from small island in West Indies and for many years I work as nursemaid or nanny to children of man who own more than half of island. I happy then, I love job, but plantation owners send sons to England to get good education when they old enough. I lucky because Mr and Mrs Grimshaw, my employers, had large family and I look after them as they arrived, from birth until they went to school in England. When last child no longer need me, I was given cottage on shore and pension.' She sighed reminiscently, and Steve saw that her liquid eyes were dark with tears. 'But I miss my children, so I decide to help at village school. Each day I walk to work . . .'

Missie proceeded to tell them how she had been walking along the shore on her way to the village when she noticed a ship anchored out in the bay, and a small boat being rowed ashore. The men on it had hailed her, asking for directions to the island's only port. Suspecting nothing, she had waited until they came ashore before beginning to explain how they must proceed. She had scarcely begun her explanation, however, when she felt a stunning blow on the back of her head which plunged her into darkness. When she recovered consciousness, the ship was at sea once more, and one of the men, the crew called him Cripple Jack because he had a wooden leg, told her that their cook had been washed overboard in a tropical storm and Captain Hogg had kidnapped her to do the work the drowned man had performed.

Missie had tried to escape and had only desisted when the captain had threatened to put her in leg irons; had he done so she would not have dared to jump overboard, knowing that she would sink like a stone. So she had promised obedience if only he would take her back to her home island when he returned to the West Indies. He promised, of course, but she very soon realised that he was not a man of his word and would do no such thing. There were still places where human beings could be bought and sold, and she knew herself to be a very good cook, and an efficient maid of all work. There were people who would be happy to have her services without having to pay her a wage. She realised she must escape as soon as an opportunity offered itself.

When the *Pride of the Sea* berthed in Liverpool, every member of the crew wanted to go ashore, for Liverpool was famous amongst seamen for its many markets and consequently many bargains. It fell to Cripple Jack to be left on board to keep an eye on Missie, and make sure she did not escape. But by this time Missie was familiar with the whole ship, for she had cleaned and scrubbed every inch of it, so when the ship was deserted, save for Cripple Jack and herself, she went to the captain's cabin and unlocked the cupboard where he kept his supply of rum. She filled a large glass almost to the brim with the spirit and took it out on deck, telling Cripple Jack that the captain had left the bottle out on his table and this was her private treat to herself.

He had immediately taken the glass from her hand and put it to his lips. She pretended to try to get it back, which made him drink all the faster. The gangway had been drawn up, but this was no bar to Missie. She waited until Cripple Jack's snores were deafening, then climbed nimbly over the ship's rail and with the aid of a loose rope lowered herself on to the quay, and simply disappeared amongst the crowds of people thronging the dockside.

Drunk with the success of her scheme, for freedom is a giddying experience after weeks of torment and imprisonment aboard a not very large merchant ship, she had trotted along, heading away from the docks. She meant to hide up somewhere until the *Pride of the Sea* had left the port, then return to the docks and stow away on any ship which was heading for the Indies. She had no money on her, of course, not so much as a penny piece, so she could not buy a passage, which was a great nuisance, since stowing away depended on her ability to find some nook or cranny where she would not be discovered. But that was for later; at present all that mattered was that she not be taken back aboard the *Pride of the Sea*.

She was some way from the docks and was wishing she had had the forethought to provide herself with some food, apart from the handful of ship's biscuits she had put into the pocket of her shabby black dress earlier in the day, when she heard a shout from behind her and, glancing back, saw the first mate pushing his way through the crowds towards her.

With her heart beating overtime she still retained enough presence of mind to knock over a box of fish awaiting collection, and saw the mate slip, try to regain his balance and then go down with an almighty crash, uttering swear words at which even the most broad-minded of seamen would raise startled eyebrows. Terrified, she had set off at her fastest pace and very soon had left the docks – and the mate – far behind, though by now panic had her in its grip. She was running from she knew not what; she simply knew that she would keep on running until her breath gave out.

It was then that she had spotted an old house with an overgrown basement and dived into the tangle of weeds and rubbish. She heard the pursuit go past but stayed in her hiding place, watching, as darkness fell and the moon came up. She saw many things, including drunken members of the crew, some accompanied by women, heading back towards the docks. Captain Hogg and his first mate had come last, but by then all thought of leaving her hidden nook had been forgotten in her anxiety not to be recaptured. Even her thirst had not been sufficient to drive her out of cover.

When eventually morning came and the danger seemed less, Missie had come out of her nook and continued to head away from the docks. She had rounded a corner and found herself amongst factories instead of houses. Missie could see nowhere to hide, but she had been pretty sure there was no need; by now the men would all be back on ship, and the *Pride* would be heading for the open sea.

Indeed, she had been beginning to relax when she had heard someone shout behind her. Her heart had redoubled its frantic beating and she had hurled herself at a huge ivy-covered wall, finding the door quite by accident and shooting through it. Then she had collapsed upon the waist-high grass, wriggling deep into cover and staring at the door as though it might presently open to reveal the entire crew of the *Pride of the Sea*, come to drag her back into captivity. Nothing had happened, however, and she eventually realised that the shout she had heard had had nothing to do with her. As the days passed she had grown more confident, though she only left her sanctuary after dark, and never lingered outside the great wall for longer than necessity dictated.

The soft, sing-song voice ceased, and Miranda and Steve stared at the old woman with considerable admiration, which Steve was the first to admit. 'Gosh, that's the most exciting story I've ever heard and you're brave as a perishin' tiger,' he told her. 'But why do you go outside the garden, Missie? Especially if you still consider it dangerous to do so.'

Missie grinned, a flash of very white teeth in her dark face. 'I need food,' she said simply. 'I only go out in dark. First I make sure Cap'n Pig's ship not there, because he bear a grudge and I worth money as slave. I also look for ship to take me home.'

'And you've not found one?' Miranda asked incredulously. 'Not in all the time you've spent in England?'

Steve was watching Missie's face; it was difficult to read her expression but he thought a look which could almost be guilt crossed her face. 'I have no money for passage; if I stow away I at mercy of captain. I too afraid.' She smiled, first at Miranda and then at Steve. 'That why I so happy when you came, and came again. I begin to tidy garden . . . once, you gave me bread and cheese. I want help yet dare not ask until I sure you good people and my friends.'

Steve and Miranda exchanged a doubtful look. Neither had any idea of how much a passage from Liverpool to the West Indies would cost but both thought it would be a great deal. However, if they could find a ship bound for the West Indies and explain to her captain how Missie had been kidnapped, then surely a man of principle would take the old woman back home? Steve said as much and Missie nodded vigorously. 'Yes, yes, but I need someone to speak for me. The *Pride of the Sea* cannot be only bad ship. If I tell wrong person, they could offer me passage then sell me at another port. I dare not, oh, I dare not!'

Steve and Miranda both nodded; in Missie's position, having suffered once from such treatment, they too would have hesitated to take any sort of risk. But Missie was gazing at them, her eyes bright with hope as she continued her story. It seemed that despite her desire to leave England she no longer visited the docks, realising that she might easily end up worse off if she asked for help from a smiling scoundrel. She pointed out, however, that her new friends might, with safety, haunt the docks during daylight hours and ask openly which captain, on a ship heading for the West Indies, was to be trusted to honour any promise he might make.

When Miranda suggested that Missie might write to her former employers, asking for their help, she pulled a doubtful face, explaining that she had been absent for so long that everyone would assume she had been taken by a shark, and would suspect a letter from a woman they had mourned for dead was a forgery by a confidence trickster wanting money.

'I see. Then of course we'll help,' Miranda said warmly. 'Though if you have to buy a passage, I don't know how we are to find the money. You see, ever since my mother disappeared more than a year ago, I've had to live with my aunt, who's not only poor but mean as well, and Steve here has a great many brothers and his parents need every penny to feed and clothe their kids.'

Missie's face, which had been full of hope, fell, but Miranda leaned forward and squeezed her hand. 'It's all right. I've a friend who's a policeman; he might be able to tell us . . .'

Missie gave a small shriek and reminded Miranda that she was here illegally, with no papers, no passport, nothing to prove her story true.

'Yes, of course,' Miranda said slowly. 'Then you have no choice but to stow away. If we can find a crew member who's willing to help you . . .'

'Someone like that would need paying, though,' Steve put in firmly. 'But I think you're right, Miranda. Missie's best bet is to leave as quietly – and illegally – as she arrived.' He turned to the little old woman, whose face promptly lit up with hope once more. 'Don't you know anyone from your home island who might be willing to give a fellow countrywoman a helping hand? Someone visiting England? What about those kids, the ones you said were sent to school in England once they were old enough to leave their family; would they help if they knew you were in trouble?'

'But if they're only kids . . .' Miranda began, only to be immediately interrupted.

'If they are at a boarding school in England, they must be at least as old as us, probably even older,' Steve said. He turned to Miranda. 'Have you an address for them?'

Missie's face, which had lit up with hope once more, fell. 'No, no address,' she said sadly. 'Master Julian and Master Gerald stay with uncle during holidays.'

Steve frowned. 'The autumn term starts in a few days, probably a week or two later for boarding schools. But we can scarcely search the whole of England for two boys when we have no idea of their address.'

Miranda leaned forward and stared hard at Missie's tired, lined little face. 'Think hard, Missie,' she urged. 'Haven't they ever mentioned a town or a city, or a street even? The Grimshaws must have mentioned something about it.'

Missie shook her head slowly. 'No, only that it's the Browncoat School . . .' She looked startled as Miranda and Steve gave a yell of triumph, and Miranda jumped up and grabbed Missie by both hands, pulling her off the stone seat and whirling her round and round until they both collapsed back on to the bench once more.

'Missie, that's all we need to know,' Miranda said breathlessly. 'The Browncoat School is famous, and it's no more than ten miles from Liverpool, which is probably why the Grimshaws chose to send their sons to it. Gosh, it looks as though we're on the right track at last. But will Julian and Gerald have enough money to buy you a passage home? Do they have some way of contacting their parents?'

Missie's face was one enormous beam, and at Miranda's question she nodded vigorously. 'Yes, yes; they can send what they call a cable. I'm certain all would be well. They are very good boys and will believe my story.'

Steve stood up. 'Right, then I think we should have a plan of action,' he said briskly. The best thing is to wait until we're sure term has started at Browncoats. Then we can go up to Crosby, which is only a bus ride away. You'll have to come with us, Missie, because otherwise we won't be able to recognise Julian or Gerald, and might start telling your story to the wrong people, which would never do. I think we should go up to the school a week on Saturday.' He scowled at Missie, who was vigorously shaking her head once more. 'Now don't say you're afraid that the crew of the *Pride of the Sea* might be lurking around the Browncoat school, because that's downright silly. They can scarcely kidnap you when you're with us and miles from the docks!'

But at the mere suggestion of leaving Jamaica House during daylight, Missie, who had been so brave, broke into floods of tears and begged them not to try to take her away from the only place she knew. Miranda and Steve begged, pleaded and argued, to no avail. Finally, Steve said, bitterly, that if she was determined not to go with them then she had better give an exact description of both boys, and also write an explanatory note which they could show Julian and Gerald if their own word was doubted.

Missie looked from one face to the other, then spoke hesitantly. 'There is a way that is used on my island to show what cannot otherwise be seen,' she said slowly. 'It is frowned upon by the Grimshaws and many others, but . . . are you willing to try? It – it is a sort of magic . . .'

'I'll try; I believe in magic,' Miranda said eagerly. 'What do I have to do, Missie?'

Missie smiled at her, but shook her head, 'Eldest first, is rule,' she said. 'Close eyes, Steve, and think of nothing; make your mind blank or think of blue sky, and little white clouds . . . then I show you Master Julian.'

As she spoke she placed both hands on Steve's temples and began to mutter, and presently, to the boy's astonishment, he saw a face. It was less a boy's face than that of a young man, with thick, light brown hair bleached by the sun, a high-bridged nose and light blue eyes. Startled, Steve gave an involuntary jump. Missie's hands fell from his head and he opened his eyes to see her staring at him anxiously. 'What you see?' Missie asked.

'I saw someone who looked a lot older than me, with very thick light brown hair and a scar just above his left eyebrow; I'd recognise him again because I suppose you might say he was very handsome,' Steve said. He stared hard at the small woman, who was now smiling triumphantly. 'How the devil did you do that, Missie? Did I really see Julian, or was it just my imagination working overtime?'

'It was Julian; he wearing his light blue shirt,' Missie said. 'Did you see shirt?'

'The one I saw was white and open at the neck . . .' Steve began, and Missie gave a crow of triumph.

'That's right, that's right; just testing;' she said, grinning broadly. She looked consideringly at Miranda. 'You see Master Gerald? Perhaps it best.'

Miranda began to say that she was longing to try, but Steve shook his head warningly. 'It made me feel sort of fuzzy for a few minutes,' he warned. 'Still, as Missie says, we ought to be able to recognise both boys. Close your eyes then, goofy; I won't tell you to make your mind a blank, because it always is.'

Miranda, who had closed her eyes, shot them open indignantly, then closed them again and sank back on the seat. Missie's small fingers touched her lightly on each temple and Steve watched with some interest, and listened too as the old woman began to mutter and to move her fingers gently in a circular motion on both sides of his pal's head. He was startled when Miranda suddenly shot upright, gave a scream and grabbed Missie by both wrists. 'I saw – I saw – I saw . . .' She had gone very pale, and her eyes kept tilting up in her head, so that only the whites showed. Then she sank back on the bench and covered her face with her hands.

Steve rounded on Missie. 'What have you done to her?' he shouted. 'What did she see that frightened her so? What have you done, you old witch?'

'I done nothing, 'cept think of Master Gerald and pass picture I see to Miranda,' Missie said. She looked as frightened, Steve realised, as he felt himself. 'I didn't do voodoo, just made picture.'

But even as she spoke, Miranda had taken her hands away from her face and was sitting upright on the bench and giving them both a watery smile. 'What's the matter? Did I startle you when I shrieked?' she asked. 'I'm so sorry, but it was such a surprise! I saw a boy with dark eyes and curly hair. Was that Master Gerald? Only he wasn't really a boy, I should think he was fifteen or sixteen.'

Missie nodded slowly. 'What colour be his shirt?' she asked, and just for a moment she sounded quite different.

'It was blue and white check.' As she spoke she got to her feet, swayed a little and then smiled reassuringly at Missie. 'I'm all right, don't worry, but I'd love to know how you work that particular sort of magic. Come to think of it, you could use it to show us the captain and crew of the *Pride of the Sea* so we'd know them if we met.'

Missie looked horrified. 'No, no; it might give them power over you. It strong magic. I only know a little of what my grandmother teach me, because when my mother found out she made Grandma promise to tell no more. But you know boys now, and will recognise them again.'

After they had left Missie, having helped her with the composition of a short note explaining the situation to the Grimshaws, Steve looked curiously at his companion. 'You needn't think you fooled me into thinking that the only thing you saw was that Gerald chap,' he said. 'You saw something that scared the life out of you, just for a moment. Come on, you can tell me.'

'Well, you know I've said quite often that I'm finding it difficult to remember my mother's face, and have to keep looking at her wedding photograph?' Miranda said at last. 'First of all I saw Gerald, plain as plain. It was odd, wasn't it? It wasn't so much like looking at a picture as looking at a real person. Behind his shoulder I could see a hill, and the branches of the trees were moving . . . really odd; quite spooky in fact.'

'What's that got to do with your mother's

photograph?' Steve said crossly. 'I take it you saw her . . . only how is that possible? Missie's never seen her, has she?'

'No, that's what makes it so very odd,' Miranda confessed. 'One moment I was looking at Gerald and the next there was my mother with a black shawl thing covering her head, and her face was white and her eyes were closed. Then, just as I was going to scream, she opened her eyes and smiled and her lips moved, and though I couldn't hear what she said I'm sure it was my name. And then I woke up.'

'Gosh, no wonder you looked sick,' Steve said prosaically. 'But it must have been your imagination . . . or maybe your mother was what you really wanted to see and perhaps Missie knew it, and kind of helped the picture to come into your mind.'

'I expect you're right, but it was bloody terrifying and I don't want it to happen again,' Miranda said firmly. She glanced behind her, then tutted. 'Look at me, expecting to see Timmy, when I know very well he stayed with Missie. They really seemed to like each other, didn't they?'

'Well, once we're in school he'd be at a loose end, so it's best that he stays at Jamaica House,' Steve said. 'I say, I don't know why but I feel most awfully tired. Let's blow tuppence on a tram ride home. We deserve it after the day we've had.'

They were in luck; the very next tram which came along took them all the way to Jamaica Close, where they went their separate ways, having agreed to meet early next morning. Miranda entered Number Six expecting her usual reception, but found the house deserted, and the fire out. Sighing, she went to the pantry to get herself some bread and jam, and found a note propped against the meat safe. *Gone to Seaforth Sands to visit Great-aunt Nell. Bread in the pantry, water in the tap.*

Miranda pulled a face. Trust them to go off to visit her favourite great-aunt without a word to her. She guessed that Aunt Vi and Beth had planned to do this deliberately and decided that she wouldn't bother with the bread and jam, but would go straight to bed. She had told Missie and Steve that she believed in magic, but she had not really meant it, and the sight of her mother's face, so pale and strange, had upset her deeply. Now all she wanted was her bed, and she felt pretty sure that it was Missie's so-called magic which had worn her out.

Without even bothering to take a slice off the loaf she made her way upstairs. In the shared bedroom she glanced with distaste at the rumpled sheets, and at the clothing slung carelessly down on the dirty linoleum. She knew they would expect her to hang up clean clothes and carry dirty ones down to soak in the sink until she had time to wash them properly, but she did neither of these things. She made the bed as respectable as she could, undressed and put on her nightgown, then rolled into bed and was asleep within seconds.

Immediately, she dreamed.

She was on a beach of wonderful golden sand. Tiny blue waves, white-fringed, hissed softly at her feet, and when she glanced behind her there were great palm trees which she recognised from pictures she had seen in books. It was beautiful, but lonely. She walked into the sea until it covered her knees; it was warm as milk, and when she looked through the clear depths she could see beautiful shells and tiny fish. She would have liked to go deeper, for since this was a dream she should be able to swim, an activity which she had never tried in real life, but something stopped her. She was on this beach for a purpose, she felt suddenly sure, and that purpose did not include testing her ability to swim. Reluctantly, she returned to shore and saw two people strolling along the hard wet sand, heading in her direction. She glanced curiously at them, and when they were within a few yards was suddenly sure that the woman was her mother. Impulsively she began to run, shouting: 'Mum! Arabella! It's me, Miranda!'

As she got closer she realised she was being completely ignored, and when Arabella's eyes met hers their expression was that of a total stranger. Pain stabbed Miranda like a knife even as her mother became as insubstantial as mist and disappeared.

Miranda found herself sitting up in bed, her cheeks wet with tears, just as the bedroom door burst open, and Aunt Vi and Beth entered the room. They took no notice of Miranda, but began to undress, talking excitedly about the day they had enjoyed, the trip on the overhead railway, the dinner they had bought themselves at the café near the Sands and the wonderful tea provided by Great-aunt Nell.

At this point Vi seemed to notice her niece for the first time. 'The old gal axed after you, seemed downright upset when I told her you'd bobbied off with some young feller rather than visit her,' Aunt Vi boomed. 'Still 'n' all, you can take yourself off to the Sands whenever you've a mind, if you can find up the money for the train fare. Except, as I telled her, you'd probably rather spend your time with a dirty thievin' young feller than with a borin' old lady.'

Miranda, still scarcely awake and still fighting tears, muttered something and hunched a shoulder. A couple of weeks previously Aunt Vi had decided that, because Beth was growing so rapidly, three in a bed was no longer possible. She had bought – second-hand of course – an ancient camp bed, provided it with sheets and blankets and told Beth that it was her new sleeping place. Beth, however, had objected vociferously, saying that her feet stuck out at the end, the covers were insufficient and she was darned if she was going to even try to sleep in such discomfort. Nothing loth, Miranda had willingly swapped with her and in fact much preferred the small creaky bed, with its inadequate bedding and rusty framework, to the big feather bed where Aunt Vi took up most of the room and Beth the rest.

So Miranda cuddled down once more and tried to wonder why, in the dream, her mother had not seemed to recognise her. When Arabella had first disappeared Miranda had dreamed of her practically every night and always in these dreams her mother's loving smile had warmed and comforted her. Sometimes they had hugged, sometimes exchanged stories of what had happened to them since they had last met, but always there had been warmth and affection flowing like a stream of happiness between the two of them. And the background to those dreams had been familiar, real; no golden sand or tropical skies. So why had this dream been so different? It was not only that her mother had looked straight through her, it was the unreality of the scene in which the dream had taken place. Looking back she realised that there had been something odd about both the shore and the sea itself. Screwing up her eyes she tried to recreate the scene.

At first it was difficult but then, all of a sudden, it came to her. The palm trees looked like cut-outs, the little waves like puffs of cotton wool, and the shells she had seen through the water were, she suddenly realised, the ones on her mother's theatrical make-up box. Despite herself, Miranda gave a relieved little smile. She did not understand why she should dream what amounted to a stage set, but it must mean that her mother, appearing not to recognise her, was as false as the setting.

Satisfied that the dream had come merely because Steve, Missie and herself had been discussing tropical islands, she turned her face into the pillow, and by the time her aunt and her cousin had stopped gloating over their day out she was fast asleep.

She did not dream.

Chapter Five

When term started, Steve and Miranda walked to and from school together, discussing many things, for, as Miranda told herself, she had no secrets from Steve. Naturally enough they talked a good deal about ways of contacting Julian and Gerald, and wondered how Missie was getting on. They guessed that she would have been out foraging each night, for now she had to feed not only herself but also Timmy, and though Miranda thought that this was rather hard on the old woman Steve disagreed. 'Having something to look after – or perhaps I should say somebody – is just about as good as being looked after yourself,' he told his friend. 'You mark my words, young Miranda, Missie will see that Timmy gets the best of everything, which means that she'll eat better herself as a result.'

'I don't see that,' Miranda objected. 'Dogs can eat raw fish, dirty old bones, scraps of food a person wouldn't look at twice.' She giggled. 'I can just picture Missie lying under the stone bench in the garden sharing a dirty great marrow bone with our little dog.'

Steve laughed too. 'Ah well, you may be right,' he conceded. 'By the way, I reckon the Browncoats have probably started classes again by now. The bus fare won't be more than a couple of bob and we've both got savings stashed away at Jamaica House, so I think we ought to go up to Crosby this coming Saturday. Have you any plans? If your aunt wants messages you'll have to slip out and let your cousin Beth do some work for once.' He raised his eyebrows. 'Where is she, incidentally? I've not seen her around since term started, come to think.'

Miranda grinned. 'Two reasons. One is that she's actually got herself a job! It's a big house on the outskirts of Speke and Beth has to be there quite early in the morning. She's a great one for her bed, which makes me wonder how long she'll stick it. She has to take a tray of early morning tea up to the old lady and help her to dress, and then she has to clean the house, cook some sort of meal at midday and take the old lady out in her wheelchair anywhere she wants to go.'

Steve whistled under his breath. 'What's the money like?' he enquired with his usual practicality. 'And how the devil did she get such a job? I've heard my mam talking about girls going into service, but usually it's live-in.'

'Well, I'll tell you, though it's rather complicated,' Miranda said. 'Aunt Vi's pal, Flo, worked for old Mrs Seymour for years and she always did it as a day job because when she started the old lady's two sons still lived with her. Ned and Barry Seymour took it in turns to bring Flo to their mother's house, though she had to make her own way home. Then the boys married and moved out, and Flo discovered the sort of money that she could earn at one of the new factories making uniforms and that for the forces. She's a marvel with a sewing machine, is Flo. She knew her job at the big house was an easy one, knew that the moment she said she was quitting there'd be a queue of applicants a mile long, so the day she gave in her notice she took Beth with her and recommended her for the job, suggesting that Beth should work there on a month's trial. The old lady was only too pleased to take Beth on since Flo had given her a good character, so that's how it happened. The only difference is that she makes her own way to and from the village; when Flo started working there there were no early buses, but there are now. And guess what . . .' Miranda giggled. 'The other reason you haven't seen her is that she's got a boyfriend. Met him on the bus going to her new job, and discovered that he was employed a couple of days a week to help in the garden. It's huge, and very well kept, Beth says. And he asked her to go to the flicks with him one evening after work, and bob's your uncle.'

Steve stared, then pretended to faint. 'What sort of feller would go for a great lumpin' girl like Beth?' he demanded.

Miranda chuckled. 'Now she's got a boyfriend Beth washes her hair once a week, same as everyone else, and means to spend her wages on nice clothes and make-up.' She sighed. 'I wonder what it's like to have a boyfriend? I wouldn't go wasting the ready on make-up or frocks, though. I'd buy cakes and ice cream and pork pies and sausage rolls . . .'

By this time they were nearing their school and Steve gave her a friendly punch in the ribs. 'You have got a boyfriend. What d'you think I am?' he asked plaintively. 'Don't I walk you to school, take you to the Saturday rush at the Derby cinema, mug you to a sticky bun when I'm in the money . . .'

Miranda gave a scornful snort. 'Huh, you're my pal

– my bezzie if you like – but you ain't my boyfriend. And Beth's feller is Spotty Wade; you must know him. When we were in primary they called him Tadpole because he had such a big head for such a little body, but now he's just fat and spotty.'

'Well, you *are* my girlfriend . . .' Steve was beginning when the school bell sounded. 'Cripes. Let's gerra move on, chuck, 'cos it'll look bad on my report if I'm late,' he said, breaking into a run as he spoke. 'Is it agreed then? That we go up to Crosby this Saturday – day after tomorrer – and see whether we can still remember what them two boys look like?'

'Are you certain the Browncoats are back, though?' Miranda said a trifle breathlessly, running along in Steve's wake. 'We'll look awful fools if we get up there and find the school's still closed – or worse, that the boys are kept on the premises even at weekends.' By now they had reached the school gates and Steve paused in his onward rush to shake his head reprovingly at Miranda.

'What a one you are for raising objections and followin' the rules,' he said airily. 'I reckon the lad weren't born who couldn't escape from a school if he wanted to. And anyhow I've been to Crosby several weekends during term time and it always seems to me that the pavements are thronged with them boys. Still, I reckon we'd best gerroff early, so your aunt can't tie you to the kitchen sink, 'cos that would ruin our chances.'

Neither Aunt Vi nor Beth worked on a Saturday so the alarm was not set. However, Miranda was rudely awakened soon after seven o'clock by her cousin briskly pulling the covers off her sleeping form to the accompaniment of a shouted 'Gerrup, you lazy little slut!' which had Aunt Vi mumbling a protest.

Miranda was about to add her own objection to such treatment when she remembered that Beth was not the only one who wanted to be up betimes, so she rolled out of bed with no more than a mumbled protest, grabbed her clothes off the hook by the window and made for the kitchen. She then realised why Beth had woken her so crossly; whoever had been last to bed the previous night had failed to make up and damp down the fire in the range, with the result that it was almost out and one could not possibly boil a kettle, let alone make the porridge, until it was brought back to life once again.

From upstairs, Beth's voice reached her. 'Bring me hot water up as soon as you've got the fire going,' she shouted. Miranda heard their bedroom door crash open and saw Beth's round, pasty face appear at the top of the stairs. 'I'm meetin' Herbert early, so's we can have a day out.' She gave Miranda an ingratiating smile. 'Sorry I had to wake you kinda rough like, but I can't abide washin' in cold water and I want to look me best for Herbert. Yesterday I seen a dress in Paddy's Market what was only twelve 'n' six; it suited me a treat, so I bought it. Herbie's callin' at eight, so if you could just make me some sarnies I'll get meself washed and dressed while you're doin' it.'

'Okay, Beth. As it happens I'm goin' out myself so I'll put up a few sarnies for me as well,' Miranda said, pulling the kettle over the now briskly burning range.

Miranda enjoyed the bus ride out to Crosby, for though she knew the early part of the journey, the rest was strange to her. Steve chatted easily as they went, and told her that if they had time they might go down to Crosby beach and paddle in the long seawater pools which formed whenever the tide went out. He seemed confident that they would soon achieve their objective, which at this stage was just to identify the two Grimshaw boys. 'If we have a chance we'll suggest that they meet us another time to discuss Missie's plight,' he explained. 'But I don't think we should rush them, because they're bound to be suspicious of two total strangers trying to get them away from their schoolfellows.'

When the bus drew up in the middle of the small town, Steve and Miranda hopped off and turned towards the street where the school was situated, looking for brown blazers trimmed with gold braid with a very imposing crest upon the breast pocket. They saw boys large and small, boys fat and thin, boys who wore their caps tilted rakishly on the backs of their heads and boys who pulled them so far forward that they had to raise their chins to look before them. In fact after five minutes Miranda grabbed Steve's arm and pulled him into a convenient doorway. 'We're never going to find them, not if we search for a hundred years,' she hissed. 'There are hundreds of them and they all look exactly alike. Oh, if only Missie would come with us, finding them would be so simple. She could point them out and then go and hide herself somewhere . . .'

'Yes, but you know very well she won't come out in daylight, let alone travel on a bus which goes perilously close to the docks at times. And, you know, I don't altogether blame her. She had a real horrible experience with them men on the *Pride of the Sea*; it's only natural that she don't want to walk into trouble again,' Steve said.

'If only there were some sign that we could look for,' Miranda moaned. 'If one of them had a wooden leg or an eye missing . . .'

Steve laughed and gave her a friendly shove. 'Don't give up so soon, Miranda,' he urged. 'What do you remember about the pictures of the lads which Missie put into our heads? I'm sure Julian's hair was light brown and I think he had a scar above one eyebrow, and didn't you say Gerald had curls?'

'I can't remember,' Miranda wailed. She had been thrown completely off balance by the fact that, in uniform, all the boys looked so similar. 'All I really remember is the colour of his shirt, and . . . oh!'

A small group of boys was approaching them, the tallest two in earnest conversation which stopped abruptly as Miranda grabbed one of the boys' arm. 'Are you Gerald Grimshaw?' she asked breathlessly. 'I've a message for you from an old friend.' The other boys were staring at her curiously – one or two sniggered – and she felt a hot blush burning up her face, but continued to cling doggedly to her target's arm. 'You are Gerald Grimshaw, aren't you? It's – it's a private sort of message . . .'

But the boy was shaking her off and frowning, his cheeks also beginning to burn. 'I don't think I know you, young woman,' he said coldly. 'Good day.'

Miranda, feeling the most almighty fool, fished the sheet of paper upon which Missie had written her message out of her pocket and tried to thrust it into the boy's hand, but he evaded her. She thought that he had cold eyes and a superior expression and wished very much that she had asked Steve to speak to him. Then she remembered that of course he had not seen the same image as she, and fixed the cold-eyed one with her most pleading expression. 'I'm sure you are Gerald Grimshaw, aren't you? This letter is most awfully important; I promised the – the writer that I would hand it to you personally. Oh, please, please read it!'

The boy, however, clapped his hand firmly over his breast pocket so that she could not insert the letter. 'I'm *not* Gerald whatsit,' he said, and then snatched the paper from her, screwed it into a little ball, and dropped it down the grating at his feet. 'We aren't allowed to talk to girls, especially ginger-headed gypsies,' he said nastily. 'Please go away; if I were seen talking to you I should be in real trouble.'

Miranda, her whole face burning by now, dropped to her knees and peered through the grating, but the note had disappeared. Scrambling to her feet, she fired one parting shot. 'You're a nasty stuck-up snob!' she said furiously. 'I was only asking you to read a letter from someone you're supposed to be fond of. When I tell Missie how horrible you've been she'll be disgusted.'

If she had expected the boy to show some sign of interest when she spoke the name she was disappointed. He simply continued to walk, speeding up slightly, and when he had got well ahead poor Miranda gave vent to her pent-up feelings in a burst of angry tears. She turned back to where she had left Steve, but could not see him anywhere and for a moment sheer terror gripped her. Steve had provided the money for the bus fares and had the two return tickets in his pocket. To be sure, she had a packet of jam sandwiches in her own pocket, but she could scarcely use them to bribe a bus conductor to take her home. And she had played her cards all wrong! She should never have tried to engage Gerald – if indeed the boy had been Gerald – in conversation whilst he was with a group of his schoolmates. Now she had spoiled the whole thing and they would have to return to Jamaica House this evening with only failure to report. Of course, it was Missie's own fault for refusing to accompany them, but Miranda understood how she felt, particularly now she had been so comprehensively snubbed. But perhaps if they told Missie what had happened she would pluck up her courage and accompany them to Crosby on their next visit.

But right now Miranda had a problem of her own, and she was about to start searching for Steve when she saw him strolling along the pavement towards her, a broad grin on his face. 'You got lucky, didn't you?' he asked as they met. 'I saw you talking to that boy – was it Gerald? Apparently they're on their way to the school playing fields, so they've got teachers with 'em, keepin' an eye; I guess you didn't have time to explain much. Shall we follow 'em up to the playin' fields and wait until Gerald's had time to read the letter? I thought I saw you put it in his pocket. Hey up, what's the matter? Don't start cryin', you idiot! What have I said? You done well. I didn't see anyone who looked like Julian.' He took her hand and gave it a squeeze. 'Look, there's a seat by that monument. If you don't want to follow them now, then we might as well have a sit down while you tell me what's upset you.'

Miranda gave an angry sniff and knuckled her eyes

to get rid of the tears which were forming. It wasn't fair! She had done her very best, had tried to explain . . . and the boy had called her nasty names and refused to listen. She had put on her only halfway decent dress and had braided her hair into two thick plaits besides having a jolly good wash, yet he had called her a ginger-headed gypsy; oh, how she hated him! But the thought of having to admit her total failure brought the tears rushing back into her eyes and she realised she was in no state to approach the Browncoat boys again, even had she wished to do so, so she followed Steve to the bench and sat down beside him. Without further preamble she told her story, including the fact that the letter over which she, Missie and Steve had taken such pains had been thrown down the grid before she had a chance to rescue it.

She half expected Steve to say she should not have offered the letter until she was certain that the boy she had accosted really was Gerald, but instead he fished out of his pocket an extremely dirty piece of rag, pressed it into her hand and told her to mop up her tears. 'It weren't your fault; we should have remembered that uniform kind of changes people,' he said comfortingly. 'Of course we'll have to rewrite the letter – or get Missie to do so, rather – but at least it will be a case of repeating what the first letter said which will be much easier than writing a new one. And next time it might be best to go straight up to the playing fields and ask someone, quietly, to point out the Grimshaws, then wait until they've been bowled out or wharrever and ask for a quiet word. So cheer up, kid; we're all but home an' dry.'

Miranda gave a watery sniff. 'So it probably wasn't even a Grimshaw who chucked our letter down the drain,' she said. 'I'm an idiot, I am! What's that thing about rushing in where angels fear to tread? That's me, that is. But I'll make up for it next week, I promise.'

Steve cleared his throat and Miranda saw that he looked distinctly uncomfortable. 'Look, queen, you've been great, much braver than what I was, but next week I think I'd do better by meself. The teachers have got it into their heads that the boys shouldn't talk to girls . . . well, you told me that the boy you spoke to said he'd be in trouble if someone saw him with a girl. So I honestly think I'd stand a better chance if I came alone.'

Miranda sighed. She had not enjoyed her encounter with the snooty Browncoat boy, who had not only insulted her – ginger-headed gypsy indeed – but made her feel small. Yet even so she did not want to be left out of the adventure, if adventure it could be called. But Steve was looking at her anxiously, probably guessing how she felt, and waiting for her reaction, so Miranda forced a smile. 'I know you're right, so next Saturday I'll spend the day with Missie,' she said with as much cheerfulness as she could muster. 'I do hope we can get her away before winter comes, though.'

Steve looked doubtful. 'It don't do to rush things,' he said, pulling her to her feet. 'You're a grand girl, you are, so let's go down to the beach and have a paddle before setting off for home.'

I never expected it to be easy, but I never thought it would be this perishin' difficult, Steve said to himself as he approached the playing fields a week later. Missie had been bitterly disappointed that they had not managed to contact one of the Grimshaw boys on their first attempt, but when Steve had explained his plan she had agreed that it was a good one. Even so, she had been reluctant to write out the letter again. She thought it would be very much easier for Steve to persuade Julian and Gerald to come to Jamaica House so that they could see for themselves that she really was in Liverpool. Steve and Miranda, however, had explained that the boys were strictly guarded and must be convinced that Missie really needed their help before they would even begin to consider venturing so far from school.

Now, Steve knew that he was unlikely to be mistaken for a Browncoat boy as they marched through the streets towards their destination, but he thought it would be easier to mingle once they were in their sports gear. He had persuaded his mother to give him a short haircut, borrowed – without his brother's knowledge – Joe's Sunday shirt, and was wearing his most respectable kecks.

Once they reached the playing fields, there was a good deal of milling around and shouting and at one point Steve rather feared he might be picked for one side or the other, but they managed to get two teams together, with half a dozen boys left disconsolately on the sidelines, and it was one of these whom Steve approached. He was a short, red-faced, cheery-looking boy, and responded at once to Steve's friendly overture. 'Gerald Grimshaw is second row forward . . .' He pointed. 'He's in the upper fifth. His brother's in the upper sixth.'

'Which one is he?' Steve said quickly. 'I'd like a word with both of 'em, but I dunno if that's possible.'

The cheery one grinned. 'I can see you don't know much about the Browncoats,' he observed. 'We have the playing fields by years; today is upper and lower fifth, next Saturday will be upper and lower fourth, and so on. The mighty men of the sixth play midweek; they get much more freedom than the rest of us, so you might find it easier to have a word with Julian than with Gerald.'

'But I don't know him from Adam. I shan't be able to recognise him even if I could get up here during the week, which is real difficult,' Steve said miserably. He suddenly thought of the letter, and fished the folded sheet out of his pocket. 'Look, if you could get this to Gerald, he could show it to Julian and they could decide what's best to do.'

The boy took the sheet of paper rather gingerly. 'I reckon I'll have to read it,' he said apologetically. 'For all I know you might be telling him to blow up the Houses of Parliament, or to aim a rocket straight through the windows of the headmaster's study.' He laughed but raised his brows. 'But you don't know me from Adam either – I'm Henry Prothero, Hal to my pals. So – shall I read it, or shall I give it back to you so you can give it to Gerald yourself?'

Steve did not even hesitate. 'Read it!' he commanded. 'And if you can see any reason for not handing it to Gerald, you tell me here and now. It's a rather complicated story, though, and if you agree to pass on the letter I'll explain anything you don't understand.' The two boys had been standing on the sidelines, watching the game in progress, but now Hal jerked his head towards a clump of trees and bushes at the perimeter of the field.

'Let's go over there where we're less likely to be spotted,' he said. 'After the first half, those who didn't play to begin with have to swap with someone who's had a game already. I hate rugger – I hate most sports, actually – and Mr Elliot, the games master, knows it, so I'll be first substitute if he catches my eye.'

Steve followed his new friend into cover and watched with some interest as Hal spread out the sheet and began to read. Watching his face, Steve saw perplexity but no trace of disapproval, and when Hal looked up and grinned at him he raised his brows. 'Well? Do you feel you can pass it on to Gerald? Is there anything in it which worries you?'

Hal shook his head, then began to read the letter aloud.

'Dear Julian and Gerald, I trust you have not forgotten your old friend Missie. I write because I am in Liverpool, having arrived here without money or papers and thus with no means of returning to the island we all love. I know your parents would help me if they knew of my plight, but they are far away and you are near.

I am writing this letter to ask for your help and have entrusted it to my friend Steve. He and his friend have helped me write this letter and supported me, but it is to you I turn for the means to buy a passage back to the West Indies. I am living quietly but long to see you both and explain how I came to be here.

You know I would not ask for your help except in great need and I pray to God you have not forgotten your old nurse.'

'Well, what more explanation do you need?' Steve said rather impatiently, as Hal came to the end. 'She's not a young woman – Missie, I mean – and she needs their help to get home.'

'Yes, but how did she end up in Liverpool? Did she come to England to look for work?'

Steve took a deep breath, trying to sort out how best to explain, then decided that it was unnecessary. Instead, he smiled and nodded. 'That's it. But her new employers were unscrupulous and mean. When she told them she wanted to leave they confiscated her papers and wouldn't pay her the money they owed her. So my friend and I helped. But we don't have the money to get her a return passage to the Indies . . .'

He stopped speaking as Hal nodded understandingly. 'Ah yes, I see. She'll want papers, a passport and so on, which you obviously cannot provide. But I expect the Grimshaws' uncle could help there. He's an old Browncoats boy and I know he's a lawyer.' As he spoke he was refolding the letter and pushing it into his trouser pocket. 'I say, that poor woman! I'm sure the Grims will be glad to help. Gerry's a wizard fellow and Julian's okay, though he's the quiet studious type, unlike his brother. But how to get you together I really don't know, because apart from coming to and from the playing fields we can't officially leave the school premises, except for some definite reason.'

'Like what?'

'Oh, a trip to the dentist, a Scout meeting, or sometimes a special exeat to see a relative of whom the school authorities approve. Tell you what, when Mr Elliot blows the whistle I'll go straight across to Gerry, pass the letter over and tell him you're in the bushes. Maybe you can arrange something then.'

Steve was so delighted that he could have hugged the other boy but contented himself with uttering profuse thanks. 'You're brilliant, you are; I never thought I'd meet someone so willing to help,' he said. 'When it's all over and Missie has been seen off safely back to her island, then I'll tell you the whole story. I wish I could do something to repay you in the meantime, though.'

'I wish I could help you more,' Hal said, his rosy face split by a wide grin. 'Wish I had a relative in Liverpool and could go a-visiting a couple of times a term. I s'pose you couldn't arrange that?'

Steve pulled a face. 'I wish I could,' he said sincerely, 'but though my mam's a grand woman, I doubt your teachers would think her respectable enough to entertain a Browncoats boy. Still, I'll see what I can do.'

Just as they emerged from the bushes the whistle blew and Mr Elliot began charging about and shouting. Hal made his way straight to Gerald Grimshaw and gripped his arm. Steve did not actually see the folded paper change hands, but guessed that it had done so when Gerald's eyes turned in his direction and he began to nod. He walked off the pitch, exchanging remarks with the other lads, and presently he joined Steve and shot out a hand. Steve shook it, taking a good look at his new companion. Gerald Grimshaw was a hefty young man who looked more than his fifteen years. He had short curly hair which stood up all over his head, broad cheekbones and twinkling brown eyes, a thick neck and broad shoulders. He grinned, then fished the letter out of his pocket. 'Are you certain sure that the woman you've been helping is really our Missie? Melissa Grundy? Only when we were at Uncle Vernon's for the Easter vac he told us that Missie had disappeared in a bad thunderstorm on her way to help at the village school. The locals said she must have gone into the sea for some reason and been taken by sharks – it does happen, especially during a storm when they have what we call a feeding frenzy – but she was certainly no longer on the island. Her house was given to someone else, and it did seem as though something like a shark attack must have been the reason for her disappearance, because nothing was missing, not so much as a pair of shoes or a teapot. And there was no – no body.'

Steve pulled a face. 'She was afraid people would think that,' he said ruefully. 'But you'd better read the letter first and then I'll fill you in on what we felt was too complicated to try to put into writing.'

'Right,' Gerald said unfolding the paper. 'How did you come to know Hal, by the way? He's a decent chap, one of the best, but he comes from somewhere north of the border and doesn't have any friends outside school so far as I know.'

'Luck,' Steve said. 'Read the perishin' letter, or your teacher will blow the whistle and our chance to arrange another meeting will be gone. And Missie is very much alive, as you'll see.'

Gerald scanned the page quickly, whilst a slow smile spread across his face. 'That's the best news I've ever had, and it'll be the same for Julian,' he said happily. 'But look here, lad, it's been a long while since Missie disappeared. How the devil did she get to Liverpool? She don't know a soul here apart from us. Can you explain a bit more?'

'Well, I could, but I think it might be better coming from Missie herself,' Steve said rather apologetically. 'But Hal mentioned that you had a relative in the legal profession. I wonder why Missie didn't think of him.'

'Oh, she wouldn't,' Gerald said at once. 'She never knew him. He's a great gun. If anyone can sort out papers, passports and so on it's our uncle, and I'm sure he'll do it as quick as a flash when we explain that it's for Missie. They never met, but he knows all about her, of course. And now you'd best explain to me what she's doing in Liverpool.'

Steve hesitated. The more he thought about Missie's capture and slavery aboard the *Pride of the Sea* the less likely it seemed. He was sure that if he told the tale he would not be believed, or at any rate a listener would take it with a grain of salt, as the saying went. They had all agreed on this, even Missie, and tempting though it was to tell all to this cheerful and friendly young man, Steve decided he had better stick to their original plan. 'Look, I promised Missie she should tell her own story,' he said firmly. 'I'm here to arrange a meeting, if that's possible. For reasons she'll explain when you see her, she will only leave her refuge after dark.'

Gerald grinned. 'Yes, Missie always was a snappy dresser. She loved brilliant colours and exotic materials,' he said reminiscently. 'I suppose she would stand out like a parrot amidst sparrows in Liverpool, where people tend to wear black or dark brown.'

Steve sighed. This was going to be even more difficult than he had supposed. 'No, it's not like that at all. Missie wears the only clothing available to her, which is black and pretty much in rags. She wouldn't stand out at all in the area near the docks, but . . . oh dear, when you meet her you'll see for yourself. And honestly, it should be as soon as possible. My pal and I worry all the time that someone will start to take an interest in Jamaica House and Missie will find herself . . .'

'Jamaica House? Our family used to run a business of some description, in Liverpool, and I think their head-quarters were called Jamaica House – in fact I'm sure of it. So that's where Missie is holed up, is it? I've never seen it myself, the family haven't been involved in that particular trade for generations, but from what I've heard the house is little better than a ruin. Look, I don't know the way there but I do agree with you that we must meet Missie, and the sooner the better. Julian is a prefect, so though he would do everything in his power to help he won't want to break any rules.'

'In that case it might be best if you came to Jamaica House on your own, preferably after it's begun to get dark,' Steve said. 'Fortunately your brown blazers and grey kecks can look pretty anonymous, so if you take your cap off and get hold of a dark-coloured muffler you're unlikely to be spotted as a Browncoat boy. I guess you think I ought to bring Missie to you, but it would be really difficult. I'll tell you what bus to catch and which stop to get off at, and I'll meet you there and take you straight to Jamaica House. But can you get away? Without being caught, I mean.'

Gerald thought the matter over. 'If Hal covers for me after the supper bell – we're in the same dorm – I can be with you by say half past eight in the evening. Then I can spend an hour or so with Missie and still get back to the dorm before anyone has checked that it's me curled up under the covers and not my pillow.'

'Well, if you're sure, I'll meet all the buses from Crosby between eight and nine o'clock. If you're not on any of them, we'll have to think again,' Steve said. 'Now, do you need to know anything else? Missie felt that the letter she wrote might not be enough to convince you that we weren't playing what you might call an under-game, though why she would want to entice a couple of bleedin' Browncoats into a ruined house is more than I can tell you.'

He expected his companion to laugh scoffingly, but Gerald did not do so. 'Extortion,' he said briefly, then grinned. 'But you don't look the type to drag me off, chuck me into a cellar and demand a ransom from parents a thousand miles away. So you can tell Missie that one of us, at least, will be with her . . . what day did we say?'

Steve laughed. So that was what 'extortion' meant! 'We didn't, but what about Monday? Or would tomorrow be better for you?'

They were still discussing the details of their plan when Mr Elliot's whistle shrilled and the boys, both players and spectators, began to amble back towards the wooden building. Gerald started to follow them, turning at the last minute to say: 'Monday evening, eight to nine. Cheerio for now.'

Steve did not hang about until the boys were back in uniform once more, but set off immediately towards the nearest bus stop. He was elated with the success of his plan, and looking forward to Monday evening. He and Miranda had grown fond of Missie, but Steve realised more than ever now that she was a real responsibility. He worried that someone would spot her when she went down to the docks to pick up any food she could find. He worried she would be seen leaving or entering the walled garden, or that one of the factory workers might follow her into her retreat, or perhaps inform the scuffers that a vagrant had taken up residence in the old house.

No, though he and Miranda would miss her, the happiest outcome of their strange friendship must be that Missie should return to the West Indies and the home she loved.

As he climbed aboard the bus which would take him into the city centre, Steve remembered Timmy. He could not go with Missie when she left, nor could he stay at Jamaica House by himself. He could imagine the screams of outrage from her aunt if Miranda tried to introduce a dog into Number Six, and whilst his own mother and father were both easy-going and generous, they would say that they needed every penny they earned to feed and clothe their own family, and could not afford the luxury of a dog. But now that he was regularly fed, groomed and exercised, Timmy was an attractive little chap. I dare say Mum and Dad would take to him if I promised to pay for all his food out of the money I earn doing odd jobs, Steve told himself, moving down towards the back of the vehicle as it slowed at his stop. He jumped down and was delighted as well as surprised to find Miranda, hands in pockets, strolling idly up and down the pavement, with Timmy close at her heels. She grinned at him as he joined her.

'Fancy meeting you!' she said gaily. 'I guess it were you who got lucky this time, judging by your grin.' She drew him out of the hurrying crowd. 'Here, Timmy! Don't you go wandering off; the butcher gave me a lovely marrowbone for you, so just you stick close to your pals, and you shall have it, as soon as we reach home.'

Back at the old house, Missie was waiting anxiously for them, knowing that Steve had believed he would meet the Grimshaws today. Despite the chill in the air she was sitting on the curved stone bench in the garden, and jumped to her feet eagerly, her big liquid eyes full of hope. 'Did you meet my young gentlemen?' she asked. 'Oh, but I can see you did. Tell me! I expect you told Miss Miranda already; it good news, it written on your face.'

By the time Steve had finished his story it was getting dark and Missie led the way down the garden and into the kitchen. This was now a much cosier and pleasanter room altogether, for a small paraffin stove stood in the hearth and the three of them had brought comfortable cane chairs through from the rest of the house. Missie and Miranda had ransacked drawers, chests and cupboards, and the result was cushions, rugs, and old-fashioned cloaks, which they had hung over the shutters at the windows. There was also food; Missie had told them she had found a bakery whose workers at the end of the day threw out cakes and loaves which they felt were no longer saleable, so now the three of them settled down to eat and chat and to discuss the future. Miranda enjoyed the cakes, despite a lurking fear that Missie had probably stolen them. Well, so what? Everyone has to live, and a baker wouldn't go hungry because of the loss of a few sticky buns, a small loaf and some cake, whereas Missie must eat to live.

'So, Gerald is coming here on Monday to meet you, just to make sure that the letter isn't a cunning forgery,' Steve said. 'Then nothing much will happen until next Saturday, when Gerald and Julian get this exeat thing and go off to their uncle's house to tell him the story.' He turned to Missie. 'Would you go with them? I really think you should. After all, you'll be heading away from the docks, not towards them, and the chances of anyone recognising you are pretty slight. I know the village where the Grimshaws' Uncle Vernon lives; it's very quiet and rural, not at all the sort of place wandering seamen want to visit.' Missie looked doubtful but Steve, catching Miranda's eye, gave an encouraging smile. 'I think we must somehow provide Missie with more suitable clothing than the things she's wearing at present before she meets Mr Grimshaw,' he said tactfully. 'I know dark clothing is fine for raiding the docks but it really won't do for visiting Holmwood.' He turned to Missie. 'I'm afraid you'd be far too conspicuous.'

Miranda had not thought of it before, but now she nodded vigorously. 'Steve's right, Missie. But even if we go to Paddy's Market, we don't have the sort of money to buy a decent dress. Oh, if only we'd thought of it earlier Steve could have arranged to borrow some cash from Gerald. I suppose we could ask your mam if she could borrow us a skirt and blouse, Steve, but . . .'

But Steve was grinning, flapping a hand at her. 'I've a better idea. I've heard two of the lads talking about the big rubbish skips at the back of Paddy's Market. It's a sort of yard at the corner of Maddox Street and Bevington Hill. The stallholders chuck anything they think they won't be able to sell into the bins on a Saturday night and on Monday morning the dustcarts collect them and carry them away. But the lads say some of the stuff is quite decent. They go there Sunday nights and either cram a sack with rags to sell to the rag and bone man – Packinham's or King's – or pick out the best stuff and sell it cheap to anyone willing to buy. If Miranda and meself nip down there tomorrow night with a couple of sacks, we can either help ourselves to anything we think will fit you, Missie, or we can fill the sacks and sell the stuff next day, like the fellers do, and by a dress wi' the gelt.'

'I'm surprised no one's twigged what's going on,' Miranda said, giggling. 'If old Kingy only knew, he'd cut out the middle man and go straight to the rubbish bins himself. He's far too mean to want to part with his money needlessly.'

Steve laughed too. 'You're right there. The fellers were sayin' someone were bound to find out soon, but I reckon if you and me go as soon as it gets dark tomorrow night, Miranda, we'll clean up.'

Missie beamed from face to face. 'Shall I come too?' she asked eagerly. 'I know where Paddy's Market is, on Scotland Road. I been there often.'

Both Miranda and Steve shook their heads firmly, however. 'No, Missie. You'll have to trust us to pick something respectable,' Steve said firmly. He gestured to Miranda. 'Time we were off. With a bit of luck your aunt and Beth will be in bed by the time you get home, and won't start asking questions.'

They said their farewells and made their way out to the main road to catch a tram back to Jamaica Close. As Miranda had expected, Number Six was in darkness, so she said goodbye to Steve and crept quietly to her bed.

Next day, in order to lull any suspicions that her aunt might be harbouring, she helped prepare and cook Sunday dinner and spent the rest of the day cleaning the house. Aunt Vi, coming in through the back door and narrowly avoiding the bucket of water with which Miranda was scrubbing the kitchen floor, swore loudly and would have given her a cuff, except that Miranda ducked and raised her brush threateningly. Aunt Vi took evasive action, grumbling as she did so. 'What ails you, you miserable little bugger? If you want to clean the place up you should do it on a Saturday. I'm in me best coat and shoes; if they've got splashed I'll know who to blame.'

Miranda finished the floor with a final swirl of her cloth and stood up. 'I'm always busy on a Saturday, earning meself a few pence, so if you want floors scrubbed and cooking done it's got to be on Sunday,' she said firmly. She glanced at the clock above the mantel, which was showing five o' clock. 'I'm off now, Aunt Vi. I won't bother to stay for tea.'

Vi had been heading across the kitchen, clearly intending to go to her room and change out of her decent Sunday clothing, but at her niece's words she stopped in her tracks. 'You're going nowhere, not unless you tell me what you're up to . . .' she began, but Miranda was already out of the back door and hurrying across the yard. Heading for Steve's house, she felt quite excited. If they could acquire a decent skirt and some sort of blouse, Missie would be able to meet Mr Grimshaw, and then it was just a matter of time before her troubles would surely be over.

Chapter Six

Despite their hopes it was almost a month before the Grimshaws managed to arrange to take Missie to Holmwood, and Missie insisted that Miranda and Steve should accompany them. 'I shall want Mr Vernon to meet my friends,' she said firmly. 'We shall be respectable group, all in Sunday things, and Mr Vernon will arrange my passage home at once.'

Sitting on the bus which would take them to Holmwood, Miranda thought back over the past four weeks. The raid on the rubbish bins had started it, she thought, and that had not been all plain sailing by any means. For a start, it had begun to rain as they arrived at their destination, heavy rain which soon had both Steve and herself soaked to the skin, and had made the clothing they had crammed into their potato sacks extremely heavy. They had intended to select respectable garments both for Missie and for Miranda herself, but they soon abandoned that idea, simply filling their sacks with any clothing they could reach, for the bins were huge and deep. They had been heading back towards the big wooden double doors which led on to the road when these had creaked open and four boys, all a good deal larger than Steve, had shouldered their way in and stopped, staring with disbelief at Steve and Miranda.

Steve had tried to push past, but the biggest boy had

shoved him in the chest and kicked the door shut behind him. 'You ain't goin' nowhere, Steve Mickleborough,' he had said gruffly. 'You've been listenin' at doors you have, you sneaky little bastard. Me and the fellers ain't told no one about this here back yard so you'll hand over them sacks and clear orf before I clacks you so hard you'll be asleep for a week.'

'Aw, come on, Muffler, there's plenty for all of us,' Steve had wheedled. 'As for listenin'. . . well, I admit I did hear someone say as how the yard door wasn't locked, but you can't call that listenin', exactly . . .'

The large boy had given a scornful laugh. 'Oh no?' he had said jeeringly. 'I'll call it what I bleedin' well like, and I say you've been earwiggin'.'

But Miranda, seeing that the other three boys were already digging into the bins and shouting to their leader to get a move on so that they could get out of the perishin' rain, had sneaked round behind Muffler, pulled open the door, screamed to Steve to follow her and set off at a gallop. Her loot had been fearfully heavy and she might easily have been caught had not Steve swung his sack at Muffler's legs, causing him to crash to the ground. Horrified, for she guessed that Muffler would take it out on her pal next time they met, Miranda had hesitated, wondering whether she ought to help the big fellow to his feet and let him have her sack of clothing, but Steve had had no such qualms. 'Gerra move on, you idiot, and don't you *dare* leave that sack behind,' he had screamed, clearly guessing her intention. 'If we get a fair sum from old Kingy, I'll give Muffler a couple of bob to keep him sweet. Come *on*, Miranda Lovage!'

Soaked to the skin and fighting a wild desire to burst

into tears, for the rain had been so heavy that she could scarcely see more than a few feet ahead, Miranda had obeyed. She was panting and breathless, but when they reached Jamaica Close and lugged their sacks round the back jigger and into Steve's yard they had both been grinning. They knew they would have to dry the clothes out before they could present them to be weighed at the rag and bone man's yard, but that could be dealt with the following day. They had pushed their sacks into the shelter of the coal shed, exchanged promises to meet as usual the following morning, and made their weary way up to bed.

It had taken longer than they had anticipated to dry everything out because Monday and Tuesday had also been wet, but by Saturday it was dry at last and, as Miranda remarked, it was also very, very clean. They had sold most of it, save for a grey pleated skirt and a green jumper for Miranda, and then they had gone to a stallholder in Paddy's Market who was a friend of Steve's mother, who had agreed to lend them both clothing and shoes in different sizes, so that Missie might choose which she felt suited her best. Then Steve had returned to the market with the unwanted garments while Missie peacocked about Jamaica House, admiring her reflection in the long cheval glass in one of the bedrooms, and persuading Miranda to brush out her greying black hair and braid it into a coronet on top of her head.

'You look like a queen, dear Missie,' Miranda had said, astonished at what decent clothing and a new hairstyle could do for their little friend. Now, as Missie sat between Steve and Miranda on the bus, she presented quite a respectable appearance. Oddly enough, she seemed to have cast all her worries and doubts to one side, and had climbed aboard the bus quite merrily, chatting away to Miranda and Steve, though she did keep her voice very low, and appeared to be eager not to stare at her fellow passengers. The Grimshaw boys, who were already aboard, had grinned at them, but they had arranged not to join forces until they reached Holmwood, where Vernon Grimshaw and his family lived. No matter how respectable she, Steve and Missie might appear in their own eyes, she guessed that folk would stare to see two Browncoat boys in such odd company.

Soon the bus was drawing to a halt and Julian and Gerald were getting up from their seats, so the others followed suit. It was not raining, but the sky was overcast, and as Miranda alighted from the bus she looked around her with interest. They were in a village street with half-timbered thatched cottages on either side of the road, several of which were small shops. Miranda saw a black-smith's, a bakery and what looked like a post office, but Steve was catching her hand, pulling her forward to where Missie and the boys stood. 'We'd better introduce ourselves,' he said briskly. 'Gerald we know, but . . .' he grinned at the older of the two boys, 'my vivid intelligence tells me that this tall feller must be Julian. Am I right?'

Everyone smiled; Julian nodded, but looked around him rather uneasily. 'We're a bit obvious standing about in the middle of the village street,' he observed. 'Let's wait until we reach Holmwood Lodge.' To Miranda's astonishment, he bent down and kissed Missie's cheek. 'It's grand to see you alive and well, dear Missie,' he said gently. 'But we're not out of the wood yet, so let's waste no more time. Uncle's house is about a quarter of a mile outside the village, so we'd best get going. Auntie is going to have tea and crumpets waiting . . .' he smacked his lips, 'and if I know my aunt there'll be a big fruit cake and scones with jam and cream as well.'

When the small group reached Holmwood Lodge, Miranda hung back. She had imagined a neat, detached house with a small front garden and a brightly painted front door; instead, Holmwood Lodge was set well back from the road, at the end of a long gravelled drive which was lined with tall trees. Steve too had not expected anything as imposing as the house they presently approached, but he grabbed Miranda's arm and gave it an admonitory shake. 'Don't look so scared, you silly twerp,' he hissed. 'It's not as though they ain't expectin' us. We're here by invitation and don't you forget it.'

'Oh, but it's huge,' Miranda said distractedly. 'I've never even imagined a garden could be so big, let alone a house.'

'Oh, don't be so daft,' Steve said crossly. 'You haven't come to buy the perishin' place, you've come to have tea, and talk about Missie. Or were you thinkin' about puttin' in an offer? I dare say they'd mebbe accept a couple of thousand quid, if you've got that much to spare.'

Miranda giggled. She did like Steve; he gave her courage, made her see her fears for what they were: groundless. So when they reached the front door – a solid slab of oak with a long bell pull and a knocker – she tugged on the bell pull so hard that even outside the house it sounded as though a fire engine was approaching. Gerald laughed. 'It is a big house, but I'm pretty sure the bell rings in the kitchen, and will be heard by the maids, so you've no need to tug the thing off the wall,' he said cheerfully. 'Of course in the old days a butler would have come to the door but now, because everyone says there's going to be a war quite soon, my uncle was telling me it's just about impossible to get domestic staff. But they've got a couple of girls who come up from the village each day, and a cook-housekeeper who makes wonderful fruit cake . . .'

'Shut up, blabbermouth,' Julian hissed. 'Someone's coming!'

Miranda listened, and heard footsteps approaching the front door. As it creaked open, she felt Missie's hand clutch hers, and realised that the older woman was even more nervous than she was herself. Missie was used to big houses all right, but only in what you might call a menial capacity. Now she was entering as a guest and felt just as awkward and embarrassed as Miranda did.

The Grimshaw boys must have realised how the old woman felt for they both turned to smile at her, and Gerald took the hand that was not gripping Miranda's even as the door swung wide and a fat, elderly woman with crimped grey hair, gold-rimmed spectacles and a broad smile appeared in the aperture, beckoning them inside. 'Come in, come in,' she said cheerfully. 'Mrs Grimshaw said to take you straight in to the drawing room, because it's a chilly day and you'll all be glad to get close to a good log fire. I've got the kettle on the stove and the crumpets will be cooked to a turn in another five minutes, so you won't have long to wait for your tea.' She ushered them into a large hallway, with a woodblock floor and elegant paintings on the panelled walls. Then she threw open the door, saying as she did so: 'Here's your guests, sir and madam. It's chilly outside, and no doubt they'll be glad of a warm whilst you talk.'

Steve and Miranda were at the back of the group, and found themselves entering a very large room indeed. Wide windows overlooked a glorious garden at the back of the house, but Miranda had no eyes for the view, the roaring log fire or the elegant furniture. She was staring very hard at Mr Vernon Grimshaw and his wife, both of whom came forward, smiling, clearly intent upon putting the visitors at their ease.

Julian performed the introductions, whilst Miranda could still only stare. The solicitor was a small thin man with a sharp intelligent face and a determined chin. Despite the fact that the boys had referred to him several times as elderly, he did not seem so to Miranda, for he had thick brown hair neatly trimmed, and a pair of very shrewd brown eyes which looked her over thoughtfully and were then lightened by a charming smile. 'It's very nice to meet you, Miss Lovage,' he said as they shook hands. 'Let me assure you that any friend of Missie's is a friend of ours. But you must let me introduce you to my wife. Mrs Grimshaw has never visited the West Indies, but she has heard me speak of Missie many times, and was as distressed as I was to learn that Missie had been only a few miles away and in great distress for all this time. Had we but known, she could have come to us straight away – heaven knows our home is big enough – and perhaps even remained here until we had managed to sort out her papers, and to get her a passage back home.' He turned to the lady at his side. 'Fiona, my dear, this is the little lady we've heard so much about: Miranda Lovage.'

Mrs Grimshaw looked taller than her husband, with a mass of beautiful dark red hair, which she wore in a French pleat. She had a heart-shaped face and very large red-brown eyes, the same colour as her hair, and when she smiled, revealing perfect white teeth, Miranda thought her truly beautiful. She was elegantly dressed in a coffee-coloured lace dress and shoes of exactly the same colour, with very high heels, which was probably why she seemed so much taller than her husband. She held out one hand to Miranda and one to Missie, and led them to a comfortable sofa.

'Sit down and make yourselves at home while I go and help Mrs Butterthwaite to bring through the tea,' she said. 'We sent the maids home, since we felt that the fewer people who knew about Missie's plight the better. Butterthwaite, of course, has been with the family for many years and is totally to be trusted.' She turned to the three boys, who were holding out icy hands towards the blazing logs. 'You must be Steve. Julian told me that you were the first to discover that someone was living in Jamaica House.' She gave a little purr of amusement. 'My husband tells me you thought Missie was a ghost, which makes it all the more impressive that you continued to visit the place, and of course eventually you met each other. When you're warm enough, come and sit down, because I think we won't discuss ways and means until we've all enjoyed Mrs Butterthwaite's cooking. Ah, I think I hear her approaching now. Open the door for her, Julian, and you can help hand plates and cups . . . dear me, Mrs Butterthwaite, I can see you've done us proud.'

Miranda looked at the heavily laden tea trolley, almost unable to believe the lavishness of it; there were cakes and scones, long plates filled with various sandwiches, and when Mrs Butterthwaite lifted the lid from a large silver salver piles of buttered crumpets, steaming gently, were revealed. 'Please help yourselves, only start off with the crumpets because they're hot,' their hostess commanded them. 'I very much hope that when Mrs Butterthwaite pushes the trolley back to the kitchen it will be a good deal lighter than it is now.'

Miranda doubted that this was likely, but when she saw the enthusiasm with which the boys and Missie attacked the food, she realised that she would only be conspicuous if she failed to take advantage of her hostess's kindness, and very soon – far sooner than she would have believed possible – Mrs Grimshaw's hopes were realised. Mrs Butterthwaite was rung for to wheel out the remnants of the feast, and Mr Grimshaw gestured them to take their places around a large and shiny table.

'And now to business,' he said. 'To start with, I want Missie's story from the very first moment she saw the *Pride of the Sea* putting out a boat to come ashore, right up to when you knocked on my front door.' He smiled round at them, a small, rather sharp-featured man who somehow inspired confidence.

Miranda had taken care to sit between Missie and Steve, though she had decided that she liked Gerald Grimshaw very much and did not feel at all awkward in his company. Julian on the other hand was still very much an unknown quantity. He had not addressed her once, and though his brother had said that he was shy, she felt that he thought himself superior to everyone in the room, save his uncle and aunt. But Missie was beginning to speak, and Miranda saw that Mrs Grimshaw, seated opposite her, appeared to be writing something in a large notebook. Mr Grimshaw must have noticed Miranda's stare for he raised a hand to stop Missie speaking whilst he explained. 'Many years ago, when I was a young solicitor just starting up in practice, I had a young secretary named Fiona Sayer. She was quite the prettiest and brightest girl I had ever met, and after a couple of years we decided that we were made for each other, and got married. Fiona's excellent shorthand has come in useful several times, so now, if you don't object, she's going to take down everything Missie tells us. Then she will go into my office, which is the room opposite this one, and transcribe it on to the typewriter. She will do the same when each of you tells your story, so then we shall have a complete record. I trust this is agreeable to everyone?'

Everyone nodded and Miranda, watching Mrs Grimshaw's pencil fly across the paper, thought that she would like to be a secretary one of these days, especially if it meant marrying one's boss and becoming mistress of a beautiful and elegant house.

Missie's recital was a long one, but it was amazing how the questions put to her by Mr Grimshaw clarified things. By the time everyone, even Miranda, had told their own story the sequence of events became clear; clearer than they had ever been before. Indeed, Miranda began to get quite excited, and decided she must ask for a transcript of Missie's story, so that she could be sure of certain facts. When Mrs Grimshaw returned with a sheaf of neatly typed pages, she was beginning to pluck up her courage to ask if she might have one when she realised there was no need to do so. Mr Grimshaw gave everyone a copy of the transcript, asking them to add or delete as necessary, for, as he said, reading it over one of them might well remember an important fact which someone else had missed. Then he told Missie that he had arranged for her to live in a property he had heard was coming vacant, until such time as she could be repatriated to the West Indies. 'You need a respectable address,' he told her. 'It's nothing very grand, my dear, just a couple of rooms above a bicycle shop on Russell Street, owned by a young man I used to employ. My wife would prefer that you remain with us – and so would I, of course – but I'm afraid that would not help your cause. We shall visit you frequently, and if you do exactly as I tell you we'll have you on a ship bound for the West Indies before you know it.'

Miranda thought that Missie would be delighted at not having to live at Jamaica House any more, but her friend looked terrified. 'I best where I know,' she said obstinately. 'Jamaica House not good address?'

Mr Grimshaw laughed. 'It's a very good address if you don't know Liverpool, but any Liverpudlians who know the house associate it with bygone days and assume it to be a total ruin. No, no, Missie my dear, you must be guided by me. I'm going to ask our young friends Miranda and Steve to keep you supplied with food and to take you around with them at weekends so that folks get used to seeing you. Don't worry, Russell Street is a good way from the docks so you won't be spotted by wandering sailors. I intend to make enquiries about the *Pride of the Sea*, but I should be very surprised indeed to find that they have ever returned to Liverpool.' He smiled at Missie. 'Why should they come back here? They will assume that you have reported their behaviour to the police and that they would be hauled before a judge and jury on a charge of kidnapping should they ever return. They might have abandoned Britain altogether and traded from the West Indies to North America, or Mexico; almost anywhere other than here. They might have changed the name of the ship. But whatever they have done, I'm certain you need no longer fear them.' He glanced at the ornate clock on the mantel. 'Time is getting on. Missie will remain here for a few nights since I can't take possession of the flat until Monday or Tuesday.' He turned to Miranda and Steve. 'I'm going to give Missie a sum of money which should last her until she leaves England, but I've written down the name, address and telephone number of my office so that if you need to contact me for any reason, such as Missie needing more money or some other worry, then you can do so.' He gave Steve a folded piece of paper as he spoke, then turned to his nephews. 'You're quite capable, I'm sure, of getting back to Crosby on public transport, but since I want to show Miranda and Steve where Missie will be living for the next few weeks, you might as well come with us in the car. Then I'll run you back to Crosby and make sure that the school understands that you will be visiting me on a regular basis.'

Missie cleared her throat. 'It very good of you, Mr Vernon, very kind,' she said timidly. 'But I rather live in Jamaica House until time to move into flat. I have little dog who waits for me. I shut him in dining room with bowl of water and biscuits, so I must return to Jamaica House. When I leave, Timmy come too.'

Mr Grimshaw's eyebrows shot up. 'A dog! Well, I shall do my best to find a good home for him, because if you were hoping to take him with you I think that is more than I can arrange,' he said. 'Very well, once I've shown you the flat in Russell Street, I'll drive you round to Jamaica House, and when I've made all the arrangements I'll return there to pick up you and your little companion.'

Julian cleared his throat. 'I've not liked to ask before, but did our family once own Jamaica House?' he asked. 'And if so did they benefit from the slave trade?'

There was an uncomfortable silence before Mr Grimshaw nodded reluctantly. 'Yes, Julian, I'm afraid you've guessed the truth. It's a period of our history of which our family are rightly ashamed, so it is never mentioned. But the family had ceased trading in slaves long before it became illegal to do so, I can promise you that.' He smiled across at Missie, who was staring at him, round-eyed. 'It was a filthy trade, dear Missie, which makes it even more important to see you a free woman, and back in your own place once more.'

Miranda, watching Julian closely, saw the worry fade from his face. 'Thank you for telling me, Uncle,' he said quietly. 'And now let us get on with the business in hand, which is making Missie comfortable and returning her to her island.'

Later that evening, as she made her way across to Number Six, Miranda reflected that everything had gone according to plan. Not knowing the area as well as Steve did, she had not realised that they would pass Russell Street every time they went to the city centre, though Steve had pointed this out to Missie. 'We'll be able to visit you on our way to and from Paddy's Market and that,' he had told her. 'And after what Mr Grimshaw said, you needn't fear meeting anyone from the *Pride of the Sea*.' He had shaken his head in self-reproach. 'Weren't we daft not to realise that the last place on earth Captain Hogg would want to visit would be Liverpool? It might be different if he had realised you'd be too afraid to go to the authorities, but I don't suppose that even crossed his mind. No, Mr Grimshaw was right. Probably this is the one place on earth that the *Pride of the Sea* dare not visit.'

Miranda approached Number Six with rather less than her usual caution, because her mind was full of the happenings of the afternoon and their plans for the future. At first her aunt had nagged her about her frequent absences, but when she realised that her niece was still doing her share of the housework, yet was seldom present at mealtimes, she had stopped expecting her to come straight home from school. The fact that Beth's boyfriend often accompanied her cousin home also made Miranda's life easier. In front of Herbert Wade, her aunt was on her best behaviour, treating Miranda, if not with affection, at least with civility, and anyway she was usually in bed by the time Miranda returned to the house.

This evening, however, when she went to open the back door, it was locked. Miranda stared. True, she was a good deal later than usual, but her aunt had never locked her out before. Naturally lazy and knowing that there was nothing worth stealing in Number Six, she never bothered to lock up. Miranda stepped back and looked up at the bedroom windows. No light showed, and she hesitated to knock. If she could have roused Beth without waking Aunt Vi, she would have done so, but there was little chance of that. Miranda heaved a sigh; one way and another she had managed to keep on the right side of her aunt recently, but she knew that if she woke her the least she could expect was a clack round the ear. She glanced towards the coal shed; she didn't much fancy trying to sleep in there, nor in the noisome little privy.

It was beginning to rain, and it was both cold and windy, which meant a night in the open was out of the question. The only alternative was to walk back to Jamaica House, wake Missie, wrap herself in one of the blankets and spend the night there. Miranda glanced hopefully at the downstairs windows, but they were all tightly shut. Oh well, it's a walk I've done often enough, and as I go I'll try to think of some solution to the problem of Timmy, she told herself. She wondered if the Grimshaws might take him in. They had a marvellous house but no pets, as far as she had been able to tell, and surely once they had seen Timmy they would be as eager to give him a home as she had been herself. She would still have loved to keep him, but knew that that would be impossible. Later, when I've got a proper job, I really will have a dog of my own, she mused as she walked, but until then I must just make sure that Timmy doesn't lose out.

By the time Miranda reached Jamaica House, the light rain had turned heavy and she was glad to open the door in the wall, cross the garden at a tired trot and approach the kitchen door. She knew Missie slept in a tiny box-like attic room on the top floor because she said she felt safer up there, and she knew that Timmy usually occupied the foot of Missie's bed. Normally he would rush downstairs, tail going nineteen to the dozen, eyes bright, ears flattened in welcome, but she had no idea how he would greet someone coming in the middle of the night. She hoped he wouldn't bark and scare Missie out of her wits, but perhaps it was not as late as she had imagined, for when she opened the kitchen door and slipped inside she saw that the room was lamp-lit, the fire glowed in the hearth and Missie was sitting at the big kitchen table eating some sort of stew from a large plate, whilst Timmy, at her feet, was destroying a large bone which Steve had wheedled from the butcher on Scotland Road.

Missie looked up and beamed when she saw who had entered, and Miranda, smiling back, thought how the visit to Holmwood Lodge had calmed all her friend's fears. Once, she would have shot out of her seat and disappeared into the rabbit warren of other rooms, but now she simply greeted Miranda as though night-time visits were commonplace.

'Have some stew, Miranda. Late for visiting,' she chuckled. She got up and fetched a second plate from the sideboard, then ladled stew into it and pushed it towards her unexpected guest. 'Go on, take bread,' she said. 'Timmy got bone; he ate his stew. Why you here?'

Miranda explained and Missie nodded wisely. 'I thought it something like that,' she said. 'Your aunt holy terror. When you finished, I get you blankets.' She beamed at Miranda; a small face shining with childlike happiness. 'It be nice and warm here; we damp down fire and both sleep on floor. Mr Vernon take me away soon.'

'I'll come with you and help you carry the blankets,'

Miranda said eagerly as she finished the stew on her plate. It was just a mixture of vegetables, but Missie had been living mostly on vegetables over the summer and knew how to make them tasty.

The two of them climbed the stairs by the light of the lantern Missie carried, and very soon the pair were back in the kitchen and making a bed on the floor, well supplied with blankets and cushions. Then they settled down, with Timmy curled up between them. Rather to her surprise, however, Miranda did not feel tired, but found herself wanting to talk over the events of the past couple of days. 'I wonder why you didn't sleep down here in the warm before, Missie?' she said, snuggling down. 'Were you too afraid of Captain Hogg and his merry men to sleep on the ground floor?'

Missie nodded. 'Yes. Mr Vernon, he no understand. Those men bad through and through; ship is evil. On very night I escape from ship, before I find Jamaica House, I make myself sort of nest in basement of other house, some way from docks. Moon was shining like daylight and I saw Captain Pig and first mate pulling woman along. She wore long white gown, hair loose. She not look bad woman, yet she with bad men . . .'

Miranda had only been half listening but on hearing those words she jerked upright and interrupted without ceremony. 'Missie, that poor woman might have been my mother! Can you recall what day it was? What street? Was the lady very beautiful? Oh, Missie, you know I live with my aunt? Well, I only moved in with her because my mother had disappeared – I don't think I told you because it upset me when people said she had gone away with a man. I knew that wasn't true. If she had wanted to go away with someone she would have taken her clothes, her books, all the things she loved, and me as well, of course, but she left in the middle of the night and I couldn't see anything missing from her wardrobe, so she might have been wearing just her nightdress. Oh, Missie, I'm sure you must have seen my mother being kidnapped by Captain Hogg! Was she bound or gagged? Were they carrying her? Please, Missie, tomorrow morning you must come to the police with me and tell them what you saw!'

Missie looked confused and worried. 'She not cry for help. Men have arms round her,' she said.

'Are you sure she was walking and not being carried?' Miranda said desperately. 'If only you will come to the police station I'm sure they will ask the Port Authority when the *Pride of the Sea* tied up at the quay, which would tell us for certain whether it was the day my mother disappeared. Oh, Missie, I beg of you to come to the police with me. Or if you won't do that, would you tell Mr Grimshaw what you saw?'

Miranda watched as the worry slowly cleared from her companion's face, to be replaced by a tentative smile. 'Yes, that good idea,' Missie said, clearly relieved. 'Mr Vernon would say I must not go to police.'

Miranda opened her mouth to argue, then shut it again. She suddenly realised that the first thing the law would ask would be for Missie's name and address. Also, it would be useless for her, Miranda, to tell the police what Missie had seen; that was not evidence, but hearsay. No, Missie was right. Mr Grimshaw would know what to do. Miranda settled back in her blankets. Missie had doused the lamp and the two had been talking in the fire's glow and now Missie turned to Miranda, her face alive with curiosity. 'It long time ago; have you been with your aunt long time?' she asked.

'Yes, I have; it seems like a lifetime,' Miranda said gloomily. 'Oh, my poor darling mother! What will they have done with her? Would they keep her on the ship as they kept you, to cook and clean for them?' She smothered a chuckle. 'If so I imagine they would very soon regret it. She isn't much of a cook and she hates housework.'

She glanced at Missie as she spoke and saw how Missie's eyes refused to meet her own. 'If was your mother, she mebbe escape, like me,' she said evasively.

'Yes, but if she did escape, why hasn't she come home?' Miranda said uneasily. 'I suppose it might take time to get people to help her if she's in a foreign country where they don't speak English, but as you say, a great deal of time has passed. Oh, Missie, I can't wait to tell Mr Grimshaw what you saw, and to get his opinion on what we should do next.'

Next day Miranda was so excited that she would have gone straight to Holmwood, but this Missie refused to do. 'You must go to your aunt's home and find out why she lock you out,' she said. 'There could be many reasons.'

The two of them were drinking tea and eating toast in the kitchen. Outside, the rain had really got into its stride and was pelting down and Miranda did not fancy the long walk back to Jamaica Close in such weather, but Missie produced the purse of money which Mr Grimshaw had given her and insisted that she should take the tram fare. 'And if your aunt ask where you spend night, tell her it with a school friend,' she instructed, and went on to explain that though she knew Miranda wouldn't give her away on purpose, she was so excited over the possibility that Missie had seen her mother that night that she might give something away. 'If you leave at once you be back here in time for us to catch two o'clock bus out to Holmwood. Perhaps rain will have stopped by then. Are you going to tell Steve what I saw?'

Miranda shook her head. 'I won't tell him today. As it is, we're going to have our work cut out to convince Mr Grimshaw.' She stood up, drained her teacup and headed for the back door. 'I'd best be making tracks.' Timmy shot across the room, his tail wagging so fast that it became a blur, for he did love a walk. However, Miranda had to disillusion him. 'Not today, old chap; you stay with Missie until I get back,' she said. She turned to the older woman. 'Do you think we could take him to Holmwood Lodge this afternoon? Only if they fell in love with him it would solve at least one of our problems.'

Missie laughed. 'You never know luck,' she said. 'See you later, Miranda.'

A couple of hours later Miranda, now clad in an old mackintosh with a scarf tied round her head, scarcely bothered to look round her before approaching the door in the ivy-covered wall. Quite apart from the fact that the rain was so heavy she could only see a couple of yards ahead, she knew that the factories did not work on Sundays, so did not fear being seen. The trees dripped and the flowers hung their heads so that the garden was no longer a paradise but looked neglected and rather sad. And neglected it soon would be, Miranda mused ruefully, for once Missie was gone she did not suppose that she and Steve would come here often. Steve would shortly be leaving school and getting a job, and she herself intended to follow his example as soon as she could. There were hostels for girls working in Liverpool, and once she found work she meant to leave the house in Jamaica Close, move into a hostel and start looking for Arabella in earnest.

As soon as she opened the back door Timmy rushed to meet her and Missie, peeling potatoes at the low stone sink, turned to give her a smile. 'Well?' she said eagerly. 'Why they lock you out?'

Miranda chuckled. 'As you know, we are Number Six. Further up the road at Number Ten there's a family with three sons, all working. It being Saturday they took themselves off for a river cruise and apparently had a grand day out, which included a great many bevvies – that means drinks – and a great deal of grub . . .'

'That mean food,' Missie said, giggling. 'So why your aunt locking door?'

Miranda laughed as well. 'Whilst they were out their house was done over – robbed – so they alerted the scuffers and one of the young constables came round to the Close. He visited every house, including Number Six of course, warned them all that the McDonalds had been robbed, and advised everyone to lock up with special care. Of course Aunt Vi swore they thought I'd come in earlier, which would have meant they were locking me in, not out. I won't say Aunt Vi apologised, because she didn't, but my cousin Beth said she were real sorry and why hadn't I chucked gravel at the bedroom window or battered on the kitchen door to be let in. She's not bad, Beth; I do believe if it wasn't for Aunt Vi she and I could have been friends. So you see it wasn't just spite, as I thought. In fact, if they hadn't locked me out you and I might never have spent the night talking, so I should be grateful to them.'

Missie nodded. 'Well, that one mystery solved,' she said cheerfully. 'We will have some of that vegetable stew for midday meal. Mrs Vernon will give us supper once we've told story to Mr Vernon.'

On their way to school next morning, Miranda regaled Steve with her doings. 'Mr Grimshaw didn't scoff once, but listened to every word Missie had to say,' she told him. 'And now that they've got the name of the ship, the police will go to the Port Authority and find out when the *Pride of the Sea* put in at Liverpool.'

Steve pulled a face. 'But it's so long ago, Miranda! I don't want to put you off or make you miserable, but if I were a detective in a book I'd say the trail had gone cold.'

Miranda scowled at him. They were both members of the nearest library and enjoyed detective stories but, as she pointed out, these were works of fiction, and what she and Steve were discussing was real life.

'Ye-es, but you can't deny that a year is a long time, and memories are short,' Steve argued. 'Still, if the ship has returned to the 'Pool, at least we'll know about it.'

'Yes. Mr Grimshaw's a man of his word, and the police will take him seriously, which is more than they would have done had you and I turned up on their doorstep,' Miranda agreed. 'And as for Missie telling her story herself . . .'

By now they were approaching their school gates and

Steve shouted to a group of boys ahead of them to wait for him. Then he turned to Miranda. 'Are we going to Jamaica House after school?' he asked. 'I know it's going to take Mr Grimshaw a day or two to fix up the flat in Russell Street – especially now you've given him another job of work, poor man – but there might be something we can do to help Missie get ready.'

In fact it was some time before Missie moved into her new abode. She was very nervous at first and begged Mr Grimshaw to allow her to share her grand new premises with Miranda and Timmy. 'Miranda very unhappy with aunt and Timmy unhappy without Miranda,' she said, and went on to explain that she still feared Captain Hogg would discover her whereabouts and burst in to carry her off.

Miranda had listened hopefully, for already she loved the neat little flat and would have been happy to live in it even for a few weeks, but Mr Grimshaw, though he understood their feelings, had shaken his head reluctantly. 'No, no, my dear Missie. Her aunt may not value Miranda as she should, but she would be as curious as anyone else if her niece suddenly found a flat share with an unknown West Indian woman! Now, it seems your Captain Hogg is suspected of a good many misdemeanours, though the Port Authority knew nothing about any kidnapping activities. Apparently, he only came into Liverpool for an engine part. That was his declared reason, anyway, and he left on the tide the day following his arrival, so very little interest was taken by the authorities on this occasion. But the date matches your mother's disappearance, Miranda, and once they started asking questions it soon became clear that the ship was notorious for slipping in and out of harbour without paying her dues, for loading shipments meant for other vessels, and similar offences.' He had smiled kindly at Miranda, and patted her on the shoulder. 'I think it's quite possible that your mother was seized by the captain, my child, but until we can trace the ship's movements we have no way of ascertaining her present whereabouts, if indeed it was Mrs Lovage Missie saw that night.'

Later, when Steve, Missie and Miranda were alone in the flat, with Timmy curled up on the hearthrug, they decided that discussing the matter was pointless. Instead, they would wait for solid news of the ship's first port of call, for Mr Grimshaw had promised that his investigations would start there. 'And as soon as we've seen you off on a ship bound for home, Missie, I shall leave school and get a job in one of the factories, and start saving up,' Miranda planned. 'I know there's been a depression – still is – but everyone seems convinced that there's a war coming and factories are being built to make uniforms and guns and wireless sets, that sort of thing. Beth is talking about leaving her job and going into either the services or a munitions factory, because they pay twice what she's getting from old Mrs Seymour, so I mean to do the same. If my mother is like you, Missie, desperate to get home but unable to raise the cash, then I shall jolly well get on a ship as soon as I've saved enough, and take her the money myself.'

'Three cheers for Miranda Lovage!' Steve said ironically. 'I never knew your mother, but that scuffer, the one who caught you sleepwalking, told me she was a real beauty with primrose-coloured hair, clear blue eyes and a very curvy figure. If you ask me she could get a job even if she'd landed on the moon!'

Miranda noticed Missie giving Steve a warning look, and for the first time it occurred to her that her mother's beauty might not be the asset she had imagined. She gave Steve a penetrating stare but he met her eyes frankly, his own faintly puzzled, and she realised that he had not understood Missie's glare either.

'What's up?' he asked, and then, as neither of his companions answered, he shrugged. 'Have your secrets then,' he said huffily. 'And it's time we were heading home, Miranda.'

As Mr Grimshaw had warned them, arranging for Missie to travel legally from England to her home took time. She had been presumed dead and had to prove that she was not an impostor, though this seemed daft to Miranda; what was the advantage in perpetrating such a fraud? Autumn was well advanced when at last Missie's passage was arranged, and when Mr Grimshaw disclosed that his brother had been overjoyed to hear that Missie was still alive, and had immediately offered to take her back into his employment when she returned, Miranda knew that her visits to the little flat above the bicycle shop would soon be a thing of the past. Regretfully, she guessed that this would also mean she could scarcely keep popping over to Holmwood Lodge; she did this a lot, particularly at weekends when the boys were visiting, and she had grown friendly with them both. Julian and Gerald seemed to enjoy Steve and Miranda's company, despite their different stations in life. For one thing, Steve had got a job upon leaving school, at one of the big factories making parts for aero engines, and talked of joining the Royal Air Force as soon as he was eighteen, whereas Julian and Gerald knew nothing of the world of work, though they had both joined the junior division of the OTC.

Steve had always been generous, and now that he was earning he bought little presents for Miranda and took her on theatre and cinema trips, for meals in cafés and similar treats. Miranda felt guilty for accepting his hospitality so often and confided in Mrs Grimshaw her plan to leave school and apply for a factory job as soon as Missie had gone home. 'At first I thought of getting a room in a hostel, but there are lots of girls in the city looking for a flat share,' she told the older woman. 'Perhaps two or three of us could club together and take on Missie's place. I wonder if my cousin Beth might want to join us. Of course living at home is much cheaper because she doesn't have to pay her mum rent, and not a great deal for her keep either, but there was a big row the other day over Beth's telling whoppers. She told Aunt Vi she'd been to a dance at the Grafton with Spotty Wade, and then Aunt Vi discovered that Herbert had been working that night so Beth had gone by herself and picked up some foreign sailor whose ship was in port. Aunt Vi wouldn't have known anything about it only Curly Danvers, who lives further up the Close, met her in the fish shop and commented that Beth seemed to have got herself an officer, and a good-looking one at that.' Miranda hesitated; there was something she longed to ask but she was not sure whether it would be polite to do so. However, she and Mrs Grimshaw were companionably washing up the tea things whilst the boys played snooker in the games room, and she decided to take a chance. She and her hostess had grown easy with one another during the past weeks, so now Miranda braced herself and voiced the question. 'Mrs Grimshaw, would you mind telling me what sort of rent the owner would ask for the flat?'

'My dear child, I've no idea what the rent of the flat would be, but I'm sure my husband could tell you,' Mrs Grimshaw said. 'But, you know, Mr Grimshaw and I have talked about your future many times, and we think it would be a great waste for you to abandon your education without even attempting to get your School Certificate. I can understand your wanting to earn money of your own . . .'

Miranda interrupted her. 'I wouldn't be abandoning my education, honest to God I wouldn't,' she said eagerly. 'My mother was always on about the importance of what she called "that little bit of paper", so I thought I'd enrol at the technical college for evening classes. You can get all sorts of qualifications from there whilst earning at the same time.'

Mrs Grimshaw nodded. 'Yes, I know.' She emptied the water in her bowl down the sink, dried her hands on a tea towel and patted Miranda's cheek. 'My dear, Mr Grimshaw and I are willing to help you establish yourself with a career and a place of your own; so we would arrange for Mr Huxtable – he's the young man who owns the bicycle shop – to let you take on the flat at a reasonable rent. Mr Grimshaw needs an office girl, and though the salary is small the hours are nine till five, much more suitable than a factory for a girl studying for her certificate.'

Miranda stared at Mrs Grimshaw open-mouthed, and when she spoke her voice was husky. 'You've been so good to me already that I feel quite guilty,' she said. 'But I can't accept a cheap rent at your expense, it really wouldn't be fair. And I know all about key money! If you can tell me how much we should be expected to pay, I'm sure I can get two or three girls interested in flat sharing; then we could pay the rent between us. And I'd work very hard at my evening classes, honest to God I would.'

Mrs Grimshaw began to collect the clean cutlery and crockery and replace it on the shelves. She said, without looking round: 'Suppose we were to call the key money a loan? Would you feel more comfortable with that? I think a flat share is a grand idea, but not with three or four of you sharing the place. You and one other could be comfortable, couldn't you?'

'Oh *yes*,' Miranda said eagerly. 'And we'd pay you back just as soon as we could.'

Miranda awoke. She twitched back the bedroom curtains to let in the early sunshine, then wondered for a moment why she had not immediately rolled out of bed, for usually she liked to be downstairs and making some sort of breakfast for herself before Beth and her aunt woke up. Then she remembered. Today was leaving day; Missie's passage was booked, her packing done, and the little flat cleaned to within an inch of its life, for Missie was determined that the Grimshaws should not find one speck of dust in her dear little flat. They had all arranged to be down at the docks when Missie left, although it meant that the boys would have to sag off school. However, Steve had arranged to get a day off from his factory and Miranda herself was what you might call 'in between', since she had left school at the end of the previous week and would not start her job in Mr Grimshaw's office until the following Monday.

Since the Grimshaws had been determined to do everything properly, Mr Grimshaw had visited Aunt Vi to explain that he and his wife intended to help Miranda as she began to gain her independence. He had somehow made it appear that he had known Miranda's mother and was doing it for Arabella's sake; at any rate, that was the explanation which Aunt Vi gave to everyone, adding that the kid had certainly fallen on her feet, since the Grimshaws were also giving her a job and had offered to pay for her to attend evening classes.

So now Miranda lay on her back contemplating the pale sunshine and the blue of the sky which she could see through the crack in the curtains, and thinking that Missie would at least start her voyage in cold but pleasant weather conditions. But presently, despite telling herself that she deserved a lie-in, for the ship did not depart until noon, she rolled out of bed, padded to the washstand and began vigorously washing. She had ironed her best cotton frock the night before and thought that she would wear the little red jacket which Steve had bought her from Paddy's Market with his very first wages. She had noticed how his face lit up whenever she wore it, and she reflected that meeting Steve and becoming his friend was the best day's work she had ever done. He had never let her down, and continued to accompany her to the Port Authority when she went each week in the hope that the *Pride of the Sea* might have berthed somewhere along the British coast. Others had given up, but Miranda knew that Mr Grimshaw had not, and was beginning to believe that Captain Hogg must have changed the name of the ship. 'I've written fifty or sixty letters and contacted just about everyone who might be able to give me some information,' he had told Miranda. 'But ships need papers, just as people do, and sooner or later, whatever they call her, we'll root her out and bring Hogg to account. No doubt he'll claim ignorance, but with a crew such as his there's bound to be one of them who can be bought. Yes, once we've run the ship to earth, I'm very hopeful we shall find out what happened to your mother.'

But that day had not yet arrived, although Miranda still could not help connecting Missie's plight with Arabella's. Missie had remained hidden for a very long time, so why should not Arabella also be tucked away somewhere out of sight? Accordingly, Miranda had got one of the actresses who had worked with her mother to sketch Arabella's likeness and had pressed the picture into Missie's hand. 'If you see anyone, anyone at all, who looks like this, will you ask her if she's Arabella Lovage?' she said urgently. 'Steve said the captain and his mate might have given her some sort of drug, and she might have lost her memory. If you do see her, Missie, and tell her about me, surely that would be enough to make her remember?'

Now, having washed and dressed as quietly as possible so as not to wake Beth and Aunt Vi, she tiptoed down the stairs and into the kitchen. It was the work of a moment to put the kettle on the range and cut herself a thick wedge of bread which she spread with the jam Missie had made from the fruit in the garden of Jamaica House. Having breakfasted, Miranda made a pot of tea and carried it upstairs. Beth had just woken and greeted the tea with enthusiasm, but Aunt Vi just grunted and rolled over. 'I aren't gerrin' up yet,' she mumbled. 'Bring me some hot water up, and mebbe I'll have a wash.'

Miranda bit back the words 'That'll be a first' and went quietly out of the room. She did not wish to get on the wrong side of Aunt Vi, for in a couple of days she would be taking over the flat, and once that happened she doubted she would return to Jamaica Close, except to visit Steve.

She let herself out of the kitchen, closed the door gently behind her and headed across the back yard, then along the jigger and out into Jamaica Close. It was early but men and women were already walking briskly towards the main road, where they would catch the trams or buses which would take them to work.

Steve answered her knock, one cheek bulging, and pulled her into his mother's kitchen. 'Here, have some brekker,' he said thickly. 'It's a bacon sarnie; that'll line your belly until dinner.'

His mother, frying bacon, smiled a greeting. 'Mornin', queen,' she said cheerfully. 'Today's the great day, I gather. Done your packin' yet?'

Miranda giggled. 'Missie leaves today, but I shan't move into the flat until the weekend,' she explained. 'As for packing, I've got my old school skirt and jersey, my winter coat and the dress I've got on, and some underwear, so I don't think I'll need a suitcase to carry my belongings from Jamaica Close to Russell Street.' She smiled at Mrs Mickleborough. 'As soon as I'm settled I hope you'll come a-visitin', you and Mr Mickleborough. I'll get a big pot of tea ready, 'cos I know what big tea drinkers you two are, and a couple of dozen penny buns, the sort with pink icing on the top, and we'll have us a little party.'

'And you'll see Timmy, Mam,' Steve said, his tone reproachful. He had begged his mother to take the little dog in, but, whilst she was still considering, Mr Huxtable had asked Miranda if he might become Timmy's new owner.

'He's a grand little chap,' he had said appreciatively. 'I've always wanted a dog, and livin' above the shop you'll be able to visit him reg'lar like.'

Both Steve and Miranda were very grateful to the dark-haired young man, but Steve put into words what they were both thinking. 'That's real kind of you, Pete, but what will happen if you're conscripted into one of the forces?' he asked. 'Or have you already volunteered?'

Pete grinned. 'I volunteered right at the start, but they turned me down 'cos I'd broken my ankle and were still in plaster when I went for the medical. They said when the hospital released me as fit they'd be in touch again, and I dare say they will, but in the meantime I'm sellin' cycles and doin' repairs, and if I do go into the services I've a cousin who'll take over here. He's gorra dog of his own and will look after Timmy here like a mother, don't you fret.'

So very soon now they would all be settled: Missie on the ship which would take her home, Miranda in her brand new flat, and Timmy in the bicycle shop, and though Steve had said he would leave home if his mam wouldn't take Timmy in, everyone knew it was an idle threat. No family was happier than the Mickleboroughs. Not even my mother and me, Miranda thought to herself, and was surprised and even slightly shocked when the thought entered her head. Naturally she remembered Arabella through rose-coloured spectacles, but she was a practical girl and knew there had been times when her mother had voiced the wish that she did not have to work every hour God sent in order to keep her daughter and herself. Then there had been all the usual arguments as Miranda grew up, which came, she supposed, from two females sharing a house. Arabella had grumbled over the state of her daughter's bedroom, saying that at her age Miranda should not simply sling dirty clothing down on the floor, but should take it downstairs, possibly even wash it. Miranda realised, guiltily, that she had not been a very good daughter; in fact she had been both selfish and lazy. Now that she had begun to think back, she thought of all the things she might have done to make her mother's life easier, some of the things her aunt had taken for granted she would do as a sort of return for living in her house. Only Aunt Vi had carried it to extremes; Miranda had been expected to do not only her own washing, but that of Beth and her aunt as well. Aunt Vi had expected her to make the bed and to do all the housework, yet even then it had not occurred to Miranda that she had treated her mother as unfairly as Aunt Vi treated her. Oh, when Arabella comes back I'll wait on her hand and foot, Miranda dreamed. I'll cook beautiful meals, keep the house clean as a new pin and buy her little presents from my salary at the end of each month. When she comes home . . .

'What are you thinkin' about, dreamy? You've gorra real soppy look on your face.' Steve's voice cut across her musing. 'What'll we do till it's time to fetch Missie?

We could go to Jamaica House and collect any windfalls so's my mam can bottle them, or make jam. Unless you want to spend the time with Missie, that is.'

Miranda jumped, then turned to smile at him. 'Sorry, Steve. I was thinking how much you help your mum, and realising how little I helped mine. You're a lad, and a lot of lads do next to nothing in the house, not even the messages. But you do all sorts without even having to be asked. It makes me ashamed that I wasn't a better daughter when I had the chance.'

Steve looked gratified. 'There you are, Mam, a recommendation,' he said, laughing. 'Ain't you glad you've got me?'

He puffed out his chest as he spoke and smirked, but Mrs Mickleborough gave him a shove. 'You ain't a bad lad, but if I'd had the good sense to give birth to a girl first I reckon you'd be like all the other young fellers round here, and wouldn't raise a finger whilst your sister was there to run messages, clean the house and do a bit of cooking on the side, so you can take that silly grin off your face and fetch my marketing bag down off its hook. I don't want a deal of stuff, just a big bag of spuds, a cabbage and Mrs Evans's laundry delivered, so mind you don't go buyin' the spuds first an' lettin' the laundry get dirty.'

Steve groaned. 'Oh, Mam, can't I do the messages later?' he asked hopefully. 'We meant to go straight round to Russell Street to see whether Missie needed any help in gettin' her stuff down to the quayside.'

Mrs Mickleborough laughed, but shook a reproving finger. 'And this is the feller who asked his pal what she wanted to do until it was time to take Missie aboard her ship,' she said. 'Oh, go on with you! Take the laundry round for me, there's a good lad, and I'll fetch the veggies myself. It'll do me good to get a breath of fresh air on such a lovely day.'

'Well, if you really wouldn't mind . . .' Steve was beginning, but Miranda cut him short.

'We'll take the laundry on our way to Russell Street and fetch your messages on the way back,' she said, smiling at Mrs Mickleborough.

Miranda, who had never been aboard a ship, was assured by Steve that they would have a good chance to look round the vessel whilst all the passengers boarded, and she was glad she'd put on her best dress and her most respectable pair of sandals. When they got to the flat, having dropped the laundry off at Mrs Evans's small tea room, she saw that Missie, too, was clad in her best. When they had first known the little woman, she had been dressed in black clothing which was little better than rags, but the Grimshaws had seen to it that she had decent garments for her stay in Liverpool, and a case of lighter clothing for the voyage and her return to the island. When Steve and Miranda ran up the metal staircase which led directly to the flat they were greeted by Missie, incredibly smart in a navy coat and skirt and a crisp white blouse. She had said she would be happy with clothing from Paddy's Market which she could wash, iron and darn where necessary, but the Grimshaws had taken her to T J Hughes and kitted her out with the very best. Miranda congratulated her on her appearance and Steve agreed that she was as smart as any lady of his acquaintance.

Missie beamed. 'I knew you would come, best of my

friends,' she said gratefully. 'Mr Vernon said he would call, but I say no need; my friends will come. But first we will have cup of tea and bun and I show you special cake, Miranda, so when I am gone you must come back here and have tea and cake.'

Missie bustled about, pouring boiling water from the kettle on the Primus into the teapot and producing some buns, which she said proudly she had made herself. Once the buns were eaten and the tea drunk, Missie fetched her hat and coat and Steve leaned towards Miranda, his brows rising. 'There's no oven in the flat,' he whispered. 'She couldn't possibly have made those buns, could she?'

Miranda giggled. 'It just shows how little you know,' she said derisively. 'Folk without ovens take their cake or bun mix, in its tin, round to Sample's, the bakery, and pay a small sum to have it cooked for them. Aunt Vi did that once in a while, when she was too lazy to light the oven.'

Steve leaned back, satisfied, then got to his feet and went over to the sink. 'I'll just wash up these few things . . .' he was beginning, when Missie came back into the room. Her hat was perched on her head and she was pulling on her gloves.

'All set; let's go!' she said briskly, then glanced around the kitchen. 'I happy here,' she said musingly as they headed for the stairs, 'yet I glad to leave. Mr Vernon take me to Jamaica House yesterday evening and I said my goodbyes. Now I must forget past and think of future.'

The three of them clattered down the stairs, Steve swinging the suitcase, and Missie with her handbag clutched beneath one arm. It was a leather one, shiny and new, a last present from Mrs Grimshaw, and Miranda knew that her little friend valued it highly. Accordingly she warned her not to wave it around when they neared the docks, and suggested that Missie should walk between herself and Steve. 'It's better to be safe than sorry,' she said sagely. 'Goodness, how the morning has flown! If we don't hurry, we'll be the last people to board the ship and I shan't have a chance to look round before they're pulling up the anchor and saying that all visitors must leave.'

When they reached the quayside, however, the Grimshaws were waiting and they all boarded the ship together. She was called the *Island Princess*, and though she was not a large craft Mr Grimshaw had been assured that her crew were experienced, her captain friendly and the passengers' quarters both comfortable and commodious. Unlike Miranda, Steve did know ships, since one of his brothers was in the Royal Navy, aboard a sloop, and Steve had visited several times when it had been in port, but he was very impressed by the *Island Princess* and told Missie that she was a lucky dog to have quarters so luxurious. 'My brother slings his hammock along with a dozen or so others, with almost no room for his own stuff,' he assured them. 'Missie's cabin could hold half a dozen, I'm sure; and she'll eat her dinner at a proper table with a white cloth and silver knives and forks. Oh aye, this is the way to travel!'

Miranda, thinking of her mother, asked Missie whether this ship was very different from the *Pride of the Sea*, but Missie shook her head. 'I dunno; it a long time ago and I a slave aboard her,' she muttered, and when a member of the crew shouted through a megaphone that they would soon be casting off and advised visitors to leave the ship, Miranda was aware that Missie was relieved.

Reaching the quayside once more, Julian and Gerald said they would stay to wave Missie off, but Mr Grimshaw wanted to get back to his office and said that if the boys could leave at once he would run them back to Crosby in his car. Julian looked thankful and Miranda guessed that his strong sense of propriety had made him reluctant to sag off school, but Gerald shook his head.

'I'm going back to Russell Street with Miranda and Steve,' he said firmly. 'Missie told me she'd left one of her magnificent fruit cakes and I just fancy a slice of it.'

'You're a greedy pig; that cake was left for me, not you,' Miranda said, but she spoke without much conviction, and even as she did so the senior Grimshaws said their goodbyes and moved away to where the car was parked.

Miranda gave them one last wave and turned back to the quayside. 'Oh, look, the ship's beginning to swing away from the quay; your parents and Julian might just as well have stayed!' she said. 'Missie is on the deck; can you see her waving? Oh, I forgot to remind her to show everyone the sketch of my mother Betty Prince made! But I'm sure she'll remember; she's not the sort to forget her friends.' She turned to Steve. 'She's promised to write, and will post a letter as soon as she can. Oh, isn't it sad saying goodbye to a friend you'll probably never see again? Oh, dear, and I was so determined not to cry . . . '

Gerald flung an arm round her shoulders and gave her a squeeze. 'Everyone cries when they're waving a friend off, even if they're going to meet again in a few months,' he said reassuringly. Seeing the look on Steve's face without fully understanding it, Miranda wriggled out of Gerald's embrace and smiled at Steve, though her eyes were still brimming with tears.

'It's all right, I'm okay now,' she said huskily. 'Let's get back to that cake; crying always makes me hungry!'

Chapter Seven

By the time Christmas was over, Miranda had received several letters from Missie, only one of which had come whilst she was still aboard the ship. On an international level, the war which had been spoken of vaguely when Miranda had first joined Grimshaw, Scott and Carruthers, Solicitors and Commissioners for Oaths, was now thought by most people to be inevitable, despite Mr Chamberlain's 'piece of paper' announcing peace for our time. And Miranda had not wasted her time at work. With a good deal of help from Mrs Grimshaw at weekends, she had learned to type and to take down simple letters in shorthand and Mr Grimshaw had increased her salary accordingly. 'Not that you're liable to be with us for long, because I dare say the government will want young women to do war work as well as young men,' he told her. 'But for the time being at least, the firm will take advantage of your many abilities.'

Miranda had beamed, delighted with the praise which she honestly felt she had earned, for despite attending evening classes in both typing and shorthand she had continued to study for her school certificate, and was always working at her desk or doing some other necessary job well before nine o'clock in the morning.

Since moving into the flat and on Mrs Grimshaw's advice, she had spent a good deal of her salary on the sort of clothes she could not have dreamed of buying before – not dance dresses, though she intended to purchase one as soon as she felt she could afford it – but what she thought of as sensible office clothing: a green pleated skirt, a crisp white blouse and a dark green cardigan. Steve, still working in his factory, also spent some of his wages on what he thought of as 'suitable clothing' for taking a young lady – Miranda – out to the cinema or the theatre, or for similar treats.

And Steve was not the only young man who took her about. Gerald Grimshaw, though still at school, managed to see her at least once a week and made it plain that he enjoyed her company. Miranda thought Steve did not altogether approve of this friendship, though he never said so, and Miranda did her best not to favour one above the other, though, as she told him, Steve would always be her bezzie.

Right now, however, the two were in the tiny kitchenette of the flat in Russell Street engaged in the tear-jerking task of pickling onions. Miranda had procured a promise from a stallholder in the Great Homer Street market to sell, on Miranda's behalf, as many jars of pickled onions as she could provide, and naturally she would make a small profit herself on every jar. When she had told Steve that this was going to be her way of paying for various little extras, like a dance frock, he had agreed at once to come round on weekends and evenings and give her a hand. So now the two sat on opposite sides of the kitchen table, packing the peeled onions into jars, adding vinegar, and sealing and labelling the jars ready to be ferried to the market on the stallholder's handcart.

Steve topped the jar he was filling with vinegar, closed

the lid and got up. 'I'll put the kettle on; I reckon we deserve a cup of tea after so much hard work,' he said. 'And just you remember, queen, who it is what's ruinin' his eyesight so's you can buy a dance dress; it's Steven Mickleborough, not Gerald Grimshaw.'

'Well, I enjoy going around with Gerald because we talk about lots of things I'd never have heard of if he hadn't told me,' Miranda explained. 'You're much more practical, Steve.' She chuckled. 'You took me horse racing, and to the football matches, so now I'm an Everton supporter and I know a bit about racing as well. But Gerald's helped me to understand why we're liable to go to war quite soon, for instance.' She grinned at her old friend. 'So you see, I value you both very highly, but in different ways. And Gerald will be off to university in a couple of years, so no doubt he'll lose interest in a little shorthand-typist and take up with an undergradu-ette, if that's what they call them.'

Steve sniffed. 'Well, so long as you don't let him take you dancing, I suppose I can't grumble.'

'Why don't you take me dancing yourself?' Miranda asked, knowing the answer full well. 'I know I don't have a decent dress yet, but I'm sure I don't mind going to the Grafton or the Daulby Hall in my office skirt and jumper.'

Steve grinned but shook his head. 'What, make a fool of myself in front of half Liverpool?' he said derisively. 'I can't dance; me brother Ted, the one what's in the Navy, says he'll learn me next time he's ashore for more than a few days . . .'

'*Teach* me, not learn me,' Miranda said instructively. 'If I've told you once, I've told you a hundred times.'

'What does it matter? You nag on when I asks you to borrow me half a dollar, but you know full well what I mean,' Steve said crossly. 'Stop tryin' to educate me, woman, or I'll forget meself and give you a clack round the ear. Oh, that reminds me, your horrible Aunt Vi stopped me as I was coming home from work yesterday and axed me why you'd not been to see them, nor you hadn't give them your new address. I lied in me teeth and telled her I didn't know and she give me a right glare, and nodded so hard that her chins wobbled. Then she said it weren't right, that woman keepin' you away from her kith and kin. She meant Mrs Grimshaw, of course. Then she said Beth wanted to know, because you cousins had always been fond of one another.' He pulled a face at Miranda. 'How I kept meself from laughin' out loud I'll never know, but I just managed it. Anyhow, she puffed off, mutterin', but I thought I'd better warn you.'

'Thanks, Steve, you're a real pal,' Miranda said gratefully. 'But in a way Aunt Vi's right; she really ought to have my address, and I wouldn't mind Beth seeing my new place, especially since I've got a flat share, which means Beth can't expect to be taken in.'

Miranda had met Avril Donovan at her shorthand and typing classes. Avril was a very large girl indeed, both tall and broad, with flaxen hair cut in a shining bob and merry blue eyes. She had been brought up in children's homes since her parents had been killed in a road accident when she was thirteen, and she was living in a hostel, but as soon as Miranda mentioned that she was looking for a flat share Avril had begged to be allowed to see the flat and, if Miranda was agreeable, to share it on a month's trial. Very soon the two girls realised that they were getting along famously, for Avril was an easy-going, hard-working girl, always willing to do more than her fair share of the work, since she was so grateful to Miranda for letting her live in the flat. To add to her other accomplishments, Avril was a good cook, having worked in a big bakery, so they took it in turns to prepare meals, and once they had had a small party, the guests being Steve, Julian and Gerald and, to make numbers even, one of the girls who worked with Avril at her clothing factory.

Very much to Miranda's surprise, Julian had liked Avril, and Miranda, who had secretly thought of him as rather a snob, had to change her mind. Avril was sweet, but she talked with a broad Liverpool accent and knew nothing of books, seeming almost proud of the fact that reading was a chore she had never really cared for, whereas Julian, who was working hard for his exams and hoping to go to university in the autumn, talked of things that had even Gerald mystified.

The party had been a great success but it had also cost a bit more than the girls expected. Since both of them were saving up, though for different reasons, they decided that parties would have to be rare events.

Very early in their relationship – in fact when Avril, sprawling across the kitchen table, had been writing a letter to one of her pals – Miranda had told her new friend all about her mother's mysterious disappearance. 'So whilst I'm saving up for a dance dress, it'll come from Paddy's Market, the same as all my clothes have,' she had admitted. 'Because what I'm really saving up for is my mother's return. I know she's not disappeared for ever, but I do think she may be in a similar condition to that of the friend who lived in this flat before I took over. Missie was kidnapped . . .'

When the story was finished, Avril had nodded understandingly. 'Of course, if your mother was kidnapped, like your pal Missie, and is now in a foreign country, she might well find it real hard to make folk believe her story, and lend her money to buy a passage home,' she had agreed. 'But if you find out where she is and go over there with all your cash, you'll be able to rescue her. That's what you're hopin', ain't it?'

'That's right,' Miranda had said after an appreciable pause. 'The thing is, when she first disappeared I was frantically worried and cross, so that when people thought she'd just gone off with a man of her own free will I stopped thinking logically. You see, I – I wasn't a very good daughter to her, only I didn't realise it until quite recently. My friend Steve – you've met him – does all sorts for his mother, and never a word of complaint. I took it for granted that Arabella would do all the housework, even iron my clothes, and give me pocket money for doing nothing but grumble when things didn't go my way. She liked me to call her Arabella, by the way, instead of Mum.'

Avril, laughing, had said she understood. 'I were real difficult at that age; I can't think how me mam stood me,' she had assured Miranda. 'If she said black, I'd say white; if she said go, I'd say stay; and if she asked me to do something – shoppin' or givin' a hand wi' the cleanin' – I'd do me best to wriggle out of it somehow. But I'm sure your mam wouldn't have run off to escape from you, kiddo. So if that's what's botherin' you . . .'

'Oh, it's not,' Miranda had said at once. 'As I told you,

I'm ninety-nine per cent sure she was kidnapped. No, I'm a hundred per cent certain that it was Arabella Missie saw being dragged down to the docks. But whatever happened, I'm sure she's alive and well, though naturally I can't explain why she doesn't seem to have made any effort to come home . . . or perhaps I should say that her efforts haven't been successful.'

'You mentioned memory loss, and the fact that she was probably sleepwalkin' at the time of her disappearance,' Avril had said thoughtfully. 'Oh, I'm sure you're right and she'll turn up again sometime . . .' she had grinned at her friend, 'and then I'll lose me lovely flat share and be cast out on the world. Or perhaps you'll let me have a shakedown in the livin' room until your mam sets you up like a queen in a proper house like the one you lived in before she disappeared.'

Now, however, Steve was handing her a steaming mug of tea and suggesting that they might take the jars of pickles along to the Great Homer Street market whilst there was still some daylight left. Miranda agreed that this was a good idea. 'Avril's gone to have tea with a friend, so we've got the flat to ourselves until nine or ten this evening,' she said. 'So when we've dumped the pickles, what do you say to fish and chips for supper?'

Steve agreed that this sounded good and the two set off, carrying the many jars of pickled onions down the stairs and stacking them on the borrowed handcart.

'Good thing you've got a pal with plenty of muscles around,' Steve said, tapping his chest with a forefinger. 'You'd of been hard put to it to get this thing over cobbles without cracking any of the jars, if I hadn't been with you.'

Miranda, heaving manfully at one of the handles, reminded him that Avril was pretty strong and that, at a pinch, she might have persuaded Gerald to give a hand, but as they reached the market and puffed to a halt beside Mrs Inchcombe's stall Steve made a derisive noise. 'Oh, ha, ha, that's a likely one!' he said. 'As you said yourself, earlier, Gerald is a good one to talk, but it's me that's good at doing.'

A lively argument might have developed, but at that moment the stallholder came out to greet them, and began to unload the handcart on to her stall. She was an enormously fat woman clad in a voluminous striped overall, with a thick scarf tied cornerwise over her hair, a muffler round her neck and large boots on her feet. She made admiring remarks about the onions, said they would all be sold within a week and waved them off with promises to take any more that they might produce, as soon as the ones that they had delivered were sold.

They were turning away from the stall, well satisfied, when Mrs Inchcombe called them back. 'You'll want some cash to buy more onions and vinegar,' she said breathlessly. 'Here's ten bob.' She chuckled richly. 'Shows I trust you, so don't you go lerrin' me down, queen.'

Miranda pocketed the money gratefully and tucked her hand into Steve's arm. 'When we get the money for the first lot of onions I'll share it with you,' she said. 'And you're right, of course; Gerald's a good pal in many ways but I can't see him pickling onions whilst tears plop on to his hands.' She pointed to the brightly lit window of a baker and confectioner's shop. 'Seeing as how I've got some money and it's a bit early for fish and chips,

I'll pop into Scott's and buy half a dozen sticky buns. We can have them as pudding after the fish and chips.'

Emerging from the shop, Miranda was unprepared when Steve suddenly shouted: 'Race you to the next lamppost!'

'Anyone would take us for a couple of kids,' she panted as they hurtled along the crowded pavement, causing a good few outraged shouts as they dodged folk hurrying along. They galloped into Russell Street, Miranda remarking that the run would have done them good after being shut up in the flat for most of the day, and saw a slim figure standing at the foot of the staircase which led to the flat. For one unbelieving moment Miranda thought it was Arabella, but the woman turned her head to smile, and even in the faint glow from the streetlamp she recognised Mrs Grimshaw. They stopped at the foot of the stairs and Miranda addressed her friend.

'What's up, Mrs Grimshaw? I wasn't supposed to be coming out to Holmwood today, was I? I'm pretty sure I told you that Steve and I were going to pickle onions . . . but how rude I am! Do come up to the flat, and we can boil the kettle and have a couple of the buns I've just bought. How nice it is to have a visitor! But I'm afraid the whole place probably reeks of onions, though it won't be quite so bad in the sitting room as in the kitchen.'

Smiling, Mrs Grimshaw followed them up the flight and into the small flat. After the fresh air the kitchen did indeed smell strongly of onions and Steve flung all the windows wide, though they only remained so for a few moments since the cold was crippling. Then he carried the tea tray through into the living room, whilst Miranda lit the lamp and Mrs Grimshaw arranged the buns on a pretty plate. She said nothing about her reason for calling on Miranda until the tea was poured and the buns handed round, but when she spoke her face was serious. 'Miranda, my dear, have you ever heard of a typhoon?'

The secret hope that Mrs Grimshaw had cheerful tidings to impart began to fade. 'Yes,' Miranda said, her voice no more than a whisper. 'Go on.'

The story did not take long in the telling. Apparently Missie had had cause to go with her employer to a neighbouring island, on plantation business. Once there, she bought some of the shellfish for sale in the market whilst Julian and Gerald's father went off with his manager, leaving Missie to wander around the harbour. True to her promise, she began to ask natives of the island whether they knew anything of the *Pride of the Sea*. Several of them did; indeed they seemed surprised that Missie had not heard. 'She foundered in a typhoon, two days out from her last port of call,' the harbour master had told her. 'Lost with all hands. There was one survivor, but he was just being given a lift from one island to another, so was not a member of the crew. But it's all history; it happened ages ago, and memories are short. No one was truly sorry that the *Pride* had gone, and the survivor, Ned Truin, said that for the short time he was on board most of the crew were drunk. They'd taken on a consignment of rum and someone had broached a bottle or a barrel, I don't know which. If you want more details, Ned Truin's working aboard a fishing boat which will be in harbour before dark. These old seamen never go far from the sea, but when he comes ashore I'll point him out and he'll tell you the story as he experienced it.'

Missie had sought out Mr Grimshaw and explained that she owed it to her English friends to get the full story, and Mr Grimshaw had agreed to delay their departure from the island until she had had a chance to do so.

The full story, as heard from Ned Truin, was a mixture of foolishness, downright wickedness and bad weather, for though Ned admitted that most of the crew were drunk and incapable, he thought there was little they could have done to save the ship once the typhoon had hit them. Within moments the sea, which had been blue and relatively calm, had become a raging inferno of ten-foot white-capped waves, which smashed down on the *Pride* until she was little better than matchwood. When the ship went down – largely in pieces – he himself had managed to cling on to a spar. He had had a terrible and frightening time over a period of two days and nights, for sharks were busy in the vicinity and he thought he had only been saved from being torn apart by managing to scramble into the ship's dinghy, whence he was rescued at last by a passing fishing boat.

Naturally, Missie's first hope had been that Arabella might already have left the ship, but when she asked Ned Truin if he knew of anyone's doing so he could only shrug. Mr Grimshaw had explained that they were searching for a woman who they believed had been kidnapped by the captain and his mate, but again Ned Truin could not say for certain what had happened on board the ill-omened ship before the typhoon blew up. 'I had only been aboard two days when the storm came,' he had told Missie. 'I realised the crew were a bad lot, but that was all.'

Mrs Grimshaw rose from her chair as her sad story

ended and went to sit beside Miranda on the couch, putting a comforting arm around her shoulders. 'My poor child, I've dreaded giving you this appalling news ever since Missie's letter and the report from the harbour master arrived in the mail this morning. At first Mr Grimshaw wanted to keep it from you, wanted to let you to continue to hope, but in his heart I'm sure he knew that to say nothing would have been cruel in the long run.'

Miranda did not speak, but the slow tears formed and fell, formed and fell. She knew Mrs Grimshaw's arm was round her shoulders, but she could not feel it. Arabella could not have drowned! She would not believe it, no matter how convincing the story. But Steve was speaking – she must listen. 'But suppose, like Missie, Miranda's mum escaped and hid herself away whilst the men were loading or unloading somewhere, and then could not be found?' Steve said at last, and even in her deep distress Miranda could hear the quiver in his voice. 'That's possible, isn't it?'

Mrs Grimshaw heaved a deep sigh. 'You must understand, my dears, that the islands which the *Pride* visited are all small, with few inhabitants. It seems to both my husband and myself highly unlikely that she could have got ashore unseen by anyone and stayed hidden for even the smallest amount of time. If such a thing had happened someone must have helped her, and why should such a person not admit to their good deed? Saving anyone from the sea and from men such as Captain Hogg is surely something to boast about, not to keep quiet? I'm afraid, my dear, that such hopes have no basis in reality. According to Missie's letter, my brother-in-law carried out a rigorous search on all the islands within reach of the one to which Ned Truin was taken, and found no indication that any stranger had landed on any of them.'

There was a silence. Miranda sat on the couch as if turned to stone, her wide eyes fixed unseeingly on Mrs Grimshaw's face as though it were a picture on the cinema screen; as though if she stared hard enough she would see her beautiful golden-haired mother being pulled ashore and rescued.

Steve, having given the matter some thought, went over to Miranda and knelt beside her, taking her cold hands and squeezing them comfortingly. 'No one can be certain that your mam was still aboard,' he said bracingly. 'And no woman's body was cast ashore. Isn't that proof of a sort that she wasn't aboard when the *Pride* went down?'

'No; Missie said there were – were sharks,' Miranda mumbled. She gave a convulsive shudder, then straightened and glared defiantly from Steve's anxious face to Mrs Grimshaw's. 'I can't – and won't – believe Arabella is dead,' she said loudly. 'If she is, I'm sure I would know in my heart, because Arabella and I were close, even though we had our bad moments when we shouted at one another and – and said things we didn't mean.'

'Of course you did; mothers and daughters are always falling out and then falling in again,' Mrs Grimshaw said comfortingly. 'And I'm sure you're right; but at least we now know that it is useless to try to find the *Pride of the Sea* or any member of her crew. However, there are a great many islands in the Caribbean. Your mother might have swum from the wreckage to any one of those islands, so we still have a great deal of ground to cover before we need give up.'

Miranda gave the older woman a watery smile. 'My mother can't swim, any more than I can,' she said sadly. 'She wasn't a very practical woman, not in that way. But you're right; I shall never give up hope of finding her alive.'

After Mrs Grimshaw had left them Steve looked at his friend's woebegone face, and decided that she must not be allowed to mope. After all, her mother had disappeared a long while ago, and though his pal claimed to think of Arabella every day Steve knew that this was probably her conscience talking. She had entered the world of work, was meeting new people and changing from an awkward child to a striking young woman. Her carroty curls had darkened to a shade between chestnut and auburn, the dusting of golden freckles across her nose gave warmth to her complexion, and she was developing a proper figure. Like it or not, he was sure her obsession with her mother's disappearance had begun to fade, though now of course the discovery that the *Pride of the Sea* had been lost with all hands had brought Arabella to the forefront of her daughter's mind once more. Probably she'll never quite lose the hope that her mother will miraculously turn up again and claim her, Steve told himself. But the Grimshaws are good people; they'll see that she lives her own life, and stops living in a fool's paradise.

Steve took his coat from its peg, slipped it on and helped Miranda into hers. 'You were goin' to buy us fish 'n' chips, Miss Moneybags,' he reminded her. 'Oh, but we've ate the buns what were intended for our pudding, so shall us pop along to the market and buy a couple of them big oranges you're so fond of?'

Miranda shrugged. 'I don't care,' she said listlessly as they left the flat and clattered down the iron stairs.

Steve blew out a steaming breath into the icy air, then glanced up at the lowering grey sky above. 'Reckon we'll have snow before morning,' he remarked. 'If there's a decent fall, shall us take my old sledge up to Simonswood and see how far we can travel on it?'

'Whatever you like,' Miranda said shortly, and Steve couldn't help giving an inward grin. She was clutching her unhappiness to her bosom, trying to make him see that the news Mrs Grimshaw had given them had affected her deeply. Well, he knew it had, of course, but he also knew that she was in the same position after Mrs Grimshaw's news as she had been before it. True, she now knew that the *Pride of the Sea* had foundered, and that there was a possibility that her mother had drowned with the rest. But if you were honest she was really no worse off than she had been before Mrs Grimshaw's revelations.

Steve sighed. 'Miranda? If it snows all night . . .'

He was interrupted. 'Snow? What does it matter? I don't care if it snows ink,' Miranda said dully. 'I keep thinking of my poor Arabella, struggling in an icy sea, perhaps even seeing approaching sharks . . .'

Her voice ended on a pathetic hiccup, but this was too much for the practical Steve. 'Oh, for God's sake, be your age and use your brain,' he said crossly. He took hold of her hand, tucking it into his elbow. 'However your mam died – if she *did* die – it wasn't in icy water. Okay, this typhoon thing blew up, but the water would be warm, probably quite pleasant . . .'

Miranda tore her hand away from his and turned on

him, eyes flashing. 'How dare you speak to me like that when I'm in such distress! I hate you, Steve Mickleborough, you're cruel and wicked and unfeeling! If it was your mother eaten by sharks you wouldn't be so offhand about it.'

Steve gave a smothered giggle; he couldn't help it. Just the thought of his cosy, smiling mother struggling in a Mersey full of enormous sharks was so absurd that he could only laugh. 'I can just see me mam punching a shark right on its hooter,' he said, trying to choke back the laughter and failing dismally. 'Anyway, you don't know that your mam was eaten by sharks. I thought you believed she was still alive and kicking somewhere. You said . . .'

Miranda rounded on him, her cheeks flushed with anger and her tear-filled eyes bright with rage. 'I *do* think she's alive, I do, I do,' she said vehemently. 'And you're cruel and hateful to scoff.'

Once again, laughter bubbled up in Steve's throat. 'If we're going to talk about scoff, let's buy them fish 'n' chips, take 'em back to the flat and scoff them, instead of scoffing at each other,' he said. 'Don't be an idiot, Miranda. You can't have it both ways: either you're going to mourn your mother as dead, which is understandable, or you're going to insist she's alive and safe on some island or other, but simply hasn't managed to get in touch. Now tell me, which is it to be?'

Miranda tightened her lips and said nothing. She speeded up, and when the fish and chip shop was reached she joined the queue, fishing out the money the stall-holder had given her. Steve chatted amiably as they inched up towards the counter, saying that he would buy a bottle of Corona to go with their meal, and asking Miranda whether she would like him to buy a slab of cake to take the place of the buns they had eaten earlier.

Miranda, however, still clearly in the grip of annoyance, tightened her lips once more and said nothing, and Steve fell silent as well. In fact they bought the chips, a bottle of cherryade and a slab of plain cake and carried everything back to the flat without exchanging another word. When they got there Miranda unlocked the door, ushered Steve inside, and divided the fish and chips between two china plates. Then she went into the small pantry – it was more like a cupboard – and produced salt and vinegar and a couple of glasses for the cherryade, all of this in complete silence. Steve, beginning to be really annoyed with his old friend, decided to follow her example and did not say anything either whilst they polished off the food and drink in record time, for it had been a long day and they were both extremely hungry.

When all the food was gone and the kettle hopping on the hob, Steve used half the water to wash up their plates and cutlery. Then he turned to Miranda. 'I can see you're still in a nasty mood, but I was brought up to be polite even when others were rude,' he said calmly. 'Good night, Miranda, and thank you for my share of the fish and chips. I'm sorry if I upset you by saying the wrong thing, but I truly meant it for the best. You're me bezzie, so that means I ought to be able to speak me mind and trust you not to take it wrong. Will you forgive me?' He had already put on his coat and hat and had his hand on the doorknob waiting for – indeed expecting – Miranda to speak, but she said nothing. Steve sighed. He supposed she had a reason for behaving so badly but none of it was his fault, so why was she taking her ill humour out on him? It was scarcely because of him that the *Pride of the Sea* had foundered. All he had really done was try to make her see that she was behaving illogically and making her situation worse. He turned to open the door and glanced back over his shoulder, but Miranda was now at the sink collecting the plates and mugs to replace them on the dresser, and took no notice of him even when snowflakes blew in through the doorway. She just stood with her back to him, stacking the plates, and he felt maliciously pleased when the cold wind roared into the room and attacked Miranda's pinafore-clad form. He saw her give a little shiver, and for a moment was tempted to go back and give her a hug. Perhaps he had been wrong to try to make her choose between accepting that her mother was dead and believing that she was still alive, but even as he hesitated, wanting to turn back, his pride rose up and refused to let him eat any more humble pie than he had already digested. He went out on to the top of the steps, closing the door softly and gently behind him. She'll have come to her senses by tomorrow, he told himself. Poor old girl. Although we've all been half expecting such news, it's obviously hit her hard. But she's sensible, is Miranda; I bet by tomorrow she'll be full of plans. She'll talk about setting off for the West Indies as soon as summer comes, and why not? If she doesn't go soon the war they're all talking about will start and she won't be able to go anywhere.

Sighing to himself, Steve clattered down the flight and into the snowstorm. Tomorrow's Sunday, so if the snow builds up real good then I reckon it'd be worth a gang of us making our way out to Simonswood and taking my sledge and any sturdy trays we can lay hands on, he told himself. Miranda will have got over her sulks by then; she loves sledging. We went last year and she loved every minute. If I get up early enough I'll get Mam to pack up a carry-out. She's bound to have bread and jam and that, and I can buy another slab of cake and another bottle of Corona. Oh aye, if the snow continues, Miranda won't go on bearing a grudge. He grinned to himself. She'd better say she's sorry, 'cos I've done it once and now it's her turn.

Making his way along the snowy and deserted streets, he decided that he would tell his mother what had transpired as soon as he reached home. She was a grand woman, his mam, and always knew what was the right thing to do. She'd feel rare sorry for Miranda, of course, but that wouldn't stop her seeing his point of view. Thinking back, he was glad he had apologised and tried to make things right, because he knew his mother would tell him to do just that. He guessed that she would also tell him off for pointing out that Miranda had got the temperature of the sea all wrong. He really shouldn't have said that; he was lucky she had not battered him across the ear, even though it was true.

Steve turned the corner and the full force of the storm hit him, hurling snowflakes into his face with stinging force. He turned up his collar and pulled his cap lower over his brow. Not much further, he told himself. Soon be out of this horrible weather and in Mam's kitchen. Wonder what she's got for supper? Hope it's scouse. He plodded on, all memory of the fish supper he had recently eaten disappearing under the onslaught of the storm. Scouse would be nice, but what he most wanted at the moment was a big mug of hot tea with two sugars and possibly one of Mam's shortbread fingers. He turned into the jigger and actually had difficulty in recognising his own back yard through the whirling flakes, but he made it at last and burst into the kitchen looking, no doubt, just like a snowman for his mother, seated comfortably by the fire in her old wicker rocking chair, gave a squawk of protest, and his stepfather, seated in the chair opposite and working away at his weekend task of mending the family's shoes, begged him tersely to 'Gerrinto the yard, lad, and brush off that perishin' snow; us don't want the kitchen like a pond when it melts.'

Steve obeyed. Then he came back into the kitchen, hung his outer clothing on a peg by the door and turned to his mother. 'Have you had supper yet, Mam?' he asked hopefully. 'I'm that hungry me belly thinks me throat's been cut. But if you've et . . .'

'I saved you a dish of scouse and two big boiled potatoes,' Mrs Mickleborough said at once. 'It's on the back of the stove keeping warm. I guessed you'd be glad of a bite after fighting your way from your young lady's place to Jamaica Close.'

'Thanks, Mam, but she ain't my young lady, nor likely to be,' Steve said gloomily, emptying the contents of the saucepan on to a tin plate. 'There's been news of that ship – the *Pride of the Sea* – what Miranda thinks her mother may have been aboard . . .'

When the story was finished – and the scouse also – Steve looked hopefully at his mother. 'I reckon you'll say I did wrong to try to make her see she weren't no worse off than before,' he said apologetically. 'Lookin' back, I can't think what come over me. I said I was sorry of course, but she never said a word, not even when I thanked her for the fish 'n' chips . . .'

His stepfather, who had not appeared to be listening with undue attention to the story, looked up, brows rising. 'Fish 'n' chips?' he said indignantly. 'And then you come here and guzzle a big plate of scouse and spuds! You've got hollow legs, young man.'

Steve laughed, but his attention was fixed on his mother. 'I'll go round tomorrer and tell her I'm sorry and mebbe we'll sit down and write a lot of letters for Missie or the Grimshaws to hand out to any islanders they think might know something,' he said. 'Poor old Miranda; she feels guilty, you know, because she wasn't nicer to her mam when she had the chance.'

Mrs Mickleborough sniffed, but Mr Mickleborough nodded slowly. 'That's what you call *what might have been*,' he said. 'It's allus the same when someone goes out of reach; those that are left wish they'd been kinder. Ah well, no doubt your little pal will come to terms with what's happened. And now, my lad, you'd best wash up that plate and mug and gerrup to bed, 'cos I know you. Tomorrer bein' Sunday, a whole gang of you will go off to Simonswood, snowballin', mekkin slides and sledgin', so you'd best get a good night's sleep.'

'Okay, Dad,' Steve said, but his eyes were still fixed on his mother's face. 'I thought I'd ask Miranda to come sledging with me; we could have a whole day away if you'd make up a carry-out for us. I don't mind takin' Kenny if you think I ought.'

He was relieved, however, when his mother shook her head. 'You'll have your work cut out to get back on the right side of young Miranda,' she said sagely. 'And now gerroff to bed, young man; I'll let you have a bit of a lie-in, but if the snow's still thick I'll wake you around nine o'clock. And once you're in bed you can work out how best to make up with your pal.'

After Steve had left, Miranda simply sat in the kitchen fighting the despair which threatened to overcome her. She acknowledged that she had probably overreacted to Mrs Grimshaw's news, and she knew in her heart that it had been no reason to turn on Steve the way she had. He was her bezzie, had never faltered in his championship of her, had listened patiently whilst she went over and over the last day that she and her mother had spent together. He had never criticised her for her behaviour, and even after Mrs Grimshaw's dreadful news he had been supportive. In fact the only thing she could blame him for was his callousness regarding the water in which her mother had drowned – *if* there had been a woman aboard, and if that woman had been her mother, of course. Going out for the fish and chips and feeling the cold wind trying to tear the hair from her head, it was natural that she had thought of her mother struggling in an ice-cold sea, but it was also foolish. She and Steve both knew from talking to Missie and the Grimshaw boys that the weather in the West Indies was tropical, that the sea was blue and warm as milk, and that in any case sharks would not venture into the icy waters that surrounded the British Isles.

Yet still she could not help feeling furious with Steve. He simply did not realise that her mind was still in shock from the story she had been told. He had been right when he had pointed out that she could either mourn her mother as dead or believe that she was still alive somewhere, but he should have understood that she couldn't think logically at the moment.

When Avril returned from her evening out, she was so full of chat that Miranda did not have to open her mouth, and presently Avril made both of them a cup of cocoa, and then went to bed. If she was surprised at Miranda's short answers to her questions she gave no sign of it and presently, sitting on the hard chair in the kitchen, her mind aching with worry and confusion, Miranda looked up at the clock and saw that it read midnight. Sighing, she damped down the fire and went through to bed, suddenly realising that she was totally exhausted, too tired even to prepare herself properly for bed. She slid between the sheets in her underwear and was asleep almost as soon as her head touched the pillow.

First there was a sensation of falling which seemed to go on for a long time, and then she was in the water. Waves as high, it seemed, as a house picked her up and threw her from one to another as though she were the ball in some wild, cruel game. She started to cry out and was gagged by the water pouring into her open mouth. Something hit her a numbing blow and she grabbed for it just as another wave, bigger than the rest, smashed down on her, but she hung on, thinking how often she had heard of a drowning man clutching at a straw, wondering whether that was what she was doing, but continuing to cling nevertheless. When the next wave crashed over her she realised she was holding on to a plank of wood; wood floats and will stay on the surface, she told herself, even in the worst and most violent sea.

Then for an instant she felt her foot touch something; was it land? But just as she was beginning to hope, a huge wave snatched her up and once more there was only darkness and water, though she was aware that there was flotsam all around her; the remains of the ship on which she had been travelling when the storm hit.

But she had no time for conjecture; the only thing that mattered was clinging to the spar of wood and praying that someone would find her before her strength gave out, before her numb fingers were torn from the spar by the strength of the attacking waves, and she was dragged into the depths.

Mostly she had scarcely bothered to look around her in the pitch dark, but presently she thought she saw a lightening of the sky overhead, and it seemed to her that the sea grew calmer as dawn, cool and grey, lit the sky. She was beginning to hope, to think that she might drag herself ashore if she were lucky enough to be carried on her friendly plank to terra firma, when she felt something nudge her dangling legs. For a moment she remembered stories of friendly dolphins helping shipwrecked mariners to gain the nearest land, but then another image arose, and she kicked out convulsively, terror in every movement. Sharks!

Desperately, she tried to haul herself aboard the plank and almost succeeded, but then her weight tipped the plank right over. For a moment she clutched it, but then the water entered her gaping mouth and she spiralled down into darkness.

Miranda awoke. She had a vague feeling that she had been dreaming and suspected that it had not been a particularly pleasant dream; why should it be pleasant, after all? Mrs Grimshaw and Steve had tried to make light of the fact that the *Pride of the Sea* had foundered in a storm somewhere in the Caribbean and that her mother might possibly have been aboard. There had been one survivor, the man who had paid to be taken aboard as supercargo in order to reach the next island at which the *Pride of the Sea* would drop anchor. Miranda sighed and sat up, glancing towards the window. For a moment she was honestly surprised to see, through a crack in the curtains, snowflakes whirling past; odd! For some reason she had expected to see bright sunlight and blue skies, and as she jumped out of bed to feel warm linoleum beneath her feet. Instead the whole room was freezing cold, and when she went over to the washstand ice had formed on the jug.

Miranda frowned. The events of the previous evening were somewhat vague, but she did remember that she had been very angry with Steve because he had not seemed to sympathise with her conviction that her mother was still alive. However, she also remembered – or thought she did – that he had promised her some sort of treat; whatever had it been? Judging by the weather she could see through the window it must have been some sort of indoor activity, and since today was Sunday she supposed that the most she could expect would be an invitation to share the Mickleboroughs' Sunday dinner, which was nice but not her idea of a special occasion.

Having ascertained that she would have to go and boil some water in order to get a wash, Miranda donned dressing gown and slippers and went through to the kitchen. She had not wound the alarm clock the previous night and had no idea of the time, but as she entered the kitchen she saw that it was nine o'clock, and when she tapped the kettle it was warm, so she guessed that Avril had been up at the usual time, breakfasted and gone off to church, no doubt guessing that her friend had been late to bed.

Miranda carried the hot water to her room, washed and dressed and returned to the kitchen. She made herself a mug of tea and several slices of toast, still aware that she was confused as to just what had been arranged the previous evening. In fact she was on her last piece of toast when she heard feet clattering up the outside stair and she got up and opened the door, imagining that it would be Steve.

But she was wrong; it was Gerald, pink-cheeked and breathing hard. He grinned at her, then knocked the snow off his cap and brushed it from his shoulders before entering the kitchen. 'Morning, Miranda. You all right?' he said, and Miranda heard the anxiety behind his cheerful words, and was grateful. He had obviously been told by his aunt or uncle about the *Pride of the Sea* and had guessed she would need cheering up. However, she did not intend to let Gerald know how desperately unhappy she had been, so she smiled and went over to the teapot.

'Want a cuppa?' she asked brightly. 'You can have toast an' all – I've cut plenty of bread – but you'll have to make it yourself. Why have you come round so early?'

'I wouldn't mind some toast,' Gerald said, rubbing his hands together. 'It's most dreadfully cold out there, what we call brass monkey weather at Browncoats. And I'm early because I thought you might like to go sledging; the buses are still running, so the roads can't be too bad. We could get out to Simonswood and I thought it might take your mind off – off your troubles. Julian and I are spending the weekend at Holmwood Lodge which is how I came to hear about the *Pride of the Sea*.' He patted her arm. 'Poor old Miranda. What a frightening story. But Auntie told me you believe your mother is still alive, and I'm sure you're right. It may take time, but us Grimshaws know all sorts of people in the West Indies, and I'm sure if your mother is on one of the islands we'll hear about it in due course. So you're to stop worrying and start getting on with your life.'

'Oh, Gerald, you are kind, and sensible as well,' Miranda said gratefully, but the mention of Simonswood had brought Steve's suggestion rushing back. He had wanted her to go to Simonswood with him so that they could sledge. Well, she hadn't said she would, though she hadn't said she wouldn't either. She decided it was time that Steve was taken down a peg or two; taught that he was not the only person on whom she relied. Accordingly, she gave Gerald a big smile. 'That would be lovely. Where's your sledge? And shall I make a carry-out? I've got a flask which I can fill with tea so we can have a hot drink . . .'

'You'll come? Oh, that's wizard,' Gerald said. 'As for my . . . er, my sledge, it's in the boot of Uncle's car. He's letting Julian drive it now he's passed his test. Don't bother with a carry-out – Uncle telephoned one of his tenants to see if she was still doing farmhouse teas and light lunches, and she is. So he booked a meal for four people and we'll eat at her place.'

'Four?' Miranda squeaked. 'Who's the fourth? You aren't going to suggest taking Steve, are you?'

Gerald looked surprised. 'Why not? But actually we thought Avril might enjoy a day out; if she's got no other plans, that is.'

'She's gone to early service so she should be home in about ten minutes, but I'm sure she'll come with us,' Miranda said. She knew she was being mean by excluding Steve, but whenever she thought of his behaviour the previous evening she felt sore and upset. And she was sure he had not dreamed of inviting Julian or Gerald on his sledging trip, so it was fair enough that they should plan a trip and not invite him. But Gerald was talking, and Miranda dragged her mind back to the present.

'. . . and you'll need warm clothes, your wellington boots and a good solid tray. That tin one advertising Guinness would be fine,' Gerald was saying. He read her startled look and grinned apologetically. 'We do have a sledge, a great big old-fashioned thing, but it won't fit into the boot of the Rover, so Auntie is letting us use a couple of her trays. We thought it would be more fun if we could have races, which means we'll need a tray each. I told Julian to give me ten or fifteen minutes to persuade you and then to come round here to pick us up, so maybe this is him arriving,' he added, as they both heard the clang of someone beginning to climb the stairs.

Miranda shot open the back door, suddenly wondering what on earth she would say if it was Steve, but it was not. Avril cast off her snowy coat and headscarf, then went across to the fire. 'Brrrr, it's perishin' icy out there,' she said breezily. She turned to Gerald. 'You're early, ain't you? And your brother's sitting in a car a couple of doors down, readin' a book. What's up?'

'Oh, Avril, they've come to ask us if we'd like to go sledging and have our dinners at one of those farmhouses who do food,' Miranda said happily. At the thought of the treat in store, all the misery she had felt the previous evening had disappeared. She still felt very cross with Steve, though, and thought it would serve him right when he discovered she had gone sledging with somebody else. 'Are you on?' Avril was thrilled, and in an incredibly short space of time the four of them – and their trays – were packed into the Rover and Julian was driving with great care along the snowy streets towards their destination.

Despite his mother's promise to wake him if it continued to snow, it was quite ten o'clock before Steve, wrapped up to the eyebrows, ascended the metal stairs and rapped on Miranda's door. Then as he always did he tried to fling it open, only to meet resistance. Steve grinned to himself; she was probably still in bed, lazy little monkey. Well, he would keep knocking until she answered, because he was sure by now she would have got over her temper and be as eager for the treat as he was himself. Five minutes later, with a worried frown, he was descending the stairs again, his feet touching the pavement just as Pete Huxtable, with Timmy at heel, came out of the shop and turned to lock the door behind him. Turning back, he spotted Steve and broke into speech. 'Mornin', Steve! As you can see I'm takin' his lordship for his mornin' constitutional. I let him out earlier – bein' Sunday there were no one much about – and he played in the snow as though he'd never seen such a thing before; well, I bet he hasn't, at that. He were tryin' to eat it and when Miranda chucked a snowball at him he thought it were a real ball and kept tryin' to pick it up. We all had a rare laugh, I can tell you.'

'Mornin', Pete; hello, Timmy,' Steve said. 'I've been up to the flat, but though I knocked real loud no one came. Are the girls out, then?'

'Oh aye; they're all out all right. When I sez all, that includes them two chaps from the Browncoat school,' Pete informed him, looking wistful. 'I don't know what Avril sees in the la-di-da one, but there's no accountin' for tastes.'

As he spoke he pinched the bridge of his nose with thumb and forefinger, a gesture which Steve had seen him use before when troubled. Steve smiled to himself: he had suspected before that Pete had fallen for Miranda's flatmate; now he was sure of it.

'I axed 'em where they were off to,' Pete went on. 'The la-di-da one was drivin' a car and Miranda said they was goin' to Simonswood to go a-sledgin' an' have their dinners at a farmhouse.' He pulled a rueful face. 'No wonder the gals was all pink and excited. All I can offer is a ride on the carrier of me racin' bike, which don't compare with a Rover.'

For a moment Steve was literally bereft of speech, and stared at the other man, his jaw dropping. Then he pulled himself together. 'Ah well, if she's gone off with the Grimshaws there's no point in my hangin' around,' he said. 'And you say they're havin' dinner somewhere and will be out for the whole day? Then I'd best look up one of me other pals.' He gestured towards his sledge. 'As you can see, I'm off to find a good slope meself.'

Pete had been looking rather anxious, but now he smiled. 'That's right, Steve, why not gerron a bus an' join 'em?' he enquired jovially. 'But I mustn't forget me duty to his lordship here.' He jerked a thumb at Timmy, who was now straining at the leash and whining. 'He's a right knowing one, is Timmy. I gives him a good walk every day afore I opens up the shop, but Sundays is special. We go all the way to Toxteth Park and I lets him off the lead and throws the ball until he's tired of retrievin' it. Then we goes to my Aunt Eva's and she makes us a Sunday dinner fit for a king. She's rare fond of Timmy so he always has his share, roast spuds, veggies an' all. She even gives him a bit of apple pie and custard for his afters, and he gobbles it up like winkin'.'

He paused, evidently expecting a reply, and Steve dragged his mind back from what he'd like to do to Miranda for her treachery to the present. 'Lucky old Timmy,' he said hollowly. 'Well, as Miranda's not about I'll be on my way. Enjoy your dinner, Pete.'

Heading for Jamaica Close once more, Steve grew angrier and angrier. It was true that the Grimshaws had arrived earlier at the flat than he, but he knew jolly well that his invitation had been extended first. True, Miranda had not accepted it, but neither had she refused it. In fact she had been in such a nasty mood that she had not even acknowledged the suggestion. For a moment Steve wondered if she had simply gone with the Grimshaws because they had a car and could take her out in style. But by this time he knew the boys well enough to guess that they would willingly have included him in their day out had Miranda explained the situation. That she had not seen fit to do so was evident, so although he felt no animosity towards Julian or Gerald he felt a good deal towards Miranda. Girls, he thought with disgust. You couldn't trust them, not where their emotions were concerned. A lad would never behave so shabbily, but that was women for you. They could take offence over the most trivial thing – he seemed to remember it was a disagreement over the temperature of the water in the Caribbean which had made Miranda screaming mad – and how they could bear a grudge! He could remember various occasions when Miranda had been so pigheaded that he had wanted to shake her, only good manners did not allow a feller to shake a girl, unless they were related, of course.

Striding out along the pavement, which was still covered by a good six inches of snow, he all but walked into someone striding in the opposite direction, and would have passed by without a word, save that the other pushed back the hood of his duffel coat and grabbed Steve's arm, saying as he did so: 'Hello–ello–ello, where's you off to in such a rush that you don't reckernise your ol' pal?'

Steve stared; then a slow grin spread over his face. 'Cyril Rogers, by all that's wonderful! Where the devil have you sprung from? I've not seen you since school. You joined one of the services, didn't you? I keep sayin' I'm goin' to do just that, though I've not got round to it yet. But we can't stand here talkin' whilst we freeze to the spot; come back to Jamaica Close and we can have a good old jangle in the warm.'

'Grand idea,' Cyril said, falling into step with Steve. 'I'm on leave, as I reckon you've guessed, but today me family have gone off to visit me gran what lives over the water in Birkenhead. She's a right miserable old codger, so I thought I'd call round and visit young Emily Sutcliffe, the gairl what I used to take dancin' when I lived at home. I thought mebbe I'd tek her sledgin' in Prince's Park, but she had other plans, it seems.' He pulled a face. 'I can't blame her I suppose, but she's found herself another feller, one who lives a good deal closer than two hundred odd miles, so I'm at a loose end. Wharrabout you, Steve? Gorrany plans of your own?' His eyes fell on the sledge which Steve was still dragging behind him. 'Oh, I see you have.'

'Well, I were goin' to go sledgin' if I could find someone to come with me,' Steve admitted. 'Tell you what, I know a couple of girls, good sports, what'd come sledgin' like a shot if you and me was to ask 'em. Remember Pearl and Ruby? Them sisters what live near the school? If we paid their bus fares and bought 'em a meal, they'd come along, no question. What d'you say we give it a go?'

Miranda kept telling herself that she was having the time of her life. She and Avril had each brought along a tin tray, but when they reached the slope which they'd judged best for sledging down, they found several people were before them and somehow this made the expedition even more fun. They organised some races, descending both singly and in pairs, but if the truth were told Miranda was missing Steve and was miserably conscious that she had behaved badly. However, she would not let her companions down by showing that she was not perfectly happy. She felt quite envious of Avril who clearly was having the time of her life, teasing the rather staid Julian until he was in fits of laughter and behaving,

Miranda thought, just like any other young fellow out with his girl. So when she happened to glance to where a new party were clambering on to their trays, she was momentarily thrilled to recognise Steve. In fact she was walking towards him, a broad smile on her face, eager to apologise for having come on ahead of him, when he flung his arms around a girl she remembered from school, gave her a kiss on the cheek and a smack on the bottom, and then jumped on the back of her tray so that the two of them disappeared down the hillside in a flurry of snow and shrieks.

Miranda turned away, misery speedily swamped by fury. How dared Steve kiss another girl when he was supposed to be her bezzie? In all the time they had known one another Steve had never kissed her, nor had she expected him to do so. Friends, she reminded herself, did not do anything as soppy as kissing.

'What's up, Miranda?' Gerald's voice cut across her thoughts. 'I see Steve's arrived. Are you going to suggest that he come to lunch with us? I'm sure there'll be plenty of food for one or two extra. By the look of it, that girl in the blue knitted cap is with him, so he'd probably want to bring her along.'

Miranda gritted her teeth but managed to reply airily, 'You mean Pearl? Yes, I think he's with her. She and Ruby – they're sisters – were in my class at school. But no, I wouldn't dream of suggesting that Steve come along. In fact it's the last thing I'd do.'

Gerald looked mildly surprised. 'Really? Well, you're probably right. Now, are you going to share my tray for one last swoop before we go to the farm for something to eat?'

Despite the best of intentions, Miranda could not help watching Steve, an older feller she also remembered from school, and the two girls, whenever she thought herself unobserved. And the more she watched, the crosser she grew. In fact she gave an inward sigh of relief when Julian and Gerald insisted that she and Avril leave the slope so that they might drive to the farmhouse. 'Mrs Higginbottom will be expecting us,' Julian reminded them. 'If I know her she'll make us a hot meal, for though she only provides salads in the summertime she'll guess we need something to keep the cold out and will cater accordingly. Gosh, if this lot knew that a hot meal was being prepared only a quarter of a mile or so away they'd probably insist upon coming along as well.'

As they climbed into the car, red-cheeked and bright-eyed, Miranda cast a glance around her and spotted Steve in earnest conversation with the feller whose name she could not remember, but then they were all in the Rover and Julian was driving carefully along the snow-covered road, and very soon they were in the Higginbottom farmhouse enjoying the magnificent meal which their hostess had prepared.

Chapter Eight

For the rest of the day Miranda brooded, trying to decide how she should treat her pal when they next met, for he had never before shown any interest in Pearl or Ruby; in fact he had never shown an interest in any girls. True, he was certainly interested in Miranda, but she now realised that this was not the same thing at all as the interest he had been showing in Pearl. Both sisters had the reputation of being what they called 'good time girls', and if anything Steve had rather despised them, yet here he was taking them sledging and ignoring Miranda completely. The thought that Miranda was also ignoring him occurred, only to be dismissed. She had walked towards him, smiling in the friendliest fashion, had she not? She told herself, untruthfully, that she had intended to ask him to accompany them to Mrs Higginbottom's, had only not done so when she saw him kissing Pearl. Well, she hoped that by now he was regretting his behaviour and would apologise to her the next time they met. The trouble with this pious hope was twofold, however. First, she knew very well that she could not possibly have extended an invitation to Steve without first discussing it with Julian and Gerald, and second that she had been at fault from the moment she had accepted their invitation, knowing full well that Steve had asked her first.

Despite the excellence of the meal Mrs Higginbottom put in front of them, Miranda found that her usual hearty appetite had fled, and she had to force herself to eat. They did not leave the farmhouse until darkness had fallen and Julian crept along, headlights blazing, clearly worried that the car might skid and deposit them all in the ditch. However, this worry proved groundless, and soon enough Miranda and Avril were thanking the brothers sincerely for a wonderful day and promising to entertain them, in their turn, to what Avril described as a 'splendiferous high tea' in the flat the following weekend.

'And with a bit of luck you'll of got out of your bad mood by then and be pals wi' Steve again,' she said airily, filling the kettle at the sink. 'I dunno what were the matter wi' you and Steve, but I could see you'd both got a cob on when not a word was exchanged, and I wasn't the only one to notice; Julian asked me what was up.'

Miranda felt her cheeks grow hot. 'I don't know what you mean,' she said feebly. 'What makes you think I was annoyed with him? He's my best pal . . .'

Avril gave a disbelieving laugh. 'No one treats their best pal the way you treated poor Steve,' she said roundly. 'And no matter how hard you tried not to show it, any fool could see you were in a bate. For a start, whenever you thought no one was looking you had a face like a smacked bum, and so did Steve.'

Miranda began to mutter that Avril had misread the situation but, having started, Avril did not intend to let the matter lie. 'Don't try to pull the wool over my eyes, 'cos it won't work,' she said firmly. 'I don't know what's been goin' on betwixt the pair of you but it's pretty obvious you've had an almighty great quarrel, probably your first from what I know of you, and I guess seeing poor old Steve give that girl a peck on the cheek just about put the lid on it.' She grinned widely, then stretched across the table and tapped Miranda's hot cheek. 'No use getting in a rage with me, 'cos I've read the situation like a perishin' book,' she said breezily. 'I don't know who was in the wrong to start with, but you couldn't get a sweeter-tempered feller than that Steve, so if I were you I'd go round to his house early tomorrer mornin', before he sets off for work, and admit you were in the wrong and apologise.'

Miranda was about to say that she knew Avril was right and would do as she suggested when, all unbidden, a picture rose up before her inner eye. It was a picture of Steve – *her* Steve – kissing Pearl's infuriatingly pink cheek and then slapping her resoundingly on her neat little bottom. 'Shan't!' she almost shouted. 'It's up to him to say he's sorry for kissing that little tart. Why, everyone knows she'll do anything for a bag of crisps and a bottle of fizzy lemonade, and if that's the sort of girl he wants . . .'

Avril was beginning to reply when the kettle reached the boil, and she took it off the Primus and began to pour the contents into Miranda's hot water bottle. She pressed the bag until all the air was out, then screwed the top on tightly and handed it to her still simmering flatmate, before beginning to fill her own bottle. 'Don't go losing your temper wi' me, luv, or you'll end up wi'out a friend in the world,' she advised kindly. 'It started last night, didn't it? The row, I mean? I knew you were upset about summat; was it the letter you and the Grimshaw boys were talking about at teatime? If so, I'm awful sorry, but it won't do you no good to turn on your pals, you know.' She squeezed the air out of the second hot water bottle, made to head for the bedroom and then turned and gave Miranda an impulsive hug. 'Oh, Miranda, I'm sure your mam's alive and kickin' somewhere,' she said gently. 'But when you're in trouble that's the time to value your friends, not drive them away from you. Just you take my advice – remember, I'm older than you, with a great deal more experience of life – and make it up wi' Steve first thing tomorrer. Unkind words fester and produce more unkind words; you can do wi'out that. Will you promise me you'll go round to Steve's place as soon as possible?'

At Avril's kind and understanding words, the ice seemed to melt around Miranda's heart and with a choking sob she ran round the table and cast herself into her friend's welcoming arms. She wept convulsively for several moments, then stood back and gave a watery smile. 'I'm really sorry I was horrid to Steve and you're quite right, I should tell him so,' she admitted. 'We had a stupid quarrel over something so trivial that I'm ashamed to mention it, but I'll go round as soon as I'm up and dressed and tell him he was right and I was wrong. Will that do, do you think?'

Avril thought that it would do very well, but unfortunately the best laid plans usually go awry. First Miranda overslept on Monday morning, and though she hurled her clothes on, snatched a slice of bread and butter to cram into her coat pocket and ran all the way to Jamaica Close, Steve had already left when she arrived. Considerably flustered, and fearing that Steve had probably told his mother how badly she, Miranda, had behaved, she left no message, merely saying that she would meet him at the factory after work. That afternoon she hung around Steve's workplace and was both cold and cross by the time one of his workmates stopped by her, eyebrows rising. 'Hello, queen. Who's you waitin' for?' the young man asked curiously. 'You're young Mickleborough's pal, ain't you? He come in late this mornin' an' went straight in to see the boss and got give a day off. Gone to London, I gather. I dare say he'll be here tomorrer, but there's no point in you waitin' now.'

Miranda mumbled her thanks and left, wondering why Steve should have gone to London now, particularly since he worked shifts and she knew that he would not be at the factory towards the end of the week. However, there was nothing she could do about it, so she returned to Russell Street and when Avril came in she had prepared vegetables to go with the two mutton chops she had bought for their tea. Avril bounced into the kitchen, slung her thick coat on the hook by the door and sniffed at the delicious smell of cooking. 'You've got the tea on early; does that mean Steve's comin' round later to take you to the flicks?' she asked, peeping into the oven of the Baby Belling Mr Grimshaw had given Miranda as a house-warming present. 'Hey, mutton chops! Is there any of that dried mint what the old lady on the Great Homer Street market give us a couple of days ago?'

It was tempting to pretend that she had made her peace with Steve, but Avril was far too canny to be taken in. As the other girl straightened up, Miranda nodded. 'Aye, there's some mint, and I didn't catch Steve, though it wasn't for lack of trying,' she assured the other girl. 'I went round to his place first thing this morning but he'd already left, so I went to the factory as soon as I'd finished work and one of his mates told me that he'd gone to London and wouldn't be in till tomorrow.'

Avril's brow puckered. 'Very odd,' she said slowly. 'I wonder why he's gone? Not with either of them girls he were with yesterday, I'd put money on it. Oh well, tomorrow he'll be full of whatever scheme he's hatched, and eager to bend your ear with his doings. But if I were you I'd set the alarm for six, lay out your clothes all ready and be on his doorstep by the time he wakes up. He's a good bloke is Steve; you don't want to lose him to young Pearl.'

Miranda sighed, but she nodded too. 'I reckon you're right, and I'll do as you say. I just wish I knew what it was all about, though. Me and Steve have never had secrets from one another, and I can tell you I don't like it.'

But though she took Avril's advice and hung around Jamaica Close until well after Steve's normal leaving time he did not appear, and though she contemplated going to the house and asking Mrs Mickleborough when he would be back her pride would not allow her to admit that she was no longer in his confidence. Instead she returned to the flat and did a few small tasks before setting off for the office, wishing the quarrel had never happened. With no other course of action open to her, she simply settled down to her work, and waited.

Steve had felt just as furious with Miranda as she had with him; probably more so. He had spotted her on the sledging slope before she had seen him and had deliberately plonked a kiss upon Pearl's hot cheek, knowing how it would infuriate his old bezzie. He had been truly hurt by the fact that she had spurned his invitation, but accepted a later one from Julian and Gerald. It was a dirty trick to bring them to the same spot where he had intended to take her, and from what he had seen of her a good deal of her animation had been put on to upset him. He and Cyril had talked for a long time when they got back to Jamaica Close after seeing the girls home and Cyril had laughed when Steve had told him how he longed to join the air force, as Cyril himself had done. 'Then why not do it?' his old friend had said. 'I took me uncle's advice – he were in the Royal Flying Corps during the last lot – and he said the sensible thing were to get in early because once war was declared there'd be a rush and them as was already in would get the plum jobs.'

Steve had nodded wisely, agreeing that he had heard other fellers say the same thing, but had Miranda come a little earlier to Number Two on Monday it is doubtful whether Steve would have gone off early to call for Cyril, who had offered to go along to the recruiting office with him. There he had filled in many forms and answered many questions, and the feeling of resentment and pain which had haunted him over Miranda's defection began to lessen. He was doing what he should have done all along, refusing to let her affect his life. He was a man, wasn't he? Well, he looked old enough to join the Royal Air Force, at any rate.

The helpful sergeant behind the desk had advised him to take his completed papers along to somewhere called Adastral House, in London, not very far from Euston

Station. Handing in his papers personally might speed things up a bit, the sergeant thought.

Feeling that his future was mapped out for him, he hurried to work to see his boss. Mr Richmond was not best pleased, but agreed that it was every fit young man's duty, in time of war, to do his best for his country. Steve was rather startled to hear his boss talking as though war were already a fact, but when he saw the hum and bustle at Adastral House he knew that he was doing the right thing. Cyril, who had accompanied him to London and was looking forward to a night on the town with his old pal, reminded him of the old saying 'One volunteer is worth ten pressed men', and he thought that this was probably true. He was given papers to take to a medical centre the next day so that his health could be checked. If all was well he might find himself in uniform within the month.

When he got home on Wednesday morning, full of excitement, Mrs Mickleborough cried, Mr Mickleborough clapped him on the shoulder and wished him success in this adventure, and his brothers stared round-eyed, though Reg and Joe reminded the family that they both intended to follow Ted into the Navy, and Kenny wept bitterly at the thought of being the only boy living at Number Two.

Steve laughed, and Kenny's tears disappeared as if by magic when his brother reminded him that he would soon have a new baby to play with, and promised that on his next trip to London he would bring back a model Spitfire for his little brother; a toy which Kenny had longed for.

'And now all I've got to do is tell Miranda. Has she

been round asking for me?' Steve said with pretended indifference.

Mrs Mickleborough wrinkled her brow. 'She came round Monday morning, after you'd left for Cyril's,' she said rather doubtfully. 'She said she would meet you at the factory after work. Didn't you tell her what you were going to do?'

'No,' Steve said airily. 'Didn't want her hangin' round me neck in floods of tears and beggin' me not to leave her.' He grinned at his mother. 'Some perishin' chance o' that! The mood she was in she'd probably have said good riddance to bad rubbish!'

Mrs Mickleborough tutted. 'What a horrible thing to say! She's a grand girl your Miranda, and when she does hear I dare say she'll be upset. She'll miss you something awful – so will us, won't us, Dad? But there, Steve luv, I'm sure you've done the right thing. You'll find your carry-out by the back door, so off you go and don't be late this evenin' 'cos it's Lancashire hotpot, and I know you love that.'

Having learned that Steve had gone to London, apparently for some reason which he had not seen fit to confide either to his pals at work or to herself, Miranda fully expected him to come thundering up the stairs which led to the flat on Tuesday evening. But this did not happen. In fact Miranda lost patience and decided to go round to Jamaica Close the next day, ostensibly to visit Aunt Vi and Beth, but really so that she might meet Steve by accident on purpose, so to speak. But on Wednesday morning Gerald telephoned her at work, suggesting that they might go to the cinema together that night. It was a film she very much wanted to see, and she was tempted to leave visiting Jamaica Close till the following day. She wondered how Gerald had got permission to leave school and come into the city, but he explained that his teachers thought he was going with his classmates to see another film, one which was part of their School Certificate curriculum and so would be helpful to them. 'But surely the other boys will report that you left them?' Miranda objected.

Gerald laughed. 'It's clear you know nothing about fellers at public school,' he said reprovingly. 'We drew lots; one of the fellers will actually go to the other film and take notes. Then, on the bus going back to Crosby, he'll fill the rest of us in. Everyone else wants to see *A Day at the Races*, but luckily the chap who drew the short straw is a swot, so he's quite happy to miss the Marx brothers and watch boring old Shakespeare instead.' His tone changed from explanatory to wheedling. 'Do say you'll come, pretty Miranda! I've already told the fellers that my girl will be one of the party. I'll look the most almighty fool if you turn me down.'

Miranda sighed. She would have loved to see the film, especially in Gerald's company, but she was forced to shake her head. 'Thank you very much, Gerry, but it's out of the question, unfortunately. I've not seen Steve since he got back from London and I must do so this evening.'

Gerald's voice sharpened with interest. 'He went up to London? Did he go with Julian? My big brother means to go to Sandhurst for officer training, and had an interview last week. Don't say your Steve was doing the same?'

'He's *not* my Steve,' Miranda said crossly. 'You say I don't know nothin' about public schools; well you don't know nothin' about Liverpool, if you think that havin' a bezzie is the same as having a boyfriend, 'cos it bleedin' well isn't. In fact I'm not even sure that Steve's my bezzie any more. If he was he wouldn't have gone off to London without a word to me.'

'Aha, I thought there was a rift in the lute when we went sledging. The pair of you were glaring at each other like a couple of angry cats quarrelling over a mouse,' Gerald said. He spoke rather unwisely, as it happened, since Miranda shouted into the receiver that he shouldn't leap to conclusions and now she certainly would not accompany him to any cinema, no matter how badly she wanted to see the film. Gerald began to apologise, but at that moment a member of staff entered the hallway where the telephone hung on the wall and Miranda slammed the receiver guiltily back on its rest and turned to face Mr Hardy, who was coming towards her, eyebrows raised.

'I trust you were not taking a personal call, Miss Lovage,' he said reprovingly. 'You know we frown on personal telephone calls. Whilst you are on the line our clients might be clamouring to get through.'

'No, it was a business call for Mr Lawrence, only he's not come in yet,' Miranda said, crossing her fingers behind her back. 'I gave the caller Mr Lawrence's extension number and told him to try it in about half an hour.'

Mr Hardy grunted, then handed Miranda a sheaf of papers. 'I'll take your word for it,' he said grumpily. 'And now have these typed up for me, please. If you're too busy to do it yourself give them to Miss Okeham; she's always very accurate and quick.'

'Certainly, sir,' Miranda said through gritted teeth. It was just her luck that Mr Hardy had been the one to catch her using the telephone for a personal call. She knew he disliked her, and thought she had got the job of office junior not through excellence but because she was some connection of Mr Grimshaw's. Unfortunately there was enough truth in this assumption to make it impossible for Miranda to deny it, so now she took the papers from Mr Hardy's hot little paw and hurried back to the typing pool, where she had a desk at the extreme end of the long room.

All that day she worked hard and tried to forget that Gerald must be wondering why she had put the phone down on him, but it was the sort of day when things keep going wrong. As office junior, she pushed a trolley round from department to department at eleven in the morning, offering cups of tea or coffee to the assembled staff, and because she was in a hurry to get back to her desk – Miss Okeham was too busy to take on Mr Hardy's work – she forgot to avoid the loose board at the entrance to the typing pool. She grabbed the tea urn just in time to stop a real calamity but, alas, not quickly enough to prevent tea from puddling all over the trolley. She had only just finished mopping up the mess when several of the men sent her out for sandwiches. She was supposed to buy two ham and pickle, one egg and cress and four beef with mustard, and she would have done so had the baker and confectioner not sold out of beef. He assured her that her customers would like pork just as well, so she followed his advice and bought pork and mustard, only to discover on her return to the office that Mr Rosenbaum, because of his religion, was not allowed to devour any part of the pig.

Miranda sighed, and her friend Lucy, who sat at the next desk, came and took some of the letters which Miranda should have been typing, and gave her friend a sympathetic grin. 'Haven't you ever noticed old Rosie wears a little cap thing in his hair?' she asked. 'He explained to me once – he's ever so nice is Mr Rosenbaum – that Jewish men call that cap thing a yarmulke and they're supposed to wear it all the time; well, not when they're in bed I s'pose, but whenever they're up and doing. Anyway, Jewish people aren't allowed to eat pork, so do you want me to type up some of your letters while you go and buy him something else?'

Miranda thanked her sincerely and scurried off to the bakery to buy another sandwich; at Mr Rosenbaum's suggestion, another egg and cress.

Naturally enough this made her late and being late made her cross, and being cross led to mistakes in her typing, which normally never happened, so by the time she was about to start her last task – collecting and stamping all the letters that had been typed that day – she was simmering with annoyance, very unfairly directed at Steve because he had not told her, his best friend, either that he was going to London, or the reason for his trip.

She was somewhat mollified on finding, when she eventually left the building, that Steve was waiting for her on the pavement. She was carrying an enormous sack of stamped mail to be posted in the nearest pillar box, and managed to give Steve a small smile and a mutter of thanks as he began helping her to push the letters through the flap. But even this friendly act could not remove her sense of ill usage nor make her forget what a horrid day she had had. During the course of it she had actually wondered if Mr Hardy might demand her dismissal, for she knew very well that Mr Hardy had hoped one of his nieces would get her job. However, until today he had really had nothing to complain about so far as her work went, so she tried to dismiss such thoughts from her mind and turned expectantly to Steve. 'Well? Where have you been?' And then, before Steve could open his mouth, she added: 'Not that I need to ask; you've been to perishin' London for some reason, so are you going to tell me, or would you rather tell that horrible Pearl?'

Steve's eyes opened wide with astonishment. 'Now what makes you say that?' he asked in a wondering tone. 'I've not seen the girl since Sunday.'

'Nor you've not seen me,' Miranda interrupted ungrammatically. 'You've made a right fool of me, Steve Mickleborough. I thought we was bezzies, but . . .'

'So we were,' Steve said. 'I asked you to come sledgin' but you chose to go with Gerald instead. Of course he's gorra car and I've only got buses and trams, but I asked you first, you can't deny it.'

'I never said I'd go, though,' Miranda said huffily. 'You'd been horrible to me, so why should I go sledging with you?'

The two had been standing on the pavement by the letter box, but now Steve took her arm and turned her towards the busy main road. 'I can see you're still in a bad mood, so if we're going to quarrel we might as well do so over a cup of tea and a bun,' he said resignedly. 'Oh, Miranda, do come down off your high horse and admit it was a rotten thing to do, to go sledgin' with the

Grimshaw boys in the very same place that you knew I wanted to take you.'

Miranda tried to snatch her arm away, but Steve hung on. 'No, you aren't goin' to walk away from me until we've had our talk, so make up your mind to it,' he said grimly. 'You must have guessed that Cyril and meself only invited Pearl and Ruby to come along because we thought you'd give me the go-by; well you had, hadn't you? You thought you were punishin' me for darin' to argue with you; well, I suppose I thought I was punishin' you by taking the girls sledgin'.'

Miranda stopped short and drew herself up to her full height. 'You know very well that Gerald and Julian are just friends, but from what I've heard Pearl and Ruby are a different matter altogether. Why, if anyone wanted to punish anyone else it was you, kissing that horrible Pearl. Not that I care,' she added quickly. 'You can kiss anyone you bloody well please, so long as it isn't me.'

Steve shook her. 'I'd as soon try to kiss a spitting wild cat, which is what you are,' he said grimly. 'Here's the tea room; furious though I am with you I'm prepared to mug you to tea and a bun whilst we sort things out. Oh, Miranda, don't be a fool. Don't just chuck away months and months of good friendship just because of one little falling out.'

Miranda began to protest but Steve ignored her. He pulled her into the small tea room and made her sit at a quiet table in the furthest corner. Then he ordered tea and cakes and the two sat in brooding silence until their order was delivered, when Miranda almost forgot her grievance at the sight of the cream cakes temptingly displayed on a three-tier stand. Her hand hovered between an éclair positively bulging with cream and a meringue, but when Steve advised her to take the éclair first and to have the meringue next she returned her hand to her lap and glared at him. 'Perhaps you're confusing me with that little tart you took sledging,' she said frostily. 'I've heard it said that she'll do anything for a packet of crisps and a fizzy drink; well I'm not like that so just in case you get the wrong impression I'll take the custard tart.'

If Steve had merely passed her the custard tart all might still have been well, but instead he gave a loud guffaw, snatched the éclair and plonked it on her plate. 'Don't be so daft, Miranda Lovage, and don't be so unfair to Ruby and Pearl. I don't know what folks say about them but to my way of thinkin' they're just a couple of girls full of energy and fun, without an ounce of vice. And since you'd been invited to come sledging and didn't even have the good manners to say yes or no, why shouldn't I ask a couple of girls I've known most of me life? Now, for God's sake eat it, and drink your tea; here's hoping it'll sweeten your temper. And then you can tell me what's wrong.'

Miranda ignored the tempting éclair. 'All right, I was wrong to fall out with you and not agree to go sledging,' she muttered. 'But next day I went round to your house to say I was sorry only you'd already gone to work. I did try to catch you there but I had no luck. So go on, I know you were in London but you've been away for three days and I don't know why you had to go there at all.' Despite her intention to treat his trip with indifference she could feel her brows beginning to draw together. 'Well? Are you going to tell me or aren't you?'

Steve took one of the cakes and bit into it. He chewed and swallowed infuriatingly slowly, before picking up his cup of tea and taking a long swig. When he spoke it was slowly and distinctly, as though to a small child. Miranda gritted her teeth and took a bite out of the chocolate éclair, not deigning to say a word, but waiting for Steve to speak first.

'Well, after I'd called for you on Sunday and you weren't there, I were walking along the Scottie headin' for Jamaica Close when someone shouted me. It were Cyril Rogers; do you remember him? Tall feller, wi' a big conk and what you used to call a puddin' basin haircut.'

Miranda giggled. 'He's changed a lot,' she observed. 'I saw him on your sledge. He's got himself a proper haircut for a start and he was wearing pretty nice clothes considering he was sledging with you and those two – young ladies.'

'Yes, well, he's joined the air force,' Steve explained. 'We talked about it all the afternoon – when we weren't actually on the sledge, I mean – and then he came home to Jamaica Close and Mam gave us both pie and chips and we went on talking. He's rare keen on the service, and it made me think I could do worse than join up as well. You see, everyone knows there's a war comin' despite what Mr Chamberlain said, and Cyril told me what I've heard others say – that them as volunteers before war is declared get the best choice of jobs – so I went to the recruiting office and filled in about a hundred forms . . .'

Miranda gasped. She suddenly realised that if she had missed Steve so badly when he was only away for three days, she would miss him a whole lot worse if he joined the forces and left Liverpool, if not for good, then for a very long time. 'Steve Mickleborough, if you've joined the Royal Air Force then it's the most unfair thing I ever heard,' she interrupted, her voice rising. 'It's not fair! I can't do the same because I'm too young. Oh, do say you're just kidding. Do say you've not committed yourself!'

Steve grinned. 'Well if I said it, it'd be a lie,' he announced cheerfully. 'I took the recruiting sergeant's advice and went up to London with Cyril. We booked ourselves into a YMCA hostel – it was quite cheap – and I went to a place called Adastral House where I filled in even more forms, and had an interview, and then they sent me to somewhere in the suburbs where I had a medical. I passed A1 – well I would, wouldn't I? – and I'll get a letter telling me where to report for training in a few weeks.'

Miranda's mouth dropped open. 'Without telling me?' she said. 'Without a word to your bezzie, just because we'd had a teeny little falling out? Steve, how *could* you? Oh, if only I were a couple of years older . . .'

Steve began to say that he had only forestalled the authorities by a few months because he was sure they would start recruiting his age group very soon, but Miranda was not listening. She pushed her teacup and the plate with its half-eaten éclair away from her, put her head down on her arms and began to weep in earnest. Steve, clearly alarmed, for everyone in the tea room was staring at them, reached across the table and tried to brush the hot tears from Miranda's reddened cheeks. 'Stop makin' an exhibition of yourself, and me too,' he hissed. 'Everyone will be thinkin' I've done or said somethin' bad to make you carry on so. What's so wrong with me joinin' the air force anyway? I don't want to go into the Navy, 'cos I'm always seasick, and I don't fancy the army either. But I'm interested in aero engines, because that's what we make at the factory. Oh, Miranda, do stop!'

Miranda sat up; she was red-eyed and the tears still brimmed over, but she muttered something inaudible and reached for her cup.

'What did you say?' Steve asked, rather apprehensively. 'Look, Miranda, it's no use blamin' me because what's done can't be undone . . . oh, dear, don't start again! Here, take this.' He offered her a moderately clean handkerchief, with which Miranda began mopping-up operations, whilst continuing to mutter.

'It's always the same,' she said in a small, hoarse voice. 'Nobody really likes me, not enough to stay with me, at any rate. First it was my mum; she pushed me away by making me call her Arabella, and left. Then it was Missie, who went off to her island, then Pete Huxtable took Timmy, and now it's you!'

'And next it will be you,' Steve pointed out. 'You've said yourself that as soon as you're old enough you're going to join one of the forces. So all you've got to do is wait a while, and you'll be off yourself. And remember, I'm joining the air force. From what I've heard the chaps in the air force don't necessarily go abroad. I might be posted to somewhere within a few miles of Liverpool; think of that!'

Miranda gave her eyes one last rub then handed the now sodden handkerchief back to Steve. Then she picked up the remainder of the éclair and began to eat it. 'You're right, of course,' she said as she finished the last delectable mouthful. 'I was being silly. The truth is, knowing that you had kept something a secret from me made me feel left out, rejected if you like. Why *didn't* you tell me, Steve? You could have come round to Russell Street before you left, or you could have come to the office.'

'Oh yeah? And have you either bury your fangs in my throat or burst into floods of tears and try to stop me going?' Steve said, grinning. He leaned across the table and rumpled Miranda's already rather untidy hair. 'Besides, I wasn't sure whether I'd be accepted or not.' He eyed the remaining cakes on the stand. 'Want another one?'

Miranda shook her head. 'No thanks; now that I've pulled myself together I really should be getting back to the flat, since it's my turn to do the spuds and get some sort of a meal together. Want to come to tea with Avril and me? If so I dare say we could run to fish and chips.'

Steve paid the bill, agreeing to forgo his mam's Lancashire hotpot and have supper in Russell Street, and they left the tea room. Outside on the pavement Steve gave Miranda's hand a squeeze. 'Are we pals again? Bezzies? Or are you still cross?'

Miranda gave a watery giggle and shook her head. 'No, I'm not cross; I was a fool to be annoyed. Of course you should join up, and I'll do the same when I'm old enough. Can you come straight round to the flat now, or do you want to go home first?'

Steve considered. 'I'd best nip back to Jamaica Close and tell Mam I shan't be in for tea,' he said. 'Come back with me, why don't you? Mam's always glad to see you and you can have a good old moan about me leavin' home, 'cos Mam was just as upset as you were when I told her I'd joined the RAF.'

Miranda suspected that he was crossing his fingers behind his back, for she thought Mrs Mickleborough far too sensible to object to her son's joining up; his elder brother was in the Royal Navy, after all. But as he had said, she did like Steve's mum, so the two of them set out together for Jamaica Close, the best of friends once more, their differences forgotten.

Chapter Nine

Miranda got into bed on the night of 3 September, aware with an uneasy chill that what everyone had talked and conjectured about was now a fact: they were at war with Germany. According to the popular press Hitler would start by overrunning France and the Low Countries, and would, within a matter of weeks, have an invasion force ready to cross the Channel and occupy Great Britain, whilst the skies above would be full of paratroopers disguised as nuns, carrying the war into even the remotest parts of the country.

Cuddling down, she allowed herself a little smile at the thought of a burly paratrooper landing on one of the Liver Birds, or having to disentangle his skirts from the tower of St Nicholas's Church, for she found it impossible to believe that even Hitler, clearly a madman, would be fool enough to send a force of men disguised as women across the Channel.

Soon her mind drifted to other things; to Steve, who was being trained as a mechanic, and to the fact that she meant to go and meet him at the village nearest his airfield as soon as it could be arranged. He was in Norfolk, rapturous about some sort of lake or river called the Broads, insisting that she should come over when he could get a forty-eight. Together, they could explore the countryside, prowl round the old city of Norwich, reputed to have a pub for every day of the year, and spend time on the beach; for though the government intended to sow all the shores with landmines they had not yet done so.

Dreamily her thoughts moved on; to the moment when she would be old enough to join the WAAF and meet Steve on his own ground, so to speak. She imagined herself in the blue cap, tunic and skirt, her legs in grey stockings, her feet in neat black lace-ups. How amazed Steve would be the first time he saw her in uniform! But of course if Hitler really did send paratroopers and an invasion fleet the war might be over before she was old enough to join up. She had heard a stallholder on the Great Homer Street market saying that he remembered how folk had thought the Great War would be over by Christmas. 'And now I hear fools sayin' the same about this little lot,' he had said bitterly. 'But that war, the last 'un, went on for four perishin' years and I reckon Hitler and his Panzers and his Lootwharrever – his air force, I mean – are a deal tougher than the Huns, so I reckon we're in for a hard slog before we've kicked 'em back over the Channel where they belongs.'

Miranda burrowed her head into her pillow. So mebbe I'll get a chance to show myself off in uniform to Steve and his pals before we've kicked 'em back over the Channel, she told herself now. I don't want a war, I'm sure nobody does, but we've got no choice; war has arrived and we've all got to do our bit towards winning it, because judging from the newsreels living under the Nazi jackboot would be a terrible thing; we'd be better off dead.

But by now excitement and tiredness had caught up

with Miranda and she sank into slumber with the words *better off dead, dead, dead* ringing in her ears.

Miranda was preparing a meal in the flat's small kitchen when she heard someone running up the metal stairs and grinned to herself. She guessed that it would be Avril, whose shift had ended half an hour ago, eager to gobble her supper so that the two of them could go Christmas shopping at Paddy's Market, for the holiday was rapidly approaching and they had not yet managed to get all their presents bought.

Despite the dire warnings in the press and on the wireless, nothing much had happened since the start of the war three months earlier. No paratroopers had descended from the sky, no invasion fleet had begun to cross the Channel, and no bombs had rained down on them from the Luftwaffe. Steve, now a fully trained mechanic on Wellingtons, would be coming home for a forty-eight over Christmas, and she and Avril were looking forward to hearing what he thought was about to happen. Folk were already referring to the first three months of the so-called 'conflict' as the phoney war, but Steve had warned Miranda in his letters that this was unlikely to last. Hitler and his generals must have some reason for delaying their onslaught upon Great Britain and the Commonwealth and Steve, who was in daily contact with the men who flew the big bombers over France, the Low Countries and Germany, had heard them say that the delay was due, not to a lack of preparation, but to Hitler's declared wish to join forces with the British against the rest of the world. Whilst he still hoped, Steve had written, whether Hitler knew it or not he was giving

Britain time to arm, train and begin to work on their defences, which at the moment were almost non-existent.

Trust us to do nothing to build up our own war machine despite knowing that Hitler's forces were already infinitely superior, both in strength and experience, to our own, he had written. *But it's always the way, so the chaps tell me. The British Bulldog lies quiet and watches until it's ready to pounce.*

Miranda had thought this downright comical since Mr Jones up the road owned a bulldog, a lazy animal, bow-legged and obese, who waddled slowly up and down the road at its master's heels, its stertorous breathing audible half a mile away. The thought of its pouncing on anyone or anything was so ludicrous that Miranda had to smile, but just at that moment the stair-climber rattled the door, then opened it, and Avril entered the kitchen, laden with paper carriers. She grinned widely at her friend, dumped her carriers on the kitchen table and sniffed the air. 'I smell Lancashire hotpot with a load of spuds and the rest of that jar of pickled cabbage,' she said dreamily. 'You're home early. I came up Great Homer and since I didn't think you'd be back yet I bought a couple of them pasties for us teas. Still, we can take one each to work tomorrow, save us makin' sarnies. Any word from Steve? Wish I had a boyfriend in the air force what could give us news of what's goin' on.'

Miranda, who had been laying the table, stared at her friend, wide-eyed. 'Avril Donovan, you've got half the crew of that corvette – the *Speedwell* – writing to you; what more could you want? And yes, I had a letter from Steve this morning. He has to be careful not to give any classified information, of course, but he did say that it's mostly leaflets which get dropped at present and not bombs.' She peered inquisitively at the nearest paper carrier. 'Looks like you've been buying up everything you could lay hands on. Heard any rumours? All I know is rationing will start in earnest once Christmas is over. And even before that no one's allowed to buy icing sugar. Fortunately, however, we had a bag left over from your birthday cake last summer so if we just ice the top and not the sides of the cake I made last week, it'll do very well for Christmas.'

'Clever old you; and I got some made up marzipan from my pal what works in Sample's,' Avril said happily. 'And being as it's only a couple of days till Christmas the boss paid us all a bit of a bonus so I spent it on goodies from Great Homer . . . look!'

As she spoke Avril had seized the largest of the paper carriers and tipped its contents on to the table, making Miranda give a protesting yelp as various items rolled and bounced across the cutlery and crockery already set out. But then she gave a squeak of excitement, for Avril had bought a packet of balloons, another of tinsel and some candy walking sticks to decorate the tiny tree which stood in their living room. 'Oh, Avril, you are clever! I particularly wanted it to be really Christmassy because Steve seems certain that the phoney war will soon become a real one, and future Christmases will be pretty thin on treats,' she said as her friend drew from another carrier a bottle of some sort of spirit, three large oranges and a bunch of bananas. When Miranda put out a hand to the next bag, however, Avril pushed her away, shaking her head.

'No, no, you mustn't look in that one, it's me Christmas presents,' she said proudly. 'I couldn't get anything much, but I don't mind tellin' you Steve's gettin' ten Woodbines, only you ain't to tell him, understand?'

'As if I would,' Miranda said indignantly. She peeped into the remaining paper carrier. 'Oh, you bad girl. The government have told us not to hoard goods against rationing starting and I spy sugar and butter – oh, and that looks like quite a lot of bacon – gosh, Steve will think he's died and gone to heaven because meals in the cookhouse are pretty basic, he says. They get dried egg but not the sort of eggs you can fry – I think they call them shell eggs – and great chunks of fried bread to make up a decent plateful. Oh, and I didn't tell you, did I? He'll be home late on Christmas Eve and has to leave again by lunchtime on Boxing Day. It's not long, but apparently they're giving the chaps with wives and young families longer.' She turned to her companion, knowing she was grinning like a Cheshire cat. 'Oh, Avril, telephone calls are all very well – and letters, of course – but it'll be grand to see Steve face to face again. He tells me he's talked to one or two Waafs and they say that provided you aren't already doing war work a girl can sign on before she's even seventeen. It's not as if girls will be actually engaged in conflict, though if you ask me the jobs they do will take them into just as much danger as the men. Now, let's get on with this meal because Steve will be back in two days' time and I want to have everything ready for him.'

Avril began to shovel her purchases back into their paper carriers and looked across at her companion, her expression a touch guilty. 'I've a confession to make, chuck. The young feller what works as a supervisor at my factory, the one who was in that dreadful accident where he lost his leg and the use of one eye, won't be goin' home for Christmas. Well, as you know, he's not got a home to go to no more. So I – I axed him back to our place, knowin' you wouldn't mind. He's okay is Gary; you'll like him. He says he'll bring some of the holly he cut for the girls in the factory, and a piece of ham which he meant to have for his own Christmas dinner. Since he'll be sharin' our chicken now, he says we can have the ham for Boxing Day with a tin of peas and a baked potato.' She gazed anxiously at Miranda. 'You don't mind, do you, chuck? It 'ud be downright mean to condemn him to a lonely Christmas after all he's gone through.'

'Of course I don't mind,' Miranda said at once. She knew Gary's story, knew that he had been working in a timber yard when something had gone wrong with the mechanism of the machine he was using and he had been dragged into the works. He had been in hospital for months, and had been fitted with a wooden leg, but according to Avril never referred to it and was always cheerful and optimistic. He had tried to join the Services – all of them – but had been turned down, so had gone to Avril's factory and started work on the bench, speedily rising to his present position as supervisor. So now she grinned encouragingly at her friend. 'Tell him he's as welcome as the flowers in May, and you can tell him as well that he won't be playin' gooseberry 'cos Steve and I are just bezzies, so there!'

Steve telephoned Miranda by dialling the number of the box on the corner at the agreed hour, for though the Mess was on the telephone the flat was not. Sometimes he was unlucky and someone at Miranda's end who was already waiting for a call snatched the receiver off its hook, breathing some other caller's name. This called for diplomacy to make sure that at the sound of an unfamiliar voice the girl, or feller, did not crossly slam the receiver down, thus cutting the connection before Miranda was able to intervene. Tonight, however, it was Miranda's own small voice which came to him as soon as the operator said 'You're through' and left them to get on with their conversation, having first reminded them sternly that it was wartime and many other people were waiting for a chance to use the instrument.

'Steve? Oh, it *is* you! I've got so much to tell you, but since we'll be together in a couple of days I won't waste telephone time. Avril's asked her supervisor to join us on Christmas Day itself, and since he's providing the food for Boxing Day I suppose he'll have to come along then too. I've never met him myself but Avril says we'll get along, and I'm sure she's right. Have they told you what time your train gets into Lime Street? And how's your mam and the little 'uns?'

Mrs Mickleborough, Kenny and the baby had been evacuated way back in September when the war had started and were now comfortably ensconced in a farmhouse somewhere in Wales, which was why Steve would be having his whole forty-eight with Miranda. Naturally, Steve would have liked to see his mam, Kenny and the baby – his stepdad had joined the Navy – but he quite agreed with the government feeling that Liverpool, once the war really got going, would be a major target, and anyone living there ran a far greater risk than if they allowed themselves to be sent to the relative safety of the countryside.

Steve cleared his throat. 'Mam's doin' fine, Kenny loves the local school and Flora has settled down well,' he said. 'I can't say much about Dad, or the others – classified information, I guess – but I'll spill the beans when we meet. As for train times, cross-country journeys are hell; I could have up to five changes, but I reckon I should be home before midnight.'

'Oh dear, and you'll have to leave on Boxing Day . . .' Miranda was beginning when the operator's voice cut in.

'You've had your three minutes, caller. Others are waiting for the line. Please replace your receiver.'

Miranda and Steve began simultaneously to say their farewells, while the operator, infuriatingly, tried to shut them up. In fact she did so just as Steve bawled 'Love you Miranda' into his receiver, and he crashed it back on its rest before Miranda could remind him that they were supposed to be just good friends.

Miranda and Avril's preparations for Christmas proceeded smoothly. Miranda was one of the few people still left in the typing pool at Mr Grimshaw's office. There was an elderly lady, a Miss Burton, and another known as Miss Phyllis, who had been called out of retirement as the other typists either joined the forces or went to work in the factories which paid very much better than even the most generous of office jobs. Miranda had missed her friends at first but soon realised that Miss Burton and Miss Phyllis were well up to the work, and proved both faster and more efficient than the staff they had replaced. Miranda might have been lured by the high wages one could earn in, for instance, a munitions factory, save that she had it on good authority that applying to join one of the forces whilst employed in such a post might well be doomed to failure. As it was, she and her two elderly companions managed to share out the work to everyone's satisfaction. They even bought each other tiny presents – Miranda gave each of her colleagues a very small bar of scented soap and they clubbed together to buy her rose geranium talcum, whilst Mr Grimshaw presented each woman with a ten shilling note.

'It may not be much of a bonus, but it's all the firm can afford at the moment,' Mr Grimshaw had said as he handed over the money. 'And we're giving you a whole week's holiday with pay, so I trust you don't feel too hard done by.'

Delighted with even a small amount of extra money, Miranda scoured the shops for Steve's favourite, chocolate ginger, and bought him the biggest box she could find. The rest of the money was spent on extras and a length of green ribbon with which she tied her hair back into a ponytail, getting Avril to knot the ribbon into a huge bow on the nape of her neck. 'Making sure he'll reckernise you?' Avril asked derisively. 'Better ring him up and tell him you're the lass with the green ribbon in her hair, just in case he's forgot your freckly old face.' It was Christmas Eve and they were in the kitchen at the flat, Avril cutting sandwiches so that they would have something to give Steve if he was starving after his long and complicated journey, whilst Miranda donned her thick navy blue overcoat and crammed a large floppy beret on her head, for at ten o'clock it was already very cold, with frost or snow threatening.

Avril looked up from her work. 'You off already?' she enquired. 'You're daft you are; the train's bound to be late, and you'll be waiting in the cold for ages.'

Miranda pulled a rueful face. 'I don't mind waiting – better that than miss him. And once I'm on the platform there's all sorts I can do – I could even go into the refreshment room and buy a cup of coffee.'

'Oh, you!' Avril said affectionately. 'Why can't you admit you're mad about the bloke? Why d'you have to keep pretendin' that you're just good friends? He's a nice feller is Steve; you want to grab hold of him while you can.'

Miranda opened the door, letting in a blast of cold air. 'Think what you like,' she said grandly, 'but I repeat: Steve and I are just bezzies!' And with that she stepped on to the top stair and slammed the door behind her before clattering down the flight and beginning to walk with care along the frosted pavement. Everyone was always complaining that trains were late, and Steve had told her that cross-country journeys in particular were fraught with difficulties and delays, so she should arrive at the station first.

She reached the main road and turned towards the city centre. Because of the blackout, crossing side roads was a dodgy business, but she had a little torch in her pocket and flashed it discreetly each time she came to a kerb, and presently arrived at the station. The concourse was crowded despite the lateness of the hour, and though she glanced wistfully towards the refreshment room the queue at the counter was a long one. Perhaps she might go in later and buy herself a coffee, but for now she would simply stroll around and wait.

Despite Steve's hopes it was after midnight before his train drew in to Liverpool Lime Street, and though the platform was by no means deserted it was not crowded either. Hefting his kitbag from the string rack, he jumped down, then turned to help an elderly lady to alight. She had told him as the train chugged slowly towards Liverpool that she was going to spend Christmas with her daughter and three grandchildren, and was hoping to persuade them to return with her when she left at the end of the holiday. 'My grandchildren were evacuated back in September – their mum works in munitions so she couldn't get away – but since there's been no bombings, nor no landings from over the Continong, she sent for them to come home,' she had explained, as the two of them sat side by side in the crowded compartment. 'I dunno if she were right, but the kids weren't happy where they was billeted. Said the woman didn't want 'em, made no secret of the fact. The eldest, Bessie, what's nine, wrote to her mam and said they weren't gettin' enough food for a sparra. She said the 'vacuation lady didn't like boys and picked on Herbie – he's five – no matter who were really at fault. So Maud, that's me daughter, decided to bring 'em home.' She looked hopefully at Steve. 'If the bombs start, like what some folk say they will, then they can come to me. I'd treat 'em right . . . only my cottage is right up agin an airfield.'

Steve had given all the right answers to reassure her and had confided that his mother, his little brother, and Flora, his baby sister who was four months old and a great favourite, had also been evacuated. 'They'd have liked to come home for Christmas once they knew I'd got leave – me brothers and me dad are in the Navy so no tellin' when they'll be in port again – but our dad got real angry when she wrote suggestin' it. So Mam give up the idea and I'm the only one of us Mickleboroughs who'll be in dear old Liverpool for Christmas.' He had grinned sheepishly at his companion. 'I'm goin' to stay with me girl,' he said proudly. 'She's only young but she's gorran important job as secretary to a firm of solicitors. Mind you, she's goin' to join the WAAF as soon as she's old enough; wants to be in the same bunch as me, of course.'

The old lady had murmured that everyone must do their best because old 'uns like herself could still remember the horrors of the Great War. 'I dunno how it come about that we ever let Germany get strong enough to take on the world again,' she had said sadly. 'Don't us British never learn nothin'? It's plain as the nose on your face that the Huns has been armin' and gettin' ready ever since the Spanish Civil War; why, I remember . . .'

The carriage had contained not only themselves but five soldiers, all of whom appeared to be asleep, and a woman whose nurse's uniform could just be glimpsed beneath her heavy overcoat. As the old woman said the words Spanish Civil War, one of the soldiers, older than the rest, opened a lazy eye. 'Careless talk costs lives,' he said reprovingly. He opened his other eye and fixed Steve with an admonitory glare. 'You should know better, young feller. Why, you all but give away where your mam and the kids have gone, and you mentioned where you'll be spendin' Christmas. Accordin' to what I've heard, perishin' Hitler's got his spies everywhere, so don't you forget it.'

The fat little woman who had been chattering so freely to Steve swelled with indignation and Steve could scarcely hide his amusement, for she reminded him of one of his mother's plump little broody hens when disturbed on the nest. Even so, though, he knew that the soldier was in the right even if his elderly companion was scarcely spy material. So he addressed the soldier in his most apologetic tone. 'Sorry, mate, you're absolutely right,' he said humbly. 'But I didn't lerron where me mam's stayin', nor what ship . . .'

'Leave it,' the soldier said easily, but there was a warning glint in his eye. He sat up straighter and pulled a pack of cards from the pocket in his battledress. 'How about a game of brag?' He lifted the blind a little to peer out into the pitch dark. 'There's no tellin' when we'll arrive at Lime Street, but I guess a game of cards will help the time to go faster.'

The little old lady gave the soldier the sort of glare he had given Steve, then settled back in her seat and folded her plump little hands over her shabby handbag. 'You can count me out, young feller. I's goin' to have a nap,' she said firmly, and spoke not another word until the train drew into the station. Then she had let everyone else get off the train before creaking to her feet and accepting Steve's offered hand. Having descended to the platform she looked all around her, then lowered her voice. 'Walls have ears, so they say,' she muttered. 'That perishin' soldier! Does I look like a spy, young feller? If he hadn't been so big I'd ha' been tempted to clack him across the lug. But thanks for your company and I wishes you a very merry Christmas.'

Steve, who had put his kitbag down on the platform whilst he helped his fellow passenger to descend, wished her the same. 'And I don't think that brown job meant he suspected *you* of spying,' he said, trying to conquer a quivering lip. 'There were others in the carriage, you know, all listening. I think he meant one of them.'

The old woman sniffed. 'Oh aye, I s'pose he were lookin' at that nurse, thinkin' she might be one of them paratroopers what they warned us about when the war first started,' she said. 'And her pretty as a picture! But there you are, I suppose; anything's possible in wartime.'

Agreeing, Steve hefted his kitbag up on one shoulder and, suiting his pace to her leisurely one, with her small suitcase in his free hand, made his way towards the concourse. Glancing up at the clock when he drew level with it he saw that it was a quarter past midnight, and the faint hope that he might be met disappeared. He knew Miranda would have been working all day – no one got Christmas Eve off – and having seen his companion trot towards the taxi rank he was about to start walking towards Russell Street when he heard his name called and, turning in the direction of the voice, was just in time to slip his kitbag from his shoulder and hold out his arms so that Miranda might fly into them. Hugging her tightly he began to kiss her upturned face, but instead of returning his kisses she gave a breathless giggle, put a hand across his mouth and told him not to be so soppy. 'I've been waiting since ten o'clock, you horrid person, so if you want cocoa and a bun before bed, we'd better get on the end of the taxi queue,' she said. 'Hey, Steve, there's someone waving at you.' She giggled again. 'So you've got yourself a girlfriend already? That's a nice state of affairs, I don't think!'

Steve grinned and raised a hand in response to the frantic beckonings from his erstwhile travelling companion. 'That old lady and meself were in the same compartment on the train,' he explained. He stretched and yawned. 'Lord, I'm that tired, and stiff as a board into the bargain. Shall we walk to Russell Street? It's not far and that queue's awful long, and I don't feel like standing around getting colder and colder. If we walk, it'll keep our circulation going, 'cos this is what we in the RAF call brass monkey weather.'

Miranda, clutching his arm, informed him crisply that it was not only the RAF who described the weather thus. Then she agreed that walking was by far the better option and the pair set off.

Steve slung an arm round her waist, pulling her close. 'If we keep in step we'll go faster, like in a three-legged race,' he informed her. He slid his hand a little lower and patted her bottom. 'My oh my, I do believe you've put on a bit of weight. About time if you ask me.'

He half expected Miranda to take offence, for she had always tried to keep him at arm's length, but either because she was so pleased to see him, or because she was too tired to quibble, she just chuckled sleepily and snuggled against him. 'Oh, you!' she said drowsily. 'Did I tell you you'd be sleeping on our sofa? I suppose if I were a real lady I'd offer you my bed, but since I'm nothing of the kind you're condemned to the sofa, my boy. Oh, Steve, it's so good to see you again and have a bit of a laugh together. You may only be my best friend, but I'm really fond of you, honest to God I am.'

Steve heaved a deep sigh and gave Miranda's waist a squeeze. 'Oh well, I guess it's better than nothing,' he said resignedly. 'And now tell me all your news. Have you been back to Jamaica House at all? I remember someone saying that since Mr Grimshaw had the deeds somewhere in his office he would be entitled to claim it, though he wasn't particularly interested in doing so, as I recall.'

'I've been far too busy to traipse all the way round there,' Miranda said rather indignantly. 'I told you I was a fire watcher – not that there have been any fires to watch yet – and I've joined the WVS; I do all sorts, never have a moment to myself, and Avril's the same. If you were home for longer we might go round and just check up that no one's found the door in the wall. When you think about it, a spy could set up a whole wireless network inside the old house and no one the wiser. I say, Steve, I never thought of that! Do you think we ought to nip round in the morning and check up?'

Steve laughed, but shook his head. 'No I do not! To tell you the truth, Mr Grimshaw said something of the sort when I got my posting and went round to Holmwood Lodge to say cheerio. He told me then that he would arrange for someone to keep an eye on the old place and would tell the authorities to check on it every so often once the boys left the area.' He peered at the pale shape of Miranda's face, turned enquiringly up to his. 'Are the Grimshaw boys still around?'

'Well, Gerald's still at school, of course, and Julian changed his mind about going to Sandhurst. He went to Africa instead, where he's flying Stringbags and happy as a sand boy. Before he went to Rhodesia he came over to see us, to say cheerio I s'pose, and I was working late and didn't see him, but he took Avril to the flicks and then out for a meal. Nice of him, wasn't it?'

'Very,' Steve said off-handedly. He squeezed her waist again. 'Glad it wasn't you. I've enough trouble keepin' tabs on Gerald without havin' to widen my scope to include Julian as well.'

Miranda pinched his hand. 'Rubbish; you're all my friends, all equal,' she said grandly, and ignored Steve's groan.

By the time Steve snuggled down on the sofa, he felt his cup of happiness was full. They had had a marvellous Christmas Day, starting with what he called a pre-war breakfast of eggs, bacon, sausage and fried bread, to say nothing of toast and marmalade and large mugs of tea. They had opened their presents earlier and Steve had been the recipient of ten Woodbines from Avril, and an air force blue muffler and matching gloves from Miranda. He had bought both girls attractive headscarves which were much appreciated, though Miranda told him that, should she wear hers at night, the oranges and lemons emblazoned upon a navy blue background would be noticeable enough to draw enemy fire.

Soon after breakfast Gary Hamilton had arrived. Avril had forbidden him to buy presents since, as she told him with all her usual honesty, she and Miranda had been far too busy to search for something for him, not knowing his tastes. However, he had brought a large cauliflower which one of the stallholders on the Great Homer Street market had sold him cheap the previous day, and offered it to Avril, blushing to the roots of his hair. 'You said no presents, but I thought you might make use of this,' he said, thrusting it into her hands. 'It's not what you might call a present . . .'

Helping him out of his coat and scarf and sitting him down before the fire, for it was bitterly cold outside, Avril assured him that the cauliflower was much appreciated and would be served next day, and then introduced him to Steve. 'He's only here until lunchtime tomorrow,' she explained, 'so we've got to make the most of today.'

And make the most of it they did, Steve recalled happily. They spent the morning preparing the chicken dinner they were going to enjoy, and as they peeled vegetables, made gravy and boiled the pudding, they talked and laughed, getting to know one another. After dinner they listened to the King's Christmas message and then played games before setting off, well wrapped, to make room for the tea which the girls had prepared in advance.

'Let's see if we can walk all the way to Prince's Park, and see if the lake is iced over. It's a pity it's not snowing because we could have a grand snowball battle between the four of us.' Miranda had sighed reminiscently. 'When I was at the Rankin Academy I had a friend called Louise, and she had two brothers, twins they were. The four of us used to have no end of fun when it was snowy. We'd make snowmen, and then a sort of snow castle, which two of us would defend and two would attack. Usually I got the smaller of the twins, Trevor, and Louise had Philip. Then whichever couple won would have to treat the other pair to tea and scones at the little café down by the orangery.' She sighed happily. 'I suppose we're too old now for snow battles, but I wouldn't mind a slide on the lake, if the ice is bearing.'

When they set out on the long walk, well muffled up, they had flinched against the icy wind, but by the time they reached the park they were glowing with health and warmth. Despite Miranda's hopes the lake was not completely iced over, and her fear that the café would be closed proved to be justified, but even so they thoroughly enjoyed the exercise. They did not indulge in races, because it would not have been fair on Gary, but they played guessing games, Chinese whispers and the like, and despite the enormous chicken dinner they had eaten were ravenous once more when they arrived back at the flat in time for tea. When the meal was over they played more games amidst great hilarity until Avril, saying she would accompany Gary part of the way back to his hostel, put on her outer clothing and wagged a finger at Miranda. 'Don't you take advantage of our being away to get up to any naughty tricks,' she said teasingly. 'I can see young Steve there is longing for a cuddling session.' She struck her head with the back of her hand. 'There, we never played postman's knock; that's a good game for a Christmas party.'

'We don't need games; we can have a cuddle for old times' sake, can't we, Miranda?' Steve said as the door closed behind Avril and Gary. He sat down in one of the creaking wicker armchairs and pulled Miranda on to his lap. 'Oh, you're lovely and warm and cuddly,' he said, pressing his cheek against hers. 'Tell you what, if we get up early you and me can go round to Jamaica House and make sure all's well there. I'd like to see the old place again; if it hadn't been for Jamaica House you and I might never have got together.'

'We've not got together now, not in the way you mean,' Miranda objected. 'I do like that Gary, don't you? Avril pretends there's nothing in it, but if you ask me, they'll be a couple by the time the winter's over. I'd better put the kettle on, because when Avril gets back the first thing she'll want will be a nice hot cup of tea.'

'The first thing I'll want is more cuddling and perhaps a bit of kissing as well,' Steve said plaintively. 'I agree with you, though, that Gary and Avril look like becoming a couple.' He pulled a funny face, cocking one eyebrow and speaking in a transatlantic accent. 'How's about youse an' me follerin' suit, Miss Gorgeous?' he said hopefully. 'I *need* a girlfriend to keep up my reputation as a great lover. Come on, Miranda, say you'll be my girl.'

Miranda, pouring boiling water into the teapot, put the kettle back on the stove and gave Steve an indulgent smile. 'Give you an inch and you'll take a mile,' she said, and then, when Steve pulled a disappointed face, she chuckled, crossed the room, pulled him to his feet and kissed the side of his mouth. Steve moved his head quickly and was fielding another kiss when, at this inauspicious moment, the door opened and Avril and a blast of cold wind entered the kitchen. He and Miranda sprang apart as though they had been doing something far more interesting than just kissing, but Avril was oblivious. She rushed over to the fire and stood as close to it as she could, teeth chattering.

'I'm perishin' perished,' she announced, beginning to unbutton her coat, remove her headscarf and endeavour to fluff up her flattened hair. 'Does that teapot still hold enough for one?'

'It holds enough for three,' Miranda said, getting three mugs down from the Welsh dresser. 'Steve and I were just saying what a grand feller Gary is. You really like him, don't you Avril?'

Steve turned his head so that he could look at the older

girl, and saw her eyes begin to sparkle, and the pink in her cheeks to deepen. 'Yes, he's a grand chap,' she said. 'If you knew what he had to put up with when he was first in hospital . . . but no point in talking about that. He's the bravest bloke I've ever met, I admire him tremendously and – and he's invited me to go to the theatre with him when the pantomime starts in January. He says he doesn't care if he's the only feller in the audience over ten years old, and he says we'll have fish and chips afterwards. Oh, Miranda, I do like him so much!'

So now Steve, clutching his pillow and wishing it was Miranda, thought that the four of them had had a perfect day. There had not been a single disagreement and everyone, he knew, had thoroughly enjoyed themselves. Next day he would have to leave the flat no later than noon, but the girls had decided to combine breakfast and lunch, and have a meal at around eleven o' clock. Then they would all go to the station together and he would set out on the long cold journey back to his Norfolk airfield. As he contemplated the following day he found himself hoping that Avril and Gary would have enough tact to realise that he and Miranda would want to be alone – or as alone as anyone could be on a crowded railway platform – to say their goodbyes, which might have to last them for many months, since rumour had it that postings would be handed out as soon as everyone had returned from their Christmas holidays.

In fact, however, when they reached Lime Street the following day the train he meant to catch was drawing into the platform, and he almost hurled himself aboard, then let down the window and leaned out to grab as much of Miranda as he could hold. 'Write to me every week – every day – and I'll write back whenever I've gorra moment,' he gabbled. He tried to give her a really ardent kiss but even as he pursed his lips for action the train began to move, porters began to shout and Miranda was quite literally torn from his arms. Steve leaned even further out of the carriage. 'I love you, Miranda Lovage,' he bawled, not caring who was listening or what they might think. 'Take care of yourself until I come home to take care of you myself.'

He could see Miranda's lips moving but could not hear what she was saying, and decided to assume it was words of love. Why should it not be, after all? He knew she was fond of Gerald but sincerely hoped that her feelings for the other boy stopped at liking. And in the meantime, whilst he remained in Norfolk a telephone call a couple of times a month and as many letters as she could pen would have to do.

Steve withdrew from the window as the train began to pick up speed. It was a corridor train, and he had slung his kitbag on to a corner seat to save himself a place, for the train was crowded. He straightened his fore and aft, checked in the window glass that his uniform was all correct and went back to his seat, reaching up to put his kitbag on the overhead rack, and then settling into his place with a contented sigh. It had been a fantastic Christmas, the best he could remember since he was a small boy, and it occurred to him now that it was the first time Miranda had not gone on and on about Arabella; this, he thought, was a good sign. When he had first joined the air force, her weekly letters had been full of her inability to believe that her mother was dead. She had wanted constant reassurance and he had done his best to give it, because Mr Grimshaw had said that she would begin to accept her loss as time went by. Now, it seemed that Mr Grimshaw was right, for Miranda had not once mentioned Arabella from the moment she had met him off the train to the moment when he had embarked on his return journey.

Steve looked around the compartment; two sailors, four airmen, including himself, and two brown jobs, one a sergeant, all settling themselves for sleep. Steve chuckled inwardly; one thing the forces did teach you was to snatch a nap whenever you got the chance, so you would be fresh and rested for whatever trials were to come. Steve closed his eyes and began to relive his lovely Christmas. Soon, he slept.

'It's a jolly good thing we had such a wizard Christmas, because this perishin' weather looks like lasting for ever,' Miranda said discontentedly. She and Avril had quite by chance boarded the same tram, and were now hanging on to a shared strap as the vehicle began to lurch along the main road. 'Have you ever seen such conditions? Steve's last letter was full of it, but in a way he thinks it's a good thing. Norfolk is even worse than us, with the blizzards blowing the snow into huge mountains, blocking roads and breaking the branches off trees. I should think even the kids must be fed up with snowballs and snowmen when they're accompanied by freezing feet and icicles forming on your nose whenever you forget to wipe it.'

'True,' Avril agreed. 'But kids don't seem to feel the cold. I remember being indifferent to it when it meant playing in the snow.'

Miranda chuckled. 'I know what you mean. And Steve says we should be grateful, because apparently the weather's just the same on the Continent and that means no planes can take off, not ours nor the Luftwaffe. They're still calling this the phoney war, but if you ask me it's a blessing from heaven for us. It's giving us time to arm ourselves for what is to come. If the weather eases in February, which is only a few days off, then I bet there'll be floods and all sorts. Still, Steve says the weather has given us a breathing space and I reckon he's right.'

Both girls began to move towards the rear of the vehicle as the ting of the bell proclaimed their stop was approaching, and as they stepped from the comparative shelter into the teeth of the storm Miranda grabbed her friend's arm and spoke directly into her ear. 'You're out at the same time as me for once – because of the weather, I imagine – so why don't we do a flick? We might as well make the most of the opportunity because once it begins to warm up your shifts will return to normal. What do you say?'

'Good idea,' Avril said. 'Gary's taking me to the cinema at the weekend but he won't want to see a romance. He's more for action films – Errol Flynn, Douglas Fairbanks, that sort of thing.'

As she spoke they had turned into Russell Street and now they did their best to hurry along the frosted pavements, clattering up the metal stair at speed since they made a point of spreading salt on each step before they left for work in the morning.

Once in the kitchen Miranda unfolded the newspaper she had bought earlier, spread it out on the table and decided that they would enjoy seeing John Barrymore and Mary Astor in *Midnight*, because, as Avril remarked, it was bound to be a romance and she felt that they could both go for something really lovey-dovey. Avril had begun to take her coat off, then hesitated. 'It's not far to the cinema where *Midnight* is showing; we can walk there easily, so let's go out straight away. We can buy ourselves some sweets to suck during the performance, and if we hurry we won't miss more than a few minutes of the main feature.'

Miranda looked rather wistfully round the kitchen but agreed with her friend that the sooner they left the sooner they would be in the warmth of the cinema. Accordingly they clattered down the stairs once more and were shortly handing over their money and being shown to their seats by an elderly usherette. She was a friendly and garrulous woman and told them that they were bound to enjoy the film. She herself would be watching it tonight for about the tenth time, since it was the end of the week and tomorrow a new film would be showing. 'It's grand seeing all the stars for free,' she confided, flashing her torch along the almost empty rows of seats. 'Sit where you like, gairls, there ain't no one goin' to check tickets on such a night. Come far, have you?'

'Not far,' Miranda replied. She took off her damp coat and spread it out on the seat next to the one she had chosen. 'Aha, it's the newsreel, I see; we're earlier than we thought.'

'Thank goodness,' Avril muttered as the usherette moved away. 'I know Scousers are friendly but I were afraid she were goin' to plonk down in the seat next to mine, and talk all the way through the newsreel.'

Miranda chuckled, wriggling back into her seat and suddenly conscious of how tired she was. On the screen, pictures came and went. Men making battleships in a large factory up in Scotland somewhere, a warehouse blaze in the London suburbs caused by a carelessly dropped match, a number of Boy Scouts on their bicycles riding through the city streets as the new age messengers who would take the place of the members of the forces who had previously done such work.

Miranda could feel her eyelids beginning to droop as the commentator talked on. 'America may not have entered the war yet, but her citizens are working hard to show they are on our side; these women are making up food parcels for our troops . . .' The picture on the screen showed women in turbans and overalls at long benches, packing biscuits, chocolate and other foodstuffs into small brown boxes. Others were in factories, making aeroplane parts, whilst their sisters joined concert parties to raise money for their cousins across the sea.

Miranda tried to fight the desire to fall asleep and was jerked suddenly awake by Avril's voice. 'Gee whizz, ain't she just the prettiest thing you've ever seen?' Avril said. 'All that fantastic hair . . .' Miranda's eyes shot open. The screen was flickering, about to change, but she still managed to glimpse the woman to whom her friend had referred. Miranda rose in her seat like a rocket when you light the blue touch paper. She clutched Avril's arm so hard that her friend gave a protesting squeak. 'What's up, chuck?' she said.

But Miranda cut across her. 'It's my mother!' she shouted. 'Oh, won't somebody stop the film, wind it back? I was almost asleep, I just caught the merest glimpse . . . oh, Avril, did it give names, addresses, anything like that?'

But the newsreel had come to an end, the curtains swished across and their erstwhile friend came waddling slowly down the stairs at the back of the circle with a tray of sweets and ice creams round her neck. A few customers left their seats and, producing their money, went across to the usherette.

Avril, meanwhile, positively gawped at her friend. 'Wharron earth's got into you, Miranda?' she said plaintively. 'What do you mean, it's your mother? I thought you said she were dead . . . and anyway it couldn't possibly be your mam, because the feller talkin' was in America – well, I think he was – so what makes you think . . .'

Miranda gave a moan. 'Oh, Avril, don't you ever *listen*?' she demanded. 'Other people said my mother must be dead after it was discovered that the ship she had sailed on had been lost in a storm. But I never believed it, never, never, never! We were close, Arabella and I, so I was always sure that had she been drowned I would have known it in my bones and given up all hope. But I never did – give up hope, I mean – and now I'm certain sure that she's alive. Oh, how can I bear to sit through the main feature and the B film before I can see the newsreel again?' She had stood up when the newsreel was coming to a close but now she sat down with a thump and turned appealingly to Avril. 'Will you come with me to the manager's office to ask him to rerun the newsreel straight away? It's most awfully important that I have proof of Arabella's being alive, and of where she is at the moment. You say the women in the newsreel were Americans.

Well, the authorities would have to let me go to America if I explained. America's a neutral country, isn't it? Oh, surely they'll let me go on one of those ships that Steve told me about? They're taking airmen who want to become pilots over to the States so that they can be trained in a no war zone. If I swore I'd work my passage in some way . . .'

Avril cut across what she clearly regarded as her friend's ramblings. 'For God's sake, chuck, don't talk such rubbish!' she urged. 'Even if it was your mother you saw on the newsreel – and I don't think it was because I'd looked at you seconds earlier and you had your perishin' eyes shut – the authorities ain't likely to ship you halfway across the world on what would probably turn out to be a wild goose chase. And why do you want to go to her, anyway? If you're right and the woman on the screen really is your mam, then why hasn't she come home, or at least tried to get in touch? Look at you, straining at the leash to get to her, so why couldn't she have done the same? Dropped you a line, or even bought a passage and come back to Liverpool before the war started? What I mean is, I can't imagine any reason for her not contacting you and getting things straightened out. Can you?'

Miranda had tried not to think about the quarrel between herself and her mother for many months, but now it came into her mind as clearly as though it had happened yesterday. She felt her cheeks grow warm and tears rose to her eyes. 'Well, we did have an awful row the evening before she disappeared,' she admitted, and realised, with some surprise, that apart from Steve she had never mentioned the row to anyone. She had been too ashamed, because in her secret soul she had believed the quarrel might have been the cause of Arabella's disappearance. In fact her rage and blame-laying on that last evening might have been the straw which had broken the camel's back.

But Avril was shaking her head. 'No, no; it would have taken more than that to send her flying off to America,' she said. 'All mothers and daughters have barneys from time to time, but they don't go off without a word and never contact each other again. As for asking the manager to rewind the film, I wouldn't try it if I were you 'cos you'd be settin' yourself up for a dusty answer. I reckon if we just stay in our seats – hey up, the curtains are drawing back and the fire screen's rolled up – then you can see the newsreel through again. But if you really didn't see the bit about the American women giving concert parties to raise money for the war effort, then what makes you think one of them girls was your mam?'

Miranda hesitated. It sounded so daft to say that her mother's wonderful mass of curling primrose-coloured hair had been unmistakable, but now that Avril mentioned it she realised she had scarcely had time to focus on the woman's face before the picture was replaced with another. She knew that it would not do to admit this to her friend, however, and said briefly that she had recognised Arabella's glorious hair.

But now the usherette had reached the end of their row and was eyeing them curiously. Plainly she had seen Miranda leaping to her feet, probably heard the shouts as well. Miranda, blushing, opened her little purse and produced some coins. 'Two wafers, please,' she said humbly, 'and a packet of peanuts.'

It was snowing steadily by the time they left the cinema and both girls pulled their mufflers up over their mouths and linked arms as they hurried along the snow-covered pavements. It was impossible to exchange conversation under such conditions, but as soon as they were back in the flat with the kettle on the primus stove, Avril turned to her friend. 'Well? Are you satisfied now? I suppose you're still sure it was your mother and not just an extremely pretty blonde? Only if I'm honest, Miranda, that woman only looked about twenty, or thirty at the most.' She giggled. 'Unless gettin' away from you took twenty years off her age!'

Miranda sniffed. 'I shall ignore that remark,' she said loftily. 'My mother married at sixteen and had me at seventeen, or so she always claimed. But remember, the commentator said she was with a concert party, so she would have been wearing stage make-up. It can take years off you, can that.'

Avril shrugged. 'Have it your way, queen. Your mam is alive and well and living in America and I'm tellin' you straight that there's no way you're going to get there until the war's over. Even if America do decide to join in the war they won't let young women go to and fro across the Atlantic like they did in peacetime. Why don't you write? Only I'm not sure to whom.'

'That's why I want to go over myself,' Miranda said impatiently. 'As for why my mother hasn't written to me, I have a theory . . .'

Avril sighed. 'You can tell me all about it whilst I make the tea and cut some bread and butter. And you can get out them jam tarts I made yesterday. It was just our luck that they'd closed the café because of there bein' almost no customers, but we'll make the best of what we've got. Go on then, what's your theory?'

Miranda wondered how best to explain to Avril the sequence of events which had led her to believe that her mother must have lost her memory. Now that she came to think about it she realised that she had never told it from beginning to end, as though it was just a story. She knew she must have let fall bits and pieces to her flatmate, but had never told her the events in sequence. Now she really must do so if she was to gain Avril's belief. 'Well, I told you that she'd disappeared during the night,' she began. 'Next day everyone was very concerned – the scuffers as well – and at first they tried to find Arabella, tried very hard. There were advertisements in the press and notices down by the docks asking if anyone had seen her. But we got absolutely nowhere, and of course I couldn't stay in our beautiful house in Sycamore Avenue – I had no money for the rent for a start – so I was forced to move in with Aunt Vi and my cousin Beth. As the weeks passed I suppose folk forgot; then one night I was woken by somebody shaking my shoulder . . .'

Miranda told the whole story of her sleepwalking, and presently she finished off with Missie's revelation that she had seen a woman in a long white gown being dragged down towards the docks by two members of the crew of the ship which was later wrecked with the loss of all hands. When she finished she looked enquiringly at Avril, who whistled softly beneath her breath. 'Cor, that's a story and a half,' her friend said appreciatively. 'And do you mean that sleepwalkin' can be inherited, like blue eyes or freckles?' She gave a snort of amusement. 'Pity you inherited sleepwalking and not long golden curls!'

'Shut up, you horrible girl,' Miranda said, unable to prevent herself from smiling. 'So you see, if I'm right and Arabella really was sleepwalking and was kidnapped by Captain Hogg and his merry men, then I should think it's quite possible that she has lost her memory. If she knew who she was, she'd know about me, and I'm sure she'd be desperate to get in touch. As you said, mothers and daughters may fight and disagree, but underneath there's a huge well of love. So I'm sure if Arabella could have written or even telephoned she would have done so. But if she's forgotten everything since the ship went down . . .'

'How dreadful it must have been, having to swim to the nearest land when she must have known there are sharks in tropical waters,' Avril said with feeling. 'She's a real heroine; no wonder you want to find her and claim her as your mother. But I'm tellin' you, queen, you won't do it until the war's over. Oh, you can write, probably put advertisements in American papers asking Arabella Lovage to get in touch, but if she's lost her memory . . .'

'If she's lost her memory the name Arabella Lovage will mean nothing to her, and I should add that she can't swim,' Miranda said gloomily. 'But I've got to try; what else can I do?'

'Tell me, queen, why did your mother insist on you calling her Arabella?' Avril asked.

'I don't know what that's got to do with it . . .' Miranda began, and then, meeting Avril's eyes, she capitulated. 'She didn't want people to know she had a daughter in her teens because when she auditioned for a part she would always tell them she was in her mid-twenties.' She saw the beginnings of a smirk on her friend's face and hastened to disabuse her. 'All right, all right, but as you've already said she doesn't look her age, and when you're auditioning for a part it's your looks they go on rather than the number of your years. Oh, Avril, I've tried and tried to put my mother's plight out of my mind, not to keep harping on about it, but I believe I'm getting somewhere at last!'

Avril agreed that knowing that Arabella was alive and living in America was a tremendous step forward. 'But you've been patient for so long that by now being patient must be second nature to you, so don't try to rush things, but let life take its course,' she added. 'Have you finished your bread and butter? If so, we'll start on the jam tarts.'

Miranda took a tart, but did not bite into it. Suddenly she knew that she wanted desperately to speak to Steve, to tell him all about the newsreel and how she was certain, now, that her mother was still alive. She glanced at the clock on the mantelpiece, which read ten o'clock; would Steve be in bed? Would there be anybody still awake to answer the telephone in the Mess? She was telling herself that she would simply have to wait until the following day to call Steve when her hand, seemingly of its own accord, replaced the jam tart on her plate even as she got to her feet. She went across the kitchen, took her thick coat, headscarf and muffler down from their hook and began to put them on. From behind her she heard Avril's chair squeak as her friend pushed it back, but she did not even look round.

Avril's voice sounded almost frightened when she

spoke. 'Miranda? Wharron earth are you doin'? Don't you go out like your mam did and get kidnapped by a beastly Nazi. It's bedtime – oh, damn it, if you must walk I suppose I'll have to go with you.'

Miranda, already at the door, turned and smiled at her friend. 'Don't be so daft. I'm just goin' down to the box on the corner to give Steve a ring, tell him about the newsreel. Once I've told him I'll come straight back, so I shan't be more than ten or fifteen minutes at the most. And you aren't to even think about coming with me, Avril, because I'm not a child and I'm not sleepwalking either. Just stay there and watch the clock.' As she spoke she was opening the kitchen door, then glanced over her shoulder at the other girl. 'It's all right, the snow's stopped. I've got my torch, though I shan't need it. See you later.' With that she closed the door upon Avril's half-hearted objections, clattered down the stair and ran all the way to the telephone box. Putting her money into the slot when the operator demanded it, she thought ruefully that she was being daft. Steve would have been in bed ages ago and she could not possibly ask for him to be told of her call because that would mean disturbing everyone else in his hut. Yet she had a strong feeling – you could call it a conviction almost – that he had not yet gone to bed, that in some mysterious way they were on the same wavelength, despite the distance which separated them, and when it was he who picked up the receiver she was not even surprised, particularly when she did not even have to give her name, because Steve said at once: 'Miranda? What's happened? I knew it must be you, ringin' at this ungodly hour, so what's new?'

'Oh, Steve, you are wonderful, and I'm sorry to ring

so late,' Miranda gabbled. 'Only I had to tell you, because I knew you'd understand. Avril and I went to the cinema this evening . . .'

At the end of the recital there was the shortest of pauses and then Steve's voice, warm and reassuring, came over the wire. 'Don't worry about disturbing me; the chaps and I have been talking and we are all still up. It's fantastic news that Arabella is still alive, and I'm sure you'll manage to get in touch with her somehow. And you can stop feeling guilty, queen, now that you know she's all right.'

Miranda hissed in a breath; how had he known that it had been guilt over their quarrel which had made her so desperately eager to prove that Arabella was still alive? She had never admitted to a soul that the quarrel, even if it had only driven her mother to take that solitary walk, might have been Arabella's downfall. And now, having told Steve and received his understanding, she was aware that she felt as if a great weight had been lifted from her shoulders. Avril had doubted her, but Steve had accepted every word of her story. Blissfully, Miranda realised that though she still meant to try to contact her mother it was no longer as essential to her happiness as it had once been. In the very nature of things she and Arabella would, by now, have begun to take their separate paths. Of course she meant to do everything she could to trace Arabella, but even if she failed she would know at least that Arabella lived, and, what's more, lived happily. But now Steve's voice spoke urgently in her ear. 'Miranda? I was going to send you a telegram asking you to ring me, but I might have known you'd sense my urge to talk and ring me anyway. I've got some news of my own which, as it happens, will affect you. In a week's time I'm being shipped along with a great many other fellers to America, where I'll be trained as aircrew; if I'm good enough, as a fighter pilot.'

For a moment, Miranda could not even speak. She felt as if all the air had been drained out of the telephone booth, leaving her gasping like a landed fish. But Steve's voice in her ear, sharp with anxiety, brought her back to life. 'Miranda, where have you gone? Have you cut the connection? I was just telling you . . .'

Miranda and the operator spoke almost simultaneously. 'Caller, your time is up.'

And Miranda's voice, small with shock and dismay: 'Oh, but Steve, you can't go. I can't lose everyone I care about . . .'

Steve's voice echoed in her ear, sounding strangely unlike himself. 'Can't change what's already happened . . .' he was beginning when there was a decisive click and the operator said crisply: 'Replace your receiver please, caller. Others are waiting for this line.'

Very, very slowly, Miranda put her receiver back on its rest, automatically pressed button B although she knew she had used all the money the operator had required, then stumbled out of the box, apologising to the young man in naval uniform who had obviously been waiting for her to finish her call. He moved to pass her, then must have noticed her pallor because he caught her arm. 'You awright, miss?' he asked. 'Not bad news, I hope. You've gone that white . . .'

Miranda conjured up what she guessed must be a rather wan smile. 'No, not bad news. But my boyfriend is being sent to America,' she said, and was about to add the information that he was going to learn how to fly when she remembered the government posters and gave the young naval officer a watery smile. 'I'm fine, honest to God I am. It was just the shock. But thanks for your concern.'

''Sawright, gairl,' the young man said easily. 'Mind how you go.'

Miranda heard the door of the box click and stood for a moment, replacing her muffler, pulling on her gloves and doing up the top button of her coat, whilst the young man consulted a small notebook, spoke into the receiver and began to put pennies in the slot with a great clatter. Then she moved away when she saw his mouth move and knew he was in contact with the operator. No use hanging about whilst he got his call. Steve would probably be on his way to bed by now, and if the operator recognised her voice she might well refuse to put another call through; some operators were like that, thought themselves in charge of the whole telephone system.

Miranda was at the foot of the metal stair when the door above opened and Avril looked anxiously out, though the anxiety disappeared as Miranda began to climb. 'Did you get through, queen?' she asked. 'Poor old Steve, was he tucked up in his nice little bunk? I bet he cursed you, especially if whoever answered the phone had to wake the whole hut.'

Miranda trudged up the remainder of the stairs and was glad to enter the warmth of the kitchen and shut the door behind her. 'He wasn't even in bed, but he had some news of his own,' she said wearily. She took off her outdoor clothing and turned to Avril, trying to manufacture a cheerful smile and knowing that she failed. 'In fact, he was going to send me a telegram because next week he's being sent to America with a batch of other men, who'll all learn to fly fighter planes.' She turned to Avril and felt the first tears rise in her eyes to the accompaniment of a violent sob. 'Oh, Avril, it's true what I said when he first joined the air force; sooner or later, everyone leaves me. And now Steve's going so far away that there won't even be telephone calls, and letters which get sent from abroad are chopped to bits by the censor, if they arrive at all, which a lot of them don't. Oh, and convoys get attacked all the time; he could be drowned, or bombed . . . I can't bear it!'

Avril tutted. 'These things happen in wartime, to everyone, not just you, so stop feelin' so perishin' sorry for yourself,' she said crossly. 'When Steve was at your beck and call you kept denying that he was your boyfriend, but now he's going away you talk as if he were your only love. Be consistent, for Gawd's sake, you silly little Lovage. Pull yourself together!'

Miranda fished a handkerchief out from her sleeve, blew her nose resoundingly and then wiped her eyes with the backs of her hands. She gave another enormous sniff and a watery giggle, then turned a calm face towards her friend. 'First I find my mother isn't dead and am over the moon, then I find my best friend – and he's still my best friend and nothing more – is being sent half a world away. Next thing I know you'll be snatched up and sent off on a mysterious mission to Antarctica or somewhere and I'll lose you as well.'

Avril sniffed. 'And of course they'll choose me since I

speak Antarctic like a native,' she said sarcastically. She handed Miranda her filled hot water bottle, which her friend immediately cuddled gratefully. 'And now shall we go to bed before I drop in my tracks? If I'm tired – and I am – you must be absolutely jiggered.'

'True,' Miranda admitted. 'But I wonder why Steve isn't getting embarkation leave, like Julian? I remember that Julian came round and took you out for a meal before he took ship for Rhodesia. So why not Steve?'

'Can't you guess? Whilst the awful weather continues all flights are grounded, and even the ships are mainly in port, here *and* on the other side of the Channel. That means your precious Steve should have a safer crossing than if he waited for a few weeks. Be grateful, girl.'

'I *am*,' Miranda said. 'Grateful, I mean. And you're a real pal, Avril, to take the worry off my mind.'

Later, snuggling down in bed, with her hot water bottle strategically positioned to de-ice her freezing toes, she began to think about her day and realised that, though she knew she would miss Steve horribly, the warm glow which she had felt ever since seeing her mother on the silver screen had not dissipated. In fact with every moment that passed it felt stronger, and she realised that her chief feeling was a very odd one indeed. Because her mother was alive she, Miranda, would be able one day to apologise to her for all the horrid things she'd said during the course of that long ago quarrel. And of course the fact that Steve might be quite near Arabella merely made the feeling even better. If I have to wait until the war is over I shan't mind so much now, she told herself, pulling the blankets up until only her eyes were clear of them. I'll be able to give Steve money from my savings to pay for advertising in American newspapers – and he saw Betty Prince's picture, which was quite a good likeness. Yes, I'm sure Steve will run her to earth if anyone can.

Chapter Ten

1940

Miranda and Avril joined the queue for the tram, shivering and stamping their feet, for it was a freezing cold December day. Miranda, however, had more important things than the weather on her mind: namely, getting to Lime Street Station in time to meet Steve's train, for he was coming home at last, after almost a year away.

'Excited, queen?' Avril's voice was indulgent. 'I know you won't let me call Steve your feller, but you've been . . . oh, I don't know, sort of lit up . . . ever since he arrived in England.'

That had been a week earlier, a week in which he had been too busy to telephone, for on arriving from the States he had been immediately posted to somewhere called Church Stretton, where they were taking pilots who had flown bombers – Wellingtons mostly – to retrain on to Lancasters, and had not been allowed off the airfield until he had been thoroughly debriefed, whatever that might mean.

'Brrr,' Miranda said. 'It's perishing brass monkey weather again. Thank you for saying you'd come to the station with me – it'll be much nicer than waiting on my own, though I'm sure that if any of the Mickleboroughs are at home they'll be on the platform as well!'

Avril laughed. 'Well, you said his mam, Kenny and

the baby were coming home for Christmas, so if they're back by now I'm sure they'll be there. And his gran is still living in Jamaica Close, isn't she? So I take it she'll be feeding Steve whether or not his mam is here.'

Miranda shrugged. 'Who can tell? What with no trains ever arriving on time and being so crowded with members of the forces that civilians scarcely ever get a seat, you can't say for certain where anyone will be at any given time. Tell you what, if Steve's mam isn't on the platform then we might as well buy fish and chips when he arrives and take him back to the flat. He can go on to his mother's place later.'

The tram drew up beside them and the two girls got in. The long narrow bench seats were already full but the girls were used to strap hanging and continued their conversation as the tram rattled on. 'I believe the weather in Texas is really warm,' Miranda said with a shiver. 'Poor Steve, having to get used to our dear old English climate all over again! Of course I told him how lovely the weather was in the summer but there was so much I couldn't mention that I think my letters became rather stilted. And his letters were rather stilted too, because he had to admit he'd had no luck at all in finding my mother.'

'Well, you know he tried; he sent you copies of the advertisements he'd put in the papers,' Avril reminded her friend. 'And if you're talking about things like the fall of France and the evac—'

'Shurrup, you moron; loose lips sink ships,' Miranda reminded her. 'But yes, the American papers will have had all the major war news in every detail. No, what I meant was the things that had happened here – the raids last month, for instance. Liverpool will seem like a foreign city compared to the one Steve knew.'

The tram skidded to a stop on the icy rails and Avril gave a squawk as the man next to her stumbled, his elbows swinging round to catch her on her upper arm. 'Sorry, chuck,' he said, not sounding sorry at all. 'But it weren't my fault, the bleedin' tram driver needs a lesson in brakin', if you ask me. You gettin' off here? It's the station.'

'Oh, crumbs, so it is,' Avril gasped. 'You can't see a thing in the perishin' blackout, and it don't do to miss your stop with the pavements so slippery an' all.' She jerked on Miranda's arm. 'Come on, queen, gerra move on. Chances are you'll still be waitin' in an hour or two, but on the other hand the train really might be on time for once.'

The girls descended from the tram, crossed the pavement and dived into the concourse. As usual it was crowded, but Avril collared a passing porter and was told that the cross-country train for which they waited was a mere forty minutes late. 'Have yourself a cup of tea and a wad, and by the time you've queued for it and ate it, your feller will have arrived,' he said jovially.

Avril sniffed. 'I hope my feller is safely tucked up in his factory startin' the night shift,' she said, to the porter's retreating back. 'Why does everyone assume that if you're meetin' a train it must have some man on it what you're busy pursuin'?' She turned to Miranda. 'Look, love, if it's forty minutes behind time now, the chances are it'll be an hour and forty minutes by the time it gets here. There's no point in me hangin' around waitin' that long for a feller what's your concern and not mine. I'll go back to the flat, light the fire and get the place warmed through, and see if I can make some sort of meal for Steve, just in case his train don't get in till after the chippies close. Shall I make up the bed in the living room in case he wants to stay over? It'd be no trouble.'

Miranda pondered for a moment, then shook her head. 'No, don't bother. As you say, it only takes a couple of minutes. What have we got in the pantry if the fish and chips shops are all closed?'

The girls took it in turns to cook their main meal of the day, which was generally eaten at around seven o'clock in the evening, and since it was Avril's week she had done the marketing, though rationing made shopping a chore. Standing on the concourse with people all around them Avril ticked the contents of the pantry off on her fingers. 'Some sausage meat, a big onion, a few carrots and enough flour and marge to make a pastry case,' she announced. 'Will that do, chuck?' When Miranda nodded, she said, 'Righty ho; see you later.'

Glumly, Miranda headed for the refreshment room. As she went she glanced around her; how good it would be to see some member of the Mickleborough family or a friend from school, but all the faces seemed strange. Sighing, she joined the queue. At least if you bought a cup of tea you might be able to sit down whilst you drank it!

By the time Steve erupted from an overcrowded carriage it was well past ten o'clock. Miranda did not recognise him at first, seeing merely the only tanned face under an RAF cap, a tan which made his teeth look astonishingly white. He must have seen her at once, though, because she was still looking wildly around her when she felt herself seized and hugged. 'Oh, you good girl; how I love you!' Steve's voice said in her ear. 'My poor darling, you must have been here for hours, because in my telegram I said my train would be arriving at seven o'clock, not twenty past ten. Now why don't you put your arms round my neck so that you can give me a welcome home kiss? And don't start talkin' nonsense about bezzies because I'm as good as a Yank, I am, and we expect kisses and hugs from every girl we see.'

Miranda obediently put her arms round his neck, but dropped her face to snuggle against his tunic. 'I feel stupid,' she mumbled. 'You've changed. Goodness me, Steve, you've grown! You're actually taller than when you went away.'

'And broader, though it's mainly across the shoulders,' Steve said complacently. 'Oh, it's so grand to see you, Miranda. I've missed you something awful.' He caught hold of her hand as she released his neck, swung it up to his face and kissed the palm, and this made her give a little gurgle of shocked astonishment, which made Steve laugh. 'You daft kid,' he said affectionately. 'And my mam's comin' home for Christmas despite my tellin' her I'd rather she didn't. The Luftwaffe are bound to get Liverpool's measure sooner or later, and when they do, believe me, honey, they'll smash the place to smithereens. Oh, I know Churchill says we won the Battle of Britain, that two German planes were downed to every one the Royal Air Force lost, but the truth of the matter is we're still building up our defences and retraining the BEF, so I'd rather my mother and the kids were tucked away safely in Wales.'

He bent and picked up his kitbag, which he had tossed aside in order to have both arms free for Miranda, and began to lead her out of the station. 'Where am I spendin' the night?' he asked. 'I'm quite happy to share your bed, pretty lady, if that's the only accommodation available. As you know, my gran stayed in Jamaica Close when Mam and the kids were evacuated, and she's there still, but she's awful old and gets confused. A neighbour does her marketing, lights her fire and cooks her food, though Gran bustles about and helps a lot, or so she claims. But even if she was told that today was red letter day, she'll probably have forgotten by now and won't have so much as a sardine in the pantry to keep my strength up. So how about if I come back to Russell Street? Any chance of a bite? And I don't necessarily mean food either.'

'You've got awfully cheeky, Steve, since you've been away,' Miranda said reprovingly. 'Of course you're very welcome to come round to Russell Street for a meal, but no biting, if you please. I had meant to buy fish and chips but I reckon all the chippies will be closed by now. However, I think Avril means to make a sausage turnover and cook some carrots and that to go with it. Then there's the remains of a junket Avril and I had for tea, standing on the slate shelf in the pantry. What do you say to finishing that? I suppose you'll have to spend the night, because the trams will have stopped running by the time we've heard each other's news.'

Steve agreed eagerly that this was a great idea, and when they reached the flat and found Avril fast asleep in bed, but the sausage turnover still warm from the oven, he took off his greatcoat, cap and scarf and settled down eagerly to attack the plate of food Miranda placed in front of him. Whilst he ate she read him Missie's latest letter, which was almost equally divided between pleasure at being in her own home again and apprehension for her friends across the seas. After that, she asked about America, and tried not to feel jealous when Steve described the parties, dances, barbecues and picnics which had been arranged by local girls for the entertainment of their British guests. She told herself firmly that to feel jealous was absurd because Steve was not her boyfriend, but presently, when he had eaten and drunk everything Avril had provided, they settled on the couch for a nice cosy cuddling session whilst they talked into the night, and told each other of the more exciting events which they had not been able to share in letters.

Miranda was in the middle of a description of a dog fight she had watched between a Messerschmitt and a Spitfire when something in her companion's breathing made her stop speaking and stare into the deeply tanned face so near to her own. And not only deeply tanned, but deeply asleep. Miranda smiled and thought about what he'd said that night. He'd told her he loved her and she felt confused. Did she really think of him as a brother? Oh, she was too tired to think about it now. She closed her own eyes and wondered how much wearier poor Steve must be! He had come all the way from Texas in a troop-carrying plane, not renowned for its comfort. Then he had had a hectic debriefing session and an introduction to the Lancaster aeroplane. After that he was given a seven day pass and had undergone the hell of a cross-country journey in wartime. Meeting her must have been quite as much of a trial for him as it was for her, because he must have been as conscious as she of the changes that had taken place during their year apart. And now, well fed and warm, it had been the most natural thing in the world for him to fall asleep. But of course it would never do. They had not made up the sofa into a bed so the bedcovers were still rolled up beneath it, and soon enough the fire would go out, leaving the room as cold as the icy courtyard below. Clearly, it behoved her to wake him up and either set him on his way to Jamaica Close or get him to give her a hand to make up a bed on the sofa. Thinking of this, she realised that she was already feeling somewhat chilly and, with infinite care, reached under the sofa and dragged out a couple of blankets. She threw them over Steve, causing him to give a sleepy mutter, and then pulled them over herself. The sofa cushions would make a lovely pillow, but of course she could not actually lie on the sofa the way Steve would, once it was converted into a bed. Miranda wriggled into a more comfortable position and found rather to her surprise that her head fitted most comfortably into the hollow of Steve's shoulder. Anyone would think we'd been married for years, she told herself sleepily. For years and years and years and years . . . and Miranda was asleep.

Steve awoke. For a moment he lay perfectly still, thoroughly puzzled. Over the past ten days or so he had woken up in so many different places that he could scarcely count them, but this waking was different from all the rest. He shifted a fraction, forced himself to open his heavy lids and looked around him. It was still dark though he could see light coming through a gap of some sort; not very much light, and not the golden sunshine to which he had become accustomed in Texas. This was a faint bluish light, as though the moon was shining directly on the outside of what he now realised must be a blackout blind. He frowned; if he was in his hut at Church Stretton then the window had got up and moved during the night, which seemed unlikely. So if he was not in his hut, where the devil was he? He remembered the long cold journey in the train and the ecstatic moment when he had descended on to the platform at Lime Street Station, and had opened his arms to Miranda . . .

Miranda! At the mere recollection of her name, memory came flooding back. They had been too late to buy fish and chips but had returned to the flat in Russell Street and found a delicious supper which Avril had cooked for him. Avril had already been in bed and asleep, so he and Miranda had moved into the living room, intending to have a goodnight cuddle . . .

Cuddle! With the word, his arms tightened around Miranda's warm body, curled up against his chest. Guiltily he realised that the two of them must have been so tired that they had fallen asleep, and here it was, early morning, and they were still cuddled up on the sofa. Steve could not help grinning to himself. In future he would be able to claim that he and his girl had slept together, and at the very thought he felt pleasure and guilt in equal quantities assail him. She would be furious, of course, if he teased her by telling Avril that they had spent the night together, even though he would explain that it had been an accident, that sheer weariness had caused them to fall asleep. At the thought he dropped a light kiss on the side of Miranda's face, thinking he would tell her that, as in all the best fairy stories, his kiss had wakened her, but in fact he was unable to do so since Miranda slumbered on.

Steve had half risen on his elbow but now with infinite care he lay down against the sofa cushions and let his mind go back to the very first time he had seen Miranda. She had been standing in Jamaica Close staring up at the great twenty-foot wall whilst her lips moved soundlessly. He had thought she looked as though she was reciting some magical rhyme which would cause a door to open in the wall, so that she might go through. Steve remembered with shame that he had jeered at the scrawny kid with her topping of carrot-coloured hair, had teased her by pretending she was just a dog, but a dog who had managed to slip its leash. Then they had talked about their parents and he had seen the wistful resignation in her large hazel eyes and had offered her friendship, an offer she had grabbed with real enthusiasm. There were no boys in Jamaica Close around his age so palling up with the new kid was sensible, and he very soon realised that she had spunk, plenty of it. Despite the fact that she was younger than he they got on very well, and it was not long before he was proud to consider her his bezzie. In fact, he thought now, with the soft sweet-smelling length of her in his arms, he had fallen in love with her long ago without actually realising that his emotions had changed and deepened.

Her introduction to Jamaica House had been intended as a test but all it had really proved was that she was a lot braver than he, and from the moment that the two of them had begun to help Missie he had known that being bezzies would never be enough. She might not have known it then – might not know it now – but she was his girl and always would be.

The only trouble was that she did not seem to realise that he had got past mere friendship and was floundering in a sea of love which she refused to let him show. He had envied the Grimshaws – Julian must have looked so suave and handsome in the uniform of a flying officer – but Julian was in Africa, training other men to fly fighter aircraft, whilst he, at long last, was on the spot. And he intended to make the most of it. Only the elderly partners and the two old biddies Miranda had told him about were left in Mr Grimshaw's office, which meant that at least there was little fear of her becoming emotionally involved with a fellow worker. But he knew she occasionally saw Gerald, and the previous evening he had been dismayed when he saw pink colour flood her cheeks at the mention of his name, and her eyes, which had been staring straight into his, suddenly veil themselves in their long pale lashes. He had given a sheepish grin. 'I think Gerald might have his eye on you,' he said frankly. 'If only you'd let me buy you an engagement ring – just a tiny one – then I'd know he wasn't a threat.'

'Oh, Steve, what a fool you are! I like both of you, but in different ways. You've been like a brother to me.'

Infuriated, Steve had got to his feet, crossed the room in a couple of strides and plucked Miranda out of her chair as though she weighed no more than a kitten. 'I am *not* your brother, for which I thank God devoutly,' he had said crossly. 'I fell in love with you when you were a scrawny little stick of a kid climbing the trees in the Jamaica House garden and throwing the fruit down to me, and I'm in love with you still, so put that in your pipe and smoke it.'

He had waited for an indignant reply, and had been pleasantly surprised when Miranda had flung an arm round his neck, pulled his face down to her level and kissed first his cheek and then the side of his mouth, though she had moved back before he could take full advantage of her softened mood. 'Look, Steve, I'm not very old and neither are you. And Gerald is a lot of fun to be with . . .'

Steve had sighed. He had been standing with her in his arms, but then he sat her down again and took his own place at the table once more. 'All right, all right, I'm jumping the gun, but I just want you to know that you can't go off and get yourself tied up to any Tom, Dick or Harry because you're mine; get it?'

Miranda had pulled a face. 'I don't belong to anyone but myself,' she said firmly. 'And don't worry, no Tom, Dick or Harry – or Gerald or Julian for that matter – is going to want to sweep me off my feet. And now let's eat up so that we can both get to bed. I see the kettle's boiling so I'll make us both a hot water bottle as soon as I've finished my supper.'

'If you go pouring boiling water into a rubber bag you're liable to get an unpleasant shock in the middle of the night,' Steve had warned her. 'You'll wake up, thinking you've peed the bed, not realising . . .'

'Don't be so rude. I've been making hot water bottles for years and always pour cold in first,' Miranda had said reprovingly. 'And now you can stop going on about poor Gerald and tell me more about Texas.'

Now, Steve stroked Miranda's cheek, looking forward to the moment when she awoke and found herself in his arms, but though she murmured she still did not wake and Steve's thoughts returned to the past. *Why* did he love Miranda so desperately? He had to admit, though no longer quite so scrawny and with her carroty hair darkened to auburn, she was still no beauty. She had a pointy chin, a straight little nose and a generous mouth, whilst her big greenish-hazel eyes seemed almost too large for her small heart-shaped face. Steve could think of a dozen girls, many of whom he had taken around whilst in Texas, who were twice as pretty and half a dozen times as willing as Miranda Lovage. But she had, for him, an attraction which could not be put into words, and he supposed that Gerald and perhaps many other men were also aware of her charms. The thought made him jerk back on to his elbow. He was home in England now and could arrange for her to visit his airfield once he got a definite posting; then he would persuade her to start thinking seriously about marriage.

As though she had read his thoughts, Miranda gave a soft moan and sat up. She stared around her, eyes dilating. 'Where the devil am I?' she said in a bewildered voice. 'Oh my goodness, what's the time? Avril, have I missed the alarm? Oh my goodness!'

As she spoke she heaved herself clear of the blankets and wrenched herself out of Steve's embrace with such force that they both descended to the floor with a crash, Steve giggling helplessly and Miranda scolding. 'Oh, Steve, I must have fallen asleep . . . I was so tired, you wouldn't believe . . . oh, goodness, it's morning and it was my turn to make the breakfast.' She turned on him where he lay on the floor, still laughing, and punched him in the stomach. 'You beast, Steve Mickleborough, how dare you let me fall asleep! Oh, and we were both wearing all our clothes . . .'

'Not all of them; I took my tunic off so I was in shirt-sleeves, but I'm afraid you're right and my kecks are pretty crumpled,' Steve said ruefully. 'But I was about to wake you 'cos I hear sounds of movement coming from your kitchen. You'll want to wash and dress and so on in your own bedroom, whilst I'll have to make do with the kitchen sink.' He grinned at her. 'Do you realise what this means? We've spent the night together and folk will think that I must do the decent thing and marry you! What do you say?'

Miranda, trying to comb her hair with her fingers for it had got considerably tangled in the night, was beginning to tell Steve that if he breathed a word regarding where he had spent the night she would excommunicate him, when the door to the living room burst open. Avril stood there, round-eyed. 'Wharron earth . . .' she was beginning when Miranda, choking back a laugh, interrupted.

'Oh, Avril, can't you guess? We came through here to make up the couch as a bed for Steve. Only we both went and fell asleep and we've only just woken up.' She stood up, stretched and yawned. 'Thank the Lord Mr Grimshaw gave me the day off because Steve was coming home! But now we'd better get a move on because Steve will want to go back to Jamaica Close to see whether his mam really means to come for Christmas, and I intend to go with him.' As she spoke she had been tidying away the blankets, and Steve, scrambling to his feet, went to the window, pulled back the curtains and wound up the blackout blind, then turned to Avril.

'Much though I hate to admit it, nothing of an interesting nature occurred all night because we were so perishin' exhausted,' he said, grinning. 'But if I may have a borrow of your sofa again tonight I can promise you I'll stay awake if I have to prop up my eyelids wi' matchsticks.'

He was relieved when Avril laughed, came over and gave him a shove. 'Men!' she said scornfully. 'You're all talk and trousers, you. I know me pal better'n you ever did and she ain't the sort to give a feller what he wants just because she's knowed him years.' She looked at Miranda. 'It's perishin' cold still but I've put the kettle on for tea and poured hot water into the big enamel jug. So if you take that to your room you can have a wash and change. You can't wear that skirt and blouse; they look as though you've slept in 'em.' She turned her attention back to Steve. 'As for you, I'll go back to my room while you make yourself respectable. We've an electric iron and an ironing board what we got off Paddy's Market, so if you want to give your kecks a quick press you can do it whilst Miranda and meself check that our glad rags are in good repair.' She gave him a wicked grin. 'I take it you're going to invite us both out for some grub, lunchtime.' She pulled a pious face, though her eyes were still twinkling. 'You could call it buyin' me silence, or a spot of blackmail, whichever you prefer. If you treat me right I'll keep me gob shut.'

Steve sighed theatrically, but said he was very willing to mug them a meal at noon and arranged to meet outside Lewis's, though he told Avril he meant to go to Jamaica Close as soon as he'd had some breakfast. 'I think Mam's due to come back tomorrow, but I know Dad's written to her absolutely forbidding her to bring Kenny and the little 'un into danger, even for the sake of having a family

Christmas,' he explained. 'It ain't as though you can rely on the Luftwaffe to just drop the odd bomb whilst they're concentrating on wiping poor old London off the map. Any day now they could turn their attention to the next largest port in the country and begin to hand out the sort of punishment the Londoners have been facing. But you know women; once they get an idea into their heads it's powerful difficult to get it out again, and . . .'

'Shut up!' both girls screamed in unison, Miranda adding: 'Your mam's really sensible and wouldn't bring the little 'uns into danger. So shut up and give yourself a good wash whilst I do the same, then we can have some porridge and toast and start our day on a full stomach.'

Although she would never have admitted it Miranda had found waking up in Steve's arms strangely exciting, and she had been aware of a slight sense of disappointment when he had not tried to take advantage of the situation. In fact she felt quite peeved. He said he loved her, which presumably meant he wanted her, yet there she had been, in his arms and at his mercy so to speak, and he had not tried to cajole her in any way, save to suggest teasingly that, having spent the night with him, she might want to marry him, thus regularising the situation. However, she supposed that it was really a sign of Steve's respect and decided she should be grateful. She had heard various stories from girls in the factory about what happened when you 'gave your all', and it sounded rude, embarrassing, and even rather painful. Definitely not the sort of thing which one did casually, especially when one knew that the door to the room in which one lay might suddenly burst open to reveal the shocked face of one's best friend.

Having convinced herself that all was well Miranda got on with the task in hand. Only the previous week she had treated herself to a thick and far from new seaman's jersey in navy blue wool, for it was already obvious that they were going to be in for another very cold winter. The jersey had been shrunken, with both elbows out and holes in various strategic spots, but Avril had been taught the art of darning and sewing whilst at the children's home and had offered to put it right. Not one hole remained, and Miranda had embellished the garment by embroidering lazy daisies round the crew neck. She put it on now with a thick woollen skirt, also in navy, and went through to the kitchen where Avril was already dishing up the porridge, and Steve, fully dressed, was turning away from the sink. He grinned at her. 'Hello again, queen. It's perishin' cold out,' he greeted her. 'I went down to the privy for the usual purpose and there's a big puddle frozen solid right at the bottom of the stair, so if you need to go you want to watch out.'

'I'm all right, thanks,' Miranda said, having shot down to the privy before going to her bedroom to change her rumpled clothing. 'Gosh, the porridge smells good; oh, and toast as well.' She grinned at Avril. 'Good job bread isn't rationed.'

The three sat down to their meal and presently, the girls clad in their thick coats and hats, they left the flat, descended the stairs and decided to go their separate ways, since Avril, who was not on shift till the following evening, still had a couple of presents to buy and Miranda wanted to go back to Jamaica Close with Steve. Her main reason for this was to learn whether Mrs Mickleborough had decided against returning to the city for Christmas. If she had, Miranda intended to ask Steve and his gran back to the flat for the day itself, but of course she would not do so should Mrs Mickleborough and the little ones be coming home. There simply would not be sufficient room in the flat for five extra people, and though Miranda had not seen Kenny since the previous September she remembered him as being lively and demanding, to say the least, whilst Flora was surely toddling about under her own steam by now.

So when they reached the main road Avril went off towards the city centre, whilst Steve and Miranda caught a tram and were presently knocking on the door of Number Two Jamaica Close. They heard Gran's slippered feet shuffling along the front hall, and presently the old lady was exclaiming with delight and ushering them into the kitchen, where a bright fire burned in the range and the kettle was hopping on the hob. 'Eh, it's grand to see thee, lad, real grand,' Granny Granger said. She beamed at Miranda. 'And you've brought your young lady along! Eh, I'm honoured! Now sit down the pair of you and you shall have tea and a bit of me seed cake, 'cos it's mortal cold out there.' She chuckled richly. 'When I visited the privy earlier me bum near on froze to the seat; imagine that!' Her visitors laughed, but as soon as they were settled with tea and cake the question which Miranda guessed was uppermost in Steve's mind was voiced. Gran, however, shook her head. 'I dunno whether they'll take the chance, but if her good man's letter reaches her in time I reckon she'll give up the idea. If you ask me she'd be downright foolish to take the risk. It ain't as if she were unhappy in that little Welsh village, 'cos she ain't. Her letters is full of country talk, and she says after the war's over she means to try for a country cottage. I dunno as she'll ever get one, 'cos her hubby has to be near his work, but it's good that she's goin' to try. More toast? Another cup?'

Steve accepted, but Miranda, shaking her head, got to her feet. 'Thanks, Mrs Granger, but I believe I ought to visit my aunt and my cousin Beth. I've not been round since war broke out – I've been too busy – but now I'm actually in the neighbourhood I really should say hello. And I've got a little present for Beth, and one for my aunt, so if you don't mind I'll just nip up the road.'

Granny Granger nodded her understanding. Steve reminded Miranda to give a knock on the door when she was ready to leave, and then he and the old lady settled down to talk of aunts and cousins he had not seen for many months, whilst Miranda walked along to her aunt's house and knocked on the door, aware of a tiny shudder of distaste at the memory of her time spent living here under her aunt's despotic rule.

When the door was answered, however, her aunt's grim mouth softened a little, though she said accusingly: 'Slummin', ain't you?'

'Don't be nasty or you shan't have your Christmas present,' Miranda said promptly. 'I haven't come all this way to be insulted, you know.'

Her aunt sniffed. 'You haven't come all this way very often,' she said, but in a milder tone. 'If you remember, young lady, you left without givin' us your new address, so you're lucky to get any sort of present off of Beth and meself. However, bein' the souls of generosity, we've bought you a little somethin' in the hope that you might deign to come round, bein' as it's the season of goodwill and all that.'

'I'm sorry, Aunt Vi, but we're so short-staffed at the office now that it's all I can do to get my messages and have a sleep,' Miranda explained. 'Well, I reckon you must understand, because a few weeks ago I met Beth in St John's fish market, and she told me she was working in a factory making parachutes, so I guess her time off is pretty limited too. And I did tell her I lived in a flat over a bicycle shop on Russell Street; didn't she pass the news on to you?'

Her aunt sniffed again but stood aside, beckoning her niece to enter. 'I dunno as she might have done,' she admitted grudgingly. 'Fact is, Miranda, that she ain't here all that often; she kips down with a pal when she's on a late shift so she's only under my roof, oh, one week in four, I suppose.' She pulled her mouth down at the corners. 'Truth to tell, I gets lonely, so if you're ever lookin' for a place to lie your head there's a spare bed here you'd be welcome to use.'

Miranda had to bite her lip or she might have reminded her aunt of the way she had been treated when she had lived in Jamaica Close, might also have added that if the factory making parachutes was too far from Jamaica Close, her own place of work was even farther. Instead she said: 'Thanks, Aunt, I'll remember your – your kind offer.' Then she rooted around in her pocket and produced the presents, both well wrapped. 'Not to be opened until Christmas Day; yours is the one in red paper and Beth's is in the green,' she said, with a gaiety she was far from feeling. One glance round the dirty neglected kitchen and one sniff of the smell of stale food and rotting vegetables was enough to convince her that her aunt had not changed. She was still lazy, greedy and a bad housewife, and she, Miranda, would have to be desperate indeed before she crossed this threshold again.

Outside once more, she took a deep breath of the icy air and was approaching the Mickleborough house when Steve emerged from it, giving her his broadest grin. 'Didn't think you'd hang around there for long,' he greeted her. 'I bet the old biddy hasn't changed at all. Did she ask you to come over and cook her Christmas dinner? I bet that was her first thought!'

'You're not far out; apparently even Beth doesn't spend much time at home now. Did I tell you she was making parachutes at a big factory on the outskirts of the city? No, probably I didn't, because of the censor. Well she is, and Aunt Vi says she kips down with a pal when she's on late shifts. She said she and Beth had a present for me, but whatever it was she didn't hand it over. Now, what else did Granny Granger say about your mam and the kids coming home for Christmas?'

'Norra lot,' Steve said cheerfully as they swung into the main road and headed for the tram stop, 'just that Mam didn't mean to come until the day before Christmas Eve, so she's still got time to make up her mind. But I think she'll be sensible; my mam is sensible, wouldn't you say?'

'She's very sensible,' Miranda agreed. 'What'll we do today? If you're not too tired I've got some last minute shopping to do, and this evening I really would love to go dancing. It's difficult for Avril and me, because of

Gary. Those two really are in love and want to marry as soon as they've saved up enough money to rent a couple of rooms somewhere. Avril used to love dancing but of course Gary can't do even the simplest steps, though he tells Avril that he wouldn't mind if she wanted to dance with other blokes, but she won't do it. You can understand why, can't you, Steve?'

'Course I can,' Steve said at once. 'She's a grand girl, your Avril. But I take it she won't mind if you and I go dancing? I'm no great shakes, but there was a girl in Texas who took me in hand and now I can waltz and quickstep with the best of 'em, though the foxtrot and the tango are still beyond me. Do you think Avril will want to come with us? Even if she won't dance for fear of hurting Gary's feelings, I suppose she could watch.'

'And play gooseberry?' Miranda said scornfully. 'Of course she won't, you idiot. Besides, she's very pretty, you know, even if she is a tiny bit overweight. She'd be besieged by offers and turning a chap down can be really uncomfortable. No, if we go dancing it will just be you and me.'

They caught a tram into the city centre, Steve admitting that he had heard so much about the shortages in England that he had scoured Texas for any foodstuffs or luxuries he could afford, to give to all his loved ones as Christmas presents. 'So we've no need to go shopping on my account,' he assured Miranda. 'Where do you want to go for yours?' He glanced at the heavy watch on his wrist. It had several different dials, which had intrigued Miranda until he had explained its various uses. 'Ah, but it's twenty to twelve; we'd best make tracks for Lewis's and a really good, pre-war lunch!'

Avril and Miranda were in Miranda's room, Avril sitting on the bed and watching as her friend tried on a dance dress she had borrowed from a pal whose own boyfriend was on one of the ships in the transatlantic convoy and would not be back home in Liverpool for another two weeks at least. And anyway, the dress would never have fitted her, Miranda thought to herself, remembering how her plump little pal had sighed as she handed the dress over in a stout paper carrier, explaining that her mother, a first rate needlewoman, had made it herself several years before the war started, and had only worn it twice. Miranda, pulling the soft chiffon out of its bag, had gasped with pleasure. It was a smoky blue-grey shade with a low-cut bodice and floating sleeves, and with it her friend's mother had worn delicate blue silk sandals. These were too small for Miranda, but her own white sandals looked almost as good, and when she turned to Avril her friend's widening eyes was all the confirmation she needed that the dress both fitted and suited her. Carefully she picked up the gossamer stole with its embroidery of silver stars and turned once more to Avril. 'Isn't it the most beautiful thing you've ever seen?' she enquired breathlessly, 'I shan't dare to have a drink even if I die of thirst, because suppose I dropped a spot on it? I could never replace it, not if I had all the money in the world. Oh, Avril, do you think I should just let Steve see me in it when he arrives and then change into my old green dress? After all, Steve hasn't seen the green one either.'

But Avril, though she laughed, shook her head. 'No way! Your pal meant you to enjoy it, and anyway the only drink they serve at the Grafton is weak orange squash. You could probably pour a gallon of that stuff down your front and it would come out the minute you put the dress in water. So stop worrying and enjoy yourself.'

Presently a knock on the door heralded Steve's arrival and his expression, when Miranda floated into the kitchen in the borrowed dress, was almost unbelieving. 'Oh, queen, you look like the Queen,' he gabbled. 'No, you look like a film star! God, I know they say love's blind, but I'm tellin' you, you're bleedin' well beautiful and I never knew it before.'

Not surprisingly, Miranda bridled. 'They say clothes make the man, and I suppose you're telling me they make the woman, too,' she said frostily. 'It's not me or my carroty hair that's beautiful, but my pal's dress.' She regarded her swirling skirts proudly. 'It is fantastic, isn't it? Her mother made it for a Masonic function before the war, and only ever wore it twice. My pal is quite a lot heavier than either her mum or me, so I doubt she'll ever get to wear it, but I'm going to treat it like gold dust, see if I don't.' She grinned at Steve. 'So you'll have to learn to dance without actually laying your greasy hands anywhere on this wonderful creation.'

Laughing, Steve promised to scrub his hands within an inch of their lives as soon as they reached the ballroom. Then he and Miranda told Avril to be good and to have the kettle on the boil by eleven o'clock, and clattered down the steep iron stairway. At the foot of it they met Gary, carrying a parcel which he explained was a bag of sprouts. 'I've a pal with an allotment out at Seaforth, and he told me that the sprouts are ready to eat after the first frost. It's a cold old job cutting them, though, so he said if I'd give him a hand I could have a bag of them for our Christmas dinner.' He stared at them inquisitively. 'You off somewhere?'

'Oh no, I always wear my best shoes to queue for fish and chips,' Miranda said sarcastically. 'I know my dress is covered by my old winter coat but surely you can see my elegant footwear!'

Gary grinned. 'So you're off for a dancing session, are you? Great news, because that'll give me a whole evening to keep Avril company,' he said at once. 'I was supposed to be on shift this evening but because of cutting the sprouts I did a swap with Billy.'

'Nice for you and even nicer for Avril, because she thinks she's going to spend the evening alone,' Miranda said. She slipped her hand into the crook of Steve's arm and they set off across the courtyard. 'Cheerio, Gary. See you later I expect.'

The pair of them hurried, carefully, along the icy pavement. Above them the dark arc of the sky blazed with stars, reminding Miranda of the stole around her shoulders. They reached the dance hall and joined the line of people waiting for admittance. Steve greeted a couple of old friends from school further up the queue whilst Miranda rubbed her cold hands together, stamped her chilled feet and wished she had done as other girls did and worn her boots, bringing her dancing sandals in a paper carrier to change into inside. But already the queue was beginning to move and very soon she and Steve were rushing to claim a couple of the little gilt chairs set out around the gleaming dance floor. As soon as the orchestra struck up they tipped their chairs forward to indicate that they were taken, as was the small round table, and set off. It was the first time they had ever danced together and Miranda found it a very pleasant experience, but unfortunately, without thinking, she said something which spoiled the moment for them both. 'The last time I was here with Gerald . . .' she began, her cheek resting comfortably against Steve's tunic, and was astonished when she found herself suddenly pushed away from him and held at a distance.

'Did you have to say that?' Steve growled, giving her an admonitory shake. 'When did you go dancing with Gerald? Why didn't you mention it in any of your letters?'

Miranda, jerked out of her pleasant daydream, scowled at her companion. 'Don't be so silly, Steve. I've danced with all sorts of people these past months . . .'

She stopped speaking as Steve put a hand across her mouth. 'What was that noise?' he asked curiously. 'A sort of wailing noise. And why is everyone streaming off the floor?'

Miranda gasped and grabbed his hand. 'That was Moaning Minnie,' she said. 'In other words, the air raid warning. Sometimes the men on watch don't see the planes till they're almost overhead, though, so we must get a move on or we shan't get into the shelter. If we were in the flat we could go down to the basement under the cycle shop, but it's too far to go from here.'

They joined the pushing, jostling crowd and once on the pavement Miranda pointed at the moon, brilliant in the blackness of the night sky. 'See that? I expect you know it's called a bomber's moon. Well, with luck they'll be heading for some other destination, but you can't take chances. Here comes the first wave. Quick, give me your hand and run like hell.'

Steve complied, saying as he did so: 'I've often heard the expression bomber's moon, and now I understand what it means. It's as light as day, I bet those buggers up there can see us clear as clear, like ants scurrying out of an anthill when a foot comes too near the nest . . .'

He stopped speaking and Miranda, gazing up, saw that the first planes were indeed overhead. The ack-ack guns were blazing away; she saw one of the enemy aircraft stagger, then seem to recover, saw something descending to earth, and dragged Steve hastily into the shelter of a shop doorway. 'Incendiaries,' she told him, as the dreaded firebombs began to rain down. 'Oh, come *on*, Steve, run before the next lot come over. Look, there's a warden. He'll tell us which shelter to make for.'

The warden, uniformed and helmeted, came towards them, and had to raise his voice to a shout above the whistle of descending bombs. Just as he reached them there was an almighty explosion somewhere in the vicinity of the Adelphi Hotel, an explosion violent enough, Miranda knew, to have caused enormous damage. The warden reached them and grabbed Miranda's arm, then peered into her face and grinned. 'Oh, it's you. Not fire watchin' tonight, then? There's a shelter not twenty yards ahead; you'll be all right there. Gerra move on, though. This is no night to be out on the streets.'

'Thanks, Jim,' Miranda said, and would have set off at once, but Steve held her back.

'Is there anything I can do to help, mate?' he asked as the warden turned away. 'I'm on leave, but . . .'

The warden laughed. 'Get into the bloody shelter and stay there until you hear the all clear,' he commanded. 'Once the raid's over . . .'

Another enormous explosion rocked the three of them, and caused Miranda to give a yelp of impatience. 'Do as the man says and get a move on,' she commanded. 'This war doesn't need dead heroes. Ah, I can see the shelter and the feller in charge is beckoning us . . . come *on*, Steve!' To their right a large building was already in flames, the firelight competing with that of the moon, but neither Miranda nor Steve so much as glanced towards the conflagration. They pushed aside the smelly sacking curtain at the bottom of the shelter steps and entered into the usual scene of confusion: children howling, mothers trying to quiet them, and old people, eyes dark with fright, trying to pretend that this was all part of a day's work. Miranda glanced sideways at Steve, remembering that this was his first experience of a severe air raid – and she knew from the number of dark shapes overflying the city that this was a severe raid indeed. Steve caught her glance and grinned sheepishly, taking his place on one of the long wooden benches which lined the shelter. Miranda sat down beside him and took his hand.

'Awful, isn't it?' she said softly. 'Poor Steve, you really have been chucked in at the deep end, haven't you? For the rest of us it's come gradually, with each raid worse than the last. Yet somehow one never gets used to it. The kids are petrified simply by the noise, and when one of the parachute mines lands too close you get the most horrible sensation, as if your brain is being pulled out through your ears. I'm told that's the result of blast, and apparently if you're near enough blast can kill you just as effectively as a direct hit. If it weren't for the fact that while we're in the shelter we're not makin' work for the wardens I'd far rather be out in the open, and I expect you feel the same.'

Steve put his arm round her and gave her a gentle squeeze, then kissed the side of her face. 'You're right, Miranda; that's exactly how I feel,' he said quietly. 'It's an odd thing, because when I'm flying I don't feel confined in any way, but now I feel boxed in and helpless.'

Miranda chuckled. 'Everyone does, I'm sure,' she said. 'But don't worry – tomorrow, when the fire service are trying to douse the flames and the wardens and anyone else who offers are digging out survivors and roping off dangerous buildings, your help will be very much appreciated. I've never managed to sleep in a shelter, though lots of people do, so I usually go back to the flat after the all clear has sounded, get a couple of hours' kip and then go and offer my services at the nearest ARP post.' She grinned at him. 'Care to follow my example? You can have the sofa again, or you can go home to Jamaica Close and get yourself a proper eight hours.'

Steve returned her grin, then winced and ducked as a whistling roar announced the arrival of yet another high explosive bomb. 'I'll stick with you, babe,' he said in a mock American accent. 'I just hope to God my mam is still safe in Wales.'

'You said she wasn't setting out until the day before Christmas Eve, so the news that the city has been targeted will reach her in time for her to make the right decision,' Miranda pointed out. 'Oh, Steve, I'm so sorry that your first trip home looks like being spoiled. So long as the skies stay clear – and there's a building standing in Liverpool – they'll keep up the attack, because everyone says after they've flattened London it'll be the turn of the busiest port in the country, and that's us. Ought you to cut your leave short? I know you're not due to go back to your airfield until Boxing Day, but you could go tomorrow. I expect you'd be more use attacking the Luftwaffe.'

But Steve was shaking his head, his expression grim. 'I'm going to stay here and do my damnedest to help,' he said. He glanced towards the end of the shelter where the warden in charge was trying to start a communal sing-song, though at present the noise from outside made such a thing impossible, and suggested that he might just slip through the curtain, steal up the smelly dank steps and take a look around, but Miranda assured him that this would not be allowed.

'Once the warden lets one person go out there would be a concerted rush. And even if you don't realise it, Steve, it's tremendously dangerous out there. People run back into their houses to fetch a wedding photograph or a terrified cat, and never run out again. The building may collapse on them, or escaping gas from a fractured pipe catch them unawares, and there's one more death to add to the Luftwaffe's haul. So just behave like the good citizen I know you are and wait for the all clear.'

Steve sighed, but after another hour, during which Miranda leaned her head against his shoulder and actually managed to snooze, he gave her a shake.

'Miranda, I've got to go outside for a moment. I – I *need* to go outside.'

Miranda stifled a giggle. 'You want to spend a penny, don't you?' she asked. 'Haven't you noticed people getting up and going behind the curtain? There's a heavy leather one behind it, which the warden draws across as soon as the shelter's full. He keeps a couple of fire buckets in the space between them which can be used in an emergency.' She saw Steve hesitating and gave him a friendly shove. 'Oh, come on, don't be shy! When we were kids you told me you used to swim in the Scaldy in the altogether, yet now you feel embarrassed having a pee in a bucket. It's much easier for you men than us girls; at least you don't have to squat on the edge of the thing whilst the warden pretends he's got business at the other end of the shelter. Besides, why suffer? We're all in the same boat and it may be another hour or more before they sound the all clear.'

Steve sighed but got stiffly to his feet. 'If you're planning to make me look a fool . . .' he began, but before Miranda could assure him that she was telling the simple truth an elderly man in a patched army greatcoat and a much darned balaclava got to his feet and shuffled towards the warden. He was ushered through the curtain, which was swished shut behind him, and when he emerged again Steve was quick to jump to his feet and follow his example. Miranda was amused to see the obvious relief on his face as he returned to her side, but was too tactful to say so. Instead she hauled a small child, a girl of four or five, on to her lap and announced that it was story time, and that she would tell them all the tale of Timmy Tiddler, a very small fish who lived in a pond in the heart of a magic wood . . .

Soon Miranda was surrounded by tiny listeners, and though the noise from outside did not stop, it began to lessen as the roar of the aircraft overhead became fainter, though it was three in the morning before the longed for notes of the all clear reverberated through the shelter. People began to rub their eyes, for many had slept once the worst of the raid was over. Belongings were collected, children claimed by parents, and the evacuation of the shelter began.

Out on the pavement, Miranda and Steve looked around them at a scene of devastation. Fires raged, and buildings which had toppled still gave off clouds of dust. Miranda sighed and tucked her hand into the crook of Steve's elbow. 'It's worse than I thought. Those dreadful incendiaries cause fires which light up the city so that the bombers have something to aim at,' she said. 'Steve, would you be happier if we went straight to Jamaica Close and checked that your grandmother – and my Aunt Vi, I suppose – are okay? I wouldn't mind a bit of a walk in the open air, having been penned up in the shelter for hours.'

Steve began to brush at the shoulders of his greatcoat, then gave it up, because the very air was dust-laden. 'There won't be much open air as you call it, more like open brick dust,' he observed, 'but I do believe you're right. We'd better check on Gran and your horrible old aunt, and once we know they're all right we can go back to your flat, get ourselves some breakfast and snatch a couple of hours' sleep. Then I mean to offer my services at the nearest ARP post.'

'All right: Jamaica Close first, and then breakfast. Best foot forward! I wonder how Avril and Gary got on.' She chuckled. 'Poor Gary, he was so looking forward to having Avril and the flat to himself for a change; maybe the whole building if Pete Huxtable decided to trek when he realised that the skies were clear and the moon would be full. Have you heard about trekking? Londoners began it, I believe. You take some grub and a couple of blankets and as soon as your work finishes for the day you lock up your house and go as far into the country as you can get and stay with anyone who'll let you sleep on their floor until morning. The raid is always over before the sky gets truly light again, and if you're lucky you can catch a bus back into the city, though otherwise you have to walk. But at least you'll have had a proper night's sleep and be fit for work next day.'

'Yes, I've heard of it, and having suffered a night in the shelter I think trekkers are doing the right thing,' Steve said. 'I can't imagine why the government tries to discourage them . . . well, they wouldn't if they had to put up with the sort of night we've just lived through. If you ask me only a lunatic would choose to stay in a city under attack if they could possibly get away from it. But I'm just a simple sergeant-pilot.' He looked at her seriously. 'Couldn't you trek, queen? I'd feel a deal happier if I knew you were safe out of it before the bombs begin to fall.'

They were heading along Great Homer Street, already finding it difficult to breathe the dust-laden air, and Miranda coughed before she replied. 'Oh, I couldn't possibly. I'm a fire watcher. They position us on top of high buildings and give us either a messenger boy or what they call a field telephone so that we can report any fires in our vicinity as soon as they start. Besides, I don't have any friends or relatives living in the country, so for me – and many like me – trekking is out of the question.'

Steve nodded reluctantly. 'I see,' he said. 'The trouble

is, queen, what I've seen tonight has made me realise that we really are all in it together. I thought being on my station was the most dangerous job of all, but at least we don't simply sit there waiting to be shot at. We have the satisfaction of knowing we're both protecting our civilians and attacking the enemy, which is a good deal preferable to being sitting ducks.'

As they neared the turning which would lead them to Jamaica Close, there were fewer and fewer people on the pavement. Out here those who had been in communal shelters had returned to their homes and others, Miranda assumed, had come up from their cellars to snatch a few hours in bed before day dawned. They turned into the Close and went straight to the front door of Number Two, where they hesitated. Steve stared at the front door, hauled the key on its string up through the letter box and looked enquiringly at Miranda. 'Do you think it's too bad of me to wake her? Gran, I mean?'

'There's no need to wake her,' Miranda whispered, gently taking the key from his hand and inserting it in the lock. 'You can just check that she's safely asleep in her bed, and then write a little note telling her that you're fine, and will come back later. Agreed?'

Steve was happy with the idea, but as it happened their creeping about was not necessary. As soon as they entered the hallway Granny Granger appeared, coming towards them from the kitchen with a big smile. 'There's tea in the pot,' she said cheerfully. 'There's nothin' like a hot cup of tea to set me up for wharrever the new day may hold, but you're early callers, ain't you?' She had ushered them into the kitchen and now jerked a thumb at the clock on the mantel, whose hands pointed at ten past four. 'Take off your coats, else you won't feel the benefit,' she instructed. And as Miranda obeyed she looked down at herself and gasped with horror.

The beautiful borrowed dress was torn and filthy, the stole with its twinkling stars ruined. Miranda groaned. 'Oh, Steve, and I promised I'd take such care of my borrowed finery,' she said. 'Whatever shall I do?'

'You can't do anything, of course, but a dress is just a dress. Life and limb are much more important,' Steve said comfortably. 'Your pal will forgive you; she'll know there was nothing you could have done to keep the dress immaculate.'

Granny Granger bustled out of the pantry, carrying a tin with a picture of the Tower of London on the lid. 'There's still some cake left and I brewed the tea not ten minutes ago,' she said. 'Now set yourselves down and tell me if there's anything left of dear old Liverpool. Were it as bad a raid as it sounded?'

Reflecting on the resilience of the old, Miranda sank gratefully into a chair and accepted a cup of tea with eagerness, even agreeing to nibble a slice of seed cake, though it was by no means a favourite with her. 'Yes, it was dreadful. There are fires and firemen everywhere. I guess when they post the casualty lists later in the day, we'll know just how bad it was in terms of people getting killed. As for damage to property, well, the mind boggles, but it's difficult to judge in the dark.'

Granny Granger nodded. 'And you'll be glad to hear, young Steve, that I had a telegram from your mam yesterday evening saying she wouldn't be coming after all. It seems she'd had the letter from your pa, and had seen the foolishness of leaving Wales. So If you want to see her, Kenny and baby Flora, you'd best gerron a bus or train and visit them, instead of the other way round.'

They chatted with the old lady for a bit, agreed to do some shopping for off-ration food, if they could find any, and accepted her invitation to have tea with her. Then Miranda ran down to Number Six and would have tapped on the door, except that as she raised her hand to knock, Mrs Brown from Number Eight appeared on her front doorstep.

'Mornin', Miranda. You're up and about early,' she remarked. 'But if you've a mind to wake your aunt, I'd suggest you think again. She spent the best part of the night searchin' for Beth's cat what has been stayin' at Number Six whenever Beth's on shift. She found it in the end because once the raid was over it come home, the way such critters do, so she shut it in the kitchen and went off to catch up on her night's sleep.' She chuckled. 'And I pity anyone what disturbs her,' she finished.

Relieved to have got out of an encounter which she knew was unlikely to bring her anything but grief, Miranda asked Mrs Brown to tell Aunt Vi that she had been asking for her. Then she and Steve trudged wearily back to the main road, and caught the first bus heading towards the city centre, though it was crowded with folk going to work so they had to stand. As always, Miranda was impressed by their cheerful acceptance of the terrible night they had endured, and saw that Steve, too, admired their fortitude. When they reached the first of the big factories the bus almost emptied and Miranda and Steve slid on to a seat and held hands as the vehicle clattered onwards. 'I hope we don't wake Avril and Gary,' Miranda said absently, as she tried to stifle an enormous yawn.

'They won't have stayed in the flat – that would be madness – they'll have been in the basement under the cycle shop. Pete has told us to make free of it. He gave us the key when the war started, and we've used it several times.' She smiled reminiscently. 'When it starts to get noisy it seems to go to poor Timmy's bladder and he whines at the door to be let out. We always joke that the all clear should be called the free to wee, because Timmy charges up the steps and barely reaches the courtyard before his leg is lifting.'

Steve smiled and said that he would like to see the little dog again, not having done so since before the war. 'You ought to buy him wax earplugs or woolly earmuffs,' he teased. 'If he couldn't hear the bangs he'd probably go off to sleep quite happily.'

They were still laughing over the idea of Timmy in fluffy earmuffs when the bus deposited them at their stop, and they hurried along towards Russell Street, planning the breakfast which they hoped to enjoy presently. It was too early for any of the shops in the street to be open, but that was not the only reason for the unfamiliar quiet. The air was thick with dust, and despite the householders' precautions there were several glassless windows, and shop doors swinging wide. Miranda began to hurry. 'I hope to God they're all right,' she said breathlessly as she ran. 'Oh, I do hope they're all right!'

Chapter Eleven

Avril and Gary had barely settled down to their fish and chip supper when Moaning Minnie set up her wail. Timmy, under the table awaiting any scraps which might come his way, moaned softly as well, but Gary and Avril fell into their usual routine without a moment's hesitation. The fish and chips were rewrapped in their paper and shoved into Avril's air raid basket along with some rather dry cake and sandwiches from the previous day and two bottles of cold tea. Then she and Gary raided her bedroom for two blankets and a pillow each, donned their winter coats, hats and scarves and set forth.

The basement was reached from the back of the bicycle shop, through a heavy oak door at the foot of a dozen steps. This would be the first time that Gary had seen it, for usually when the warning sounded he had to hurry off either to act as a shelter warden or to take messages from one post to another on his trusty old bike, for despite the fact that one of his legs was made of wood he could ride a bicycle as well as any able-bodied man, thanks to a special pedal into which his false foot fitted.

He looked appreciatively around the underground room, which was empty as they had known it would be. Pete had warned them that he meant to go out to his uncle's farm on the Wirral and get at least one decent night's sleep, for the moment he looked up at the clear sky and the great disc of a moon he knew it was on the cards that the raiders would soon be overhead. Avril and Gary had said they would look after Timmy, since the little dog was terrified by the sound of falling bombs and would hear very little if he was in the cycle shop basement, which was deep and well protected. Avril put the basket on the small table Pete had provided and closed the door. Gary stood the little dog down on the uneven floor and began to spread his blanket out on the wooden bench which ran along the wall.

Avril smiled as she took in Pete's latest attempt to make the basement homelike: an ancient alarm clock had appeared on one of the shelves he had built some time before. There was also a Primus stove, a kerosene lamp, a couple of ancient but comfortable chairs, and wooden benches on the two longest walls, so that, when just two of you were sharing the basement, you could stretch out on a bench each, wrapped in your blanket with your head on your pillow, and make believe you were in bed. 'What do you think?' she asked. 'All the houses and shops on this side of the street have basements, but I bet no one has gone to greater lengths to make theirs comfortable than Pete has. I can never sleep in the public shelters – too much noise and too many people – but I've slept down here a couple of times. That door is solid oak; you can't hear much through it, unless a bomb drops awfully near. The only thing that really worries Pete is fire, so every now and then he just has a quick look out, but so far we've been lucky. Go on, what do you think?'

'It's grand,' Gary said appreciatively. 'Shall I light the Primus? I think the fish and chips will still be warm, but I don't fancy cold tea if we can have it hot.'

'Well, all right,' Avril said rather uncertainly. 'I don't believe anyone's ever lit it before, though. Pete always says that, what with the floor being so uneven and the stove pretty old and wonky, he's afraid it might tip over and set fire to the basement. It's really for emergencies only, so if you don't mind, Gary, I think we'll stick to cold tea.'

'Of course I don't mind,' Gary said immediately, and presently they were seated on opposite sides of the small table eating fish and chips with their fingers whilst Timmy, fears apparently forgotten, laid his head in Avril's lap and accepted chips, small pieces of fish and larger pieces of crisp golden batter. They finished their meal in record time and went to their respective beds, though Gary, looking uneasy as the noise from outside grew in intensity, did not immediately wrap himself in his blanket. 'I feel I ought to be out there, because it sounds like a bad one to me,' he said. 'I know I'm off duty tonight, but if the noise is anything to go by the fellows might be glad of an extra pair of hands.'

Avril sighed. 'You know what they say: folk wanderin' about durin' a raid, even if they're tryin' to help, simply cause the wardens more work. So just settle down and try to get some sleep. Morning comes a lot quicker if you've managed to nod off for a while at least. We'll leave the lamp on, but I'll turn the wick right down.'

For twenty minutes or so both Gary and Avril lay quiet, but Avril soon realised that sleep would not come. The noise was dreadful. The bombs seemed to be bursting all around them; several times the basement rocked, and what Pete had feared came to pass: the Primus stove fell over and rolled tinnily back and forth, whilst Timmy, who had been lying on the foot of Avril's bed, suddenly elevated his nose to heaven and howled.

Avril sighed and sat up. 'It's no use; no one could possibly sleep through this,' she announced. 'I'm going to turn up the lamp, find my book and have a read. What about you? There's yesterday's *Echo* in my basket as well as a couple of children's books – *The Secret Garden* and *Humpty Dumpty and the Princess*. When there's a bad raid I find it easier to read a children's book which I know well so I don't have to think.'

'I'll have whichever one you don't want,' Gary was saying, when someone knocked on the heavy oak door and then pushed it open. Two frightened little faces peered into the warm and well lit basement.

'Can we . . .' the older child, a boy of perhaps ten, began, but before he could say any more Avril pulled him and the little girl who clung to his hand into the basement and slammed the heavy door shut. 'Where have you come from, and what are you doing in the street when there's a really terrible raid going on?' she demanded. 'It's lucky you saw our door; lucky we were here. Where are your parents? I don't want to frighten you, but . . .' A tremendous explosion cut the sentence off short and both children jumped and winced before the boy answered, his voice coming out in a squeak.

'We was goin' home. We've been evacuated, me and Maisie, only the lady hated us and didn't feed us proper. We stuck it as long as we could, only at teatime yesterday she wouldn't give us no bread, said it were on ration now and we'd ate our share at breakfast. Maisie was so hungry she were cryin' so I telled her we'd go home – we live in Bootle – only we didn't have no money so we had to walk. We axed the way and got lifts a couple of times. We telled folk we'd missed our train . . .'

'Well, never mind that,' Avril said. 'You'll be safe enough here until the raid's over and then me and my friend will take you home to your parents. I'm sure you know your address and which tram to catch.'

The boy nodded eagerly. 'Thanks, missus,' he said. The little girl suddenly clutched him and pulled his head down to her level.

'Ask the lady if there's food,' she pleaded, and there was a wealth of longing in her voice. 'Any food 'ud do, Dickie. I's so hungry . . . and thirsty . . .'

Gary leaned forward, took the sandwiches out of Avril's basket and wordlessly handed them over, watching as the children devoured Spam, jam, and paste sandwiches indiscriminately and with every sign of enjoyment. 'You can give the crusts to Timmy,' he said, then laughed as he saw that the two little visitors were eating the sandwiches in great starved bites, indifferent to crusts.

'Fanks, mister,' the boy said, and took the offered cup of cold tea, holding it for his sister and not drinking himself until her thirst was satisfied. Then he looked up at Gary. 'Who's Timmy?' he asked curiously. 'Is that you, mister?'

'No, I'm Gary, this is Avril and the little dog is Timmy . . .' Gary began at the same moment as Avril gave a cry of dismay.

'Timmy's gone!' she said, her voice rising. 'He must have slipped out when the door opened, and we didn't notice. Oh, Gary, he'll be killed for sure! Even if the bombs don't get him he'll die of fright.' She rushed across to the door and began to tug it open, hoping that the little dog would have got no further than the foot of the stairs, but there was no sign of him. Avril climbed halfway up the flight and got the impression, in the only glance she was allowed, that the whole city was in flames and that the bombers were still attacking, black against the stars. Then she was peremptorily snatched back by Gary, who caught her round the waist and pulled her back to the relative safety of the basement.

'I'll go and call Timmy. If he's out there and I can see him I'll fetch him back,' he shouted above the whistle of descending bombs and the terrible crashes as they came to earth. 'It's all right, silly, I won't take any risks, but I know you won't be happy until you know Timmy's safe.' He was climbing the stairs as he spoke and Avril called to him not to be a fool.

'You know what they say – if you go back into a bombed house for a cat or a dog, they'll have found a safe spot but you'll wake up dead,' she cried distractedly. 'I know we all love Timmy, but he'll be hiding away somewhere . . . please, please, Gary don't go out there!'

Gary glanced back at her and grinned. 'Can you hear me, Mother?' he said in a passable imitation of Sandy Powell whose catchphrase it was. 'Get back into the cellar and look after those two kids; I shan't be a tick.'

Avril was tempted to ignore him, but when she turned and saw Dickie and Maisie she changed her mind. She closed the door on the horror outside and produced slices of cake and a bag of boiled sweets from her emergency supply. The two little faces turned so trustingly towards her were white with exhaustion and streaked with tears and dust. Of course she loved Timmy, often lured him up to the flat with scraps so that she could have a cuddle, but these two children had had an even worse time than the little dog. According to Dickie – and she had no reason to doubt his word – both he and his sister had been half starved by their so-called foster parent and had taken desperate measures. Fate had flung them in her way and now it was her duty – hers and Gary's – to see that they got safe home to Bootle, where their real parents would make sure they were fed and loved as befitted children so young.

She stared hopefully at the heavy oak door, but realised that it might take Gary five or ten minutes to search the places to which Timmy might have fled. She turned back to the children, about to suggest that she read them a story, then changed her mind. 'Take your coats and hats off and I'll wrap you up in a blanket and you can have a bit of a snooze,' she said tactfully. When the two children continued to stare blankly at her, she sat down, took Maisie on her knee and undressed the little girl down to her liberty bodice and patched knickers.

But when she put out a hand to help Dickie, masculine pride made him say, gruffly, 'I can manage, fanks, missus,' as he shed coat, balaclava and much darned jumper. Then he climbed up on to the bench where his sister was already wrapped in blankets, thumb in mouth and eyes tightly closed, and cuddled down beside her. Avril opened her mouth to bid them goodnight and closed it again. Her unexpected visitors were already fast asleep.

For the next half hour Avril read her book, but after every two or three chapters she found herself glancing towards the door. She realised she was in a difficult position. She longed to go in search of Gary and Timmy, but knew that if she did so she would be acting against her own advice, and in a thoroughly foolish manner. Besides, she could not possibly leave the two children. Gary was so sensible; she imagined he had gone further than he intended and had either found Timmy or given up the search, for the time being at any rate. Then he must have realised how far he had wandered and would either have been ordered down a shelter by a passing warden or have gone down himself, knowing that without his tin hat or his bicycle he would be of very little use to the emergency services until the raid was over and the clearing up operation was beginning.

Wondering what time it was, Avril picked up the alarm clock and examined it closely, sure that it must have stopped. But its tick was steady and when she tried the winder mechanism she realised that Pete must have set it going just before he left, which meant that the time really was around two o'clock in the morning. She knew she should get some sleep, but had to fight an almost irresistible urge to slip through the doorway and climb the stairs so that she could get some idea at least of what was going on. Surely the Luftwaffe must have dropped all their bombs and incendiaries by now? But going to investigate meant leaving the safety of the cellar, and suppose one of the children woke and followed her, or slipped out as Timmy had done? No, the sensible thing to do, and well she knew it, was to stay where she was until the all clear sounded. Then and only then could she and the two children emerge to make their way across the city to Bootle.

Avril gave a deep sigh, picked up her book and began to read, but after several more chapters she glanced at the lamp. Damnation! The wretched flame was beginning to waver, which had her chewing her fingernails. If she turned it down to save what oil there was in the hope of retaining some sort of light in the cellar, then it might go out altogether and prove difficult to relight. If she left it turned up full, however, it might still go out, and possibly at an even worse moment. She had just decided that she would turn the lamp as low as it could go without actually going out when two things happened. She remembered she always kept a small torch in her handbag, which nestled in the bottom of her emergency basket, and just as she got to her feet to fetch the torch there was an even bigger explosion than the ones she had been hearing all night, and the lamp was blown out.

Avril stood very still for a moment, her heart thundering. That had sounded far too close for comfort. She fumbled in her basket, found the torch and switched it on. Instead of being brilliant white, the torchlight was pale and yellowish, a sure sign that the battery was on its way out, but the ceiling above them, though it was raining dust, was not actually coming down. Not a direct hit, then, but something pretty near. With trembling fingers she found the matches Pete always kept within easy reach. After four or five attempts she shook the lamp and realised that it was almost out of oil. She knew Pete kept a small supply somewhere in the cellar, but could not remember exactly where, and she did not want to use the torch more than she must. She decided she would just nip over to the door, climb perhaps halfway up the stairs and see what was happening at ground level. Cautiously, she swung the beam of her torch across the children. They were both sound asleep and she guessed that if they could remain slumbering through the sort of raid the city had just suffered the chances were they would sleep the clock round; at any rate she need not worry about them for the time being.

Cautiously, she went across to the heavy oak door, put her hand on the handle and gave an experimental shove. It did not move. She stopped, puzzled. Had she locked it after the children's arrival? For that matter, had she locked it after Gary had gone in search of Timmy? But she knew very well, really, that the last thing she would have done was lock this door. How else could Gary possibly come back triumphant, with Timmy in his arms? And what if some other unfortunate soul should be looking for a place of refuge? No, she knew very well that neither she nor Miranda, nor Pete, would ever lock the door whilst they were inside, or if a raid was in progress. She gave the door another push; it was like pushing at Snowdon. Before she could stop herself, Avril hurled herself at the door, beating uselessly at the stout panels, and even as she did so she heard a crashing rumble and part of the ceiling – thank God it was the far end – came down. Bricks, rubble, a wooden beam and, oddly, a bicycle came crashing into the cellar. Avril glanced involuntarily at the two children, but though Dickie stirred and muttered neither child woke.

Relieved of one worry, for she had no wish to have two terrified children on her hands, Avril made herself sit down once more, and began to think logically. Gary knew she was here. Miranda, Steve and probably Pete Huxtable would guess. As soon as the raid was over and there was daylight the rescue services would begin their unenviable task. Damaged buildings would be cordoned off for fear somebody would try to enter and be trapped beneath falling masonry. The army would be brought in from Seaforth Barracks to sift through the rubble in search of survivors. From the glimpse she had already seen, Avril guessed that the fire service would be fully occupied and would probably be requesting aid from as far away as Manchester and Blackpool. And there must have been mayhem amongst the shipping, which meant mayhem also in the docks and the warehouses which clustered close to the water. Sooner or later Pete would come back from his uncle's place on the Wirral to find, judging from the great pile of rubble at one end of the cellar, that his beautiful shop and the flat above it were no more. And he would immediately remember the basement. It might take a fair while to move the rubble which was so effectively blocking the door, but it would be done at last.

Avril's wavering torch beam was getting fainter, so she switched it off, hoping that as soon as it was daylight – and daylight could not be long in coming now – a beam of it would somehow enter the cellar. Gingerly she crossed to the pile of rubble and stared upwards with watering eyes, for the dust here was dreadful, catching at your throat, making you long for fresh air as one usually longs for a cool drink. But to her disappointment no light came from above. Sighing, she returned to her chair but did not attempt to light the lamp or switch on the torch. Time might drag its feet, but even as she had gone over and tried the door she was pretty sure she'd heard the all clear, and she thanked God that her ordeal would soon be over. Volunteers would dig her out quickly, especially when Gary told them that there were two small children buried with her in the cellar beneath the cycle shop. Yes, release would come quite soon now.

And since she was terribly tired she leaned back into her chair and let sleep overcome her.

A soft whimpering awoke her. For a moment she thought that it was Timmy, but then the whimpering became a small voice. 'Where is we, Dickie? Oh, Dickie, I's frightened.'

Immediately the events of the night sprang fully fledged into Avril's mind. The two children seeking refuge, Timmy bolting out of the basement and Gary going in search of him. And now that she was properly awake she could see a beam of light, dust-laden to be sure, but light nevertheless. It was coming from the hole in the ceiling above the pile of rubble at the far end of the basement, and far off and faint she thought she could hear voices. Hastily she fumbled in her pocket and produced the torch, clicking it on to reveal the two children, both now wide awake and sitting up, Dickie with his arms protectively around Maisie's small shoulders. 'S'all right, nipper, the lady'll see us home now it's daytime,' he said reassuringly. He glanced curiously around the cellar in the faint torchlight. 'You said you'd take us home, didn't you, missus? Can we go now? Our mam will be worried if Mrs Grimble has writ to say we've run off.'

Avril got rather stiffly out of the chair in which she had been sleeping, and took the last slice of cake out of the basket. She broke it in two, gave the children a piece each and then spoke reassuringly. 'We can't go out just yet, because there's something against the door. I tried to open it earlier but it wouldn't budge, and I don't believe we should try to get out from where the daylight is getting in because it wouldn't be safe. But Gary – the friend who was with me when you arrived – will tell the rescue people we're here, and they'll get us out in a trice, just you see.'

Dickie swallowed a mouthful of cake, then addressed his sister. 'Do the warning, Maisie,' he commanded, and before Avril could ask him what he meant both children threw back their heads whilst from their mouths, shrill and demanding, came the sound, first, of the air raid warning and then of the all clear. It was so piercing that Avril, laughing, clapped her hands to her ears, whilst Dickie patted his little sister on the back and told her to take a deep breath and 'give 'em one more go of the warning, just in case they've not noticed the first 'un.'

Avril laughed again, ferreted in the basket and produced the remaining boiled sweets. 'You're a couple of little marvels,' she said admiringly, handing each child a Fox's glacier mint. 'Yes, I hear voices; thanks to you, we'll be out of here in no time.'

Dickie chuckled, but Maisie turned wide eyes upon Avril. 'I'd rather be out in five minutes than in no time,' she said. 'I don't like it here. There's a funny sort of smell and my hair's all dusty.' The two children had been sitting up on the bunk bed but now Maisie cast aside the blankets, slid on to the floor and went towards the door. She gave it a kick with one small, wellington booted foot, and even as she did so the door began to tremble, and a man's cheerful voice hailed them.

'You okay down there? We'll have you out just as soon as we can. Your feller didn't mention you'd got the red alert and the all clear down there as well.'

Avril was laughing and beginning to explain when the

door gave a protesting creak and opened six or seven inches. Maisie could have squeezed through, but the man's voice warned them to keep clear. 'You aren't out of the wood yet,' he told Avril. 'Let us clear the stairway. As soon as it's safe we'll tell you.'

Avril stepped back from the door. Dickie was dressing himself, Maisie was trying to struggle into the garments she had worn earlier and they were both clear of the door and able to see quite well now that daylight was pouring in through the increasing gap the rescuers were making. The work ceased for a moment while a flask of hot tea and some jam sandwiches were passed through and the three captives sat down on a bench and had what Avril called their breakfast, though the alarm clock had disappeared when the end of the cellar had collapsed so she had no idea of the time.

It seemed ages before the man who had been chatting reassuringly to them as he worked announced that they might come up now, and Avril and the children crawled up the steep stairs, getting filthier with every step, but not caring. What did a bit of dirt matter? What mattered was escaping back to normality. They were helped up the last few steps and stood in what Avril imagined had once been the courtyard, though it did not resemble its old self in any way. She cleared her throat and touched their rescuer's arm. 'Where's my pal, the man who told you we were in the basement?' she asked. 'Is he – is he hurt? Is that why he didn't dig us out himself?'

'That's right, queen, but he ain't too bad. Stood too close to a collapsing building. A brick got him on the noggin' – head wounds bleed like fury – and they reckon he's bust his arm, but he still wanted to dig you out himself; they had to all but carry him to the ambulance, protestin' all the way . . . ah, here he comes! Is that your feller, the one with the bandage round his head and his arm in a sling?'

Avril ran towards the approaching figure. 'Did you find Timmy?' she asked anxiously. 'Oh, Gary . . .' Her voice faded into silence as Pete Huxtable pushed impatiently at the bandage which hid his dark hair and obscured the sight in one of his eyes. Then he put his free arm round Avril, and gave her hand a squeeze.

'Thank God you're all right. I were that worried I tried to stop them takin' me up to Casualty, only one of the wardens said they'd heard voices . . .' He shuddered. 'And now you'd best come wi' me, queen.'

He led her back into what had once been the courtyard and over to a silent figure lying with several others on the cobbles.

Avril gasped. 'Is he much hurt?' she asked anxiously, seeming not to realise the significance of the sheet which Pete was gently folding back to reveal Gary's dirt-smudged face and, as the sheet was pulled lower, the little dog curled up in the crook of his arm.

'I'm sorry, queen,' Pete said quietly. 'I know he were your feller and a better man never lived, but there's nowt we can do about it. I reckon he went out after Timmy, ain't that so? God, I'm goin' to miss Timmy.'

Avril gulped. Tears, she knew, stood in her eyes, but she could not let them fall in front of the two children who had followed her into the courtyard and were now pressing close to her. She turned away blindly whilst beside her Maisie's voice, sounding slightly puzzled, came to her ears. 'Is they sleepin'? The feller and the little dog? They ain't hurt, are they?'

It was too much. Avril gulped back the tears, but could not answer the child's innocent question. Instead, she said huskily: 'Time to get going, little 'uns. If there's a tea room still standing I'll buy us some breakfast – oh no I won't, I haven't got any money, but I dare say someone will lend me a couple of bob – and then we'll have to make our way to Bootle.'

As she left the courtyard – what had once been the courtyard – she tripped and would have fallen but for Pete Huxtable, who grabbed her arm and pulled her to a halt. 'There's a WVS van at the end of the road what'll feed and water you for free,' he said. He lowered his voice. 'And if it's any comfort, love, they would neither of 'em know a thing. Blast's like that; it kills without leaving so much as an eyelash out of place. Who are your little friends, anyway?'

He was interrupted. 'Oh, thank God! When I saw the flat and the shop so badly damaged, with the roof gone and the windows all out, I thought . . . but of course I should have realised you'd have all gone to the basement as soon as the raid started. Steve and I spent the night in the big shelter near the Grafton Ballroom on West Derby Road. Where's Gary? That guy's incredible. I bet he went straight out and started helping the rescue teams . . .'

'Steady, Miranda; Gary's bought it,' Pete said with a brusqueness Avril had never heard in his voice before. 'And I'm afraid Timmy . . .'

Miranda put both arms round Avril and hugged her tightly. Tears ran down her face and mingled with the dirt. 'Oh, my love, I'm so sorry,' she whispered. 'I won't ask you what happened, because I can guess. Let's find a tea room where we can take stock.' She suddenly seemed to notice the children for the first time, both now clinging to Avril's skirt, and raised her brows. 'Who the devil are they?'

'They were in the basement with me when – when the place collapsed,' Avril said wearily. 'We're takin' them – I mean I'm takin' them – back to Bootle, to find their parents. Where's Steve, by the way?'

'Fighting fires down by the docks; there are several warehouses ablaze, and someone's reported an unexploded bomb. And you can forget the *I'm* takin' the children, because that *should* be we, since I don't intend to let you go off by yourself. And then I suppose we shall have to think about finding a place in a hostel. Incidentally, your beloved workplace has been badly damaged and may not be fit for work again for many weeks, if it ever is again . . .'

Avril cut across her friend's sentence. 'I'm not stayin' in the city. I couldn't bear it. I've already applied to join the WAAF; I shall pretend I got a letter of acceptance but it went up in smoke at the same time as the flat in Russell Street. You'll have to do whatever you think best, but I just want to get away from here.'

Beside them, Pete nodded his bandaged head in agreement. 'That's right, chuck, get right away from here, put it all behind you and start a new life in the air force. I'm goin' to do the same, though I guess they won't take me until my arm's out of plaster and the stitches are out of my head. But keep in touch, won't you?' His glance encompassed both girls but Miranda knew he was thinking of Avril. 'We'll all have to report to an ARP post, see if they can find accommodation for us for a few nights. I don't mean to trek tonight; I reckon I'll be needed here.' Very much to Avril's surprise he gave each girl a kiss on the cheek before turning away and disappearing in the direction of the nearest ARP post.

'Pete's real fond of you, Avril,' Miranda said gently. 'But I guess you know that.'

'As you are so fond of saying, he's just a pal,' Avril said wearily, pushing a wing of blonde hair off her forehead.

They joined the queue of dazed and dirty people at the WVS van and after some thought Miranda said that she would join the WAAF as well. 'I'm sure Mr Grimshaw will understand. And he'll still have Miss Burton and Miss Phyllis.' She gave a rather wan chuckle. 'It will solve the dilemma of what to wear now that we haven't even got a pair of knickers or a hair ribbon left. The WAAF will kit us out, feed us, find us beds and train us for whatever work needs our skills . . .' She reached the head of the queue in mid-sentence. 'Oh, can we have four mugs of tea and four sandwiches or buns or whatever, please?'

Presently the four of them, still chewing, jumped on a bus. The children were understandably excited as the vehicle upon which they were travelling reached familiar territory. Maisie, with her nose pressed to the window, was the first to shout 'Our stop's comin' up!' and but for Avril's staying hand would have bailed out before the vehicle had actually come to a halt. Dickie told his sister sternly to behave herself, but Avril saw how his eyes sparkled and guessed he was quite as excited as Maisie, just, being older, more capable of restraint.

Once on the pavement she took Maisie's hand and

Miranda took Dickie's and they followed the children's instructions through a maze of small side streets until they reached Quarry Lane where they were towed impatiently up to the front door of Number Six. Avril looked for a bell, but seeing none would have used her knuckles on the wooden panel, only Dickie bade her follow him, and went down the side of the small house. Before he could knock on the back door it shot open and a weary-looking woman with tear stains on her cheeks stumbled across the tiny cobbled yard and grabbed both children in a comprehensive embrace before turning to the two older girls.

'Oh, thank you, ladies,' she gasped. 'I had a visit from the scuffers this mornin', said the kids had run off yesterday, though their foster mother swore she'd been kindness itself, and said they was ungrateful and wicked, which, as I told the scuffers, weren't anywhere near the truth.' She lifted Maisie up and lodged her on one hip, then held out a hand to Dickie. 'Come along, big feller; I'll make a brew of tea and your new pals can tell me what's been happenin'. The scuffers was worried in case you'd reached Liverpool 'cos of the big raid last night, but I thought you'd likely found yourselves an air raid shelter or a garden shed and kipped down in it long before the Jerries had even begun to come over.'

The two girls followed her and the children into the house, but Avril, taking the lead for once, said that though they would be glad of a cup of tea they knew very little more than she about the children's reason for running away. 'They told me that their foster mother didn't feed them properly, and I gather she was pretty quick-tempered; not the type of person to look after children at all. But I expect you'll get more out of them than we had a chance to do. Only they were in Liverpool at the height of the raid and knocked on our door . . .'

She told the whole story clearly and precisely, as far as she knew it, but glossed over what had happened to Gary and the dog. Remembering her own childhood, she knew how easily Dickie might talk himself into believing that it was his fault, because had he not knocked on the basement door both Gary and Timmy might be alive today. If the dog had not scooted past them up the stairs Avril knew, ruefully, that Gary would never have left the security of the basement.

But it did not do to think like that; what's done is done, she told herself, and nothing in this world was certain, except that death comes to us all in the end. In such dangerous times she and Miranda would not be any safer than the citizens of Liverpool wherever the air force might choose to send them. Folk who stayed behind in the city, or trekked into the country when the moon rode high in the clear sky, were all at risk. And war, she told herself, was the biggest uncertainty of all.

Mrs O'Halloran proved to be a delightful person. Barely five foot in height she was correspondingly skinny, with greying hair pulled back from a tiny, bright-eyed face, and an endless fund of stories about her children. She insisted that her guests should take a freshly baked scone with the cup of tea she had already set before them, exclaimed with horror when Avril told her that their flat had had its roof blown off, and actually offered her sofa, if the girls were desperate, though the little house only had two small bedrooms, one for herself and Mr O'Halloran, and the other, little more than a box room, for Dickie and Maisie.

'And what I'll do when they's older, and it wouldn't be right for 'em to share, is more than I can say,' she admitted. 'We stays here because the rent's cheap and it's near my husband's work, but one of these days I'd like to move into the country. The only good thing about that Mrs Grimble was the village she lived in: plenty of space for kids, a nice little school with only thirty or forty pupils, and even a stream at the end of her garden where the kids could paddle or try to catch tiddlers . . .'

Avril and Miranda exchanged glances; outside it was still freezing cold, not at all paddling weather, but of course the children might have been there for some time, though they doubted it, and Dickie confirmed their doubts. 'At first we was at a lovely place, real nice, with a fat jolly farmer's wife, and a granfer what smoked a pipe and told us wizard stories about that other war, what he called the Great War. Only Auntie Ethel – that's what we called the farmer's wife – got appendic . . . appendiss . . . two months ago and couldn't keep us no longer.' He sighed heavily. 'We wanted to go and live wi' the baker's wife – she offered to have us – but Mam said . . .'

Mrs O'Halloran cut across the sentence. 'They was in Devon, what's a devil of a way off. I only visited 'em once and it took a whole day to get there and a whole day to get back, besides costing a small fortune,' she explained. 'Oh, dear, it's all my fault. I said I wanted 'em closer, so's I could visit mebbe once a month, and the authorities found Mrs Grimble what had no evacuees and sent 'em there. Oh, if only I hadn't interfered, they'd be in that little village in Devonshire, happy as Larry, and writin' regular, which they never did from Mrs

Grimble's, which should've made me wonder . . . oh, what a fool you are, Suzie O'Halloran.'

Both girls assured her that she could not have known how unsuitable Mrs Grimble was, and then, catching each other's eye once more, they rose to their feet, thanked their hostess for her hospitality, kissed the children and made them promise to become evacuees once more, for though this second experience had been horrid their mother would make sure that they went somewhere pleasant as soon as she could get them away from the city. 'If you need to escape from somewhere again, just run as far as the nearest scuffer, and tell him you're being badly treated,' Miranda instructed. 'Be good, and write to Mum every week. And don't forget us!'

Back in the city once more, the girls got beds in a hostel and went to the nearest recruiting office where they told their story and gave the sergeant in charge the address of the hostel. They were assured that because of their situation they would receive their postings within a week to ten days. Then they went down to the docks, where they found Steve working to help fight the many fires which still blazed. Before he could put his foot in it and ask about Gary, Miranda took him to one side and explained. 'It's still too raw and painful for Avril to want to talk about it, so the less said the better,' she explained. 'Later, when she's begun to accept that Gary's gone, she'll want to talk about him, but not yet.'

When she told him that they were joining the WAAF she wondered if he would think that they were running away in a cowardly fashion, but he gave his approval at once.

'Without bed or board or so much as a stitch of your own clothing, you'd be nothing but another mouth to feed if you stayed here,' he told them. 'As soon as they can spare me I shall go back to my airfield and start teaching the Jerries that they can't attack Liverpool with impunity.' He smiled at Miranda. 'And the moment you get an address you must drop me a line with the telephone number of the Mess. You'll go to a training camp for starters and be there for about six weeks while they kit you out, train you to march with a heavy pack on your back and decide what you're best suited for . . .' he grinned, 'and then they'll post you to somewhere entirely different.'

Miranda heaved a sigh. 'I can see we shall be writing a great many letters to all the people who've been kind or helpful, or both,' she said ruefully. She looked up at the sky, which was clear and filled with wintry sunshine, and turned to Avril. 'It wouldn't surprise me if there was another raid tonight, so let's get back to the hostel and have a zizz while we've got the chance.'

Chapter Twelve

1944

Miranda and her fellow Waafs were in their hut, preparing for a kit inspection. Knowing how fussy their officer was they always tried to arrive at least ten minutes before the inspection was due to take place, and today was no exception. The rest of the air force might be whispering excitedly about the invasion which was such a big secret, but which everyone knew would be taking place very soon, but the Waafs had their minds fixed on the forthcoming inspection and nothing else.

'Hey, has anyone seen my respirator? Oh, it's okay, it's under my bed.' That was Doris, whose bed was on the right-hand side of Miranda's. Doris was always in a flap about something. On Miranda's other side, Tiddles Tidsworth was trying to arrange her grey stockings so that the huge hole in one heel was out of sight. Miranda checked that her own kit was as it should be, then sat cautiously down on the end of her bed and addressed her neighbour.

'Oh, Doris, this time tomorrow Sarah will be off to the north of England and my friend Avril will be settling in here. She'll find it strange after her beloved balloon site, but oh, it will be wonderful to have her around again.'

Tiddles gave a snort. 'Isn't that just typical of the air force?' she demanded. 'First they put girls on balloons, one of the hardest jobs there is, and let them slog away at it for two or three years without apparently even noticing the casualty rates. Then, when it suits them, they decide to close just about all the balloon sites, and the ones that remain go back to the fellers.' She stood back and regarded her kit with approval. 'Still, they have played fair in one respect; they let the redundant balloon ops retrain for the trade of their choice, though why your pal should chose MT is more than I can fathom.'

Miranda puffed out her chest and seized the lapels of her tunic. 'I told her what a great thing it was to be an MT driver,' she said, grinning. 'So naturally she went off to Wheaton for training same as I did. It was just sheer luck that she got posted here, though. It's months and months since we last met. I reckon she's as excited as I am.'

'And I expect you'll want me to move my bed so that your pal and you can be next door to one another,' Doris said somewhat sulkily. She had already moved several times to accommodate friends who wanted to be together and was always threatening not to do so, but on this occasion at least the move, Miranda thought, would surely be to her advantage. Doris was a parachute packer and so was Sarah's neighbour, so Doris ought to welcome the change.

To the dismay of them both, Miranda and Avril had been separated after their initial training down in Gloucestershire, where they were kitted out with uniform and accessories such as knives, forks and spoons – usually known as 'irons' – gas masks and button sticks and taught to march, to wear the correct uniform for every occasion, and to keep everything immaculate. At Wheaton Miranda was taught to drive, to maintain engines and to become, in short, a mechanical transport driver. She and her fellow MT drivers might drive trucks, salvage wagons, ambulances, tractors or mortuary vans as well as staff cars, and very soon Miranda found herself on an airfield in Norfolk, learning the practicalities of her trade. Sitting on the end of her bed, now, and thinking about the past three years, she remembered ruefully that, upon passing out as a fully trained MT driver, she had thought it would be a cushy job. That had soon proved to be an illusion, for at times drivers had to find their way in almost pitch darkness across countryside from which all signposts and other means of identification had been removed. Furthermore, they had to find their destination with virtually no headlights, since these were masked, with only a little slit of light to make them visible to others allowed.

She soon discovered that East Anglia was covered in airfields and as a driver she had to visit all of them, sometimes carrying messages, sometimes officers and sometimes aircrew. She drove the liberty truck into the nearest big town, loaded with off-duty airmen, and on more than one occasion she drove their group captain up to London for an important meeting. On her first long drive it was winter, the snow thick on the ground, and though she managed to find her way to her destination she got hopelessly lost trying to get out of London, and was almost ready to burst into tears when, having stopped to try to find some indication of their position, she was hailed by a passing lorry driver, who had slowed and leaned out of his cab to see if she needed help. 'Are you lost, lass?' he asked in a strong Scottish accent. 'Where are you bound?'

Miranda hesitated; should she say, or would she get into trouble if she did? But a voice from the back seat reassured her. 'Tell him,' the voice said impatiently. 'He's not likely to be a spy in the middle of London with snow on the ground.'

'Righty ho, sir,' Miranda had said thankfully. She put her head out of the window and gave the required information.

The lorry driver chuckled. 'Got you,' he said cheerfully. 'Just follow me, only not too close, and I'll take you through the suburbs and out on the right road. When I pip my horn and veer off to the right you go straight on.' Miranda thanked him from the bottom of her heart, but expected a rocket from the officer when at last they drew to a halt outside his headquarters. Sometimes the men she drove scarcely bothered to acknowledge her presence at all, but this one, it seemed, was different.

'You've done very well, aircraftwoman. Despite the conditions you drove so smoothly that I was able to snatch quite an hour of sleep.'

'Thank you, sir,' Miranda said, gratified. 'But I'm sorry I got lost.'

The man chuckled. 'You weren't the only one,' he admitted ruefully. 'I'm a Londoner, but with the snow down and no lights showing you could've driven me into Buckingham Palace and I still wouldn't have known where we were. What's your name? I shall ask for you next time I'm needed for a meeting.'

Doris's voice brought Miranda back to the present with a jolt. 'Do you want me to move my bed or don't you?' she demanded. 'Honest to God, Miranda, you're such a dreamer.'

Miranda apologised hastily and admitted that it would be grand to have Avril beside her. 'Otherwise we'll keep trotting up and down the hut exchanging bits of gossip and news and disturbing everybody . . .' she was beginning when the hut door was abruptly opened by their flight sergeant and the officer was ushered into the room. Miranda jumped hastily to her feet and went and stood at the head of her bed, saluting stiffly until they were told to stand at ease, and the kit inspection began.

When it was over and no one had been called to account for missing equipment or clothing, she walked across to the cookhouse with the others, glancing at the large watch on her wrist. It was essential for drivers to know the time since their work was planned by the clock, and now she saw that she would have to get a move on or she would be late for her next job.

The girls straggled into the cookhouse, taking a plate each from the big pile at the end of the counter nearest the door. Miranda held hers out to the fat little cook who plopped a generous helping of mashed potato on to it, whilst another girl slapped on a ladle of the much despised corned beef stew. There was tea in a bucket and Miranda dipped out a mugful, then went and sat down at a table where girls she knew were already tucking into their food. 'Room for a little one, Hazel?' she asked politely, not waiting for a reply before she took her place at the table and began to eat. All around her there was clatter and chatter, and when Hazel suddenly addressed her Miranda, whose thoughts had been far away, jumped. Hazel laughed. 'I was just asking you about this pal of yours who's coming up to use her training as a driver after two years on barrage balloons,' she said. 'All the girls are leaving the balloon sites, aren't they?' She snorted. 'Now that the air force have maimed the flower of British womanhood with the beastly things, they simply change their minds and make the girls re-muster. It's too bad, so it is.'

Miranda laughed, but shook her head. 'No, you've got it wrong. Apparently, if your job simply disappears, you can choose which branch of the WAAF you transfer into. Avril – that's my pal – trained as a C and B, but went over to balloons after her first year because they were recruiting strong girls and she hated working in the cook-house. They gave them men's rations, because they were doing men's work, and men's clothing too: trousers, special gloves, balaclavas – all sorts, in fact.' She laughed. 'The fellers will like Avril; she's one of those Nordic types; blonde hair, blue eyes . . .'

'. . . and white eyelashes,' Hazel said, giggling. 'What time's she arriving? Will she come by rail?'

'I dunno,' Miranda said, shrugging, 'but I shall be hanging round the airfield until she arrives. I'm driving the liberty truck into Norwich this evening, so I just hope she gets here before then.'

Avril sat in the train, peering out through the dirt-smeared window and reflecting that although re-mustering was probably always a bit of a strain, re-mustering from balloons was weird. Balloon operatives were the only people who were allowed two kit bags because of the great mass of equipment they had to carry around with them, so travelling without the extra weight made her feel strange, almost naked. She knew that the air force was constantly posting Waafs from one station to another, seeming indifferent to the fact that this was the part of service life which the Waafs found hardest to take. To be removed from friends and from the familiarity of work and workplace seemed to them totally unnecessary; certainly the powers that be would not dream of splitting up the crew of a bomber, though she supposed the fighter pilots might find themselves flying from a variety of different airfields in the course of their work.

'Hey, Avril! Want a sandwich? I'd do a swap, because mine are all dry and curling up at the edges. I couldn't believe it when Cookie told me that all we got for the whole journey – apart from the rail pass – were two lousy Spam sandwiches, a bottle of cold tea and a bit of cake so stale you could resole your shoes with it. It's not as if we could hop off the train and buy something from the refreshment room because if we miss our connection they'll probably court martial us.'

Avril gave a snort of laughter, but turned away from the window to answer. She and the other aircraftwoman had met whilst waiting for the connection and Avril had speedily discovered that they were both heading for Norfolk airfields. Now she shook her head at the suggestion of a court martial, though it was perfectly true that arriving after your leave had expired was a punishable offence. It had to be, otherwise members of the forces would use the unreliability of the trains and the various vicissitudes which beset all travellers in war time as an excuse for prolonging their leave by a day or two.

'You're daft, you are!' she said. 'Next time the train stops we'll look out and see if there's a grub trolley on the platform. I can manage without food but I'm desperate for a drink, and if I have a drink I shall have to visit the bog, unless you think I ought to use my tin hat?'

The other girl laughed. 'Tell you what, when the train stops next we'll both hop out, I'll hold the door open – the engine can't move until every door is closed – and you can nip along to the bog, and if you see someone selling drinks . . .'

'Right you are,' Avril said. 'God, this train is barely moving at walking pace. At this rate it'll be midnight before we get in. Good thing the weather's lovely, because I've not got enough money for a taxi . . . but surely they'll send a vehicle of some sort to meet us? I saw other Waafs and aircraftmen on the train when we got on, so I'm hoping there'll be a gharry or even a bus waiting for us. I know the days are long at this time of year, but they'll want to see us into our huts and get bedding and so on sorted out whilst it's still light, don't you think?'

It was her companion's turn to shrug. 'Dunno. This is my first posting, apart from when I first joined of course, and that took place with twenty or thirty of us all heading in the same direction.' She looked curiously at her companion. 'You said you were on balloons. Did you like it? I reckon I'm too short – maybe even too fat – but I wouldn't mind having a go. They say you get special rations and have a much freer life on a balloon site, with only the odd officer prowling round a couple of times a month, than you do when you're on a real RAF station. So why did you decide to re-muster?'

'I didn't,' Avril said patiently. She felt she had already explained at least fifty times why she was heading for pastures new. 'The air force looked into the number of balloon ops who were in hospital with hernias or broken wrists or . . . oh, all sorts, and when they realised how many of us got injured one way or another they closed down most of the balloon sites, conscripted men to run the ones which were left and advised us to re-muster. I don't deny that it was hard and dangerous work – it truly was – but I think we all loved it. It wasn't too good on the city sites because it was the devil of a job to get the blimp up when it was surrounded by tall buildings, flats, churches and the like. Getting it down was even worse; that's when most people got injured. I copped a broken wrist and two smashed toes on my right foot, but apparently I'm a quick healer and was only off duty for six or eight weeks. But I loved it – as I said, I think most of us did. I'd never have re-mustered of my own accord, but of course we had no choice.' She smiled at the incredulity on the other girl's face. 'It would be hard for other people to understand, but the comradeship, the closeness, the feeling that we were all in it together, and the sheer beauty of the countryside surrounding some of the sites . . . it made up for the hard work and the danger.'

'But all the airfields are surrounded by countryside,' her companion pointed out. 'And though they're pretty dangerous places there are plenty of dugouts and shelters and such, whereas on the balloon sites you had to be outside working with the balloon all through the raid until well after the all clear had sounded. I don't fancy that, I'm telling you.'

Avril sighed, knowing that it was impossible to explain how she felt. She remembered a wild night when the cable which tethered the balloon to the ground had snapped and she, the sergeant in charge of the winch, and the entire crew of Site 36 had chased across the London suburbs in the windy darkness, finding the balloon eventually and staring helplessly up to where it roosted, like an enormous broody hen, over the roof of a fire station. Poor Belinda Boop – the girls always named the balloons – had been rescued eventually but the damage was too extensive for mending and she had been taken away on a tender. The new balloon arrived the very next day and the girls, worn out from their exertions in pursuit of the errant Belinda, had to begin the task of readying the new balloon in case a raid occurred the following night.

Avril told the story of the escaping balloon amusingly and well, and pushed to the back of her mind the sad memories which she could not bear to recall. There was Erica, who had tripped over a guy rope and failed to see the concrete block which secured it. She had bashed her head open, and because the night was wild and the concrete block in shadow had not been discovered until she had bled to death. The girls had been shocked and horrified and had not appreciated the dressing down they had received for not noticing Erica earlier. Later, their sergeant had told them that their fellow operative could never have recovered, was probably dead within seconds of her head's meeting the block, but Avril knew for a fact that two of the girls – the ones who had first found Erica – had asked for transfers to other, less hazardous work as a result.

But the train was slowing and the ghastly image conjured up by memory faded as their carriage drew to a juddering halt. Avril stood up and let the window down, then turned to her companion. 'Are you sure you'll be all right, Daisy? I'm sure if you explain to the porter that this isn't a corridor train he'll let us nip out to the bog. If we take it in turns then whoever remains here can buy a cuppa or whatever. How much money have you got? I've got two half crowns, which won't buy much, but . . .'

'I've got the same,' Daisy said, ferreting around in her gas mask case and producing a small red leather purse. She jumped down on to the platform and gave Avril, who was already down, a shove. 'Go *on*,' she urged. 'There's folk getting off but no one in uniform, so this ain't Norwich Thorpe. But there's been no announcement about changing trains, so we'd best hang on where we are.'

Avril set off at trot for the Ladies, passing a lad of fourteen or fifteen pushing a scantily laden trolley. She waited until she had swapped places with Daisy, then beckoned to the boy. 'What have you got for half a crown? A mug of tea – no, two mugs of tea – would be very welcome.' She eyed the rolls and sandwiches suspiciously, then pointed to two which looked as though they contained lettuce and tomato as well as some sort of cheese. 'I'll have two teas, please, and two cheese salad rolls, if that's what they are.' She fished around in the breast pocket of her tunic. 'What's the damage?'

Miranda spent most of the afternoon in jumpy distraction. She was on ambulance driving, but managed to swap with another girl, hoping that when she drove into the city she would find Avril waiting on Castle Meadow, where all the gharries from all the airfields congregated so that the troops might know precisely where to find them for the return trip.

She had been edgy all afternoon, but as soon as she stopped the gharry on Castle Meadow and went round to remind her passengers that she would be leaving at ten o'clock, she began to feel apprehensive as well. Suppose Avril had missed her train? It was not unlikely, since most trains would be full of troops, heading for whatever part of the coast had been selected as the jump-off point for the planned invasion. On the other hand, Avril would have been told to arrive at RAF Scratby by midnight, so in the event of something's preventing her from getting here before Miranda, and the gharry, left, she would still have two hours before she was liable to get hauled over the coals for tardiness.

Miranda was just deciding that, if the worst came to the worst, she would disable the engine in some way and claim that that was what had held her friend up, when a familiar head appeared in the window of the gharry, flaxen hair flopping over a broad forehead, light blue eyes sparkling with excitement.

Both girls squeaked each other's names and Miranda threw open the gharry door, nearly sending her friend flying, but Avril righted herself and the girls hugged exuberantly, Avril laughing whilst tears ran unchecked down Miranda's cheeks.

Miranda was the first to recover. She rubbed the tears away, then produced a handkerchief and blew her nose before shoving the hanky back in her battledress pocket. 'Oh, Avril, it's just so wonderful to see you,' she gasped. 'I couldn't believe my eyes when your letter came saying you'd re-mustered as a driver and were being posted to RAF Scratby.'

Avril laughed again. 'Then you can imagine how

flabbergasted I was when my posting came through,' she said as Miranda slammed the driver's door shut, locked it and then went round to secure the passenger door. When she re-joined Avril on the pavement she took careful stock of her friend before suggesting that they might go down to the Foundry Bridge, over the river Wensun. 'There's a food outlet, a big van, parked down by the river. All the forces personnel go there, knowing his grub's good and cheap. We can pick up a bottle of pop and a couple of sandwiches and go and sit on the river bank and talk.' She glanced at her wristwatch. 'We've got a couple of hours before I've got to drive the gharry back to the station, so we can sit and watch the boats and catch up. Agreed?'

Avril agreed with enthusiasm, saying that after twelve hours in stuffy railway carriages or on almost equally stuffy station platforms she would appreciate a quiet time in the fresh air. 'I crossed the bridge near the station, and thought the river banks, with the willows leaning over the water, looked really attractive,' she said. 'Another day, perhaps we could take a boat out . . .' But by now they had reached the van, and when they got to the head of the queue Miranda greeted the owner with a cheerful grin and asked what was tonight's special.

'Well, how hungry are you, together?' he asked, in a rich Norfolk accent, eyeing them judiciously. 'I guess you had a cookhouse meal earlier so you won't want a sausage sandwich . . .'

'A sausage sandwich will be fine, Claude,' Miranda said quickly. She knew all too well that if she did not make up her mind at once Claude would run through his entire stock, for he liked to please his customers.

Having made a decision Miranda added a bottle of pop and two paper cups, then handed over her money, and armed with a fat sandwich each the girls hurried towards the river. Presently, settled beneath the branches of a willow, Miranda watched as Avril took a big bite out of her sandwich, grinned, and nodded.

'This sausage tastes pre-war, and the bread's delicious,' she announced. 'Pour me some pop, would you?'

Miranda complied, saying as she did so: 'So you appreciate our Claude's grub, do you? I believe his mother makes the bread, or perhaps it's Claude himself; at any rate he doesn't approve of the national loaf and always serves homemade stuff. And now let me have a proper look at you.'

She scanned her friend from the top of her flaxen head to her well-polished air force issue black shoes. 'You're thinner. Now I wonder why that is? Everyone tells you that the girls on balloons get extra rations because it's such hard work; but of course the work itself might have slimmed you down. And don't think I'm criticising, 'cos you look grand. I expect you'll notice changes in me too, though I don't think I've lost much weight.'

'You look worn out,' Avril said with all the frankness which Miranda remembered. 'I guess driving is pretty tense, what with the blackout an' all.' She hesitated. 'Steve still all right? Do you realise how much we've lost touch over the past three years? Oh, I know we've exchanged scrappy little letters from time to time, and we did meet up once, but to be honest, Miranda, if it hadn't been for this posting I reckon we'd have lost touch altogether. Somehow there was always something more important to do than write letters.'

'Steve's okay, or he was last night when I telephoned the Mess,' Miranda said. 'But there's a big offensive coming up . . .' she lowered her voice, 'I expect you've heard all about it, though it's supposed to be top secret. Anyway, bombing raids over Germany are taking place whenever the weather's good, and so far this summer has been brilliant.' She looked shyly at her friend, then waved a finger under Avril's nose. 'That, dear Avril, is an engagement ring. I didn't want to get engaged. I had a silly superstitious fear that if we did something which made both of us so happy we'd be tempting fate to throw a spanner in the works. But in the end I just wanted to do whatever Steve wanted, and that was to get engaged.'

Avril seized her friend's hand and gazed at the pretty little ring on her third finger. 'How on earth did he save up the money for this?' she demanded. 'I don't know much about jewellery prices . . .'

Miranda laughed. 'He didn't buy it. Do you remember Granny Granger? I think you met her once.'

'Yes, I remember; a lovely old lady,' Avril said at once. 'Don't say she's gone for a burton?'

'Good heavens, no,' Miranda said, looking shocked. 'Steve and I had a spot of leave and decided to take it at the same time, and go home to Liverpool. While we were there Steve told Granny Granger that we wanted to get engaged and would do so as soon as he could afford to buy a ring. Whereupon the old lady trotted up to her bedroom and came down again with this dear little ring in a tiny green velvet box. She said it had belonged to her mother, so it's really old, an antique almost, and since she meant to leave it to Steve in her will he might as well have it now, so we got engaged on the spot.'

Avril whistled admiringly. 'Ain't you the lucky one? But shouldn't the ring have gone to Steve's mother rather than to Steve? It seems an odd thing to leave to a feller.'

'Not really. Mrs Mickleborough will get Granny's engagement ring and all the rest of her jewellery, which isn't saying much. Of course she gave this to Steve on impulse really, but we both took it as a sign that she thought getting engaged was a good idea, and I have to say we've never regretted it. It's – it's kind of nice to belong to someone else, to look towards a shared future . . . oh, I don't know, I'm not putting it very well, but I guess you understand.' She hesitated as a large rowboat full of RAF personnel splashed its way past, then spoke diffidently. 'Have you got a boyfriend, queen? You never mentioned one in your letters, but then you didn't write often, or at much length . . .'

Avril cut across the sentence, the colour rising in her cheeks. 'No, I've not got a boyfriend, though of course I've been out with several people over the last three years. After Gary was killed I could see all too clearly that having a boyfriend in wartime is nowt but a ticket to pain. It's why you look so worn and weary. I'll bet you spend ninety per cent of your time worrying that something bad will happen to Steve. Well, I can do without that. Maybe I'm selfish – a great many men have told me I'm hard – but I don't mean to hand over my heart for breaking twice in one lifetime.'

Miranda nodded. 'I know what you mean, because I suppose it was the reason why I didn't want to get engaged,' she admitted. 'But you're not just shutting the door on the possibility of being hurt, queen, you're shutting it on the chance of happiness. And it takes two to tango, as they say. What about the feller? Isn't he allowed a voice in this decision? And don't tell me there isn't a feller. What about Julian; what about Pete? I know you write to them both and I bet there are lots of others chasing you, because with that blonde mop you always had chaps in tow when we were living in Russell Street and I can't believe it's any different now.'

'Oh, them!' Avril said contemptuously. 'They're just pals, as you used to be so fond of remarking. As for new blokes, you obviously don't know balloon sites. They are – were, I should say – all staffed by women except the sergeant in charge who was usually a man, so us balloon ops didn't have the same opportunities that you get as an MT driver. Of course we went to RAF stations for dances and social events, but I never got close to anyone, not really close. And looking at the strain on your face, I can only say I'm grateful I never got involved.'

Miranda was in the middle of admitting that she did worry about Steve most of the time when she heard a clock begin to strike and jumped to her feet, knocking over the bottle of pop and casting crumbs to the four winds. 'Heavens, I'm supposed to be back at the gharry, loading the fellers up,' she said, beginning to scramble up the bank, with Avril in hot pursuit. 'Oh, damn, we're going to have to run. I dare not be late, because everyone in my hut knows you're arriving today and will assume I'm risking their passes because my friend missed her connection.'

Miranda had always had friends amongst the other MT drivers and mechanics who shared the care and maintenance of all the vehicles on the station, but none had suited her as well as Avril. Perhaps it was their shared background, or the fact that they were the only two Liverpudlians in their group, but whatever the reason the two girls, who had been close when they shared the flat, grew closer still. A couple of times Steve suggested that Avril might like to make up a foursome with a member of his crew, but in the end Miranda seized the opportunity, when she and Steve both got a forty-eight, to suggest that they should spend it alone together. 'I'll explain to Avril, and we can enjoy ourselves with a clear conscience,' she told Steve when she telephoned him at his Mess. 'I'm not suggesting we should share anything other than a meal and a dance at the Samson and Hercules though, so don't you go getting ideas.'

Steve said virtuously that of course he would expect nothing but friendship from a fiancée so high-minded. Chuckling, Miranda told him not to be so cheeky and replaced the receiver before he could reply.

She told Avril that she and Steve meant to spend their forty-eight together, since the weather was still blissfully fine. Indeed, it had been blissfully fine throughout Operation Overlord, as the invasion became known, and the thousands of Allied soldiers now pushing their way across German-occupied France must be grateful to have the weather on their side. All leave had been cancelled, but Steve's Lancaster, overflying occupied France in order to bomb Germany, had limped home after sustaining a good deal of damage, and this enabled the crew to ask permission to take a forty-eight whilst their Lancaster, which they had named Lindy Lou, had her many injuries repaired.

Leave usually started after work so that one might

catch the gharry either to the nearest railway station or into the city, and on this occasion Steve and Miranda met on Castle Meadow, each with a kitbag slung over one shoulder, and Steve, at least, with an anticipatory gleam in his eyes. Kissing was forbidden whilst in uniform, and one was always in uniform, but Steve had already planned what they would do. 'We'll catch a bus out of the city heading for Ringland Hills,' he said, starting to walk towards the bus station. 'There's a nice little pub in the village which will do us supper and only charge us five shillings, or ten bob for bed and breakfast,' he said, taking her arm in a proprietorial manner. 'You'll love it; all the chaps say the food's prime, the beds soft and the landlady discreet.'

Miranda, giggling, gave Steve a shove. 'Enough of that,' she said severely. 'It all sounds fine apart from the landlady. She can keep her discretion to herself.'

They reached Surrey Street and found the bus they wanted waiting, and very soon they were in the cosy little pub with a remarkably good meal on the table before them while Steve, having reluctantly booked two rooms, spent a good deal of energy trying to persuade Miranda that sharing would be much more fun than going off to their own beds after supper.

When they had first entered the pub the bar had been empty, but now it was beginning to fill up, and Steve hushed his companion when she began to argue. 'I was only teasing,' he said in an undertone. 'Of course there isn't a law against not sharing a room if you're engaged.' Then his voice sharpened. 'Oh, hell; there's a face I recognise! She's not in uniform – a bit old for that probably – but I'm sure I know her from somewhere. Oh, heck, she's coming over. I do hate it when somebody whose name I can't recall expects to be recognised and made welcome, and all you can do is wonder who the devil it is.'

Miranda was beginning to say that it was his imagination, that the woman was not really heading for them but had spotted a vacant place on the bench beside her, when she broke off short. 'Lynette!' she squeaked excitedly. 'What on earth are you doing here?'

The former member of the Madison Players approached, beaming, and Miranda jumped to her feet to give her a hearty kiss. 'I were just about to ask you the same, kiddo,' Lynette Rich said cheerily. 'It's the last place I should have expected to meet someone I know.' She dug a plump elbow into Miranda's ribs. 'We come here, me and my American feller, to have a quiet weekend away from all the fuss and botheration, and who's the first person I set me eyes on? It's little Miranda Lovage, though she ain't so little now. They say it's bad manners to ask a woman her age, but when I last seen you you were just a child, and now I suppose you must be nineteen or twenty.' She turned to stare piercingly into Steve's face. 'Do I reckernise you, young feller? I hopes as you haven't brought my little friend here with the intention of misbehavin'.'

Steve grinned. 'We've seen each other before, when Miranda took me round to the theatre a couple of times whilst she was searching for her mother,' he said. 'You're a dancer, aren't you?'

The plump, smiling lady nodded her peroxided curls vigorously. That's me; or that *was* me rather. I'm with ENSA; we entertain the troops . . . well, you know all that, and this was to be a bit of a treat between shows because once it's safe to do so they'll send us across to the jolly old Continong to entertain the troops over there. It'll be a change from . . .'

She stopped speaking as a voice hailed her, and a heavily built, middle-aged American with so many stripes on his sleeve and medals on his chest that Miranda guessed he was someone high up in the USAF crossed the room and put a hand on his companion's arm. 'Gee, honey, you find friends everywhere,' he said admiringly. 'But we're in a bit of a fix, sweetie; the landlady says they've not got a room.' He pointed an accusing finger at Steve. 'This young guy has took 'em both, so unless I can persuade your pals to give one up . . .'

After that there was much talk and much persuasion on the part of Lynette and her friend, though Steve was far too sensible to join in. He stood back, well aware that Miranda would presently bow to the inevitable, as indeed she did, though it must have been almost midnight when the two couples climbed the winding wooden stair, exchanged goodnights and disappeared into their respective rooms. Once there, Miranda allowed her annoyance to show, actually accusing Steve of having planned the whole business, though she knew very well that he had done no such thing. However, they managed to undress discreetly and climbed into bed, pulling the bolster down between them. 'A bit of a cuddle wouldn't hurt,' Steve said hopefully when they had blown out the candle and rolled up the blackout blind and were lying in the friendly summer dark. 'I won't do anything you wouldn't like, honest to God, Miranda.'

'Go to sleep!' Miranda replied smartly. 'Go straight to sleep; do not pass Go, do not collect two hundred pounds.

And just remember, all Waafs have a scream like a train whistle, so if you put so much as one finger across that bolster . . .'

'I wasn't considering a finger . . .' Steve said plaintively, and received a quick smack round the ear. 'Oh, very well. I'm tired too, so we'd best get some shut-eye, or it'll be morning and that damned Yankee will have ate up all the bacon and eggs.'

Miranda and Steve, despite the best of intentions, woke late, and by the time they took their places opposite one another at the small table in the bar the American was paying the bill and thanking the landlady for a delightful visit. He hefted a large suitcase out to the waiting taxi and Lynette, with a cheery wave, was about to follow him when something seemed to occur to her and she turned back. 'I take it you've seen your mam?' she bawled across the room. 'You could ha' knocked me down with a feather when I walked slap bang into her on Lime Street. I could see she didn't remember me – well, I weren't always blonde and I've put on a bit more weight than I should over the past two or three years. She said she were with a concert party, come over from the States to entertain the doughboys, but before I could tell her how worried we'd all been someone shouted and she gave me a big smile, said "Excuse me, but I'm wanted" and disappeared into the crowd. You knew she were back, of course?'

Sheer astonishment had caused Miranda's throat to close up, making speech impossible, but Steve seized Lynette's arm, digging his fingers into the soft flesh until she squeaked. 'Miranda don't know anything about her mother, except that she might have been living in America. She's not seen her since the day she disappeared,' he said urgently. 'Are you sure it was Arabella? Did the person who shouted use the name Arabella? Oh, Lynette, you can't just walk away, having told only half the story.'

But Lynette was shaking her head. 'I dunno. I called her Arabella but she just looked straight through me as if I didn't exist. It were only when I grabbed her arm that she looked at me. At the time I would have sworn it was Arabella, but afterwards . . . oh, I don't know, I suppose it could have been one of them lookalikes. Which twin has the Toni, sort of thing. Still, it might be worth you havin' a word with whoever runs the Yankee ENSA; see if you can trace her through them.' A bellow from the yard outside made her turn hastily away from them. 'I've gotta go,' she shouted over her shoulder. 'See you again. Sorry I can't stay . . .'

Miranda jumped to her feet just as the landlady appeared with two plates full of bacon, eggs, fried bread and sausages. She would have run out of the room but Steve caught her arm and made her sit down. 'The car went off the moment she climbed into the passenger seat,' he said cheerfully. 'And anyway there was no point in asking any more questions, because she'd already told us everything she knew. But she's given you a very good clue, queen, the best you've had so far. Now I wonder whether anyone else in Liverpool recognised her?'

'I've got to get back to Liverpool!' Miranda cried wildly, ignoring Steve's words. 'I've simply got to find her. If she's lost her memory and doesn't know who she really is, then I can tell her she's my mother, say how sorry I am that I wasn't a better daughter. And there's other things: she won't know she was kidnapped, or by whom. She won't know what happened to her in that storm, how she escaped drowning, I mean. Oh, once I've helped her to unlock her memory it will all come flooding back. I must go up to Liverpool at once!'

Steve, however, was shaking his head. 'No you mustn't. You're a member of His Majesty's forces, and you can't possibly get up to Liverpool and back in the course of a forty-eight. Besides, Lynette never said *when* she bumped into Arabella. The Yanks have been in the war now for over two years; it could have happened way back. I'm afraid you're going to have to keep on being patient and sensible, because rushing your fences will only lead to a fall. And now, darling Miranda, do let's get on with what's left of our little holiday. Going AWOL will only get you court martialled and that won't help to find your mother. I'll tell you what, though: write to Lynette, care of ENSA, and ask all the questions which you didn't have time for just now. She might remember a bit more if you give her a few days.' He dug his fork into the egg yolk. 'Aren't we lucky? This egg is cooked just as I like it with the yolk runny and the white firm. Oh, come on, Miranda, cheer up. You're on holiday and you've had a clue to your mother's whereabouts at last!'

Chapter Thirteen

Avril had waved Miranda off, gone to the NAAFI for a cup of tea and a natter, and then repaired to their hut. She undressed slowly and climbed into bed, expecting to sleep at once for she had had a tiring day, but in fact she lay wakeful, suddenly aware that she was missing the younger girl. Avril wondered how she and Steve were getting on, and cast off her blankets, for it was a hot night. She hoped they were making the most of their leave and turned and twisted, trying to find a cool spot, but finally decided to stop courting sleep and instead think back over her time at RAF Scratby.

Miranda had made it easy for her, she thought now. There had been a great many girls to meet as well as a good few young men, for, one way or another, Miranda knew practically all the personnel on the airfield and introduced Avril to each one. Everyone was friendly, the men intrigued by the combination of her Liverpool accent and Nordic good looks and the girls fascinated to learn that she had spent the last few years on a balloon site and eager for details.

But now Avril let her mind go right back to the time when she had joined the air force to get away from the streets where she and Gary had once been happy . . . she had joined in fact to forget the pain which losing him had caused her. Before she had met Gary she had never known what it was to love someone, for though she supposed she must have loved her parents she could scarcely remember them. Along with most of the children in the home, she had hated the place, the staff and a good few of the other occupants. When she had met Miranda she had been living in a hostel, working as hard as she could at her job and scarcely believing that she could ever escape from the treadmill of trying to earn enough money to be independent. Then Gary had entered her life.

Before then, Avril had had several boyfriends but had never taken them seriously. They had families – mums and dads, brothers and sisters – and whenever she was taken to a young man's home she felt panicked, like someone thrown into deep water before learning to swim. She floundered, unable to find the right attitude, always aware that she was different.

Knowing Miranda had helped, because Miranda, too, had no cosy home background. She had talked of her loving mother, but Avril secretly thought a good deal of what her friend said was wishful thinking. If Miranda's mother had truly loved her, why had she gone away and not come back? So, gradually, almost imperceptibly, Avril began to relax. And when she met Gary, and discovered that he, too, had been brought up in a children's home, she had begun to talk of her past, and to her delight had found Gary understood.

Very soon she realised she was deeply in love with him, so that the shock of his death had been almost unbearable. Running away, determined to make a career for herself in the air force, she had accepted the position of kitchen worker on an airfield in Lincolnshire, lowly and disgusting though this was to her way of thinking, because she was determined to do well, to be the best C and B the air force had ever known.

She had reckoned without Corporal Greesby, of course. She had no idea whence his dislike had sprung, but she soon discovered that it was in his power to make or break her and that the best way to escape his malevolence was to keep her head down and do as she was told. 'Never explain, never complain' was an old army saying, but apparently it also applied to the air force, and Avril and one or two other girls for whom Corporal Greesby had developed a dislike soon learned to follow its advice. So when the notice had appeared on the bulletin board in the Mess, asking for women volunteers who were strong, fit and healthy to take over from the men on balloon sites, Avril had been the first to put her name forward, and had been immediately accepted. She had been given a rail pass to Cardington, where she would be trained, along with several other girls from her hut, to fly the great unwieldy barrage balloons.

If the Royal Air Force wondered why so many girls from Corporal Greesby's kitchen applied for the balloon corps they didn't ask, and Avril suspected they didn't care, though she got a good deal of pleasure from a small revenge which she personally carried out upon the corporal, spiking his usual enormous helping of chocolate pudding with a bar of Ex-lax chocolate crumbled over the top. Grinning evilly, she told one of the other girls that the corporal would be spending the next few hours glued to the bog, and shouldered her kitbag with the feeling that honour had been satisfied.

Number One balloon training unit at Cardington was

like a breath of fresh air after the horrors of Corporal Greesby's kitchen. The course lasted ten weeks, during which Avril learned skills of which she had never previously heard. The sergeant who taught them to splice rope and wire, inflate the balloons with hydrogen and drive the winches which operated the winding gear was a sensible man in his forties, who had been a teacher in civvy street and knew exactly how to deal with his recruits. By the end of the course they appreciated not only his skills but also his kindness, and in Avril's eyes he had rescued the reputation of the air force.

After their initial training the girls spent a week at an old aerodrome actually working with a balloon. They were divided into teams of twelve Waafs and a flight sergeant, and, to their relief, when they got their posting at the end of the course they stayed with their team, though the flight sergeant would be allocated when they actually reached their balloon site.

From that moment on Avril was in her element. The work was hard, heavy and frequently dangerous, but she loved it. Most of the sites were on the outskirts of big cities or built-up areas which needed extra protection from the Luftwaffe raids. At first it was difficult to see what extra protection the balloons offered, but the girls had a talk from a flying officer who assured them that the blimps were best avoided, both by the enemy and by their own aircraft. 'The Luftwaffe fly high when they come in for a bombing raid, and do their best to keep well clear of the balloons,' he assured them. 'No doubt you've been taught that a plane which flies too near a balloon can be caught up in the cable, which moves with a sawing motion and can cut through wings, tail, even fuselage. So never think your work isn't important, because it has saved countless lives.'

By the time the order came that Waafs were to leave the balloon sites Avril viewed the prospect of re-mustering with dismay. Only when she learned that, because she had volunteered for balloons, she might choose her new trade did she begin to see that this, in fact, might not be a bad thing. Balloons were all very well, but they weren't exactly a career move; if she re-mustered as, for instance, an MT driver, then they would teach her, not only to drive, but also to repair and maintain all the many and various vehicles used by the air force, and this would still be a useful skill even when the war was over. So off she went to Wheaton, and because she was bright and hard-working she emerged at the end of the training period a fully fledged MT driver.

Naturally enough she watched the bulletin board anxiously, hoping to get a posting soon, and was almost unbelieving when she learned that she was to go to RAF Scratby, the very airfield, had she been given the choice, which she would have chosen.

And now here she was actually lying on her hard little bed feeling a fresh breeze blowing in through the window with a touch of salt on its breath, for the airfield was only a couple of miles from the sea. I wonder whether the beach is mined, Avril found herself thinking sleepily. I know most of the beaches are, particularly along the south and east coasts, but I've read in the newspapers that they have to leave an area clear of mines so that lifeboats can be launched. Oh well, I expect we'd get court martialled if we tried to so much as paddle, and there are lots of other things to do when you're on a proper RAF station. She snuggled her face into the pillow, remembering the meal they had been served that evening in the Scratby cookhouse, some sort of stew with not very much meat but an awful lot of carrots, and a syrup pudding. Tiddles Tidsworth, watching her, had laughed and asked if the food was up to balloon standards.

Avril had laughed too. On a balloon site one took turns at everything: guard duty, driving the winch, cooking the meals. When it was your turn to cook you were given the ingredients and told to go ahead; there were no such things as menus, or suggestions even. Some girls could cook naturally, others couldn't. Avril remembered Sandra, who didn't understand about boiling potatoes until they were soft, and Janette whose meals were so delicious that at first they had suspected she was buying extra grub from a restaurant somewhere. Avril had assured Tiddles that it was a treat to have food cooked for you and left it at that. No point in putting anyone's back up by saying that the stew could have benefited from some flour to thicken it or even a bit more meat. Smiling at the recollection, she fell asleep at last.

Miranda had spent the day ferrying personnel between airfields, and knew that Avril had been doing the same, so at eight o'clock, when she was free at last, she went straight to the cookhouse, hoping that someone would realise that the MT drivers on duty would not have been fed.

The large room with its many tables and chairs and its long wooden counter was almost empty, but to Miranda's relief those who were in there all seemed to be eating and there was a smell of hot food in the air.

She went over to the counter and a weary little Waaf clad in blue wrapover apron, white cap and leather clogs greeted her with a tired grin. 'Evenin', Lovage; what can I do you for? Cheese on toast, beans on toast, scrambled eggs on toast? Or a mixture of all three?'

Miranda settled for cheese on toast and was turning away with her plate of food when the girl behind the counter spoke again. 'Your mate come in ten minutes ago; she's over there in that corner. She were one of the lucky ones; got in before Corp used the last of the fried spuds. Help yourself to HP Sauce; it's by the bucket of tea.'

Miranda collected a mug, dipped out her tea and went across to where Avril was sitting. She had one of the tables to herself and Miranda was surprised to see that she had, spread out upon it, five or six sheets of cheap airmail paper. She scowled as Miranda's shadow fell across her table, then looked up and smiled as she recognised her friend.

'Wotcher!' she said cheerfully. She pushed one of the chairs towards Miranda. 'Do sit down, only don't drip that tea all over my letters.'

'Letters?' Miranda said. 'Don't you mean letter? Is it going to be an awfully long one? Or are you expecting to make a lot of mistakes?' She sat down as she spoke and eyed the other girl curiously.

'Neither,' Avril said positively. She waved a newly sharpened pencil under her friend's nose. 'I do this every week or so, and it's a real bind, but I know my duty. I quite like getting letters myself, though by the time they've gone through the censor they often look more like those lacy paper things people used to stand cakes on . . . can't remember what they're called . . .'

'Doilies,' Miranda supplied. She took a big bite out of her toasted cheese, then leaned forward so that if she did dribble brown sauce it would fall on her plate rather than on her uniform. 'Who are you writing to anyway?' She half expected Avril to tell her to mind her own business, but though her friend tapped the side of her nose in the well-known gesture she replied readily enough, whilst producing from her gas mask case several crumpled and really rather dirty pages which she smoothed out, ticked off and laid out, parade ground fashion, each one on a separate sheet of the airmail paper.

'I don't mind tellin' you, because you won't know any of them,' Avril said. She pointed. 'That's to Danny, that's to Simon, that's to Frank and that's to Freddy, and then there's one for P— Paul.' She looked challengingly across the table at her friend. 'Satisfied?'

'Yes, I suppose so. Are they all service personnel? Or are you still in touch with any of your old pals from the factory? Come to that, are you still in touch with people from the children's home? I know I ought to drop Aunt Vi and Beth a line from time to time – well, I do – but I warned Beth last time I wrote that if she didn't reply I wouldn't write again.'

'Has she? Replied, I mean,' Avril asked. She wrote *Dear Danny, Lovely to get your letter*, then looked questioningly up at her friend.

'Not yet, but Steve had a letter from his mam – they're back in Jamaica Close – and she says Aunt Vi and Beth are okay though Aunt Vi disapproves of Beth's feller and they're always having rows.' She leaned forward to stare as Avril began to write on the next sheet of paper.

'Whatever are you doing, queen? Don't you finish one letter before you start the next?'

'Course not; that'd be a waste of time,' Avril said impatiently. She pulled the next sheet towards her and proceeded to write. She had large, rather childish handwriting, and Miranda read it upside down from across the table with ease. *Dear Simon, Lovely to get your letter . . .*

Even as Miranda watched, Avril pulled forward the third sheet. *Dear Frank, Lovely to get your letter . . .* 'Aircraftwoman Donovan, what on *earth* do you think you're doing? Surely you aren't going to write exactly the same letter to all those fellers? Next thing you'll have half a dozen pencils all working together so you only have to write the once; the pencils will do the rest.' She was joking, but Avril answered her quite seriously.

'I know what you mean, and I've tried it, but it simply won't work. This method is better, because I can write quite a lot when I don't have to think about what I'm saying. If I wrote to each bloke separately I'd never have a spare moment, so this is the obvious answer.' As she spoke she was finishing off the line of papers, *Dear Frank* being followed by *Dear Freddy* and *Dear Paul*.

Miranda watched, fascinated, as her friend rapidly scrawled identical messages on the first four sheets of paper. 'What's wrong with Paul?' she asked, indicating the last sheet, still blank apart from the salutation. 'Is he special? In fact, is Paul the reason why you won't settle down with one chap, you greedy girl, you?'

'Special? Not particularly,' Avril said, but Miranda saw a flush climb up her friend's neck into her cheeks. 'But they're a long way off and all my letters to them go by sea, so as you must realise, nosy, they don't get all of them by a long chalk. Last time I wrote to Paul he wrote back to say only half my letter had arrived; some idiot in the censorship office had seen fit to tear it in two, or at any rate only half arrived on Paul's notice board. After that it seems only fair to write in a bit more detail, otherwise he's behind the rest of the blokes, if you see what I mean.' She glared across the table. 'Have you any objection? It was you who told me letters were important to fellers a long way from home, if you remember . . .'

'Oh, I don't blame you,' Miranda said quickly. 'It just seems a bit cold-blooded, that's all. I dare say you've given all of them the impression that they're the only bloke in your life, and that after the war . . .'

Avril snorted. 'I can't help what they believe, that's up to them,' she said firmly. 'And if you're going to keep talking I'll get in a muddle and repeat the same sentence twice in one letter, and that would be awful, wouldn't it? I mean, one of them might guess that he's not my only correspondent. And don't you go dribbling brown sauce over my last two sheets of airmail paper, or you can jolly well buy me another pad from the NAAFI.'

'Sorry,' Miranda said hastily, cramming the last piece of toasted cheese into her mouth, and speaking rather thickly through it. 'As I said, it just seems a bit cold-blooded. What happens if Tom, Dick or Harry suddenly stops replying to your form letters?'

This time a real flush turned Avril's pale skin to scarlet. She glared at Miranda and Miranda saw that her friend's lip was trembling. 'You mean when one of them is killed, don't you?' she said, her voice breaking. 'Someone in his flight will go through his mail and let me know. And now you can bloody well gerrout of here and leave me to finish me letters in peace.'

Miranda jumped to her feet and went round the table to give Avril a hug. 'I'm really sorry, queen,' she said gently. 'It was very wrong of me to pry and even more wrong to assume that your letter writing was some sort of game. I can see now that you're making a load of fellers happy and harming no one. Will you forgive me?'

Avril gulped and wiped her eyes with the backs of her hands, causing a couple of large teardrops to splash onto one of her letters, but she turned and gave her friend a rueful grin. 'The thing is, Miranda, I've only got one life. The letters are full of what I've been doing – except I never mention other chaps, of course – so the letters are bound to be nearly identical, even if I went to the trouble of writing on separate days. This way, I'm keeping four or five guys happy without making promises I don't intend to keep.'

'Well, bully for you,' Miranda said. 'I'm dog tired; I've been driving all day. I'll just get myself a slice of spotted dick and then I'm for bed. How long will it take you to finish your – er – letters?' Some imp of mischief made her add: 'How do you sign off? Not SWALK?'

To her relief, Avril laughed. 'Course not. I just say *Thanks again for your letter, can't wait for the next, Avril*. Does that suit your majesty's sense of what's right and wrong? It had better, because I don't intend to change my way of life just to suit you.'

'All right, you've made your point.' Miranda carried her plate across to the counter, swished her irons briefly in the barrel of lukewarm water, dried them on a rag of dishcloth and pushed them into her gas mask case. Then she waved to Avril, busily writing once more, and set off for their hut. Dead tired as she was she still forced herself to go along to the ablutions and have as good a shower as she could in cold water before getting between the blankets. She had been there only what felt like a few minutes when she was awoken by Avril crashing into her own bed. Miranda sat up on her elbow and gazed in the dimness across to where Avril was already snuggling down. 'Finished your letters?' she asked sleepily. 'There was no hot water but I managed to get a shower, though it was cold. How about you?'

'I done 'em, the letters I mean, but I've not been to the 'blutions; too late, too tired,' Avril droned, her voice already sleep-drugged. 'I'll wash in the mornin'. G'night.'

'G'night,' Miranda echoed, and almost immediately fell fast asleep.

Avril lay watching the light gradually strengthen through the small window, and thinking that she had had a narrow escape in the cookhouse the previous evening, when Miranda had come so jauntily across the room to join her at her table. How easily she might have been writing to Pete Huxtable first instead of last, and for some reason, a reason which she could not explain even to herself, she had no wish for either Miranda or anyone else to know that she was writing to Pete. He had had a very varied war so far and oddly, though they had not been particularly close when she had lived in the flat, as time went on she had grown to appreciate him and to prefer him to all her other suitors. Whilst she had been what she now thought of as a kitchen slave, she and Pete had been exchanging letters – fairly short uniformative ones – and when he had suggested a meeting she had jumped at it. She was missing Miranda, her job at the factory and the girls she had known there, and meeting Pete had been a bit like plunging back into her past. They had agreed to meet in Lincoln, since Pete was familiar with the city, being at the time at RAF Waddington, so he had telephoned her with instructions to meet him at the Saracen's Head, a pub on the high street. 'But I'll never find it. Lincoln's a huge city, and I've never been off the station,' Avril had wailed. 'Is there some sort of landmark which will tell me I'm goin' in the right direction?'

Pete had laughed. 'It's on the high street, right next door to what they call the Stonebow, which is a sort of arch under which all the traffic has to pass,' he had told her. 'Honest to God, Avril, every soul in Lincoln knows the Saracen's Head. Be there at seven o'clock and we'll snatch a meal and catch up with each other's news.' He had chuckled. 'I gather you aren't too keen on working in a cookhouse. You can tell me why not over a meal at the Cornhill Hotel.'

Avril had agreed to this and had been astonished by the flood of pleasure which broke over her like a wave at the sight of Pete Huxtable's plain but well-remembered face. They were both in uniform, but had held hands discreetly below the table at the hotel. When Pete had told her that other members of his ground crew spent their forty-eights with their girlfriends at the hotel, she had looked at him suspiciously, thinking he was about to suggest that they should do likewise, but the matter-of-fact way he spoke and his usual friendliness soon assured her that he was not going to try anything on.

He was doing an important job, servicing the engines of great bombers, and proud of his ability, but he was still the rather shy young man she had known from their Liverpool days.

They had remained friends throughout their time in Lincolnshire, always trying to time their trips to the city to coincide, and thinking about it now Avril realised that her desperation to be free of Corporal Greesby and the cookhouse had really only come to a head when Pete was posted to Malaya. She knew he would have a long and dangerous sea voyage and at their last meeting she had been prepared, if he demanded it, for them to spend their forty-eight as guests at the Cornhill Hotel. Pete, however, had merely said that he could only bear his posting if she would both promise to write and also look kindly upon him when the war was over and he was free to ask her to wed him.

At the time this had caused Avril considerable hilarity, for, as she told him, she did not intend to marry anyone, not even someone as nice as he. 'I'm goin' to have a career. Oh, I might marry when I'm really old, say thirty-five, but until then I'm goin' to earn lots of money and have lots of fun,' she told him airily. 'So don't you try and tie me down, Pete Huxtable.'

Pete had agreed meekly that he would do no such thing and said he applauded her decision to have a career. 'Though I can't think that cooking for forty and peeling potatoes far into the night is going to help your future much,' he had said, keeping his voice serious though his eyes had twinkled. 'In fact the only thing it will prepare you for is marriage – if you intend to have a great many children, that is.'

With thoughts of the children's home in mind, for the food provided there had been very similar to that which was slopped on to plates daily by the cookhouse staff, she had shuddered and assured him that she would apply for a posting as soon as she had suffered Corporal Greesby and the cookhouse for the obligatory six months, but then Pete had been posted and her whole attitude had changed. Losing her pal Miranda, and then Pete, and doing work she hated under a man she disliked, had caused her to watch the bulletin board closely, and when the request for girls to apply to become balloon operatives appeared on the board she was first in the queue. She had told no one that Pete meant more to her than any of her other correspondents, so now, chuckling to herself over her narrow escape from Miranda's curiosity, she fell abruptly asleep and was only woken when the tannoy began to shout. She had been late to bed, thanks to writing all her letters, but nevertheless grabbed her clothes, towel and soap and tore out of the hut, covering the short distance between her bed and the ablutions at greyhound speed. She bolted into the hut, which possessed three curtained-off showers, half a dozen curtained-off lavatories and a great many wash basins. For Avril, who for two years had known nothing but the primitive arrangements which balloon sites offered, the mere thought of a shower either hot or cold was always welcome, and since two were already occupied she went happily into the third, hanging her pyjamas on the hook and plunging under the water. Soon, clean and fully dressed apart from shoes and cap, she returned to their hut and there was Miranda, ready for the off. The two girls grinned at one another and set off for the cookhouse, for their day's work would begin at eight. Miranda would be driving yet more airmen to some unspecified destination and Avril was on ambulance duty, which she hoped sincerely would prove to be a sinecure that day. The British airmen only flew at night – unlike the Americans who, she knew, did daylight raids – so though the ambulance was always manned and ready, its chief work came after dark. That meant she would be free until noon and on call from six or seven o'clock, which should give her plenty of time to write to Pete, for she had not liked to do so the previous evening with Miranda's too knowing eyes upon her.

In fact, however, she had no opportunity to write letters, for she was called to the small bay to service the engine of a car which the driver was having trouble starting, and by the time she finished she was ready for a meal, so she searched out Miranda and the two joined the cookhouse queue together. They reached the counter and had just had corned beef hash, cabbage and gravy slapped on to their plates when Miranda turned to her friend. 'I forgot to ask if you ever write to Pete Huxtable?' she said airily. 'Steve says he's out in Malaya now; but I guess you know that, don't you?'

Despite her best efforts, Avril's mouth hung open for quite ten seconds before she pulled herself together. 'What makes you think that?' she asked belligerently. A sudden thought struck her. 'You looked at the letters on the board and saw the one I got from him! Miranda Lovage, you are a thoroughly sneaky person! And why shouldn't I write to Pete, anyway? He were real nice to me after Gary and Timmy died. Besides, what are you trying to make of it? I've gorra grosh of fellers what I write to and I dare say there's chaps here what'll want me to go to the flicks or to a dance with them. What's wrong wi' that?'

Miranda laughed. 'Nothing, you fool,' she said, 'so why be so secretive? Why not admit you write to Pete and actually rather like him? As you'd be the first to point out, liking someone is no sin.' As she spoke they had managed to find an unoccupied table and put their plates on it, so now they pulled up two chairs and sat down.

Avril shrugged. 'I dunno; I guess I just wanted to keep it to myself. That Pete and I are going to go steady when he comes home, I mean,' she said sulkily. 'I always swore I wouldn't get involved because it was just a pathway to pain, and so it is. I worry about Pete all the time, but I tell myself he means no more to me than the other fellers. You see, while I pretend he's not important . . . oh, I don't know, I can't explain. It's got something to do with the fact that I knew him before either of us had joined the RAF. I'm afraid I can't explain better than that, because I don't understand it myself. Only on my last balloon site we had this lovely flight sergeant. Gosh, she was beautiful, and tremendously efficient too. She'd been in the WAAF from the very beginning and a couple of months after she joined she got married to a tail gunner. He was killed six weeks after their wedding; she was devastated, but went on with the job. Her dead husband's best pal began to take her about. He was a fighter pilot trying to defend the troops when the Dunkirk evacuation began. He ditched and was presumed dead. After that she kept herself to herself for a couple of years, but then she had an affair with the boy next door who was a bomb aimer. He was killed over Cologne. Fellers started looking at her funny, and no one would take her out, though she was so beautiful! They thought she were a jinx, you see. Nothing's ever happened to none of my fellers, and I reckon that was because I didn't really love any of 'em. Only – only Pete is a bit different, so I won't risk him. He's no beauty – plain as a boot, in fact – but he means a lot to me. So he's stayin' under hatches until the war's over, understand?'

'Oh, poor Avril,' Miranda said softly. 'But I do understand, in a way. You thought you lost everything when Gary died and you're afraid of losing everything again. And I think I can imagine how that feels – even though my Steve is in England and I know he doesn't mean to worry me, some of the things he says keep me awake at nights. So don't think I don't sympathise, because I do.' She pushed her empty plate to one side as she spoke and stood up, fastened the buttons on her tunic and slapped her cap on her head. 'Are you coming to the NAAFI? And just think – there's one good thing about having your feller abroad: you don't have to join the queue for the telephone, which seems to get longer with every passing day!'

Chapter Fourteen

Miranda had become Group Captain Llewellyn's personal driver whenever he needed to be taken on a long journey, and these were happening rather frequently now, because Operation Overlord, which had started the previous June, meant a great many meetings of the top brass. Avril, on the other hand, drove whatever she was given – the blood wagon, the liberty truck, convoys carrying heavy weapons from one place to another – just about anything. Which was why, when the letter arrived, she was called in from her post as ambulance driver for the day to receive it.

Avril's forehead wrinkled into a frown. What had she done to receive an official letter? But the Waaf who had come to fetch her scowled up at her and jerked an impatient thumb. 'Come along, Donovan, you're wanted in Flight's office,' she said impatiently. 'Letters ain't always bad news . . . maybe it's a perishin' postin', or you're bein' made up to corporal, ha ha!'

But at the mere mention of a posting Avril jumped down from her seat in the ambulance and hared off across the grass to their flight officer's small room. She shot through the doorway, her heart hammering in her throat, but at a glance from the officer's chilly blue eyes she pulled herself together. She came stiffly to attention and saluted with such force that her right temple tingled.

Then she said, as coolly as she could, 'LACW Donovan reporting, ma'am.'

'Official letter, Donovan,' the flight officer said, and she must have seen the shock which Avril was trying so hard to hide, for she unbent a little. She handed it over, advising, as Avril's hand closed on the flimsy paper, 'Take it to your hut and read it in there. They won't miss you on the blood wagon for several hours yet. It passes my comprehension why we have to man the ambulance all through the day when our planes only attack by night.'

Avril could have told her; enemy planes did not work by the same rules as the British ones, which meant that the airfield could be attacked at any hour of day or night, but she realised that Flight Officer Adams was only making conversation to give her support, for she must have already guessed what the letter contained. So Avril answered accordingly. 'It's something we all query, ma'am,' she said, hoping her voice was not wobbling. She threw off another smart salute, turned with a click of her heels and strode out of the room.

She pushed open the door of their hut, glad to find it empty, and went over to her bed, slumping on to it and unfolding the sheet of paper. She found she was trembling so much that the words on the page blurred. For a moment she simply sat there, staring at the paper before her, then she took a deep breath and held it for a count of ten, releasing it slowly in a low whistle. She did this twice and then the words on the page were clear, could be calmly read.

Her eyes went first to the signature: a known name, occasionally mentioned in Pete's letters, and of course it said what she dreaded to hear, that Corporal Peter

Huxtable had not returned from a raid and was accordingly posted as missing. Since Corporal Huxtable had given her name as his next of kin it was his duty to inform her that Lancaster BT 308 had been shot down, but that the pilot of the aircraft following it in the formation had seen several parachutes open and thought that some of these had reached the ground safely.

Avril took another deep breath and expelled it even more slowly than she had the first. She thought of the dangers which Pete must face even if he had managed to get out of the plane; landing behind enemy lines in an area his aircraft had recently been bombing could mean that a trigger-happy air raid warden – if they had such things in Malaya – might blast off a round of deadly bullets without a moment's consideration. But on the other hand, there was that thing called the third Geneva convention . . .

The hut door burst open, stopping Avril's thoughts in mid-flow. The little Waaf who had instructed her to go to the flight officer came into the hut. Her face was pink, concerned, but Avril met her gaze blandly. 'In a hurry, Ellis? If you've come to find out what was in my letter . . .'

The other girl's face turned from pink to crimson and her eyes sparkled indignantly. 'Flight told me to make sure you were all right,' she said stiffly. 'But I can see there was no need for concern. God, you're a hard nut, Donovan; don't nothin' crack your shell?'

Avril made a great play of putting her letter away in her locker, so that the other girl could not see her face. When she was in full command once more, she swung round and spoke, her voice even and unemotional. 'Not while I've got nothing to moan about,' she said quietly. 'My feller's missing, but the aircraft behind his in the formation saw 'chutes opening. My feller will come out of it all right; he's like a cat, always lands on his feet.' She hesitated, then gave her fellow Waaf a tight little grin. 'But thanks for coming over, Mary; it were real good of you.'

Together the two girls left the hut and Avril began to chat of other things, the work in which she was engaged, the meal they would presently eat in the cookhouse and how she missed her best friend Lovage, who was now seldom on the airfield, but taking the top brass wherever it wanted to go. She missed her, of course she did, but Miranda would be back, probably before dark . . . The two girls chatted on, as though neither had a worry in the world.

Miranda had a perfectly dreadful day. Some senior officers were a positive joy to transport from one place to another, but Air Commodore Bailey was not one of them. He made no secret of the fact that he did not like women, did not trust women drivers and had no intention of placing his valuable life in the hands of someone he described as 'a chit of a girl'. In normal circumstances, therefore, Miranda would never have been told to drive the commodore, in his beautifully polished staff car, from the station he had been inspecting the previous day to what was described as an unknown destination in the north of England. But when the orderly officer went to wake the commodore's driver he found him writhing in his bed, sweat standing out on his forehead, obviously burning up with fever. The man had to be hospitalised at once, and within the hour was on the operating table having a burst appendix removed, and poor Miranda, looking forward to a quiet day for once, was given her new orders, reminded of the air commodore's feelings regarding women drivers and sent round to the Commodore's quarters to be given details of her destination.

Dismayed, for everyone knew Air Commodore Bailey, Miranda begged to be excused, suggesting that almost any man in the MT section might take her place. But men were at a premium and the officer who had given her her instructions raised a quizzical eyebrow. 'What do you mean, Lovage? Oh, I dare say he can be a bit difficult, and women don't like that, but I'm sure you'll charm the pants off him, if you'll forgive the expression. Just do your best and don't get lost, and we'll see you back here before dark.'

Not at this point knowing her eventual destination, Miranda could only assure the orderly officer that she would do her best, but when she read her instructions and realised she was going up to Northumberland she gave a soft whistle of dismay. She thought it extremely unlikely that she would be back at the airfield before dark, for the days were getting shorter and, though the main roads would probably be quite clear, if one came across a convoy heading in the same direction it could add hours to any journey.

However, orders were orders and Miranda nipped into the ablutions to damp her curly hair into submission, though it was cut short and little could be seen beneath her cap. Then she checked her appearance, which was as immaculate as a clothes brush and Brasso could make it, and she drove to the meeting point, where she had her first unpleasant experience of the day. The air commodore, deep in conversation with the group captain, crossed the concrete apron and paused to allow his driver to wriggle out from behind the wheel and come round to open the rear passenger door for him. He began to thank her, but then the words seemed to shrivel in his throat. 'What – what – what?' he barked. 'Where's Jones?' He put a hand out to rest on the roof of the car, but made no attempt to climb inside. Instead he swung round to face the group captain. 'I remember you telling me Jones had been carted off with a pain in his innards, but you never said . . .'

The group captain hastily cut across what he must have guessed would be an offensive sentence. 'LACW Lovage is one of the best drivers we have, so you'll be in good hands,' he said soothingly. 'She has her instructions and understands that you must reach Northumberland before the weapons trials can begin.' He turned to Miranda, still holding the passenger door open. 'You can get the air commodore to his destination without trouble, can't you, Aircraftwoman?'

'I'll do my best, sir,' Miranda said. 'So long as we don't find ourselves held up by a convoy or by closed roads . . . but I've got a map which the orderly officer assured me is up to date, so we'll hope for the best.'

The air commodore, a large man who probably weighed in at over fifteen stone, had climbed into the car and leaned back against the leather, but at her words he jerked forward, waving a sausage-like forefinger almost in her face. 'Hoping for the best is not good enough, young woman,' he growled. 'If one route is closed to us by heavy traffic or convoys we must find an alternative one.' He might have gone on at some length but Miranda closed the door smartly and got back behind the wheel. Giving her a wink, the groupie stood back and saluted smartly as Miranda put the big car into gear and drove forward, trying to take no notice of the muttered imprecations coming from the rear seat.

She had hoped that the air commodore might unbend when he realised the quality of her driving, but she hoped in vain. He criticised constantly, accused her of taking wrong turnings, complained if she drove too fast but disliked it even more when she had to slow to a crawl. He refused to leave the road for so much as a cup of coffee or what the troops called a 'comfort break', and by the time they reached the airfield where the trials were taking place Miranda was as tired as though she had driven to Scotland and back. However, she did not mean to let it show, and when the guards at the gate of their destination waved her down and examined her papers and those of her illustrious passenger she put a brave face on it. The guards told her where to go and said a trifle reproachfully that she was early, so the commodore would have to kill half an hour before a meal was served in the officers' Mess. Miranda could not help shooting a triumphant glance at her reluctant passenger as she drew to a halt and got out to open the rear door. 'There you are, sir, with thirty whole minutes in hand,' she said chirpily. 'I've been told to go to the Mess and await further instructions from you, but first I have to go to the cookhouse. I'm sure they'll find me bangers and mash, or a plateful of . . .' She stopped speaking as her passenger, ignoring her completely, marched stiff-backed into the officers' mess, slamming the door behind him with enough force to take it off its hinges.

'What a mean pig,' Miranda muttered. But some men were like that; if you proved you were as good at your job as a man, they resented you all the more. And this elderly air commodore was probably bursting for a pee – she was herself – and so had not dared to stop and throw even a word of thanks to the driver who had managed to get him to his destination with thirty minutes to spare.

Despite her hopes and everyone's expectations, however, the trials took longer than expected and it was full dark when the big car eased out of the tall gates once more and headed for the main road south. Miranda had managed to grab a second meal of sorts at the cookhouse as soon as she realised that they would not be leaving until much later than planned, and she supposed that someone must have fed her officer, so when he climbed into the car, smelling faintly of both food and alcohol, she hoped that his temper would be much improved. In her experience a man who has been well fed and watered was usually either chattier or more comatose as a result. After a mere couple of miles, a peep in the rear view mirror showed the air commodore comfortably settled in one corner of the long leather seat, eyes tightly closed, little bubbles of saliva coming from the corners of his mouth. Miranda could not help a little chuckle of pleasure escaping her. Thank God! If only he would sleep all the way to his quarters, how happy she would be. In order not to wake him she took extra care, and of course care was necessary due to the blackout, but even so she only took forty minutes longer on the return journey than she had going north.

As she drew up beside the administrative offices, she wondered for the first time how she should wake her passenger. She could imagine his rage if he realised she had known he was sleeping, had seen him dribbling – disgusting old man – on to the leather upholstery of the beautiful car. But the orderly officer, who had no doubt arranged the trip with considerable trepidation, must have been keeping a lookout for them, because he popped out of the offices like a jack-in-the-box, and when she tried to get out of her seat and go round to open the rear door he shook his head and put a finger to his lips. 'I'll wake him gently, but don't expect any thanks for your good driving,' he whispered. 'And as soon as he's awake and on his feet you'd best get rid of the car and see if the cookhouse can dream you up char and a wad, late though it is.' He patted her shoulder and even in the pale light she saw the flash of his teeth, white against tanned skin. 'Many thanks, LACW Lovage; I take it all went according to plan?'

Miranda nodded. 'Yes sir. We arrived early and left late,' she said cheerfully. She lowered her voice. 'I don't envy Corporal Jones, sir.' The orderly officer chuckled, but just at that moment there was a heaving and a muttering from the figure slumped on the rear seat and Miranda, quick to see the good sense of a speedy disappearance, only waited until her passenger was out of the car before making off without a backward glance.

She decided to see if Avril would accompany her to the cookhouse, for there are few things worse than sitting down to a plate full of lukewarm food, the only person in a great echoing room set with dozens of tables and chairs, all of them empty except one's own. Upon investigation, however, she discovered that there were only two girls in their hut, neither of them Avril. She emerged from the hut, closing the door softly behind her, and almost immediately came face to face with another Waaf. 'Hiya, Lovage,' the girl said cheerfully. 'Lookin' for your pal? She's gone to the NAAFI; said she'd wait up for you when you weren't in for a meal earlier.'

'Thanks. I hate eating alone in the cookhouse, so I'll get Avril to keep me company,' Miranda said. When she got to the NAAFI, however, expecting to find Avril the centre of a group, she saw her friend sitting alone at a small table, industriously scribbling. She had a mug of coffee before her but when Miranda got near enough she could see that the drink was cold by the skin on it, and the way Avril was hunched over the page upon which she was writing warned Miranda that something was up. She slid into the seat opposite and tapped the other girl's mug. 'You've let your drink go cold,' she said disapprovingly. 'What's happened?'

Avril said nothing but fished in her tunic pocket and handed the letter to Miranda, who read it at a glance and then whistled softly beneath her breath.

'Oh, Avril, poor old Pete! But missing doesn't necessarily mean . . .'

'I know, I know,' Avril said impatiently, 'I'm being sensible and telling myself it just means more waiting. He – he gave me as his next of kin, otherwise I really would be waiting, and wondering, too. But since his squadron leader says they saw chutes open, at least there's hope. Oh, Miranda, I wish I'd been more generous! To pretend he meant no more to me than the other fellers I'd gone with was just plain stupid, and now I'm payin' for it.' She gave her friend a watery grin. 'I'm writin' a letter to him now. I'm going to add a page or two each day and then, when he comes home – I suppose I should say *if* he comes home – he'll get a whole batch of news in one go. And I've started the letter by sayin' I won't go out with anyone else because he's the only feller that matters to me and always will be. Do you think I'm doin' the right thing?'

'Yes, of course you are,' Miranda said, keeping her inevitable reflections to herself. Avril loved dancing, the cinema and the company of young men. Miranda could appreciate her feelings, but doubted whether Avril would be able to stick to a nun-like existence. However, only time would tell, and right now her friend was undoubtedly sincere.

It was four whole months after the squadron leader's first letter telling her that Pete was missing before Avril got another letter, this time with Pete's familiar handwriting on the envelope. On their way to breakfast they had stopped off at the bulletin board in the Mess and Avril had taken down the letter, her heart hammering in her throat. Seeing Miranda's interest, she shook her head. 'It's probably been in the post for months, or stuck in the wrong pigeon hole, so I don't mean to get all excited,' she said. 'I won't wait till we reach the cookhouse, I'll read it now.'

She slit open the envelope with clumsy fingers and pulled out the printed sheet it contained. 'I told you it would be nothin',' she said bitterly. 'It's one of them forms . . . oh, my God, my God, my God!' And Avril, who never showed emotion, who had not cried even when Gary had been killed, or not publicly anyway, burst into tears.

'What is it? What is it?' Miranda asked agitatedly. 'Oh, Avril, I'm so sorry . . .'

Avril raised a tear-drenched face, her mouth beginning to form into a watery smile. 'He's a prisoner of war,' she said huskily. 'It's one of them standard letters giving his address and saying he has been in hospital but is out of it now, and he's scrawled on the bottom *Love you, Avril. Pete.*' Miranda was in the middle of telling her friend how happy she was when Avril gave a whoop and bounced across the Mess. 'I'm goin' to get that letter, the one I'd been writin' for the past four months,' she said jubilantly. 'It'll take him a month of Sundays to read it, but I'm sure he won't mind that. And I promised him that we'll get together just as soon as he's back in Britain.' She gave Miranda a defiant look. 'That means as Mr and Mrs Huxtable, even if we can't marry straight away, because I was a fool, and wasted the time we could have spent together.'

'Oh, Avril, I'm so happy for you, and I'm sure it won't be long before the war's over and Pete can come home,' Miranda said. She grinned wickedly at her friend. 'Does this mean you'll come to dances and start flirting again, the way you did before Pete went missing?'

Avril laughed with her but shook her head. 'No point,' she said. 'I'm a one man girl now, and it means just that. And now let's get to the cookhouse because I'm absolutely starving; no matter what rubbish they're handing out I'll eat every scrap.'

'How do I look?'

The war had been over for several months and Miranda

and Steve were alone in the living room of the small flat into which Avril and she had moved only the previous week, because despite Avril's brave words Pete had said that he would prefer to start their married life after the wedding rather than before it. This had made Avril go scarlet to the roots of her hair, whilst Miranda, who had been present at the time, had had to stifle a laugh.

Pete had returned from the POW camp thinner and sporting a black beard streaked with grey, and looking, for a moment, a dozen years older than the Pete she had known. Avril would have walked straight past him, and when he had grabbed her, accusing her of forgetting him, Avril, once so proud of never showing emotion, had wept bitterly. But the weeping had been of short duration, and the kissing and cuddling that followed had been quite sufficient to prove to Pete that, beard or no beard, he really was her dearest love.

Now, however, Miranda twirled until the skirt of her new-second-hand dress flew out, showing her petticoat, and Steve got up from the creaking sofa to grab her and give her a kiss whilst assuring her that she looked gorgeous; so pretty, in fact, that she would outshine the bride. Miranda smiled. She had seen Avril's dress and knew that though her own blue cotton was both fresh and attractive, it would be totally eclipsed by Avril's long white gown, borrowed from a theatrical costumiers for this special occasion.

She and Avril had decided that they would like a double wedding but this had been impossible since Pete's first action on arriving in Liverpool was to buy a special licence, something which neither Steve nor Miranda had even heard of before; they themselves would be married conventionally after the banns had been read three times in their local church, and they had arranged with Mrs Mickleborough to have a small reception at her home. It had never occurred to either Miranda or Avril that Pete owned other premises, as well as his cycle shop, in the city. They both knew of course that Pete was ten years older than Steve, and had not wasted those ten years. He had been not a spender but a saver, and before the war had gone in for property, so that now he had a comfortable sum in the bank just waiting, he told them, to be spent on a home for his wife to be.

Realising that a double wedding was out of the question, Miranda had thrown herself wholeheartedly into the preparations for her friend's great day. She had agreed to be a bridesmaid and had found a pretty dress on Paddy's Market, and she and Steve had put their gratuities together to buy a small kitchen table and two stools for the newly-weds, which had just about cleaned them out financially.

As soon as the wedding was over, Pete would move into the flat in which Miranda and Steve now waited, and the lack of somewhere of their own was the main reason why Miranda and Steve had still not settled on the wedding date. Because of the bombing every single room in Liverpool was bulging with occupants and as soon as a property came up for rent it was grabbed. When Miranda moved out of this flat she would have no option but to go back either to share with Aunt Vi or to accept a put-you-up in the Mickleboroughs' front parlour. She told herself it was unfair on Steve's mum to add yet another person to a house already bursting at the seams, but Steve assured her that his mother would take an extra non-paying lodger in her stride, especially if that person was willing to help in the house and even do a bit of cooking.

The door opening put an end to Miranda's thoughts and she beamed as Avril bounced into the room. She had always been a big, tall girl, but dressed in dazzling white satin with a wreath of lilies of the valley crowning her smooth flaxen head she looked like a princess, Miranda thought. Steve wolf-whistled, his eyes rounding. 'Avril Donovan, you look fantastic!' he breathed. 'Wait till Pete sees you; he'll be over the moon to think you're his and his alone. Can I kiss the bride? 'Cos I am acting father of the bride, after all.'

Avril curtsied. 'Ta very much; I thought I looked good, but now I'm sure of it,' she said. 'You ain't one to pay compliments you don't mean, old Steve. But just remember this 'ere bridal gown is the very same one what Miranda will be wearing in a few weeks, so just you keep your kisses for her, young feller.'

Miranda was about to make a joking remark when something occurred to her and she clapped a hand to her mouth. 'The bridegroom isn't supposed to see the bride before the wedding, because he won't be so astonished at how lovely she looks in the dress,' she said. 'Oh, hell, does that mean, if I wear that dress, we'll have bad luck?'

'No, of course not . . .' Steve began, but Avril interrupted.

'You're mad, you. It ain't the dress, it's the woman,' she explained. 'It's something to do with ancient times, when they rigged some girl up in wedding finery with a real thick veil in front of her face, and passed her off as the bride, or so I've heard tell. So you needn't worry, Steve – oh, heavens, where's me perishin' veil? Miranda Lovage, you're supposed to be helping me to get ready, and you never even noticed I'd not got me veil on yet.'

Miranda shot out of the room, fetched the veil and draped it elegantly over her friend's coronet of the tiny sweet-smelling flowers. She stepped back to admire the effect just as a taxi drew up in the street below, and sounded a toot-toot-ti-toot-toot on his horn.

Both girls squeaked and headed for the stairs whilst Steve, following, told them that they had plenty of time and reminded Avril that if she didn't pick up her skirts she would soil them on the piles of wet snow left over from the storm a week before.

The three of them bundled into the taxi and Avril grabbed Miranda's hand. 'I hope I'm doin' the right thing,' she muttered. 'I hope Pete is, for that matter. We've been apart for so long that sometimes he seems like a stranger. Partly it's the beard, but I can't expect him to shave it off just because it makes him look so different. Besides, I know he's rather proud of it.'

Miranda patted the hand which clutched her own. 'You're both doing the right thing,' she said gently. 'It's the same thing that Steve and I will be doing in a few weeks, and we have no doubts, do we, Steve?'

Steve pretended to frown and consider, but just then the taxi drew up outside the church and in his role as surrogate father of the bride he had to be first out so that he could accompany Avril to where Pete awaited her at the top of the church.

Avril tucked her hand into Steve's arm as they reached

the porch, and glanced behind her as her friend adjusted her train. Her veil was down but it was a frail and beautiful affair through which she could see quite easily. She smiled her thanks, and then the organ music swelled and they began to process up the aisle. She was clutching Steve's arm so hard that she saw him wince, but then he was pushing her gently towards her waiting bridegroom, and the three of them stood, shoulder to shoulder, as the priest began the wedding service.

Avril clutched her bouquet nervously. The sonorous words rang out. 'Dearly beloved, we are gathered together here in the sight of God, and in the face of this congregation, to join together this man and this woman in holy matrimony; which is an honourable estate . . .'

Avril had been staring straight ahead of her, waiting for her heart to stop beating so fast, knowing that the time was about to come when she would have to speak, and speak calmly what was more. For the first time, she risked a glance at Pete, standing so still and straight beside her, and a squeak of surprise emerged from her lips, just as the priest said, 'First, it was ordained for the procreation of children, to be brought up in the fear and nurture of the Lord . . .' He paused, but when Avril said nothing more he continued with the service whilst Avril caught Pete's hand and squeezed it convulsively. The black beard, of which she knew Pete was secretly proud, had disappeared, and above the clean lines of jaw and chin she saw the love in the eyes he fixed upon her. Avril smiled at him; her heart was dancing with joy. At that moment she knew without any doubt that she and Pete were about to set out on a journey together, and that, whatever might befall them, their happiness was assured.

Chapter Fifteen

Miranda woke early, because her feet were cold. For a moment she just lay there, staring at the ceiling above her head and wondering where on earth she was. Not in the Nissen hut with fellow Waafs all around her; not in the Mickleboroughs' crowded, happy house in Jamaica Close . . .

Then someone sighed gustily almost in her ear, a warm hand stole across her waist, and memory returned with a rush. She was in the Elms private hotel, the wandering hand belonged to Steve, her brand new husband, and the pair of them were having the only honeymoon they could afford before moving into the little rooms above the village butcher's shop.

Turning her head very carefully on the pillow, Miranda stared intently but lovingly at Steve's unconscious face. He wasn't handsome, but there was something sweet in the curve of his lips, and today, she remembered, something very exciting was going to happen, or so she and Steve hoped. Her very best chance of finding her mother would be between nine and ten o'clock at the Pier Head and she meant to be there in good time, come hell or high water.

She and Steve had learned about it by chance, when Steve had met an old pal from the air force, who had been rear gunner in his Lancaster. Miranda had been at work, for the solicitors had been happy to give her her old job back, so Steve and Tony had gone into the nearest pub to tell each other how the peace was treating them.

Now, Miranda imagined the scene about which Steve had told her when he met her out of the office. He had told his pal, a journalist with the *Echo* once more, how he and Miranda had married only the previous day, and in describing his wife he had added the information that Miranda was the daughter of the missing actress from the Madison Players. Tony, who had covered the original story for his newspaper, had been very interested, especially when Steve mentioned the newsreel in which Miranda had been certain her mother had appeared, and the fact that Lynette Rich, also a former Madison Player, had told them that Arabella had taken part in a revue put on for the Americans by actors and actresses from the USA.

'Well now, it's lucky you met me,' Tony had said, producing a card from his raincoat pocket. 'The Yanks who've been entertaining their troops are leaving the country in a couple of days and congregating at the Pier Head first for what they describe as a farewell photo shoot.' He pressed the card into Steve's hand. 'Tell your wife to hang on to your arm and show this to anyone who tries to stop you getting near the performers. It's my press card, but I shan't be covering that particular event, and if your wife spots her mother she'll be able to approach her.' He had looked doubtfully at Steve. 'Or do you think it's best to let sleeping dogs lie? After all, it's been a long time since Arabella Lovage disappeared. It just doesn't seem possible that she wouldn't contact her daughter . . . but I leave it up to you. Tell her and risk disappointment or keep it to yourself. The choice is yours.'

Lying now, almost nose to nose with Steve in the creaky old double bed, Miranda was devoutly thankful that Steve had decided to tell her everything, though he had warned her that her hopes would probably be dashed. 'Tony pointed out that if Arabella is alive she would surely have made some effort to get in touch,' he had said. 'But now I've told you, and as Tony said the choice is yours. Go down to the Pier Head and see if you recognise anyone, or forget all about it.'

And I made my choice without a second's hesitation, Miranda remembered. As it said in the marriage service, *for better for worse, for richer for poorer, in sickness and in health*. She would never forget Arabella, and to pass up the chance of flying into her mother's arms and hearing her story would be to forego everything she'd ever dreamed of.

So when Steve had suggested spending a couple of nights at a small hotel in the city centre before moving into the flat she had agreed eagerly. It might not be much of a honeymoon but it was all they could afford and the Elms was only a short walk from the Pier Head.

Miranda dangled one foot out of bed until it got quite cold, then pulled it back in and planted it squarely on Steve's warm body. He groaned, then turned and seized her, proving, Miranda thought, that he had been awake all along. 'Morning, beautiful!' he said, whispering straight into her ear because it seemed no one but themselves was yet stirring. 'Ready for your great day? I've booked us in for eight o'clock breakfast; what's the time now?'

Miranda reached out a lazy hand and picked up her wrist watch, lying on the bedside table. 'Ten to seven,' she announced. 'There's no point in getting up yet; the staff won't even have started their own breakfast, let alone ours.'

She snuggled down again as she spoke, trying to pull Steve down with her, but he resisted, capturing her wrists and holding them firmly. 'If we get up now we'll be first in the bathroom,' he said. 'There was a rush for it yesterday, because most of the people staying here are sales reps or office workers, and they want to be up and away by nine o'clock.'

As he spoke he scrambled out of bed, accidentally kneeling on Miranda's toes and causing her to exclaim: 'Ouch! I'll get you for that, Steve Mickleborough!' She aimed a punch at him, but he dodged, then crossed the room and reached out to where their dressing gowns hung on the back of the door.

'Better put 'em on in case the old feller in the room next door is on the prowl,' he observed. 'Go quietly, or that chap with the huge moustache will complain that he wants his room moved again, because we make more noise than all the trains arriving and departing at Lime Street Station.'

'If he does, I'll tell him that it's my husband who whistles and sings the minute the bathroom door is locked,' Miranda said. 'Oh, Steve, I can't wait till we're in our own little place, with no one listening to our every move. But even here, even on your mam's living room couch, being married is the best thing that ever happened to me. I wish we'd done it sooner.' She had been whispering as they glided softly up the corridor and let themselves into the bathroom. She looked around for the box of matches, pounced on them, and as Steve turned the gas tap on the geyser held the flame through the small aperture and blew out her cheeks in a breath of relief as it caught. 'First go off,' she said triumphantly. 'Naturally I learn how to do it properly on our last day! Fill the jug, there's a dear. That woman made it pretty plain that baths were only allowed between six and ten in the evening, so a good wash will have to suffice.'

Presently, washed, brushed and with their shared sponge bag clutched in Miranda's hand, Miranda and Steve left the bathroom. They mumbled an awkward 'Good morning' to the short queue of would-be occupants standing patiently in the corridor, and received various grunts in reply. In their own room once more, Steve consulted his watch and then put both arms around Miranda as she shed her dressing gown and reached for her clothes. 'God, you're gorgeous,' he mumbled. 'It won't be breakfast time for ages, so how about a bit of smooching? There's time, honest to God there is.'

'No there isn't, because I mean to look my best so that if we do meet Arabella she'll be proud of me,' Miranda said. 'And unlike my mother I'm not a star of the stage, so it will take me quite a while to get ready.'

Steve laughed and gave her a quick kiss on the cheek, then turned to his neatly piled clothing and began to dress. 'Don't forget we've got to put our suitcases in the left luggage at the bus depot,' he reminded her. 'And before that there's breakfast and paying our bill, and afterwards we have to walk down to the Pier Head.'

Miranda pouted. 'All right, all right, I'm doing my

best,' she said. 'Shall I wear the blue blouse or the pink one? Only I've already packed the blue one . . .'

'Shut up and get a move on,' Steve said severely. 'Are you ready? Then let's go and get breakfast eaten, and mind you eat lots because you won't get anything else until later on this evening, when we go to Mam's for our share of the big pan of scouse she's preparing.'

Miranda promised to eat up, but in fact most things were still on ration or unobtainable, and though the recently introduced bread ration was quite generous Mrs Ada of the Elms was not. She watched her guests with an eagle eye, and though more than one cup of tea was allowed it grew weaker and weaker with every cup, and Steve had made Miranda laugh the previous day by declaring that the old skinflint dried out the tea leaves given to her guests on a Monday and made tea – or something vaguely resembling tea – with those same leaves on a Tuesday.

Accordingly, breakfast was not a lengthy meal and by half past eight they had handed over the key to their room, paid their bill – checking it carefully first – and set off for the bus depot, where they left their suitcases and accepted in their place two green tickets so that they might reclaim their property later.

Despite the fact that it was sunny there was a distinct nip in the air and Miranda was glad of her old winter coat, particularly as the breeze always seemed to get stronger when one neared the docks. But today the blue sky gave an illusion of summer, and the faces of folk going about their business, though pale and war-weary, were smiling as if in anticipation of the good weather to come.

They reached the Pier Head and Miranda clutched Steve's arm tightly. She was dressed in her best and even though her green suit and pink blouse had both come from Paddy's Market she thought she looked both neat and smart. Despite the cold wind she had cast off her overcoat, which was old and patched, and Steve held it over his arm while she turned an anxious face to his. 'Is my hat on straight?' she asked. 'Is my hair tidy? Oh, I'm sure my nose must be blue with the cold. Will Arabella recognise me, do you suppose? If she does, should I run up to her and give her a big hug? But what if she doesn't? What if I run towards her and she just stands there, staring; what do I do then? Oh, darling Steve, I'm scared stiff; I almost wish I'd never come.' She tugged at his arm, and began to turn away just as a large cream-coloured coach drew up in front of them, closely followed by another. Even as they watched the doors of both coaches opened, and a great many beautiful, excited people poured out and began to take up their positions at the foot of the gangway belonging to the ship upon which they were about to embark.

Miranda and Steve both watched, fascinated, as a tall, handsome man in his forties began to try to calm the excited babble, and to arrange both the actors and actresses themselves and those members of the press wielding cameras into some sort of order.

Miranda stared. There was no thought, now, of turning to flee. As the cameras clicked and whirred her gaze went from face to face, trying to find the one she remembered from long ago. If only her mother had had some clearly visible imperfection, but Arabella's skin had always been pale and flawless, and anyway without exception all the women who had got off the coach were heavily made up.

Miranda was still scanning every fair-haired woman when Steve bent and whispered in her ear. 'See anyone you know, queen? I can't help you much, 'cos all I really know is that your mam was beautiful and very very blonde. There are one or two brunettes amongst the line-up but mostly they're blondes.'

Miranda snorted. 'Bottle blondes, that's what they are,' she said scornfully. 'Arabella despised bottle blondes. But oh, Steve, if only they wouldn't keep moving about! I no sooner begin to examine one face than its owner flicks round and turns her back on me. I wish someone would tell them . . .'

As though on cue the tall man took off his dark glasses and pinched the bridge of his nose before beginning to speak. 'Settle down, people; give the good gentlemen of the press a chance to see how us Yankees can behave ourselves. We'll have small girls in the front in a crescent and the rest of you fall in behind, whilst I fetch the star of the show from . . . ah, here she comes.'

All eyes turned to the last coach. A tall and very beautiful woman in a cream dress which clung to every curve of her slender body descended from the vehicle and appeared to drift across to where the man awaited her. She murmured something to him then turned to face the battery of cameras, and even as she gave her audience the benefit of a dazzling smile the wind tore off the tiny hat perched on her head and sent it flying towards the Mersey, whilst the great mass of her hair, released from its many pins, descended in a whirling cloud of primrose around her shoulders. The cameramen moved forward eagerly as the woman turned, pointing desperately to the neat little hat, but though there was not a man present who would not have dived into the Mersey had it been possible to catch it there was not a hope in hell of doing so, Miranda saw. The hat was gone, the lady was laughing and protesting, Miranda presumed she was saying words to the effect that she had other hats, and the tall man was putting his arm round her, drawing her close, kissing the top of that glorious primrose head.

'Is it her?' Steve was saying anxiously. 'Is it your mam, sweetheart? Don't tell me *she's* a bottle blonde, because I wouldn't believe you. Oh, damn, they're going for another photo shoot. But it'll be over in a few minutes; the captain has come to the top of the gangway to welcome his passengers aboard. Then you can nab her . . .'

But his voice was almost drowned by the eager shouts of cameramen and journalists. 'Show a leg, ladies! Do a bit of a dance for us! That's right, lass, hold out your arms as though you wanted to embrace the whole of Liverpool . . .' Someone else shouted: 'The whole of England, you mean,' and there was laughter and much bustling to and fro as the cine cameras – there were two of them – trundled across the uneven paving to snatch views of the Americans leaving Britain which would appear, Miranda guessed, in newsreels all over the world.

Then the cameramen moved back, allowing the journalists their turn, and men with notebooks began to converge on the company. The biggest crowd was around that wonderful primrose hair, and Steve took his wife's hand. 'We've got our press pass, remember,' he whispered. 'You can ask her anything you like, only it will have to be you, because she's your mother, or you think she is. Is that right?' The crowd was beginning to thin as the men and women from the concert parties headed for the gangway. But still the man in dark glasses and the woman within the circle of his arm remained. Clearly they were the most important members of the group, and intended to shepherd their flock aboard before embarking themselves. Steve tugged on Miranda's hand, meaning to lead her up to the man and woman now standing at the foot of the gangway, but Miranda shook herself free.

'You stay here please, Steve,' she whispered. 'This is something I've got to do alone.'

Steve watched the small, straight-backed figure in the green suit and the perky little hat approach the couple, who smiled graciously. Then the woman turned to her companion and he handed her something which looked like a notepad, and a pencil. She scribbled something and gave the sheet of paper to Miranda, who promptly turned round and re-joined Steve. She was very pink, and there were tears in her eyes, but when Steve asked her what had happened she would only shake her head.

When the couple had climbed the gangway they leaned on the rail, watching as preparations for departure were carried out by smartly uniformed sailors. Steve put his arm round Miranda, bent his head and kissed the side of her neck. 'Want to leave?' he asked, but she shook her head. So they stood there, almost alone on the quayside now, and Miranda gave a little wave just as the couple on board the liner turned away, and watched in silence until the ship was out of sight.

'Are you disappointed, darling?' Steve asked anxiously,

as he and Miranda began to walk slowly back the way they had come. 'I really thought it must be your mother, because of her wonderful hair. What did she give you, by the way? I saw her hand you something that looked like a piece of paper . . .'

'It was; she thought I wanted her autograph,' Miranda said bitterly. 'Oh, Steve, when my eyes met hers, when she looked at me as though she had never seen me in her life before, I could have wept. She's married to that man, you know, the one wearing dark glasses. I heard one of the chorus telling a reporter that she was Mrs Salvatore, though that isn't her stage name. He's an – an impresario and they're very wealthy and extremely happy. She's the leading lady in all his productions . . .'

'But *not* your mother,' Steve said with a chuckle. 'Oh, sweetheart, I'm so very sorry to have raised your hopes for nothing. But it was worth a try, wouldn't you say? If you'd not had the chance to discover for yourself . . .'

Miranda pulled him to a halt and turned to gaze at him, round-eyed. 'Are you mad, Steve Mickleborough?' she said. 'Of course she was my mother! We've wondered many times if she might have lost her memory, and now I'm sure that must be what happened. She looked at me so coolly, with not a trace of interest. And if I'd told her who I was – and who she was – I'd also have had to tell her that she was once a second-rate actress in a second-rate rep company, about to marry a man she didn't love just to settle all her debts and keep her head above water. Oh, Steve, it would've been the wickedest, cruellest thing! As Mrs Salvatore and her husband's leading lady she has a wonderful life, and that, after all, was what I wanted to find out. I always said that if I could know she was alive and happy I'd be content.' She looked up at Steve and saw his face wreathed in a grin, and hid the tiny stab of pain in her own heart. 'So I'm afraid you can't claim to have married the daughter of a star after all, just plain little Miranda Lovage . . .'

'. . . who is now Miranda Mickleborough,' Steve said contentedly. 'And you've done the right thing. You must know, queen, that you're quite old enough to manage very well without a mother. Most girls have left home and family by the time they're twenty-one. In fact you should be more interested in having a daughter of your own, and I'll help you do just that. So let's go and collect our suitcases and go back to the village to claim our rooms.' They were beginning to walk back towards the main road once more when Steve suddenly remembered something. 'Did you ask her for her autograph . . . no, of course you didn't, she just gave it to you. I wonder if she signed Salvatore or her stage name? Let's have a look.' Miranda delved into her pocket and produced the sheet of paper. Scrawled across it was one word.

Steve stared. 'Miranda; she signed it Miranda,' he said in an awed voice. 'Did you tell her your name, queen?'

Miranda shook her head. 'I didn't say a word, but of course it's not really odd,' she said in a low voice. 'She called me Miranda because she had always loved the name, she told me so many times.' She heaved a sigh, then took the paper from Steve and was about to push it back into her pocket when she changed her mind. Very slowly and deliberately she tore the page into tiny fragments, then opened her hand and let the wind take them. Like a cloud of confetti the tiny pieces were caught in the breeze and carried in the wake of the great liner, already, no doubt, settling into its voyage towards America, and suddenly it seemed like a message, a portent almost, to Miranda. She watched the 'confetti', blue as her mother's forget-me-not eyes, as it curtsied and cavorted higher and higher in the blue sky, and suddenly she knew she had done the right thing. It was important, she reminded herself, to let go, and unwise to cling, whether to your grown-up child or your mother. Furthermore, if at any time in the future she decided she should contact Arabella, she now had her married name, and her stage name, too.

Hand in hand, the young couple watched until the last scrap of paper disappeared, then turned and began to walk up the slope once more. We're leaving the past behind us and doing the right thing, the kind thing, Miranda told herself contentedly. After all, she had had her mother's love for the most important years of her growing up, and now, bless him, she had Steve's. She squeezed his hand and began to sing beneath her breath, so that only Steve could hear.

For this time it isn't fascination,
Or a dream that will fade and fall apart,
It's love, this time it's love, my foolish heart.

Steve returned the pressure of her hand and she saw that his eyes were wet, but he grinned at her and gave her a little push. 'Race you to the main road,' he said. 'Oh, darling Miranda, I love you, too!'

ALSO AVAILABLE IN ARROW

A Sixpenny Christmas

Katie Flynn

As the worst storm of the century sweeps through the mountains of Snowdonia and across the Mersey, two women, Molly and Ellen, give birth to girls in a Liverpool maternity hospital.

Molly and Rhys Roberts farm sheep in Snowdonia and Ellen is married to a docker, Sam O'Mara, but despite their different backgrounds the two young women become firm friends, though Molly has a secret she can share with no one.

But despite promises Ellen's husband continues to be violent, so she throws him out and years later, when Molly is taken to hospital after an accident, Ellen and her daughter Lana are free to help out. They approach this new life with enthusiasm, unaware that they are being watched, but on the very day of Molly's release from hospital there is another terrible thunderstorm and the hidden watcher makes his move at last . . .

ALSO AVAILABLE IN ARROW

The Runaway

Katie Flynn

When Dana and Caitlin meet by chance on the ferry from Ireland, they tell each other that they are simply going to search for work, but they soon realise they have more than that in common. They are both in search of new lives in Liverpool, leaving their secrets behind in Ireland. But Dana is ambitious and resourceful, and when the opportunity comes to own their own tearoom she persuades her friend to join her.

No one is willing to rent property to a couple of girls, however, especially during the Depression. So when Caitlin's new man friend says he'll back them, they are delighted and soon the tearoom is thriving.

Then fate intervenes, and soon the girls find themselves fighting to survive in a world on the brink of war.

arrow books

ALSO AVAILABLE IN ARROW

The Lost Days of Summer

Katie Flynn

Nell Whitaker is fifteen when war breaks out and, despite her protests, her mother sends her to live with her Auntie Kath on a remote farm in Anglesey. Life on the farm is hard, and Nell is lonely after living in the busy heart of Liverpool all her life. Only her friendship with young farmhand Bryn makes life bearable. But when he leaves to join the merchant navy, Nell is alone again, with only the promise of his return to keep her spirits up.

But Bryn's ship is sunk, and Bryn is reported drowned, leaving Nell heartbroken. Determined to bury her grief in hard work, Nell finds herself growing closer to Auntie Kath, whose harsh attitude hides a kind heart. Despite their new closeness, however, she dare not question her aunt about the mysterious photograph of a young soldier she discovers in the attic.

As time passes, the women learn to help each other through the rigours of war. And when Nell meets Bryn's friend Hywel, she begins to believe that she, too, may find love . . .

arrow books

Time Out Florence & Tuscany

Penguin Books

PENGUIN BOOKS

Published by the Penguin Group
Penguin Books Ltd, 27 Wrights Lane, London W8 5TZ, England
Penguin Putnam Inc., 375 Hudson Street, New York, New York 10014, USA
Penguin Books Australia Ltd, Ringwood, Victoria, Australia
Penguin Books Canada Ltd, 10 Alcorn Avenue, Toronto, Ontario, Canada M4V 3B2
Penguin Books (NZ) Ltd, 182-190 Wairau Road, Auckland, New Zealand

Penguin Books Ltd, Registered offices: Harmondsworth, Middlesex, England

First published 1998. Second edition 1999
10 9 8 7 6 5 4 3 2 1

Colour reprographics by Precise Litho, 34–35 Great Sutton Street, London EC1
Printed and bound by William Clowes Ltd, Beccles, Suffolk NR34 9QE

Edited and designed by
Time Out Guides Limited
Universal House
251 Tottenham Court Road
London W1P 0AB
Tel + 44 (0)171 813 3000
Fax + 44 (0)171 813 6001
Email guides@timeout.com
www.timeout.com

Editorial
Editorial Director Peter Fiennes
Editor Kevin Ebbutt
Deputy Editor Angela Jameson
Consultant Editor Nicky Swallow
Proofreader Marion Moisy
Indexer Jackie Brind

Design
Art Director John Oakey
Art Editor Mandy Martin
Senior Designer Scott Moore
Designers Benjamin de Lotz, Lucy Grant, Paul Mansfield
Picture Editor Kerri Miles
Picture Researcher Kit Burnet
Scanning & Imaging Chris Quinn

Advertising
Group Advertisement Director Lesley Gill
Sales Director Mark Phillips
International Sales Manager Mary L Rega
Advertisement Sales (Florence) Margherita Tedone, Sara De Martini
Advertising Assistant Ingrid Sigerson

Administration
Publisher Tony Elliott
Managing Director Mike Hardwick
Financial Director Kevin Ellis
Marketing Director Gillian Auld
General Manager Nichola Coulthard
Production Manager Mark Lamond
Accountant Bridget Carter

Features in this guide were written and researched by:
Introduction Kevin Ebbutt. **Tuscany by Season** Nicky Swallow. **History** Jonathan Cox, Mathew Spender, Glenn Haybittle, Ann Witheridge. **Florence Today** Glenn Haybittle. **Architecture** Richard Freemantle, Magda Nabb. **Sightseeing** Ros Belford, Dan Duffett, Magda Nabb, Ann Witheridge. **Museums & Galleries** Ros Belford, Dan Duffett. **Accommodation** Nicky Swallow. **Restaurants** Nicky Swallow. **Wine bars** Nicky Swallow. **Cafés & Bars** Dan Duffett, Danielle Caplan, Crimson Boner, April Rinne, Alessio Olivieri. **Shopping & Services** Nicky Swallow. Ros Belford, April Rinne. **Children** Elena Brizio. **Film** Elena Brizio, Lee Marshall, Alexandra Solomon. **Gay & Lesbian** Elena Biagini, Davide di Cosimo. **Media** Elena Brizio. **Music: Classical & Opera** Nicky Swallow. **Music: Rock, Roots & Jazz** Glenn Haybittle, Crimson Boner, Danielle Caplan. **Nightlife** Dan Duffett, Kevin Ebbutt, Glenn Haybittle, Crimson Boner, Danielle Caplan, Alessio Olivieri. **Theatre & Dance** Nicky Swallow. **Sport & Fitness** Dan Duffett, Kevin Ebbutt, April Rinne, Paul Blanchard. **Tuscany** Marco Bianchini. **Tuscan wines** Mathew McAuliffe, Gillian Arthur. **Food in Tuscany** Kate Singleton, Kate Carlisle, Monica Larner. **Around Florence** Kate Carlisle, Kate Singleton. **Pisa & Livorno** Kate Carlisle, Claudia Clemente. **Chianti & Siena Province** Monica Larner, Lee Marshall. **Siena** Monica Larner, Kate Singleton, Cosima Spender. **Massa-Carrara & Lucca Provinces** Monica Larner, Ros Belford, Lee Marshall. **Lucca** Marco Bianchini, Jonathan Cox. **Arezzo Province** Marco Bianchini, Kate Singleton. **Arezzo** Marco Bianchini, Kate Singleton. **Grosseto & South Tuscany** Kate Carlisle, Richard Freemantle, Lee Marshall. **Directory** Nicky Swallow, Dan Duffett, Glenn Haybittle.

The Editor would like to thank the following:
Giusi Contino & Emily, Massimo 'he knows his chickens' Borsini & Christina Guarducci, the Lazio girls and Roma boys (particularly Stefano), Lynn Levine, Rosa Spatola, Sarah Dallas, PJ Cresswell, Mathew Ballard, Lorien Mowat. The Editor travelled to Tuscany courtesy of Italian Connection.

Maps by JS Graphics, 17 Beadles Lane, Old Oxted, Surrey RH8 9JG.

Photography by Monica Larner except for: pages 5, 145, 148, 153, 161, 165 and 166 **Gianluca Moggi**; page 10 **AP Photos/Pietro Cinotti**; pages 13, 17, 21, 23, 24, 27 and 30 **Hulton Getty**; pages 18, 22, 26 (left) and 71 **AKG London**; pages 19, 26 right and 227 **Mary Evans Picture Library**; page 28 **The trustees of The Imperial War Museum**; pages 12 and 31 **Camera Press**; page 66 courtesy of **The Italian State Tourist Board** (ENIT) London; page 69 **Opera Museo Stibbert**; page 74 **Instituto E Museo Di Storia Della Scienza**; page 76 **Museo Ferragamo**; pages 87, 89, 91 and 93 **Mark Read**; page 138 **Merchant Ivory Productions**; page 139 **Renaissance Films**; page 150 **Lucia Baldini**. Thanks to **Danny Chau Photolabs** for black and white prints.

Contents

About the Guide

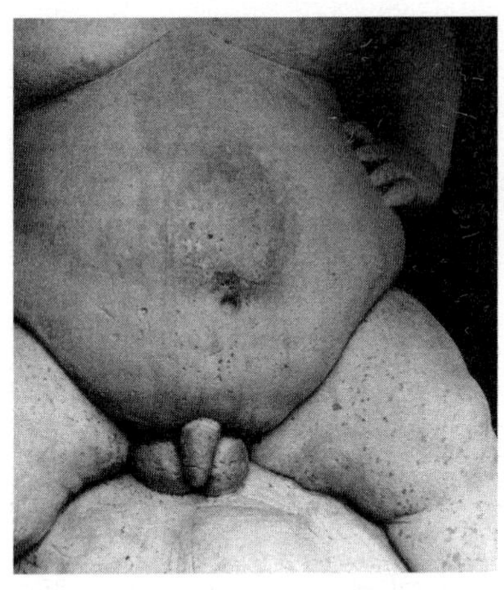

This second edition of the *Time Out Florence & Tuscany Guide* has been written by a team of Tuscany-based writers. It is one in a series of 24 city guides that includes Rome, London, Berlin, New York, Madrid, Budapest, Sydney and Venice.

Checked & correct

As far as possible, all the information in this guide was checked and correct at time of writing. However, Tuscan owners and managers can be highly erratic in their answers to questions about opening times, the dates of exhibitions, admission fees and even their address and telephone number. It's always best to phone before visiting.

Prices

The prices listed throughout the guide should be used as guidelines. Fluctuating exchange rates and inflation can cause prices, in shops and restaurants especially, to change rapidly. If prices or services somewhere vary greatly from those we have quoted, ask if there's a good reason. If not, go elsewhere and then please let us know. We try to give the best and most up-to-date advice, so we always want to hear if you've been overcharged or badly treated.

Credit Cards

Throughout the guide, the following abbreviations have been used for credit cards: **AmEx** American Express; **DC** Diners' Club; **JCB** Japanese credit card; **MC** Mastercard/Access; **V** Visa/Barclaycard.

Bold

Where we mention people, places or events that are listed elsewhere in the guide, or in detail later in the chapter, they are usually **highlighted in bold** – this means you'll find them in the index.

Buses

For places beyond Florence's *centro storico*, we have listed bus routes that serve that destination. Because the city is small and easy to negotiate on foot, we have not given bus numbers when the destination is in the city centre.

Street numbering

The street numbering in Florence is a little odd, jumping from 21 to 47 and then back to 23. There are two concurrent numbering systems, one in red (*rosso*) and the other in blue and black (*nero*). When you ask for an address, or are giving instructions to a cab driver, it is important to specify whether the number is rosso or nero, as there may be two number 21s in the same street, but a long way apart. All rosso numbers are commercial properties (although not all commercial properties have a red number) and the nero numbers tend to be residential. Red numbers are followed by a letter 'r', as you will see throughout this guide.

Telephones

At the end of 1998, the Italian telephone system changed – you must now always include an area code on dialling. If you are in Florence and wish to dial a Florence number, you have to dial 055 followed by the number.

Right to reply

It should be stressed that in all cases the information we give is impartial. No organisation or enterprise has been included in this guide because its owner or manager has advertised in our publications. We hope you enjoy the *Time Out Florence & Tuscany Guide*, but if you disagree with any of our reviews, let us know. Your comments on places you have visited are always welcome and will be taken into account when compiling the future editions of the guide. For this purpose, you will find a reader's reply card at the back of the book.

There is an online version of this guide, as well as weekly events listings for several international cities, at http://www.timeout.com

Introduction

In Santa Croce with no Baedeker.

'Tut, tut! Miss Lucy! I hope we shall soon emancipate you from Baedeker. He does but touch the surface of things. As to the true Italy – he does not even dream of it. The true Italy is only to be found by patient observation.'

This is how Miss Lavish scolds Lucy Honeychurch as they prepare for a day of Florentine sightseeing in chapter two of EM Forster's brilliant *A Room With a View.* And she's right – not about whether Baedeker only touches the surface of things, but how to find the true Italy, or, in our case, Florence and Tuscany.

I wouldn't want to discourage the reader at such an early stage in the guide book from reading on, as inside are plenty of facts, insights and observations (and where to find the best rooms with a view) to enrich your visit.

But, as is the case the world over, to find the true spirit of Florence a little patient observation is in order. Too much rushing around trying to soak in all the Renaissance heritage may leave you with a nasty case of Stendhal Syndrome – the symptoms of which are the dizziness and disorientation first described by the French novelist after he became physically ill as a reaction to the overwhelming beauty of Florence.

Tuscany is a magnet for mass tourism. People from all over the world come in huge numbers every year to see the postcard-perfect views of the rolling hills, to sup on classic Chiantis and feast on perfect pasta, but, above all, to see the artistic and architectural treasures of the Renaissance. The danger all our Tuscan team have faced in writing about these 'wonders' is slipping into cliché. But it is difficult, mainly because the clichés have become clichés because they are true.

What particularly interested me at the outset of this guide was what had happened to the Renaissance spirit. Characteristics of the Renaissance are usually considered to include intensified classical scholarship, scientific and geographical discovery, a sense of individual potentialities and the assertion of the active and secular over the religious and contemplative life, according to the *Collins English Dictionary*. Is this spirit alive today? Are the Tuscans still carrying the Renaissance torch, or are they overshadowed and inhibited in the way the children of the famous sometimes are?

A trip to the belly of the Renaissance beast, the Uffizi, left me feeling peculiarly empty, not dizzy.

During my time in Tuscany it was simple sensory pleasures that sent shivers down my spine: soaking in the steaming thermal waters of Bagno Vignoni watching the sunset; chomping on *cinghiale* and supping a glass of Chianti in the street at lunch-time in Florence; editing the guide on a laptop outside a farmhouse at the top of one of Chianti's hills when the light was just stupendous. But these experiences weren't encounters with the Renaissance spirit.

Also, before this waxing lyrical gets out of control: a trip close to the spot in Fiesole where Lucy has her first kiss with George Beebe in *A Room With a View* does afford a fantastic view of Florence – but shows the pall of pollution over the city. The racist booing of the *Viola* at a Fiorentina match was extremely depressing. And the inefficiencies of the card paying system in Florentine nightclubs was utterly exasperating.

It wasn't until my last night in Florence before returning to England to put this thing together that I felt I had finally found the true spirit of Renaissance Florence. A night out with new friends in the Oltrarno ended up in a large, amazingly ornate room of a sixteenth-century palazzo which was now home to a young couple – one half of whom we had met that evening and who had invited us to his home for a nightcap.

He made wrought-iron pieces – light fittings, hat stands and the incredible four-poster bed his girlfriend was asleep in. Around the room was a huge array of stunning hats that she was designing. They were undeniably sensing their individual potentiality and assuredly asserting the active. Not content with living in extreme beauty they were creating yet more. I started to feel dizzy and disorientated – maybe this was an attack of Stendhal Syndrome, more than likely it was one drink too many. Regardless, it certainly felt like I had found the spirit (no, not grappa) of Renaissance Florence.
Kevin Ebbutt

In Context

Tuscany by Season

Food, wine, music – Tuscans are always ready to eat, drink and be merry.

Spring

Telephone numbers listed may be operational for the duration of the festival only, in which case the local tourist office is the best place to call.

Festa della Donna

Date 8 March.

Italy seems to be one of the only countries where Women's Day is celebrated. Traditionally, women are presented with sprigs of bright yellow mimosa by almost anyone or everyone. In the evening, Florentine restaurants and clubs are packed full of gangs of girls out on the town and many places put on male strippers as part of the evening's entertainment.

Diladdarno

Santo Spirito and San Frediano, Florence. **Date** mid Mar to early Apr. **Information** 055 290 832.

Three weeks of music, exhibitions, guided tours, theatre, food and street events celebrating life, past and present, in Florence's 'Left Bank'.

Holy Week

Date March or April.

Holy week is celebrated in many small towns all over Tuscany with religious processions, many of them in Renaissance costume. Some of the more important ones are Buonconvento (near Siena), Castiglion Fiorentino (near Arezzo) and Bagno a Ripoli (just outside Florence). In Grassina, near Florence, and San Gimignano, re-enactments of episodes from the life of Christ are staged on Good Friday.

Scoppio del Carro

Piazzale della Porta al Prato to Piazza del Duomo. **Date** Easter Sunday.

Easter Sunday is one of the most important days of the Florentine calendar: it's the day of the **Scoppio del Carro**, an ancient ritual that dates back to the

Parades and pyrotechnics – the **Scoppio del Carro** *culminates in an explosion of fireworks.*

twelfth century. It's a wonderfully eccentric and colourful event. A long parade of trumpeters, drummers, costumed dignitaries and flag throwers escort the *carro* (a tall, heavy wooden cart), pulled by four white oxen with garlands of flowers around their horns, through the streets from Piazzale della Porta al Prato to Piazza del Duomo. Nearby streets are always blocked by thousands of spectators; if you want a clear view of the procession, be at Porta al Prato when it sets off at 9.30am. The *scoppio* (explosion) happens at 11am when a mechanical dove is 'lit' by the priest during mass. The dove flies along a wire stretched from the altar to the carro outside, sets off an explosion of fireworks, and returns to the altar. If all goes smoothly, it is said that the year's harvests will be good.

Settimana dei Beni Culturali

Florence. **Date** one week in Apr or Dec.
Information 055 290 832.
A cultural free-for-all (that sometimes takes place in December) when the doors of the municipal museums are opened free of charge.

Mostra Mercato di Piante e Fiori

Parterra, Florence. **Date** Around 25 Apr-1 May.
Information 055 290 832.
This huge plant and flower show held near Piazza della Libertà attracts growers from miles around.

Mostra Mercato Internazionale dell'Artigianato

Fortezza da Basso, Florence. **Date** late Apr/May.
Information 055 49721.
A vast craft fair, taking in ceramics, glassware, fabrics and wood products of varying quality.

Mostra Mercato Primaverile di Piante e Fiori

Greve in Chianti. **Date** 1st Sun in May.
Information 055 290 832.
A large horticultural show in the pretty town of Greve near Florence. Food and drink stalls too.

Palio dei Micci

Querceta, near Seravezza. **Date** 1st Sun in May.
Information 0584 869 015.
This low-key version of the Siena palio is a fine spectacle, with a parade in Renaissance costume, trumpets, drums, flag throwers and scenes of local life being re-enacted. The climax of the event is the donkey race between the various teams.

Cantine Aperte, Toscana

Date 9am-6pm, one Sun in late May. **Information** 055 290 832.
Wine-producing estates throw open their doors to the public each year for tastings and nibbles. A useful guide to the various wineries is available at tourist offices.

Maggio Musicale Fiorentino

Teatro Comunale, Florence. **Date** May/June.
Information 055 211 158.
The highlight of the musical year in Florence, with opera, concerts, ballet, and lectures by international artists. *See chapter* **Music: Classical & Opera**.

Itinerari Sconsciuti

Date May to July. **Information** 055 290 832.
The opening of Florentine churches, palaces and monuments not normally available for public view.

International Iris Show

Piazzale Michelangiolo, Florence. Bus 12, 13. **Open** 10am-12.30pm, 3-7pm daily. **Date** May.
Information 055 290 832.
Spectacular floral display, with hundreds of varieties of iris on display.

Summer

Una Sera al Museo

Various venues, Florence. **Date** June-Sept.
Information 055 290 832.
Many Florentine museums stay open in the evenings during the summer and are used as concert venues.

Giostra del Saracino

Piazza Grande, Arezzo. **Date** June, Sept. **Tickets** L15,000 (standing); L60-70,000 (sitting, June only).
Information 0575 377 6678.
One Sunday in mid-June, and on the first Sunday of September, this reconstruction of an ancient jousting tournament between the four *quartieri* of Arezzo is held in historic Piazza Grande. The event originated in the thirteenth century, and is accompanied by a parade of musicians and acrobatic flag throwers dressed in the period garb of their team's colours. The action starts at about 10am with the first of the parades. Another begins at 2.30pm and at 5pm the procession of horses, knights and their escort arrives in the Piazza, and the tournament begins.

Calcio in Costume

Piazza Santa Croce, Florence. **Date** June, early July.
Information 055 290 832.
The only fixed date for this extremely violent variation on football, in medieval costume, is 24 June. The dates of the other three matches are pulled out of a hat on Easter Sunday, but all are in June or early July. *See box* in **Sport**.

Festa del Grillo

Parco delle Cascine, Florence. **Date** June.
Held on Candlemas, this ancient symbolic event has become, like so many other events of the kind, an excuse for a big general market. However, live crickets, traditionally meant to woo sweethearts with their chirping and given as gifts to cheer them up in your absence, are still sold in tiny hand-painted cages. Because of protests by animal rights activists this singular tradition may soon be abandoned.

Palio, Magliano in Toscana

Magliano in Toscana. **Date** 1, 2 or 3 May.
Information 0564 454 510.
One of many smaller traditional events of the Tuscan year, this jousting match and *palio* takes

place in a particularly attractive town in the Maremma. The evening before the race, there's a torchlit procession through town and the horses are blessed. The actual palio, raced in a field on the outskirts of the town, is at 4pm, but various teams begin to gather and parade from 9am.

Luminaria di San Ranieri

Pisa. **Date** 16/17 June. **Information** 050 560 464.
The visually stunning Luminaria sees tens of thousands of candles lit and displayed along the Arno and on the buildings on the Lungarni. The next day, at about 6.30pm, there's a boat race along the Arno between the town's four *quartieri*.

Festa di San Giovanni

Florence. **Date** 24 June.
Florence's patron saint brings its municipality a public holiday and a huge fireworks display is held in the evening near Piazzale Michelangiolo.

Il Gioco del Ponte

Pisa. **Date** last Sun in June. **Tickets** L20,000. **Information** 050 560 464; tickets 050 910 5092.
Another bizarre-to-the-uninitiated historic event: this is a kind of 'push-of-war' dating from the thirteenth century, in which teams from Pisa and its environs fight for supremacy on the Ponte di Mezzo by trying to push a metal construction on rails against an opposing team. Processions start near the Ponte di Mezzo from 4.30pm; the competition starts at 6pm.

Festa Internazionale della Ceramica

Montelupo. **Date** 8 days from Sat to Sun in last week of June; 6pm-midnight Mon-Sat, 10am-midnight Sun. **Information** 0571 518 993.
Tuscan ceramics are world famous, and Montelupo is one of the centres of production. This event celebrates a craft very much rooted in the past, with Renaissance music and costume, and craftsmen demonstrating techniques, both past and present.

Rassegna Internazionale di Canto Corale

Impruneta, near Florence. **Date** every Sat in June. **Information** 055 231 3729.
The international choral competition held in this small town just south of Florence attracts choirs from all over the world.

International Polo Tournament

Ippodromo delle Cascine, Florence. **Date** late June/ July. **Information** 055 204 7847.
Top-flight sporting action for horsey types.

Pitti Uomo

Fortezza da Basso, Florence. **Date** early July. **Information** 055 36931.
The summer edition of the international men's ready-to-wear fashion fair (*see below*, **Winter**).

Florence Dance Festival

Teatro Romano, Fiesole. **Date** July. **Information** 055 289 276.
Three-week-long, international contemporary dance festival held in the atmospheric Roman amphitheatre in Fiesole. *See chapter* **Dance & Theatre**.

Open-air cinema

Arena di Marte (Palasport) and Il Raggio Verde (Palazzo dei Congressi), Florence. **Date** July-Aug. **Information** 055 293 169.
Two films per night are shown at these cinemas *all'aperto*.

Incontri in Terra di Siena

La Foce, Chianciano Terme. **Date** July-Aug. **Information** 0578 69101.
A festival of chamber music in the incomparable settings of Castelluccio di Pienza and La Foce (the family estate of writer Iris Origo).

Opera Festival

Batignano. **Date** July-Aug. **Information** 0564 28115; (Grosseto tourist office) 0564 454 510.
The tiny hilltop town of Batignano near Grosseto provides an idyllic setting for little-known opera productions by international artists.

Puccini Opera Festival

Torre del Lago. **Dates** July-Aug. **Information** 0584 359 322/fax 0584 350 277. **No credit cards**.
Puccini's villa on the shore of Lago di Massaciuccoli provides a magnificent setting for the staging of two or three of the maestro's operas. *See also chapter* **Music: Classical & Opera**.

Effetto Venezia

Livorno. **Date** late July to Aug.
A ten-day festival of evening shows and concerts in Livorno's 'Venetian quarter', so-called because of all the little canals in the area. Restaurants stay open late and serve local delicacies. Try the hearty Livornese speciality *cacciucco*, a thick fish soup.

Palio, Siena

Piazza del Campo, Siena. **Date** 2 July & 16 Aug. **Information** 0577 280 551. **Tickets** L250,000-L400,000 (balconies).
The famous and much criticised horse race around Siena's Piazza del Campo is Tuscan pageantry at its best. The last of the trial races is run at 9am on the big day. In the early afternoon, each qualifying horse and jockey is blessed in his team's church. At around 4.30pm, the historic procession enters the Piazza del Campo and, after an incredible display of acrobatic flag-throwing, the often violent race is run at about 7pm. It's free to stand, but you need to be in place early. Tickets for the balconies overlooking the piazza are sold from bars and cafés on the piazza, but are horrendously hard to come by.

On The Road Festival

Pelago. **Date** one weekend in late July. **Information** 055 832 6236. **Tickets** L10,000.
This lively festival of street performers, artists, musicians, actors, mime artists and fire-eaters takes place over a long weekend (Thur-Sun). Events start at around 9pm. Pelago is 25 km east of Florence.

Mostra Mercato dei Ferri taglienti e del ferro battuto

Scarperia. **Date** end Aug.

The Sagra

Every Tuscan village – even the tiniest hamlet – has its *sagra*. The word sagra means rite, and the tradition of celebrating a particular product of the land goes back many hundreds of years. Nowadays, a sagra will celebrate just about anything from wine and olive oil, wild boar, truffles, chestnuts, to tripe and *bistecca*; it is an excuse for a huge binge involving eating, drinking, music and general merry-making. The event almost always takes place at the weekend. The town's central piazza and surrounding streets will be blocked off to traffic and vendors will set up stalls selling the object of the celebrations, other local food and drink and sometimes local crafts. Most importantly, a makeshift trattoria will be set up where the local women will serve wonderful home-made food (with the magic ingredient featuring strongly) at long wooden tables. In the evening, there is often live music with a band brought in to play old-fashioned ballroom dance numbers.

Sagre are always good fun, and offer a chance to experience a taste of rural Tuscan life. Outsiders are usually made to feel welcome, and you may well find yourself in a clinch on the dance floor with the local butcher. To discover the whereabouts of the nearest sagra, ask at the local tourist office. They are also often advertised on posters and billboards around town, and the events magazine *Firenze Spettacolo* lists some of them.

Sagra della Bistecca

Cortona. **Date** mid-Aug.

If meat's your thing, don't miss this orgy of steak-eating from the Valdichiana, reputedly home to the best cuts of beef in Italy.

Festa del Uva

Impruneta, near Florence. **Date** end Sept. **Information** 055 231 3729.

A celebration of the grape: food, wine and a parade of allegorical floats.

Festa del Vino Novello

Montecarlo, Lucca. **Date** early Nov. **Information** 0583 419 689.

A celebration of food and, above all, the new season's wine, with live music, craft stalls, food and drink in the streets of Montecarlo.

Mostra Mercato del Tartufo Bianco

San Miniato. **Date** weekends in late Nov.

One of the year's top foodie events, celebrating the white truffle. Stalls sell not only bargain-priced *tartufi* but cheeses, salami, grappa and other comestibles all flavoured with the much sought-after tuber. Restaurants present special truffle menus.

A fascinating display of knives, ancient and modern, and wrought iron from the home of this art (*see chapter* **Around Florence & Pisa**).

Autumn

La Rificolona

Florence. **Date** Sept. **Information** See local posters.

Children take paper lanterns and gather in the evening in Piazza SS Annunziata and along the river. For further details, *see chapter* **Children**.

Opera and ballet season

Teatro Comunale, Florence. **Date** Sept-Dec. **Information** 055 211 158.

See chapter **Classical & Opera**.

Settembre Musica

Teatro della Pergola and various venues, Florence. **Date** Sept. **Information** 055 608 420.

A month of early music concerts.

Rassegna Internazionale Musica dei Popoli

Auditorium Flog, Florence. **Date** Oct-Nov. **Information** 055 422 0300.

An innovative world music festival.

Festival dei Popoli

Florence. **Date** late Nov to early Dec. **Information** 055 244 778.

A season of social documentary films. *See also chapter* **Film**.

Winter

Italians go in for Nativity scenes in a big way, and many churches set up cribs, some of them *viventi* (with live animals). On the island of Giglio, there is even an underwater crib at Campese. In Florence, the principal ones are at San Lorenzo, Santa Croce, Chiesa di Dante and Santa Maria de' Ricci.

Settimana dei Beni Culturali

Florence. **Date** one week in Apr or Dec. **Information** 055 290 832.

See above, **Spring**.

Florence Marathon

Florence. **Date** late Nov/early Dec. **Information** 055 572 885.

Anyone over 18 can enter the 27-mile race. First prize is around the L3,000,000 mark, which may seem worth it.

A hairy moment – one of the reasons why Siena's **Palio** *is so notorious. See also p211.*

Christmas Concerts

Various venues, Florence. **Date** Dec/Jan. **Information** 055 290 832.

The antique organs of Florence are put through their paces.

Sfilata dei Canottieri

Florence. **Date** 1 Jan.

Traditional parade of boats on the Arno in Florence.

New Year Concert by the Scuola di Musica di Fiesole

Teatro Comunale, Florence. **Date** 1 Jan. **Information** 055 599 725.

Tickets are free and available upon application to the Scuola di Musica.

Concert Season

Teatro Comunale, Florence. **Date** Jan-Apr. **Information** 055 211 158.

See chapter **Music: Classical & Opera**.

Pitti Uomo

Fortezza da Basso, Florence. **Date** Mid-Jan. **Information** 055 36931.

The first of the year's international men's ready-to-wear fashion fairs. Leading labels from all over the world bring their designs to show at this important event.

La Befana (Epiphany)

Date 6 Jan.

La Befana is a holiday throughout Italy and smaller towns hold street parties. In Pisa, parachutists dressed as the Befana, drop from the sky and bring presents to children. *See also chapter* **Children**.

Carnevale

Date ten days leading up to Shrove Tuesday, Feb.

Many Tuscan towns celebrate Carnevale during February. Most consist of parades with elaborate floats, fancy dress parties, and excesses of eating and drinking. In Florence, children get dressed up and parade with their parents in the piazzas, and especially along the Lungarno Amerigo Vespucci. The younger kids scatter confetti, but beware older children with aerosol foam who squirt anything moving. Elsewhere in Tuscany, Carnival celebrations include those in Borgo San Lorenzo (a children's event with floats, street performances, costumes and mimes), Calenzano (in medieval costumes) and San Gimignano (floats, masks and costumes). Shrove Tuesday marks the last day of Carnevale.

Viareggio Carnevale

Viareggio. **Date** Feb. **Transport** LAZZI bus from Piazza Adua, Florence (055 351 061) to Viareggio; train from Florence SMN (1478 88088) to Viareggio via Pisa. **Tickets** L17,000 (for all days); L32,000 (in stands). **Information** 0584 963 501.

The most important Carnival celebrations in Italy outside Venice. The parades take place on four consecutive Sundays in February, the last (and most important) sometimes spilling over into March. The first three parades begin at about 2.30pm, and the last at 5pm, finishing around 9.30pm. The latter, an OTT procession of gigantic and elaborate floats, often lampooning political and public figures, is rounded off with a fireworks display and prize-giving ceremony for the best float. Tickets are available at booths in the town from 8am on the day or by phone in advance.

Key Events

59 BC Foundation of Florentia by Julius Caesar.
56 BC Caesar, Crassus and Pompey form first triumvirate at Lucca.
AD 406 Stilicho holds Florence against the rampaging Ostrogoths.
541 Florence held in Totila and Belisarius campaigns.
552 Florence falls to the Goths under Totila.
568 Invasion of the Lombards.
778 Charlemagne defeats last of the Lombard kings.
c800 New walls erected around Florence.

Tenth-twelfth centuries

Pisa becomes one of Italy's wealthiest ports; Lucca, seat of the Margraves of Tuscany, is the region's most important city; Florence is still only a small trading post.
978 Badìa established in Florence by Willa, widow of the Margrave Uberto.
1027 Canossa family become Margraves but take the title Counts of Tuscany.
1076 Matilda, daughter of the Canossa Margrave, becomes Countess of Tuscany.
1078 New defences for Florence constructed.
1115 Matilda grants Florence status of independent city; on her death she bequeaths all her lands to the Pope except Florence, Lucca and Siena.
1125 Florence captures Fiesole.
1173-5 More new walls for Florence.

Thirteenth century

Increasing self-dependence and wealth of Tuscan cities causes increased inter-city conflict; the era of Guelph/Ghibelline rivalry.
1207 Florence's council is replaced by the Podestà.
1216 Murder of Buondelmonte dei Buondelmonti on the Ponte Vecchio in Florence ignites the simmering Guelph/Ghibelline conflict.
1248 Ghibellines oust Guelphs from Florence.
1250 Guelphs boot Ghibellines out of Florence.
1252 First gold florin minted.
1260 Siena beats Florence at Montaperti; Guelphs again displaced from Florence.
1261 Invasion of Italy by Charles of Anjou.
1266 Charles of Anjou conquers Naples, and in the following year becomes Florence's overlord.
1280s Guelphs back in control of Florence.
1289 Florence defeats Arezzo at Campaldino.
1293 A number of reforms are passed including the Ordinances of Justice which exclude the nobility from government and create the Signoria, drawn from the *arti maggiori* (major guilds).
1296 Foundations laid for new Florence cathedral.

Fourteenth century

The early years are marked by struggle between virulently anti-Imperial 'black' Guelphs and conciliatory 'white' Guelphs; increasing Florentine muscle flexing.
1302 Many 'white' Guelphs, including Dante, exiled.
1325 Lucchese army, under Castruccio Castracani defeats Florence at Altopascio, and goes on to besiege Florence.
1328 Castruccio Castracani dies, saving Florence.
1329 Florence takes over Pistoia.
1333 Severe floods in Florence.
1339 The Bardi and Peruzzi banks, the biggest in Florence, collapse after English king Edward III defaults on his debts.
1348 Black Death ravages Tuscany.
1351 Florence buys Prato from the Queen of Naples.
1375-8 War of the Eight Saints frees Florence from the Papal influence. The Guelphs join up with the *popolo grasso* to exclude the guilds from power.
1400 Florence threatened by Gian Galeazzo Visconti.

Fifteenth century

Flowering of the Florentine Renaissance.
1406 Florence captures Pisa.
1411 Florence gains Cortona.
1421 Florence buys Livorno from Genova.
1428 Start of war between Florence and Lucca.
1432 Rout of San Romano – Florence beats Siena in a skirmish immortalised by the artist Uccello.
1433 Cosimo imprisoned and exiled by the Albizzi during unpopular Lucchese war.
1434 Return of Cosimo from exile; overthrow and exile of the Albizzi.
1436 Brunelleschi completes the dome of the Duomo.
1437 Florence defeats Milan at Barga.
1439 Church Council moves to Florence and succeeds in bringing a shortlived reconciliation between Eastern and Western churches.
1440 Florentines rout Milanese at Anghiari.
1452 Florence abandons traditional alliance with Venice to join with Milan. Naples and Venice declare war on Milan and Florence.
1453 Fall of Constantinople to the Turks.
1454 Threat of the Turks brings Pope, Venice, Florence and Milan together in Holy League.
1464 Cosimo dies; Piero gains control of Florence.
1466 Piero quashes conspiracy to overthrow Medici.
1467 Florence, Naples and Milan defeat Venice at Imola.
1469 Piero dies; his son Lorenzo 'il Magnifico' takes over in Florence.
1472 Sack of Volterra – Lorenzo held responsible.
1478 Pazzi conspiracy, kills Giuliano de' Medici but his brother Lorenzo escapes; conspirators and supporters executed. Plot's failure leads Papacy and Naples to declare war on Florence.
1479 Lorenzo goes alone to Naples to negotiate peace treaty with King Ferrante.
1492 Death of Lorenzo; his son Piero takes over.
1494 Wars of Italy begin – Charles VIII invades Italy. Inept Piero, son of Lorenzo, surrenders Florence on his own authority and then flees.
Piero Capponi leads the government, but this is the era of the friar Savonarola's greatest influence.

He persuades Charles VIII to leave Florence, but meanwhile Pisa successfully revolts, leading to a long war with Florence.
Charles VIII dallies in Naples; meanwhile Pope Alexander VI, forms a Holy League, including the Empire and Spain, against the French.
1495 French beat the Holy League at Fornovo on the banks of the Taro, but then withdraw from Italy.
1497 'Bonfire of the Vanities' in Florence. Savonarola's criticisms of clerical corruption alienate the Pope, who raises a league against Florence.
1498 Florentines burn Savonarola.

Sixteenth century

Florence slowly declines, economically and culturally; Pisa subjugated; Siena crushed.
1502 Piero Soderini elected *gonfaloniere* for life; he is advised by Macchiavelli.
1509 Pope Julius II forms the League of Cambrai with the Empire, Spain and France to pick off the richest bits of the Venetian territories; League of Cambrai beats Venice at Agnadello.
On defeat of Venetian allies, Pisa finally sues Florence for peace.
1512 Battle of Ronco; Papacy/Spain versus France. Papal and Spanish armies sack Prato and force Florentines to kick out Soderini and allow the return of the Medici.
Giuliano de' Medici abolishes Grand Council and imposes his own rule, backed by soldiers.
1513 Giovanni de' Medici elected as Pope Leo X.
1516 Giuliano dies; his nephew, the unpopular Lorenzo, Duke of Urbino, takes over, but the real boss is the Medici Pope.
1519 Lorenzo dies. In name, Giulio, Lorenzo's bastard nephew is in charge, but Leo X continues to pull Florence's strings from Rome.
Death of Emporer Maximilian; accession of Charles V opposed by both Francis I of France and Pope. Charles V attacks France's Italian possessions.
1521 Leo dies of a 'violent chill'; Adrian VI elected.
1522 Adrian VI dies; Giulio becomes Pope Clement VII; continues to run Florence from Rome. Nominal leaders in Florence are Cardinal Passerini and the illegitimate Medicis, Ippolito and Alessandro.
1525 Charles V and the Duke of Milan defeat the French at Pavia; Francis I taken prisoner.
1526 Giovanni della Bande Nere, father of future Cosimo I, dies trying to halt German army on the Po.
1527 Horrific sack of Rome by Charles V's army. Ippolito and Alessandro de' Medici and Cardinal Passerini are expelled by the Florentines; new republic declared.
1529 Charles V, now allied with Clement VII, besieges Florence.
1530 Florence falls; end of the Republic.
1531 Alessandro de' Medici is installed as head of government by Charles V; the next year Charles creates him Duke and makes succession permanent; Spanish troops ensure obedience.
1537 Alessandro murdered by jealous cousin Lorenzaccio de' Medici.
Obscure Cosimo de' Medici chosen to succeed; Cosimo defeats Florentine rebels at Montemurlo.
1555 With Imperial help, Cosimo crushes Siena after a devastating war; Sienese power destroyed
1564 Increasingly ill, Cosimo abdicates much responsibility to son Francesco.
1569 Cosimo buys the title Grand Duke of Tuscany from Pope Paul V.
1574 Death of Cosimo I; son Francesco I accedes.
1587 Francesco dies; brother Ferdinando I accedes.

Seventeenth-eighteenth century

Wool trade finally collapses completely in the 1630s; Tuscany becoming more of a European backwater.
1609 Death of Ferdinando; Cosimo II takes over.
1621 Death of Cosimo II; Ferdinando II accedes.
1670 Death of Ferdinando II; Cosimo III accedes.
1723 Death of Cosimo III; Gian Gastone, last of the Medici rulers, takes the reigns.
1735 Treaty of Aix-la-Chapelle gives Grand Duchy of Tuscany to Francis Stephen, Duke of Lorraine. An enlightened regime is established.
1737 Death of Gian Gastone.
1743 Death of Gian Gastone's sister, Anna Maria, the last surviving Medici, who leaves all the Medici art and treasures to Florence in perpetuity.
1765 Francis Stephens dies; Peter Leopold accedes.
1790 Grand Duke Peter Leopold becomes Emperor of Austria; son becomes Grand Duke Ferdinando III.
1799 French troops enter Florence.

Nineteenth century

Revival of interest in Tuscany; it becomes a major stop for Grand Tourists.
1801-7 Grand Duchy absorbed into Etruria.
1808 Napoleon installs his sister, Elisa Bacciochi, as Grand Duchess of Tuscany.
1815 Grand Duke Ferdinando III returns to Tuscany on defeat of Napoleon.
1824 Genial Leopold II succeeds after father's death.
1859 Leopold allows himself to be overthrown in the Risorgimento.
1860 Tuscans vote for unification with Vittorio Emanuele's Kingdom of Piedmont.
1865-70 Florence becomes first capital of the united Italy until the fall of Rome.

Twentieth century

1943 Germans enter Florence; they establish Gothic Line on the Arno.
1944 Germans blow up all of Pisa's bridges and all but the Ponte Vecchio (thanks to Hitler's personal intervention) in Florence. Allies liberate Florence.
1966 The Arno floods to a height of 6.5 metres, causing huge damage.
1993 Bomb destroys Gregoriophilus library (*below*) opposite the Uffizi and damages the Vasari corridor.

History

Medicis, maestros and monsters.

Lorenzo 'il Magnifico' – his rule marked the peak of the Florentine Renaissance.

From around the eighth century BC much of central Italy was controlled by the Etruscans, who settled in Veii and Caere (Cerveteri) close to Rome and further north in (what is now Tuscany) Volterra, Populonia, Arezzo, Clusium (Chiusi) and Cortona. They entirely overlooked the site we now know as Florence, making hilltop Fiesole their northernmost stronghold. It was not until 59 BC, when Julius Caesar established a Roman colony along the narrowest stretch of the Arno, that Florentia was born. It was DH Lawrence who said, 'The Etruscans, as everyone knows, were the people who occupied the middle of Italy in early Roman days and whom the Romans, in their usual neighbourly fashion, wiped out entirely in order to make room for Rome with a very big R.' Lawrence's love of the Etruscans was almost as great as his hatred for the Romans.

The Etruscans are ideal material for mythologising: tantalisingly little evidence remains of their history and culture before they were clobbered out of existence by the Romans, allowing interpreters to make of them what they will. One of the main reasons that we can be sure of so little about the Etruscans is that they constructed almost everything from wood. Everything, that is, except their tombs. Because of this, their tombs, and the objects recovered from them, provide most of the surviving evidence on their civilisation. The frescoes of feasts, festivals, dancing and hunting that adorn many of the tombs led Lawrence to conclude that, '...death to the Etruscan was a pleasant continuance of life.' Others say the opposite: that the Etruscans were terrified of death and the seemingly carefree paintings were a desperate plea for the gods to go easy on the other side. The Etruscans were certainly a spiritual people, but they were also partial to a good war, either against other tribes or rival Etruscan cities.

The historical bones of what we know about the Etruscans is as follows. Their civilisation reached its peak in the seventh and sixth centuries BC, when their loose federation of individually distinctive cities dominated much of what is now southern Tuscany and northern Lazio.

Women played an unusually prominent role in these booming Etruscan settlements, apparently having as much fun as the lads. Writing in the fourth century BC, Theopompos says, 'Etruscan women

The people's poet

Dante Alighieri was born in 1265 into a noble family that had fallen on hard times. In common with most other minor nobles and merchants, the Alighieris were affiliated to the Guelphs and their fortunes during the thirteenth century were thus dictated by the ups and downs of their party.

Most of Dante's early life coincided with a period of Guelph domination of Florence. The young Dante did his bit to preserve peace, fighting for the city in the victory against Ghibelline Arezzo at Campaldino in 1289, and later taking part in the siege of the Pisan fortress of Caprona.

His expulsion from Florence with the other White Guelphs in 1302 was a bitter blow and, despite repeated attempts to return, he never saw the city again, dying in Ravenna in 1321.

It was while he was in exile that Dante wrote his greatest work, *La Commedia*, known to posterity as the *Divine Comedy*. This multi-levelled poetic epic is the story of Dante the Pilgrim's journey through Hell, Purgatory and Paradise to God. On the way, Dante the Poet incorporates countless references to the tumultuous events of the preceding century, railing against the injustices of the Ghibellines and lamenting the plight of Florence.

Dante was a firm believer that temporal and spiritual power should be kept separate. He viewed the Pope's increasing domination of Italian politics as an ominous sign. In Canto XVI of *Purgatorio* he warns: 'The sword is now one with the crook – and fused together thus, must bring about misrule.'

Dante was, however, deeply religious, and particularly outraged by clerical corruption (outspoken criticism of such was one of the chief causes of the split between 'Black' and 'White' Guelphs). In Canto XIX of *Inferno* he condemns the simonists (those who obtained or dispensed religious offices for money) to be shoved down tubes and have flames flicker across the soles of their feet. Popes Nicholas III and Benedict VIII (who was instrumental in bringing about Dante's exile) are found here, lambasted by Dante the Pilgrim:

'Those things of God that rightly should be wed to holiness, you, rapacious creatures, for the price of silver and gold prostitute.'

take particular care of their bodies and exercise often, sometimes along with the men, and sometimes by themselves. It is not a disgrace for them to be seen naked. They do not share their couches with their husbands but with other men who happen to be present... They are expert drinkers and very attractive.'

The Etruscan cities grew wealthy on the proceeds of trading and mining in copper and iron. Their art and superbly worked gold jewellery display distinctive oriental influences, adding credence to the theory that the Etruscans migrated to Italy from the east, possibly Asia Minor. Equally, such influences could have been due to extensive trading in the eastern Mediterranean.

The impenetrability of their language adds a further veil of mystery. The problem of Etruscan origins is probably intractable. In all likelihood they emerged from a huge number of mini-migrations within Italy. At the end of the seventh century BC, the Etruscans captured the small town of Rome and ruled there for a century before being expelled. The next few centuries witnessed city against city and tribe against tribe all over central Italy until the emerging Roman Republic finally overwhelmed all-comers by the third century BC. The Romans absorbed many aspects of Etruscan society such as Etruscan gods and divination by entrails, but a distinct Etruscan civilisation ceased to exist.

Etruscan to Tuscan

Unravelling medieval Italian history is not for the faint-hearted. The seemingly interminable progression of petty squabbles, alliances and counter-alliances, scraps and skirmishes between the bewildering number of petty statelets, leaves the head spinning.

In the fifth century, the Western Empire finally crumbled before the pagan hordes (some, incidentally, considerably more cultured than the clapped-out, dissolute Romans they displaced). Italian unity collapsed as Ostrogoths, Visigoths, Huns and Lombards successively rampaged at will through the peninsula.

In the eighth century Charlemagne crushed the last of the Lombard kings of Italy and much of the country came under (at least nominal) control of the Holy Roman Emperors. In practice, however, local warlords carved out feudal fiefs for themselves and threw their weight around much as they pleased.

Under the Canossa family, the iiperial Margravate of Tuscany began to emerge as a region of some promise during the tenth and eleventh centuries. Initially, the richest city was Lucca, but it was Pisa's increasingly profitable maritime trade that brought the biggest impetus of ideas and wealth into the region.

As a merchant class developed in cities all over Tuscany, it sought to throw off the constraints and demands of its feudal overlords. By 1200 the majority had succeeded and Tuscany had become a patchwork of tiny, but increasingly self-confident and ambitious, city states. The potential for conflict was huge, and by the thirteenth century it crystallised into the notorious and intractable struggle between Guelph and Ghibelline.

GUELPH V GHIBELLINE

In the beginning the names Guelph and Ghibelline actually meant something. The words are Italian forms of Welf (the family name of the German Emperor Otto IV) and Waiblingen (a castle of the Welfs' rivals, the Hohenstaufen). By the time the appellations crossed the Alps into Italy (probably in the twelfth century) their meanings had changed.

The name Guelph became attached primarily to the increasingly influential merchant classes. In their continuing desire to be free from Imperial control, they looked around for a powerful backer. The only viable candidate was the Emperor's old enemy, the Pope, who believed that the fourth-century Roman Emperor Constantine had assigned not just spiritual but also temporal power in Italy to the Papacy. The Guelphs, therefore, were able to add a patriotic and religious sheen to their own self-interest. Anyone keen to uphold Imperial power and opposed to Papal designs and rising commercial interests (mainly the old nobility) became known as Ghibellines. That was the theory.

Although the conflict had been simmering for decades, the murder in 1215 of Florentine nobleman Buondelmonte dei Buondelmonti is traditionally seen as the spark that ignited flames across Tuscany. It soon became clear that self-interest and local rivalries were of far greater importance than theoretical allegiances to Emperor or Pope.

Florence and Lucca were generally Guelph-dominated cities, while Siena and Pisa tended to favour the Ghibellines, but this had as much to do with mutual antagonisms as deeply held beliefs. Siena started off Guelph, but couldn't bear the thought of having to be nice to its traditional enemy, Florence, and so swapped to the Ghibelline cause. Similarly, the Guelph/Ghibelline splits within cities were more often class- and grudge-based than ideological.

Throughout the fourteenth century, power ebbed and flowed between the two (loosely knit) parties across Tuscany and from city to city. When one party was in the ascendant its supporters would tear down its opponents' fortified towers (the Guelphs' with characteristic square crenellations, the Ghibellines' with swallow-tail ones), only to have its own towers levelled in turn as soon as the pendulum swung back again. In Florence, the Guelphs finally triumphed in 1267 but, as if to prove the meaninglessness of the labels, the party soon started squabbling internally. Around 1300, open conflict broke out between the virulently anti-Imperial 'Blacks' and the more conciliatory 'Whites'. After various to-ings and fro-ings, the Blacks booted the Whites out for good. Among those sent into exile was Dante Alighieri (*see* **The people's poet**).

Eventually, the Guelph/Ghibelline conflict ran out of steam, or, rather, everyone admitted that the labels no longer meant anything and invented new ones to slap on their enemies. It says much for the energy, innovation, graft and skill of the Tuscans (or for the relative harmlessness of much medieval warfare in Italy) that throughout this tempestuous period, the region was booming economically. The stage was being set for the explosion of curiosity, creativity and achievement that was to characterise fifteenth-century Tuscany.

The birth of the new

By the beginning of the fourteenth century Florence was one of the five biggest cities in Europe, with a population of about 100,000. The city's good fortune was due in no small part to its woollen cloth industry. In the mid-1380s the three guilds that were formed in the wake of the rising of the Ciompi 'wool-carders', began to lose ground to the *popolo grasso*, a small group of wealthy middle-class merchant families, who had united with the Guelphs and formed an oligarchy in 1382. The popolo grasso held sway for 40 years. During this time, early in fifteenth century, intellectuals and artists were becoming increasingly involved in political life.

From time to time, one of the heads of the merchant families was sent into exile to prevent any one person from gaining too much power. It was Cosimo de' Medici's popularity among the city's merchants that caused so much resentment toward him with other powerful families that, in 1433, the Albizzi had him exiled on trumped-up charges. A year later he returned to Florence by popular consent and was immediately made first citizen of the people. As one contemporary commented, he was 'king in all but name'.

Medici who's who

Medici is a name all but synonymous with Florence and Tuscany from the fifteenth to the early eighteenth centuries. As their name suggests, the family's origins probably lie in the medical profession – doctors or apothecaries – although their later wealth was built on banking. The Medici had risen to some prominence in Florence by the end of the thirteenth century but declined in wealth and influence thereafter, before their fortunes revived again towards the end of the fourteenth century. From then on, there was no turning back.

Giovanni di Bicci (1360-1429)

In a sense, Giovanni could be called the first Medici. It was the fortune that he quietly built up through his banking business (boosted immensely by handling the papal account) that was to be the foundation of the Medici's prominence in the fifteenth century. Giovanni concentrated on making cash and always acted with the utmost discretion, wary of the Florentines' habit of picking on those who got above themselves. It was his son Cosimo who really shot the Medici into the big time.

Cosimo 'il Vecchio' (1389-1464)

The name 'il Vecchio' was bestowed as a mark of respect for his role in fifteenth-century Florence. When he died, the Florentines inscribed on his tomb the words *Pater Patriae* (father of the nation), a distinction once accorded to Roman statesman Cicero. Cosimo ran Florence informally from 1434 and, in so doing, presided over one of its most prosperous and prestigious eras.

He was even more astute a banker than his father and managed to expand the fortunes left to him. At the same time Cosimo pacified opponents and his conscience by spending lavishly on charities and public building projects, introducing a progressive income tax system and balancing the interests of the volatile Florentine classes relatively successfully.

He also brought much prestige to the city by persuading the General Council of the Roman and Greek churches to meet in Florence, where they achieved a (short-lived) reconciliation. As well as being an astute politician and businessman, Cosimo was an intellectual, and the most admirable feature of his rule was his enthusiasm for the new humanist learning and exciting developments in art that were sweeping Florence. He built up a magnificent public library (the first in Europe), encouraged and financed the activities of scholars and artists, gave architectural commissions and founded an academy of learning based on Plato's Academy. In fact, he was the Renaissance epitome of *uomo universale.*

Piero 'il Gottoso' (1416-69)

Cosimo's son Piero had the rather unfortunate nickname of 'the Gouty one'. All the Medici suffered from it, but poor Piero's joints gave him such gyp that he had to be carried around for half his life. He wasn't expected to survive his father, and didn't last long after Cosimo died, but proved a surprisingly able ruler. He crushed an anti-Medici conspiracy, maintained the success of the Medici bank and generously patronised Florence's best artists, sculptors and architects.

Lorenzo 'il Magnifico' (1449-92)

Upon Piero's death his son Lorenzo took the reins. Lorenzo was the big Medici, famous in his own time and legendary in later centuries. His rule marked the peak of the Florentine Renaissance, with artists such as Botticelli and the young Michelangelo producing superlative works. Although much of Lorenzo's glory was reflected, he did all he could to foster talent and reward achievement. He was an accomplished poet himself, and gathered round him a supremely talented collection of scholars and artists.

It was also a period of relative peace. Lorenzo's diplomatic skills were vital in keeping relations between the perpetually squabbling Italian states on a relatively even keel. As a businessman, however, Lorenzo was not a patch on his predecessors and the Medici bank suffered a severe decline during his lifetime (although this was also related to a general slump in Florence's economic fortunes). Lorenzo maintained a façade of being no more than *primus inter pares* (first among equals) but he made sure he always got his way and could be ruthless with his enemies. The citizens of Florence always remained loyal to Lorenzo, and the general climate of toleration and intellectual freedom he supported was a major factor in some of the greatest achievements of the Renaissance.

Piero di Lorenzo (1471-1503)

Unfortunately, Piero couldn't quite live up to his father's name. He was ruthless, charmless and tactless with a violent temper, no sense of loyalty and an unpopular haughty wife. His own father described him as 'foolish'. He did nothing to help his cause when he surrendered the city to Charles

VIII of France in 1494 and then fled when he realised he'd cocked up. Piero spent the rest of his life sulking his way around Italy, trying to persuade unenthusiastic states to help him regain power in a Florence that had no wish to see his duplicitous mug again. He drowned while fighting for France against Spain.

Giuliano, Duke of Nemours (1478-1516)

After the ascetic rule of Savonarola (*see p20* **Twisted firestarter**) and a spell under Piero Soderini (aided and abetted by Machiavelli), the Medici were restored in 1512. Giuliano was the third son of Lorenzo il Magnifico and an improvement on his brother only in the sense that he was more nonentity than swine. He was ruler of Florence in name only – being little more than a puppet of his older brother Cardinal Giovanni, later Pope Leo X.

Lorenzo, Duke of Urbino (1492-1519)

Son of Piero di Lorenzo, Lorenzo was puny, arrogant, high-handed and corrupt. No one was anything but relieved when he succumbed to tuberculosis, aggravated by syphilis.

Giovanni (Pope Leo X) (1475-1521)

Lorenzo il Magnifico's second son was not such a loser as his brothers. The night before his birth his mother dreamed she would give birth not to a baby but a huge lion. Lorenzo decided early on that Giovanni was destined for a glittering ecclesiastical career. Serious papal ear-bending saw Giovanni enter the monkhood at the age of eight, become the youngest ever cardinal when he was 16, and elbow his way into the papacy in 1513. Indirectly, he was ruling Florence from this time.

Pope Leo (spot the lion reference) was a remarkably likeable, open character, and although portly, lazy and fond of the good life ('God has given us the Papacy so let us enjoy it', he is reported to have said), he was a generous host and politically conciliatory. However, his shameless exploitation of the sale of indulgences to ease his permanent debts added further fuel to the fires of critics of papal corruption, including Martin Luther. And a chronic anal fistula made him not entirely the most fragrant company.

Giulio (Pope Clement VII) (1478-1534)

Although he was the illegitimate son of Giuliano, Lorenzo il Magnifico's brother, in the ancient Italian tradition of nepotism, Giulio had honours heaped upon him by his cousin Pope Leo. This did not win him many friends among the other cardinals and his 'rather morose and disagreeable' personality didn't help much either. His management of Florence was astute, however, and he managed to swing the Papacy in 1524.

After a while Clement became notorious for his indecision, irresolution and disloyalty. He abandoned his alliance with France only to regret it when the Emperor Charles V invaded Italy and sacked Rome in 1527 (the Pope's umm-ing and ah-ing delayed the city's defensive works for weeks). In the meantime, the Republic was re-established in Florence and Clement agreed to crown Charles in return for his help in retaking the city for the Medici. Florence fell in 1530.

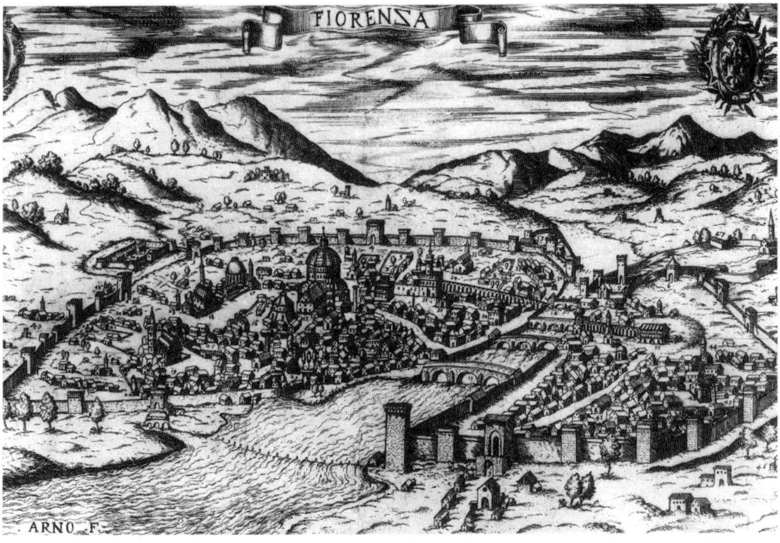

A view of Florence in 1580, with the Duomo dominating the city as it still does today.

But while he may have triumphed for his family, when Clement died in 1534, Rome celebrated. The words 'Clemens Pontifex Maximus' were obliterated on his tomb, to be replaced by 'Inclemens Pontifex Minimus'.

Alessandro (1511-37)

When Clement installed the frizzy-haired Alessandro in power in Florence in 1530 and Charles V made him hereditary Duke, the city entered one of its darkest and most desperate periods.

Thought to be Clement's illegitimate son, Alessandro proved to be bastard by name, bastard by nature. He abandoned all pretence of respecting the Florentines' treasured institutions and freedoms. He became increasingly authoritarian, tortured and executed his opponents, and outraged the good Florentine burghers by his appalling rudeness and sexual antics.

He had a penchant for dressing in women's clothing, riding about town with his bosom buddy (and sometime bed partner), the equally alarming Lorenzaccio (a distant cousin), screeching insults at the populace. A deputation of senior figures officially complained to Charles V, but to no avail. It was left to Lorenzaccio to put everyone out of their misery by luring Alessandro into bed and then stabbing him to death.

Cosimo I (1519-74)

Since there was no surviving heir in the direct Medici line, the Florentines chose this obscure 18-year-old (grandson of Lorenzo il Magnifico's daughter, Lucrezia), whom they thought they could manipulate. They were mistaken. Cosimo was the classic dark horse. Cold, secretive, cunning but effective, he knew exactly how he wanted to rule Florence and set about it with calculated, merciless efficiency – Machiavelli (*see* **The prince of darkness**) would have loved him.

He may have been unlovable, but he did restore stability within Florence and international respect for the city. He built up a Florentine navy (which proved its worth against the Turks at Lepanto in 1571), threw off the dependence on Spanish troops to maintain order and, after relentless lobbying, was made Grand Duke of Tuscany by Pope Paul V in 1569. Unfortunately he could do nothing to halt Florence's continuing economic decline (due largely to the drying up of raw materials for the city's core cloth trade) and he involved Florence in a protracted and devastating war with Siena that destroyed Sienese power for ever, and left half its population dead and the city fit for nothing.

Francesco I (1541-87)

Short, skinny, graceless and sulky, Francesco had little in common with his father, Cosimo I. During his rule (1564-87) he managed to keep Florence out of trouble, but retreated into his own little world at any opportunity, to play with his pet reindeer and dabble in alchemy. Francesco was not without talent: he became an expert in making vases from metal and crystal, and invented a new process for making porcelain.

Alessandro (without the women's clothing).

All things considered, he was a pretty harmless character, especially when compared to his younger brother Pietro, an unbalanced sponger who strangled his wife for grieving for the lover whom Pietro had had executed.

Ferdinando I (1549-1609)

Ferdinando was a huge improvement on his brother Francesco: he was more gregarious and ruled Tuscany (from 1587) efficiently and responsibly. He reduced corruption, improved trade and farming, encouraged learning, and further developed the navy and the port of Livorno. By acts such as staging lavish popular entertainments and giving dowries to poor girls, Ferdinando became the most loved Medici since Lorenzo il Magnifico.

Cosimo II (1590-1621)

Cosimo II was the son of Ferdinando I and he ruled Florence from 1609. His protection of Galileo (*see p29* **The appliance of science**) from a hostile Italy was about the only worthwhile thing he did.

Ferdinando II (1610-70)

By the time Cosimo II's son climbed into the driving seat in 1621, Tuscany had lost all pretence of being anything more than an Italian backwater. Florence was described by a contemporary visitor as a sad place 'much sunk from what it was [...] one cannot but wonder to find a country that has been a scene of so much action now so forsaken and so poor'. Porky, laid-back, moustachioed Ferdinando did nothing to arrest the trend. He loved to hunt, eye-up the boys and collect bric-a-brac. A lightweight compared to his learned brother Leopoldo, but not as bad as another brother, Gian Carlo, a prodigious glutton and lover who had at least one of his rivals murdered.

Cosimo III (1642-1723)

Things were going rapidly downhill for the Medici and Tuscany, with trade drying up and plague and famine stalking the land. It was at this stage, in 1670, that Cosimo III began to rule, but in all his 53 years at the helm he never even made the pretence of trying to improve Tuscany's lot. He was a joyless, gluttonous loner who preferred hanging around with monks to girls (although his sulky wife, Marguerite-Louise, must take some responsi-

The prince of darkness

If one response to the perceived decadence of Renaissance Florence was Savonarola's fundamentalist crusade, then Niccolò Machiavelli's cynicism was another. Machiavelli was a complex, confusing character.

In many ways, this largely self-educated lawyer's son was a product and beneficiary of the rebirth of classical learning. The statesman and writer had little esteem or affection for most of his contemporaries, however. Shrewd, sarcastic, arrogant and aloof, he believed the achievements of the Renaissance were worth nothing if they were not backed by force. He had been in Florence in 1494 when Charles VIII's troops had marched in and he had been horrified by the city's abject inability to oppose them. The theory of the pursuit and maintenance of power became his obsession.

On the fall of Savonarola, Machiavelli (1469-1527) took up a relatively minor post in the Florentine government, but gained influence when his friend Piero Soderini was appointed Gonfaloniere (the most powerful position in the administration) for life in 1502. One of Machiavelli's new responsiblities was war and he took the revolutionary step of forming the Republic's first national militia. The first bands paraded in Piazza della Signoria in 1506. Their first test came in 1512.

In an effort to regain his family's power base, Cardinal Giovanni de Medici (the future Pope Leo X) advanced on Florence with Spanish troops. The Tuscan militia was called to arms and garrisoned Prato. But when the Spanish attacked, the militia lost its nerve and fled. Florence capitulated without a fight and Machiavelli's cynicism deepened.

He would have been happy to serve the Medici, but was forced into exile at his villa at Sant'Andrea in Percussina, where he wrote his most celebrated book, *The Prince,* a year later.

By that time, he had become convinced that the best form of government was that provided by a strong leader and maintained by armed force. 'It is better to be feared than loved if you cannot be both.'

While Machiavelli's response to Florence's military weakness and loss of prestige was understandable, he failed to see that the city's achievements grew out of the very principles he saw as weak: republicanism, civic responsibility, democracy (of a sort) and tolerance.

Machiavelli never managed to practice what he preached and died bitter and unappreciated. He had no idea of the notoriety his work would one day attract; in his own time he was far more successful a playwright than politician. His satirical and irreverent plays, such as *Mandragola,* were big hits and are well regarded today.

Twisted firestarter

On Shrove Tuesday, 1497, the Florentines erected an 18-metre pile of wood in the **Piazza della Signoria**. On it they placed tapestries, wigs, perfumes, tailored clothes, ivory chessboards, volumes of poetry, works by Boccaccio and Petrarch, paintings by Botticelli and Fra Bartolomeo (willingly donated by the artists) and, on the top, an effigy of a Venetian merchant who had offered to buy the lot for a huge sum. People cheered as this 'Bonfire of the Vanities' was lit and some of the finest achievements of the Renaissance were burned to ashes.

The man responsible for this conflagration was Girolamo Savonarola (1452-98). He was born 45 years earlier into a medical family; his grandfather and father had been court physicians for the Duke of Ferrara, but Girolamo had no interest in court life. Miserable and insular, he spent most of his depressed youth reading the scriptures and composing tunes for the lute; his innate gloominess reinforced when his advances to the daughter of a Florentine exile were bluntly rejected.

In 1475, Savonarola joined the monastery of San Domenico in Bologna, living a life of austerity for seven years. After being sent out to preach all over Italy, Savonarola ended up in Florence, where he settled at the Monastery of San Marco.

Savonarola believed that the world was going down the pan. Church and society were corrupt and in need of a good scourging. Simplicity, austerity and purity were the goals, and could only be achieved by casting aside worldly goods and pleasures. He railed against the new trend in painting that made 'the Virgin Mary look like a harlot', and against prostitutes ('pieces of meat with eyes'). As for sodomites, it was straight into the fire with them. That Savonarola should have exerted such a powerful grip in what was probably the most liberal and enlightened city in Europe seems paradoxical.

It wasn't just the uneducated masses who flocked to hear him preach, either. His most passionate supporters included members of Lorenzo de' Medici's close circle of humanist thinkers and artists, such as Pico della Mirandola and Sandro Botticelli. Savonarola's success underlined the (often ignored) deep religiosity behind many of the greatest achievements of the Renaissance, while at the same time capturing a general end-of-the-century public mood of unease and foreboding.

After Lorenzo's death in 1494, Savonarola's prophecies of doom became ever more intense. He told of his visions of the 'Sword of the Lord' hanging over Florence, threatening to wreak revenge and disaster on the evil city. When Charles VIII of France invaded Italy later that year, the prophecy seemed to have been fulfilled.

Savonarola welcomed the invaders, and for the next three years, became *de facto* ruler of Florence. He despatched bands of child informers, dressed as angels, to snitch on those wearing fancy clothes or make-up, playing games, boozing or whoring. The people fasted, the people prayed.

The Borgia Pope, Alexander VI, became alarmed at Savonarola's growing independence and excommunicated him in 1497. Meanwhile plague, famine and an unsuccessful war against Pisa were leaving the Florentines looking for a scapegoat.

The Franciscans challenged the Dominican Savonarola to prove his divine favour and an

bility for this). He was not uneducated, but as he got older he grew more and more prudish and antisemitic. Intellectual freedom took a nosedive, taxes soared, public executions were a daily occurrence.

Gian Gastone (1671-1737)

When Cosimo III finally snuffed it in 1723, he left his disaster of a son in control: this was to be the last of the Medici rulers. Neglected, lonely and miserable, Gian Gastone was forcibly m arried to a spectacularly offensive woman, Anna Maria Francesca, daughter of the Duke of Saxe-Lauenberg, who dragged him off to her gloomy castle near Prague.

He drowned his sorrows in the taverns of Prague, whoring about with stable boys and students before escaping back to Florence in 1708. He was shocked to find himself Grand Duke in 1723. The start of his rule was surprisingly coherent, he tried to relieve the burden of taxation, increase tolerance and reinstate citizens' rights, but he soon lapsed into chronic apathy and dissolution.

When his relations tried to get him back on the straight and narrow he disgraced himself by, for instance, vomiting into his napkin at a respectable dinner, then taking off his wig and wiping his mouth with it. Eventually he couldn't even be bothered to get out of bed, and had troops of rowdy boys known as *ruspanti* entertain him by cavorting about and shouting obscenities. He only ever came out of his bedroom to prove to his subjects that he wasn't dead. The poor bugger was so derided that the Treaty of Aix-la-Chapelle in 1735 gave the Grand Duchy over to Francis Stephen of Lorraine without even consulting Gian Gastone.

ordeal by fire was agreed upon. On 7 April 1498, lines of oiled sticks were laid out in readiness, but then the whole thing descended into farce as no-one knew the correct procedure. Eventually heavy rain brought an end to the squabbling.

The mob saw red. They wanted blood, and rioting broke out the next day. The ruling council, bowing to public pressure, arrested Savonarola, tortured a confession out of him, and sentenced him to death for heresy and schism.

On 23 May 1498, the Florentines piled wood on the same spot that, only a year before, had witnessed the Bonfire of the Vanities. Savonarola was hanged and burned, along with two of his followers. It was a martyrdom, and one with clear biblical overtones. The authorities were aware of the possibility of devotees salvaging relics and ensured everything was burned to ashes and scattered in the Arno.

A year later, Botticelli, still tormented by the disgrace of his hero, asked one of Savonarola's examiners what the friar had done to be brought down so ignominiously. 'We never found any sin in him [...] if the prophet and his colleagues hadn't been put to death [...] the people would have rushed on us and cut us to pieces. It was their lives or ours.'

Anna Maria (died 1743)

Gian Gastone had a sister – the very last surviving Medici, who was as much a contrast to her brother as can be imagined. Every visitor to Florence since the mid-eighteenth century has reason to be grateful to the strait-laced, solemn and pious Anna Maria. In her will she bequeathed all Medici property and treasures to the Grand Duchy in perpetuity – on the one condition that they never leave Florence.

The Renaissance

Although the most visible manifestation of the Renaissance was the astonishing outpouring of art emanating from fifteenth-century Florence, the spark that lit the Renaissance fire was undoubtedly literary. The word 'Renaissance' (rebirth) is most properly applied to the rediscovery of ancient Greek and Roman texts and the new view of the world and mankind they revealed. A few classical works had never been lost, but those that were known were usually corrupted versions only available to clerics who forbade their dissemination or discussion.

It was the inquisitive Florentines who first decided to take matters into their own hands. Their wealth paid for dedicated manuscript detectives such as Poggio Bracciolini to dig through neglected monastery libraries across Europe. The volume of unknown works discovered was astonishing – and their effect was intellectual dynamite, causing the Florentines to reassess the way they thought about almost every field of human endeavour. Within the first few decades of the fifteenth cen-

The rebirth of art

It was Giorgio Vasari who first used the term *rinascita* (rebirth), in *The Lives of the Most Eminent Painters, Sculptors and Architects* (1550). Vasari – his portrait of Lorenzo (1534) is above – refers specifically to the rebirth of art under the classical influence; it is not solely a copying of classical form that developed in the arts but a referral back to nature with a deeper understanding and inquiry into mathematics and science.

From Vasari's example it is generally accepted that the Renaissance period in art consisted of two phases: an Early Renaissance from 1400-1500, a time of learning and discovery, and a High Renaissance from 1500-27, where a perfect harmony was achieved between the intellectual side of anatomy, perspective and light and the beauty of drama, colour and expression.

There are several reasons why this rebirth took place in Florence. In 1400 the Florentines resisted the attacks by the Duke of Milan, and established themselves as the 'New Athens'; with increased economic power the Florentines were feeling confident and ready to embellish their city.

At the same time, there was a shift in attitude towards art itself; it was no longer viewed as a mere craft, but as a liberal art, one that involved learning, creativity and expression of ideas. Artists started mingling with scholars and poets, and writing their own treatises exploring science, anatomy and geometry. This was *uomo universale*: the artist no longer necessarily specialised in one particular art form. Even Giotto, working a century earlier, and whom Vasari saw as the first artist to break away from the art of the Middle Ages, was both a painter and architect. Today he is regarded by many as the founder of modern painting, but he was also supervisor of the **Duomo** and worked on the Campanile.

ARCHITECTURE

It was Brunelleschi (1377-1446) who first incorporated classical philosophy into architecture. He developed a new system of linear perspective, which enabled him to prepare ground plans. This did not mean, however, that he rejected the Gothic tradition (his work on the dome of the Duomo demonstrates his knowledge of Gothic vaulting), but adapted it, adding a classical vocabulary to Christian iconography. The classical language was adapted to domestic architecture by Alberti in **Palazzo Ruccelai**.

SCULPTURE

The development from Gothic to Renaissance sculpture can be traced in the work of Ghiberti on the doors of the Baptistery, from the Gothic set on the north side to the Renaissance set on the east. It is, however, in the work of Donatello that the Renaissance spirit is most keenly apparent. His work does not just copy classical formulae, but has an added vitalism and naturalism. Compare the strength and power of his *St George* at **Orsanmichele** to the freshness of his *David* in the **Bargello** or the tenderness of the *Penitent Magdalene*. Renaissance sculpture culminated in the work of Michelangelo as seen at the Medici tombs at **San Lorenzo**.

PAINTING

The pictures in the **Uffizi** show the development of the Renaissance in painting and the artists mastering perspective and the effects of light and expression. Giotto's *Maestà* adds a dignity and human reality to the image. Where Giotto's figures have a carved solidity, Masaccio's have a sense of flesh and form. Masaccio was the great forerunner of the Renaissance. His work at the Brancacci Chapel shows an ability to narrate through images. At **Santa Maria Novella** Masaccio used the linear perspective as set out by Brunelleschi.

Pope Julius II arrives to give his verdict on Michelangelo's latest sculpture.

tury, there came to light Quintilian's *The Training of an Orator,* which detailed the Roman education system, Columella's *De Re Rustica* on agriculture, key texts on Roman architecture by Vitruvius and Frontinus, and Cicero's *Brutus* (a justification of republicanism). Very few Greek works were known in Western Europe; suddenly, almost simultaneously, most of Plato, Homer, the plays of Sophocles, Aeschylus, Euripedes, Aristophanes, histories by Herodotus, Xenophon, Thucydides, the speeches of Demosthenes and many other Classics were discovered.

FLORENTINE PRE-EMINENCE

The Renaissance didn't just happen. Much groundwork had already been laid by the turn of the fifteenth century (and some argue that there was a mini-Renaissance as early as the twelfth century). Giotto, for instance, had made a decisive break from Byzantine formality in art towards naturalism as early as the late thirteenth century; Petrarch, Boccaccio and Dante had all collected Latin manuscripts. However, such men as these were exceptions, and it was undoubtedly in the city on the Arno in the fifteenth century that the intellectual ideas of the Renaissance really took hold. Magnificent while it lasted, Florence's pre-eminence was, nevertheless, abruptly snuffed out on the death of Lorenzo il Magnifico in 1492 and the invasion of Italy by Charles VIII of France in the 1490s. In the early sixteenth century, the cutting edge switched to Rome, where Michelangelo, Bramante and Raphael were creating their finest works; and thence, after Emperor Charles V sacked Rome in 1527, to Venice later in the century, where masters such as Palladio and Titian practised their arts. Meanwhile, Gutenberg's invention of movable type and the widespread introduction of the printing press across Europe in the mid fifteenth century meant that the new learning reached into the farthest corners of the continent, inspiring the people of cities as distant as Lisbon and Krakow.

SPIRITUAL MATTERS

Unlike in the eighteenth-century Enlightenment, God was not under threat from the Renaissance. Although scholars started to look for explanations beyond the Scriptures, these were seen as complementary to accepted religion rather than as a challenge to it. Much effort was made to present the wisdom of the ancients, in a pre-Christian age, as a hitherto forgotten precursor to the ultimate wisdom of God. Many of the foremost figures of the time were deeply religious and saw no conflict between God and Plato. Even Lorenzo Valla's exposure of the document known as the *Donation of Constantine* (on which the Pope's claim for temporal power in Italy was based) as a fake was intended to focus the church on spiritual matters rather than discredit the institution itself.

The Renaissance should not be confused with the Reformation of the early sixteenth century, which heartily disapproved of many of the (as the Germans saw it) flowery, frivolous and indecent Italian fripperies of Renaissance artists, writers and architects.

A PRE-SCIENTIFIC AGE

The rarified world of the educated and wealthy may have been electrified by the new learning and exciting achievements in the arts, but the lives of the vast majority of people didn't change at all. Pretty paintings and handsome buildings were one thing, but real practical advances that would alter and improve their lives, in fields such as sanitation and understanding of disease, were still centuries away. Even among the privileged, it was clear that the Renaissance was a pre-scientific age. The fifteenth century was an era when ideas were still paramount. Science, as a process of deduction based on observation and experimentation, didn't really get going until the seventeenth century. Leonardo (*see p26* **Pure genius**) may have produced marvellous anatomical drawings but the ancient (and, for practical purposes, useless) medical theory of the four humours was still widely accepted; astronomy and astrology were all but synonymous; mathematics was seen in a Pythagorean way as an almost mystical art; alchemy, the attempted transformation of base metals into gold, was flourishing.

Uccello was obsessed by perspective as is apparent in *Rout of San Romano* (Uffizi), a masterpiece of foreshortening. Piero della Francesca wrote a treatise on the rules of perspective for painters and his expertise shows in his fresco cycle at San Francesco, Arezzo which portrays the *Legend of The True Cross* in an uncluttered, selective manner.

You can't discuss the Renaissance without mentioning Botticelli. In his *Birth of Venus*, while he would not have actually believed in the goddess of love, he depicts her as a symbol – an approach which could not have been taken prior to the Renaissance.

EM Forster muses on rooms and views.

Florence in the Risorgimento

Florence never wanted to be capital of Italy. Vittorio Emanuele II, King of Sardinia-Piedmont and leader of the Risorgimento – the movement to unify the country – never wanted to reign from Florence. The Piedmontese people were outraged by the idea.

When, in 1865, with Rome still holding out against the nationalists, the Convention of September declared Florence the capital, the people of Turin rioted and were subdued only after 200 had been killed. It was the culmination of an extraordinary few decades for Florence and Italy.

Tuscany in the 1820s and 1830s had been an agreeable, benign place. Under the laid-back, if not overly bright, Grand Duke Leopold II, the region enjoyed a climate of toleration that attracted intellectuals, dissidents, artists and writers from all over Italy and Europe. They would meet in the Gabinetto Scientifico-Letterario in the Palazzo Buondelmonti in Piazza Santa Trinità, frequently welcoming distinguished foreigners such as Heine, Byron and Chateaubriand.

For a time, Leopold and his ministers managed to keep the reactionary influence of the Grand Duke's uncle, Emperor Francis II of Austria, at arm's length, while playing down the growing populist cry for unification. By the 1840s, however, it was clear that the two-pronged nationalist movement, represented by the Piedmontese monarchy and Giuseppe Mazzini's republican Giovane Italia movement, had become a serious threat to the status quo. Even relaxed Florence was swept up in nationalist enthusiasm, causing Leopold to clamp down on reformers and impose some censorship.

In 1848, the tumultuous year of revolutions, insurrections in Livorno and Pisa forced Leopold to grant concessions to the reformers, including a Tuscan constitution.

When news reached Florence that the Milanese had driven the Austrians out of their city, and that Charles Albert, King of Sardinia-Piedmont, had determined to push them out of Italy altogether, thousands of Tuscans joined the cause (including Carlo Lorenzini, better known as Carlo Collodi, author of the *Adventures of Pinocchio*). However, the better-trained Austrians beat the Tuscans at Montanara and the Piedmontese at Novara in 1849.

The pendulum seemed to be swinging back in Austria's favour, but the radicals in Florence dug their heels in and bullied the Grand Duke into appointing the activist reformer Giuseppe Montanelli, a professor of law at Pisa University,

A head of his time

Leon Battista Alberti epitomises one of the most significant changes wrought by the Renaissance: the reawakening of man's interest in himself and belief in his own potential (women, alas, still had several centuries to wait). It is a view that has been fundamental to our thinking, and actions, ever since.

Alberti was born in 1407, the illegitimate son of a wealthy banker. A sickly child, he systematically toughened his body by riding, jousting, rock climbing and archery to become a noted athlete. Alberti went on to study Latin in Padua and Greek in Bologna, where he took a degree in law, while devouring every classical text he could find. While still a student he wrote a comedy in Latin, *Philodoxus*, that he successfully passed off as a lost Roman text for several years.

Devious cousins swindled Alberti out of his inheritance and he took a job as a writer of briefs for the papacy, coming to Florence with Pope Eugenius IV in 1434. The creative energies of the city were the catalyst for an astonishing outpouring of works. Alberti taught himself music, wrote songs, sonnets and mastered the organ. In 1435 he wrote the first treatise on the art of painting, *Della Pittura*. Along with Brunelleschi and Michelozzo, he was one of the leading architects of his day, putting the rediscovered principles of classical architecture into practice. The **Palazzo Rucellai** and the joyful façade of **Santa Maria Novella** in Florence are perhaps his most celebrated works. 'Tell me, is there anything this man doesn't know?' wrote an incredulous contemporary.

Seemingly not. Alberti hung out with blacksmiths and shipbuilders to learn their trades; he made a diorama of Rome that doubled as a planetarium; he invented machinery to raise sunken Roman galleys from Lake Nemi. His books included works on horsebreeding, oratory, orthographics, ciphers, sculpture, mathematical puzzles, fables, the secrets of a lady's toilet and a far-sighted manual for judges which urged that criminals should be reformed rather than punished.

As Alberti himself wrote: 'Man is born not to mourn in idleness, but to work at magnificent and large-scale tasks, thereby pleasing and honouring God, and manifesting in himself perfect *virtù*, that is, the fruit of happiness.'

to head a new government. Montanelli asked the extremist Francesco Guerazzi to join him. They went to Rome to attend a constituent assembly, but the alarmed Pope Pius IX threatened to excommunicate anyone attending such an assembly.

GRIM TIMES

Leopold panicked, and fled Florence in disguise for Naples. Montanelli, Guerazzi and Mazzini set up a provisional government but, in the absence of armed support, it collapsed.

Preferring the devil they knew to the Austrians, the Florentines invited Leopold back; he returned in July 1849, but brought with him Austrian troops to keep order. Grim times followed for a city just recovering from one of its worst ever floods. Seemingly now content to be an Austrian puppet, clamping down on the press and dissent, Leopold's one-time popularity dissipated.

Elsewhere in Italy, the fighting continued, with the Piedmontese Count Camillo Cavour persuading Napoleon III's France to join with him in expelling the Austrians. Eventually they goaded the Emperor into action, and war was declared in April 1859.

The French and Piedmontese swept the Imperial armies before them, while, in Florence, nationalist demonstrations organised by the *Società Nazionale* forced the government to resign. Leopold refused to formally abdicate but, on 27 April, he left Florence for the last time with his family, while his former subjects watched in silence. The following year, the minister of justice announced that the Tuscan people had voted for unification with Vittorio Emanuele's Kingdom of Piedmont.

The Florentines greeted their new king with enthusiasm when he arrived in February 1865 to take up residence in the Palazzo Pitti. The influx of northerners, though, was met with mixed feelings: business boomed, but the Florentines didn't take much to Piedmontese flashiness.

Huge changes were wrought in the city. Ring roads encircled the old centre, avenues and squares (such as Piazza della Repubblica) were built, residential suburbs constructed and parks laid out (Giardino dei Semplici, for example). Intellectuals and socialites crowded the salons and cafés. In Via Cavour, the Caffè Michelangelo was the favoured hangout of the painters known as the *Macchiaioli*, the Italian version of the Impressionists.

When war with Prussia forced the French (who had swapped sides) to withdraw their troops from Italy in 1870, Rome finally fell to Vittorio Emanuele's troops and Italy was united for the first time since the fall of the Roman Empire.

Pure genius

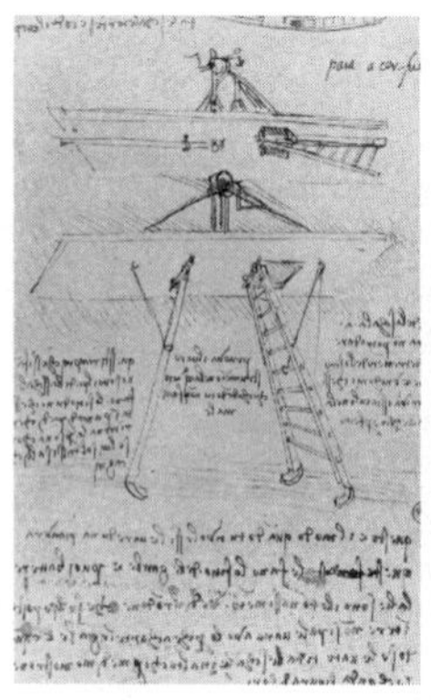

'In the normal course of events many men and women are born with various remarkable qualities and talents; but occasionally, in a way that transcends nature, a single person is marvellously endowed by heaven with beauty, grace and talent in such abundance that he leaves other men far behind, all his actions seem inspired, and indeed everything he does clearly comes from God rather than from human art.'

This quote from Vasari's *Lives of the Artists* refers to Leonardo da Vinci (1452-1519), a veritable *uomo universale.* With Michelangelo and Raphael, he is considered one of the three great artists of the High Renaissance and yet he was much older and a contemporary of Raphael's teacher, Perugino. He is best known as a painter even though few of his works were ever finished due to his impatience and low boredom threshold. His drawings far outnumber the paintings he produced. He was fascinated by science and the natural world, believing that to see was to know; his observations from life and his recordings through drawings are testimony to his inventiveness. He practically discovered the circulation of blood, the growth of the embryo in the womb, man-powered flight. He was a keen geologist, botanist, musician and writer. He performed numerous dissections to gain a greater insight into anatomy, and designed buildings, fortifications, canals and locks.

He was born in Vinci near Florence and was apprenticed to Verrochio's studio in about 1469. He helped on Verrochio's *Baptism* (now in the **Uffizi**). You can see his hand in the angel on the left and in parts of the landscape. The draperies of the angel are not modelled in line but through chiaroscuro; he does not have a set formula for drapery but has actually observed how the cloth would fall across the forms of the body. The expression of the angel exudes grace and calmness. Vasari wrote that, having seen Leonardo's work on the painting, 'Verrochio never touched colours again, he was so ashamed that the boy understood their use better than he did.'

Leonardo's earliest drawing *Arno Landscape* (Uffizi) is dated 1473; he was left-handed and the date is written right to left. He often wrote like this in his notes on his drawings, perhaps as a game, but also so that his notes would not easily be copied.

The authorship of the *Annunciation* (Uffizi) has been questioned and is now believed to be an early work by Leonardo. The carpet of flowers demonstrates his great interest in botany, the wings of the angel are meticulously painted and are accurately modelled on those of a bird.

He soon gained a great reputation and as early as 1481 received a commission from the monks of San Donato at Scopeto near Florence for the *Adoration of the Magi.* The work was never finished, though the cartoon remains in the Uffizi. It is a masterpiece in itself and offers a wonderful insight into his working practices. The composition is geometrically mapped out; the figures and landscape are not separate but work together as a harmonious whole. Drawings survive for particular poses of the various figures, and a preparatory perspectival study of the whole (also in the Uffizi) shows lines ruled in silverpoint with figures drawn on top in ink. It is incredible how much preparatory study went into the design of one painting.

In 1482, after payments were stopped, Leonardo set off for Milan where he worked on a number of important works including the *Last Supper* (Santa Maria delle Grazie). He returned to Florence in 1500 and was commissioned, among other work, to paint the walls of the Salone dei Cinquecento with a scene celebrating Florence's victory of the Battle of Anghiari. Michelangelo also received a commission for work in the same room though neither artist completed his work. Michelangelo left for Rome and Leonardo for Milan; from there he went to France where he died in 1519.

Though little of his work survives in Florence, it is worth visiting the Uffizi to view the great advances Leonardo made in painting and to experience a small aspect of his immeasurable genius.

Florence's brief reign as capital ended, but the Florentines remained phlegmatic. As a popular epigram of the time declared:

Turin sheds tears when the King departs
And Rome's exultant when the King arrives.
Florence, fount of poetry and the arts,
Cares not one whit in either case – and thrives.

The twentieth century

Has the twentieth century even arrived yet in Florence? Though the tourist, a twentieth-century archetype, has a field day in the Tuscan capital, it might appear to the naked eye that it has more or less succeeded in remaining immune to the fireworks and fads of this precipitous and debriefed century. This, after all, is the city which, for years, refused McDonald's permission to establish an outlet in the city centre. So, while the rest of the world is frantically rummaging for the remedy to an as yet unspecified ailment, Florence seems happy to sit back on its laurels and give this pockmarked century the cold shoulder.

Florence began the twentieth century much as it ended it – as a thriving tourist centre. Its allure in the early 1900s was essentially confined to an exclusive coterie of writers, artists, aesthetes and the upper middle classes. Queen Victoria, Oscar Wilde, Henry James, EM Forster and DH Lawrence were among its most famous visitors. An entire English-speaking industry sprung up to cater for the needs and excesses of these wealthy foreign visitors.

FUTURISM & FASCISM

During the first half of the twentieth century, Florence bore the same cross to which the political and social fate of Italy was nailed. Though the city had remained relatively unaffected by World War I – it was neither occupied nor attacked – it inevitably suffered the social repercussions of the conflict. Post-war hardship and chaos, together with the mounting threat of Bolshevism, inspired a fierce middle-class rage for order, which found expression in the black shirt of Fascism. Groups of *squadristi* were already forming in 1919 and with the support of the Futurists and their prophet, the novelist and dramatist Filippo Marinetti, for whom the recent war had constituted 'the most beautiful poem', began organising parades and demonstrations in the streets of Florence. Italian Fascism began its existence as a narcissistic spectacle for the eye rather than a coherent political system: it provided an appearance of law and order in the manner of the old medieval love of pageant and procession.

When Bennito Mussolini came to power and the resistance to Fascism died down, there began in Florence a campaign to expunge the city of its foreign elements and influences. Hotels and shops with English names were put under pressure to sever their Anglo-Saxon affiliations; non-Italians were given a harder time. The Florence which had been described as a *'ville toute Anglaise'* by the social historian De Goncourt brothers was under threat.

Buildings constructed during the Fascist reign include the exhibition centre at the Parterre to the

Benito Mussolini and Adolf Hitler share a joke as they are driven through Florence.

north of Piazza della Liberta, the Biblioteca Nazionale (1935), the Ponte Sospeso (1932), the Stadio Communale at Campo di Marte designed by Pier Luigi Nervi and opened in 1932 and the new railway station of 1935. In the spring of 1938 Mussolini and Adolf Hitler appeared on the balcony of the Palazzo della Signoria together. In general the Florentines are reputed to have not taken to the Führer, though Florence was said to have been his favourite Italian city.

THE ART OF WAR

Italy entered the war at Germany's side on 10 June 1940. Mussolini's declaration of war had been expected and plans had already been made for the protection of the city's monuments and works of art. Confident in the love of the British and Americans for the city, few Florentines considered an aerial attack a realistic prospect. Florence itself was an open-air museum, a testament to man's artistic evolution and, as such, a patrimony which belonged to the entire world. The city's monuments became its best protection against bombardments. Nevertheless, the Fascist regime, perhaps for propaganda reasons, immediately began protecting Florence's works of art. Photos of the period reveal the statuary of the famous piazzas disappearing inside grotesque, comically inefficient, corrugated-iron or wooden sheds. The Baptistery doors were hidden behind bricks. In truth, the precautions taken would have saved very little had the Allies decided to carpet bomb the streets of Florence. Many of the principal treasures from the Uffizi and the Pitti Palace, including Botticelli's *Primavera* and Giotto's *Madonna,* were taken to the Castello Montegufoni in the Tuscan countryside for safe keeping.

Though Florence was important to the Germans' route from Rome back to Germany, it was saved from major bombardments by the express wish of the Allied Command. Only when it became necessary to hinder the Nazis' communication line to Rome were these aesthetic scruples set aside. In September 1943 a formation of American bombers took off, intent on wiping out Bologna's railway station. Thick, low cloud put an end to that idea. The target was switched and Florence's Campo di Marte station became the new target. The city was caught unaware. The American bombers made something of a mess of their mission, in fact, and 218 civilians died in the air raids while the station remained in perfect working order.

The decision to prohibit further air raids on the city was taken at the highest level. Clearly no one was willing to go down in history as the man responsible for destroying the artistic treasures of a universally loved cultural heritage, and there were no more air raids on Florence for the remainder of 1943. However, the station at Campo di Marte became instrumental to the Nazi war effort

The ruins of Ponte alle Grazie, destroyed by the Nazis in 1944.

The appliance of science

Galileo Galilei, the 'founder of modern science', was born in Pisa in 1564. The son of a court musician and descending from a noble Florentine family, he entered the University of Pisa as a medical student having previously received an early education at the monastery of Vallombrisa near Florence. He was to abandon medicine for mathematics and physics but was unable to finish his degree because his father could no longer afford the fees.

In 1589 he was given a post at the University of Pisa where he taught mathematics. In 1590 he completed a book, *De Motu* (On Motion), in which he took exception to the Aristotelian doctrines of motion based on lightness and heaviness. In 1592, by then well known for various revolutionary scientific treatises, he was given a chair at Padua.

In 1609 news came to him of a Dutch invention: the telescope. He quickly built one of his own and before the year was out had produced a telescope that enabled him to see mountains on the moon and identify four stars circling Jupiter. In 1610 he published these discoveries in a book entitled *The Sidereal Messenger,* which became the basis for his scientific reputation.

Also in 1609, Galileo was called upon to do the astrological chart for the Grand Duke Ferdinando I. In the best high-street tradition, he predicted a long, happy life for the Grand Duke. Unfortunately Ferdinando died a few months later and thus ended Galileo's cursory career as a fortune teller.

Some years later he demonstrated his telescope at Rome. By then, however, he had offended and alarmed the ecclesiastical authorities by his defence of Copernican theory of the solar system in contradiction of the Scriptures. It was at this stage of his career that he was invited by Ferdinando's son Cosimo, who had once been a pupil of his at Padua, to come to Florence as First Philosopher and Mathematician to the Grand Duke of Tuscany. Grateful for the opportunity to continue his studies and experiments under Ducal protection, Galileo moved, as the Medici's guest, to a house in Bellosguardo near Florence and, having discovered the satellites of Jupiter, repaid his patron's kindness by naming them Sidera Medicea.

His book *The Assayer* incensed the Jesuits who were then enjoying a certain power in the Papal Court. The Thirty Years' War was in full swing and accusations of heresy abounded as the Counter-Reformation struggled to spread its influence.

It was Galileo's next book, *Dialogue on Two World Systems,* which really got him into trouble. In it he stated that the ebb and flow of the tides is due to the three-fold Copernican motions of the Earth. For this he was summoned to Rome to stand trial for heresy, the Jesuits having insisted that his theories would have more catastrophic consequences for the Church than 'Luther and Calvin put together'. On 22 June 1633, Galileo was pronounced 'vehemently suspected of heresy' and condemned to formal imprisonment. He was forced to sign a recantation of his theories: 'I abandon completely the false opinion that the sun is at the centre of the world and does not move and that the Earth is not the centre of the world and moves…' But his sentence was commuted by the Pope and later that year he was allowed to return to Tuscany under house arrest. Here he spent the last eight years of his life on a small estate at Arcetri.

His last book *Discorsi* discusses the problems of matter and local motion. Galileo attributed the internal cohesion of solids to the pressure of intercorpuscular gaps – a vacuum. He discovered that liquids, not possessing vacuums among their particles, did not have an appreciable internal cohesion.

Galileo died on 8 January 1642. The Church forbade a Christian burial, but in 1737 the Medici arranged for his remains to be transferred to the Novice's Chapel at **Santa Croce**, where a memorial can be seen today. There is also a room devoted to him in the **Museo di Storia della Scienza** where the bones of his right middle finger are displayed (*pictured above*). These were removed from his tomb when his remains were being moved in 1737. A Vatican commission cleared Galileo of heresy in 1992.

The flood of November 1966 killed 39 people and wrecked 15,000 cars.

and army generals tried to convince their superiors to lift the ban to bomb Florence. As Florence became increasingly more important to the Nazis, it was eventually decided to carry out an attack using only the most experienced and expert squadrons and only in ideal weather conditions. On 11 March 1944, the Americans unleashed their bombers on Florence. This attack was followed by several more, all directed at incapacitating the Nazi communications system. Casualties were inevitable but the *centro storico* remained unviolated – saved by its art.

A REIGN OF TERROR

The Germans entered Florence on 11 September 1943, a matter of weeks after Mussolini's arrest and the armistice was signed. They established their headquarters in Piazza San Marco.

During the 11 months of their occupation, the Fascists came out of the woodwork and established a special police force known as the *Banda Carità* after its chief Mario Carità. *Carità* in Italian means charity; Mario Carità was known for his systematic brutality. A German officer inspecting the *Banda*'s headquarters found it so drenched in the blood of torture victims that he insisted the unit leave town. A new reign of terror began for the Florentines, especially those of Jewish descent.

In 1938 Florence had a Jewish population of 2,326. The chief rabbi after 1943 was a man called Nathan Cassuto. He was instrumental in saving the lives of many Jews in the city, who, following his advice, hid themselves in convents or little villages under false names.

The night of 27 November was one of terror in Florence with at least three brutal raids. In the largest attack, Nazis and Fascists invaded the Convent of the Franciscan Sisters of Mary in the Piazza del Carmine. About 30 Jewish women and children were hiding there. All were deported. The second train to leave Italian soil bound for the gas chambers was the one that left Florence containing at least 400 Jews from Florence, Siena and Bologna. Only 85 of these are now known by name. Of the 400, 13 men and 94 women passed the infamous selection and escaped immediate gassing. Not a single one is known to have returned.

On 1 August 1944, fighting broke out in various parts of the city but the Florentine patriots were poorly armed and could not prevent the Germans from destroying all the Arno bridges except Ponte Vecchio. About 150,000 people were affected by the evacuation order before the mines were detonated. Along with the bridges, the old quarter around Ponte Vecchio was razed to the ground.

The British and American infantry did not arrive to reinforce partisan lines on the Arno until 1 September. The German army abandoned Fiesole on 7 September. When the Allies finally reached Florence they found a functioning government formed by the Committee of National Liberation (CLN). Within hours of the Germans' departure, work started in what has become typically Florentine fashion to put the bridges back into place. Ponte Santa Trinità was rebuilt, stone by stone, in exactly the same location.

BURSTING BANKS & BOMBS

It was not long before the Florentine capacity for restoration was forced into action again. This time for a calamity of an altogether different nature. In the early hours of the morning of 4 November 1966, the Arno burst its banks, allowing its waters to crash through the houses, galleries and workshops of Florence.

People awoke to find their homes invaded by the enraged river. At 9.45am the flood burst into the Piazza del Duomo. Florence became Venice for a day: all the main piazzas were under water, the water level rising in some places to over 6m.

The damage was substantial; the flood had more impact on Florence than either Napoleon or the Nazis. An estimated 15,000 cars were destroyed; 6,000 shops put out of business; and almost 14,000 families left homeless. Many works of art, books and archives were damaged by the flood: treasures in the refectory of Santa Croce were blackened by the mud; on the right wall of the nave of the church Donatello's *Cavalcanti Annunciation* was soaked with oil to the level of the Virgin's knees.

As word of Florence's flood spread around the world, public and private funds were pumped into repairing and restoring some of the damage. Thirty years down the line, work is still far from finished. Naturally, measures have been put into place should history ever attempt to repeat itself; the river bed beneath Ponte Vecchio has been deepened, for example, and videos and computer equipment have been installed to monitor changes in water level.

No one could have foreseen the car bomb explosion of 1993, however. Thought to have been placed by the Mafia, the bomb went off in Via Lambertesca, killing five people. It caused structural damage to the Uffizi, destroying the Gregoriophilus library and damaging the Vasari Corridor. The culprits were never caught.

Today, Florence expends much of its energy on catering for the tourist though in true Tuscan style manages to conceal the stress and sweat of the endeavour very well. So unmarked is it by the vicissitudes of the twentieth century it might almost seem to the irreverent post-modernist eye a kind of Renaissance theme park.

In 1993, a Mafia bomb killed five people and destroyed the Gregoriophilus library.

Florence Today

But is it the real world?

An insidious misgiving of the long-term visitor to Florence is that they might be running away from something. This 'something' will inevitably end up being generically classified under the heading 'reality'. But what's reality nowadays? A gratuitous fist in the face? A groping hand in a dark alley? Who is willing any more to grant reality to anything that doesn't call on every reserve of aggression, ambition and administrative prowess? If reality has come to be synonymous with grunge, grind, clenched fists, broken glass, scorched earth and wailing sirens, Florence can easily seem at first glance a therapeutic haven from the ills of the modern world.

Some maintain that even Florence is slowly contracting some of the diseases of the modern world and even a couple of the carcinogenic internal ones. The drug-runners, for instance, who patrol the streets at night like contraband shadow foes of the forces of law and order. Or else there's the perpetual mushroom of ozoned smog that hangs over the city like an injunction – you can metabolise twice as many painkilling compounds here as in London. The city is so badly polluted, the air so full of toxic impurities, that it's often necessary to ban cars from the city centre in an attempt to ferry away the alarmingly thick deposits of low level pollution.

Then there are the tourists. Look! There's Miho, Kiko, Yoko and Hoho again, this time grinning for the lens in front of the Duomo while another wagon train of Mid-West American fast-food junkies all appearing to be in an advanced stage of pregnancy waddle their way back to the air-conditioned coach and a pair of girls jog their deodorised, desexed bodies along the river, flaunting such scrupulous standards of hygiene that you wonder if they were born and raised in a laboratory. The tourists, though bringing their own paranoias and detergents to Florence, do nothing to alleviate the idea that the city is some kind of weekend getaway exempt from the pressures and polystyrene packaging of the real world.

Florence's *centro storico* is as much an open-air museum as a mapped grid of shop-lined streets and thus tends to be infected by the rather strained, glassy atmosphere that pervades and sterilises art galleries. Florence tourists are also likely to be part of a tightly scheduled tour group and officiously ushered about like schoolchildren on an outing. This too – grown-ups in adolescent elasticated Dayglo sports costumes surrendering up all personal initiative to a follow-the-leader mentality – enervates the central nervous system of the city.

Restoration work is ubiquitous in Florence. Workshops proliferate in every old quarter of the city where the new generation of craftsmen following in their father's father's footsteps alchemically restore all kinds of artifacts to their original state. Florence is thus a city which expends a great deal of energy on preserving the past; a city which holds in great esteem the healing process.

In Florence it's not birdsong that heralds the arrival of spring but the omnipresent cacophony of pneumatic drills. Florentine workmen have a habit of getting all the noisiest work over first thing in the morning. Perhaps so that by eleven o'clock when the sun's getting into its stride they are free to bask in the ozone rays and wolf whistle to their hearts' content.

Florence is full of foreign women for the workmen to whistle at. Lured here by who knows what magnetic charge. The myth of the Latin Lover? A more civilised way of life? A nostalgia for the days when the father still imparted some exemplary fabric of spiritual integrity. Or perhaps simply to learn the salty swelling and subsiding rhythms of a Mediterranean language?

And yet it might be said that Florence is a very masculine city. Female nature is certainly kept under wraps, cloistered and domesticated inside courtyards and monastic structures. In Piazza della Signoria, Perseus has cut off the head of Medusa, marking the end, according to Robert Graves, of the era of the female mysteries; the Sabine women are being raped, as is Polixena. Only Judith flaunting the head of Holofernes anticipates the decline and fall of patriarchal administration.

Florence is also a belligerently chaste city in appearance. Butter wouldn't melt in its mouth. But despite its painstakingly assembled montage of treasures and high-principled emblems, through its heart there sometimes rages a recalcitrant force of nature, the Arno, prone to flooding its banks and swamping the streets like some Jungian metaphor of untreated insurgent appetites.

The rhythm of life is slower in Florence; there's little gratuitous violence; children are less likely to take issue with their parents and many families remain in the same house their entire lives. You rarely come across drunk and disorderly inferiority complexes at night. So does Florence have credibility in the rat race reality stakes? Martin Amis wouldn't set a novel here. Or if he did he might be tempted to have one of his characters say, 'It's just like a Euro Disney Renaissance theme park'. It's just surprising they don't dress up some of the locals in medieval costume and pay them to poke pigs to the market. You can almost persuade yourself that the values represented here still have some bearing on the way you might live your life – but then the streets are, of course, bristling with the usual Eurotrash and it becomes quite clear the divine comedy consists not in how you choose to confess your sins but in how you choose to advertise them.

If reality bites in London, or Manhattan tests your capacity to absorb ugliness and countenance violence, Florence perhaps flings you back on a less worked-out part of your sensibility: your capacity to withstand an onslaught of raw beauty. Your resources of wonder and reflection and your attention span are all put through their paces.

Apparently some people have panic attacks because they're unable to recycle so much mind-altering beauty in one go. The condition has been given a name: Stendhal Syndrome. Stendhal almost went mad in Florence: the onset of so much beauty was all too much for the French writer.

So is Florence still part of the real world? Let's face it, your own particular fear or poison will find you wherever you go. And wherever you end up cannot but be the real world.

Architecture

The harmonious, simple and simply magnificent buildings of Firenze.

As with everything else in Florence, the watershed year is 1530. Before that, Florentine architecture – as befitted a commercial republic anxious to do business in an efficient and profitable way – searched for freedom and truth. After 1530 elegance and finish replaced curiosity, effect displaced content. The Spanish army led by Charles V that conquered Florence in 1530 installed the Medici family as absolute rulers. From that time forward the once-free city which had been foremost in the birth of modern Europe became more and more of a backwater.

Florentine architecture – as opposed to architecture in Florence – began in the eleventh century at the time of the completion of the Baptistery, the green-and-white structure just in front of the Duomo (*see page 46* **The Duomo**). It ended at the time of the death of the last male Medici in 1737. After that Florence was owned by the Austrians, then the French, then the Austrians again, and finally, after the unification of Italy in 1860, by the Italians.

The roots of Florentine builders are primarily Etruscan. It was the Etruscans, in the third or fourth century before Christ, who first used the arch. And it was their sense of proportion and colour that reappeared during the Middle Ages on buildings like the Baptistery.

Great architecture began with the **Baptistery**...

The Romans were important too, but since all the early kings of Rome were Etruscans, the distinction is somewhat blurred. Besides, Rome is located on the southern border of Etruria – on the Tiber – and near many of the main Etruscan centres. Rome may have originally been an Etruscan city. So when, during the Renaissance, Imperial Rome and Christian Rome infused Florentine architecture, it was to a great extent a rebirth.

The names of all the prominent architects who worked in Florence are local names: Giotto (1266/7-1337); Filippo Brunelleschi (1377-1446); Michelozzo di Bartolommeo Michelozzi (1396-1472); Leon Battista Alberti (1404-72); Giuliano da Sangallo (c1445-1535); Il Cronaca (1454-1508); Michelangelo Buonarroti (1475-1564); Giorgio Vasari (1511-74); Bartolommeo Ammanati (1511-92); Bernardo Buontalenti (1531-1608). Even the best modern building in Florence, the railway station at Santa Maria Novella, was built in the 1930s by a local fellow: Giovanni Michelucci (1891-1991) from Pistoia.

Florentine architecture is characterised by a search for harmony. The buildings are balanced and simple. They are sharp-edged, with wide, overhanging roofs. The almost black shadows they cast onto the hard stone streets have no gradation at all between light and dark. Any baroque that you may see in Florentine architecture is certainly an import from Rome.

Long before the existence of the Baptistery, there was an Etruscan city at Fiesole, on the hill to the north of Florence. Extensive sections of walls survive there – some with the massive blocks of stone for which the Etruscans were famous – and there are considerable remains from both Etruscan and later Roman times. The Roman theatre is still used for performances in the summer.

Fiesole was one of the league of major Etruscan cities and, as such, would have been built to protect the pass coming south out of the Apennines, and the crossing point over the Arno, more or less where the **Ponte Vecchio** now stands. Only later when the Romans began to absorb Etruscan civilisation did Roman Florence come to be built. Laid out in the grid pattern still visible on any map, the town was apparently founded by Julius Caesar in 59 BC. Not much of Roman Florence remains above ground, but it is known that the theatre was just behind **Palazzo Vecchio**, while the

... *and ended at* **Santa Maria Novella** station?

amphitheatre's shape can still be seen just west of Piazza Santa Croce.

It was along one of the main axes of Roman Florence, now Via dei Calzaiuoli, that medieval Florence grew up. At one end of the axis was the religious centre with the Baptistery and Santa Reparata (the church that once stood where the Duomo now stands). At the other end, the civil centre of **Piazza della Signoria**, where Palazzo Vecchio stands. Between the two, just as today, was the commercial centre, now **Piazza della Repubblica**.

ROMANESQUE & GOTHIC

The Baptistery of San Giovanni, **San Miniato al Monte** – the wonderful green- and white-faced church which looks down on the city from above **Piazzale Michelangelo** – and **Santissimi Apostoli** are the principal Romanesque churches in Florence. The first was built some time between the sixth and the eleventh centuries. Both the stupendous mosaics inside and the marble decoration outside seem to have been finished in the late twelfth or early thirteenth century, indicating that the building was completed by that time.

San Miniato is an eleventh-century building, also finished at the beginning of the thirteenth century and, together with the Baptistery, among the finest Romanesque churches in Europe. Santissimi Apostoli (c1080) is hidden away on the north bank of the Arno, between Ponte Vecchio and Ponte Santa Trinita. It's also an early building, less spectacular perhaps, but purely Romanesque in its plan and in the way it conveys the beauty of medieval culture.

Gothic construction followed, using a pointed arch instead of the earlier half-moon Roman one. The pointed arch carries the weight of the roof and of the arch itself more directly through the columns below and into the ground. There are five major Gothic churches in Florence, four of which were influenced by the one built slightly earlier. This first one is a French pilgrims' church of the twelfth century, San Remigio, located just behind Palazzo Vecchio. It retains, as does much Florentine building, a simplicity on the outside which belies its interior. In 1278 the building of **Santa Maria Novella** was started. This vast and beautiful Domenican church near the railway station, is perhaps the loveliest structure ever put up by that order of monks.

The cathedral of Santa Maria del Fiore, better known as the Duomo, was begun in 1297. It carried medieval construction to a yet higher and larger scale, while retaining the essential Gothic principles of construction. The size of the building's enormous cupola was not actually envisaged in the original plan.

The fourth major Gothic church in Florence is **Santa Croce** (1298). Although this Franciscan building has wide, pointed arches along both sides of the nave, springing diagonally across it, the flat, timber ceiling inside Santa Croce, supported on the two rows of parallel nave arches means that, upon entering the church, the eye is drawn along the nave to the main altar and to the wall of stained glass behind it, rather than upwards.

At the end of the fourteenth century, the grain market and store that was San Michele in Orto (now known as **Orsanmichele**) had its ground-floor loggia closed on all sides to create a small, rather gloomy church for the guilds of Florence. At the beginning of the fifteenth century each guild commissioned a statue to place in each of the 14 niches around the building's exterior. These statues, modelled as they were on humans rather than on traditional medieval Christian figures, were an important impetus to the development of the early Renaissance. Many of the originals are housed in the **Museo di Orsanmichele** and the **Bargello** and have been replaced here by replicas.

Another Gothic structure is the belltower of the Duomo, the Campanile. Designed and begun by Giotto in about 1330, it was completed only after his death. The Bargello (originally the Palazzo del Popolo, begun 1250) and the Palazzo Vecchio (begun 1299) are two more civil structures that were built in the Gothic period.

EARLY RENAISSANCE

Brunelleschi, Michelozzo and Alberti are the three most important names of early Renaissance architecture in Florence. Brunelleschi not only gave the Duomo its cupola – the largest such construction since Ancient Roman times –, he also designed two of the city's finest churches: **San Lorenzo** (constructed 1422-69), including its especially fine, almost independent Old Sacristy (1422-9) and **Santo Spirito** (1444-81). He also built the Pazzi Chapel (begun 1442), a small private family building in the garden of Santa Croce. Breaking with the past, these buildings embrace human thought even more than Christian faith. They turn back to ideas and forms of the pagan world before Christianity. Their very roots spring from a new, lay Christianity, centred on the individual.

The long slog up to **San Miniato al Monte**.

The cupola of the Duomo is really already the ideal Renaissance central-plan church, built on top of an earlier fourteenth-century structure. Many later churches, dating from the High Renaissance and even baroque periods, descend directly from this amazing structure. St Peter's cupola in Rome, begun about 100 years later by Michelangelo, has roughly the same interior diameter: 42 metres. But both structures are marginally less wide than the dome of the Pantheon in Rome, built over 1,200 years earlier.

Michelozzo worked often for Cosimo de' Medici (Cosimo il Vecchio), the grandfather of Lorenzo il Magnifico and founder of the Medici family's fortunes. Michelozzo built Cosimo's town residence, now called **Palazzo Medici Riccardi** (1444), where he developed the traditional Florentine palazzo so that it had two façades, as well as strongly rusticated orders. He also built for Cosimo a number of castellated villas in thirteenth-century style: Cafaggiolo (25km north of Florence at San Piero a Sieve, 1451), Careggi (7km west of Florence, 1457) and Trebbio (visible from Cafaggiolo, 1461).

Although Florentine, Alberti grew up elsewhere and worked mostly outside Florence. His usual taste tended almost to ape the architectural forms of Ancient Rome, but in Florence he completed the façade of Santa Maria Novella (1470) in such a harmonious manner that it has remained a symbol of the city to this day. He also built for the Rucellai family the palazzo in the Via della Vigna Nuova (c1446-51), where they still live, and the lovely loggia opposite (1463). To the palazzo's façade Alberti introduced pilasters and capitals of the three classical orders which appear to support the three storeys, strongly separated with carved friezes. He completed the tribune started by Michelozzo at the church of Santissima Annunziata in an ornate style more compatible with Rome than Florence.

LATER RENAISSANCE

Other architects, especially Il Cronaca (Simone del Pollaiolo) and Giuliano da Sangallo, the preferred architect of Lorenzo il Magnifico, carried Brunelleschian and Albertian ideals to the end of the fifteenth and even into the sixteenth century. These were then developed in both Florence and Rome, principally by Michelangelo, whose work spanned the tense years in Florence before, during and after its subjugation in 1530. Michelangelo left for Rome in 1534 never to return, but he was followed in Florence by three main Medici court architects who all worked for Cosimo I, the first Duke of Tuscany after the siege and conquest of Florence: Vasari, Ammanati, and Buontalenti.

The statuary of **Orsanmichele**.

Il Cronaca built the Santo Spirito vestibule and sacristy (1489-94), structures that carry the Renaissance imitation of the Ancient World almost to a culmination. He also built the **Museo** (formerly Palazzo) **Horne** (1495-1502), returning to an earlier, less rustic Florentine style. Sangallo could be a builder of great delicacy, as demonstrated by his cloister in Santa Maria Maddalena dei Pazzi (1492) in Borgo Pinti. He also built the relatively plain Palazzo Gondi (c1490), as well as two grand structures outside Florence: the beautiful Medici Villa at Poggio a Caiano (begun 1480), and the tiny Renaissance church of Santa Maria delle Carceri, in Prato (1484-95).

Michelangelo was certainly the greatest of these architects. He took the bold, classicising style that Giuliano da Sangallo and Il Cronaca had inherited from Alberti and instilled it with a sense of uncertainty, but also of great energy and rhythm. Instead of the exterior reflecting Ancient Rome, it was the very soul of his creations that was pagan, oriented toward man's emotional state, rather than his Christianity. In this sense Michelangelo's architecture moved beyond the Renaissance.

In both the projects he undertook in Florence, the so-called New Sacristy (begun c1520) at the church of San Lorenzo – a mausoleum for the Medici, as well as for Florence as a republic – and the Laurentian Library (begun 1524), there is not even the slightest reference to Christianity. In the former, the use of levels that have nothing to do with floor structure, non-load-bearing columns and arches, and windows that don't give light, instills a sense of the unreal. The overall effect is enhanced by large areas of cold, white wall. With its cupola so reminiscent of the Pantheon, the structure draws the curtain on that part of the Renaissance where the idea that resurrecting the Antique would provide a new truth sufficient to supplant God. The Laurentian Library too, with its evocative vestibule, calculated to raise the spirits of readers before they entered the reading-room, is a structure so modern as to be mysterious.

Many fine things were built in Florence during the sixteenth and seventeenth centuries – churches, private palazzi, gardens, loggias, villas – but certainly nothing that may be called the essence of Brunelleschi and Michelangelo. The tenure of the age is expressed by the two fortresses built during the sixteenth century: the **Fortezza da Basso** (1534), which, symbolically, has its strongest side facing the city, and the **Forte di Belvedere** (1590), which dominates from just above Ponte Vecchio. These, together with the vast **Palazzo Pitti** (1457), where the Medici moved in the mid-sixteenth century, express the total dominance the Medici had attained over their fellow Florentines at this time.

Vasari built the **Uffizi** (1560) for Cosimo I, and with Buontalenti's help, filled it with offices and workshops for the city's administration. On the top floor was located the Gallery, which remains there still for the ever-expanding Medici collections. Vasari also built the raised corridor which runs from their office building to their home at Palazzo Pitti, so that the family could travel without the dangers of the streets of Florence. Ammannati built the lovely **Ponte Santa Trìnita** over the Arno to replace an earlier bridge which had collapsed in 1557. It was he who began to enlarge Palazzo Pitti, and the expansion continued after his work for some 300 years. Buontalenti, besides extending Palazzo Vecchio (1588) to its present eastern limits, and building the Forte di Belvedere, built for the Medici the lovely villas at Petraia (1587), Artimino (1596), and (later demolished) Pratolino (1568).

THE LONG DECLINE

Not much happened in Florence, architecturally, between 1600 and 1860, at least not compared with the previous three centuries. Gardens and palazzi were enlarged, grottos were fitted into hillsides, piazzas were decorated with fountains and statues, the vast and questionable Cappella dei Principi in San Lorenzo (c1604) was built. A few fine but unspectacular churches, necessarily in a Roman baroque style, were built: San Gaetano (1604), in Via dei Tornabuoni, San Frediano in Cestello (1680-9), on the Lungarno Soderini, San Giorgio alla Costa (1705-8), just up the hill from Ponte Vecchio, and San Filippo Neri (1640-1715), in Piazza San Firenze. Eventually, in the nineteenth century, the railway arrived in Florence and two stations were built: the Leopolda (1847, outside the walls) and the Maria Antonia (1848, inside the walls, near Santa Maria Novella). Only the Leopolda still stands, just outside Porta al Prato. But the period from 1600 to the death of the last Medici ruler in 1737, is a long decline. And even after the Grand Duchy of Tuscany became property of the Hapsburgs, with their capable reforms, the city remained a provincial appendage of the Austrian Empire. Napoleon, who destroyed so much, did little to damage Florence. Perhaps he felt at home? His family had come from just near Florence and had been minor Florentine nobles from the fourteenth century onwards, until their move to Corsica – when it was still part of Italy.

DESTRUCTION & DEVELOPMENT

Beginning with the period just before the unification of Italy in 1860, the city of Florence underwent a series of enormous architectural changes. First, much of the open, as yet undeveloped land inside the city walls was used for housing. Then, on the north side of the Arno, the walls themselves were pulled down (1865-9), leaving only some of the gates standing isolated, as they still do today. Where there had been walls, *viali* (avenues) were built for the carriages of the new householders, and two large open spaces were left as breaks in the *viali*: Piazza C Beccaria and Piazza della Libertà. The *viali* were continued on the south side of the river, up towards another large open space for carriages and past more new villas, to Piazzale Michelangelo (1875) – just below the church of San Miniato.

In these same years, parts of the old city were pulled down to make space for three covered, cast-iron market buildings. This was followed, from 1890 onwards, by the most thoughtless devastation of all: the area that had been the centre of the Roman and medieval city, that is, nearly everything in what is now Piazza della Repubblica, and all the streets near it, was pulled down so that the city centre could be redeveloped. Then, soon after World War I, the central government at Rome, with much the same speculative mentality, pulled down yet more large sections of the city, particularly around the new station of Santa Maria Novella, and near Santa Croce.

Only 50 years after the centre of Florence had been gutted, yet another large area of destruction took place, once again removing scores of beautiful and irreplaceable ancient buildings. The Germans, partly out of fury with their former allies, who had changed sides in the middle of World War II, and partly in a hopeless attempt to stem the Anglo-American advance, blew up all the bridges over the Arno except Ponte Vecchio (1944). They also destroyed all the buildings to the immediate north and immediate south of Ponte Vecchio.

Brunelleschi's **Santo Spirito**.

This means that, whereas just over 100 years ago most of the old centre of Florence was still intact, made up of buildings going back to the early Middle Ages, on foundations that went back at least to Ancient Rome, today you can walk all the way from the Duomo, down Via Roma, across Piazza della Repubblica, through Via Calimala and Via Por Santa Maria, right down to the Ponte Vecchio without passing more than two or three buildings which are not late nineteenth- or twentieth-century structures. What's more, the buildings you pass, erected to replace those destroyed are, at best, banal. Only two modern structures in or near Florence can be regarded with any respect: the 1936 railway station of Santa Maria Novella, mentioned earlier, and the stadium at **Campo di Marte**, built in 1932 – although even this has already been altered for commercial reasons.

Unfortunately, the same total lack of quality in modern building exists all along the flatlands of the Arno valley, particularly to the west, where the city has expanded enormously. No doubt greed and speculation, combined with the dishonesty rife among public officials, means that there's more degradation to come. There are plans, for example, to develop new areas – whole towns, really, like the Firenze Nova area near Rifredi – on open land beyond the Peretola airport. Distinguished, internationally known architects have submitted proposals for these. But if the past is anything to go by, these plans are merely for show. The areas are likely to be developed piecemeal, even chaotically, to the financial advantage of a few interested parties and to the detriment of many others. One of the largest of these projects is backed by La Fondiaria, an insurance firm. But the fact that massive, nineteenth-century insurance office buildings dominate both Piazza Signoria and Piazza Repubblica where once there were medieval buildings in the centre of Florence, gives an idea of how the project may develop.

One extremely bright note in this somewhat bleak picture is that the beautiful green landscape on three sides of Florence has been preserved. Although the past 50 years have been an almost total architectural disaster, somehow the speculation and ugliness have not spread to building on the hills. When you consider that no other major town in Italy, or perhaps even Europe, can boast the preservation of three quarters of its green area, this is a major achievement on the part of modern Florentines.

Murder she wrote

The first question everybody asks a writer is, 'Do you write with a pen or a computer?' Why do they care? The second question, in my case, is usually, 'Why do you write about murder when you have such a beautiful, romantic setting as Florence?' That one I can answer. I love my adopted city. It is beautiful. Its architecture inspires murder.

I've never been a tourist here but I can imagine getting into a taxi at Santa Maria Novella station, whizzing past elegant shops, glimpsing a slice of the Duomo at the end of a picturesque street, the tumble of jewellers' shops on the Ponte Vecchio, arriving at a charming hotel with frescoes on the bedroom ceiling.

But I live here. The Walt Disney Castle charm of the Palazzo Vecchio is inextricably bound up with endless, sweating queues for documents, the Ponte Vecchio with the bitter – sometimes physical – fight between the influential jewellers and proliferating street vendors. Floodlit palace façades look different once you know that they are not façades, that the great houses turn their backs on you and hug their real, decorated façades, their gardens, fountains and statuary, to themselves, beyond those formidable studded carriage doors designed to keep out foreign foes, usually Pisans. ('Better a dead man in your home than a Pisan at your door.')

Juliet called to her Romeo from a Veronese balcony. In Siena they hang embroidered cloths from the windows of elegant, rose-coloured palaces. Florentine architecture is designed for the pouring of boiling oil. This is masculine architecture. The greatest attraction might be museums now, but they were built as fortresses, prisons and monuments to the temporal power of the church. It is an architecture of forts, bulwarks and secret passages, of war, money, power, aggression. There is nothing romantic about having to tunnel your way from one building to another (as in the Vasari corridor) because to walk in the street would mean being stabbed to death. The Florentines didn't hang embroidered cloths from the windows, they hanged men. Material for a Leonardo drawing.

And Leonardo wished to be considered a military engineer: 'I have plans for bridges… and plans for destroying those of the enemy. Also I have ways of arriving at a certain fixed spot by caverns and secret winding passages. I can supply an infinite number of different engines of attack and defence.' Florentine architecture shapes Florentine character. Or vice versa? Chicken or the egg? The last man to be tortured, murdered and hanged out of his own window was a baker named Angelo Carbone. That was about 10 years ago.

After 24 years, my own mentality has been deeply influenced and I would be unhappy to have nothing but the flimsy front door of an English semi between me and the 'Pisans'. So I stay here in my personal fortress, ready to do the boiling oil bit if under attack. I'm just by the Roman gate. No, that's not my façade you can see, though it is my house number. My garden is visible only to me. I'm in here, concealed by vegetation under a pergola, plotting a new murder.

Magda Nabb is the author of a series of crime books set in Florence

The heavily rusticated home of Cosimo de'Medici: **Palazzo Medici Riccardi**.

CODA

Early morning, when the light is full but low, is a wonderful time to view the architecture in Florence. The city contains more than 200 private palazzi, among the most beautiful buildings anywhere. Among the best streets to see some of these are: Via Maggio, Via di Santo Spirito, Via dei Tornabuoni, Via dei Gori and Via San Gallo, and Borgo degli Albizi. There are many beautiful loggias and porches, often hidden away in private courtyards or monasteries, but many can also be seen from the street. The loggias in Piazza della Signoria and Piazzale degli Uffizi, in Piazza della SS Annunziata, in Piazza San Marco, behind the Uffizi at the corner of Via dei Neri, and at the **Mercato Nuovo** are all easily accessible.

There are also a number of medieval towers still standing, the oldest of which is the round Torre della Pagliazza in Via Santa Elisabetta, just off Via del Corso. There are others in Via Dante Alighieri, opposite Dante's house, in Piazza di San Pier Maggiore, and in Borgo San Jacopo, near Ponte Vecchio. Besides the one by Michelangelo, there are two libraries of merit: the beautiful one by Michelozzo in the **San Marco** monastery (after 1437), and the less beautiful **Biblioteca Nazionale** (begun 1911) – the largest in Italy – at Piazza Cavallegeri. The cast-iron markets near piazzas San Lorenzo and Sant'Ambrogio are two fine nineteenth-century structures. Two other relatively modern buildings worth visiting are the large Jewish Synagogue (begun 1874) in Via LC Farini, and the smaller, exquisite Russian Church (1902) in Viale Leone X. There are also the gardens, of which the **Boboli**, behind Palazzo Pitti, are the largest, as well as one of the finest formal gardens in Europe. There are others (some of which are open by appointment only) not far from the centre at Villa Gamberaia (Settignano, 055 697 205), Villa La Pietra (Via Bolognese, 055 50071) and Villa I Tatti (Ponte a Mensola, 055 603 251).

UP AT THE VILLAS

Last but not least, there are the villas, the country houses big and small that dot the countryside for many miles all around Florence: some of these are among the loveliest, most harmonious buildings in the world. It was the *borghi* that first produced these villas – really townhouses transferred to the country. The borghi were suburban areas (our word is the same, from the Latin *sub* – under, and *urbana* – town) that grew up chiefly along the roads leading out of early medieval towns. As is still the case today, these were commercial and industrial sites with buildings on the road and large storage spaces and room for expansion behind. As medieval cities grew, Florence among them, new walls were raised and old ones knocked down. In Florence this happened principally between 1259 and 1333. The borghi suddenly became fairly straight, wide streets within the walls. And the owners of industrial buildings and plots became owners of 'prize development land'. Many of them moved their commercial premises outside the new walls, knocked down the old ones, now inside the city, and built large townhouses in their place – eventually to be called palazzi – with ample gardens behind. Then, of course, as the borghese acquired even greater wealth and success, they desired country estates, and so simply transferred their idea of a large city dwelling to the country. This is why the elegant architecture of Tuscan villas often has little to do with the country surrounding it. And just as the palazzi inside the city walls began as relatively small, simple structures, developing in the Renaissance into bigger, better, more classical symbols of wealth, so too did the country villas.

Sightseeing

Sightseeing

Firenze's finest features.

Sights are arranged in a suitable order for a walking tour.

Central Florence

Home to the Duomo, Piazza della Signoria and the Uffizi, there are probably more tourists per square centimetre in central Florence than in any other city in Italy. Even in November, it's virtually impossible to walk down a street without hearing an English, American or Aussie gushing over gelato, Gucci, Giotto or gigolos. Piazzas are full of backpackers snacking on take-away pizza; café terraces are packed with the middle classes of northern Europe and America lingering over L10,000 cappuccinos; and all over, vying with one another to lighten visitors' purses, are gaudy fast food and ice cream joints, fake Louis Vuitton, fake Gucci and fake Chanel vendors, and shops selling posters, postcards and T-shirts printed with images from Botticelli, Leonardo and, of course, Michelangelo.

Orsanmichele & the Museo di Orsanmichele

Via Arte della Lana (055 284 944). **Open** *church* 9am-noon, 4-6pm, daily. **Museum tours** 9am, 10am, 11am. **Closed** 1st & last Mon of the month. **Admission** free.

The relationship between art, religion and commerce hardly gets closer than in the church of Orsanmichele. The site was first occupied by a church, San Michele in Orto, then by a grain market where traders mingled with money lenders, beggars and locals who'd come to seek solutions to life's problems from a miracle-working painting of the Madonna. In 1336, the city council decided to replace the ancient market hall with a building that contained an oratory on its ground floor and a store for the city's emergency grain supplies on its two upper storeys. In 1380 the arcades of the lower storey were walled in.

From the outset, the council intended Orsanmichele to be a magnificent advertisement for the wealth of the city's guilds and, in 1339, each guild was instructed to fill one of the loggia's niches with a statue of its patron saint. Only the wool guild obliged (with a stone statue of St Stephen) so, in 1406, the council presented the guilds with a ten-year deadline. In 1412, the Calimala, the wealthiest guild (of cloth importers) commissioned Ghiberti to create a life-sized bronze of John the Baptist, the largest statue ever to have been cast in Florence. From then on, the other major guilds fell over themselves to produce the finest statue. The guild of armourers were represented by a tense *St George* by Donatello (now in the **Bargello**), one of the first psychologically realistic sculptures of the Renaissance; the Parte Guelfa had Donatello gild their bronze, a St Louis of Toulouse, later removed by the Medici to **Santa Croce** (*see below*) in their drive to expunge all memory of the Guelphs from the public face of the city. Most of the statues are now replicas – the originals are on display either in the museum or in the Bargello. Inside the church a restored elaborate glass and marble Orcagna tabernacle frames a *Madonna* by Bernardo Daddi (currently undergoing restoration itself), painted in 1347 to replace the miraculous Madonna which was destroyed in a fire in 1304.

SS Apostoli and Piazza del Limbo

Piazza del Limbo (055 290 642). **Open** 10am-noon, 3-6pm, Mon-Sat; 10am-noon, 3-6pm Sun.

SS Apostoli is one of the oldest churches in the city, still retaining much of its original eleventh-century façade. The church's design, like that of the early Christian churches of Rome, is based on that of a Roman basilica: rectangular, with columns and a flat ceiling. The church used to hold pieces of flint reputed to have come from Jerusalem's Holy Sepulchre, which were awarded to Pazzino de'Pazzi for his bravery during the Crusades (though his name, Little Mad Man of the Mad Men might suggest his actions were more foolhardy than brave). These flints were used on Easter Day to light the 'dove' which sets off the fireworks display at the Scoppio del Carro (*see chapter* **Tuscany by Season**). Piazza del Limbo outside is so-called because it occupies the site of a graveyard for unbaptised babies. Note, it has a tendency to close in the afternoon without prior notice.

Badia Fiorentina

Via del Proconsolo. **Open** 4.30-6.30pm Mon-Sat; 10.30-11.30am Sun. **Admission** free.

The Badia, a Benedictine abbey founded in the tenth century by Willa, mother of Ugo, Margrave of Tuscany, was the richest religious institution of medieval Florence. Willa had been deeply influenced by Romuald, a monk who travelled around Tuscany denouncing the wickedness of the clergy, flagellating himself, and urging the rich to build monasteries. Eventually Romuald persuaded Willa to found an abbey within Florence, which she did in 978. Ugo also lavished money and land on the abbey, and was eventually buried there in a Roman sarcophagus, later replaced by a tomb by Renaissance sculptor Mino da Fiesole. It was in the Badia, just across the street from Dante's probable birthplace, that the poet

Mannerist monstrosity? Ammanati's Neptune *fountain in* **Piazza della Signoria**. *See p45.*

first set eyes on Beatrice Portinari attending a May feast in 1274. He was nine, she eight, and he fell instantly in love with 'the glorious Lady of my mind'. His life was for ever blighted when her family arranged her marriage at the age of 17 to one Simone de Bardi. Beatrice died seven years later at the age of 24 and Dante attempted to forget his pain by throwing himself into war, fighting in battles against Arezzo and Pisa. As for the Badia, it has been rebuilt many times since Dante's day, but still retains a graceful Romanesque campanile. The Chiostro degli Aranci, where the Benedictine monks grew oranges (*aranci*) dates from 1430 and is frescoed with scenes from the life of St Bernard. Inside the church Bernard is again celebrated, this time in a painting by Filippino Lippi. At time of writing the Badia Fiorentina was closed owing to restoration works being carried out.

Piazza della Signoria

Florence's civic showpiece, Piazza della Signoria is dominated by the crenellated and corbelled **Palazzo Vecchio** (formerly Palazzo della Signoria), built at the end of the thirteenth century (probably to a design by Arnolfo di Cambio) as the seat of the Signoria, the top tier of the city's government. The piazza itself was the focus of civic activity. Life in medieval Florence was beset with political and personal vendettas, and it didn't take much to ignite a crowd. On one occasion in the fourteenth century, a man who aroused the hatred of the crowd was actually eaten to death.

More constructively, whenever Florence was threatened by an external enemy, the bell of the Palazzo della Signoria (known as the 'Vacca', after its moo-ing tone) was tolled to summon the citizens' militia. Part of the militia's training included playing Calcio, a rough ball game, which is still played in costume every June on the Piazza. It was here that the religious and political reformer Girolamo Savonarola lit his famous Bonfire of the Vanities in 1497. In 1924, a Fascist march through the city, intended to intimidate people mourning the murder of anti-fascist politician Giacomo Matteotti, ended up in the piazza.

In the 1970s it was decided to take up and restore the piazza's ancient paving stones. In the course of the work, the ruins of twelfth-century Florence were discovered beneath the piazza, built over bits and pieces of Roman and Etruscan Florentia. The state-run Soprintendenza di Bene Archeologica ordered the excavation of the ruins; local government, faced with the prospect of their showpiece piazza becoming a building site, and losing them valuable tourist income, objected.

The result was a shambles. The company charged with restoring the ancient slabs turned out to have won the contract by bribing the city's chief engineer. They not only had no idea how to restore stone properly, but managed to 'lose' some of the slabs, now apparently gracing the courtyards of various Tuscan villas.

Brunelleschi's **San Lorenzo**. *See p61.*

Mercato Nuovo*'s lucky boar. See p52.*

The Duomo

Nowhere in Italy is there a city centre quite as magnificent as Florence's Piazza del Duomo. The cathedral itself, lacily inlaid with pink, white and bottle-green marble, soars above the surrounding buildings, so huge that there is no point nearby from which you can see the whole building.

Il Duomo

(Ufficio del Duomo 055 215 380). **Open** *church* 10am-5pm Mon-Fri; 10am-4.45pm Sat; 1-5pm Sun; 10am-3.30pm 1st Sat of month; *cupola* 9.30am-5.20pm Mon-Fri; 9.30am-5pm Sat; 9.30am-3.20pm 1st Sat of month. **Admission** *church* free; *cupola* L10,000. **No credit cards.**

In the thirteenth century a hugely successful and expanding wool industry gave the Florentine population such a boost that several new churches had to be built, among them Santa Croce and Santa Maria Novella, but most important of all Santa Maria del Fiore or the Duomo, which replaced the small church of Santa Reparata. The construction was commissioned by the Florentine Republic, who saw the project as an opportunity to show Florence as indisputably the most important Tuscan city. A competition was held to find an architect and the commission was given to Arnolfo di Cambio, a sculptor from Pisa who had trained with Nicola Pisano. The first stones were laid on 8 September 1296 around the exterior of Santa Reparata (to allow its continued use) and building continued for the next 170 years though the church was consecrated 30 years before its completion in 1436. As Arnolfo was obviously unable to supervise the project from start to finish the work saw the guidance and revision of three further architects. The visionary Francesco Talenti had sufficient confidence in future architectural achievements to enlarge the cathedral and prepare the building for Brunelleschi's inspired dome. The last significant change to be made came in the nineteenth century when Emilio De Fabris designed a neo-Gothic style façade to replace the bland temporary façade left over from 1588.

The dome is undoubtedly the cathedral's most celebrated feature. To really experience its magnificence though you need to distance yourself from it. Only then is it possible to appreciate how it towers above the city and is, as Alberti put it, 'large enough to cover every Tuscan with its shadow'. But the dome is not just visually awe-inspiring, it is also an incredible feat of engineering, thanks to the genius of Brunelleschi, who had dreamed of completing the dome since childhood and studied architecture in Rome specifically with the dome in mind. Brunelleschi made the dome support itself, realised by employing two domes, one on top of the other, and more importantly by laying the bricks in herringbone-pattern rings to integrate successive layers and consequently support themselves. As innovative as the design were the tools used and the organisation of the work: Brunelleschi designed pulley systems to winch materials up to the dome. Between the two shells of the dome he installed a canteen so the workers wouldn't waste time going down to ground level to eat, measures that helped keep the construction time down to a mere 16 years (1420-36).

After the splendour of the exterior, the interior looks dark and dreary. But decorating the fourth largest cathedral in the world was never going to be easy. It is actually full of fascinating oddities, notably the clock on the inner side of the Paolo Uccello façade, a clock which marks 24 hours, operates anti-clockwise and starts its days at sunset; expect it to be between four and six hours fast. Also by Uccello is a monument to the English mercenary Sir John Hawkwood, painted in 1436, the portrait is somewhat of a muddle and has a perspective problem. Far more coherent is Andrea del Castagno's work of *Niccolo da Tolentino,* painted in 1456 and illustrating the heroic characteristics of a Renaissance man. Beyond these two is Domenico di Michelino's well-known *Dante Explaining the Divine Comedy*, featuring the poet dressed in pink and the recently completed Duomo vying for prominence with the Mountain of Purgatory. A couple of strides forward and across puts you directly underneath the dome – possibly more breathtaking inside than out. The lantern in the centre is 90m above you and the diameter of the inner dome is 43m across, housing within it one of the largest frescoed surfaces in the world, covering 3,600 square metres. Brunelleschi had intended, however, that the cupola be mosaic, so it would mirror the Baptistery ceiling, but interior work began some 125 years after his death in 1572. The frescoes were started under the supervision of Giorgio Vasari, who died two years after starting and was succeeded by Federigo Zuccaro, who worked for a further five years until completion. The subject of the frescoes is the Last Judgement, which uses the huge space of the dome to suggest visitors are looking up into Heaven.

To get to the top of the dome, there's a separate entrance at the side of the church, where you can trek up the 463 steps for 20 minutes and earn yourself fantastic views of the city.

Campanile

Open *Apr-Oct* 9am-6.50pm daily; *Nov-Mar* 9am-4.20pm daily. **Admission** L10,000. **No credit cards.**

The Campanile was originally designed by Giotto in 1334, though its completion did not follow his design faithfully, as shown by comparison with his original drawing, held in the **Museo**

dell'Opera Metropolitana in Siena (the drawing can be seen on request). Subsequent changes were made by Andrea Pisano, who continued the work three years after Giotto's death and took the precaution of doubling the thickness of the walls, while Francesco Talenti saw the building to completion in 1359 and was responsible for inserting the large windows high up the tower. Inlaid, like the Duomo, with pretty pink, white and green marble, it is decorated with 16 sculptures of prophets, patriarchs and pagans, (the originals are in the **Museo dell'Opera del Duomo**), bas reliefs designed by Giotto and executed by Pisano recounting the *Creation* and *Fall of Man* and his *Redemption Through Industry*. Look carefully and you can make out Eve emerging from Adam's side and a drunken Noah. There are great views of the Duomo and city from the top.

Baptistery

Open 1.30-6pm Mon-Sat; 9am-12.30pm Sun.
Admission L10,000. **No credit cards**.
For centuries, Florentines (including such well educated characters as Brunelleschi and Alberti) believed that the Baptistery was converted from an ancient Roman temple dedicated to Mars. In fact, although there are the relics of an ancient pavement below the building, these probably belonged to a bakery. The Baptistery of St John the Baptist was actually built to an octagonal design between 1059 and 1128 as a remodelling of a sixth- or seventh-century version. The octagon reappears most obviously in the shape of the Cathedral dome, but also on the buttresses of the Campanile, which constitute its corners. Today, the gaily striped octagon is best known for its bronze doors, though you might want to go inside to see the vibrant *Last Judgement* mosaic lining the vault.

In the 1330s Andrea Pisano completed the south doors, with 28 Gothic quatrefoil-framed panels depicting stories from the life of St John the Baptist and the eight theological and cardinal virtues. In the winter of 1400, the Calimala guild held a competition to find an artist to create a pair of bronze doors for the north entrance, and eventually, having seen trial pieces by Brunelleschi, Ghiberti and five others gave the commission to Ghiberti, then only 20 years old. Relief panels displaying a masterful use of perspective, retell the story of Christ, from the Annunciation to the Crucifixion. The eight lower panels show the four evangelists and four doctors.

Even more remarkable are the east doors, known as the Gates of Paradise. No sooner had the north doors been installed than the Calimala commissioned Ghiberti to make another pair. The doors you see here are actually copies (the originals are in the Museo dell'Opera del Duomo) but the casts are fine enough to appreciate Ghiberti's achievement.

Viva la Vespa!

There are two sounds that are intrinsically Florentine – the chime of bells from Giotto's Campanile and the buzz of scooters. In Florence there are more scooters per capita than in any other Italian city.

The scootermania that now exists in Italy started on 23 April 1946 when Piaggio, a Tuscan firm based in Pontadera, near Pisa (now part of Fiat), released the Vespa-98, designed by Corradino D'Ascanio. D'Ascanio was a visionary: he realised that a cheaper, more agile form of transport than the car was need to remobilise Italy in the immediate post-war period. His scooter was the perfect solution. It could scoot round bomb craters, debris and make its own tracks wherever required (hence the first model's name *vespa*, the wasp) and, more importantly, it was simpler and cheaper to make than a car. Soon it was heralded as 'the symbol of our industrial miracle' as it championed Italy's post-war industrial rehabilitation. In the years that followed, Piaggio's success grew, as did its prestige. In 1949, an official Vespa Club was formed, and three years later the Vespa made its first cinematic appearance in the film *Roman Holiday*. But perhaps the most illustrious accolade came from the novelist Umberto Eco, who wrote an account of his youthful lusting for a Vespa, a desire that was never realised and became for him 'un simbolo di un desiderio non soddisfatto' (a symbol of unfulfilled desire).

Fifty years on, scooters are still a thoroughly convenient means of transport in Italy and nowhere more so than in Florence, where the maze of narrow streets, insane one-way system and plethora of tight corners make the scooter the epitome of practical. It has found favour in all sectors of society – professionals, pensioners and teenagers and not just for their practicality; Vespas have found a firm foothold in fashion. Scooter fashion is characterised by the same smoothness that made the world ogle at the Vespa 50 years ago. Old-school scooters like Piaggio's Si or Honda's Sh-50 have made way for the softer 1990s lines that define Aprilia's Scarabeo, Italjet's Torpedo, and Piaggio's Vespa ET4. Unsurprisingly given its illustrious past and instant credibility it bestows on its rider, the Vespa ET4 is Italy's most popular scooter.

However, scooters have their enemies, among them the Italian Minister for the Environment, not to mention an EU directive. The principal complaint concerns the bike's effect on pollution; current estimates suggest that scooters con-

tribute around 40 per cent to total fuel emissions in Florence. Many scooters are uncatalysed and the smallest, *motorini* (with 50cc engines), use highly pollutant two-stroke engines.

The Italian government has been trying to remedy the problem. In 1997/8, the government initiated their *rottamazione* project to rid the streets of old scooters by offering incentives; part exchange your old scooter for a new, cleaner and cheaper model. Simultaneously, a push was made towards electric bikes. The city of Florence installed 11 free recharge points for electric bikes and will now contribute L500,000 to the price of a new electric bike. As yet, these bikes have not seen great success, due to their slow acceleration, weak battery and higher price (around L6,800,000). A more realistic promise for a cleaner Florence has come from Piaggio's development of the Vespa ET2 iniezione (L4,600,000), which uses a cleaner fuel injection engine, cutting previous emissions by up to 70 per cent. It's also the first scooter on the market to meet the EU standards on pollution emissions.

Despite these moves, Florence and other major Italian cities will, for the foreseeable future, still buzz to the sound of one of Europe's greatest bikes – Piaggio's Vespa.

"And then there were tourists that thought they could leave without..."
...International Phone Cards.

Faking it: **Piazza della Signoria***'s* David *copy.*

The art of the matter – a tribute to Botticelli.

The Piazza's statues

Dominating the piazza are a copy of Michelangelo's *David*, and an equestrian bronze of Cosimo I by Giambologna, who also created some sexy nymphs and satyrs for Ammanati's *Neptune* fountain, a Mannerist monstrosity of which Michelangelo is said to have said 'Ammanato, Ammanato, che bel marmo ha rovinato' (Ammanati, what beautiful marble you have ruined). Even Ammanati eventually admitted the piece was a failure. This was in part because the block of marble used for Neptune lacked width, forcing Ammanati to give the god narrow shoulders and to keep his right arm close to his body. Beyond is a copy of Donatello's *Marzocco* (the original of the city's heraldic lion is in the **Bargello** and his *Judith and Holofernes* (the original is in the **Palazzo Vecchio**). Judith, like David, was a symbol of the power of the people over tyrannical rulers, a Jewish widow who inveigled her way into the camp of Holofernes, Israel's enemy, got the man drunk, then sliced off his head. Beyond *David* is a *Hercules and Cacus* by Bandinelli, described by rival sculptor Benvenuto Cellini as a 'sack of melons'.

Cellini himself was represented by another monster-killer, a fabulous *Perseus* holding the snaky head of Medusa. The statue stood in the adjacent Loggia dei Lanzi but has been removed for restoration. The loggia was built in the late fourteenth century to shelter civic bigwigs during ceremonies. By the mid-fifteenth century it had become a favourite spot for old men to gossip and shelter from the sun, which, the architect Alberti noted with approval, had a restraining influence on the young men engaging in the 'mischievousness and folly natural to their Age'. Also in the Loggia is Giambologna's spiralling *Rape of the Sabine Women*, carved in 1582, a virtuoso attempt by the artist to outdo Cellini.

Mercato Nuovo

The Mercato Nuovo is a fine stone loggia erected between 1547 and 1551 on a site where there had been a market since the eleventh century (the Mercato Vecchio, or old market, occupied the area now covered by Piazza della Repubblica). It now houses stalls selling expensive tourist tat, but in the sixteenth century it would have been full of silk and gold merchants and money-changers. The market is popularly known as the Porcellino, or piglet, after a bronze statue of a boar, a copy of an ancient statue now in the **Uffizi**. It is considered good luck to put a coin in the animal's mouth and get it to drop through the grille below – all proceeds go to a charity for abandoned children.

Palazzo Antinori

Not open to the public (apart from the wine bar).

This austere mid-fifteenth century palace of neat stone blocks was bought by the Antinori family in 1506, and today houses an upmarket wine-bar/restaurant selling wines from the extensive Antinori estates. There is a pretty courtyard inside.

Michelangelo's Doni Tondo *in the* **Uffizi**.

Take it to the bridge – **Ponte Vecchio**.

Piazza della Repubblica

In 1882, the ancient heart of Florence was demolished and replaced with Piazza della Repubblica. Now the only remnant from before that time is the Colonna dell'Abbondanza, which used to mark the spot where two principal Roman roads crossed; it was reinstated to its original position after World War II. The piazza is an urban space that would be more at home in Milan or Turin, surrounded by pavement cafés (*see chapter* **Cafés & Bars**) and dominated at night by a neon Martini ad clamped to an ersatz triumphal arch. The ancient Roman Forum once occupied about a quarter of the piazza, while nearby there were two bath complexes. In the medieval period the area covered by the piazza was given over to a huge market where you could change money, buy a hawk or falcon, pay over the odds for a quack remedy, or pick up a prostitute (distinguished by the bells on their hats and their gloves).

Ponte Vecchio

There has been a bridge spanning this point of the Arno – its narrowest point within the city of Florence – since Roman times. The current structure, however, was completed in 1345 to replace a bridge swept away by a flood in 1333. By the thirteenth century there were wooden shops on the bridge. These frequently caught fire and, consequently, when the bridge was reconstructed, the shops were built of stone. Now occupied by gold and gem merchants, the Ponte Vecchio was originally favoured by butchers and tanners. As the latter trade involved soaking the hides in the Arno for eight months, then curing them in horse urine, the bridge was a pretty smelly place. Eventually, in 1593, Grand Duke Ferdinando I, fed up with retching every time he walked along the Corridoio Vasariano (*see below,* **Santa Felicità**) on his way to or from the Pitti Palace, decided to ban all vile trades, as he called them, and permit only jewellers and goldsmiths on the bridge.

Palazzo Strozzi

Piazza Strozzi (055 288 342). **Open** varies according to exhibitions; *library* 9am-1pm, 3-6pm, Mon-Fri; 9am-1pm Sat.

Mercantile Florence was at its zenith in the 1400s, and, in the course of the century, over 100 palaces were built. The largest and most magnificent was Palazzo Strozzi, whose three tiers of golden rusticated stone still dominate Via Tornabuoni. Work began on the palace in 1489 on the orders of Filippo Strozzi. The Strozzi family had been exiled from Florence in 1434 for opposing the Medici, but made good use of the time, moving south and becoming bankers to the King of Naples. By the time they returned to Florence in 1466, they had amassed a fortune. In 1474 Filippo began buying up property in the centre of Florence, until he had acquired enough to build the biggest palace in the city. Fifteen buildings were demolished to make room for it, playing

Trading places

There are more than 300 African street traders in Florence selling anything from tissues, lighters, and Raphael reproductions to African carvings and fake Prada bags. Of these, about 70 actually have permits from the *Comune* of Florence. Most Africans working in Florence come from Senegal, the Ivory Coast and North Africa. They tend to be students or recent graduates; some are qualified doctors or engineers: 'Our main reason for coming to Italy is financial. Not only is there more job security, but we can often earn more money than as graduates at home.' The comune explains: 'The qualified ones hope to find work in their profession in Italy. Last year we managed to find a job for a computer engineer in Milan, it was one of the first instances, but we're optimistic.' Most intend to come here for a couple of years but many stay longer. Within five to ten years they've usual managed to save enough money to secure their futures.

Mild-mannered and approachable, the African street seller knows exactly who to target and when to strike. They expect a good haggle, of course, and you can get them down to about a third of the original quote. The haggle may involve full concentration on your behalf while they spend most of their time looking over their shoulder for the carabinieri. It is pretty rare to see the carabinieri stopping them, firstly because the salesmen are too swift, and secondly, the carabinieri tend to turn a blind eye. Few Italians really object to them; but there's a lot of resentment among local shopkeepers. They're the ones paying taxes to sell wares, and it's their livelihood that's affected by illegal traders blocking their window displays and undercutting their prices. In the early 1990s the street sellers suffered a brief series of racial attacks, but these were quickly stamped out and nothing of the kind has happened since.

He may not be part of the idealised and overromanticised vision of Italian life, but the African street seller has become just as much part of the sightseeing scene as the Japanese coachloads or your pasty T-shirted tourist.

havoc with local traffic and covering the city in dust, according to local shopkeeper and diarist Landucci. Finally an astrologer was asked to choose an auspicious day on which to lay the foundation stone: 6 August, 1489. Conveniently, a few months earlier, Lorenzo de' Medici had passed a law exempting anyone who built a house on empty sites from 40 years of communal taxes. Three architects were involved in the design of the palazzo, Giuliano da Sangallo, Benedetto da Maiano and Simone del Pollaiuolo. When Filippo died in 1491, he left his heirs with the responsibility of completing the project; it eventually bankrupted them. The palace now houses several institutions and stages prestigious exhibitions. Incidentally, the huge iron rings embedded in the façade were for tethering horses, and the spiky iron clusters on the corners are torch holders.

Oltrarno

Oltrarno literally means 'on the other side of the Arno', and this area was first the working-class and then the alternative centre of the city, despite the fact that the Medici's gargantuan Palazzo Pitti was bang in the middle. Nowadays, while there are still plenty of artisans' workshops, a couple of trattorias serving cheap food, and a monthly fleamarket, gentrification is well underway. The bars and restaurants of Piazza Santo Spirito are among the hippest in town, the fleamarket alternates with an organic produce market, and opening among the neighbourhood household and food shops are boutiques selling trendy crafts, clothes and jewellery. An air of rusticity is retained by the daily food market as farmers come into town to sell their pro-

The laid-back and utterly charming **Piazza Santo Spirito**. *See p58.*

duce. The area immediately around Palazzo Pitti is devoted to shops selling expensive paper, crafts and jewellery, while Borgo San Jacopo is lined with a mix of clothes and food shops.

Over towards the church of Santa Maria del Carmine (frescoed by Masaccio and Masolino) and stretching down to the Porta Romana at the start of the road to Rome, and west to Porta San Frediano, is the area of Borgo San Frediano, where locals live in terraced cottages. If you stop for a bite in one of the osterias and trattorias here, you're likely to be the only foreigner. It's the best area in the city for getting the sense of Florence as a medieval town.

Santa Felicità

Piazza Santa Felicità (055 213 018). Bus D. **Open** 9am-noon, 3-6pm Mon-Sat; 4-6pm Sun.

This little church occupies the site of the first church in Florence, founded in the second century AD by Syrian Greek tradesmen who settled in the area. There are, however, no traces of its ancient beginnings – the interior is largely eighteenth-century. The portico was built by Vasari in 1564 to support the Corridoio Vasariano, an overhead walkway that connected the **Palazzo Pitti** with the **Palazzo Vecchio** and the **Uffizi**. The main reason to step inside is to see Pontormo's *Deposition* altarpiece.

Palazzo Pitti

Piazza Pitti, Via Romana. (See chapter **Museums & Galleries** for opening times of individual museums.)

Palazzo Pitti's chunkily rusticated façade bears down on its sloping forecourt, dwarfing the tourists who've come to visit its museums or wander around the Boboli Gardens behind. It was built in 1457 for Luca Pitti, a rival of the Medici, probably to a design by Brunelleschi that had been rejected by Cosimo il Vecchio as too grandiose. It was also too grandiose for the Pitti, and less than a century later they were forced to sell out to the doubtless gleeful Medici. The palace was more luxurious than the draughty old Palazzo Vecchio and, in 1549, Cosimo I and his wife Eleonora di Toledo moved in. Huge as it was, it wasn't big enough for the Medici, and Ammanati (he of the hideous *Neptune* fountain, *see above* **Piazza della Signoria**) was charged with remodelling the façade and creating the courtyard, a manic Mannerist space, with columns threaded through huge stone doughnuts. The façade was extended in the seventeenth century and two further wings were added in the eighteenth century. The palazzo now holds the vast, opulent Medici collection.

Boboli Gardens

Piazza Pitti, Via Romana (055 218 741). **Open** *Nov-Feb* 9am-4.30pm daily; *Mar* 9am-5.30pm daily; *Apr, May, Sept, Oct* 9am-6.30pm daily; June-Aug 9am-7.30pm daily; closed 1st and last Mon of month.

Admission L4,000 (includes entrance to Museo di Porcellana).

The Boboli, the only park in central Florence, was laid out by a number of artists for Eleonora di Toledo and Cosimo I. Bandinelli created a grotto for Eleonora, complete with casts of Michelangelo's *prigionieri* and Ammanati- and Giambologna-designed fountains. The gardens run up to the Forte di Belvedere (there is no access to the fortress from the gardens) and down to the Porta Romana. Beautifully kept, it makes the most of its hilly site. Be sure to wander along the Viottolone, a long avenue lined with cypresses, and stop at the rococo Kaffeehaus (1776), to gaze out over the city. Other highlights include the L'Isolotto, a miniature island in a circular lake with a copy of Giambologna's *Oceanus* charging through the waters; the Amphitheatre, created in the gap left after stone had been quarried for the Palazzo, and where Jacopo Peri's opera, *Euridice*, was staged for the Medici in 1600 (his earlier *Dafne* is widely acknowledged to be the first ever opera); and the repulsive *Bacchus* fountain, a copy of a six-

Police and thieves

Borgo Ognissanto 48. Big carriage doors, a high arched passage whose huge flagstones make your footsteps echo, and then out into a sunny cloister. A fountain cools the air and the shadows under the colonnade are deep and delightful when the heat of the Florentine summer is asphyxiating. On the right, a staircase leads to an upper floor where red tiled corridors are highly polished, the large plants neat and shiny. Across the cloister to your left you can see the refectory. To your right, Gothic arched doors lead into cell after cell where you might glimpse a fragment of a fresco or the heavy frame of a seventeenth-century painting from an overflowing museum. No prizes for guessing that this is a monastery – but what's that noise? Look down from the windows of the tranquil shining corridor. Church bells are ringing the midday angelus and the noise is drowned by that of an engine revving up, roaring through the cloister and out into the street, blue light spinning and siren wailing.

As a tourist, there are two ways of getting to see this cloister and ex-monastery: commit a crime or have one committed against you. The choice is yours. I don't recommend the former because the slammer on the ground floor is next to the boiler room. Noisy, stuffy and no view of the fountain. As a victim you get the view and – according to my sister, who fetched up here minus her handbag – a really good-looking young carabinieri who speaks excellent English.

So, what's the difference between the police and the carabinieri? The carabinieri are the first army of Italy. They have infantry and cavalry regiments and provide the presidential guard as well as having a judiciary police force parallel to the civil one but bigger, because the carabinieri police every tiny village in the country, much like the French Gendarmerie. Policemen have blue uniforms and will arrest you but not go to war for you. The men in the tall white helmets and Pucci-designed uniforms are municipal police who will tell you the way to go to Borgo Ognissanti and perhaps leave a parking ticket on your car for when you get back.

There are about ten other kinds of police, but you will not encounter them if you're lucky. If disaster strikes during your visit you can call 112 for the carabinieri or 113 for the police, and if in your moment of panic you forget the difference, don't worry about it. Either will do, but the carabinieri have sexier uniforms and, since they got there first, buildings like the one described above.

When I started writing about Florentine murders, the carabinieri headquarters for the left bank of the Arno was in Borgo Ognissanti. The carabinieri are still there, but that particular command has moved downriver into a new, purpose-built barracks.

I refused to move with them and give up my sirens in the cloister, so Marshal Guarnaccia (my fictional hero) can still leave his own little station, housed in the Palazzo Pitti (that station is still there, thank goodness), walk across the Ponte Santa Trinità or Ponte alla Carraia and call in on his captain to ask for advice or extra manpower – he never gets either but it's a pleasant walk. Try it.

You can't see much of Guarnaccia's station at Palazzo Pitti, but if you are going into the Boboli Gardens anyway, take the entrance on the left and go in under the archway beneath the great iron lantern. Above the parkkeeper's entrance immediately on your left is a carabinieri shield. The real marshal's car will probably be parked on the gravel there near the famous statue of naked Silenus riding a turtle.

Many visitors to the Boboli gardens like to eat their sandwiches on the steps of the Roman theatre. If you do, spare a morsel for the Boboli cats and watch your handbag... unless you are going over to Borgo Ognissanti anyway...

Magda Nabb is the author of a series of crime books set in Florence

teenth-century statue showing Cosimo I's dwarf as a nude Bacchus. In the Rose Garden, at the far end of the Boboli is the **Museo di Porcellana**.

Santo Spirito

Piazza Santo Spirito. Bus D, 11, 36, 37. **Open** 8am-noon, 4-6pm, Mon, Tue, Thur-Sun; 8am-noon Wed.

Santo Spirito is one of Brunelleschi's most remarkable buildings, although you wouldn't know it from the yellow eighteenth-century façade, blank and featureless as a slab of marzipan. Step inside, however, and you enter a world of perfect proportions, a Latin-cross church surrounded by a continuous colonnade of dove grey *pietra serena* columns. There had been an Augustinian church on the site since 1250, but in 1397 the monks decided to replace it. To finance the project, they cut out one meal a day. Eventually they commissioned Brunelleschi to design it. Work started in 1444, two years before Brunelleschi died. The façade and exterior walls were never finished; Vasari reckoned that if the church had been completed to Brunelleschi's plans it would have been 'the most perfect temple of Christianity'. It is hard to disagree. To the left of the church is the **Cenacolo di Santo Spirito**.

Piazza Santo Spirito

Bus D, 11, 36, 37.

Piazza Santo Spirito is a low-key, laid-back space that – by day at least – still very much belongs to the locals. Furniture restorers have workshops just off the square; nearby trattorias serve good, cheap food and there is a daily morning market, an organic food market on the third Sunday of the month, and a huge fleamarket that spills over the piazza on the second Sunday of the month. Until quite recently the square was full of dope dealers, but it has recently been cleaned up (the dealers simply moved a few blocks away), and it has become a popular rendezvous point for the city's pre-clubbers (*see chapter* **Nightlife**).

Santa Maria del Carmine & the Brancacci Chapel

Piazza del Carmine. Bus D, 11, 36, 37. **Open** *Brancacci Chapel* 9am-5pm Mon, Wed-Sat; 1-5pm Sun. **Admission** L5,000 (M).

The church of Santa Maria del Carmine is a blowsy baroque edifice. It's dominated by a huge single nave, adorned with pilasters and pious sculptures overlooked by a ceiling fresco of *The Ascension*. It was built in 1782 as a replacement for a medieval church belonging to the Carmelite order, most of which burnt down in 1771.

Miraculously, the Brancacci Chapel, matchlessly frescoed in the fifteenth century by Masaccio and Masolino, escaped. The two were an odd pair with little in common other than the fact that they were both born in the Val d'Arno. Masolino was a court painter, his style graceful, and still in tune with the decorative International Gothic traditions of artists like Gentile da Fabriano (*see chapter* **Museums & Galleries: Uffizi**). Masaccio was a more modern, innovative painter, who worked mostly for monks and local priests – his work is more realistic, driven and emotive. Compare Masolino's elegant Adam and Eve in *The Temptation*, with Masaccio's horror-stricken couple in *Expulsion from Paradise*, or Masolino's dandified Florentines in their silks and brocades with Masaccio's simple saints. There are two themes to the paintings: the redemption of sinners, and scenes from the life of St Peter. Masaccio died aged 25, and work on the frescoes stopped for 60 years, when it was taken up again by Filippino Lippi, whose most striking contribution was *The Release of St Peter*.

The frescoes were restored during the 1980s, financed by Olivetti, and there are strict rules about how many people can visit, and how long they are allowed to stay (15 minutes).

Chilling in the **Boboli Gardens**. *See p56.*

Piazzale Michelangiolo

Bus 12, 13.

Popular with lovers in cars, Piazzale Michelangiolo is the city's balcony, a large, open square with views over the entire city. Laid out in 1869 by Giuseppe Poggi, it is dominated by a bronze replica of Michelangelo's *David*, and crammed all day with coaches. The most pleasant way of approaching from the lower city is to walk along Via San Niccolo until you reach Porta San Miniato, and climb up Via del Monte alle Croci, winding between the gardens of villas. Alternatively, walk up the rococo staircase Poggi designed to link Piazzale Michelangiolo with his namesake, Piazza G Poggi below.

Forte di Belvedere

Via San Leonardo (055 27681). Bus B, C, then 10-minute uphill walk. **Open** Grounds *summer* 9am-7pm daily; *winter* 9am-6pm daily. **Admission** free.
This star-shaped fortress was built by Bernardo Buontalenti in 1590. Originally intended to protect the city from foreign enemies or insurgent natives, it soon became a place of refuge for the Medici Grand Dukes. The fortress is open only when an exhibition is being held there. The views over the city from the ramparts are stupendous.

San Miniato al Monte

Via delle Porte Sante 34 (055 234 2731). Bus 12, 13. **Open** *summer* 8am-noon, 2-7pm, daily; *winter* 8am-noon, 2.30-6pm, daily.
The exquisite façade of the church of San Miniato, delicately inlaid with white Carrara and green Verde di Prato marble, looks down on the city from high; a quietly confident landmark, visible throughout the west of Florence. There has been a chapel on the site since at least the fourth century, erected on the spot where, according to legend, the recently beheaded San Miniato took up his head and walked from the banks of the Arno up the hill, where he finally expired. The chapel was replaced with a Benedictine monastery in the early eleventh century, built on the orders of the reformer, Bishop Hildebrand. The interior of the church is one of the most beautiful in Tuscany, its walls patchworked with faded frescoes, its choir raised above a serene eleventh-century crypt. Occasionally a door from the crypt is open, leading down to an even earlier chapel. One of the church's most remarkable features is the marble pavement of the nave, inlaid with signs of the zodiac and stylised lions and lambs.

Whipping boys? **Santa Maria Novella**.

Santa Maria Novella to Ognissanti

Stretching from the striking modernist main railway station (designed by Michelucci in 1935), through a maze of dark, twisting backstreets to the river, this is a richly varied area of Florence. Round the railway station (as in virtually every European city) sleaze is conspicuous, with a chaos of beggars, tramps, men-on-the-pull, chestnut vendors, bewildered backpackers, buses and taxis. Across from the station, Alberti's façade for the church of Santa Maria Novella looks out on a piazza where tour groups thread their way through Africans, Asians and Filipinos hanging out. Down below the church, narrow streets twist down to the designer clothes shops of Via della Vigna Nuova.

Santa Maria Novella

Piazza Santa Maria Novella (055 210 113). **Open** 7am-12.15pm, 3-6pm Sun-Fri; 7am-12.15pm, 3-5pm Sat.
Santa Maria Novella was the Florentine seat of the Dominicans, a fanatically inquisitorial order, fond of leading street brawls against suspected heretics and encouraging the faithful to strip and whip themselves before the church's altar. The piazza outside, one of Florence's biggest, was enlarged in 1244-5 in order to accommodate the crowds who came to hear St Peter the martyr, one of the viler members of the saintly canon, who made his name persecuting so-called heretics in the north of Italy (and ended up with one of their axes in his head).

The interior of the church, designed by the order's own monks, is appropriately cheerless, but the façade is a light, elegant green and white marble affair. This is thanks to Alberti, who in 1465, at the request of the Rucellai family, incorporated the Romanesque lower storey into a refined Renaissance scheme. To the right of the church is a cemetery surrounded by the grave niches of Florence's wealthy families. Until Vasari insisted they were whitewashed in the mid-sixteenth century, the walls of the church were covered with frescoes. Fortunately Vasari left Masaccio's *Trinity*. Painted in 1427, this was the first time that Brunelleschi's mathematical rules of perspective were applied to a painting, and the result is a solemn triumph of *trompe l'œil*, with God, Christ and two saints appearing to stand in a niche, watched by the two patrons, Lorenzo Lenzi and his wife. The inscription above the skeleton on the sarcophagus reads 'I was what you are and what I am you shall be'.

Over the next few decades the Dominicans appear to have loosened up a bit. In 1485, they allowed Ghirlandaio to cover the walls of the Cappella Tornabuoni with scenes from the life of John the

Baptist, featuring lavish contemporary Florentine interiors and a supporting cast from the Tornabuoni family. At about the same time, Filippino Lippi was at work next door in the Cappella di Filippo Strozzi, painting scenes from the life of St Philip.

To compare Masaccio's easeful use of perspective with the contorted struggles of Paolo Uccello, pop outside to the Chiostro Verde, to the left of the church. The cloister is so-called because of the green base pigment Uccello used, giving the flood-damaged frescoes a chill, deathly hue. The best preserved example of how not to do perspective is *The Flood*, looking as if it was painted from down a plug hole. Beyond the Chiostro is the Cappella degli Spagnoli, named because Cosimo I's wife Eleonora di Toledo reserved it for the use of her Spanish cronies, and decorated it with vibrant scenes celebrating the triumph of Dominicans and the Catholic Church. There is also a small **Museo di Santa Maria Novella** just off the Chiostro Verde.

Palazzo Rucellai

Via della Vigna Nuova.

When Alberti created the façade of Santa Maria Novella for the Rucellai family, he had already designed their palazzo, the most refined in the city. Its subtle façade was inspired by Rome's Colosseum: the pilasters that section the bottom storey have Doric capitals, those on the middle storey Ionic, and those on the top storey based on the Corinthian. There is no rustication: Alberti loathed it, considering it pompous, arrogant and fit only for tyrants. The Rucellais were wool merchants who had grown rich by importing from Majorca a red dye derived from lichen, known as *oricello*, from which their surname derives.

A load of balls

The Medici have long been associated with a load of balls. Their family emblem – a number of red balls, the *palle*, on a gold shield – is prominently displayed on buildings all over Florence and Tuscany that have Medicean connections or that were financed with Medici money. One outraged contemporary of Cosimo il Vecchio declared that 'He has emblazoned even the monks' privies with his balls.' In times of danger, Medici supporters were rallied with cries of *Palle! Palle!*

The most romantic (and far-fetched) explanation of the origin of the *palle* is that the balls are actually dents in a shield, inflicted in the Mugello by a fearsome giant on one of Charlemagne's knights, Averardo. The knight eventually vanquished the giant and, to mark his victory, Charlemagne permitted Averardo to use the image of the battered shield as his coat of arms. Rather more probable is that, as the name Medici suggests, the balls have a medical connection, perhaps representing pills or cupping-glasses.

Santa Trìnita

Piazza Santa Trinita (055 216 912). **Open** 8am-noon, 4-7pm, Mon-Sat; 4-7pm Sun.

Santa Trìnita is a plain church built in the thirteenth century over the ruins of two earlier churches belonging to the Vallombrosans. The order was founded by San Giovanni Gualberto Visdomini in 1038, following a miraculous incident almost 20 years earlier in the church of San Miniato al Monte. While kneeling in front of a crucifix, Giovanni saw the head of Christ nod in approval of his prayer. This incident started his conversion from a nobleman to a monk – a riches-to-rags story that explains why he spent a great deal of time attempting to persuade pious aristocrats to surrender their wealth and live a life of austerity. The said crucifix was supposedly that held in the Ficozzi Chapel moved to Santa Trìnita in 1671. The order became extremely wealthy and powerful, reaching a peak in the sixteenth and seventeenth centuries when their huge fortress abbey at Vallombrosa was built. The church is worth a visit for the Sassetti Chapel, frescoed by Ghirlandaio, with scenes from the life of St Francis, including one set in the Piazza della Signoria and featuring Lorenzo il Magnifico and his children.

Piazza & Ponte Santa Trìnita

Piazza Santa Trìnita is little more than a bulge in Via Tornabuoni, used as a taxi rank and dominated by an ancient column taken from the Baths of Caracalla in Rome, a gift to Cosimo I by Pope Pius I in 1560. The statue of *Justice* on top was designed by Ammanati. Ponte Santa Trìnita is an elegant bridge with an elliptical arch, linking Piazza Santa Trìnita with the Oltrarno. It was built by Ammanati in 1567, possibly to a design by Michelangelo. The statues at either end represent the Four Seasons and were placed there in 1608 to celebrate Cosimo II's marriage to Maria of Austria.

Ognissanti

Via Borgognissanti 42. **Open** 8am-noon, 4-7pm daily; *cenacolo* 9am-noon Mon, Tue, Sat.

Ognissanti, or All Saints, was founded in the thirteenth century by a group of monks from Lombardy known as the Umiliati. They were responsible for introducing the wool trade to Florence and, as the city's subsequent wealth was built on wool, it could be argued that without the Umiliati there would have been no Florentine Renaissance. As well as building their church and monastery, the Umiliati

Duomo *domination. See page 46.*

had 30 houses that they rented out to wool workers. They also built a sturdy bridge across the Arno to Borgo di San Frediano, where most wool workers lived. It is still known as the Ponte alla Carraia after the *carri* or carts that carried fleece back and forth across the Arno. By the fourteenth century, the Umiliati were so rich they commissioned Giotto to paint the *Maestà* (now in the **Uffizi**) for their high altar. Fifty years later they decided they needed a flashier altar, and commissioned Giovanni da Milano to create an altarpiece with more gold (now also in the Uffizi).

Ognissanti was also the parish church of the Vespucci, a family of merchants from Peretola (near the airport) who dealt in silk, wine, wool, banking and goods from the Far East. One of their number was the fifteenth-century navigator, Amerigo, who sailed to the Venezuelan coast in 1499 and ended up having two continents named after him. The church has been rebuilt on numerous occasions, and is visited now mainly for paintings by Ghirlandaio. Amerigo himself appears as a young boy dressed in pink in the *Madonna della Misericordia*. Other frescoes worth seeing include *St Augustine* by Botticelli, a *St Jerome* by Ghirlandaio, and on a wall of the refectory, a *Last Supper,* also by Ghirlandaio. *See p70* **Cloisters & crucifixions**.

San Lorenzo & San Marco

This is a vibrant, colourful area, stretching north from the huge market around the church of San Lorenzo, with hundreds of stalls selling identical wares, to the student area of San Marco.

San Lorenzo

Piazza San Lorenzo (055 216 634). **Open** 7am-noon, 3.30-5.30pm, Mon-Sat; (for prayers only) Sun.

San Lorenzo was the parish church of the Medici, who largely financed its construction, and for centuries the ruling family continued to lavish money on the place. It was built between 1419 and 1469 to a design by Brunelleschi. Its huge dome is almost as prominent as that of the Duomo, and the building itself sprawls, heavy and imposing, between Piazza di San Lorenzo and Piazza di Madonna degli Aldobrandini.

Despite the fortune spent on the place, the façade was never finished, hence the digestive-biscuit-bricks. In 1518, the Medici Pope Leo X commissioned Michelangelo to design a façade (the models can be seen in the **Casa Buonarroti**). The Pope decided that the marble should be mined at Pietrasanta, which was part of Florence's domain. Michelangelo, however, wanted to use high-quality Carrara marble. In the end it didn't matter as the whole scheme was cancelled in 1520.

San Lorenzo was the first church to which Brunelleschi applied his theory of rational proportion. Like Santo Spirito, this is a church to stroll around and savour, though there are a couple of artworks you might want to look at more closely. First of these is Donatello's bronze pulpits, from which Savonarola snarled his tales of sin and doom. The reliefs are pretty powerful too: you can almost hear the crowds scream in the *Deposition*. On the north wall is a *Martyrdom of St Lawrence* by Mannerist par excellence Bronzino, a decadent affair in which the burning of the saint is attended by musclebound men and hefty women with masculine shoulders and red-gold hair, dressed in pink, lime green, yellow and lilac. In the second chapel on the right is another mannerist work, a *Marriage of the Virgin* by Rosso Fiorentino. In the north transept is an *Annunciation* by Filippo Lippi, with a clarity of line and depth of perspective that make it perfect for this interior.

Opening off the north transept is the Sagrestia Vecchia (old sacristy) another Brunelleschi design, with a dome segmented like a tangerine, and proportions based on cubes and spheres. The doors, by Donatello, feature martyrs, apostles and church fathers, while to the left of the entrance is an elaborate tomb of serpentine, porphyry, marble and bronze filled with the remains of Lorenzo il Magnifico's father and uncle, and designed by Verrocchio. The Biblioteca Laurenziana was built to house the Medicis' considerable library and is reached via the door to the left of the façade and up one of Europe's most elegant stairways, a slick Michelangelo Mannerist design in *pietra serena*.

There are more Medici tombs in the Cappella dei Principi, entered from the side of the church on Piazza Madonna di Aldobrandini. Designed by Michelangelo as the Medici mausoleum, the floorplan was based on that of Florence's Baptistery, and possibly of the Holy Sepulchre in Jerusalem. It is inlaid with brilliantly hued *pietra dura,* which kept the workers of the **Opificio delle Pietre Dure** busy for several centuries. It is made of huge hunks of porphyry and ancient Roman marbles hauled into the city and sawn into pieces by Turkish slaves. At one time it was hoped that the tombs of the Medici would be joined by that of Christ, but unfortunately for the Medici, the authorities in Jerusalem refused to sell it. The adjoining Sagrestia Nuova is dominated by the tombs of Lorenzo il Magnifico's far-from-magnificent cousins, Giuliano, Duke of Nemours, and Lorenzo, Duke of Urbino (*see chapter* **History**: **Medici Who's Who**), designed by Michelangelo with ghastly figures of Night and Day, and Dawn and Dusk reclining atop.

Giardino dei Semplici

Via Micheli 3 (055 275 7402). Bus 11, 17. **Open** 9am-noon, 2.30-5pm, Mon, Wed; 9am-noon Fri, four Sundays in Apr, May. **Admission** free.

The Giardino dei Semplici, or garden of samples, was planted in 1545 on the orders of Cosimo I, on lands seized from an order of Dominican nuns, for the cultivation of exotic plants and research into their uses. Essential oils were extracted, perfumes distilled and cures sought for various ailments and as antidotes to poisons. Nowadays it makes a pleasant place to wander in spring or summer, an escape from both crowds and high culture.

Palazzo Medici Riccardi

Via Cavour 1 (055 276 0340). **Open** 9am-1pm, 3-5pm, Mon-Sat; 9am-noon Sun; also *summer* 3-6pm Sun. **Admission** free. *Capella dei Magi* open 9am-1pm, 3-6pm, Mon-Tue, Thur-Sat; 9am-1pm Sun. **Admission** L6,000.

A demonstration of both Medici muscle and Medici subtlety, Palazzo Medici Riccardi was home to *La Famiglia* until they moved into the Palazzo Vecchio in 1540. Not wishing to appear too ostentatious, Cosimo il Vecchio rejected a design by Brunelleschi as too extravagant. He plumped instead for one by Michelozzo, with a heavily rusticated lower storey in the style of many military buildings, but a smoother, more refined, first storey and a yet more restrained second storey, crowned by an overhanging cornice. The palazzo doubled as fortress and home, and was widely copied throughout Italy. It was massively expanded and revamped in the seventeenth century by its new owners, the Riccardi, but retains a chapel frescoed by Benozzo Gozzoli, featuring a vivid *Journey of the Magi*. The palace now hosts various cultural exhibitions.

San Marco

Piazza San Marco. Bus 1, 6, 11, 17. **Open** 7am-12.30pm, 4-6.30pm, daily.

The Medici lavished even more money on the church and convent of San Marco than they did on San Lorenzo. In 1434, Cosimo il Vecchio returned from exile and organised the handing over of the monastery of San Marco to the Dominicans. He then funded the renovation of the decaying church and convent by Michelozzo. Whether he did it to ease his conscience (banking was still officially forbidden by the church), or to cash in on the increasing popularity of the Dominicans, is uncertain, but Cosimo agreed to foot the bill. He also founded a public library, full of Greek and Latin works, which had a great influence on Florentine humanists. Ironically, later in the fifteenth century, San Marco became the base of religious fundamentalist Savonarola.

The **Museo di San Marco** is housed in the various buildings of the convent alongside the church, and is largely dedicated to the ethereal paintings of Fra Angelico, arguably the most spiritual artist of the fifteenth century. You are greeted on the first floor of the convent by one of the most famous images in Christendom – an *Annunciation* that is, for once, entirely of another world. The same is true of the other images Fra Angelico and his assistants frescoed on the walls of the monks' white, vaulted cells. Most of the cells on the outer wall of the left corridor are by Fra Angelico himself. Particularly outstanding are a lyrical *Noli Me Tangere* showing Christ appearing to Mary Magdalene in a field of flowers, and the surreal *Mocking of Christ,* in which Christ's torturers are represented simply by relevant fragments of their anatomy: a hand holding a whip, another holding a sponge, a face spitting. The cell that was occupied by Savonarola is adorned with portraits of the rabid reformer by Fra Bartolommeo.

On the ground floor, there are more works by Fra Angelico in the Ospizio dei Pellegrini (pilgrims' hospice) many of them collected from churches around the city: his first commission, the *Madonna dei Linaiuoli*, painted in 1433 for the Guild of Linen Makers, is here, along with a superb *Deposition* and a *Last Judgement* in which the Blessed dance among the flowers and trees of Paradise, while the Damned are boiled in cauldrons and pursued by monsters. By way of contrast, pop into the refectory, dominated by a Ghirlandaio *Last Supper,* in which the disciples – by turn bored, praying, crying or haughty – pick at a frugal repast of bread, wine and cherries against a typically Ghirlandaio iconographic background of orange trees, a peacock, a Burmese cat and flying ducks. The peacock symbolises the Resurrection, the oranges are the fruits of paradise, the cat is a symbol of evil (hence near Judas), the ducks represent the heavens.

There's plenty to reflect on in ***Piazza dei Ciompi****'s market.* *See page 64.*

SS Annunziata

Piazza SS Annunziata (055 239 8034). Bus 6, 31, 32. **Open** 7am-12.30pm, 4-7.30pm, Mon-Sat; 7am-12.30pm, 4-9.30pm, Sun.

SS Annunziata, the church of the Servite Order, is a place of popular worship rather than perfect proportion. Cosy and candlelit, it has a frescoed baroque ceiling and an opulent shrine built around a miraculous icon of the Madonna, said to have been painted by a monk called Bartolomeo in 1252 and finished by angels. It is from this legend that the church derives its name. Surrounding the icon are bouquets of flowers, silver lamps and pewter body parts – ex-votives left in the hope that the Madonna will cure the dicky heart or gammy leg of a loved one. Despite its baroque appearance, the church was actually built by Michelozzo in the fifteenth century, as can be seen in the light, arcaded atrium. It was frescoed early the following century by Pontormo, Rosso Fiorentino and, most strikingly, Andrea del Sarto, whose *Birth of the Virgin* is set within the walls of a Renaissance palazzo, with cherubs perched on a finely carved mantelpiece and on the festooned canopy of the bed. There is another fresco by del Sarto in the Chiostro dei Morti (Cloister of the Dead), so-named because it was originally a burial ground, but you need to get permission from the sacristan to see it.

Piazza SS Annunziata

Bus 6, 31, 32.

Piazza SS Annunziata is one of the most pleasing piazzas in the city, surrounded on three sides by delicate arcades, and with a powerful equestrian statue of Grand Duke Ferdinando I by Giambologna in the centre. Opened in 1445, the Spedale degli Innocenti on the eastern side was the first foundling hospital in Europe, commissioned by the Guild of Silk Weavers and designed by Brunelleschi (a member of the guild). The powder blue medallions in the spandrels, each showing a swaddled baby, are by Andrea della Robbia. Babies, many of them the offspring of the city's numerous domestic slaves, were left in a small revolving door, set into the wall on the left. Brunelleschi envisioned creating a perfectly symmetrical piazza, which would have been modern Europe's first, but died before he could realise the dream.

However, in the seventeenth century, the porticos were continued around two further sides of the square, giving the piazza a human scale and unity absent elsewhere in the city. By day it's a popular hang-out for students from the nearby university and mums waiting to collect children from the school, but by night it provides shelter for the city's down and outs.

Santa Croce & Sant'Ambrogio

The streets leading from central Florence to the church and piazza of Santa Croce are devoted to tourism – at least every other shop is a leather-goods emporium. Behind Santa Croce, however, it's a totally different scene with a funky alternative element manifesting itself in ads for tattooists, graffitied self-advertisements for conceptual artists and flyers for gigs and benefits at the *centri sociali*. At the heart of the district is the fruit and vegetable market of Sant'Ambrogio, best seen on a Saturday, followed by an aperitif at **Caffè Cibreo**.

Santa Croce

Piazza Santa Croce (055 244 619). Bus 14. **Open** *summer* 9.30am-5.45pm Mon-Sat; 3-5.45pm Sun; *winter* 8am-12.30pm, 3-6.30pm, Mon-Sat; 3-6pm Sun.
Santa Croce is filled with the tombs of the city's illustrious; oddly so, given that it belonged to the Franciscans, the most unworldly of the religious orders. They founded the church in 1228, ten years after they arrived in the city. A recently established order, the Franciscans were supposed to make their living by manual work, preaching and begging. At the time, Santa Croce was a slum, full of the city's grossly underpaid dyers and wool-workers. Franciscan preaching, with its message that all men were equal, had a huge impact on the poor people of the quarter. It was doubtless in part due to the confidence given them by the Franciscans that, in 1378, the dyers and wool-makers revolted against the all-powerful guilds and were allowed to organise their own guilds. As for the Franciscans, their vow of poverty slowly eroded. By the late thirteenth century, the old church was felt to be inadequate, and a new one was planned – intended to be one of the largest in Christendom, and probably designed by Arnolfo di Cambio, architect of the Duomo and the Palazzo Vecchio. It was financed partly by property confiscated from Ghibellines who had been convicted of heresy.

Santa Croce remains the richest medieval church in the city, with frescoes by Giotto, a chapel by Brunelleschi, and one of the finest of all early Renaissance tombs. At first sight, however, the interior of the church is a bit of a disappointment, too big, too gloomy and with too many overbearing marble tombs clogging the walls. Not all the tombs contain bodies: Dante's (right aisle) is simply a memorial to the writer, who is buried in Ravenna. In the niche alongside is the tomb of Michelangelo – he died in Rome, but his body was brought back to Florence, and further down, the tomb of Leonardo Bruni by Bernardo Rossellini. Back at the top of the left aisle is Galileo's tomb, a polychrome marble confection created in 1737 more than a century after his death, when the Church finally permitted him a Christian burial.

The Cappelle Bardi and Peruzzi, completely frescoed by Giotto, are more interesting. Unfortunately, they are not in great condition – a result of Giotto painting on dry instead of wet plaster (a technique known as *a secco*), and of them being daubed with whitewash in the eighteenth century. The most striking of the two chapels is the Bardi, with scenes from the life of St Francis, in haunting, virtual monotone, the figures just stylized enough to make them other-worldly, yet individual enough to make them human. On the far side of the high altar is the Cappella Bardi di Vernio, frescoed by one of Giotto's most interesting followers, Maso di Banco, and recently restored in fresh, vibrant colours.

To get to the Cappella dei Pazzi, Brunelleschi's geometric *tour de force*, you have to leave the church, and pass through the cloister. Planned in the 1430s, and completed 40 years later, it is based on a central square topped by a cupola, flanked by two barrel-vaulted bays with decorative arches on the white walls echoing the structural arches. Across the courtyard is **Museo dell'Opera di Santa Croce**, a small museum of church treasures, including a thirteenth-century crucifix by Cimabué badly damaged in the 1966 flood and Donatello's *St Louis of Toulouse* from **Orsanmichele**.

Ponte alle Grazie

Until they were demolished in the nineteenth century, the Ponte delle Grazie had several oratories and chapels built upon its piers. One of them, devoted to Santa Maria delle Grazie, was much visited by distraught lovers seeking solace, and gave the bridge its name. Also on the bridge was a tiny convent where several nuns cloistered themselves for life. The architect Alberti died in another of the bridge's chapels. The original stone bridge, built in 1227, was the only one in Florence to survive a flood in 1333. It was destroyed during World War II, and replaced by the present structure in 1957.

Piazza dei Ciompi

Bus B.
Named after the dyers and wool-workers revolt of 1378, Piazza dei Ciompi is now given over to a junk/antiques market during the week, and is flooded by a huge day-long fleamarket on the last Sunday of every month. It is dominated by a loggia, built by Vasari in 1568 for the Mercato Vecchio, which occupied the site of Piazza della Repubblica. It was dismantled in the nineteenth century and re-erected here. It now shelters a book cart which often has some good-value art and history books.

One for the road

Certosa di Galluzzo

Via Senese. Bus 37. **Open** Tue-Sun, closed noon-3pm; **Admission** by donation.
Some 5km to the south of Porta Romana lies the Certosa del Galuzzo. Sitting like a fortress above the busy arterial road that leads out of town towards Siena, the imposing complex was founded in 1342 as a Carthusian monastery by Niccolò Acciaiuoli and is the third of six Certosas to be built in Tuscany in the fourteenth century. Inhabited since 1958 by a small group of Cistercian monks, it is a spiritual place full of artistic interest. The main entrance leads into a large courtyard and the Church of San Lorenzo, said to be by Brunelleschi, who is also thought to be responsible for the double-arched lay brothers' cloister. Although the church itself is not that interesting there are some imposing tombs in the crypt. Sixty six *majolica tondi* decorate the Chiostro Grande (the main cloister) around which are constructed the twelve monks' cells. These are more like mini-houses, each with a well, vegetable garden and study room.

Museums & Galleries

The art behemoths and a clutch of eclectic collections.

Florence's museum collections are unrivalled, and it would take several weeks and much shoe leather to see them all properly. Many have private collections at their core: whether that of a mega-family like the Medici (**Uffizi** and **Palazzo Pitti**) or of a lone connoisseur (Museos **Bardini**, **Horne** and **Stibbert**). Add to these the museums founded to preserve treasures too precious to expose to the elements (**Accademia**, **Bargello** and the **Museo dell'Opera del Duomo**), to say nothing of the scholarly collections you would expect to find in any university town, and you have a selection as refined as the Renaissance itself.

Administratively, Florentine museums fall into three categories: private, state or municipal. A collective ticket is available for municipal museums which entitles you to a 50 per cent discount on entry to all the museums on paying an initial L10,000; the ticket is valid for one year and allows one visit to each museum. Municipal museums where this discount scheme applies have (M) after the admission fee in our listings.

The state museums don't give concessions, save the two weeks (which vary) of the year when they are all free. For general information on the state museums (*Firenze Musei*) and booking call 055 294 883.

For some of the state museums, such as **Appartamenti Reali** of the **Palazzo Pitti**, booking is sometimes the only means of viewing, while for others, such as the Uffizi, it is often far more convenient. Booking costs L2,000 and the tickets are collected from an office in the corner of the Palazzo Pitti courtyard. But don't expect to be able to book tickets there directly, you will be told to phone the central number.

Temporary exhibitions are regularly held at a few locations in Florence, such as **Palazzo Vecchio**, **Palazzo Medici Riccardi** and **Palazzo Strozzi** (*see chapter* **Sightseeing**) and the Istituzioni di Architettura on Via Ricasoli.

Last issuing times for tickets vary – try to get to the ticket office an hour before the museum closes. Closing time for at least half the city's museums is 1.50pm and Mondays see a number of museums closed all day.

Donatello in the **Bargello**. *See page 67.*

The Uffizi

Piazzale degli Uffizi 6 (055 23885). **Open** 8.30am-6.50pm Tue-Sat; 8.30am-1.50pm Sun. **Admission** L12,000. **No credit cards.**

If you're at all fond of Renaissance art prepare to step into heaven. A crowded heaven maybe, but one that is dressed to the nines in the most gorgeous daubings. Picking a time when the gallery won't be busy is difficult, but try lunchtime and early evening, booking will avoid the queue but won't mean inside is crowd-free.

The collection begins, gloriously, with three *Maestàs* by Giotto, Cimabué and Duccio in **Room 2**, painted in the thirteenth and early fourteenth centuries. All three are still part of the Byzantine tradition: even Giotto's Virgin, painted for Ognissanti, is still very much otherworldly. Stepping into **Room 3** is to enter the world of fourteenth-century Siena, most exquisitely evoked by Simone Martini's *Annunciation* with breathtakingly beautiful angel, coy yet fearful Virgin, and a Room with a marble floor, marquesite throne and lilies standing in a gold vase. Such delight in detail reached its zenith in the international Gothic movement (**Rooms 5 & 6**), most particularly in the work of Gentile da Fabriano (1370-1427), whose *Adoration of the Magi* (otherwise known as the Strozzi altarpiece) seems a wonderful excuse to paint sumptuous brocades and intricate gold jewellery.

It is something of a surprise, then, to turn to an almost contemporary *Madonna and Child with Saint Anne* by Masolino and Masaccio (1401-1428) in **Room 7**. Although Masolino was not averse to a little international Gothic frivolity (note some of the costumes he dreamed up for the **Brancacci Chapel**), here he is totally restrained. Masaccio painted the Virgin, whose severe expression and statuesque pose make her an indubitable descendant of Giotto's *Maestà*.

In the same room is the *Madonna Enthroned with Saints Francis, John the Baptist, Zenobius and Lucy* by Domenico Veneziano (1400-61), a Venetian artist who died a pauper in Florence, and had a remarkable skill for rendering the way in which light affects colour. If you are familiar with his pupil Piero della Francesca's work, his influence on the younger artist will be clear, represented in the portraits of the *Duke and Duchess of Urbino*. Still in

At the time of going to print much work was underway in the museums of Florence in preparation for the year 2000 and opening times may change – telephone before setting out to avoid disappointment.

Major collections

Accademia

Via Ricasoli 58-60 (055 238 8609). **Open** 8.30am-6.50pm Tue-Sat, 8.30am-1.50pm Sun. **Admission** L12,000. **No credit cards.**

They queue and they queue. In fact they queue so much that the street outside has been pedestrianised. And what they queue to see is Michelangelo's *David* (1504). The sculpture started life as a serious political icon, an example of strength and resolve, designed to encourage Florentines to support their fledgling constitution. Michelangelo, however, undoubtedly considered it a monument to his genius – a triumph of skill in carving a figure from a slab of marble 5m high, but exceptionally narrow. Not without reason has it been suggested that *David*'s arrogant and self-satisfied smugness reflects the image that Michelangelo saw in the mirror. The Accademia is not all about *David*. There's also Michelangelo's so-called slaves – unfinished sculptures struggling to escape from being encased in marble. They were intended for Pope Julius II's tomb, a project that Michelangelo was eventually, much to his irritation, forced to abandon in order to paint the Sistine Chapel ceiling in Rome. And the Salone dell'Ottocento is full of sculptural reproductions – intended to provide budding artists with examples to copy.

Room 7, Paolo Uccello (1396-1475) is represented by one of three original panels of the *Battle of San Romano*. A work of tremendous energy and power, it further reinforces the chaos of battle with its intense, distorted perspective.

Rooms 8 & 9 are dominated by Filippo Lippi and the Pollaiuolo brothers. The Madonna in Lippi's *Madonna and Child with Angels* is a portrait of the astonishingly beautiful Lucrezia Buti, a nun, whom he abducted and married. The more talented of the brothers, Antonio, was one of the first artists to dissect bodies in order to study anatomy. His small panels of the *Labours of Hercules* evidence his familiarity with the skeletal form and musculature.

The two most famous paintings in the Uffizi and in Italy are in **Room 10**. Botticelli's *Birth of Venus*, the epitome of Renaissance romance, in fact depicts the birth of the goddess from a sea impregnated by the castration of Uranus; an allegory of the birth of beauty from the mingling of the physical world (the sea) and the spiritual (Uranus). As for the meaning of the *Primavera* – scholars have been squabbling about that since it was painted in 1478, but most now agree that it is intended to signify the triumph of Venus (in the centre), with the Three Graces representing her beauty, and Flora her fecundity.

Beyond, in **Room 15**, are several paintings by Leonardo da Vinci, including a collaboration with his teacher Verrocchio in il Battesimo di Cristo, after which Verrocchio never painted again, reputedly because his work paled in comparison to Leonardo's. The octagonal **Room 18**, with its mother-of-pearl ceiling, is dominated by portraits by Bronzino, most strikingly that of Eleonora di Toledo, assured, beautiful and very Spanish in an opulent gold and black brocade gown. In **Room 25** the gallery makes its transition to Mannerism, championed by Michelangelo's *Holy Family*, which shows the sculptural bodies, virtuoso composition and luscious palette which characterised the new wave. The Sala del Pontormo e del Rosso Fiorentino again show Michelangelo's legacy, evidently developed further in *Moses Defending the Children of Jethro* by Rosso Fiorentino, famous for his fiery red hair and angular, tortured style.

Room 28 has works by Titian including his masterpiece *Venus of Urbino* (*pictured left*), whose questionably chaste gaze has disarmed viewers for centuries. For more Venetian works skip to **Rooms 31-35**, but en route don't miss the visually-challenging *Madonna with the Long Neck* by Parmigianino (*pictured above*).

Bargello

Via del Proconsolo 4 (055 238 8606). **Open** 8.30am-2pm Tue-Sat; 2nd & 4th Sun of month; 1st, 3rd & 5th Mon of month. **Admission** L8,000. **No credit cards**.

This dour, fortified building started life as the Palazzo del Popolo in 1250, and soon became the seat of the *Podestà*, the chief magistrate. In the fourteenth century the bodies of executed criminals were displayed in the courtyard and, in the fifteenth century, law courts, prisons and torture chambers were set up inside. It didn't get its present name until the sixteenth century, when the Medici made it the seat of the chief of police, known as the Bargello. In 1865, the Bargello was opened as a museum.

The collection is one of the most eclectic and prestigious in the city, ranging from prime sculptures by the likes of Michelangelo, Donatello, Cellini and Giambologna, to Scandinavian chess sets and Egyptian ivories. The most famous works are Michelangelo's androgynous *Bacchus* and Giambologna's fleet-of-foot *Mercury*. The first-floor loggia in the courtyard has Giambologna's virtuoso aviary of bronze birds, including a madly exaggerated turkey. This leads to the Salone Donatello with his two triumphant *David*s and tense-looking *Saint George*. Also fascinating are the two panels of the *Sacrifice of Isaac*, sculpted by Brunelleschi and Lorenzo Ghiberti for a competition to design the north doors of the Baptistery.

Museo dell'Opera del Duomo

Piazza Duomo 9 (055 230 2885). **Open** 9am-6.50pm Mon-Sat; 9am-1.30pm Sun. **Admission** L10,000. **No credit cards**.

This recently enlarged and improved museum con-

Collezione della Ragione: *Marini's* Cavallino *looks out over Piazza della Signoria. See p70.*

tains instruments used to build the Duomo and sculptures deemed too precious and vulnerable to be left to the mercy of the elements.

On the ground floor are the recently restored Baptistery doors, *La Porta del Paradiso* (the Gates of Paradise), sculpted by Lorenzo Ghiberti. There are also bits and pieces from Santa Reparata, an earlier church on the site, including a classical-style *Madonna* with spooky glass eyes by Arnolfo di Cambio.

Halfway up the stairs is a *Pietà*, a late work by Michelangelo showing Christ, dead and disjointed, slithering from the grasp of Nicodemus. The sculpture was never finished, supposedly because Michelangelo got so frustrated by his servant nagging him about it, and with the poor quality of the marble, that he eventually smashed off the arm of Christ in frustration. According to Vasari, Nicodemus is a self-portrait.

Upstairs are brick stamps and forms, the pulleys and ropes by which building materials (and workers) were winched up to the dome. Also, the extraordinary wood sculpture of *Mary Magdalene* by Donatello, dishevelled and ugly, with coarse, dirty hair so realistic you can almost smell it. His *Habbakuk*, bald, emancipated and caught in vision is another uncomfortable work: indeed Donatello himself is said to have gripped the statue and screamed at it 'Speak, speak, speak!'

It's a relief then to turn to the *cantorie* (choir lofts). One is by Donatello, carved with cavorting putti, the other full of angel musicians by Luca della Robbia. Beyond are the reliefs that Giotto carved for the campanile.

Palazzo Pitti

Galleria d'Arte Moderna *(055 238 8616)*. **Open** 8.30am-1.50pm daily (last entry 1.15pm). **Closed** 2nd, 4th Sun & 1st, 3rd, 5th Mon of month. **Admission** L8,000.

The 30 rooms on the top floor of Palazzo Pitti, which now constitute Florence's modern art museum, were a set of royal apartments until 1920. The collection comprises works bought by the state, those belonging to the Florentine Grand Dukes and paintings donated by private collectors. The collection is varied, housing anything from neo-classical to early twentieth-century art. Among the highlights are Giovanni Dupré's forceful bronze sculptures of Cain and Abel in Room 5 and Ottone Rosai's simple Piazza del Carmine in Room 30. There are also some veritable disaster areas; Room 18 is dedicated to the Macchieaioli school, paintings built up using dots (*macchie*).

Museo del Costume Closed until April 2000.

Housed in the Palazzina della Meridiana, which periodically served as residence to members of the Lorraine family and the House of Savoy. To preserve the exhibits the collection rotates and at the time of publishing no precise details were available on the future collection. The archives, however, include clothes from early eighteenth-century *robe a la française* to *fin de siècle* clothes by Rosa Genoni, inspired by Botticelli and Pisanello.

Galleria del Palatina & Appartamenti Reali *(055 238 8614)*. **Open** 8.30am-6.50pm Tue-Sat; 8.30am-1.50pm Sun. **Admission** L12,000. **No credit cards**.

The **Galleria del Palatina** has paintings hung four or five high on its damask walls, in rooms busy with *pietra dura* and malachite tables. Included in the collection are a beautiful Filippo Lippi, *Madonna and Child*, which shows his sophisticated understanding of line, colour and form, and several works by Raphael – the coyly sweet *Madonna della Seggiola*, the serene *Madonna del Granduca* and the most innovative *Holy Family*, his last painting, showing his susceptibility to the contagious influences of Michelangelo. In addition, there are some inspired works by Titian and *Consequences of War* by Rubens.

The Galleria runs into the **Appartamenti Reali**, or royal apartments. These were lavishly decorated in the nineteenth century, first by the Lorraine Dukes, then by Italy's first royals, King Umberto I and Queen Margherita (of pizza fame), who lived here during Florence's brief stint as capital (1865-70). Rooms are walled with garish silk brocade, anything that can be gilded is gilded, and anything not gilded is smothered in precious gems and marbles. Look out for the two grotesque ebony *prie dieu* (kneeling desks for prayer), one in each of the royal bedrooms, the King's adorned with ghoulish porcelain dolls' heads and the Queen's encrusted with gilded bronze and *pietra dura*.

Museo degli Argenti *(055 238 8710)*. **Open** 8.30am-1.50pm Tue-Sat; 2nd & 4th Mon of month; 1st, 3rd & 5th Sun of month. **Admission** L4,000. **No credit cards**.
The two floors of this museum are full of treasures amassed by the Medici. These range from beautiful vases and ornate crystal cups to a breathtakingly banal collection of miniature animals. There's also a display of Chinese and Japanese ceramics.

Museo di Porcellana Admission L4,000 (incl in ticket for Boboli Gardens – *see chapter* **Sightseeing**).
At the top of the Boboli Gardens, this former reception room for artists, built by Leopoldo de' Medici, offers appropriately inspiring views over the Tuscan hills. The museum displays china used by the various occupants of Palazzo Pitti and includes the largest selection of Viennese china outside of Vienna. Look out for the rare oyster stand from Sèvres and the teapot in the shape of a hen from the Meissen factory.

Palazzo Vecchio

Piazza Signoria (055 276 8465). **Open** 9am-7pm Mon-Wed, Fri, Sat; 9am-2pm Thur; 8am-1pm Sun. **Admission** L10,000 (M). **No credit cards**.
Still Florence's town hall, the thirteenth-century Palazzo Vecchio (*see chapter* **Sightseeing**) was the seat first of the Signoria, the city's ruling body, then, for nine years, of the Medici (1540-9). The Medici's stay may have been brief, but they instigated a massive Mannerist makeover of the palace's interior, under the direction of Giorgio Vasari, court architect from 1555 to 1574.

The Salone dei Cinquecento (hall of the 500), where the members of the Great Council held meetings, should have been decorated with battle scenes by Michelangelo and Leonardo, not the zestless scenes of victory over Siena and Pisa by Vasari that actually cover the walls. Leonardo, frustrated with failed attempts to develop new mural painting techniques, abandoned the project. Michelangelo had only completed the cartoon for the *Battle of Cascine* when he was summoned to Rome by Pope Julius II. One of Michelangelo's commissions did end up here: *Victory*, a statue carved for the Pope's never-finished tomb.

Off the Salone is the Studiolo di Francesco I, where Francesco hid away and conducted alchemical experiments. The room, also decorated by Vasari, includes a scene from the Alchemist's laboratory and illustrations of the four elements, while, from the vaulted ceiling, portraits of Francesco's parents, Cosimo I and Elenora di Toledo by Bronzino look down.

Upstairs, the Quartiere degli Elementi contains Vasari's allegories of the elements. The Quartiere di Eleonora (the wife of Cosimo I) has two entirely frescoed chapels; the first was partly decorated by Bronzino, who uses intense pastel hues to depict a surreal *Crossing the Red Sea*, while the Capella dei Priori is decorated with fake mosaics and an idealised *Annunciation*.

Beyond is the garish Sala D'Udienza with a carved ceiling dripping in gold; more subtle is the Sala dei Gigli, so named because of the gilded lilies (the sym-

Dressed to kill at **Museo Stibbert**. *See p72.*

Cloisters & crucifixions

In the late fifteenth century there were 30 monasteries in and around Florence. The richer fraternities could afford to commission the most celebrated artists to decorate their monasteries. Fundamental to each was a *cenacolo* (a painting of the Last Supper, often with a picture of the crucifixion above for added dramatism) for the refectory, to give the dining monks a little thought for food. These paintings traditionally depicted either the delivery of the Eucharist or the more popular declaration by Christ that he will be betrayed by one of the disciples. Today, many of these are accessible to the public:

Cenacolo di Sant'Apollonia

Via XXVII Aprile 1 (055 23885). Bus 4, 28. **Open** 8.30am-1.50pm Tue-Sat; 2nd & 4th Sun of month; 1st, 3rd & 5th Mon of month. **Admission** free.

The works in this Benedictine refectory, such as the frescoes of the passion of Christ, were covered over during the baroque period and only came to light during a restoration process. The most important piece is Andrea del Castagno's *Last Supper* (1445-50) (*pictured right*) in which the painter reverts back to a fourteenth-century seating plan, with Judas alienated on our side of the table. The vibrant colours and enclosed space of the room intensify the scene. There are also other works by del Castagno, including a *Pietá*.

Cenacolo di Ognissanti

Via Borgo Ognissanti 42 (055 239 6802). **Open** 9am-noon Mon-Tue, Sat. **Admission** free.

Off the cloister is Domenico Ghirlandaio's most famous *Last Supper* (1480). Like his work in San Marco (*see chapter* **Sightseeing**), here he uses religious iconography to load the work with deeper significance. Unlike in San Marco, however, his Apostles' expressions are noticeably more realistic. There's also a museum of Franciscan nick-knacks.

Cenacolo di Santo Spirito

Piazza Santo Spirito 29 (055 287 043). **Open** 10am-1.30pm Tue-Sat; 9am-12.30pm Sun. **Admission** L4,000 (M). **No credit cards**.

The *Last Supper* by Andrea Orcagna is not the foremost reason for visiting this former Augustinian refectory. The fresco was butchered by an eighteenth-century architect, commissioned to build some doors into it so it could be used as a carriage depot. Today only the fringes remain although above there is a more complete but heavily restored *Crucifixion*. But the museum houses an eclectic collection of sculptures given to the state in 1946 on the death of its owner a sailor called Salvatore Romano. He considered his body in its sarcophagus a worthy partner to sculptures by Tino Di Camaino and reliefs by Donatello.

bol of the city) that cover the walls. Decorated in the fifteenth century, it has a ceiling by Guiliano and Benedetto da Maiano, and frescoes of great Roman statesmen by Ghirlandaio opposite the door. Equally appealing is Donatello's *Judith and Holofernes*, rich in political significance; Judith representing Savonarola's virtuous new republic triumphing over the iniquitous Medicis.

Individual collections

Collezione Contini-Buonacossi

Uffizi, entrance Via Lambertesca (055 294 883). **Open** by appointment only. **Ticket** included in Uffizi ticket. Closed for refurbishment; due to re-open in 2000.

It's worth trying to save some energy during a tour of the **Uffizi** (*see listings*) for this impressive collection, which was donated to the state by the Contini-Buonacossi family in 1974. There's Madonna and Childs by Duccio, Cimabué and Andrea del Castagno and a room of artistic VIPs, with works by Bernini, Veronese and Tintoretto. Foreigners prestigious enough to find their way into the collection include El Greco, Velázquez and Goya.

Collezione della Ragione

Piazza Signoria 5 (055 283 078). **Open** 9am-1.30pm Mon, Wed-Sat; 8am-12.30pm Sun. **Admission** L4,000 (M). **No credit cards**.

The collection of Alberto della Ragione, an engineer from Sorrento, follows the Italian artistic movements that fought the restrictions of Fascism and challenged the success of modern art in France and Germany between 1920 and 1960. There's Futurist and surrealist works, including a De Chirico in Room 9, though not one of his trademark dreamscapes. More interesting are Ottone Rosai's works, which are indicative of a post-Fascist artistic freedom. This sense of freedom can also be seen in works by Emilio Vedova, labelled the Venetian brother of Kline and Pollock, whose Tintoretto-inspired works display a disarming array of colour and form.

Museo Bardini

Piazza dei Mozzi 1 (055 234 2427). **Open** 9am-2pm Mon, Tue, Thur-Sat; 8am-1pm Sun. **Admission** L6,000 (M). **No credit cards.** Closed for refurbishment; due to re-open Sept 2000.

The art dealer Stefano Bardini bequeathed his huge collection to the city on his death in 1922. Bardini

Museo del Cenacolo di Andrea del Sarto

Via San Salvi 16 (055 238 8603). Bus 3, 6. **Open** 8.30am-1.50pm Tue-Sun. **Admission** free.

Another refectory cum museum, formerly part of the monastery of San Salvi used by the Vallombrosan order, with a peculiar charm which makes the visit out of town worthwhile. The highlight is the *Last Supper* (1526-7) by Andrea del Sarto, a godfather of Mannerism, whose careful study of form, movement and colour give the work a tangible tension. Among other works by Andrea del Sarto are those by Pontormo, his pupil, whose Mannerist tendencies are much stronger than those of his teacher.

Museo dell'Opera di Santa Croce

Piazza Santa Croce 16 (055 244 619). **Open** *summer* 10am-12pm, 2-6.30pm daily; *winter* 10am-12pm, 3-5pm, daily. **Admission** L5,000. **No credit cards**.

A ticket into the cloisters of Santa Croce is worth it, even if the museum is not the highlight. The backbone of the collection is in the former refectory with Taddeo Gaddi's *Last Supper*, the impact of which is reduced due to its bad condition and the imposing, yet poetic *Albero della Vita* (tree of life) above. In equally bad condition is Cimabué's *Crucifixion* which used to hang in the basilica until the flood of 1966. On the opposite wall is a pious *St Louis of Toulouse* cast in bronze by Donatello. There's also a small permanent exhibition of the woodcust and engravings of Pietro Parigi, whose reawakening of Tuscan realism in religious illustrations earned him his fame.

built the palazzo in 1881 on the foundations of a ruined thirteenth-century church, using ceilings, doors and fireplaces salvaged from other palaces. The collection is partly uncatalogued – Bardini, no fan of writing, saw no need to record details. The eccentric pieces on display include muskets, daggers, musical instruments and Persian and Anatolian carpets. There's also some pleasing Etruscan sculpture and two unusual Donatello *Madonnas* (Room 14).

Museo di Casa Siviero

Lungarno Serristori 1-3 (055 234 5219/guided tours 055 293 007). **Open** 9.30am-12.30pm Mon; 3.30-6.30pm Sat. **Admission** free.

This museum was previously the house of Rodolfo Silviero – the James Bond of art, so called for his relentless efforts to prevent the Nazis plundering Italian masters during the war; those that were he subsequently retrieved. The collection pales in comparison to others in the city, but does present an honest image of a Florentine gentleman's house in the middle of the twentieth century. The paintings and antiques on display reflect his appreciation of various artistic styles. Visits are supervised by informed and friendly guides.

Museo Horne

Via dei Benci 6 (055 244 661). **Open** 9am-1pm Mon-Sat. **Admission** L8,000. **No credit cards**.

The fifteenth-century Palazzo Corsi-Alberti was bought by English architect and art historian Herbert Percy Horne in the late nineteenth century. When he died he left the palazzo and his vast magpie-ish collection to the state, and in 1922 it opened as a museum. Objects on the ground floor range from ceramics and Florentine coins to a coffee grinder and a pair of spectacles.

Upstairs is a damaged wooden panel from a triptych attributed to Masaccio, relating the story of San Giuliano, a medieval Oedipus who came home early one day to find his mother in bed with a man. He killed the both of them before bothering to find out that the man was his father. In repentance, Giuliano cut off his right arm and became a devout Christian. Also seen here is an exorcism by the Maestro di San Severino and, pride of the Horne collection, a gold-backed *Santo Stefano* by Giotto. Other famous works include a statue of a limbless athlete by Giambologna, a painted wedding chest by Filippino Lippi and a diptych by Simone Martini.

Museo Stibbert

Via Stibbert 26 (055 486 049). **Open** 10am-2pm Mon-Wed, Fri; 10am-6pm Sat, Sun. **Admission** L8,000 (M). **No credit cards.**

The collection of Fredrick Stibbert (1838-1906), a brother-in-arms with Garibaldi in the name of Italian unification. He was born of an English father and Italian mother, who left him her fourteenth-century house. Considering it too small, he bought the neighbouring mansion and had the two joined together to house his collection. The linking room between the palazzi (Sala della Cavalcata) houses a troop of horses with fully clad knights and footmen – Stibbert had a penchant for war memorabilia and weaponry. The 64 rooms are crammed with around 50,000 items ranging from a hand-painted harpsichord to

State of the art

Florentine art is inescapably linked with the Renaissance – but has this unique heritage rubbed off on its artists of today? 'The last 30 years of Tuscan art have been the most plentiful of the twentieth century,' insists Tommaso Paloscia, former art critic for *La Nazione*. During this time talents such as Daniela de Lorenzo, Maurizio Nannucci and Carlo Guaita have established themselves on the international scene; emerging names include Mauro Falzoni, Gianni Galli and Lorenzo Pizzanelli.

But where can you see this art in Florence? Not one of the city's museums is dedicated to contemporary art. The closest the city gets is the modern art on show in the **Collezione della Ragione**, the **Museo Marino Marini** and the **Museo dell'Arte Moderna**, though in the latter, there is no work after 1945.

'If a Michelangelo were born here today he'd have to go somewhere else in the world,' says Professor Antonio Paolucci, director of Musei Statali Fiorentini (Florence state museums).

The importance of the tourist industry to the local economy dictates – visitors come for the Renaissance art. The city spends an estimated L20,000,000,000 a year on restoration work.

But, as Massimo Pieratelli, one of Tuscany's most important contemporary art patrons, points out: 'Florence especially, cannot survive only on the greatness of its illustrious past'.

The Comune di Firenze does periodically organise exhibitions and work is being carried out to convert a former factory in Refredi on the city outskirts into a centre for contemporary art. No date has been given for its opening, but given that the first proposals to create the museum were forwarded in 1966, don't hold your breath.

In the meantime, get a feel for Florence's contemporary art by touring bars such as **Zoe**, **Sant'Ambrogio** and **Dolce Vita**. Alternatively, try some of the private galleries listed. But for the most impressive and exhaustive collection, take a trip out of town to the excellent Centro per L'Arte Contemporanea, Luigi Pecci, on the outskirts of Prato (*see chapter* **Around Florence**).

La Corte Arte Contemporanea *Via de'Coverelli 27r (055 284 435).* **Open** 4-7pm Tue-Sat. **No credit cards.**
The 20 or so exhibitions per year here showcase a diverse range of artists. The smallness of the gallery intensifies the often confrontational images.

Galleria d'Arte Spagna *Via Ghibellina 97r (055 292 969).* **Open** 10am-12.30pm, 4-7.30pm Tue-Sat; 4-7.30pm Sun. **Credit** V.
A small gallery specialising in post-World War II Italian artists. There are four exhibitions a year between autumn and the end of spring.

Galleria Biagiotti Arte Contemporanea *Via delle Belle Donne 39r (055 214 757).* **Open** 3-7pm Mon-Sat. **Credit** AmEx, DC, MC, V.
New to the scene and probably your best bet for contemporary Italian art in Florence. Director Carole Biagiotti scouts out the new talent. There's a permanent collection and about six exhibitions a year in this 1980s New Yorkesque sala.

Ken's Art Gallery *Via Lambertesca 17r (055 239 6587/wmcbell@ats.it).* **Open** 10am-1pm, 3-8pm Mon-Sat. **Credit** AmEx, DC, JCB, MC, V.
Walter Bellini runs an exciting gallery with several artists in residence and an exhibition programme with a rapid turnover. The works are fiercely contemporary and all by Florentine residents.

Galleria Pananti *Piazza Santa Croce 8 (055 244 931/fax 055 245 849).* **Open** 10am-7pm daily. **Credit** AmEx, DC, JCB, MC, V.
Exhibits contemporary Italian artists, and holds modern art shows and retrospectives.

Galleria Masini *Piazza Goldoni 6r (055 294 000).* **Open** 9am-1pm, 3-7pm Tue-Sat. **Credit** AmEx, DC, JCB, MC, V.
Boasts the largest collection of original modern paintings in Florence. Paintings, yes. Modern and original? Quaint and picturesque would be fairer.

Galleria Santo Ficara *Via Ghibellina 164r (055 234 0239).* **Open** 9.30am-12.30pm, 3.30-7.30pm Mon-Sat. **Credit** AmEx, DC, JCB, MC, V.
This large gallery has five exhibitions annually.

Varart *Via dell'Oriuolo 47-49r (055 213 827).* **Open** 10am-12.30pm, 4-7.30pm, Tue-Sat. **No credit cards.**
A full-on commercial gallery with a spacious layout.

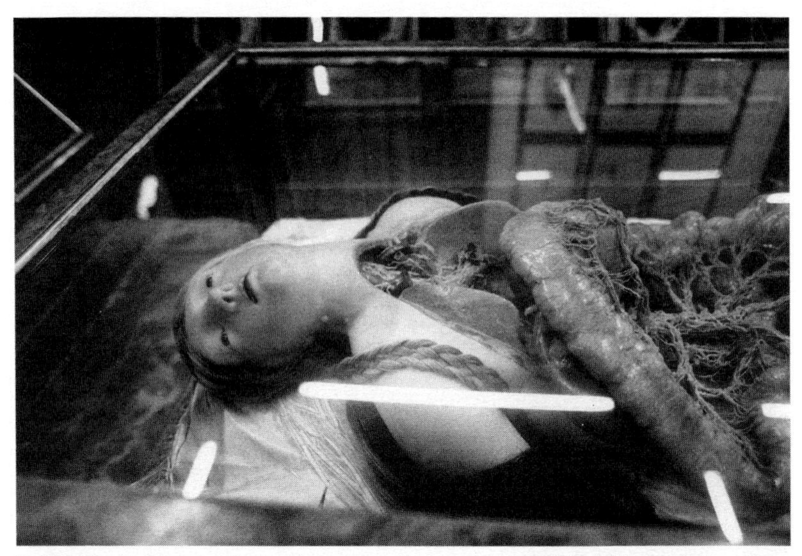

Inside out – **La Specola***, Florence's zoology museum, is not for the faint-hearted.* *See p74.*

chalices and crucifixes. Look out for the painted leather covering the stairwell and the Sienese Palio banners on the ceiling in the Sala delle Bandiere.

Florence life

Museo dl Bigallo

Piazza San Giovanni 1 (055 230 2885). **Open** 8.15am-1.30pm Mon-Sat. **Admission** L5,000. **No credit cards**.

The tiniest museum in the city is situated in a beautiful Gothic loggia built for the Misericordia, a charitable organisation which cared for unwanted children and plague victims. The loggia was later renovated for another fraternity, the Bigallo, and the Misericordia moved across the road, where another small museum is housed. The main room has frescoes depicting the work of the two fraternities, though the two scenes on the left wall as you enter were badly damaged while being transferred from the façade in the eighteenth century. The *Madonna della Misericordia,* an anonymous work of 1342, shows the Virgin suspended above the earliest known depiction of Florence, with the Baptistery, the original façade to the domeless Duomo and an incomplete campanile.

Museo Firenze com'era

Via dell'Oriuolo 24 (055 261 6545). **Open** 9am-2pm Mon-Wed, Fri, Sat; 8am-1pm Sun. **Admission** L5,000 (M). **No credit cards**.

This charmingly named museum of 'Florence as it was' houses a collection of maps, paintings and archeological discoveries that trace the city's development. There's: a room devoted to Giuseppe Poggi's plans from the 1860s to modernise Florence by creating Parisian-style boulevards; the famous lunettes of the Medici villas painted in 1599 by the Flemish artist Giusto Utens; and a room charting the history of the region from 200 million years ago to Roman times.

Museo dello Spedale degli Innocenti

Piazza Santissimi Annunziata (055 249 1708). **Open** 8.30am-2pm Mon, Tue, Thur-Sun. **Admission** L5,000. **No credit cards**.

This museum is located in the former recreation room of Brunelleschi's foundlings hospital. The collection received a substantial blow in 1853 when several important works were auctioned off (for a relative pittance) in order to raise money for the hospital. What remains constitutes a harmonious collection, with an unsurprising concentration of Madonna and Child pieces, including a Botticelli, and a sparkling version by Luca della Robbia worthy of Jeff Koons. The highlight is Ghirlandaio's beautifully balanced *Adoration of the Magi*, which was commissioned for the high altar of the hospital's church.

Museo del Rinascimento

Piazza Santa Croce 12 (055 263 8732). **Open** 10am-7pm daily. **Admission** L12,000. **Credit** AmEx, DC, JCB, MC, V.

This waxworks museum, opened in the spring of 1999, offers an illustrated stroll through the Renaissance; you can peek over the shoulder of Masaccio as he paints the disproportioned bodies of Adam and Eve in the *Expulsion from Paradise,* or look up at Michelangelo's backside as he paints the

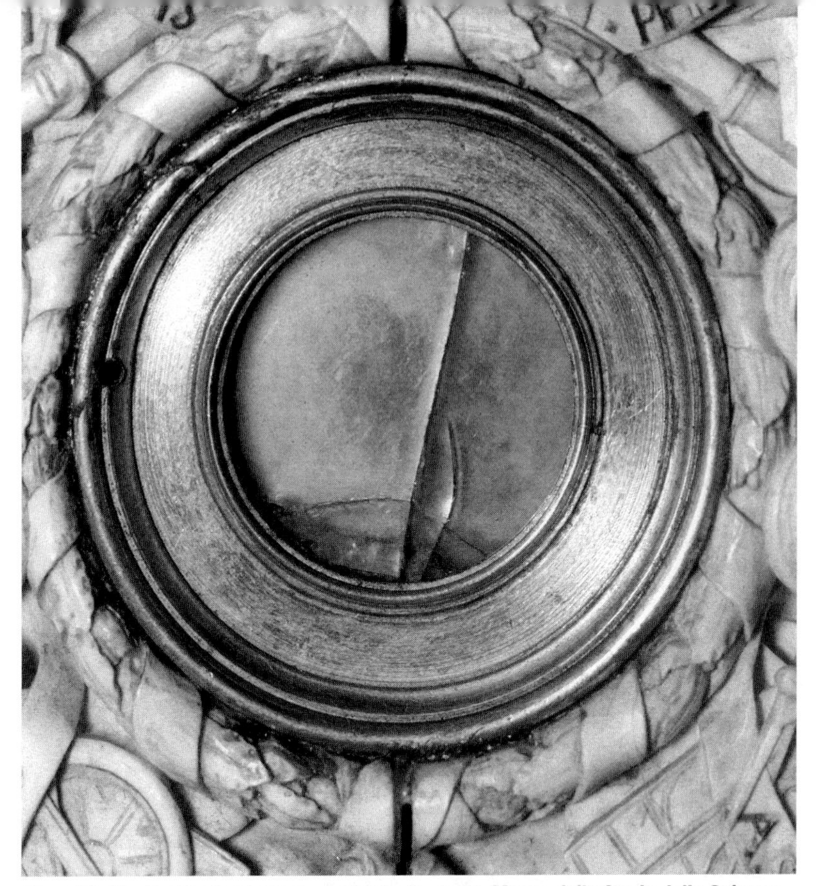

One of Galileo's objective lenses – he broke it – in the **Museo della Storia della Scienza**.

Sistine Chapel. Cringeworthy as the experience is, the museum does give interesting contextual information about the masters. Leonardo gets a raw deal, as does Botticelli, while Savonarola looks like the grim reaper.

Science & natural history

Museo di Geologia e Paleontologia

Via la Pira 4 (055 275 7536). **Open** 2-6pm Mon; 9am-1pm Tue-Sat; 9am-12.30pm 2nd Sun of the month. **Admission** L5,000; L8,000 double ticket incl Museo di Minerologia e Lithologia. **No credit cards**.

This old-fashioned museum has one of the best fossil collections in Italy – and it looks like an unusually ordered hoard belonging to an eccentric uncle. Towering above every visitor are the remains of an elephant-like creature found in the Valdarno (Room 4).

Museo di Mineralogia e Lithologia

Via la Pira 4 (055 275 7537). **Open** 9am-1pm Mon-Fri; Sat by appointment only; 9am-12.30pm 2nd Sun of the month. **Admission** free Mon-Sat; L5,000 Sun; L8,000 double ticket incl Museo di Geologia e Paleontologia. **No credit cards**.

The simple arrangement and clear explanations of the exhibits in this museum make its collection accessible to the least scientifically minded. It is packed full of strange and lovely gems, including a display of 12 huge Brazilian quartzes opposite the entrance. Fantastic agates, chalcedony, tormaline, opals and iridescent limonite line the cabinets. There are also glass models of famous stones such as the Koh-i-noor and items from the Granducale collection of Cosimo III.

La Specola

Via Romana 17 (055 228 8251). **Open** 9am-1pm Mon, Tue, Thur-Sun. **Admission** L6,000. **No credit cards**.

Known as La Specola because of the telescope on the roof, this is actually Florence's zoology museum. The first 23 rooms are crammed with stuffed and pickled animals, including a hippopotamus given to Grand Duke Pietro Leopoldo, that used to be kept in the Boboli Gardens. Room 9 has a charmless collection of hunting trophies donated by the Count of Turin, including an elephant-skin sofa. From Room 24 onwards, the exhibits become more grotesque. In a laboratory fit for Frankenstein, wax corpses lie on satin beds. Each corpse is a little more dissected than the last, walls are covered with dismembered body parts: limbs, organs and body slices – all perfectly realistic. They were crafted between 1771 and the late 1800s by artist Clemente Susini and physiologist Felice Fontana to be used as teaching aids. Also look out for the gory tableaux devoted to Florence during the plague, made by the Sicilian wax sculptor Giulio Gaetano Zumbo. Not for sensitive souls.

Museo della Storia della Scienza

Piazza dei Giudici 1 (055 239 8876). **Open** 9.30am-1pm Tue, Thur, Sat; 9.30am-1pm, 2-5pm, Mon, Wed, Fri. **Admission** L10,000. **No credit cards.**

This is one of the best museums in Florence, offering a view of the Renaissance and beyond, that, for once, is not limited to stone and pigment. Two of the most fascinating rooms are those devoted to Galileo and include a reliquary of his right-hand middle finger (the rest of his body is in Santa Croce) and one of his telescopes, bound in leather. *See also p29* **The appliance of science**.

In the following rooms are a collection of prisms and optical games. Art continues to mingle with science in Room 7, which is devoted to armillary spheres and dominated by a gold-leaf-decorated model commissioned by Federico II in 1593. Most of them have the earth emphatically placed at the centre of the universe, surrounded by seven spheres of the planets.

The second floor comprises an eclectic mix of machines, mechanisms and models, including a nineteenth-century clock (a *pianola*) which writes a sentence with a mechanical hand, and a selection of electromagnetic and electrostatic instruments (Room 14). More pleasing are the pneumatic pumps decorated with inlaid wood by Nollet (famous for his globe machine) and the carefully constructed illustration of the mechanical paradox of two spheres ascending a plane. Less pleasing is the display of surgical implements used for amputation and the models of foetuses adorning the walls.

Anthropology & archaeology

Museo Antropologia e Etnologia

Proconsolo 12 (055 239 6449). **Open** 10am-1pm Mon, Wed-Sun. **Admission** L6,000. **No credit cards.**

A mixed bag of goodies from all over the world: a collection of Peruvian mummies; an Ostyak harp in the shape of a swan from Lapland (Room 13); an engraved trumpet made from an elephant tusk from the former Belgian Congo (Room 5); Ecuadorian shrunken heads complete with a specially designed club (a tupinamba) to beat the skull; and a Marini-meets-Picasso equestrian monument in Room 7.

Museo Archeologico

Via della Colonna 38 (055 23575). **Open** 9am-1.50pm Tue-Sat; 1st, 3rd & 5th Mon of month; 2nd & 4th Sun of month. **Admission** L8,000. **No credit cards.**

With its Etruscan, Egyptian and Greek collections, this is the place to come for a break from the Renaissance. The Etruscan art on show includes jewellery, a large collection of funerary sculpture and a selection of bronzes. The Egyptian rooms exude a pyramidal mysticism with their sedate cube-statues from the Middle Kingdom and their precisely decorated tombs, complete with mummified bodies. On the second floor is an extensive collection of Greek ceramics, which painstakingly follows their artistic development.

Museo Fiorentino di Preistoria

Via Sant'Egidio 21 (055 295 151). **Open** 9.30am-12.30pm; guided tours by appointment. **Admission** L6,000. **No credit cards.**

This museum traces man's development from the Paleolithic to the Bronze Age. The first floor follows prehistoric man's physical changes and also examines his artistic legacy in Italy, the first discoveries found as late as 1905. Unfortunately the evidence is for the greatest part in caves, so the museum has to make do with photos and illustrations. The second floor covers the rest of the world and houses a collection of stone implements found by Frenchman Boucher de Perthes who ascertained that rocks previously believed to have been shaped by weathering and glacial movement were actually the work of prehistoric man.

Artists & writers

Casa Buonarroti

Via Ghibellina 70 (055 241 752/fax 055 241 698). **Open** 9.30am-1.30pm Mon, Wed-Sun. **Admission** L12,000. **No credit cards.**

Michelangelo never actually lived in this house, although he did own it, and this collection of Michelangelo memorabilia, put together by his great-nephew Filippo, is a little contrived. Among the attributions and reproductions are interesting scenes from the painter's life painted on the walls of La Galleria and two original works, a bas-relief *Madonna della Scala*, breast-feeding at the foot of a flight of stairs, and an unfinished *Battaglia dei Centauri*.

Museo Casa di Dante

Via Santa Margherita 1 (055 219 416). **Open** *summer* 10am-6pm Mon, Wed-Sat; 10am-2pm Sun. *winter* 10am-4pm Mon, Wed-Sat; 10am-2pm Sun. **Admission** L5,000. **No credit cards.**

Barely worth the entrance fee. The museum, located where Dante is thought to have lived, is full of facsimiles of archive material. 'Treasures' include: a photocopy of a document in which the poet's great, great grandfather promised to cut down a fig tree; a photograph of a field where Dante may have fought at the battle of Campaldino in 1289; and copies of the *Divine Comedy* in German and Greek.

If the shoe fits – **Museo Ferragamo***.*

Modern arts & ancient crafts

Museo Ferragamo

Via Tournabuoni 2 (055 336 0456). **Open** 9am-1pm, 2-6pm Mon-Fri, by appointment only. **Admission** prices vary. **No credit cards.**

The small museum above Ferragamo's shop in Palazzo Spini Ferroni displays a fraction of the company's 10,000 archive shoes, and affords an opportunity to drool over some of the most beautiful shoes in the world. Ferragamo, born in a small village outside Naples in 1898, opened his first shop at the age of 14, emigrated to the US at 16, and was soon designing shoes for the movies. Commissions for anything from Roman sandals to shoes for Cecil B DeMille's *Cleopatra*, gave him the opportunity to experiment. In 1927 Ferragamo moved to Florence, to put together a factory that could produce handmade shoes *en masse*. Momentarily set back by bankruptcy in 1933, he recovered by 1938 to buy the Palazzo Spini Ferroni. Ferragamo continued to make fantastic footwear for the rich and famous until his death in 1960.

Museo Marino Marini

Piazza San Pancrazio (055 219 432). **Open** *summer* 10am-5pm Mon, Wed, Fri, Sat; 10am-11pm Thur; *winter* 10am-5pm Mon, Wed-Sat; 10am-1pm Sun. **Admission** L8,000 (M). **No credit cards.**

This Albertian church was redesigned to accommodate the work of sculptor Marino Marini (1901-80). As a result, the works' equine rigidity and monumentality are reflected in the building's design and spaciousness. Many of the first floor sculptures are a variation on the theme of horse and rider, championed by the central exhibit *Composizione Equestre* which stands 6m high. The second floor has a series of other sculptural subjects including the hypnotic *Nuotatore,* along with some fabulous paintings of dancers and jugglers.

Opificio delle Pietre Dure

Via degli Alfani 78 (055 265 111/055 287 123). **Open** 9am-2pm Mon-Sat. **Admission** L4,000. **No credit cards.**

Founded in 1588 by Grand Duke Ferdinando I, the name literally means the workshop of hard stones. *Pietra dura* is the craft of inlaying gems or semi-precious stones in intricate mosaics. Nowadays most work undertaken is restoration, but some fine pieces are exhibited in this small museum.

Sculture Olandesi del XX Secolo

Istituto Universitario Olandese di Storia dell'arte, Via Torricelli Evangelista 5 (055 221 612). **Open** 10am-1pm; 3-6pm Mon.-Fri. **Closed** holidays; 15 Dec-15 Jan & 1 Aug-10 Sept. **Admission** free. **No credit cards.**

Set on a hill on the outskirts of Florence, the Dutch institute's garden of twentieth-century sculpture seems in perfect harmony with its surroundings – most notably Leo Vroegindewey's interpretation of land art in *Untitled* and Yvonne Kracht's post-Mondrian sculpture *Acute Angles*. A breath of fresh air, culturally and literally.

VINS EN EXPOSITION PEUVENT ETRE ACHETES DANS LE RESTAURANT
TERRE BRUNE
TIGNANELLO
Vigorello
Ca del Pazzo

WEINE IN DER AUSSTELLUNG WERDEN IM RESTAURANT VERKAUFT
BARBI
BRUNELLO

IE WINES ON DISPLAY ARE AVAILABLE FOR SALE IN THE RESTAURANT
CASTELLO DI VOLPAIA
MILLENNIO

Consumer

Accommodation

Florence hotels are not short of views, if you're not short of cash.

Surpassed only by Venice, Florence is one of the most expensive cities in Italy when it comes to staying overnight. On the positive side, however, many of its hotels, even the cheaper ones, are wonderfully atmospheric and there is a merciful lack of international chains. Prices have shot up since the last edition of this guide, although some hotels have been honest enough to keep rates contained. Enormous disparity exists in price and standards (especially in budget categories), even among hotels of the same star rating, so it pays to shop around. Once you have picked a hotel, it is your right to ask to see the room before accepting it and, if for some reason you don't like what you are shown, ask to see another. Don't be intimidated by grumpy Florentine hoteliers. If, after your stay, you feel you have been taken for a ride, you are entitled to complain to the tourist board. Ask at the local tourist office about the best way to go about this.

Something to look for if you are visiting during the summer is a hotel terrace or garden; it can make a huge difference after a long day's sightseeing to be able to relax al fresco with a Campari.

As in any tourist-orientated city, there are plenty of hotels in each price category that are anonymous, unfriendly or just plain nasty. The hotels listed here have been chosen either for the good value they offer (not that common in Florence) or for some characteristic that elevates them above the norm. Italian hotels are classified on a star-rating system (one to five), which may give you some idea of what to expect, but, since many hotels use a lower rating than they deserve (to incur lower taxes), it is only a rough guideline and no indication of the atmosphere.

Few establishments have even heard of no-smoking areas, so people seeking nicotine-free rooms are unlikely to get much joy. Facilities for the disabled are improving a little, partly due to a law which requires hotels to have a certain number of adapted rooms. This law does not extend to all facilities, however, resulting in the ridiculous situation where many new rooms for the disabled are only accessible by a lift too narrow to fit a wheelchair. Staff are willing to help, but the nature of many buildings in Florence is such that most places have so many steep stairs there's not much they can do. We have indicated the few places that do have special facilities.

Hotels are in either the tourist-packed *centro storico*, the quieter, often cheaper, but still convenient residential outskirts, or away from the crowds in the relative cool and calm of nearby hills. As with many European cities, the area around the railway station can be unsavoury at night, but is packed with cheap *pensioni* (particularly in Via Faenza). Few central hotels have their own parking and car parks are pricey.

Many hotels reduce prices by as much as 50 per cent off-season. In Florence, this means roughly January to March, a couple of weeks before Easter, late July and August, and a few weeks in November. Even outside these times, you may find that a hotel will give you a better price if it has plenty of room; it's worth haggling.

Our listings are in the following categories: The sky's the limit (over L500,000); Expensive (L300,000-L500,000); Moderate (L200,000-L300,000); Budget (L100,000-L200,000); Very cheap (under L100,000); Hostels; Camp sites; Long-term accommodation.

The old and rotund **Brunelleschi**. *See p80.*

ADVANCE BOOKINGS

Always book well in advance, whatever time you are visiting, as Florence is busy with visitors for most of the year. The city is trying to come up with more bed space in anticipation of the crowds expected for the millennium, and moves are afoot to create B&Bs, a new type of accommodation for Italy. Just how much extra room this will actually create, however, is still unknown.

If you arrive without a place to stay, go to the **APT** office (*see chapter* **Directory**), the **Ufficio Informazione Turistiche** in Piazza Stazione or at Peretola airport, where they provide hotel lists but not a booking service, or directly to the **ITA** office in the station where they will find and book you a hotel for a fee.

Unless stated, prices (which are subject to change) are for a room with en suite bathroom, and include breakfast. Nearly all hotels and *pensioni* will put at least one extra bed into a double room – you'll have to pay extra, but it's cheaper than an extra single room. The breakfast provided in cheaper hotels is rarely worth eating: the cardboard roll and undrinkable coffee bears no resemblance to the warm, buttery brioche and steaming cappuccino you can find at the stand-up *pasticceria* on the corner. The latter should cost about L3,000.

The sky's the limit

Brunelleschi

Via dei Calzaiuoli, Piazza Santa Elisabetta (055 290 311/fax 055 219 653). **Rates** *single* L380,000; *double* L510,000; *triple* L610,000; *suite* L800,000. **Credit** AmEx, DC, JCB, MC, V.

It is hard to believe that the Byzantine tower that now forms part of this centrally located hotel was once a prison, and it is thought to be the oldest standing structure in Florence. Many objects of archaeological interest were unearthed during reconstruction in the 1980s and are displayed in a museum in the basement. The 95 bedrooms are comfortably, if uniformly furnished. Part of the restaurant is in the tower, and two penthouse suites on the fifth floor enjoy 360° views of the city.

Hotel services *Air-conditioning. Babysitting. Bar. Car park (nearby garage, extra cost). Conference facilities (up to 140). Currency exchange. Fax. Laundry. Lifts. Multilingual staff. Non-smoking rooms. Restaurant.* **Room services** *Hair dryer. Jacuzzi (penthouse suites). Minibar. Radio. Room service (24 hours). Telephone. TV (satellite).*

Excelsior

Piazza Ognissanti 3 (055 264 201/fax 055 217 400). Bus B. **Rates** *single* L566,000-L632,000; *double* L860,000-L950,000; *suite* L1,140,000-L3,700,000; *supplement for view of Arno* L121,000; *breakfast* L36,000. **Credit** AmEx, DC, JCB, MC, V.

More old world in style than the Grand (*see below*), the hotel offers luxury without being stuffy; the green-liveried staff are pleasant and helpful. The restored public rooms have floors of polished marble, neo-classical columns, painted wood ceilings and stained glass. The 163 bedrooms are sumptuously adorned. Those on the fifth floor have been recently renovated and some boast terraces with views over the river to the rooftops of Oltrarno.

Hotel services *Air-conditioning. Babysitting. Bar. Car park (nearby garage, extra cost). Conference facilities (up to 180). Currency exchange. Fax. Laundry. Lifts. Multilingual staff. Non-smoking rooms. Restaurant. Tours arranged.* **Room services** *Hair dryer. Minibar. Radio. Room service (24 hrs). Safe. Telephone. TV (satellite).*

Grand Hotel

Piazza Ognissanti 1 (055 288 781/fax 055 217 400). **Rates** *single* L566,000-L632,000; *double* L860,000-L950,000; *suite* L1,140,000-L3,000,000; *supplement for view of Arno* L120,000; *breakfast* L29,000. **Credit** AmEx, DC, JCB, MC, V.

The two sister hotels facing each other across Piazza Ognissanti (*see* **Excelsior** *above*) are equal in grandeur, but different in character. The smaller Grand was renovated five years ago and glories in its unashamed luxury. The vast hall, with its fifteenth-century stained-glass ceiling, marble floor, pietra serena columns, brocades, statues and palms, comprises restaurant, bar, salon and piano bar. Many of the 107 bedrooms look over the Arno and are decorated in early Florentine style with frescoes.

Hotel services *Air-conditioning. Babysitting. Bar. Car park (nearby garage, extra cost). Conference facilities (up to 200). Currency exchange. Fax. Laundry. Lifts. Multilingual staff. Non-smoking rooms. Restaurant. Safe. Tours arranged.* **Room services** *Hair dryer. Minibar. Radio. Room service (24 hours). Telephone. TV (satellite).*

Grand Hotel Villa Cora

Viale N Machiavelli 18 (055 229 8451/fax 055 229 086). Bus 13. **Rates** *single* L460,000; *double* L750,000-L860,000; *suite* L1,100,000-L1,900,000. **Credit** AmEx, DC, JCB, MC, V.

Although a luxury hotel, the relatively small size (49 rooms) and friendly staff of Villa Cora enable it to maintain the feel of a grand country house. The nineteenth-century villa is set in spacious gardens just above Porta Romana; a courtesy limo service provides transport into town. Downstairs, the public rooms are lavish with ornate plasterwork, lashings of gold, frescoes, Venetian chandeliers, huge mirrors, intricate woodwork and rich fabrics. The bedrooms vary in style from the clean and classical to formal and grand.

Hotel services *Air-conditioning. Bar. Car park. Conference facilities (up to 120). Currency exchange. Fax. Garden. Laundry. Lifts. Multilingual staff. Non-smoking rooms. Pool. Restaurant.* **Room services** *Hair dryer. Minibar. Radio. Room service (24 hours). Telephone. TV (satellite). Video (on request).*

Helvetia & Bristol

Via dei Pescioni 2 (055 287 814/fax 055 288 353). **Rates** *single* L380,000; *double* L440,000-L580,000;

The luxurious **Excelsior** in Piazza Ognissanti.

suite L730,000-L950.000; *breakfast* L34,000. **Credit** AmEx, DC, MC, V.
With such illustrious names as Stravinsky, Gabriele d'Annunzio, Luigi Pirandello and Bertrand Russell among past guests, the Helvetia & Bristol preserves a long, distinguished history. It is arguably central Florence's finest and, with just over 50 rooms, manages to maintain a sense of intimacy. While undeniably exclusive, it avoids any hint of stuffiness. The salon has a welcoming fireplace and velvet sofas and armchairs; breakfast and lunch are served in the delightful Winter Garden, once a meeting place for 1920s intelligentsia. Bedrooms are sumptuous (sometimes to excess) with swathes of ornate fabrics everywhere.
Hotel services *Air-conditioning. Bar. Car park (nearby garage, extra cost). Currency exchange. Fax. Laundry. Lift. Multilingual staff. Non-smoking rooms. Restaurant.* **Room services** *Hair dryer. Jacuzzi (some). Minibar. Radio. Room service (24 hrs). Safe. Telephone. TV (satellite). Video.*

Lungarno

Borgo San Jacopo 14 (055 264 211/fax 055 268 437). **Rates** *single* L390,000; *double* L560,000-L590,000; *suite* L760,000-L1,000,000. **Credit** AmEx, DC, JCB, MC, V.
The most coveted rooms in this recently refurbished hotel have terraces overlooking the Arno. The 1960s building incorporates a medieval tower and is in the smart part of the Oltrarno. The sitting room and bar area has huge picture windows, which take full advantage of the waterside setting, as does the elegant ground-floor restaurant, serving principally fish dishes. Bedrooms are not particularly spacious, but comfortable and tasteful in blues and cream; those in the medieval tower have original stone walls.
Hotel services *Bar. Babysitting. Currency exchange. Car park (nearby garage, extra charge). Fax. Laundry. Lifts. Multilingual staff. Restaurant.* **Room services** *Hair dryer. Minibar. Radio. Room service. Safe. Telephone. TV (satellite).*

Expensive (L300,000-L500,000)

Hermitage

Vicolo Marzio 1 (Piazza del Pesce) (055 287 216/fax 055 212 208). **Rates** *double* L330,000-L350,000; *triple* L410,000; *quad* L470,000. **Credit** MC, V.
As one of the most popular small hotels in Florence, rooms at this delightful hotel are always in demand, so book early. The superb location (practically on the Ponte Vecchio), warm welcome and superior facilities make it a winner. In summer, breakfast in the plant-filled roof garden is a fabulous start to the day. The reception area and public rooms are on the top floors, while the comfortable and intimate bedrooms occupy the lower three floors. Some bedrooms enjoy a view of the river but, in spite of double-glazing, these are not the most peaceful. Prices are a little above average for this category, but worth the outlay.
Hotel services *Babysitting. Bar. Currency exchange. Fax. Laundry. Lift. Multilingual staff. Non-smoking rooms. Roof garden.* **Room services** *Hair dryer. Jacuzzi (in eight rooms). Room service. Telephone. TV.*

J and J

Via di Mezzo 20 (055 234 5005/fax 055 240 282). Bus A to Piazza dei Ciompi. **Rates** *double* L400,000-L450,000; *suite* L530,000-L630,000. **Credit** AmEx, DC, MC, V.
The simple façade of this former convent, in a quiet residential street in the old city near Sant'Ambrogio, gives little clue to the the luxury accommodation within. Throughout the designer-chic interior, old and new are effectively combined with many original architectural features visible in the public rooms and in the cool, arched cloister, where breakfast is served in the summer. No two bedrooms are alike – some are enormous, with split levels and seating areas. Supremely comfortable and discreet for those who appreciate individual attention.
Hotel services *Air-conditioning. Babysitting. Bar. Car park (nearby, extra cost). Fax. Laundry. Multilingual staff. Safe.* **Room services** *Hair dryer. Minibar. Room service. Telephone. TV (satellite).*

Kraft

Via Solferino 2 (055 284 273/fax 055 239 8267). Bus B, D. **Rates** *single* L350,000; *double* L450,000-L520,000; *triple* L580,000. **Credit** AmEx, DC, JCB, MC, V.
This 80-room hotel is situated west of the city centre, near the Arno and convenient for Santa Maria

Yes, the rooms have great views at the popular **Hermitage**. *See p81.*

Novella station. It is an excellent choice if you are here for the opera as the Teatro Comunale is just across the road; indeed, conductors and singers frequently number among the guests. The bedrooms are traditionally furnished in bright, warm colours; the five junior suites enjoy panoramic views. One unusual feature, and a major bonus in the summer, is the roof-top pool where you can escape from the city heat.
Hotel services *Air-conditioning. Babysitting. Bar. Conference facilities. Currency exchange. Fax. Laundry. Lift. Multilingual staff. Non-smoking rooms. Pool. Restaurant. Roof garden. Safe.* **Room services** *Hair dryer. Minibar. Room service. Telephone. TV (satellite). Safe (in some rooms).*

Loggiato dei Serviti

Piazza SS Annunziata 3 (055 289 592/fax 055 289 595). Bus 6, 31, 32. **Rates** *single* L220,000; *double* L325,000; *suite* L380,000-L680,000. **Credit** AmEx, DC, JCB, M, V.
This delightful, 29-room hotel occupies a wonderful position in one of Florence's most beautiful piazzas, now, thankfully, enjoying traffic-free status. The front rooms look over the square on to the famous Della Robbia *tondos* on the façade of Brunelleschi's foundling hospital. The hotel building was a convent in the sixteenth century, and the interior décor tastefully combines original architectural features and antique furniture with all the comforts of an upmarket hotel. Bedrooms vary in size and style; the four suites are ideal for families. Breakfast is served in a bright, elegant room with vaulted ceilings, and there is an additional cosy bar area.
Hotel services *Air-conditioning. Babysitting. Bar. Car park (nearby garage, extra cost). Fax. Laundry. Lift. Multilingual staff.* **Room services** *Hair dryer. Minibar. Radio. Room service (24 hrs). Safe. Telephone. TV (satellite).*

Monna Lisa

Borgo Pinti 27 (055 247 9751/fax 055 247 9755). Bus A. **Rates** *single* L300,000; *double* L480,000-L520,000. **Credit** AmEx, DC, JCB, MC, V.
Florence is full of grand *palazzi* hiding behind plain façades; the upmarket Monna Lisa, on a narrow street north of Santa Croce, is a prime example. The maze of public rooms, many of which have original waxed terracotta floors and wood ceilings, is crammed with the owners' collection of paintings, sculptures and furniture. It's not the friendliest hotel in Florence, but has one great asset: the delightful courtyard garden. The 30 bedrooms range from huge and ornate to cramped and ordinary; the best look on to the garden; some have balconies.
Hotel services *Air-conditioning. Babysitting. Bar. Car park (extra charge). Laundry. Lift (in annexe). Multilingual staff. Non-smoking rooms. Safe.* **Room services** *Hair dryer. Jacuzzi (in 6 rooms). Minibar. Room service. Telephone. TV (satellite).*

Montebello Splendid

Via Montebello 60 (055 239 8051). Bus B. **Rates** *single* L335,000; *double* L485,000; *triple* L500,000; *suite* L600,000. **Credit** AmEx, DC, JCB, MC, V.
A solid, old-fashioned hotel in a residential street ten minutes' walk from the station. The entrance hall is pale grey marble and there is a pleasant bar with a conservatory restaurant. Bedrooms are traditionally furnished with lots of dark mahogany; those on the top floor, with sloping ceilings and floral wallpapers, are more intimate. Some rooms have generous terraces looking over the garden.
Hotel services *Air-conditioning. Babysitting. Bar. Car park. Conference facilities (up to 100). Currency exchange. Fax. Garden. Laundry. Lift. Multilingual staff. Restaurant.* **Room services** *Hair dryer. Jacuzzi (some). Mini bar. Radio. Room service. Safe. TV (satellite).*

Porta Faenza

Via Faenza 77 (055 217 975/fax 055 210 101). **Rates** *single* L300,000; *double* L340,000; *triple* L450,000; *suite* L340,000. **Credit** AmEx, DC, MC, V.
Rising from the ashes (not literally) of Tony's Inn (a former pitstop for budget travellers), Porta Faenza opened its three-star doors in 1997. Photographer Antonio Lelli ran Tony's with great charm and the warm welcome still remains. The eighteenth-century building has been gutted and revamped and the result is a comfortable hotel with good facilities for business travellers. The 25 spacious rooms are soundproof and comfortable with excellent bathrooms.
Hotel services *Air-conditioning. Babysitting. Bar. Car park (extra cost). Currency exchange. Fax. Laundry. Lift. Multilingual staff. Non-smoking rooms.* **Room services** *Hair dryer. Room service. Telephone. TV (satellite).*

Torre di Bellosguardo

Via Roti Michelozzi 2 (055 229 8145/fax 055 229 008). Bus to Porto Romana then 15-min walk. **Rates** *single* L290,000-L340,000; *double* L450,000; *suite* L550,000; *breakfast* L35,000. **Credit** AmEx, DC, MC, V.
Just above the traffic hell of Porta Romana roundabout lies Bellosguardo, a collection of villas among olive groves and cypresses, which is an appealing retreat from the summer heat. Amerigo Franchetti has lovingly restored the Renaissance villa that has been in his family for generations, preserving its historic atmosphere while offering supreme comfort. The suite in the top of the tower enjoys a 360° view of the Florentine hills. The staff can be exceptionally rude though.
Hotel services *Babysitting. Bar. Car park. Fax. Garden. Laundry. Lift. Multilingual staff. Pool. Safe.* **Room services** *Air-conditioning (three suites). Room service. Telephone.*

Villa Belvedere

Via Benedetto Castelli 3 (055 222 501/502/fax 055 223 163). Bus 11. **Rates** *single* L240,000; *double* L300,000-L340,000; *suite* L450,000. **Closed** mid Nov-mid Mar. **Credit** AmEx, DC, MC, V.
The Villa Belvedere is set in an attractive garden on a quiet residential street above Porta Romana, and enjoys some wonderful views of Florence. Essentially a family-run hotel housed in a plain 1930s building; the 25 rooms are comfortable, spacious and have parquet floors and wood furnishings.
Hotel services *Air-conditioning. Bar. Car park. Currency exchange. Fax. Garden. Laundry. Multilingual staff. Pool. Restaurant (light meals). Tennis court.* **Room services** *Hair dryer. Radio. Room service. Safe. TV (satellite).*

Villa Villoresi

Via Campi 2, Colonnata di Sesto Fiorentino (055 443 692/fax 055 442 063). Bus 2, 28. **Rates** *single* L160,000; *double* L250,000-L350,000; *deluxe double* L450,000; *half-board* L180,000-L230,000 (L280,000 deluxe) per person. **Credit** AmEx, DC, MC, V.
Contessa Cristina Villoresi's aristocratic family home was once a country retreat. It has now been engulfed by the sprawl of Florentine suburbia, but remains an oasis of calm elegance. It has the air of a grand, if faded, private home. Courses on Italian Renaissance culture are also organised at the villa.
Hotel services *Babysitting. Bar. Car park. Fax. Laundry. Pool. Restaurant.* **Room services** *Room service. Telephone. TV.*

Moderate (L200,000-L300,000)

Annalena

Via Romana 34 (055 222 439/fax 055 222 403). Bus 11, 36, 37 to Boboli Gardens. **Rates** *single* L190,000; *double* L270,000. **Credit** AmEx, DC, MC, V.
If buildings could speak, the fifteenth-century *palazzo* that houses the Annalena would have many stories to tell. Annalena, a young Florentine noblewoman, inherited the house from the Medici, but tragic circumstances (outlined in the hotel brochure) obliged her to donate it to nuns to use as a refuge for young widows. In the 1940s later, during the Mussolini years, refugees from the fascist police were lodged here. Today it is a comfortable, old-fashioned *pensione*. Bedrooms vary in size, but the best have balconies and views over the adjacent horticultural centre.
Hotel services *Bar. Car Park (nearby, extra cost). Currency exchange. Fax. Laundry. Multilingual staff. Safe.* **Room services** *Room service. Telephone. TV*

Aprile

Via della Scala 6 (055 216 237 or 055 289 147/fax 055 280 947). **Rates** *single* L180,000; *double* L260,000. **Credit** AmEx, JCB, MC, V.
The bust of Cosimo I above the entrance of this hotel is a reminder that the building was once a Medici palace. Convenient for the station, the place has an old-fashioned feel, and some of its bedrooms feature frescoes and scraps of fifteenth-century graffiti; others are a little gloomy. There is an attractive bar and breakfast room and a shady courtyard.
Hotel services *Bar. Babysitting. Car park (nearby garage, extra cost). Currency exchange. Fax. Lift. Multilingual staff. Safe.* **Room services** *Air-conditioning (15 rooms). Hair dryer (15 rooms). Minibar. Room service. Telephone. TV.*

Bencistà

Via Benedetto di Maiano 4, Fiesole (tel/fax 055 59163). Bus 7. **Rates** *per person, half-board* L140,000; *without bath* L120,000; *half-board* (lunch or dinner) obligatory; full board L15,000 extra. **No credit cards**.
This former convent has been run as a *pensione* by the Simoni family since 1925. Its setting on a hillside just below Fiesole is unparalleled. There are three salons furnished with antiques; one has a fireplace and shelves stuffed with early editions of English books. The 47 rooms are arranged off a rabbit warren of passages and stone stairways. Those at the front of the building enjoy fabulous city views. Prices are based on half-board: you are expected to take lunch or dinner in the restaurant overlooking Florence.
Hotel services *Bar service. Car park. Exchange.*

Fax. Garden. Laundry. Multilingual staff. Restaurant. Safe. TV. **Room services** *Telephone.*

Classic Hotel

Viale N Machiavelli 25 (055 229 351/fax 055 229 353). Bus 11, 36, 37 to Porta Romana. **Rates** *single* L152,000; *double* L224,000; *suite* L324,000. **Closed** one week mid-Aug. **Credit** AmEx, MC, V.

In a lush garden just outside the old city walls at Porta Romana, is this attractive villa, which has been carefully refurbished with tasteful, pristine results. A conservatory leads to the garden of tall trees. For romantics, an annexe suite with its own terrace is tucked away in a corner of the garden. The friendly, helpful staff and high standard of accommodation make the Classic a bargain.

Hotel services *Bar. Babysitting. Car park. Currency exchange. Fax. Laundry. Garden. Lift. Multilingual staff.* **Room services** *Room service. Safe. Telephone. TV.*

Guelfo Bianco

Via C Cavour 29 (055 288 330/fax 055 295 203). Bus 1, 11, 17. **Rates** *single* L205,000; *double* L285,000-L335,000; *triple* L385,000; *family* L430,000; *suite* L630,000. **Credit** AmEx, MC, V.

An attractive hotel with helpful staff, situated just north of the Duomo. The renovation of the two adjacent fifteenth-century houses has preserved many original features. The 39 rooms are comfortable, the more spacious ones allowing for a lounge area or two extra beds. Those on Via Cavour are soundproofed, but the ones at the back are quieter. One single room has a terrace; be prepared to fight for it. Two courtyards offer respite from city noise.

Hotel services *Air-conditioning. Babysitting. Bar. Bicycle hire. Car park (nearby garage, extra cost). Currency exchange. Fax. Laundry. Lift. Multilingual staff. Non-smoking rooms.* **Room services** *Hair dryer. Minibar. Radio. Room service. Safe. Telephone. TV (satellite).*

Liana

Via Alfieri 18 (055 245 303/fax 055 234 4596). Bus 8, 80 to Piazza Donatello. **Rates** *single* L180,000; *double* L240,000; *triple* L320,000; 20% discount in low season and four nights for the price of three; anyone arriving with a copy of this guide will get a 5% discount. **Credit** AmEx, DC, MC, V.

Once the British Embassy, this nineteenth-century house is worth considering if you want to be within reach of the sights, but not in the centre. The hotel moved from two- to three-star status and its rooms are now more comfortable, especially in the case of the elegant Count's Room. Classical music is played in the first-floor breakfast room, and there are lots of fresh flowers about.

Hotel services *Bar. Car park (extra cost). Currency exchange. Fax. Laundry. Hair dryer. Multilingual staff. Garden. Safe.* **Room services** *Room service. Telephone. TV.*

Mario's

Via Faenza 89 (055 216 801/fax 055 212 039). Bus to Santa Maria Novella station, then 10-min walk. **Rates** *single* L210,000; *double* L260,000; *triple* L330,000; *quad* L400,000. **Credit** AmEx, DC, MC, V.

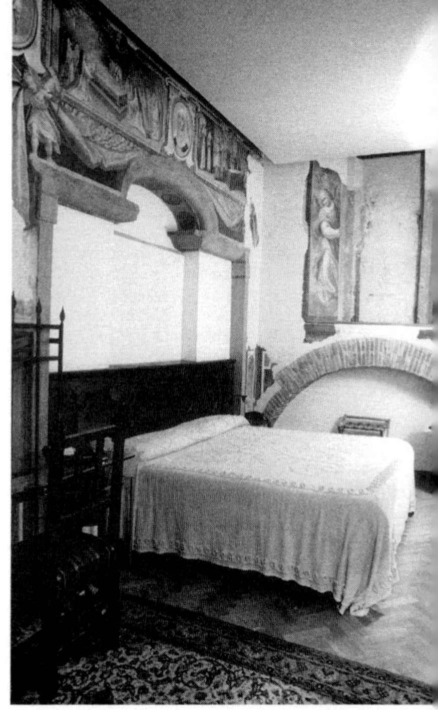

Morandi alla Crocetta – *a former convent.*

A short walk from the train station, Via Faenza is full of hotels, most pretty basic, but Mario's is an exception. On the second floor of an unremarkable building, the welcome is friendly. The traditional, rustic reception and bar set the scene and there are lots of fresh flowers. The 16 bedrooms follow the same lines. Those looking on to the street are double-glazed, but others at the back are quieter.

Hotel services *Bar. Car park (nearby garage, extra cost). Currency exchange. Fax. Laundry. Safe.* **Room services** *Air-conditioning. Hair dryer. Room service. Radio. Telephone. TV (satellite).*

Morandi alla Crocetta

Via Laura 50 (055 234 4747/fax 055 248 0954). Bus 6, 31, 32 to Piazza della SS Annunziata. **Rates** *single* L140,000; *double* L240,000; *triple* L310,000; *breakfast* L18,000. **Credit** AmEx, DC, MC, V.

Book well in advance for a bed in this quiet ten-room hotel housed in a former sixteenth-century convent in the university area. Kathleen Doyle Antuono and her family offer friendly, comfortable accommodation yet keep prices reasonable. You will have to fight for one of the two rooms with a private terrace.

Hotel services *Air-conditioning. Babysitting. Bar. Car park (nearby garage, extra cost). Fax. Laundry. Multilingual staff.* **Room services** *Hair dryer. Minibar. Radio. Room service. Safe. Telephone. TV (satellite).*

La Residenza

Via dei Tornabuoni 8 (055 284 197 or 055 218 684/ fax 055 284 197). **Rates** *single* L180,000; *double* L300,000; *triple* L390,000; *dinner* L45,000. **Credit** AmEx, DC, MC, V.

Step off Via dei Tornabuoni into an old-fashioned wood and glass lift with brass rails that will bear you, creakily, up to the top three floors of the palazzo that houses this hotel. Apart from the location, one of the hotel's pluses is its roof garden and adjacent lounge. It is one of the few Florentine pensioni to offer half board. Double-glazing keeps out the worst of the noise from Via dei Tornabuoni.

Hotel services *Air-conditioning. Bar. Babysitting. Car park (nearby garage, extra cost). Currency exchange. Fax. Laundry. Lift. Multilingual staff. Restaurant. Roof terrace. Safe.* **Room services** *Hair dryer. Room service (24 hours). Telephone. TV.*

Silla

Via dei Renai 5 (055 234 2888/fax 055 234 1437). Bus D. **Rates** *single* L180,000; *double* L250,000; *triple* L300,000. **Credit** AmEx, DC, MC, V.

This old-fashioned pensione is housed in an elegant sixteenth-century palazzo south of the river. Its terrace looks over the Arno. Public areas have an almost Venetian feel to them, but bedrooms are furnished in traditional style and are spotlessly clean. Those facing the Lungarno can be noisy.

Hotel services *Air-conditioning. Bar. Car park (extra cost). Fax. Lift (within hotel, but not up the two flights to get to it). Multilingual staff. Terrace.* **Room services** *Air-conditioning. Hair dryer. Minibar. Room service. Telephone. TV.*

Splendor

Via San Gallo 30 (055 483 427/fax 055 461 276). Bus to Piazza San Marco. **Rates** *single* L160,000-L215,000; *double* L180,000-L240,000; *triple* L250,000-L290,000. **Credit** AmEx, MC, V.

Windowboxes brighten up the façade of this modest nineteenth-century palazzo near Piazza San Marco; inside, the public rooms are lavish with original parquet floors, frescoed ceilings and chandeliers. The lounge is painted floor-to-ceiling in rich, deep reds, while the sunny breakfast room looks onto a pretty terrace. All but a few of the 31 bedrooms have private bathrooms. The triples are huge and light with views over San Marco.

Hotel services *Car park (nearby garage, extra cost). Fax. Multilingual staff. Terrace.* **Room services** *Air-conditioning (most). Hair dryer. Room service. Safe. TV (satellite).*

Torre Guelfa

Borgo SS Apostoli 8 (055 239 6338/fax 055 239 8577). **Rates** *single* L170,000; *double* L270,000. **Credit** AmEx, JCB, MC, V.

This hotel boasts the tallest privately owned tower in Florence. From the top you can enjoy an aperitif while marvelling at the 360° view. In spite of the building's great age, the décor lends it a contemporary air; bedrooms have wrought-iron beds (several four-posters), white cotton curtains and bedspreads, and hand-painted Florentine furniture. One room has its own roof garden. Popular with the designer crowd who come for the fashion shows.

Hotel services *Bar. Car park (nearby garage, extra cost). Fax. Lift. Multilingual staff. Terrace.* **Room services** *Air-conditioning (eight rooms). Minibar. Room service. Telephone. TV (five rooms).*

Villa Betania

Viale del Poggio Imperiale 23 (055 220 532/055 222 243/fax 055 220 532). Bus to Porta Romana. **Rates** *single* L180,000; *double* L260,000; *triple* L300,000. **Credit** AmEx, DC, MC, V.

Hidden away in a secret garden, ten minutes' walk from Porta Romana, this fifteenth-century building is immersed in trees and flowers. It had become rather dilapidated until 1998, when extensive redecoration brought it up to scratch. The most pleasant of the 15 rooms are in the tower. A generous breakfast buffet can be taken on one of two shady terraces.

Hotel services *Air-conditioning. Bar. Car Park. Currency exchange. Fax. Garden. Multilingual staff. TV (satellite).* **Room services** *Room service. Safe. Telephone. TV.*

Budget (L100,000-L200,000)

Alessandra

Borgo SS Apostoli 17 (055 283 438/fax 055 210 619). **Rates** *single* L100,000-L150,000; *double* L150,000-L200,000; *triple* L220,000-L270,000; *quad* L260,000-L330,000. **Credit** AmEx, MC, V.

This modest hotel is well located on a quiet back street between Santa Trinità and the Ponte Vecchio. The 25 rooms (only some have en suite bathrooms) are spacious and many have polished parquet floors.

Hotel services *Currency exchange. Fax. Non-smoking rooms. Safe.*
Room services *Air-conditioning (seven rooms). Room service. Telephone. TV.*

Belletini

Via dei Conti 7 (055 213 561/055 282 980/fax 055 283 551). Bus 11, 17. **Rates** *single* L140,000; *double* L190,000; *triple* L246,000; *quad* L300,000. **Credit** AmEx, DC, MC, V.

This bustling hotel near to the Medici Chapels and San Lorenzo represents a real bargain. Dating from the fifteenth century, it has an interesting past and holds one of the oldest hotel licences in the city. Signora Gina is a warm hostess and goes out of her way to please, offering games and videos for bored children, a theatre-booking service and travel arrangements. The 27 rooms are simply furnished and the two at the top afford a close-up view of the Duomo.

Hotel services *Babysitting. Bar. Car park (nearby garage, extra cost). Currency exchange. Fax. Laundry. Lift (to first floor). Multilingual staff. Non-smoking rooms. Video.* **Room services** *Air-conditioning. Room service. Telephone. TV (most rooms).*

Casci

Via C Cavour 13 (055 211 686/fax 055 239 6461). Bus 1, 11, 17. **Rates** *single* L140,000; *double* L190,000; *triple* L255,000; *quad* L320,000. **Closed** three weeks in Jan. **Credit** AmEx, DC, JCB, MC, V.

This fifteenth-century palazzo once belonged to Giacomo Rossini; it is now run by the Lombardi family as a cheerful pensione. There are 25 bedrooms, a breakfast room and bar with frescoed ceilings and shelves are stocked with guide books and maps. A real bargain with a welcoming family atmosphere.
Hotel services *Babysitting. Bar. Car park (nearby garage, extra cost). Currency exchange. Fax. Laundry. Lift. Multilingual staff. Safes.* **Room services** *Air-conditioning. Hair dryer. Telephone. TV (satellite).*

Cimabue

Via B Lupi 7 (055 471 989/fax 055 475 601). Bus to Piazza San Marco. **Rates** *single* L140,000; *double* L190,000; *triple* L220,000; *quad* L260,000. **Closed** two weeks in Dec. **Credit** AmEx, DC, MC, V.
This two-star hotel ten minutes' walk north of the Duomo is at the upper end of its category thanks to the Rossis, who go to a lot of trouble to create a welcoming atmosphere for guests. The 16 rooms all have their own bathroom. The generous breakfast buffet is served in a bright, little ground-floor room.
Hotel services *Babysitting. Bar. Currency exchange. Fax. Multilingual staff. Safe. Car park (nearby garage, extra cost).* **Room services** *Hair dryer. Room service. Telephone. TV.*

Dei Mori

Via D Alighieri 12 (tel/fax 055 211 438). **Rates** *single* L110,000-L130,000; *double* L150,000; reduced rates for longer stays. **Credit** AmEx, MC, V.

Scoti's *wonderful sitting room.* *See p91.*

Daniele and Franco welcome guests into this fifteenth-century town house as they might friends into their home. The traffic-free location near Dante's house is extremely central. Rooms are small, but attractively decorated. Nice touches (unusual for the price) include feather duvets and dressing gowns, but only two rooms have private baths. The sitting room has a TV, a stereo, books and magazines. There is a small terrace from which you can just see the top of the Duomo.
Hotel services *Fax. Kitchen. Laundry. Multilingual staff.* **Room services** *Telephone.*

Firenze

Via del Corso/Piazza Donati 4 (055 268 301/fax 055 212 370). **Rates** *single* L90,000; *double* L130,000; *triple* L180,000; *quad* L225,000; *quin* L260,000. **No credit cards**.
This central hotel has been completely modernised over the past few years and offers clean, if not very imaginative, accommodation at budget prices. All 60 rooms have private bathrooms; those on the top two floors have more light.
Hotel services *Car park (nearby garage, extra cost). Currency exchange. Fax. Lift. Multilingual staff. Safe.* **Room services** *Hair dryer. Telephone. TV.*

Pensione Maxim

Via dei Medici 4 (055 217 474). **Rates** *single* L130,000; *double* L140,000; *triple* L180,000. **No credit cards**.
A small hotel offering basic but clean accommodation in the busy shopping area between the Duomo and Piazza Signoria. The two- and three-bedded rooms all have private bathrooms, many new.
Hotel services *Telephone. Multilingual staff.* **Room services** *Hair dryers (some).*

Residence Johanna

Via B Lupi 14 (055 481 896/fax 055 482 721). **Rates** *single* (no bath) L60,000; *double* L110,000 (L100,000 no bath). **No credit cards**.
A different kind of hotel in a residential area, this discreet home-from-home offers comfortable, stylish accommodation at rock-bottom prices. Each room has tea- and coffee-making facilities. Mobile phones are available to rent and there is a good supply of books and magazines.
Hotel services *Car park (nearby, extra cost). Fax. Lift. Multilingual staff. Safe.* **Room services** *Kettle.*

Residence Johanna Cinque Giornate

Via delle Cinque Giornate 12 (055 473 377). Bus 4, 28 to Via dello Statuto opposite UPIM store. **Rates** *double* L135,000. **No credit cards**.
Under the same directorship as Residence Johanna (*see above*) and offering the same kind of set-up, this small villa (in another residential area, north-west of the town centre) has its own garden, which also allows for free parking. Each of the six bedrooms has its own bathroom and breakfast trays are provided.
Hotel services *Car park. Fridge. Laundry (external). Multilingual staff.* **Room services** *Air-conditioning (three rooms). Kettle. TV.*

Grand ceiling – **Grand Hotel**. *See p80.*

La Scaletta

Via de' Guicciardini 13 (055 283 028 or 055 214 255/fax 055 289 562). Bus C. **Rates** *single* L140,000 (L80,000 no bath); *double* L200,000 (L140,000 no bath); *triple* L240,000 (L180,000 no bath); *quad* L260,000; *dinner* L20,000. **Credit** MC, V, JCB.

The fifteenth-century building that houses this budget hotel is located between Palazzo Pitti and Ponte Vecchio and has two bonuses: its vicinity to the Boboli Gardens and its delightful roof garden with two terraces. It is a simple, friendly, family-run hotel, which has a lived-in and labyrinthine feel. It is one of the few small hotels in Florence to provide meals. Rooms on the noisy Via de' Guicciardini have double-glazing, while others have views on to the Boboli Gardens.

Hotel services *Bar. Car park (garage nearby, extra cost). Currency exchange. Fax. Lift. Multilingual staff. Restaurant. Roof garden. Safe.*
Room services *Hair dryer. Telephone.*

Sorelle Bandini

Piazza Santo Spirito 9 (055 215 308/fax 055 282 761). **Rates** *double* L162,000 (L127,000 no bath); *triple* L219,000 (L172,000 no bath); *breakfast* L16,000. **No credit cards**.

Occupying the top floors of a fifteenth-century palazzo, Sorelle Bandini enjoys a superb situation on Piazza Santo Spirito. The hotel offers shabby charm in a wonderful setting, and the loggia which runs along two sides of the building (ask for room No.4 if you want direct access) makes up for the dilapidated interior with its faded mirrors and dusty chandeliers. Several of the 12 rooms enjoy superb views of the Florentine skyline. Afficionados of this simple pensione would not even consider staying elsewhere, despite the discomfort involved: you can't rely on getting blankets or having the central heating on in winter, and don't be surprised if your bed feels damp.

Hotel services *Currency exchange. Fax. Lift. Telephone. Safe.* **Room services** *Room service (breakfast).*

Villa Natalia

Via Bolognese 106-110 (055 490 773/fax 055 470 773). Bus 25. **Rates** *single* L95,000; *double* L160,000; *triple* L190,000. **Credit** AmEx, MC, V.

Villa Natalia (once home to Queen Natalia of Serbia) is an impressive, if slightly crumbling, ochre-coloured building in a formal *giardino al'Italiano*. The public rooms are a bit institutional (the canteen is shared by employees of the nearby Olivetti headquarters), but bedrooms are comfortable. The prices make it a bargain, but, as the hotel has an arrangement with one of the American universities, rooms are hard to come by.

B&B

Borgo Pinti 31 (tel/fax 055 248 0056). **Rates** *single* L90,000; *double* L130,000. **No credit cards**.

Florence's only women's hotel is tiny and allows no smoking, but offers great value. The four rooms on the top floor of an old palazzo are light, airy and quiet with views over an internal garden and surrounding rooftops. It is a simple but stylish retreat from the city heat and dust. The two communal bathrooms are spotless. Breakfast is a help-yourself affair.

Hotel services *Multilingual staff. No-smoking hotel.*

Palazzo Vecchio

Via B Cennini 4 (055 212 182/fax 055 216 445). **Rates** *single* L100,000; *double* L180,000; *triple* L220,000; *quad* L260,000. **Credit** AmEx, DC, MC, V.

A surprisingly pleasant hotel given its two-star status and vicinity to the station. It has been given a facelift in the past couple of years resulting in modern, spacious bedrooms with spruce bathrooms; standards are high for the price.

Hotel services *Car park. Lift. Multilingual staff.*
Room services *Telephone. TV.*

Hotel Bodoni

Via Martiri del Popolo 27 (055 240 741/fax 055 244 432). Bus A. **Rates** *single* L115,000; *double* L180,000; *triple* L243,000; *quad* L299,000. **Credit** AmEx, DC, MC, V.

On the fourth floor of a modern building next to the Piazza dei Ciompi fleamarket, the Bodoni offers reasonable, clean, two-star accommodation. The 44 rooms are done out in rather dreary brown and beige, but are comfortable; about a third have a private terrace looking over Santa Croce.

Hotel services *Bar. Fax. Lift. Multilingual staff. Safe. TV.* **Room services** *Air-conditioning (15 rooms). Telephone.*

Lungarno – *another 'rooms with best view' contender.* *See p81.*

Very cheap (under L100,000)

The accommodation booklet *Guida all' ospitalità* published by the **APT** and available from tourist offices is a good source of cheap accommodation. It gives a list of *affittacamere* (private houses with rooms to let) and religious institutions (often single sex with a curfew) that provide beds.

Anna

Via Faenza 56, 2nd floor (055 239 8322). **Rates** *single* L65,000; *double* L100,000; *triple* L120,000. **No credit cards.**

In the same building as Azzi (*see below*), Anna has only eight rooms, none with a private bathroom. As in so many old Florentine buildings, the basic level of accommodation is offset by the occasional frescoed ceiling. Some rooms are quite spacious, others decidedly pokey, but everything is clean.

Hotel services *Car park (nearby garage, extra cost). Multilingual staff.*

Azzi

Via Faenza 56, 1st floor (tel/fax 055 213 806). **Rates** *single* L65,000; *double* L130,000 (L100,000 no bath); *triple* L150,000 (L120,000 no bath). **No credit cards.**

A simple, friendly pensione near the train station in a crumbling building, which houses six such places. Rooms are geared towards students, but one or two stand out from the rest. Breakfast is served in the homely sitting room and there is a big terrace which offers a breath of air in the summer.

Hotel services *Bar. Car park (nearby garage, extra cost). Multilingual staff. Telephone.*

Istituto Gould

Via dei Serragli 49 (055 212 576/fax 055 280 274). Bus 11, 36, 37 to Serragli. **Open** *office* 9am-1pm, 3pm-7pm Mon-Fri; 9am-1pm Sat; closed Sun. **Rates** *single* L55,000 (L48,000 no bath); *double* L78,000 (L72,000 no bath); *triple* L105,000; *quad* L132,000; *quin* L140,000. **No credit cards.**

Superior budget accommodation near Santo Spirito. The seventeenth-century palazzo, with its courtyard, stone staircases, white walls and terracotta floors has plenty of atmosphere. If you want to avoid noisy Via dei Serragli, ask for a room at the back; some have access to a terrace. You have to check in during office hours, but once that's done, you get your own key. Popular, so book well ahead.

Hotel services *Multilingual staff. Safe. Wheelchair access.* **Room services** *Telephone.*

Locanda Orchidea

Borgo degli Albizi 11 (tel/fax 055 248 0346). Bus 14, A. **Rates** *single* L60,000; *double* L90,000; *triple* L130,000; **Closed** 6-22 Aug, 3 days over Christmas. **No credit cards.**

Dante's wife was born in the twelfth-century palazzo that houses the simple, cosy Locanda Orchidea. The hotel has seven bright rooms, the best of which overlook a wonderful, overgrown garden. Only one room has a private shower; the rest share two communal bathrooms. Friendly Anglo-Italian owners.

Hotel services *Multilingual staff. Telephone.*

Pensionato Pio X

Via dei Serragli 106 (055 225 044). Bus 11, 36, 37 to Serragli. **Open** 24 hours. **Rates** *single* L25,000; *doubles, triples, quads & quins* L22,000 per person. Minimum stay 2 days. **No credit cards.**

This state-owned pensione (in a thirteenth-century former convent) provides a quiet, pleasant alternative to a youth hostel. Single rooms are amazing value, but most rooms are three and four-bedded. There is a cheerful sitting room and a dining room where guests can picnic. There is a midnight curfew, but the place has one huge advantage over the hostels: it is open all day.

Hotel services *Hair dryers. Safe. Telephone. Vending machine (hot and cold drinks).*

Scoti

Via Tornabuoni 7 (tel/fax 055 292 128). **Rates** *single* L60,000; *double* L90,000; *triple* L120,000; *quad* L150,000. **No credit cards.**

This simple pensione, housed on the second floor of a fifteenth-century palazzo, is one of the best bargains in town if you are interested in atmosphere rather than creature comforts. Bedrooms are light and airy, if basic, and none have private baths. The sitting room, with its nineteenth-century floor-to-ceiling frescoes, is out of this world. Book well ahead to secure one of the more intimate single rooms.
Hotel services *Lift. Multilingual staff.*

Hostels

Hostel Archi Rossi

Via Faenza 94r (055 290 804/fax 055 230 2601). **Open** 6.30-11am, 2.30pm-12.30am daily. **Rates** *per person* L24,000-L26,000 in dorm; L35,000 in quad with bath (L30,000 no bath); *breakfast* L3,000-L4,000; *dinner* from L12,000. **No credit cards.**

A purpose-converted hostel only ten minutes from the station. You can leave your mark on the walls of the reception area and corridors which are covered in colourful graffiti. Rooms are spacious and light and some have bathrooms. There's a terrace at the back of the building, a restaurant, and a vending machine with microwave for snacks. Facilities for the disabled are unusually good for Italy.
Services *Disabled: lift, toilet, wheelchair access. Restaurant. Vending machine.*

Ostello per la Gioventù (YHA)

Viale A Righi 2/4 (055 601 451/fax 055 610 300). Bus 17a or 17b. **Rates** *per person* L25,000 in dorm; *family rooms* (double) from L64,000; *extra meals* L14,000. **No credit cards.**

Not as central as other hostels, but more pleasant in the heat, this YHA hostel lies just below Fiesole in an impressive setting with a loggia and ranks of lemon trees in its extensive grounds. Most accommodation is in shared dormitories, but there are smaller rooms for families. There are also camping facilities. Worth the 20-minute bus ride (it's a trek up the hill from the bus-stop) from the centre of town if you want peace and quiet. Midnight curfew.
Services *Bar. Disabled: toilet, wheelchair access. Restaurant. TV.*

Santa Monaca

Via Santa Monaca 6 (055 268 338/fax 055 280 185). Bus 11, D to Carmine or Santa Spirito. **Rates** *per person* L21,000. **No credit cards.**

This convent building dating from the fifteenth century was converted to a hostel about 30 years ago. It provides convenient accommodation for those wanting to stay south of the river, in trendy Oltrarno, but is a little gloomy. Curfew is 1am.
Services *Kitchen. Laundry. TV.*

Youth Residence Firenze 2000

Viale Raffaello Sanzio 16 (055 233 5558/fax 055 230 6392). Bus 12, 13. **Rates** *per person* L50,000. **No credit cards.**

A spanking new hostel hoping to cater for the influx of young and budget-conscious tourists expected for the millennium. Aiming to capture a more discerning

Torre di Bellosguardo. *See p83.*

clientèle than a standard hostel, the facilities are superior: all rooms (2-5 beds) have bathrooms; sheets and towels are changed daily, there's an indoor pool and a lounge area with vending machines. Rooms must be pre-booked and groups of ten or more get free breakfast. There is a blanket no-smoking policy.
Services *Car park (limited, extra cost). Currency exchange. Disabled: lift, toilet, wheelchair access. Fax. Multilingual staff. No-smoking hotel. Pool. Reception (24hrs). Vending machine.*

Camp sites

Camping di Fiesole

Via Peramondo 1 (055 599 069). Bus 7 and walk. **Rates** *per person* L13,000; *per tent* L23,000; *per camper van* L26,000; *electricity hook-up* for vans only. **Open** office 8am-10pm daily.

Probably the most picturesque camp site within easy reach of Florence, this is about 8km out of town. It gets packed in the summer.

Camping Italiani e Stranieri

Viale Michelangiolo 80 (055 681 1977). Bus 12, 13. **Rates** *per person* L13,000; *children* 5-12 yrs L8,000; *under-4s* free; *per tent* L9,000; *per camper van* L18,000; *electricity hook-up incl.* **Open** *office* 7am-midnight daily.

Not the most peaceful of sites owing to the disco that

podere Casato
The Podere Casato is located
just 20Km from Siena, on the hills
of the Chianti Classico Region.
It is the ideal place for a comfortable
and relaxing vacation.
Strada Castelnuovo Berardenga (Siena) Italy
Tel: +39 0577352002 Fax: +39 0577352900
Email: casato@chiantinet.it
SUPERSTRADA SIENA -FIRENZE
Strada Chiantigiana
Greve
Uscita A1
VALDARNO
Montevarchi
Bucine
podere Casato
Castelnuovo
Berardenga
Colonna
del Grillo
SIENA

Torre Guelfa *(p85) has the city's tallest private tower; it wins our 'rooms with the best view' prize.*

goes on until 1am, but the views over the city are fabulous. It has its own bar and supermarket.

Villa Camerata

Viale Righi 2-4 (055 601 451). **Rates** *per person* L9,000; *per tent* L8,000/L16,000 (depending on size); *per camper van* L16,000; *electricity hook-up incl.* **Open** *office* 7am-midnight only.
In the grounds of the YHA hostel below Fiesole (*see above,* **Hostels**).

Long-term accommodation

Florence & Abroad

Via San Zanobi 58 (055 487 004). Bus to Piazza Independenza. **Open** 10am-12.30pm, 3-6.30pm, Mon-Fri. **No credit cards**.
The English-speaking staff do their best to find you an apartment. Expect to pay from L3,000,000 to L5,000,000 per month on a holiday let, or upwards of L1,500,000 for longer rentals in the city centre.

Milligan and Milligan Rentals

Via degli Alfani 68 (055 268 256/fax 055 268 260). **Open** 9am-noon, 1-4pm, Mon-Fri. **No credit cards**.
This office is staffed by English speakers, and specialises in student-type accommodation.

YAIF

Piazza Santo Spirito 2r (055 282 899). **Open** 10am-6pm Mon-Fri. **Credit** AmEx, DC, JCB, MC, V.
The name stands for Your Agency In Florence, and the staff specialise in finding modestly priced accommodation in the city.
Branch: Via Ghibellina 72r (055 263 8727).

Restaurants

Buon appetito!

Osteria Santo Spirito – *a fashionable and stylish spot in the Oltrarno. See p103.*

A visitor to Florence runs the risk of being disappointed as far as food is concerned, since the most obvious eateries in the touristy parts of the city know they have a captive market – all they need to do is hang some hams, salamis and the odd Chianti flask from the beams, and the tables will fill up. The fact that the food is not up to scratch seems to be of minor importance.

But these places can easily be avoided by seeking out the restaurants where Florentines eat. Culinary standards in the city have improved enormously in recent years with the emergence of mid-priced, 'new generation' restaurants, where the food is based proudly on Tuscan traditions, but given a contemporary interpretation. There has also been a revival of traditional *trattorie* and *osterie* – no longer run by archetypal round-faced mammas, but by their sons and daughters. Dishes stick faithfully to traditional recipes, the atmosphere will be rustic (if sometimes antiseptic), and the bill shouldn't be excessive.

Foreign food has become increasingly popular in Florence. Fifteen years ago, the only non-Italian options were the few Chinese restaurants. Now there is much more choice. There are more than 20 Chinese restaurants (granted, most are mediocre); several Indian, Japanese, Middle Eastern and Mexican joints, an African and a Vietnamese restaurant.

The situation has also improved for vegetarians. Many a waiter will still look aghast when

Al fresco dining at **Borgo Antico**. *See p104.*

The legendary **Cibrèo**. *See p99.*

faced with 'Sono vegetariano' (I'm vegetarian), and will insist the plate of *salsicce e fagioli* (sausage and beans) is suitable as the sausage has been fished out. However, most Florentine restaurants offer plenty of pasta and rice dishes that are vegetable-based, the non-meat choices among the *secondi* have improved and there are plenty of salads and side-vegetables (*contorni*) to choose from.

So how does a first-time visitor to Florence avoid being ripped off? Well, to start with, carry this guide. Try and find somewhere that seems to be full of locals – the oldest trick in the book. There is a series of respected Italian restaurant guides, whose stickers are often displayed in the window of their recommended establishments, and these are a way of gauging the standard of a place. The most widely known of these are: Gambero Rosso's *Ristoranti d'Italia*; Veronelli; L'Espresso, and Slow Food's *Osterie d'Italia*.

With the odd exception, places that announce a special *Menu Turistico,* or where everything is translated into English and German, are to be avoided. Do not feel pressured into eating multiple courses from *antipasto* through to *dolce*, unless you see a sign saying *solo pasti completi* (only complete meals served) ; there are a few of these.

Bills usually include a cover charge (*pane e coperto*) per person of anything from L2,000 to an outrageous L6,000 – this is to cover your bread consumption. There will also be a service charge (by law included in the bill, but sometimes listed separately). Some places now include both of these in the price of the meal. One consolation for these extras is that you are not expected to leave a hefty tip. Leave ten per cent if you are truly happy with your service, or round the bill up a few thousand lire in a modest place. By law you should be given a *ricevuta fiscale*, and must keep it when you leave.

Italian restaurants are, on the whole, refreshingly informal. This means dress codes are not strict and you can be casual in all but the most upmarket establishments. Children are almost always welcome, and staff do their best to find something for them to eat even if it is not listed on the menu. A simple *pasta al pomodoro* is never a problem, neither are half-portions (*una mezza porzione*). Booking is advisable in most of the listed restaurants, especially in summer, and certainly if you want a table outside.

The restaurants are listed in price brackets – the price covers *antipasto* or *primo*, *secondo*, *contorno* and *dolce*; it does not include wine or water.

The ultimate splash-out

Enoteca Pinchiorri

Via Ghibellina 87 (055 242 777). **Open** 7.30-10pm Mon, Wed; 12.30-1.45pm, 7.30-10pm, Tue, Thur-Sat. **Credit** AmEx, MC, V.

Famous throughout Italy and in possession of two Michelin stars, L'Enoteca Pinchiorri is in a class of its own. The setting is totally captivating; a palazzo near Santa Croce with an internal courtyard scented with jasmine and roses, several elegant rooms laid with the finest linens, porcelain and crystal. It's hovering waiter and silver domes-ville; if that kind of thing bugs you, don't bother. The food is exquisite, although the running local joke is that you need to book a table at a pizzeria after a meal here; the portions, in true nouvelle style, are tiny. There are several set menus, all of which involve at least eight or nine superbly executed and beautifully presented courses. As much as for the food, the Enoteca is famous for its wine cellar, and Giorgio Pinchiorri has amassed a collection second to none, including labels unavailable elsewhere.

Over L80,000

Alle Murate

Via Ghibillina 52r (055 240 618). **Open** 7.30pm-midnight Tue-Sun. **Credit** AmEx, DC, MC, V.

Alle Murate is definitely on Florence's 'most desirable' restaurant list. The atmosphere is intimate and discreet, the staff efficient and professional (although the reception can be brusque), and the food creative. You can eat à la carte or choose one of two set menus (only served if everyone at the table participates), the Menu Toscano and the Menu Creativo; the staff maintain a rather exaggerated secrecy about the

A bite between sights

A hard day of culture can be exhausting on both the mind and the feet. When it comes to finding something to eat in the middle of the day, the last thing you want to do is expend energy on a search for the perfect trattoria. Many of the obvious places in the city centre are a mediocre mix of fast-food joints, *tavola calda*, expensive bars or places posing as cosy trattorie; they will fleece you for poor-quality food as quick as you can sprinkle parmesan over your plate of rubbery pasta.

But there are places to eat in the centre of Florence where you can find a reasonably priced snack or light meal. The following suggestions are made because of their proximity to the city's main sights (in brackets after the name). Wine bars are also good places for a fast, inexpensive snack and a glass (*see chapter* **Wine bars**) and many local bars or *latterie* also serve a small selection of hot and cold dishes at lunchtime.

Trattoria Bordino

(Ponte Vecchio, Palazzo Pitti)
Via Stracciatella 9r (055 213 048). **Open** noon-2.30pm Mon-Sat. **Credit** AmEx, DC, MC, V.
This little trattoria is tucked away, off a piazza just south of the Ponte Vecchio. Lunch is a bargain, and for L10,000, you can eat *primo*, *secondo* and *contorno* – dessert and drinks are extra. There's a choice of four first courses, four main courses and a couple of vegetable dishes. Bookings are not accepted for lunch. There are a few tables outside.

Caffè Italiano

(Uffizi, Palazzo Vecchio)
Via Condotta 56r (055 291 082). **Open** 8am-8pm Mon-Sat; *lunch served* 12.30-2.45pm. **No credit cards**.
Under the same ownership as the excellent **Alle Murate**, this elegant bar near Piazza Signoria is a good lunch stop. Downstairs is a dark, wood-panelled bar with a few tables, and upstairs is more like an old-fashioned English tea-room than an Italian trattoria, where light lunches are served. The menu changes daily and seasonally. In summer, there is a choice of more than 20 different salads along with some interesting *primi* and *secondi*. It gets very crowded between 1pm and 2pm.

Nerbone

Mercato Centrale (055 219 949). **Open** 7am-2pm Mon-Sat. **No credit cards**.
If it's local colour you're after, this combination of food stall and trattoria dating from 1872 within the covered part of the central market is the place to come. It is always full of market workers breakfasting on a *lampredotto* sandwiches (*see p106* **A load of tripe**) and a glass of wine. A bowl of simple pasta or soup, an offal sandwich and a glass of cheap red plonk costs around L10,000.

Tavola Calda da Rocco

(Sant'Ambrogio market)
Mercato di Sant'Ambrogio (no phone). **Open** noon-2.30pm Mon-Sat. **No credit cards**.
Rocco has recently jazzed his joint up; the tiny kitchen and rows of Formica-covered tables and benches in the middle of Sant'Ambrogio market is now enclosed in a kind of glasshouse. It is still a great place for a no-frills lunch. You will be seated wherever there is space. Prices are rock-bottom: pastas and soups start at L6,000 (the *pappa al pomodoro* is good), while for secondi try the *polpette*. The house wine is just the right side of drinkable.

Caffè dei Ritti

(Orsanmichele)
Via dei Lamberti 9r (055 291 583). **Open** 7am-11pm daily; *lunch served* noon-2.30pm. **Credit** AmEx, MC, V.
A cut above most of the *tavola calda* in the centre of Florence and at lunchtime frequented as much by a Florentine business crowd as by tourists. It is always busy and turnover is fast. There is a wide variety of hot and cold dishes and good sandwiches. Point to what you want, pay at the till, and carry it to the table (if you can find one).

latter until the dishes actually appear. Most dishes are a triumph, although on our last visit the *polpette di pollo e ricotta* was rather bland and solid and the *faggottini* (parcels) of beef with creamy robbiola cheese didn't work at all; not good enough at the price. Desserts are impressive: try the *torrone di pistacchio* served with an acacia honey sauce. The wine list has more than 140 labels, predominantly Tuscan, ranging in price from L30,000 for a 1994 Chianti Classico (La Massa) to L250,000 for a 1988 Brunello di Montalcino.

Cibrèo

Via de'Macci 118r (055 234 1100). **Open** 12.50-2.30pm, 7.30-11.15pm, Tue-Sat. **Credit** AmEx, DC, JCB, MC, V.

Cibrèo is a legend among the world's foodies (there is even a branch in Tokyo), for once justifiably so. The food is a refreshingly unpretentious combination of traditional Tuscan and creative cuisines, based on the use of prime ingredients. Owner Fabio Picchi understands that people who love food want to relax and enjoy it, not feel under pressure to pose. Cibrèo has two dining rooms: one, a trattoria (known locally as *Cibreino*) with marble-topped tables and where no bookings are taken; the other, an elegant, panelled restaurant where prices are at least double. The restaurant is so popular that you may have to wait for your table, even if you have booked. You can drink in the Cibrèo Caffè opposite while you wait, and a member of staff will get you when your table is ready. There are no antipasti at Cibrèo, but a generous selection of *amuse-gueules* is included in the price. These could include a triumphant soft, tomato jelly, gently spiced with basil and chilli, a ricotta and parmesan soufflé, and a gelatinous, spicy tripe salad. Unusually, the menu does not offer pasta but a fantastic selection of soups and polentas. For secondi, look out for *inzimino*, a Tuscan dish that sounds horrible, but is delicious: a spicy stew of squid, spinach and chard, served with triangles of toast. Dessert is a must: cheesecake with tangerine marmalade, the famous flourless chocolate cake, and the *torta di pere* are such that you will probably remember them on your deathbed.

Da Stefano

Via Senese 271, Galluzzo (055 204 9105). **Open** 7.30-10pm Mon-Sat. **Credit** AmEx, DC, JCB, MC, V.

Charismatic Stefano's motto is 'Solo pesce, solo la sera, solo fresco' (only fish, only in the evening, only fresh) and it's worth making the short drive to Galluzzo to eat in his excellent restaurant. The atmosphere is casual, noisy and slightly chaotic. There's a fixed menu but it is advisable to put yourself in Stefano's hands, as dishes depend on the catch of the day – he will talk you enthusiastically through the possibilities. Triumphs include *spaghetti allo Stefano*, a steaming platter of perfectly cooked spaghetti, with buttery, chilli-spiked lobster, langoustines and prawns, and the aptly named *gran piatto*, a mountain of steamed seafood. There is a jasmine-scented terrace for summer eating al fresco.

L60,000-L80,000

Caffè Concerto

Lungarno C Colombo 7 (055 677 377). Bus 31, 32. **Open** noon-2.30pm, 8-11pm, Mon-Sat. **Credit** AmEx, DC, MC, V.

Gabriele Tarchiani lived in the US for some years, and the décor of his riverside restaurant reflects this; lots of warm wood, huge picture windows on three sides, intimate lighting, background jazz and informal service. The menu, which changes every two months, is inventive without being fussy, based on seasonal variation and freshest ingredients. If you want fish, the hearty traditional soup from Livorno, *cacciucco*, is lightened with the addition of spring vegetables and herbs, or try the pasta with mullet, ham and sage. The *pasticcio di piccione* resembles a pork pie, but is filled with pigeon, or try duck breast stuffed with artichokes. The dessert menu includes a hot chocolate soufflé with fresh strawberry jus which is worth leaving room for.

Dulcamara

Via Dante Da Castiglione 2, Località Cercina (055 425 5021). **Open** 8-11pm Tue-Sun. **Credit** AmEx, DC, MC, V.

Nine kilometres north of the city centre and popular with a young crowd, Dulcamara enjoys a lovely setting among the trees with a fine view of Florence and you can eat out in summer. The inventive menu is based on Tuscan traditions, using fresh, seasonal ingredients. Its antipasti are always interesting; delicately flavoured *sformati* (flat terrines), griddled goat's cheese with strawberries or smoked duck breast. Courgette flowers are flavoured with star anise to dress taglierini, or spaghetti is served with mackerel. The *fonduta di mare* (fish fondue) is served to a minimum of two people and consists of salmon, shrimp, swordfish and monkfish cooked at the table and dipped into one of four sauces. Leave enough room for the wonderful desserts (crème brûlée is recommended). The wine list is excellent and there is a wide choice of grappas for the *colpo finale*.

Momoyama

Borgo San Frediano 10r (055 291 840). **Open** 7.30pm-1.30am Tue-Sat; 12.30-3pm, 8pm-1.30am, Sun. **Credit** AmEx, MC, V.

One of the 'new-generation' Florentine restaurants, Momoyama is sleek and chic. Downstairs, you are faced with two huge glass chandeliers, a long beech wood table and the Japanese sushi chef slicing away behind glass. Other tables are arranged in a series of intimate rooms. The clientèle is a mix of Japanese diners (a good sign) and well-heeled trendies. The restaurant offers 'Sushi Bar + Inventive Food'. The sushi and sashimi are beautifully presented and there is tempura on Tuesdays. The Inventive part of the menu is perplexing and overpriced; there is a choice of four or five dishes for each course. On our visit the shrimp and onion soup was bland, and the rabbit with tomato and rosemary, while good, was incongruously accompanied by peppered goat's cheese.

The Menu

GENERAL

Posso vedere il menù? – May I see the menu?
Mi fa il conto, per favore? – May I have the bill, please?
Dovè il bagno? – Where's the toilet?
Aceto – vinegar
Al forno – cooked in an oven
Affumicato – smoked
Arrosto – roast
A vapore – steamed
Bottiglia – bottle
Brasato – braised
Burro – butter
Fatto in casa – home-made
Focaccia – flat bread made with olive oil
Fritto – fried
Ghiaccio – ice
Griglia – grill
Miele – honey
Nostrali – locally grown/raised
Olio – oil
Pane – bread
Panino – sandwich
Panna – cream
Pepe – pepper
Ripieno – stuffed
Sale – salt
Salsa – sauce
Senape – mustard
Uovo – egg

ANTIPASTI

Antipasti misto – mixed hors d'œuvres
Bruschetta – bread toasted and rubbed with garlic, sometimes drizzled with olive oil. Often comes with tomatoes or white tuscan beans
Crostini – small slices of toasted bread, *crostini toscani* are smeared with chicken liver pâté.
Crostone – big crostini
Fettunta – the Tuscan name for bruschetta
Prosciutto crudo – cured ham, either *dolce* (sweet, similar to Parma ham) or *salato* (salty)

PRIMI

Acquacotta – cabbage soup usually served with a bruschetta, sometimes with an egg broken into it
Agnolotti – stuffed triangle-shaped pasta
Brodo – broth
Cacciucco – thick, chilli-spiked fish soup: Livorno's main contribution to Tuscan cuisine
Cecina – flat, crispy bread made of chickpea flour
Fettuccine – long, narrow ribbons of egg pasta
Frittata – type of substantial omelette
Gnocchi – small potato and flour dumplings
Minestra – soup, usually vegetable
Pappa al pomodoro – bread and tomato soup
Pappardelle – broad ribbons of egg pasta, usually served with *lepre* (hare)
Panzanella – Tuscan bread and tomato salad
Passato – puréed soup
Pasta e fagioli – pasta and bean soup
Ribollita – literally a twice-cooked bean, bread, cabbage and vegetable soup
Taglierini – thin ribbons of pasta
Tordelli/Tortelli – stuffed pasta
Zuppa – soup
Zuppa frantoiana – literally, olive press soup; another bean and cabbage soup, distinguished by being served with the very best young olive oil

FISH & SEAFOOD

Acciughe/Alici – anchovies
Anguilla – eel
Aragosta – lobster
Aringa – herring
Baccalà – salt cod
Bianchetti – little fish, like whitebait
Bonito – small tuna
Branzino – sea bass
Calamari – squid
Capesante – scallops
Cefalo – grey mullet
Coda di rospo – monkfish tails
Cozze – mussels
Fritto misto – mixed fried fish
Gamberetti – shrimps
Gamberi – prawns
Granchio – crab
Insalata di mare – seafood salad
Merluzzo – cod
Nasello – hake
Ostriche – oyster
Pesce – fish
Pesce spada – swordfish
Polpo – octopus
Ricci – sea urchins
Rombo – turbot
San Pietro – John Dory
Sarde – sardines
Scampi – langoustines
Scoglio – shell- and rockfish
Sgombro – mackerel
Seppia – cuttlefish or squid
Sogliola – sole
Spigola – sea bass
Stoccafisso – stockfish
Tonno – tuna
Triglia – red mullet
Trota – trout
Trota salmonata – salmon trout
Vongole – clams

MEAT, POULTRY & GAME

Agnellino – young lamb
Agnello – lamb
Anatra – duck
Animelle – sweetbreads
Arrosto misto – mixed roast meats

Beccacce – woodcock
Bistecca – beef steak
Bresaola – cured, dried beef, served in thin slices
Caccia – general term for game
Carpaccio – raw beef, served in thin slices
Capretto – kid
Cervo – venison
Cinghiale – wild boar
Coniglio – rabbit
Cotoletta/costoletta – chop
Fagiano – pheasant
Fegato – liver
Lepre – hare
Maiale – pork
Manzo – beef
Ocio/Oca – goose
Ossobucco – veal shank stew
Pancetta – like bacon
Piccione – pigeon
Pollo – chicken
Porchetta – roast pork
Rognone – kidney
Ruspante – free-range
Salsicce – sausages
Tacchino – turkey
Trippa – tripe
Vitello – veal

HERBS, PULSES & VEGETABLES

Aglio – garlic
Asparagi – asparagus
Basilico – basil
Bietola – Swiss chard
Capperi – capers
Carciofi – artichokes
Carote – carrots
Castagne – chestnuts
Cavolfiore – cauliflower
Cavolo nero – red cabbage
Ceci – chickpeas
Cetriolo – cucumber
Cipolla – onion
Dragoncello – tarragon
Erbe – herbs
Fagioli – Tuscan white beans
Fagiolini – green, string or French beans
Farro – spelt (a hard wheat), a popular soup ingredient around Lucca and the Garfagnana
Fave or baccelli – broad beans (NB 'Fava' in Tuscany means the male 'organ'; so use 'baccelli')
Finocchio – fennel
Fiori di zucca – courgette flowers
Funghi – mushrooms
Funghi porcini – ceps
Funghi selvatici – wild mushrooms
Lattuga – lettuce
Lenticchie – lentils
Mandorle – almonds
Melanzane – aubergine
Menta – mint
Patate – potatoes
Peperoncino – chilli pepper
Peperoni – peppers
Pinoli – pine nuts
Pinzimonio – selection of raw vegetables to be dipped in olive oil
Piselli – peas
Pomodoro – tomato
Porri – leeks
Prezzemolo – parsley
Radice/ravanelli – radish
Ramerino/rosmarino – rosemary
Rapa – turnip
Rucola/rughetta – rocket (UK), rugola (US)
Salvia – sage
Sedano – celery
Spinaci – spinach
Tartufo – truffles
Tartufato – cut thin like a truffle
Zucchini – courgette

FRUIT

Albicocche – apricots
Ananas – pineapple
Arance – oranges
Banane – bananas
Ciliege – cherries
Cocomero – watermelon
Datteri – dates
Fichi – figs
Fragole – strawberries
Lamponi – raspberries
Limone – lemon
Macedonia di frutta – fruit salad
Mele – apples
Melone – melon
More – blackberries
Pera – pear
Pesca – peach
Pompelmo – grapefruit
Uva – grapes

DESSERTS & CHEESE

Cantuccini – almond biscuits, to dunk in Vin Santo
Castagnaccio – chestnut flour cake, made around Lucca
Cavallucci – spiced biscuits from Siena
Gelato – ice-cream
Granita – flavoured ice
Mandorlata – almond brittle
Panforte – heavy cake of dried fruit
Pecorino – sheep's milk cheese
Ricciarelli – almond biscuits from Siena
Torrone – nougat
Torta – tart, cake
Zabaglione – egg custard mixed with Marsala
Zuppa Inglese – trifle

DRINKS

Acqua – water; *gassata* (fizzy) or *senza gas* (still)
Birra – beer
Caffè – coffee
Cioccolata – hot chocolate
Latte – milk
Succo di frutta – fruit juice
Tè – tea
Vino rosso/bianco/rosato – red/white/rosé wine
Vin Santo – dessert wine

Oliviero

Via delle Terme 51r (055 212 421). **Open** 7.30pm-1am Mon-Sat. **Credit** AmEx, DC, MC, V.

Oliviero has a strange *Dolce Vita* atmosphere, but the food is great: generous portions of inventive Tuscan and southern Italian dishes, executed with real skill. Service is formal, and a glass of prosecco will arrive while you peruse the menu. There is always something interesting to start; duck terrine subtly flavoured with black truffle or *sformatino* of fluffy polenta stuffed with tongue and porcini mushrooms. To follow, there's an unusual leek soup with frogs' legs, superb *gnudi* (like ravioli without the pasta) of courgette flowers and poppy seeds, and pigeon stuffed with chestnuts or minced rabbit *polpettine* with artichokes.

Osteria del Caffè Italiano

Via Isola delle Stinche 11/13r (055 289 368). **Open** noon-1am daily. **Credit** AmEx, DC, MC, V.

On the ground floor of Palazzo da Cintoia, this is one of the most beautifully appointed restaurants in Florence. Its three rooms are the epitome of elegant rustic; high, vaulted ceilings, wrought-iron light fittings, the odd well-placed oil painting and sparkling crystal. It is the latest project of Umberto Montano, owner of **Alle Murate** (*see above*) and **Caffè Italiano** (*see p98* **A bite between sights**), who set out to provide simple Tuscan dishes of the highest quality in beautiful surroundings. Indeed, all the classics are there in the short menu; four soups, penne with a smooth duck sauce, tagliatelle with funghi porcini, roasted veal shank, *rosticciana*, *bollito misto* (served with pungent *salsa verde*). The wine list is exceptional with many Tuscan labels from L22,000, to the great vintages at L400,000-L500,000 a bottle. Snacks – salamis, prosciutto, and cheese – are served all day.

Osteria dei Cento Poveri

Via Palazzuolo 31r (055 218 846). **Open** 12.30-2.30pm, 7.30pm-midnight, Mon-Thur, Sun; 7.30pm-midnight Wed. **Credit** AmEx, DC, MC, V.

Try not to be put off by the number of tourists squeezed into this tiny restaurant, or go late, when they've all finished. The food – mainly Tuscan with a creative twist – is excellent. There are two menus, the permanent and the seasonal; both feature lots of fish. Antipasti are delicately flavoured and beautifully presented. The primi include fabulous *gnocchi all'astice* (with lobster) and subtle taglierini with mussels and courgette flowers. *Tortellacci* are stuffed with ricotta and nettles, and served with a tasty sauce of minced quail and fresh peas. Or try the pan-fried duck breast laced with a strong balsamic vinegar jus, bound with a drop of cream. The wine list includes some Super Tuscans and other extravagances. But avoid the house red; it is disgusting.

Pane e Vino

Via San Niccolò 70r (055 247 6956).
Open 7.30pm-midnight Mon-Sat. **Credit** AmEx, DC, JCB, MC, V.

A calm, informal restaurant that started out as a wine bar and enoteca, with amenable staff, good wines and an enticing menu. The day's multi-course *degustazione* menu is recommended and excellent value at L50,000; you can choose wines by the glass to match each course. Highlights include the porcini mousse, and a smoked duck salad; exceptionally good miniature dumplings of *cavolo nero* (red cabbage) with olive oil and smoked tuna roe; deep-fried courgette flowers; and tender young lamb with rosemary-spiked broad bean purée. For dessert, there is an excellent pear and almond tart. The wine list is ample and one advantage for solitary diners is that you will only be charged for what you consume of a bottle.

Sushi and style at **Momoyama**. *See p99.*

Taverna del Bronzino

Via delle Ruote 25r (055 495 220). **Open** 12.30-2.30pm, 7.30-10.30pm, Mon-Sat. **Average** L90,000 incl a bottle of wine. **Credit** AmEx, DC, MC, V.

The sixteenth-century palazzo that houses the Bronzino is in an unremarkable street ten minutes' walk north of San Lorenzo. The interior is classic Tuscan: vaulted ceilings and terracotta floors. Much-frequented by well-heeled tourists, it was also a favourite haunt of Sandro Pertini, late ex-president of Italy. The regular menu offers such classics as *bistecca alla fiorentina*, deep-fried brains and artichokes and *ossobuco alla fiorentina*. The daily menu is more adventurous; *insalata di pesce spada e gamberetti* is a delicate dish of smoked swordfish on a bed of fresh shrimp and spring vegetables. And primi worth a try include *spaghetti al fiorgorgo*, with courgette flowers, gorgonzola and tomato; and *cappelacci* (a kind of ravioli) in a delicate lemon sauce.

L40,000-L60,000

Alla Vecchia Bettola

Viale Ariosto 32/34r (055 224 158). **Open** 7.30am-3.30pm, 7.30-10.30pm, Tue-Sat. **No credit cards**.

Just over the viale from Piazza Tasso in the Oltrarno,

Alla Vecchia Bettola is popular with locals. You sit on stools and benches at marble tables, and are given a flask of house wine – you pay for what you drink. The menu changes daily, but regular fixtures include *taglierini con funghi porcini*, *topini* (literally 'little mice'-gnocchi) *al pomodoro* and what is possibly the best carpaccio in Tuscany. On Fridays there is *baccalà alla Livornese* (salt cod in tomato sauce), or go for a simple and excellent *bistecca*. For dessert, try the ice-cream, which comes from **Vivoli** (*see chapter* **Cafés & Bars**).

Baldovino

Via San Giuseppe 22r (055 241 773). **Open** 11.30am-2.30pm, 7-11.30pm, Tue-Sun. **Credit** AmEx, DC, MC, V.

Baldovino is the type of restaurant that is appearing ever more frequently in Florence; a place you can eat just about anything from a salad to a full meal and no one will hassle you. It has an atmosphere all of its own thanks to David Gardner, one of the few foreigners in the city to make a success in the restaurant business. The décor is a refreshing change from plain walls, white linen and straw wine flasks: colours are contemporary and there is interesting art on the walls, mostly by a Sicilian artist friend of David Gardner. Part of the menu changes monthly, so, depending on the season, you may find crab gazpacho, *orechiette* with red cabbage pesto, papardelle with pigeon sauce, veal with asparagus sauce or mixed fish kebabs. Pizzas (Napoli-style), excellent *bistecca* (with Chianina beef) and main course salads are always 'on'.

Beccofino *Piazza degli Scarlatti (055 290 076).* **Open** *wine bar* 11.30am-3.30pm, 6pm-midnight, daily; *restaurant* noon-3pm, 6.30-11.30pm, daily. Gardner's latest project was heaving with the Florentine beau-monde at its opening in May 1999. Once a gallery, most recently a mosque, it is situated on a tiny *piazzetta* looking onto the Lungarno. The food promises to be interesting, given that talented chef Francesco Berardinelli has been lured here.

Bibe

Via delle Bagnese 1r (055 204 9085). **Open** 12.30-1.45pm, 7.30-9.45pm, Mon, Tue, Fri-Sun; 7.30-9.45pm Thur. **Credit** AmEx, V.

Three kilometres from Porta Romana, this restaurant is worth the trip. An old *casa colonica* (farmhouse) in a lovely flower-filled garden (with outside tables in summer), it serves traditional food. There is always something interesting on offer – *torta di caprino e olive nere* (black olive paste sandwiched in goat's cheese) or oven-baked, garlicky tomatoes. One of the best primi is the *zuppa di porcini e ceci* (cep soup with chick peas), but homemade spinach and ricotta ravioli is excellent, as is the *pappardelle alla lepre* and the stuffed courgette flowers. Secondi are classic Tuscan: excellent steak or veal done over an olive wood grill, roast pigeon or deep-fried chicken or brains. Puddings are a creative dream – the home-made ice-cream with a honeycomb case is fantastic. The wine list is unusually good for such a rustic place, but the fruity house red is worth trying.

Latini

Via dei Palchetti 6r (055 210 916). **Open** 12.30-2.30pm, 7.30-10.30pm, Tue-Sun. **Credit** AmEx, DC, MC, V.

Latini is a legend in Florence although the quality of the food has deteriorated recently. In spite of this, there is always a huge crowd clamouring to get in; it's difficult to book. Once inside, Narciso Latini (the head of the family and well into his eighties), may be slicing a huge ham and will slosh you out a glass of house wine if you are in for a wait. Once seated, things happen fast, and often without a menu. The fare is standard Tuscan of gargantuan portions; most of it is unremarkable until you arrive at the secondi where the meat is of the highest quality. The Latini family are prolific producers of a fine, sludgy green olive oil, and of some very good wines – the house red is very drinkable. A meal here is definitely an experience, but not a peaceful one, so don't choose Latini for a romantic *cena à due*.

Mastrobuletto

Via Cento Stelle 27r (055 571 275). Bus 11, 17. **Open** 12.30-2.30pm, 7.30-10.30pm, Mon-Sat. **No credit cards**.

You won't find many tourists in this trattoria near the stadium. Your fellow diners are more likely to be members of the Fiorentina football team and journalists who come for the Florentine cooking and lively atmosphere overseen by extrovert Marco and his wife Roberta, the chef. The menu features just about everything you would want from a Tuscan meal. Meat (from the Valdichiana) is excellent here, so try the *bistecca alla Fiorentina* or a *tagliata con rucola*. A plate of *biscotti da Prato* dunked in Vin Santo winds up the meal nicely.

Osteria dei Benci

Via de'Benci 13r (055 234 4923). **Open** 12.45-2.25pm, 7.45-10.45pm, daily. **Credit** AmEx, DC, JCB, MC, V.

Young and lively management run this restaurant, where you dine in brick vaulted rooms. The food is delicious and the menu, which changes every month, is imaginative. During warmer months, the emphasis is on light, fresh ingredients; *carpaccio di zucchine con scaglie di parmigiano* is a plate of thinly sliced, raw courgette topped with parmesan and dressed with olive oil. In autumn and winter months, don't miss the *crostone di piccione* – hot toast heaped with a warm pigeon pâté. There are also good soups, stews and grilled meats. Desserts include a fantastically light, towering baked cheesecake.

Osteria Santo Spirito

Piazza Santo Spirito 16r (055 238 2383). **Open** 12.30-2.30pm, 7.30-11.30pm, daily. **Credit** AmEx, MC, V.

Instead of the usual white tablecloth trattoria style, this popular osteria has flame-red walls and contemporary lighting. The fixed menu features a series of salads and cold dishes, such as Lardo di Colonnata with bruschetta, or lobster salad with rocket. The gnocchi in truffle-scented cheese is sublime. The daily menu reflects the season, and there is always lots of fish. The choice of wines is reasonable, with some excellent reds. In the summer, tables are set outside in the piazza. While you wait for your meal, you can amuse yourself with the absurd spelling on the English menu; 'gratinated fresh roockloobster with …' or 'Cremy ice crem with hot cioccolate'.

La Pentola dell'Oro

Via di Mezzo 24r (055 241 821). **Open** 7.30-11.30pm Mon-Sat. **Credit** MC, V.

Giuseppe Alessi once had a posh restaurant in Fiesole that specialised in historic Tuscan dishes. Fed up with cooking for the nobs, he moved into a more lowly neighbourhood near Santa Croce, where his menus are still full of intriguing dishes. He is extraordinarily knowledgeable about food, and happy to talk about it all night long. In his (somewhat uncomfortable) basement, you are likely to eat combinations of tastes never before experienced. Warm crostini topped with herring and bitter greens, penne with fresh broad beans, *linguine mare incantato* (charmed sea) with crab, calimari and prawns. Main courses include classic Florentine *seppie in inzimino* (squid and spinach stew) and *il peposo* (originating from the time of Brunelleschi), a beef stew where the meat is braised for hours and flavoured with black pepper and pears. There is also a number of vegetarian choices.

Under L40,000

All'Antico Ristoro Di Cambi

Via Sant'Onofrio 1r (055 217 134). **Open** noon-2.30pm, 7.30-10.30pm, Mon-Sat. **Credit** MC, V.

The only negative aspect of this popular, noisy trattoria near the river in the Oltrarno, is the incredibly uncomfortable wooden seating. Otherwise, it's great. The *bistecca* are displayed raw in the fridge cabinet and you may be asked which one you want. Cooked properly, the steak will be well-done on the outside and almost raw in the middle; if you don't like it that way, ask for *ben cotta*. The house wine (L12,000 a litre) slips down nicely.

Ashoka

Via Pisana 86r (055 224 446). **Open** 7pm-midnight Mon-Sat. **Credit** AmEx, DC, MC, V.

Om Parkash was new to the restaurant business when he opened Florence's only Indian restaurant in October 1998, and this could explain the feeling of chaos that greeted the first customers. He has learned fast, however, and things are running smoothly now; the place is always packed. The food is basically north-Indian and tandoori, and of a decent standard (with a slight doubt over a dahl that tasted of Italian cooking cream).

Borgo Antico

Piazza Santo Spirito 6r (055 210 437). **Open** 12.45-2.30pm, 7.45pm-midnight, daily. **Credit** AmEx, DC, MC, V.

This pizzeria-trattoria is one of the most popular hangouts for the young Florentine beau monde, who seem to disregard the fact that the service is often shoddy and unprofessional. The menu of pizzas (not the best), salads and a selection of pasta, meat and fish dishes has something for everyone. For vegetarians, the grilled vegetables with camembert is a good choice, and salads are fresh and generous. Don't go if you object to noise; the music is almost always too loud to converse. In the summer, tables are laid outside where relative peace reigns. Be prepared to wait – Borgo Antico gets very crowded.

La Casalinga

Via del Michelozzo 9r (055 218 624). **Open** noon-2.30pm, 7-9.45pm, Mon-Sat. **Credit** AmEx, DC, MC, V.

One of the best neighbourhood restaurants in the city, run for decades by a family that are now an essential part of the Oltrarno. Increasingly full of tourists (it is in all the guide books), there are still plenty of regulars to save the atmosphere, and it's a vibrant, bustling place. Not every dish is good; the bland *penne all'arrabbiata,* for example, but the *ribollita* and *pappa al pomodoro* are excellent, the lasagne and cannelloni are homemade, the roast meat good (try the guinea fowl), and the *bollito misto* comes with a deliciously fresh and pungent *salsa verde*. The tiramisù is delectable.

Da Ruggero

Via Senese 89r (055 220 542). Buses 11, 36, 37 to Porta Romana. **Open** noon-2.30pm, 7.30-10.30pm Mon, Thur-Sun. **No credit cards**.

Don't risk the trek to Porta Romana without booking at this tiny and popular trattoria; you will almost certainly be disappointed. The food is local and home-cooked, and the prices are low. Traditional soups are always on the menu, the *ribollita* is very good, as is the *paperdelle alla lepre*. Puddings are homemade, and there is a short wine list.

Ruth's

Via Farini 2a (055 248 0888). **Open** 12.30-2.30pm, 8-10.30pm, Mon-Sat. **No credit cards**.

Next to Florence's synagogue is Ruth's kosher restaurant, a pleasant, brightly lit room with the kitchen in full view. Vegetarian in this case includes fish, and the cooking has a strong Middle Eastern influence. The *Piatto Ruth's* (L16,000) consists of falafel, houmous, potato cake, rice, spicy Tunisian salad and various sauces; enough for lunch on its own. Then there is fish couscous, spicy fish soup and crisp-fried kefté. There are always vegetarian pasta choices and lots of salads.

Trattoria del Carmine

Piazza del Carmine 18r (055 218 601). **Open** noon-2.30pm, 7-10.30pm, Mon-Sat. **Credit** AmEx, DC, MC, V.

This trattoria has had a welcome facelift; pristine white walls and wood have replaced the dingy brown, Formica interior. Luckily the informal atmosphere is still there, and prices have remained reasonable. Piazza del Carmine would be more peaceful if it weren't for the car park that now occupies it, but the

Vinesio *packs in the punters for its Pugliese pasta and prime steak.*

few outside tables are still a pleasant place to sit and enjoy a meal. The menu is long (including dishes of the day), with plenty of choice. Try the *coniglio alla Maremmana* (rabbit stewed in a rich tomato sauce), tasty roast pork or octopus stewed with celery and tomato. The dolci are all homemade and delicious.

Vinesio

Borgo San Frediano 145r (055 223 449).
Open 8-11pm Tue-Sun. **Credit** AmEx, DC, MC, V.
Situated in the increasingly trendy San Frediano area south of the Arno, this little restaurant specialises in Pugliese dishes. The long, narrow room is usually packed with a predominantly young crowd, attracted by good food, reasonable prices and the *simpatico* owners, Gianluca and Marco. The mixed antipasto plate is generous enough for two and the star attraction is the fresh mozzarella. If you want a taste of Puglia, try the *orecchiette alle cime di rape* ('little ears' of pasta with garlicky greens spiced with chilli). The meat is excellent, and the *tagliata di Manzo* (while not sticking to the regional theme) is a juicy piece of prime steak, chargrilled and dressed with parmesan shavings, rocket, olive oil and lemon juice. Fridays and Saturdays are fish nights.

Under L25,000

Da Mario

Via della Ruosina 2r (055 218 550).
Open 11am-2.30pm Mon-Sat. **No credit cards**.
Behind the market stalls in San Lorenzo, the Colzi family has been serving lunch for over 40 years. This is the right place for a simple, cheap and tasty meal with a 'real' Florentine feel. The menu varies little and there are no frills; *pappa al pomodoro, ribollita* or *minestra di farro* followed by roast beef, roast veal or *bistecca alla Fiorentina*. There is always tripe on Mondays and Thursdays, and fish on Fridays. The only dessert is *cantucci e vin santo*. There is no coffee machine, so you have to go to a nearby bar.

Nin Hao

Borgo Ognissanti 159r (055 210 770).
Open 11.30am-3pm, 6.30-11pm, daily. **Credit** AmEx, DC, MC, V.
One of the best Chinese restaurants in the city, with a more upmarket atmosphere than most. If you don't waste energy on comparisons with London, Paris or New York, you can have a cheap, satisfying meal. The menu is yards long, the dim sum tasty, *gamberoni* (giant prawns) cooked in various ways are a good bet as is the duck. Fish, chicken or meat cooked *alla piastra* come sizzling to the table on a grill.

Il Pizzaiuolo

Via de'Macci 113r (055 241 171). **Open** 12.30-2.30pm, 7.30-midnight, Mon-Sat. **No credit cards**.
Book ahead as Il Pizzaiuolo is nearly always full. People come here to eat the Neapolitan pizzas (although there are plenty of other choices) as it is one of the few places in Florence where you can get the genuine article. Pizza base in Florence is usually thin and crisp; the Neapolitan version comes steaming from the wood oven with light, puffy edges and a thin, slightly soggy middle. There is a choice of about 20 (from L8,000-L15,000). Ask specially for *mozzarella di buffala,* which makes a huge difference to the taste.

Sabatino

Via Pisana 2r (Porta San Frediano) (055 225 955).
Open noon-2.30pm, 7.30-10pm, Mon-Fri; closed Aug.
No credit cards.
Sabatino's, a San Frediano institution, is moving. As the result of an eviction, it is to move 200 metres down the road to a place directly beneath the ancient gateway into the city. The Buccioni family are determined, however, to maintain the unique atmosphere of their trattoria, which has been in the family for 43 years. The pre-war fridge, the flood-damaged chairs, the 1950s tiles and, most likely, the same regular customers will all be moved too. Hopefully the standard

Italian and Florentine specialities they serve will remain the same high quality.

Santa Lucia

Via Ponte alle Mosse 102r (055 353 255). Bus 30, 35. **Open** 7pm-1am Mon, Tue, Thur-Sun. **No credit cards**.

Some say the pizza here is the best in Florence; the fact that you rarely get a table on spec supports that theory. Once seated, you have to wait patiently. The service is notoriously slow, and if you complain, you are likely to be relegated to the bottom of the list – all Florentines know this. The pizza is authentically Neapolitan, with the sweetest tomatoes and the milkiest mozzarella. If you don't want pizza, the seafood is excellent. It used to be torture in the summer (almost like sitting in the pizza oven itself), but air-conditioning has improved things.

I Tarocchi

Via dei Renai 12/14 (055 234 3912). **Open** noon-2.30pm, 7pm-1am, Tue-Sun. **Credit** MC, V.

This lively, perennially popular pizzeria is a great place for a good, cheap, late-night pizza (take-away too), a plate of pasta and a beer. Pizzas are Florentine-style (crisp, thin, slightly charred crusts) and cost from L7,000 to L10,000. A daily menu has a few pasta dishes, salads and the odd seafood or meat secondo.

Il Vegetariano

Via delle Ruote 30r (055 475 030). Bus 11,17. **Open** 12.30-2.30pm, 7.30-10.30pm, Tue-Fri; 7.30-10.30pm Sat, Sun. **No credit cards**.

Run by a co-operative and rather reminiscent of vegetarian restaurants in 1970s Britain, this eaterie is included here mainly because it is a rare breed in Florence. It's a pleasant and cheap option, though more interesting vegetarian dishes are often on offer at many ordinary restaurants. Take your pick from the long list on the blackboard, pay at the desk and get a written receipt, then show your order at the counter and carry it to your table. The food is standard vegetarian fare but the salad bar is fabulous.

A load of tripe

Tripe stands are Florentine open-air fast food. These mobile stalls are stationed throughout the city, and are laden with a series of bubbling cauldrons and heated trays containing steaming masses of (to the uninitiated) unidentifiable innards, a pile of bread rolls and a series of condiments. They are certainly not for the faint-hearted.

Nowadays, their clientele ranges from factory workers to shop assistants, bank managers to builders, all anxious to partake of and preserve an ancient Florentine culinary tradition, which, until relatively recently, was in danger of extinction. Originally, however, this was *mangiare dei poveri* (food for the poor). Just about any parts of the cow that remain after the best bits have been removed are cooked in various ways, the most basic and traditional being in a stock flavoured with onion, parsley, celery and carrot. In the old days, when the meat was finished in the evening, rice and *cavolo nero* would be added to the stock to make a nutritious soup; nothing was wasted.

The *tripperie* are enjoying something of a revival. In Florence, exclusively cow offal is served. Tripe itself is either eaten cold (mixed with pickles and dressed with olive oil, salt and pepper), or hot, *alla Fiorentina* (in a rich tomato sauce and topped with a sprinkling of Parmesan). *Lampredotto* (the lining of the last stomach of the cow) is often simmered for hours in a vegetable stock and served either on a *panino* or in a little tray to be eaten with a plastic fork. You may also find *nervetti,* tendons simmered in stock; *budelline*, intestines served in a rich sauce; *poppa*, the udder boiled and served cold, and *lingua*, tongue. It is a very economical way to eat. A *lampredotto* sandwich accompanied by a glass of plonk will only cost about L5,000.

Listed below are the tripe stands nearest the city centre. Most open at around 8.30am and close at 7pm; some close after lunch for a couple of hours.

Loggia del Porcellino, west side (closed Sat in summer); **Piazza dei Cimatori** (outside the American Express office); **Piazzale Porta Romana** (in the car park), the oldest tripe vendor in town; **Via dell'Ariento** (just outside the main entrance to the covered part of the Central Market); **Via de'Macci** (near Sant'Ambrogio market); **Via Masi Fineguerra**; **Piazza dei Nerli** (south of Ponte A Vespucci).

Wine bars

Fiaschetterie, enoteche, mescite and vinerie.

There have been wine bars of some description in Florence for hundreds of years, places where you could grab a glass of wine, a bite to eat and have a chat – every neighbourhood had one. The most minimal of wine bars comprised a little hole in the wall at the side of the street, usually a stone arch at waist level; a door would open from within, a few coins would be thrown on the counter and a glass of wine would emerge – a quick slurp and the customers would be on their way. These stone arches are still in evidence in parts of the city, especially in the Oltrarno.

Wine bars in Florence are enjoying something of a revival, particularly among the young. There are various types of wine bars in the city, from the tiny booths on the street with no seating, which serve basic Tuscan wines and rustic food, to the new, upmarket places that offer a huge range of labels from all over Italy (and beyond). Here, the food (and the clientele) will be more sophisticated and the ambience convivial to a whole evening's drinking and eating. *Fiaschetteria*, *enoteca*, *mescita* and *vineria* all denote wine bar of some kind.

All these places will have a selection of wine by the glass (*alla mescita*), and eats of some description, from basic *panini* to complete meals. The old-fashioned places tend to be open during the day until dinner time, whereas the new ones will stay open until late. For the tourist, they are an ideal stop-off on the museum trail (*see also page 98* **A bite between sights**) and should cost considerably less than one of the ghastly *tavola calda* joints in the city centre.

L'Antico Noè

Volta di San Piero 6r (055 234 0838). **Open** 9.30am-9pm daily. **No credit cards.**

In a pedestrian area near Santa Croce is a seedy passageway frequented by winos, junkies, and scruffy dogs, who all hang out round the falafel shop, second-hand clothes store and this tiny squeeze of a wine bar. A predictable range of Tuscan reds at reasonable prices are served with snacks at the stand-up bar. Drinkers spill out into the passageway, and there is a cheap trattoria next door.

All'Antico Vinaio

Via dei Neri 65r (055 282 738). **Open** 8am-8pm Mon-Sat. **No credit cards.**

One thing you won't find in this old-fashioned wine bar is many tourists. Refreshingly un 'done' – furnishings are basic (dark wood tables and chairs), walls are white, lighting is not designed to invite you in or make you want to linger, and there is not a designer nibble in sight. However, you will find a genuine taste of Florentine life, and a fair spattering of sozzled, florid-faced locals propping up the tables. Wines by the glass range from a really cheap plonk, through Chianti Putto, Gallo Nero, a decent Vino Nobile. All reasonably priced. Accompany your glass with a *panino*, a doorstep of salt-less Tuscan bread topped with a slab of Pecorino, or one of the excellent *affettati*; peppery *salame toscano*, prosciutto or finocchiona.

Balducci

Via dei Neri 2r (055 216 887). **Open** 9am-10pm Mon-Sat. **No credit cards.**

Dusty bottles are stacked on dark wood shelves, the counter is laden with edible goodies, there is a fair spattering of local life, including various canine customers (especially in the early evening), and the *padrone* is *simpatico*; Balducci's has a traditional feel to it, and is a popular quick lunch place for a range of Florentines, from builders to bank directors. The choice of wines by the glass (from cheap plonk out of a plastic flask to Brunello) is fairly run-of-the mill, but the munchies are excellent (crostini with various toppings, salads, a couple of daily pasta dishes and truffle panini).

Cantinetta dei Verrazzano

Via dei Tavolini 18-20r (055 268 590). **Open** 8am-9pm Mon-Sat. **Credit** AmEx, DC, MC, V.

Located in the centre of town, this wine bar belongs to the Castello da Verrazzano estate, one of Chianti's major vineyards. The wood-panelled rooms serve several purposes and are always crowded. On one side is the bakery (complete with wood oven) and coffee shop, on the other, the wine bar serves exclusively estate-produced wines. These are excellent value, both by the glass (from L3,000 for a simple Tuscan Trebbiano to a robust Riserva Gran Cru at L10,000) and by the bottle. These start from L18,000 for a Rosso Toscano and go up to L150,000 for a Riserva '90. Snacks, unusual crostini and sandwiches, are prepared behind the bar, or try a filled *focaccia*, straight from the oven.

Casa del Vino

Via dell' Ariento 16r (055 215 609). **Open** 9am-2pm, 4.30-8pm, Mon-Fri; 9am-2pm Sat. **Credit** MC, V.

Tucked behind the stalls outside the busy Central Market, this is a lively place to come and drink a glass of wine, have a snack or choose from the excellent selection of bottles on the laden shelves. Surprisingly given its situation, it is not usually too touristy and

Le Volpe e L'Uva *is typical of the new generation of enoteche in the city.*

is frequented above all by Florentines. Stand or sit at one of the tall stools at the bar, chat to owner Gianni Migliorini about wine and munch on a variety of crostini and panini with *finocchiona* (sausage flavoured with fennel), *prosciutto* and various cheeses.

Coquinarius

Via delle Oche 15r (055 230 2153). **Open** 9am-11pm Mon-Sat. **Credit** MC, V.

You can eat or drink just about anything at any time of the day at this cosy wine bar in the heart of tourist land, a stone's throw from the Duomo. There is a wide-ranging menu for lunch and dinner; various kinds of snacks to accompany a glass of wine, or hot pasta dishes such as asparagus crêpes, fettucine with hare sauce or ravioli with sage and butter. *Carpaccio* (slivers of raw fillet of beef) with artichokes and parmesan shavings is light and delicious, or you can opt for one of the main-course salads. Of course, there is a good selection of wines available by the glass or the bottle.

Enoteca Baldovino

Via San Giuseppe 18r (055 234 7220). **Open** *summer* noon-midnight Tue-Sun; *winter* noon-4pm, 7pm-midnight Tue-Sun. **Credit** AmEx, DC, MC, V.

Alongside Santa Croce, Enoteca Baldovino (annexe to the popular **Baldovino** trattoria, *see chapter* **Restaurants**) has recently been expanded. In the bright serving area, the marble-topped counter is backed by shelves laden with big jars of olives, sun-dried tomatoes, interesting-looking bottles of olive oil, vinegars, capers, sauces; salamis and hams hang from butchers' hooks. Hot crostini are prepared on the spot (try the Taleggio cheese and bitter red *radicchio trevigiano*), and dishes of the day are written on a blackboard. Bright ceramic-topped tables, warm wood floors, mellow lighting and honey-coloured walls show off bright paintings; there are tables outside in the summer. The choice of wines – all Italian – is not geared towards the true connoisseur, but there is a decent selection.

Enoteca Le Barrique

Via del Leone 40r (055 224 192). **Open** 4.30pm-1am Tue-Fri, Sun; 4.30pm-2am Sat. **Credit** AmEx, DC, MC, V.

In the heart of the Oltrarno, on an unassuming side street, this little wine bar has a 'new rustic' atmosphere. Hot and cold dishes of the day (such as pasta with rocket and speck or duck-breast salad flavoured with citrus) are listed on a blackboard and will cost around L35,000 for two courses; there is also a great selection of cheeses (both Italian and French) and other snacks. You can have a quick glass of wine from a selection of open bottles at the wooden counter, or enjoy a bottle from the list *con calma* at one of the tables in the back. There's a varied choice

of wines ranging from Tuscan to Californian, both recognised labels and lesser-known names.

Enoteca de' Giraldi

Via dei Giraldi 4r (055 216 518). **Open** 11am-4pm, 6pm-1am, Mon-Sat. **Credit** MC, V.

Opened in December 1996 by Tuscan Andrea Moradei and his Swiss wife, Giraldi is hidden in a narrow street off Via Ghibellina and occupies what was once the stables of Palazzo Borghese. Andrea is passionate about seeking out lesser-known wines, especially from Tuscany and central Italy (Umbria, Le Marche, Lazio, Campania), and the result is a refreshing collection of bottles. Recommended purchases include a perfumed Tuscan Chardonnay '97 Le Murelle (L16,000) and a fabulous pure Sangiovese from I Selvatici (Colli della Toscana Centrale) Capitolare di Cardisco '90 (L40,000). Some 25 wines are sold by the glass, and a range of hot and cold snacks and light meals is served all day. The atmosphere is pleasing, and art is always displayed on the walls. Wine tastings and courses are also on offer.

Fuori Porta

Via Monte alle Croci 10r (055 234 2483). Bus D. **Open** 12.30-3.30pm, 7pm-12.30am, Mon-Sat. **Credit** AmEx, MC, V.

Just outside one of the old city gates in the San Niccolò district south of the river, Fuori Porta is the most famous wine bar in Florence and nearly always full. The wine list consists of more than 600 labels (from Italy and further afield), plus a formidable number of grappas and Scotch whiskies. Every six days, the choice of some 40 wines available by the glass (from L3,500 to L10,000) changes. The daily menu offers hot dishes, but food is mostly a suitable range of nibbles and snacks to complement the wine. Best of all, and just the thing to pad out that second bottle of wine, is the huge choice of *crostoni*, vast slabs of Tuscan bread topped with, for example, Asiago cheese and sun-dried tomatoes and scattered with peppery rocket leaves. In warm weather, the few tables outside are in great demand.

Vini

Via dei Cimatori 38r (no telephone). **Open** 8am-8pm Mon-Sat. **No credit cards.**

Founded in 1875 and, literally, a hole in the wall, this *vinaio* is one of the last few of its kind left in the city. There is something truly delightful about stopping off at its wine counter, squeezed between a brass engraver and a jeweller, on a warm summer's evening. You can join the other customers standing on the road or even squatting on the pavement for a glass of whatever is open and a liver-topped *crostino*, *bruschetta* with sweet, red tomatoes and fresh basil or a great slab of *porchetta* – rosemary-flavoured roast pork – on a hunk of bread.

Le Volpi e L'Uva

Piazza dei Rossi 1r (055 239 8132). **Open** 10am-8pm Mon-Sat. **Credit** AmEx, MC, V.

Tucked away in a little piazza just behind the Ponte Vecchio in the Oltrarno, this new generation enoteca always looks inviting from the outside with its mellow-looking clientele perched on high stools around the marble-topped bar. If you are looking for unusual labels, this is a good place to start, and experts Emilio and Riccardo take great pride and pleasure in giving advice and recommending a wine. They search out small, little-known producers that supply the best value for money. Some 40 or 50 wines are usually available by the glass at any given time, and these rotate as bottles get finished. There is a particular leaning towards northern Italian labels. The nibbles are delicious; a great selection of French and Italian cheeses, marinated fish, *panini tartufati* (stuffed with truffle cream), smoked duck breast and rich patés, all designed to *stuzzicare* (whet) the appetite.

Zanobini

Via Sant'Antonino 47r (055 239 6850). **Open** 8am-2pm, 3.30-8pm Mon-Sat. **Credit** AmEx, MC, V (for purchases over L50,000).

In a narrow street that leads from the station to the Central Market, right opposite the *friggitoria* (fried food stall), this wood-panelled bar is always crowded with early-starting locals. Good for a quick slurp and a snack before you repair to the back room with its shelves full of interesting bottles to buy.

Cafés & Bars

Delicious dolce, gigantic gelati and creamy cappuccinos.

Café society didn't take off in Florence until the beginning of the twentieth century, relatively late in comparison with other European cities. Prior to this time, the only café of note was Caffè Michelangelo in Via Cavour, which was an artists' and intellectuals' haven between 1848 and 1866.

Although most cafés of the time, especially those on Piazza della Repubblica, had artistic, literary and social connections (Caffè Giocosa was a favourite with aristocrats and **Caffè Concerto Paszkowski** was a haunt of musicians), **Giubbe Rosse** was the best known. Founded as a German beer hall in 1897, it got its name from the red jackets the waiters wore. Montale and Futurist leaders such as Marinetti and Papini treated Giubbe Rosse as their own intellectual enclave, actually launching the movement from there in 1909, with the publication of the Futurist Manifesto.

Today Florence has a huge variety of venues where you can get a caffeine fix. There are any number of fairly generic coffee bars, usually reasonably cheap, and selling alcohol and decent food. It is here you'll find Florentines downing espressos at the bar: take their lead because more often than not it is much cheaper to shoot the breeze there than at a table. Alternatives include *pasticcerie*, which sell freshly baked biscuits, cakes and other delicacies. *Fiaschiatterie* specialise in wines and food, but will always serve an espresso. Depending on their licences, some cafés sell fresh milk products (*latterie*), cigarettes (*tabacchi*) and groceries (*drogherie*). Many can provide a full, three-course lunch menu.

Caffè Amerini

Via della Vigna Nuova 63r (055 284 941). **Open** 8.30am-8.30pm Mon-Sat. **No credit cards**.

An elegant, cosy place in which to breakfast, lunch or take an aperitif. Black-and-white photographs of Florentine streets cover stippled eggshell walls; the abundance of mirrors and comfy seats mean you could hole up here all day, watching brusque locals mingle with ladies who shop. Sandwiches and cakes are all around L6,000; a cappuccino costs L1,800 at the bar; L5,000 seated.

Caffè degli Artigiani

Via dello Sprone 16r (055 287 141). **Open** 10am-midnight Tue-Sun. **Credit** AmEx, DC, JCB, MC, V.

On the corner of one of Florence's least known piazzas, this café is worth seeking out. It is extremely charming and there is always room on its two floors to sit down in chic-rustic surroundings. The young, hip, multilingual staff entertain an art-school clientele, making it a rare example of the less frantic side to Florentine café life. Cappuccino is L3,000 at the bar; L5,000 seated.

Caffèllatte

Via degli Alfani 39r (055 247 8878). **Open** 8am-midnight Mon-Sat. **No credit cards**.

Caffèllatte was originally licensed in 1920 as a shop to sell 'coffee and milk beverages'; prior to that it was home to a butcher's shop (a bas-relief cow is still visible on the large marble counter). The café's primary function was to supply the neighbourhood's milk, a task which it continues to perform. In 1984, an organic bakery was added and the current Caffèllatte was born. The café consists of one tiny room kitted out with rustic wood tables and chairs. Jazz music plays, and there are exhibits and magazines to peruse. In line with its name, Caffèllatte's caffèlattes are the city's best (L2,000 at the bar; L3,500 seated), served piping hot in giant coffee bowls.

Capocaccia

Lungarno Corsini 12/14r (055 210 751). **Open** noon-4pm Mon; noon-2am Tue-Sun. **Credit** MC, V.

Is it a bar? Is it a café? Is it a bistro? Who knows, but it is certainly something else. The smart interior, which includes a lovely fresco in the breakfast room, is complemented with excellent *panini* (L6,000-L24,000), an extensive whisky selection and friendly, cosmopolitan clientele. Different lunch menus are offered every day, except Sunday when a rehabilitating brunch is served. There's another branch in Monte Carlo. A cappuccino costs L3,000.

Caffè Cibreo

Via Andrea del Verrocchio 5r (055 234 5853). Bus B, 14. **Open** 8am-1am Tue-Sat; lunch served 1-2.30pm. **No credit cards**.

Founded in 1989 as the third Cibreo outpost in this street (*see chapter* **Restaurants**). Around the corner from the Sant'Ambrogio market, it's a peaceful, non-touristy place. The café benefits from the Cibreo kitchen, which turns out phenomenal desserts, notably a dense chocolate torte and a cheesecake served with an *arancia amara* (bitter orange) sauce made from a secret recipe. If you call the café a day in advance, they will make you a cake (from L25,000) to take home. A cappuccino costs L1,800 at the bar; L4,000 seated. Outside seating in the summer.

Caffè Concerto Paszkowski

Piazza della Repubblica 31-35r (055 210 236). **Open** 7am-1.30am Tue-Sun. **Credit** AmEx, DC, JCB, MC, V.

Caffè Concerto Paszkowski was founded in 1846 as a beer hall, and during the second half of the nine-

The **Giubbe Rosse** *– the former hangout of Florence's Futurists.* *See page 112.*

teenth century it was a meeting point for artists, performers and writers. Its name commemorates the nightly concerts given here in summer; alas, now it is just another overpriced café on the Piazza della Repubblica. It's less popular than both Caffè Gilli and Giubbe Rosse (*see below*), so at least you can always find a seat. The café was declared a national monument in 1991. A cappuccino costs L1,800 at the bar; L6,000 seated. There's outside seating in summer.

Caffè Curtatone

Borgo Ognissanti 167r (055 210 772). **Open** 7am-1am Mon, Wed-Fri, Sun; 7am-2am Sat. **No credit cards**.

A vast, stylish café serving a decadent selection of pastries, cakes and savouries. You can take a three-course meal here from 12.30-2.30pm or sip on a selection of liqueurs and aperitifs. The faux-Gothic frescoes may not be to your taste, but the local business people and stylish Florentines don't seem to mind. Always busy, but service is efficient. A cappuccino costs L1,800 at the bar; L5,000 seated.

Caffè Fiorenza

Via dei Calzaiuoli 9r (055 216 651). **Open** 7am-1am daily. **No credit cards**.

The Fiorenza lures you into its compact mirrored premises just when you thought you had overcome your desire for a little light refreshment in the nearby Piazza Signoria. Resistance is futile, especially with 24 home-made ice-cream flavours to choose from (L8,000 if you sit at one of the few tables). Aperitifs, coffee and cakes are also available. A cappuccino costs L1,800 at the bar; L5,000 seated.

I Fratellini

Via dei Cimatori 38r (055 239 6096). **Open** 8am-8.30pm Mon-Sat; *Apr-June, Sept, Oct, Dec, 1st 2 weeks Jan* 8am-8.30pm daily. **No credit cards**.

A real hole in the wall, serving tasty sandwiches, crostini and wines from the best vineyards in Italy. Outside, there are shelves built into the wall where you can rest your wine glass as you stand in the street and enjoy your grub. Look out for wild boar salami, artichokes in olive oil and a delicious selection of cheeses and truffle and parsley sauces. Classy fast food. A sandwich and a glass of wine will set you back L6,000; coffee is not served.

Giacosa

Via Tornabuoni 83r (055 239 6226). **Open** 7.30am-8.30pm Mon-Sat. **Credit** MC, V.

Under the same management as the **Rivoire** (*see below*), Giacosa offers similarly sumptuous chocolates and cakes, however its greatest asset is undoubtedly the famous Negroni aperitif. During the nineteenth century the café was a popular watering hole for Florentine nobility and today the café's clientele can be equally sophisticated. A cappuccino costs L2,000 at the bar; L7,000 seated.

Caffè Gilli

Piazza della Repubblica 36-39r (055 213 896). **Open** 8am-midnight Mon, Wed-Sun. **Credit** AmEx, DC, JCB, MC, V.

Caffè Gilli's history dates back to 1733, when a *pasticceria* of the same name was founded on Via degli Speziali. It moved to its present site in 1910. The *belle époque* interior and furnishings are original. Not to be missed are Caffè Gilli's rich hot chocolates: cacao, *gianduia*, almond, mint, orange and coffee. The spread of mouth-watering *spuntini* (nibbles) on the bar at *aperitivo* time are among the best in town and the waiters among the most cordial in Florence. A cappuccino costs L2,000 at the bar; L6,000 seated. Outside seating in warm weather.

Giubbe Rosse

Piazza della Repubblica 13-14r (055 212 280). **Open** 7.30am-2am daily. **Credit** AmEx, DC, JCB, MC, V.
This café dates from the end of the nineteenth century and was in its heyday between 1910 and 1920, during which time one of its back rooms served as the editorial office for the avant-garde (predominantly Futurist) journal *Lacerba,* founded in December 1912. Always popular with international literati, it nevertheless declined after World War II and the trend was only arrested when new management took over in 1991. The food and drink are fairly standard (but pricey); the reasons to come here are more historic and social than gastronomic. A cappuccino at the bar costs L2,000 and at a table it's L7,000. Outside seating in the summer.

Hemingway

Piazza Piattellina 9r (055 284 781). **Open** 4.30pm-1am Tue-Thur; 4.30pm-2am Fri, Sat; 11am-8pm Sun. **Credit** AmEx, DC, JCB, MC, V.
The owners of this beautiful café have decked it out with anglocentric décor. Walls are painted in duck-egg blue with cabinets of Fortnum & Mason tea, wicker chairs and giant black-and-white prints of Ernie. The menu is extensive, with a huge selection of teas, at least 20 different types of coffee and stunning tea cocktails. The bar's star attraction (for chocoholics, at least) is that owner Monica Meschini is the secretary of La Compagnia del Cioccolato (Chocolate Appreciation Society) so the cakes and choccies here are to die for. It won the Campionato Mondiale di Pasticceria (world cake championships) in 1997 with its *sette veli* chocolate cake (L8,500). Prices are fair considering the quality: from L1,900 for a cappuccino (but L8,500 at a table) to L10,000 for a cocktail and L8,000 for a tea. The handmade chocolates go for around L9,000 for 100g. There's also a Hemingway high tea (L23,000) from 6-7.30pm which includes ten different nibbles and a buffet brunch on Sundays (11.30am-2.30pm; L32,000; booking advisable). It is a no-smoking café.

Caffè Italiano

Via della Condotta 56r (055 291 082). **Open** 8am-8pm Mon-Sat; *lunch served* 1-3pm. **No credit cards**.
Caffè Italiano is one of Florence's hidden secrets: centrally located, but tranquil and yet to be overrun by tourists. It's popular with locals at lunchtime. The café is on two levels: the lower is reserved for stand-up service and the upper is for those wishing to dally awhile. Dark wood tables, red velvet seats and mellow sounds create a classy atmosphere. Regularly changing exhibitions line the walls and there are newspapers and books to browse. Coffee and desserts are superb, but service can be poor. The *caffè-choc,* espresso laced with pure bitter chocolate powder, is a must. A cappuccino costs L1,800 at the bar; L5,000 seated, but if you're seated, drinks come with a complementary plate of delicious home-made *biscotti.*

Caffè Megara

Via della Spada 15-17r (055 211 837). **Open** 8am-2am Mon-Sat; *lunch served* 11.30am-3pm. **No credit cards**.
At Caffè Megara you can lose yourself among the mounds of international newspapers and magazines and enjoy impeccable friendly service. The café attracts a large (primarily Italian) lunch crowd, who flock for such dishes as *farfalle con pomodori, melanzane e noci* (pasta butterflies with tomato, aubergine and walnut sauce) for L8,000. They also serve substantial breakfasts and a mean cheesecake. Happy hour is 5-8pm, when cocktails are L5,000 and there are student discounts after 9pm. A cappuccino costs L1,800 at the bar; L5,000 seated.

Caffè Notte

Via delle Caldaie 28r (055 223 067). **Open** 8am-2am Tue-Thur, Sun; 8am-3am Fri, Sat. **No credit cards**.
Offering an invitingly earthy, friendly and nicotine-stained ambience, Caffè Notte is a great little place to drop in – whether for a wake-up call, to put away a plate of pasta at lunchtime, or best of all, to sip at a glass of port until the early hours of the morning. Alternatively, settle down to a board game at one of the large wooden tables or pull down one of the old theatre seats for a prime view of the television. A cappuccino costs L1,800 until 8.30pm.

Caffè Nuove Poste

Via G Verdi 73r (055 248 0424). **Open** *Sept-June* 7am-1am Mon-Sat; *July, Aug* 7am-1am daily. **No credit cards**.
Popular with gregarious local students, the Nuovo Poste has spooky blue strip lighting and huge patio windows that open out on to the street. There is a seating area outside in warmer weather, unfortunately on a busy road. Prices are average: a cappuccino is L1,800 at the bar, L4,000 at a table and it's L3,000 for a pizza slice or sandwich.

Perche No!

Via Tavolini 19r (055 239 8969). **Open** *summer* 10am-1am Mon, Wed-Sun; noon-1am Tue; *winter* 10am-8pm Mon, Wed-Sun. **No credit cards**.
This gelateria has been operating since 1939, and is probably the best in Florence. At the moment, there is a bank of 56 flavours (more than double the national gelateria average of 24), but which 30 of these flavours are made available varies with the day and the season. Portions are a good size for L2,500. The ice-cream is truly excellent, in fact the pistachio is so good you can hardly believe it's ice-cream. It's busy at lunchtime, so if you can, control your craving until later. A cappuccino costs L1,800.

Caffeteria Piansa

Borgo Pinti 18r, nr Piazza G Salvemini (055 234 2362). **Open** 7am-8pm Mon-Sat; lunch served noon-3pm. **No credit cards**.

The **Caffè Notte** *is a fine locale for late-night drinking – you can even buy one each.*

Unobtrusively located on a quiet street, this is a favourite with students, local business folk and the occasional tourist. Wooden tables line the walls, and seating is rarely a problem outside the lunch period. Because it's self-service, prices are reasonable: cappuccino L1,800, sandwiches L3,000-L5,000, pasta L5,500 and a filling set lunch for L14,000.

Bar La Ribotta

Borgo degli Albizi 80/82r (055 234 5668). **Open** 9am-1am Mon-Sat. **No credit cards.**
A friendly, busy café, with plenty of tables. The sandwiches are delicious, while more substantial hot food and salads are served at lunchtime. Seats are in alcoves so, despite the bustle, you can have a fairly peaceful meal. Staff are lively and efficient and there is always information here about local clubs, music and events. A cappuccino costs L1,700 at the bar; L4,000 seated. Discounts for students with student cards.

Caffè Ricchi

Piazza Santo Spirito 9r (055 215 864). **Open** *summer* 7am-1am Mon-Sat. *winter* 7am-8pm Mon-Sat. **Credit** MC, V.
One of the most pleasant settings for al fresco drinking in Florence is traffic-free Piazza Santo Spirito. Café Ricchi has been a local hangout for years, and is central to life in the area. Check out the art in the back room – dozens of images of Brunelleschi's famous façade of Santo Spirito. The lunch menu changes daily but the prices remain reasonable. At aperitif time, there is a tray of 'nibbles' to help the Campari go down. A cappuccino costs L1,800 at the bar; L5,000 seated.

Il Rifrullo

Via San Niccolò 53/57 (055 234 2621). **Open** 8am-2am daily. **Credit** MC, V.
Away from the bustling centre, in the peaceful quarter of San Niccolò, you can sit and relax in the pub-like atmosphere of this bar. Newspapers are available in the mornings for lingering over your cappuccino, but things liven up later: the music comes on and you can watch the amazing acrobatics of an expert cocktail barman. From 6 till 9.30pm the counter groans with dips and appetisers, which are included in the price of your drink. An inviting fire is lit on winter evenings in the back room. A cappuccino costs L1,800 at the bar; L5,000 seated.

Caffè Rivoire

Piazza della Signoria 5r (055 214 412). **Open** 8am-midnight Tue-Sun. **Credit** AmEx, DC, JCB, MC, V.
Caffè Rivoire was founded in 1872 as a steamed chocolate factory and is still famous for its chocolate concoctions. It has a picturesque location directly across from the Palazzo Vecchio. Aside from the chocolate, the food and drink are standard fare, though the ice-creams are better than most (at prices up to L20,000, they should be). A cappuccino costs L2,000 at the bar; L8,000 seated. Outside seating.

Ruggini Pasticceria

Via dei Neri 76r (055 214 521). **Open** 7.30am-8pm Tue-Sat; 7.30am-1.30pm Sun. **No credit cards.**
This much-loved pasticceria is packed with glass display boxes, fridges and shelves crammed with exquisite selections of gastronomic delights – delicious handmade chocolates, pastries, ice-creams, gateaux and cakes. At the far end of the shop there's a curved coffee bar (no seating) where you can neck an espresso (L1,400), a cappuccino (L1,700) or grab a bowl of *tagliatelle rucola e gorgonzola* (L6,000).

Bar San Firenze

Piazza di San Firenze 1r (055 211 426). **Open** *summer* 7am-8pm daily; *winter* 7am-8pm Mon-Sat. **Credit** DC, MC, V.
This bar is located within a fifteenth-century Renaissance palace built by Giuliano da Sangallo. There's ample seating and the high ceilings create a cool atmosphere. The vast range of culinary delights includes chocolates, ice-creams, pizzas and three-course meals. You can also buy *cantucci* (almond biscuits) to dip in Vin Santo (*see chapter* **Tuscan Wines**) and the Sicilian speciality of marzipan fruits. A cappuccino costs L1,800 at the bar; L5,000 at a table.

Bar Tiratoio

Piazza dei Nerli 1 (055 213 578). **Open** 6.30am-8pm Mon; 6.30am-midnight Tue-Sun. **No credit cards.**
A stylish bar near Porta San Frediano in the Oltrano. Staff are congenial and efficient and, as Tiratoio is not particularly central, prices are low. They serve delicious *dolce* and a changing rota of savouries. The bar has most liqueurs, aperitifs, coffees and cold drinks. The hot chocolate with cream (L4,000) is so rich and thick you have to eat it with a spoon and comes in flavours such as *cioccolata all' amaretto*. A cappuccino costs L1,800 at the bar; L4,000 seated.

Valentino (Festival del Gelato)

Via del Corso 75r (055 294 386). **Open** *summer* 9am-12.30am daily; *winter* 9am-12.30am Tue-Sun. **No credit cards.**
Offers a huge range (80) of commercial (Nutella and Mars) and surreal (spinach, carrot and truffle) flavours – but it's not a patch on the others (*see above*).

Vivoli

Via Isole delle Stinche 7r (055 292 334). **Open** 7.30am-1am Tue-Sat; 9.30am-1am Sun. **No credit cards.**
One of the most famous *gelaterie* in Florence and not without reason. The ice-cream is good, their fruit flavours are light and refreshing verging towards a sorbet, while the chocolate selection such as *aranciotti al cioccolato* (chocolate orange) or special recipes including *millefoglie* and tiramisú are creamier and richer. Ice-cream flavours are seasonal, though traditional ones can be found all year round along with the most popular like *pera al caramello* (caramelised pear). Vivoli's reputation precedes it and recently it has put the prices up (or made portions smaller, whichever way you prefer to look at it). However, you can sit down at tables at the back for no extra charge. A cappuccino costs L1,800.

Shopping & Services

Views and culture are all well and good, but this is what any self-respecting consumer needs to know.

One of the most effective ways of combating Stendhal Syndrome (an illness caused by sensory overload – too much art, culture, beauty) is with a little retail therapy, so it's just as well that Florence is a good place to shop. The city centre is compact and full of designer boutiques. Shopping in Florence is particularly popular with the Japanese (and, to a lesser extent, Americans), who come here to pay less for designer gear than they would at home. Year round, the shopping streets are mobbed with large groups clutching clusters of designer-labelled bags: Ferragamo, Gucci, Armani, Prada.

Many designer clothes shops are concentrated around Via Tornabuoni (*see p125* **Chic to chic**), Via della Vigna Nuova, Via dei Calzaiuoli and Via Roma. There are some interesting shops around the **Mercato Centrale**. Via Panzani (between the Duomo and the station) is worth a browse too, and Borgo San Lorenzo is full of reasonably priced shoes. As for street or club fashion, there's barely any to speak of, but there are plenty of little shops to bargain-hunt in (*see p118* **On a shoestring**).

One of Florence's big pluses is its strong artisan tradition. Leather goods and hand-marbled paper are specialities and, although some of what you see is mass-produced, there are still genuine craftsmen and women at work in the city, many of them in the Oltrarno. For leather goods, the obvious places to look are the markets (Mercato Centrale and **Mercato Nuovo** in particular), as prices here tend to be lower. Be wary of temptation in the form of leather jackets at astoundingly low prices in the market: they are usually made from poor-quality hide and will fall apart. For wider choice, better quality and better value for money, go to Santa Croce and hunt around the hundreds of shops scattered around the area.

Of course, there is plenty in the way of food and drink and you can buy it for a fraction of what you would pay in a deli back home. Dried porcini mushrooms, locally produced olive oil, balsamic vinegar, local cheeses (such as pecorino, a sheep's cheese), salamis (try *salame di cinghiale,* made from wild boar) and prosciutto, fresh pasta, wines, vin santo and grappas. *See also chapter* **Food in Tuscany**. Let your nose take the lead and you're bound to end up in the maze of little streets around San Lorenzo, which is packed with tempting delicatessens and food shops; the Florentines do their shopping here, so prices are reasonable. There are not many such shops right in the centre of town and those that there are tend to be expensive. Most things can be picked up in a local supermarket, but most of these are a bit out of town.

Unless the lira is extremely weak, prices in Florence tend to be on the high side. The two major sales periods in January/March and July/August make a huge difference, and bargains can be had. Keep your official receipt (*scontrino*) as non-EC visitors are entitled to a VAT rebate on purchases

Get hip to the Beat in **City Lights**. *See p116.*

of goods over L300,000 if exported unused. The shop will give you a form to show to customs when leaving Italy (*see also p266* **Tax-free shopping**).

OPENING HOURS

While supermarkets and the larger stores in the centre of Florence now stay open throughout the day (*orario continuato*), most shops still operate standard hours – closing at lunchtime and (food shops excepted) Monday mornings. Standard opening times are: 5pm to 7.30pm on Monday; from 8.30am to 1pm, and 5pm to 7.30pm Tuesday to Saturday. With the rise in popularity of Sunday shopping, many central stores open for at least part of the day.

Clothes shops tend to open later in the mornings, and food shops are open on Monday morning but closed on Wednesday afternoon. Hours change slightly in mid-June until the end of August, with most shops staying open a bit later on weekday evenings and closing on Saturday afternoons. Small shops tend to shut completely at some point during July or August, for anything from a week to a month.

The opening times listed below apply for most of the year. Please note, however, that times do vary, and shops, especially small, privately owned ones may well open or close at other times.

E-MAIL, FAXES AND PHOTOCOPIES

For computer-related services, e-mail, faxing, photocopying and mobile phone hire, please *see chapter* **Directory**: **Business**.

Department stores

COIN

Via dei Calzaiuoli 56r (055 280 531). **Open** 9.30am-8pm Mon-Sat; 11am-8pm Sun. **Credit** AmEx, DC, MC, V.

COIN's middle-of-the-road clothing is also middle-aged, but the young collections are interesting; look out for the in-house Koan label. Florentines come here for socks and bargain make-up. Good quality bedlinen, towels and kitchenware fill the basement.

Rinascente

Piazza della Repubblica 1 (055 239 8544). **Open** 9am-9pm Mon-Sat; 10.30am-8pm Sun. **Credit** AmEx, DC, MC, V.

A touch more upmarket than COIN; Rinascente's Misaky womenswear label occasionally comes up with the goods. Kitchenware and bedding are on the top floor, underwear is in the basement.

Standa

Via Pietrapiana 42/44 (055 234 7856). Bus A. **Open** 2-8pm Mon; 7.30am-8pm Tue-Sat. **Credit** AmEx, DC, MC, V.

This shabby supermarket is good for cheap toiletries or basic foods. It is the only place in central Florence where you can buy food on a Wednesday afternoon.

Branch: Via Panzani 31r (055 239 8963).

Books

Many bookshops in Florence stock English-language books, but prices are about 25 per cent higher than in the UK. For children's books, *see chapter* **Children**.

After Dark

Via de' Ginori 47r (055 294 203). **Open** 10am-2pm, 3-7pm, Mon-Sat. **Credit** AmEx, DC, MC, V.

Norman's English-language bookstore stocks Florence's best selection of magazines. There are a number of novels set in Italy, and reasonable psychology, philosophy, new age and gender sections.

Alinari

Largo Alinari 15 (055 23951). **Open** 9am-1pm, 3-7pm, Mon-Sat. **Credit** AmEx, DC, V.

The Alinari brothers' photographic firm, established in 1852, was the world's first. The shop stocks photography books, exhibition catalogues and will order prints of virtually anything in the Alinari archives.

City Lights

Via San Niccolò 23 (055 234 7882). **Open** 5.30-10.30pm Tue-Thur; 4pm-midnight Fri, Sat; 4-9pm Sun. **Credit** AmEx, DC, MC, V.

Modelled on the San Francisco bookstore of the same name, City Lights stocks Beat Generation literature, much of it in English. A cultural reference point in the city, it organises readings and other literary events.

Feltrinelli Internazionale

Via Cavour 12-20r (055 219 524). **Open** 9am-7.30pm Mon-Sat. **Credit** AmEx, DC, MC, V.

Branch of Italy's foremost chain, owned by radical publishing group Feltrinelli. Modern, well organised, and with strong art, photography and Italian comic book sections.

Branch: Via Cerretani 30r (055 238 2652).

Website: http://www.vol.it/icone

Libreria del Cinema e dello Spectacolo

Via Guelfa 14r (055 216 416). **Open** 9.30am-1pm, 3.30-7.30pm, Mon-Sat. **Credit** MC, V.

Tuscany's only bookshop specialising in the cinema. It stocks books, magazines, videos (also in English), posters and film memorabilia. *See also chapter* **Film**.

Libreria delle Donne

Via Fiesolana 2b (055 240 384). Bus A. **Open** 3.30-7.30pm Mon; 9am-1pm, 3.30-7.30pm, Tue-Fri; 11.30am-1pm, 3.30-7.30pm, Sat. **Credit** MC, V.

Florence's women's bookshop is a good reference point for women visiting the city. The feminist literature is mostly Italian. There is a useful notice board.

Paperback Exchange

Via Fiesolana 31r (055 247 8154/fax 055 247 8856/papex@dada.it). **Open** 9am-1pm, 3.30-7.30pm, Tue-Sat; also Mon mid-Mar to mid-Nov. **Credit** AmEx, DC, MC, V.

An imaginative selection of new English-language fiction and non-fiction, particularly art, art history and Italian culture. It is a meeting point for anglophones in Florence, and has a useful notice board.

Seeber

Via Tornabuoni 70r (055 215 697). **Open** 9.30am-7.30pm Mon-Sat. **Credit** AmEx, DC, MC, V.
A good selection of Italian and foreign-language books – travel, food, art, fiction.

Il Viaggio

Borgo degli Albizi 41r (055 240 489). Bus 14, 23. **Open** 3.30-7.30pm Mon; 9.30-1pm, 3.30-7.30pm, Tue-Sat; *summer* also 2.30-6pm last Sun of month; closed Sat afternoon. **Credit** AmEx, MC, V.
The best travel bookshop in town. Stock includes English-language guides to Italy and elsewhere; walking maps and travel literature.

Dress sense

For sports clothes and equipment, *see chapter* **Sport**; for children's clothes, *see chapter* **Children**; for designer clothing *see p125* **Chic to chic;** for second-hand and budget gear *see below* **Markets** and *p118* **On a shoestring**.

Il Guardaroba

Via Verdi 28r (055 247 8250). **Open** 1-7.30pm Mon; 9.30am-7.30pm, Tue-Sat. **Credit** AmEx, DC, MC, V.
Last-season designer gear at decent prices.
Branches Via Castellani 26r (055 294 853); Borgo degli Albizi 85/87 (055 234 0271); Via Nazionale 38r (055 215 482).

Geraldine Tayar

Sdrucciolo dei Pitti 6r (055 290 405). **Open** 9am-1pm, 3-7pm, Mon-Sat. **Credit** MC, V.
Clothes and accessories in jewel-coloured raw silks, cool linens and crisp cottons. Geraldine also offers a made-to-measure service.

Stroll

Via Romana 78r (055 229 144). **Open** 4-8pm Mon; 9.30am-1pm, 3.30-7.30pm, Tue-Sat. **Credit** AmEx, DC, MC, V.
An Aladdin's cave stuffed full of designer end-of-lines. You may root out Max Mara, Byblos, Gigli, Kookaï, Maska and much more at reasonable prices.

Dry cleaners & launderettes

Some cleaners (*tintorie*) in Florence are cheaper than others, so do look around. Most launderettes will do your washing for you, charging by the kilo.

Lucy & Rita

Via della Chiesa 19r (055 224 536). **Open** 7am-1pm, 2.30-7.30pm, Mon-Fri. **No credit cards**.
Not the cheapest (L5,000 for a shirt, L18,000 for a suit), but it does a fine job. Wet laundry is done by hand.

Serena

Via della Scala 30r (055 218 183). Bus to Santa Maria Novella station. **Open** 8.30am-8pm Mon-Sat. **No credit cards**.
Serena charges about L5,000 to wash and iron a shirt and around L17,000 to dry clean a suit. There's also a self-service laundry facility.

Wash & Dry

Via Nazionale 129r (055 291 504/freephone 167 231 172). **Open** 8am-10pm daily; *last wash* 9pm. **No credit cards**.
This new chain of self-service laundrettes offers machines that wash and dry in 50 minutes. Charges are L6,000 for 8 kilos, plus L6,000 for a dry.
Branches: Via dei Servi 105r; Via della Scala 52/54r; Via dei Serragli 87r; Via Ghibellina 143r; Via del Sole 29r.

Jewellery

Altri Mondi

Via degli Alfani 92r (no phone). Bus to Piazza San Marco. **Open** 3.30-7.30pm Mon; 9.30am-1.30pm, 3.30-7.30pm, Tue-Sat. **Credit** AmEx, V.
Indian and its own contemporary designs in silver and semi-precious stones.

Aprosio e Luthi

Via dello Sprone 1r (055 290 534). **Open** 9.30am-1pm, 2-7pm, Mon-Sat. **Credit** AmEx, MC, V.
Intricately designed necklaces, bracelets, brooches, earrings, evening bags and belts, all made from tiny glass beads.

Il Gatto Bianco

Borgo SS Apostoli 12r (055 282 989). **Open** 3.30-7.30pm Mon; 10am-1.30pm, 3.30-7.30pm, Tue-Sat. **Credit** AmEx, DC, MC, V.
Original contemporary designs are crafted in the shop using silver, gold, and other metals, precious and semi-precious stones. Prices start from L80,000.

Papillon

Via dei Neri 21r (055 215 222). **Open** 10am-7pm Mon-Sat. **Credit** AmEx, DC, MC, V.
A squeeze of a shop where three jewellers – one Colombian, one French, one Italian – sell their wares. These include filigree copper chokers, coloured aluminium bracelets, quartz and turquoise necklaces, glass rings and hair slides. Prices start from L18,000.

Parsifal

Via della Spada 28r (055 288 610). **Open** 10am-2pm, 3.30-7.30pm, Mon-Sat. **Credit** AmEx, DC, MC, V.
Striking contemporary jewellery, including some wacky cut-outs, in silver plate and aluminium.

Pepita Studio

Borgo degli Albizi 23r (055 244 538). Bus A. **Open** 10am-7.30pm daily. **Credit** MC, V.
Fun, chunky plexiglass, wood and glass jewellery. Prices for rings and hatpins start at L15,000 and go up to a maximum of L50,000.

Seven Stars

Borgo degli Albizi 45r (055 234 0566). Bus A. **Open** 3.30-7.30pm Mon; 9.30am-1pm, 3.30-7.30pm, Tue-Sat. **Credit** AmEx, DC, MC, V.
Classic as well as some innovative contemporary designs, mostly in silver. Most pieces are Italian. Prices start at L40,000.

On a shoestring

Italians are into image and a large proportion of their income is spent on clothes and accessories; Italians usually renew at least half of their wardrobe each season. While the very idea of wearing someone else's cast-offs would appal most, attitudes towards cast-offs and second-hand gear gradually appear to be changing – hence the increasing number of second-hand clothes shops.

Market stalls are the best source of cheap and second-hand clothes, but quality is variable. The Mercato Centrale is the main event (8.30am-7pm Mon-Sat; closed Mon in winter), but the weekly Cascine market is where the Florentines search for bargains. Look out for the most crowded stalls; you might find a load of designer wear that has just fallen off the back of a lorry. Many residential areas of Florence have a morning market with, among other things, new or used clothes stalls; Piazza delle Cure, Piazza Santo Spirito, Isolotto, Galuzzo are just a few. They are usually open between 8am and 1pm Mon-Sat. *See also* **Markets**.

Florence is not big on factory outlets, but there are a couple. **Gucci** (Via Aretina 63, 055 865 7775) stocks unsold sales items for about 60 per cent of the normal retail price; a pair of classic loafers costs about L175,000. **Prada** sells ends of lines, samples and overstocks from its outlet in Montevarchi, some 30kms south of Florence (Località SS Levanella 69, 055 91901). If outlet shopping is your thing, Prato makes a productive trip. It is a world centre for textile production and home to a number of outlet stores, offering cloth lengths, cashmere knitwear and made-to-measure items.

In Florence proper, try Via Nazionale, Via dei Neri, Via Panzani, Corso Italia and around Borgo San Lorenzo and other streets near the central market, with the latter offering probably the funkiest gear. Recommended women's shops (all

Repairs

Anna Maria Sernesi

Via dei Serragli 82 (no phone). Bus 11. **Open** 9am-12.30pm, 3.30-7pm, Mon-Fri. **No credit cards**.

This miniscule workshop carries out alterations and repairs on all garments, including leather.

Guido

Via Santa Monaca 9 (no phone). Bus 11. **Open** 7am-1pm, 3-6pm, Mon-Fri. **No credit cards**.

Guido lived in Australia for 25 years, and is pleased to speak English to anybody who brings their museum-weary shoes in to him for repair.

Brovelli

Borgo San Frediano 11r (055 213 840). Bus D. **Open** 3.30-7.30pm Mon; 9am-1pm, 3.30-7.30pm, Tue-Sat. **Credit** AmEx, DC, MC, V.

Repairs to all leather goods (except shoes).

Presto Service

Via Faenza 77 (no telephone). **Open** 3.30-7.30pm Mon; 9am-12.30pm, 3.30-7.30pm, Tue-Sat. **No credit cards**.

While-you-wait heel bar and key-cutting service.

Time Out

Via dei Bardi 70r (055 213 111). **Open** 3.30-7.30pm Mon; 9.30am-1pm, 3.30-7.30pm, Tue-Sat. **Credit** AmEx, DC, JCB, MC, V.

Time Out (no relation) specialises in antique watches.

Walter's Silver and Gold

Borgo dei Greci 11Cr (055 239 6678). Bus 23. **Open** 9am-6pm daily. **Credit** AmEx, DC, MC, V.

English-speaking Walter does all jewellery repairs.

Shoes & leather goods

Bisonte

Via del Parione 31r (055 215 722). **Open** 3-7pm Mon; 9.30am-7pm, Tue-Sat. **Credit** AmEx, DC, JCB, MC, V.

Bisonte started out just down the road; his distinctive label, a bison stamped on the leather, has since acquired world renown. Prices are sky-high but the goods are made to last.

Francesco da Firenze

Via di Santo Spirito 62r (055 212 428). Bus 11, 36, 37. **Open** 9am-1pm, 3-7.30pm, Mon-Sat. **Credit** AmEx, DC, MC, V.

Handmade shoes are made in thick, supple leather on the premises and, amazingly, are sold at prices not much higher than you would expect to pay for mass-produced shoes.

JP Tod's

Via Tornabuoni 103r (055 219 423). **Open** 3-7pm Mon; 10am-7.30pm Tue-Sat. **Credit** AmEx, DC, JCB, MC, V.

Americans crowd this shop out for the simple reason that the shoes and bags are cheaper than in the US.

Madova

Via Guicciardini 1r (055 239 6526). **Open** 10am-7.30pm Mon-Sat; *winter* Tue-Sat. **Credit** AmEx, MC, V.

A shrine to leather gloves. Every style and colour, made at the factory behind the shop. Prices start from L39,000 for a pair of unlined women's gloves and go right up to L350,000 for an exquisite, hand-made and silk-lined evening edition.

are in Borgo San Lorenzo) include **Donna** (26r; 055 289 850) and **Clash** (5r; 055 215 061), while for men there's **Desii** (4-6r; 055 211 222/055 292 321). Casual clothing for both sexes is available at **14 Once** (9r; 055 239 6074) and funkier, younger styles at **Ritratto** (53r; 055 295 091). All the above shops are also open on the last Sunday of the month.

A little more upmarket, **Luisa Via Roma** (Via Roma 19/21r, 055 217 826) is an Alta Moda super store whose interior design is as pleasing as its clothing. Big-name designers (Donna Karan, Calvin Klein, Dolce & Gabbana, Romeo Gigli, Gaultier) rub shoulders with lesser names; they also sell interesting shoes and accessories. Possibly the closest thing to hip street fashion is **Gerard** (Via Vacchereccia 18/20r; 055 215 942), where there are also some gorgeous Romeo Gigli suits.

A stroll down the Corso or Via dei Neri is also likely to turn up some clothing bargains. **The End** chain of stores (Via del Corso 39r; 055 215 948) and **Solomoda** (Via dei Neri 51r; no phone) are good places to start.

For second-hand clothes: **La Belle Epoque** (Borgo degli Albizi 78r; 055 234 0537) offers a little bit of everything, including Levis and some rather fetching antiquey items; and an unnamed shop at **Borgo Pinti 37r** stocks a good range of 1970s and other retrowear.

One final recommendation for women is **Echo** (Via dell'Oriuolo 37r; no phone), whose excellent range of striking sweaters, skirts and eveningwear, made-to-order or off-the-rack, carry incredibly low price tags. As a last resort, perhaps (and they're actually not that bad), there's always the clothing superstores **La Rinascente, COIN** or one of the numerous Benetton or Sisley outfits in town.

Peppe Peluso

Via del Corso 1/11r (055 268 283). **Open** 10am-1.30pm, 3.30-7.30pm, daily. **Credit** MC, V.
Classic leather shoes cost from L50,000, but more interesting are the contemporary designs.

Stefano Bemer

Borgo San Frediano 143r (055 211 356). Bus 6. **Open** 9am-1pm, 3.30-7.30pm, Mon-Sat **Credit** AmEx, DC, JCB, MC, V.
This tiny shop in the Oltrarno sells luxury hand-made shoes fashioned by a young shoemaker.

Vigna Nuova

Via della Vigna Nuova 81r (055 284 607). **Open** 3.30-7.30pm Mon; 10.30am-1pm, 3.30-7.30pm, Tue-Sat. **No credit cards**.
What? A cheap shop in designer land? Moccasins in mock leopardskin and velvet cost about L40,000.

Florists

Calvanelli

Via della Vigna Nuova 24 (055 213 742). **Open** 8am-1pm, 3.30-7.30pm, Mon, Tue, Thur-Sat; 7am-1pm Wed. **No credit cards**.
There is no charge for delivery within the city.

La Fioreria di Gabriele Carnovale

Borgo degli Albizi 29r (055 234 0860). **Open** 8am-1pm, 3.30-7.30pm, Mon,Tue, Thur-Sat; 8am-1pm Wed. **Credit** MC, V.
A wonderful place with something a little different to offer. L5,000 is charged for delivery within the city centre, L10,000 for further afield.

Galli

Via Guicciardini 11 (055 294 742). **Open** 7.30am-7.30pm Mon-Sat; some Sun mornings. **Credit** MC, V.
Delivery in Florence costs from L5,000 on top of the price of the flowers.

Food & drink

For food markets, *see below* **Markets**.

Arte Alimentare Meridionale

Piazza Ghiberti 33r (055 234 2696). **Open** 8.30am-8pm Mon-Sat. **No credit cards**.
A recently opened shop which stocks wonderful *mozzarella di bufala*, brought up regularly from Salerno, near Naples. Other excellent cheeses include *provolone*, smoked *casciotta* and fresh buffalo ricotta. Try the ricotta and parsley ravioli.

Bottega della Frutta

Via della Spada 58r (055 239 8590). **Open** 8am-7.30pm Mon, Tue, Thur-Sat; 8am-1.30pm Wed. **Credit** MC, V.
Fabulous fruit and veg shop, with carefully sourced produce from all over Italy.

Colivicchi

Via San Agostino 24 (055 210 001). **Open** 7.30am-1.30pm, 4-8pm, Mon, Tue, Thur-Sat; 7.30am-1.30pm Wed. **No credit cards**.
Prices are the lowest you can expect to find outside a market. You occasionally find a rotten apple in your bag, but it's still worth it. Colivicchi olive oil is extraordinary value at under L10,000 a litre.

La Dolciaria

Via de' Ginori 24r (055 214 646). **Open** 9am-1pm, 4-7.30pm, Mon-Sat. **Credit** MC, V.
Foods to quash ex-pat homesickness, from Tiptree jams to Jacobs' Crackers. Sweet Italian goodies too.

Gastronomia Galanti

Piazza della Libertà 31r (055 490 359). Bus to Piazza della Libertà. **Open** 8am-2pm, 5-8pm, Mon-Sat. **No credit cards.**
The mouth-watering delicacies laid out in this deli are ideal for picnic supplies.

Morgani

Piazza Santo Spirito 3r (055 289 230). **Open** 8.30am-1pm, 4.30-8pm, Mon, Tue, Thur-Sat; 8.30am-1pm Wed. **Credit** AmEx, DC, MC, V.
Morgani sells anything from cat food and loo roll to straw hats. It also sells basmati and Thai rice and a great dried soup mix called *Zuppa di Santo Spirito.*

Pegna

Via dello Studio 8 (055 282 701). **Open** 9am-1pm, 3.30-7.30pm, Mon, Tue, Thur-Sat; 9am-1pm Wed. **No credit cards.**
Upmarket grocery store selling just about everything, including Cheddar and Stilton cheeses.

Procacci

Via Tornabuoni 64r (055 212 656). **Open** 8am-1pm, 4.30-7.45pm, Mon, Tue, Thur-Sat; 8am-1pm Wed. **No credit cards.**
This is *the* place to buy truffles. They come in every day at around 10am during the season (Oct-Dec). The wood-panelled, stand-up bar is a genteel place to stop off for a glass of *prosecco* and a *panino tartuffato.*

I Sapori del Chianti

Via dei Servi 10 (055 238 2071). **Open** 9.30am-7.30pm daily. **Credit** AmEx, DC, V.
Food and drink from Chianti. Wines, grappas in fancy bottles, olive oils, *cantuccini*, *cavallucci* and *ossi di morto* biscuits, salami from the Falorni shop in Greve, and jars of pestos, condiments and vegetables preserved in extra virgin olive oil.

Stenio del Panta

Via Sant'Antonino 49r (055 216 889). **Open** 5-7.30pm Mon; 7am-1pm, 5-7.30pm, Tue-Sat. **Credit** AmEx, DC, MC, V.
Founded early this century, Stenio's deli is famous for its preserved fish (salt cod, high-quality canned tuna, Spanish sardines and marinated anchovies), but also sells hams, cheeses, olives, artichokes and capers. Ask them to construct a sandwich (of focaccia, country bread or *schiacciata*) around the fillings of your choice.

Sugar Blues

Via dei Serragli 57r (055 268 378). Bus 11, 36, 37. **Open** 9am-1.30pm, 4-7.30pm, Mon, Tue, Thur-Sat; 9am-1.30pm Wed. **No credit cards.**
Being one of the few such sources in town, Sugar Blues can afford to charge outrageous prices for organic vegetables, grains, pulses, breads and cakes plus natural cosmetics and beauty products.
Branch: Via XXVII Aprile 46/48r (055 483 666).

Bakeries

Il Fornaio

Via dei Guicciardini 6r (055 219 854). **Open** 7.30am-7.30pm Mon, Tue, Thur-Sat. **No credit cards.**
A great selection of all kinds of breads, focaccias, pizzas, cakes and biscuits straight from the oven.
Branches: Via Faenza 39r (055 215 314); Via Palmieri 24r (055 280 336).

Forno Top

Via della Spada 23r (055 212 461). **Open** 7.30am-1pm, 5-7.30pm, Mon, Tue, Thur-Sat; 7.30am-1pm Wed. **No credit cards.**
An excellent bakery: try the takeaway pizza, the *schiacciata*, and the *castagnaccio* (a crisp cake of chestnut flour and pine nuts, spiked with rosemary).

Deliveries

Ciao

Via Masaccio 101A (055 574 485). **Open** 10.30am-2.30pm, 5.30-10.30pm, daily. **Credit** V.
A good Chinese takeaway that will also deliver (minimum order L30,000). A set combination costs from L8,500, and a full meal will cost about L18,000.

Pronto Pizza

(055 716 767/055 716 768). **Open** 7-11pm daily. **No credit cards.**
Pizzas here start at L8,000 for a straightforward Margherita and increase to L15,000 for a creation with just about everything on top.

Runner Pizza

(055 333 333). **Open** noon-2pm, 6.30-11pm, Mon-Fri; 6.30-11pm Sat, Sun. **No credit cards.**
Pizzas cost L8,000-L12,000, and this includes a 'free' drink or ice cream. Delivery is L2,000 if you order one pizza; free if you order more.

Totoya

Via del Campuccio 12r (055 222 404). Bus to Santo Spirito. **Open** 11am-2pm, 6-10pm, Mon-Sat. **No credit cards.**
A new Japanese takeaway that also offers free home delivery. The menu changes according to the season.

Ethnic

Asia Masala

Piazza Santa Maria Novella 22r (055 281 800). **Open** 9.30am-8pm daily. **Credit** AmEx, DC, JCB, MC, V.
A wonderful source of foods from Asia with an increasing number of fresh ingredients.

Vivimarket

Via del Melarancio 17r (055 294 911). **Open** 9am-1pm, 3.30-7.30pm, Mon-Sat. **Credit** V.
Indian, Chinese, Japanese, Thai, Mexican and North African specialities weigh down the shelves in this popular shop. You can also get hold of rarer (for Italy) ingredients tofu, lemongrass, fresh coriander and ginger and a good stock of kitchen equipment.

Il Fornaio – *where all the cakes sell like, erm... hot cakes.* *See page 121.*

Pasta

Bianchi

Via del Albero 1r (055 282 246). **Open** 9am-1pm, 4.30-7.30pm, Mon, Tue, Thur-Sat; 9am-1pm Wed. **No credit cards**.

Spinach-and-ricotta ravioli and potato gnocchi are among the delights on offer in this modest shop.

La Bolognese

Via dei Serragli 24 (055 282 318). Bus 11, 36, 37. **Open** 7am-1pm, 4.30-7.30pm, Mon-Fri; 7am-1pm Sat. **No credit cards**.

As well as the bog-standard tagliatelle and spaghetti, fresh pasta here includes *ravioli di zucca gialla* (pumpkin), plus versions stuffed with porcini, potato or truffles (in season), as well as tortellini with smoked salmon, gnocchi and black squid-ink pasta.

Pasticcerie

Most *pasticcerie* have a bar, so they are good for breakfast coffees and snacks, but all cakes and savouries can also be take-away (say '*da portare via*'). If you are fortunate enough to be invited to dine in an Italian home, a tray of small cakes is a standard gift; they are usually sold by weight.

Cennini

Borgo San Jacopo 51r (055 294 930). **Open** 7.30am-7.30pm Tue-Sun. **No credit cards**.

A pleasant, family-run bar that does not charge you to sit down. Pastries and cakes to take away include an excellent *panettone* and the Easter *colomba*.

Dolci e Dolcezze

Piazza Beccaria 8r (055 234 5458). Bus 31, 32, B. **Open** 8.30am-8.30pm Mon-Sat; 8.30am-1pm, 4-8.30pm, Sun. **No credit cards**.

Possibly Florence's finest; known for its delectable, flourless chocolate cake. Don't limit yourself to that, however, the orange flan and the raspberry cake are also superb.

Branch: Via del Corso 41r (055 282 578).

Fabiani

Via Gelsomino 39r (055 232 0017). Bus 36, 37. **Open** 6am-9pm Tue-Sun. **No credit cards**.

Strategically placed on the road out of town to Siena, Fabiani's melt-in-the-mouth, buttery pastries are a fabulous start to the day as you head out of town. On the way back, try the *bomboloni caldi* (filled, hot doughnuts, freshly made at around 4pm).

La Loggia degli Albizzi

Borgo degli Albizzi 39r (055 247 9574). **Open** 7.30am-8pm Mon-Sat. **No credit cards**.

Not particularly inviting from the outside, this shop has superb small cakes; the individual *torta della nonna* (grandmother's tart) will melt in your mouth.

Marino

Piazza Nazario Sauro 19r (055 212 657). **Open** 6am-8pm Tue-Sun. **No credit cards**.

The pastries here have an extraordinarily high butter content. Sample them at their best at breakfast and tea time, when fresh batches are pulled steaming from the oven. The owners are Sicilian, so specialities include *cannoli siciliani* (ricotta and candied fruit pastry tubes), rum babas and cassata ice-cream cake.

Robiglio

Via dei Servi 112r (055 214 501). **Open** 7.30am-7.30pm Mon-Sat. **No credit cards**.

An old-fashioned pasticceria with superb pastries. Try their *cioccolato caldo*, hot chocolate thick enough to stand a spoon upright in it.

Branch: Via Tosinghi 11r (055 215 013).

Rosticcerie

Cheaper than eating out, easier than cooking for yourself – *rosticcerie* are a wonderful concept. They're basically take-away joints, but offer everything you need for a full meal, from crostini to roast meats (spit-roasted chickens are a favourite, you can buy them by the quarter, the half or the whole bird), vegetables and desserts. There's always a basic selection of wines. They often shut on Mondays.

Ramraj

Via Ghibellina 61r (055 240 999). **Open** 11.30am-3.30pm, 5-11pm Tue-Sun. **No credit cards.**
This Indian rosticceria's specialities are tandoori and moghul dishes. Prices start at L5,000 with a set menu at L15,000. An *à la carte* feast costs L23,000.

Rosticceria Alisio

Via dei Serragli 75r (055 225 192). **Open** 7am-2pm, 5-9pm, Tue-Sun. **No credit cards.**
Free home delivery within central Florence.

Rosticceria Giuliano

Via dei Neri 174r (055 238 2723). Bus 23. **Open** 8am-3pm, 5-9pm, Tue-Sat; 8am-3pm Sun. **Credit** AmEx, MC, V.
Relatively central place selling a huge selection of roasted meats and other savoury goodies.

Rosticceria Le Due Strade

Via Senese 161/163 (055 204 7594). Bus 36, 37. **Open** 9am-2pm, 5-9pm, Tue-Sat; 9am-2pm Sun. **No credit cards.**
Useful as a stop-off on your way into or out of town if you are heading in the Siena direction.

Supermarkets

There are no decent supermarkets in the centre of town, but it's worth the trek into the suburbs to stock up on biscuits, olive oils, vinegars and salamis at lower prices than in the specialist shops. There are two main supermarkets in Florence, each of which has several branches:

Esselunga

Via Pisana 130/132 (055 706 556). **Open** 2.30-9pm Mon; 8am-9pm Tue-Sat. **Credit** DC, MC, V.
Plenty of excellent fresh fruit and veg, some fresh fish, a groaning deli counter, good fresh meat and poultry and in-house bakery. All have free parking.
Branches: Via Masaccio 274/276 (055 573 348); Viale Gianotti 75/77 (055 683 613).

Co-Op

Viale Talenti 94/96 (055 702 073). Bus 1, 5. **Open** 8am-8pm Mon, Tue, Thur-Sat; 8am-1.30pm Wed. **No credit cards.**
Slightly more expensive than Esselunga (*see above*), the biggest of the Co-Ops has fresh vegetables and fruit, excellent fresh fish and deli counters and own-brand products.
Branches: Via Cimabue 49 (055 246 0199); Via Nazionale 32r (055 282 135).

Tea & coffee

Peter's Tea House

Piazza Strozzi 12-13r (055 213 879). **Open** 3.30-7.30pm Mon; 9am-7.30pm Tue-Sat. **Credit** AmEx, DC, MC, V.
A tea-drinker's delight: more than 240 types of teas, from Earl Grey to exotic herbal blends, infusions, spice blends – the choice is vast.

Torrefazione Fiorenza

Via Santa Monaca 2r (055 287 546). **Open** 8am-1pm, 5-7.30pm, Mon, Tue, Thur-Sat; 8am-1pm Wed. **No credit cards.**
An old-fashioned, aromatic little shop which grinds its own selection of coffees and sells all sorts of sweets and spices by weight as well.

Wine

See also chapter **Wine Bars.**

Enoteca Murgia

Via dei Banchi 55/57r (055 215 686). **Open** 3.30-7.30pm Mon; 9am-1pm, 3.30-7.30pm, Tue-Sat. **Credit** AmEx, V.
Long-established *enoteca* with a fine selection of olive oils, limoncellos and grappas as well as wines. Service is courteous, and you will be guided towards the best wines and oils for your money.

Gola e Cantina

Piazza Pitti 16 (055 212 704). **Open** 10am-1pm, 3-7pm, Tue-Sun. **Credit** AmEx, DC, MC, V.
An inviting shop with a good choice of wines, from a simple Chianti Putto for L10,000 to some superb Super Tuscans. Wine tastings and tasting courses are held regularly. There is also a selection of olive oils, designer chocolate, mustards and cookery books.

La Fiaschetteria

Via dei Serragli 47r (055 287 420). **Open** 8am-1pm, 3.30-8.30pm, Mon-Sat. **Credit** AmEx, MC, V.
An old-fashioned little place with a marble counter where the local soaks go for a glass in the evening. The shelves are stacked with fine wines with the more mundane plonk in big bottles on the floor.

Gifts & crafts

Animalmania

Via il Prato 38r (055 213 065). **Open** 3-8pm Mon; 10am-8pm Tue-Sat. **Credit** AmEx, DC, MC, V.
Pet shop which sells tarantulas, snakes and lizards.

Disney Store

Via dei Calzaiuoli 69r (055 291 633). **Open** 10am-8pm Mon-Sat; 11am-8pm Sun. **Credit** AmEx, MC, V.
If you really want to buy Disney in Florence.

Fornasetti

Borgo degli Albizi 70r (055 234 7398). Bus A. **Open** 3.30-7.30pm Mon; 9.30am-1pm, 3.30-7.30pm, Tue-Sat. **Credit** AmEx, MC, V.
Nothing but Fornasetti. A set of six espresso cups and saucers for L180,000, plates cost from L1,250,000.

Marchi

Borgo degli Albizi 69-71r (055 234 0415). **Open** 3.30-7.30pm Mon; 9.30-1pm, 3.30-7.30pm, Tue-Sat. **Credit** AmEx, DC, MC, V.

Guatamalan textiles, Indian bedspreads, Nepalese lamps as well as clothes, toys and other nick-nacks.

Messico e Nuvole

Borgo degli Albizi 54r (055 242 677). **Open** 3.45-7.45pm Mon; 10am-1.30pm, 3.45-7.45pm, Tue-Sat. **Credit** AmEx, MC, V.

This bright shop (run by an Italo-Mexican couple) stocks colourful Mexican and Native American jewellery, ceramics, pipes and some furniture.

Mineral Shop

Via dei Servi 120r (055 218 281). **Open** 3.30-7.30pm Mon; 9.30am-1pm, 3.30-7.30pm, Tue-Sat. **Credit** AmEx, DC, MC, V.

Fossils, chunks of minerals, and jewellery made of semi-precious stones.

Progetto Verde

Piazza Tasso 11 (055 229 8029). Bus 12, 13. **Open** 3.30-7.30pm Mon; 9am-1pm, 3.30-7.30pm, Tue-Sat. **Credit** AmEx, DC, MC, V.

Anyone seriously green should know about this shop; it sells everything from non-toxic paints to recycled paper, essential oils and futons.

Siddhartha

Via Cesare Battisti 5r (no phone). **Open** 4-8pm Mon; 10am-1pm, 4-8pm, Tue-Sat. **No credit cards.**

Hippy trail textiles, bags, tarot cards and jewellery.

Farmacia di Santa Maria Novella.

Health & beauty

Body Shop

I Gigli Shopping Centre, Via San Quirico 165, Campi Bisenzio (055 896 9600). Bus 30, 35 to Campi Bisenzio, then bus 60. **Open** 2-9pm Mon; 9am-9pm Tue-Sat, and 1st Sun of month. **Credit** MC, V.

A branch of the English cruelty-free cosmetics chain. Prices are roughly 30 per cent more than in the UK.

Erboristeria Aux Herbes Sauvages

Via dei Cimatori 2r (055 217 570). **Open** 9.30am-1pm, 4.30-7.30pm, Tue-Sat. **Credit** MC, V.

A herbalist based in the historic centre of Florence, which makes its own line of essential oils and other herbal infusions.

Farmacia del Cinghiale

Piazza del Mercato Nuovo 4r (055 212 128). **Open** 9am-1pm, 3.30-7.30pm, Mon-Fri; Sat according to rota. **Credit** AmEx, MC, V.

Cinghiale was founded in the eighteenth century by a herbalist named Guadagni. His laboratory was upstairs, where experiments were conducted and cures were sold to the public downstairs. Now it has its own line of natural cosmetics.

Farmacia Franchi

Via de' Ginori 65r (055 210 565). **Open** 9am-1pm, 4-8pm, Mon-Fri; Sat according to rota. **Credit** DC, MC, V.

Although it occupies the site of a fourteenth-century pharmacy, Franchi's interior décor is early twentieth-century in origin (but the wrought-iron sign in the window is original). It specialises in herbal remedies and homeopathic treatments.

Farmacia Molteni

Via dei Calzaiuoli 7r (055 215 472). **Open** 24 hrs daily. **Credit** AmEx, MC, V.

A lavishly carved and gilded eighteenth-century pharmacy on the historic centre's main drag.

Farmacia di Santa Maria Novella

Via della Scala 16 (055 216 276). **Open** 3.30-7.30pm Mon; 9.30am-7.30pm Tue-Sat. **Credit** AmEx, DC, MC, V.

An ancient pharmacy housed in a thirteenth-century frescoed chapel, which makes up lotions and potions similar to those concocted by sixteenth-century friars. Aqua di Santa Maria Novella for its calming properties, aromatic vinegar for treating fainting ladies, as well as more mundane things such as shampoos and soaps are made on the premises. Staff are knowledgeable and helpful, and it is a wonderful place for (expensive) gifts.

Sigillo

Via Porta Rossa 23r (055 287 732). **Open** 3.30-7.30pm Mon; 10am-1pm, 3.30-7.30pm, Tue-Sat. **Credit** AmEx, DC, MC, V.

The only source in town for Neal's Yard oils, unguents and soaps plus Zarvis bath oils and other wonderful smelly stuffs.

Chic to chic

Most of the city's international designer shops are strung along Via Tornabuoni and Via Vigna Nuova. Addresses are as follows:

Armani *Via della Vigna Nuova 51r (055 219 041).* **Open** 3.30-7.30pm Mon; 10am-7.30pm Tue-Sat. **Credit** AmEx,DC, JCB, MC, V.
All the usual Armani favourites; ultra understated, ultra elegant.

Bulgari *Via Tornabuoni 61/63r (055 239 6786).* **Open** 3-7.30pm Mon; 10am-1pm, 3-7.30pm, Tue-Sat. **Credit** AmEx, DC, JCB, MC, V.
A lot of the jewellery here is really vulgar, and it is all astronomically priced. Scarves, accessories and perfume as well.

Emporio Armani *Piazza Strozzi 16r (055 284 315).* **Open** 3.30-7.30pm Mon; 10am-2pm, 3.30-7.30pm, Tue-Sat. **Credit** AmEx, DC, JCB, MC, V.
Not all the clothes are as well-made as they should be in Armani's diffusion line; check the seams before you hand over the cash.

Enrico Coveri *Via Tornabuoni 81r (055 211 263).* **Open** 3.30am-7.30pm Mon; 10am-1.30pm, 3.30-7.30pm, Tue-Sat. **Credit** DC, MC, V.
Prato creator of loud, brash clothes. The diffusion line is just next door in Via della Vigna Nuova.

Ferragamo *Via Tornabuoni 14r (055 292 123).* **Open** 3.30-7.30pm Mon; 9.30am-7.30pm Tue-Sat. **Credit** AmEx, DC, JCB, MC, V.
Fantastic shoes from the company founded by Salvatore Ferragamo in the 1920s. Nowadays they also design clothes and accessories, but it's the shoes that are worth splashing out on.

Gucci *Via Tornabuoni 73r (055 264 011).* **Open** 3-7pm Mon; 9.30am-7pm Tue-Sat. **Credit** AmEx, DC, JCB, MC, V.
Gucci has a more contemporary look these days – there's not a stirrup or headscarf in sight in their cool window displays. It remains popular with Japanese shoppers, who are standing outside the doors first thing in the morning.

Louis Vuitton Via Tornabuoni 24-28r (055 214 344). **Open** 3-7.30pm Mon; 9.30am-7.30pm Tue-Sat. **Credit** AmEx, DC, JCB, MC, V.
Buy the fakes on the Ponte Vecchio or go for the genuine, brown, orange-peel bags and accessories; only you will know the difference.

Prada *Via Tornabuoni 67r (055 283 439).* **Open** 3-7pm Mon; 10am-7pm Tue-Sat. **Credit** AmEx, DC, JCB, MC, V.
Chic, minimalist styles from the darling of the Japanese. Their carrier bags are cute, too…

Pucci *Via Vigna Nuova 97r (055 294 028).* **Open** 3.30-7.30pm Mon; 10am-1pm, 3.30-7.30pm, Tue-Sat. **Credit** AmEx, DC, MC, V.
Psychedelic printed shirts and leggings, little changed since the first 1950s designs by aristocrat Emilio Pucci.

Trussardi *Via Tornabuoni 34/36r (055 219 902).* **Open** 3-7pm Mon; 10am-7pm Tue-Sat. **Credit** AmEx, DC, JCB, MC, V.
Niccolò Trussardi's recent death in a car crash has fixed his name in fashion history books. Italians think his classic leather bags, jackets, tweed trousers and overcoats very English; the English think it looks *molto italiano*.

Hairdressers

Hairdressers in Florence are closed on Mondays.

Carlo Bay Hair Diffusion

Via Marsuppini 18r (055 681 1876). **Open** 9am-7pm Tue-Sat. **Credit** AmEx, DC, MC, V.
This unisex salon has English-speaking staff, who specialise in colour. It costs L62,000 for a cut and blow dry.

De Stijl

Via Cavour 170Ar (055 578 295). Bus 1, 11. **Open** 9.30am-6pm Tue-Thur; 9am-6pm Fri, Sat. **Credit** AmEx, MC, V.
This lively, unisex salon leans towards the young and trendy, but caters to all. A wash and cut costs L38,000, a blow dry L22,000. English is spoken.

Mario's

Via della Vigna Nuova 22r (055 294 813). **Open** *hairdresser* 9am-6pm Tue-Sat; *beauty salon* 9am-7pm Tue-Sat; *profumeria* 3.30-7.30pm Mon; 9am-7.30pm Tue-Sat. **Credit** AmEx, DC, JCB, MC, V.
This shop combines a *profumeria* (selling perfumes and cosmetics), a beauty parlour and a hair salon. It is popular with well-heeled signoras. L50,000 will cover the cost of a haircut (blow drying is extra), a full leg wax or a facial. Some staff speak English.

Stefano Pavi

Via dei Serragli 17 (055 287 636). Bus 11. **Open** 9am-8pm Tue-Sat. **Credit** DC, MC, V.
A predominantly men's hairdresser located in an old palazzo just south of the Arno. A wash, cut and dry will cost from L50,000.

Health centres

Acquabel

Piazza Pier Vettori 12 (055 229 434). Bus 6. **Open** 10am-8.30pm Mon-Fri; 10am-3pm Sat. **Credit** AmEx, DC, MC, V.

A beauty salon, gym, sauna, Turkish bath, Jacuzzi and hairdresser. Prices for a facial begin at L80,000, a haircut and dry starts at L50,000. Day membership, which entitles you to use all facilities, costs L40,000.

Hito Estetica

Via de' Ginori 21 (055 284 424). Bus 11, 17. **Open** 9am-8pm Mon-Sat. **Credit** AmEx, MC, V.

Hito specialises in treatments using natural products, including Yurvedic techniques. Prices start from L35,000 for a facial and L55,000 for a full leg wax.

Istituto Freni

Via Pasquale Villari 6B (055 676 686). **Open** 9.30am-1pm, 3-7pm, Mon-Fri; 9am-1pm Sat. **Credit** AmEx, MC, V.

If your feet give out after all those museums, come to the Freni for a foot treatment. Other treatments are available: facials are L80,000; leg waxes are L60,000.

Opticians

Camera and optical lenses go hand in hand in Italy: photography shops sell glasses and opticians sell basic photo equipment. *See below* **Photography**.

Pisacchi

Via Condotta 22/24r (055 214 542). **Open** 4-8pm Mon; 9am-1pm, 4-8pm, Tue-Sat. **Credit** AmEx, DC, MC, V.

This contact lens specialist carries out eye tests.

Sbisa

Piazza Signoria 10r (055 211 339). **Open** 3.30-7.30pm Mon; 9am-7.30pm Tue-Sat. **Credit** AmEx, DC, MC, V.

Armani, Gucci, Ralph Lauren, Valentino, Versace; this shop has them all, plus a good range of optical and photographic equipment.

Home accessories

See also **Gifts & crafts**.

Arredamenti Castorina

Via di Santo Spirito 13/15r (055 212 885). **Open** 9am-1pm, 3.30-7.30pm, Mon-Fri; 9am-1pm Sat. **Credit** AmEx, DC, MC, V.

This extraordinary shop, over 100 years old, has all things baroque: carved and gilded mouldings, frames, cherubs and candelabra, trompe l'œil tables and fake malachite and tortoiseshell obelisks.

Giraffa

Via Ginori 20r (055 283 652). **Open** 3.30-7.30pm Mon; 9am-1pm, 3.30-7.30pm, Tue-Sat. **Credit** AmEx, DC, MC, V.

Good source of presents for the home: brightly coloured silk lamps, Italian and Moroccan ceramics, candles, candelabra and heavy glazed earthenware.

Oltrefrontiera

Via Mazzetta 14r (055 213 496). **Open** 10am-1pm, 3.30-8pm, Tue-Sat, 2nd Sun of month. **Credit** AmEx, DC, MC, V.

The Florence branch of a franchise chain selling furniture, lighting, basketware and *objets* from India, Indonesia, Africa, and the Philippines.

Patti

Borgo degli Albizi 64r (055 243 610). **Open** 3.30-7.30pm Mon; 10am-1pm, 3.30-7.30pm, Tue-Sat. **Credit** AmEx, DC, MC, V.

A cosy little shop selling African textiles, Japanese lacquerware and ceramics, silver-trimmed Moroccan ceramics, Japanese teapots, Persian carpets, along with the odd antique piece from Burma or Tibet.

Sakura

Via del Melarancio 4r (055 264 045). **Open** 4-7.30pm Mon; 9am-7.30pm, Tue-Sun; *winter* closed Sun. **Credit** AmEx, DC, MC, V.

Among the tourist fare are some tasteful Japanese goods: tea sets, lacquer bowls, brushes, calligraphy pens, cotton kimonos and handmade paper.

Le Stanze

Borgo Ognissanti 50/52r (055 288 921). Bus 12, C. **Open** 3.30-7.30pm Mon; 10am-1pm, 3.30-7.30pm, Tue-Sat. **Credit** AmEx, DC, MC, V.

Stylish design emporium selling desirable objects like cerulean-glazed clay pots, cubic candles and canvas magazine racks.

Zona

Via di Santo Spirito 11 (055 230 2272). **Open** 9.30-7.30pm Mon-Sat. **Credit** AmEx, JCB, MC, V.

The emphasis is on natural, handmade materials including textiles, glassware, furniture, wrought iron and pewter, candles, books, toys and clothes. Sale time is about the only chance of a bargain.

Ceramics

La Botteghina del Ceramista

Via Guelfa 5r (055 287 367). **Open** 3.30-7.30pm Mon; 9.30am-1pm, 3.30-7.30pm, Tue-Sat. **Credit** AmEx, DC, JCB, MC, V.

Superb, hand-painted ceramics in intricate designs and vivid colours. It is not your common or garden stuff: prices go up to L780,000 for a plate. There are plenty of cheaper, still stunning alternatives, though.

Sbigoli Terrecotte

Via Sant' Egidio 4r (055 247 9713). Bus A. **Open** 3.30-7.30pm Mon; 9am-1pm, 3.30-7.30pm, Tue-Sat. **Credit** AmEx, DC, MC, V.

Handmade Tuscan ceramics and terracotta, mostly in traditional designs. Terracotta casseroles (known for their heat-retaining qualities) start at L20,000.

Il Tegame

Piazza Salvemini 7 (055 248 0568). Bus A. **Open** 3.30-7.30pm Mon; 9.30am-1pm, 3.30-7.30pm, Tue-Sat. **Credit** AmEx, MC, V.

A nicely cluttered shop, whose every inch of shelf space is filled with ceramics, terracotta and glassware.

Leonardo Romanelli *plys his trade in the Oltrarno, an area still full of artisans.*

Kitchenware

Bartolini

Via dei Servi 30r (055 211 895). **Open** 3.30-7.30pm Mon; 9am-1pm, 3.30-7.30pm, Tue-Sat. **Credit** AmEx, V.

A good all-round kitchen shop stocking everything from Alessi and Le Creuset to woks and mincers.

La Ménagère

Via Ginori 4r-8r (055 213 875). **Open** 3.30-7.30pm Mon; 9am-1pm, 3.30-7.30pm, Tue-Sat. **Credit** AmEx, DC, MC, V.

Stock ranges from Starck's designs for Alessi to ceramic roasting dishes in the form of a gaudy duck.

Open House

Via Barbadori 40r (055 212 094). **Open** 10am-1pm, 2.30-7.30pm, Tue-Sat. **Credit** AmEx, MC, V.

A dream of a kitchen shop for anybody with a generous budget interested in contemporary design.

Locksmiths

Avoid the 24-hour emergency locksmiths listed under *Fabro* in the Yellow Pages; their charges are abusive. To get back into a flat, call the fire brigade; into a car, call the **ACI** (*see chapter* **Directory: Driving in Florence**).

SOS Casa

(055 434 030/434 445). **Open** 8am-8pm daily. **No credit cards**.

Expensive, but useful for any kind of household emergency, SOS Casa's prices start with a call-out charge of L30,000 on weekdays and L40,000 on weekends. Add to this L40,000 per hour and the cost of any materials used, and you have a hefty bill, but it's reassuring to know they are there. Plumbers, locksmiths, carpenters, electricians are all on call.

Picture framers

Leonardo Romanelli

Via Santo Spirito 16r (055 284 794). **Open** 9am-1pm, 3-8pm, Mon-Fri; 9am-1pm Sat. **No credit cards**.

Framing is generally cheap in Italy and the friendly Mr Romanelli offers both excellent frames and workmanship. A small frame costs about L30,000.

Markets

Cascine

Parco dell Cascine, Viale Lincoln. Bus 1, 9, 12. **Open** 8am-1pm Tue.

A better bet than the Mercato Centrale as few tourists venture out here. Over 300 stalls selling everything from live chickens to shoes. Lots of cheap tack, but you can find the odd designer bargain.

Mercato Centrale

Piazza del Mercato Centrale and adjacent streets. **Open** *clothes* 8.30am-7pm Mon-Sat; *food* 7am-2pm Mon-Fri; Sat afternoons in winter.

Fruit, vegetables, meat, fish and deli items are sold in the nineteenth-century covered market, and clothes, gloves, bags, Botticelli T-shirts, souvenirs and accessories in the sprawl of stalls outside.

Mercato Nuovo (Mercato del Porcellino)

Loggia Mercato Nuova. **Open** 9am-7pm Mon-Sat.

The sixteenth-century loggia (*see also chapter* **Florence by Area**) is now devoted to the tourist tat of the Straw Market: plastercasts of Michelangelo's *David*, mass-produced leather goods, cheap jewellery and suchlike.

Mercato di Sant'Ambrogio

Piazza Ghiberti. Bus A. **Open** 7am-2pm Mon-Sat.

Florence's foremost and cheapest produce market.

Fish, meat, cheese, salamis, hams, and all manner of fruit and veg in and around a decaying nineteenth-century building. Outside are cheap clothes stalls.

Mercato delle Pulci

Piazza dei Ciompi. Bus A. **Open** 9am-7pm Mon-Sat.
A good fleamarket with plenty of genuine household and wardrobe throw-outs as well as cheap hippy trail tat, and antique/bric-a-brac stalls.

Plant Market

Piazza della Repubblica. **Open** 8am-1pm Thur.
A sweet-smelling, colourful, good value plant market under the arches outside the main post office.

Santo Spirito

Piazza Santo Spirito. **Open** 8am-6pm 2nd Sun of month.
A lively fleamarket with bric-a-brac, used clothes, handmade jewellery and ceramics, old prints, ethnic jewellery and garments… and a fair amount of tat.

Photography

Bongi

Via Por Santa Maria 82/84r (055 239 8811). **Open** 3.30-7.30pm Mon; 9am-1pm, 3.30-7.30pm, Tue-Sat. **Credit** AmEx, DC, MC, V.
One of the biggest and best-equipped shops in the centre of the city. It carries a wide range of second-hand photographic equipment.

It's all gone quiet at **Kaos**.

Foto Levi

Vicolo dell'Oro 12/14r (055 294 002). **Open** 9am-1pm, 3.30-7.30pm, Mon-Fri; 9am-1pm Sat. **Credit** AmEx, MC, V.
Tucked away behind the Ponte Vecchio, this tiny shop is a useful, central place to have film developed. Ready in 60 minutes, a 24-exposure colour film will cost L15,000.

Foto Ottica Fontani

Viale Strozzi 18/20A (055 470 981). Bus 4, 13. **Open** 3.30-7.30pm Mon; 9am-1pm, 3.30-7.30pm, Tue-Sat. **No credit cards**.
This family-run shop prints over 3,000 films per day and is a mecca for all photography enthusiasts. The prices for processing and developing are the lowest in Florence: L9,000 for 24 exposures, overnight service. They also stock glasses by Armani, Byblos and Ralph Lauren.

Records

Data Records

Via dei Neri 15r (055 287 592). **Open** 3.30-7.30pm Mon; 10am-1pm, 3.30-9.30pm, Tue-Sat. **Credit** MC, V.
An amazing shop packed with vinyl, from old 78s to 12" singles. There are over 80,000 titles in stock with some emphasis on psychadelic, blues, r&b, jazz and soundtracks, both new and second-hand. They specialise in finding the unfindable.

Disco Emporium

Via dell Studio 11r (055 295 101). **Open** 3.30-7.30pm Mon; 9am-1pm, 3.30-7.30pm, Tue-Sat. **Credit** MC, V.
Hidden in a little side street behind the Duomo, this misleadingly named record shop that specialises in historic opera recordings.

KAOS

Via della Scala 65r (055 282 643). **Open** 10.30am-1pm, 3.30-7.30pm, Tue-Sat. **Credit** AmEx, MC, V.
The hippest record shop in town, stocking a great range of UK and US imports. It is especially strong on drum'n'bass and 1970s vinyl. Naturally it is much frequented by DJs.

Rock Bottom

Via degli Alfani 43r (055 245 220). **Open** 10am-1pm, 3.30-7.30pm, Mon-Fri; 10am-7.30pm Sat. **Credit** DC, MC, V.
Eclectic second-hand CD and record store with a strong world music section, and sections devoted to medieval, avant garde and experimental stuff, as well as the more predictable selection of metal, grunge and 1960s classics.

Setticlavio

Via Guelfa 19r (055 287 017). **Open** 3.30-7.30pm Mon; 9am-1pm, 3.30-7.30pm, Tue-Sat. **Credit** DC, MC, V.
A well-stocked classical record shop with over 30,000 titles. Operatic repertoire is well-represented.

Weighty matters – **Mercato Centrale**, *p127.*

Stationery & artists' supplies

Cartoleria Ecologica La Tartaruga

Borgo Albizi 60r (055 234 0845). **Open** 1.30-7.30pm Mon; 9am-7.30pm Tue-Sat. **Credit** MC, V.
Unusual stationery made from recycled paper.

Manzani

Piazza San Felice (055 229 8936). **Open** 9am-7.30pm Mon-Fri; 9am-1pm Sat. **Credit** AmEx, DC, MC, V.
Paper from East Asia and India along with paints, enamels, brushes, stencils and other artists' supplies.

Pineider

Piazza della Signoria 13r (055 284 655). **Open** 3.30-7.30pm Mon; 10am-7.30pm Tue-Sat. **Credit** AmEx, DC, JCB, MC, V.
There has been a stationery shop on this site since 1774, when Francesco Pineider opened his business. Unfortunately the original interior was destroyed in the 1966 flood, but the family firm continues to be famous for high-quality paper and writing accessories.

Romeo

Via Condotta 43r (055 210 350). **Open** 9am-7.30pm Mon-Sat. **Credit** AmEx, DC, MC, V.
An excellent general stationers with some upmarket leather and paper goods as well.

Zecchi

Via dello Studio 19r (055 211 470). **Open** 8.30am-12.30pm, 3.30-7.30pm, Mon-Fri; 8.30am-12.30pm Sat. **Credit** AmEx, DC, MC, V.
Heaven for artists, this fascinating shop sells everything from pencils to gold leaf and is worth visiting even if you are not interested in buying art supplies.

Handmade, marbled paper

Several Florentine workshops produce decorative papers (often used as fly papers in books) using age-old methods. A gelatine solution is made up of water and marine algae and poured into a shallow tray. Coloured inks are dropped in which float on the gelatine solution. Forms are made by drawing metal combs through the liquid, and when the design is finished, a sheet of paper is placed on top. This absorbs the inks and is then hung up to dry. Each sheet will take about ten minutes to make once the solution is mixed.

A Cozzi

Via del Parione 35r (055 294 968). **Open** 9am-1pm, 3-7pm, Mon-Fri. **Credit** AmEx, MC, V.
This bookbinders has a selection of books with marbled paper covers, some bound in leather.
Branch Via Sant'Agostino.

Take home some cantuccini to soak up your Vin Santo.

Hands up for **Madova** *gloves. See p118.*

Giulio Giannini e Figlio

Piazza Pitti 36r (055 212 621). **Open** 9am-7.30pm Mon-Sat; *winter* Tue-Sat. **Credit** AmEx, DC, MC, V.
This book-binding and paper-making company was founded in 1856 by the Gianninis and the family still runs it from the workshop upstairs on the first floor. They stock marbled books, leather desk accessories, and unusual greetings cards.

Il Torchio

Via dei Bardi 17 (055 234 2862). Bus D. **Open** 9am-7.30pm Mon-Fri; 10am-1pm Sat. **Credit** AmEx, MC, V.
This is a working business and you can see book-binding being done on the big, central table. The handmade paper comes in all colours and designs, and the books, boxes, stationery and albums are reasonably priced. Il Torchio also supplies Liberty's.

Shipping

Fracassi

Via Santo Spirito 11 (055 283 597). **Open** 8.30am-12.30pm, 2.30-6.30pm, Mon-Fri. **No credit cards**.
Not the cheapest movers in town, but they are very central and will move anything, anywhere.

Gondrand

Via Baldanzese 198 (055 882 6376). Bus 28C. **Open** 8.30am-12.30pm, 2.30-6.30pm, Mon-Fri. **No credit cards**.
Gondrand provides reliable international or local shipping and moving. It has offices throughout Italy, storage facilities and free estimates. English spoken.

Ticket agencies

When booking tickets over the phone, make sure that the arrangements for the collection or delivery of the tickets are specified clearly.

Box Office

Via Alammanni 39 (055 210 804). **Open** 10am-7.30pm Tue-Sat; 3.30-7.30pm Mon. **No credit cards**.
Tickets for concerts, theatre and exhibitions in Florence, Italy and abroad. There are 20 branches in Tuscany. Go in person: the telephone will be busy.
Branch: Chiasso de Soldanieri 8r (055 293 393).

Travel agents

Belvedere Viaggi

Via dei Serragli 38r (055 290 558). **Open** 9.30am-1pm, 3-7.30pm, Mon-Fri; 9.30am-1pm Sat. **Credit** MC, V.
A small, friendly and helpful travel agent that is especially sympathetic to student needs. They book air, train and boat tickets and have a change service.

CTS (Student Travel Centre)

Via dei Ginori 25r (055 289 570). **Open** 9.30am-1.30pm, 2.30-6pm, Mon-Fri; 9.30am-12.30pm Sat. **No credit cards**.
The official student travel service offers discounted air, coach and train tickets to all destinations. Some discounts are only available for students, but you do not need to be one to take out obligatory membership (L45,000 for non-students, L15,000 for students).

Intertravel

Via Lamberti 39r (055 217 936). **Open** 9am-6.30pm Mon-Fri; 9am-noon Sat. **Credit** AmEx, MC, V.
A busy and efficient travel agent offering a full range of services, a currency exchange and a DHL service.

Lazzi Express

Piazza Adua/Piazza Stazione (055 215 155). Bus to Santa Maria Novella station. **Open** 9am-6.30pm Mon-Fri; 9am-2pm, 3-6pm, Sat. **No credit cards**.
Lazzi has information and tickets for coach services within Italy, and for Euroline international services.

Nouvelles Frontières

Piazza N Sauro 17r (055 214 733). Bus 11. **Open** 9am-1pm, 2.30-6.30pm, Mon-Fri; 9am-1pm Sat. **Credit** AmEx.
Some of the cheapest air tickets available in Florence. It is also an agent for the Corsica/Sardinia ferry line.

Video rental

Blockbuster

Viale Belfiore 6A (055 330 542). Bus 4, 14, 23. **Open** 11am-11pm Mon-Thur, Sun; 11am-midnight Fri, Sat. **Credit** V.
Finally, a decent video store in Florence with a good number of films in English. Registration is L10,000 and films cost L6,000-L8,000 for 48 hours.
Branch: Via di Novoli 9/11 (055 333 533).

Punto Video

Via San Antonino 7r (055 284 813). **Open** 9am-8pm Mon-Sat. **No credit cards**.
Over 500 English titles to choose from. Membership is free, and videos cost L5,000 per night.

Arts & Entertainment

Children

Florentine family fun.

Admiring art is not exactly a child's idea of having a good time; to avoid your kids developing a permanent aversion to churches and museums in general, and to the Renaissance in particular, it's worth discovering what else Florence has to offer. Italians love children, so they are welcomed almost everywhere, in fact, they'll be pampered and smiled at much more than at home. Florence itself has many child-friendly attractions; gardens with merry-go-rounds and swings, swimming pools and museums with wax figures, mummies and stuffed animals (*see chapter* **Museums & Galleries**). Older children will appreciate the Internet centres, games stores and outdoor clothes markets.

When the old town centre was built the principal means of transportation was by horse. A good game can be made of finding and counting the rings used to tie horses that often remain on buildings. The quiet streets around Piazza Santo Spirito provide a pleasant respite from all the shop windows. While you're meandering, it's fascinating to peek into workshops to see artisans applying gold leaf, carving wood or polishing silver.

Though many children love pizza and spaghetti there are familiar fast-food joints in the city, and your children's eyes will probably pop out when they see the ice-cream choices.

If your kids like nature there's plenty of easily accessible countryside near the city, and farmers usually tolerate a discrete invasion of their olive groves for walks and picnics. The prospect of a day at the sea or the hot springs tends to make kids more tolerant about visiting monasteries and Etruscan tombs along the way.

Every Thursday *La Repubblica*, in the Florentine edition, has a page called Happy Days which carries information on events for children. For numbers to call in case of emergencies, *see chapter* **Directory**.

Babysitting

Check the notice boards of the children's lending library in **St James' American Church**, British Institute (*see chapter* **Directory**), Paperback Exchange (*see chapter* **Shopping & Services**) and **Ludoteca Centrale**.

Canadian Island

Via Gioberti 15 (055 677 312/canadian@ats.it). Bus 3, 6, 14. **Open** 3-6.30pm Mon-Fri; 9.30am-1pm Sat. **Admission** L40,000 per afternoon (package deals available for longer periods). **No credit cards**.

Children can be left here for hours to play in an English-speaking environment, while mixing with Italian children learning English. English-speaking summer camps are also organised on farms.

Bookshops & libraries

In addition to places listed here, **Paperback Exchange** has an excellent children's section plus toys to distract little ones while you browse (*see chapter* **Shopping: Books**).

After Dark

Via de'Ginori 47r (055 294 203). **Open** 10am-2pm, 3.30-6.30pm, Mon-Sat. **Credit** AmEx, DC, JCB, MC, V.

Sells a huge range of British and American magazines, comics and books.

Biblioteca dei Ragazzi Santa Croce

Via Tripoli 34 (055 247 8551). **Open** 9am-1.30pm Mon, Wed, Fri; 9am-1.30pm, 2.30-5.30pm Tue, Thur.

Anyone can borrow or browse the books, CDs, videos and magazines in this peaceful library for children aged two to 16.

Natura e...

Via dello Studio 30r (055 265 7624). **Open** 3.30-7.30pm Mon, Sun; 10am-1pm, 3.30-7.30pm Tue-Sat. **No credit cards**.

Nature maniacs' shop, selling everything from scientific toys, experiments, optical illusions to outdoor trekking gear. Also has pamphlets on WWF activities and parks in Tuscany.

St James' American Church

Via Bernardo Rucellai 9 (info: Kathy Procissi 055 577 527; Mary Diamond 055 714 779). **Open** 10-11.30am, 3.30-5.30pm Wed; 11.30am-1pm Sun. **Membership** *books* L15,000; *videos* L15,000; *books & videos* L25,000.

A friendly place with a good selection of English-language books, videos and games. On Saturdays before festivals children are invited to small parties where they make and paint decorations and masks.

Festivities

During **Carnevale**, on Sundays especially, you'll see children in fancy dress in the piazzas and on the Lungarno Amerigo Vespucci. During the **Diladdarno Festival** children of all ages can enjoy excellent open-air puppet shows in the

Piazza di Cestello. For this and other festivals and events, *see chapter* **Tuscany by Season**.

La Rificolona

One day in September every year, children make paper lanterns with a candle in the centre or buy them in the local stationery shops. They gather in the evening either in Piazza SS Annunziata or along the river (posters give details of the gatherings). After dark, with their lanterns lit and bobbing up and down on long bamboo poles, the children parade about singing. Traditionally boys use peashooters to blow paper darts into the little girls' lanterns to set them on fire. You will often see a delighted boy and wailing girl holding a burning lantern with onlookers laughing.

La Befana

In the past, it was at Befana (Epiphany), not Christmas, that children in Italy got their presents (that's when the magi brought theirs). The story goes that on the eve of 6 January a poor, tattered old woman (*la befana*), riding a donkey (or a broom) and carrying a sack full of toys, fills children's stockings with toys and sweets (or coal, if they have been naughty). On the eve of Befana children leave biscuits and milk out for the old lady and some hay for her donkey near where they have hung their stockings. Christmas is more celebrated now, but there is lingering affection for La Befana (there was uproar when this public holiday was cancelled a few years ago; it was rapidly restored).

Food

Florentine mothers give fingers of *schiacciata all' olio* (white pizza with salt and olive oil) to babies to chew on and the taste clearly stays with them, since children buy big squares of it before school, stuffed with a little ham or mortadella. Every season has its speciality: during September's grape harvest it's *schiacciata all'uva* (with grapes) and *castagnaccio* (a flat cake made with chestnut flour with pine nuts and raisins); try *panettone* at Christmas, *schiacciata alla Fiorentina* or *cenci* ('rags', sweet, deep-fried strips of pastry doused with icing sugar) during Carnevale, and for Easter it's *colomba* (dove-shaped sponge cake with almonds). Italian ice-cream is sold all year round at the *gelaterie*. The best ones for kids are **Festival del Gelato, Perchè No!** and **Vivoli** (*see chapter* **Cafés & Bars**).

Il Cucciolo

Via del Corso 25r (055 287 727). **Open** 7.30am-8.30pm Mon-Sat. **No credit cards.**

This bar is famous among Florentine children because in a first-floor room *bomboloni* (pastries, plain or filled with cream, chocolate or jam) are made and dropped down a tube to the bar below and served hot.

Kenny's

Via dei Bardi 64r (055 214 502). **Open** 11am-11pm daily. **Credit** MC, V.

This fast-food joint serving hamburgers and pizzas has a breathtaking view on to the Ponte Vecchio.

McDonald's

Santa Maria Novella Station (055 292 040). **Open** *outside station* 24hrs daily; *inside station* 6am-midnight. **No credit cards.**

There are branches inside and outside the station and in Via Cavour.

Mr Jimmy's American Bakery

Via San Niccolò 47 (055 248 0999). Bus D. **Open** 10am-8pm Tue-Sun. **No credit cards.**

Mr Jimmy's has American-style apple pie, chocolate cake, cheesecake, muffins, brownies and bagels.

Pit Stop

Via F Corridoni 30r (055 422 1437). Bus 14, 28. **Open** 7.30pm-1am, 12.30-2.30pm Mon, Wed-Sun. **No credit cards.**
An amazing 128 different *primi* (starters) and 90 different kinds of pizzas.

Pizza Taxi

North Florence (055 434 343); South Florence (055 234 4444). **Open** 12-3pm, 6.30pm-midnight, daily. **No credit cards.**
You get a free drink with every pizza.

I Tarocchi

Via dei Renai 12/14r (055 234 3912). Bus 23D. **Open** 12.30-2.30pm, 7pm-1am Tue-Fri; 7pm-1am Sat, Sun. **Credit** AmEx, DC, JCB, MC, V.
A friendly place that serves child-sized pizzas.

Games & toys

Avalon

Via Cavour 40r (055 267 0134). **Open** 3.30-7.30pm Mon; 10am-2pm, 3.30-7.30pm, Tue-Sat. **Credit** AmEx, DC, JCB, MC, V.
Selection of role-playing games (Dungeons & Dragons, Vampires) for sale and playing.

Centro Giovani

Corner of Via Pietrapiana and Via Fiesolana (055 276 7648/giovani.s.croce@comune.fi.it). **Open** 5-11pm Mon, Wed-Sat; 4-8pm Sun.
Youth centre which offers free access to computers (including the Internet), shows films and videos and has information on courses and events.

Città del Sole

Borgo Ognissanti 37r (055 219 345). **Open** 3.30-7.30pm Mon; 9am-1pm, 3.30-7.30pm Tue-Sat. **Credit** AmEx, MC, V.
Well-made children's toys – the wooden ones are particularly nice – as well as a selection of board games and puzzles.

La Co-operativa dei Ragazzi

Via San Gallo 27r (055 287 500). **Open** 3.30-7.30pm Mon; 9am-1pm, 3.30-7.30pm Tue-Sat. **Credit** V.
A great shop with a large selection of books and an even better choice of toys.

Ludoteca Centrale

Piazza SS Annunziata 13 (055 248 0477). **Open** 9am-1pm, 3-6.45pm, Mon, Tue, Thur, Fri; 9am-1pm Sat.
Free play centre with books and toys to borrow, play rooms, library and comfy sofas to fall into. One room is beautifully frescoed and next door is the Museo dello Spedale degli Innocenti (*see chapter* **Museums & Galleries**).

Menicucci

Via Guicciardini 51r (055 294 934). **Open** 9.30am-7.30pm daily. **Credit** AmEx, MC, V.
A good all-round toy shop remarkable for its window display of soft toys and wooden Pinocchios in all sizes.

Gardens & parks

Boboli Gardens

Labyrinths, grottoes, fountains, statues and hiding places: the Boboli offers plenty of diversions for children and magnificent views of the city.

Le Cascine

Florence's largest park, the site of regular fairs and markets, is at its most animated on Sundays. You go swimming in the pool or rent rollerblades. Playgrounds dot the park, and there are snacks and balloons for sale.

Forte Belvedere

When not hosting an exhibition (when you have to pay) Forte Belvedere is a wonderful place to go for free. It has a 360° view over the city and surrounding countryside and lots of grass to laze or play on.

Giardini d'Azeglio

With a merry-go-round, swings, slides and games, this shady park is peaceful during the day, but fills up after school, at about 4.30pm. There's a small used-toys market and other activities.

Giardino di Borgo Allegri

A former parking lot near Santa Croce transformed by local senior citizens into a charming garden full of flowers, with games for small children.

Mondobimbo Inflatables

Parterre, Piazza della Libertà (0330 909 150). **Open** 10.30am-7.30pm daily. **Admission** day ticket L8,000. **No credit cards.**
Under-tens can let off steam here on huge inflatable castles, whales, dogs and snakes. It's wise to bring spare socks (you can buy them at the entrance).

Out of town

The best way of escape is by car, although buses and trains run to most major destinations. The most immediate way to get into the Tuscan countryside is to take either bus 7 to Fiesole or bus 10 to Settignano (15 minutes from Santa Maria Novella). There are numerous walks around these two towns. Another option is a one-day bike ride, organised by I Bike Italy (055 234 2371 or 0474 198 288).

Giardino Zoologico

Via Pieve a Celle 160, Pistoia (0573 911 219). **Open** 9am-7pm daily. **Admission** L14,000; L10,000 3-9-yr-olds; under-3s free. **No credit cards.**
Giraffes, rhinos, crocodiles, jaguars and a growing gang of Malagasy lemurs in a large park with palm and banana trees. No entrance after 6pm.

Parco Giochi Cavallino Matto

Via Po 1, Marina di Castagneto Donoratico, Livorno (0565 745 720). **Open** *Mar, Oct* 10am-8pm Sun; *Apr, last 2 weeks Sept* 10am-8pm Sat, Sun & holidays; *May, June* 10am-8pm daily; *July, Aug, 1st 2 weeks Sept* 10am-midnight daily. **Admission** L20,000. **No credit cards.**
The largest fun fair of the coastal region.

Parco Preistorico

Peccioli Via Cappuccini 20, Pisa (0587 636 030). **Open** 9am-noon, 2pm-sunset daily. **Admission** L7,000; L5,000 children; free tours in Italian (English information sheet). **No credit cards.**

This park, about 50 kilometres from Pisa, has impressive life-size models of 18 different dinosaurs, a play area, bar and picnic facilities. The tour lasts an hour.

Hot springs

Bagni Vignoni

Hotel Posta Marcucci, Via Ara Urcea 43 (0577 887 112). **Open** 9am-1pm daily, 2.30-6pm Mon-Wed, Fri-Sun. **Admission** *day* L18,000; *afternoon* L12,000. **Credit** AmEx, DC, JCB, MC, V.

To enjoy the spa waters, go to this outdoor pool which has wonderful views. All-day ticket holders are not allowed to swim during the lunch break.

Calidario

Via del Bottaccio 40, Venturina, Livorno (0565 851 504). **Open** 8.30am-midnight daily. **Admission** L22,000; L11,000 2-10s; under-2s free. **Credit** AmEx, MC, V.

One of the most organised hot springs, with wonderfully clear water. The immense swimming pool has a slide, a restaurant, pizzeria and evening disco.

Saturnia

Just outside the village is an abandoned mill and a river of hot sulphurous water. The waterfalls and steaming pools can be enjoyed any time (free).

Water fun

Le Pavoniere

Viale della Catena 2 (055 333 979). Bus 17. **Open** *end May-Sept* 10am-6pm daily. **Admission** L12,000 adults; L9,000 children. **No credit cards.**

This peaceful pool in Cascine park is not suitable for toddlers unless they can swim. A bar sells snacks and ice-cream and in the evening a restaurant opens.

Piscina Bellariva

Lungarno Aldo Moro 6 (055 677 541). Bus 14. **Open** *summer* 10am-6pm daily; 8.30-11pm Mon-Fri; *winter* 8.30-11pm Tue, Thur; 9.30am-12.30pm Sat, Sun. **Admission** L10,000; L9,000 members. **No credit cards.**

Great for little ones: safe pools, grassy lawns, trees and a separate pool for older kids and adults.

Piscina Costoli

Viale Paoli, Campo di Marte (055 678 841). Bus 10, 17, 20. **Open** *June-early Sept* 10am-6pm daily. **Admission** L10,000. **No credit cards.**

A huge swirling water slide makes this pool a big hit with older kids. Due to re-open in 2000.

Rowing on the Arno

Ponte San Niccolò (next to tourist bus park).

From May to September the Lido rents little rowing boats for L20,000 an hour.

Film

Location, location, location.

'Tuscany has a great attribute: if you plant a nail in the ground and you extend a string for a radius of about 50km you find everything.' This is how Giorgio Galliani, location manager on 92 films shot in Tuscany, including Anthony Minghella's *The English Patient*, speaks of the region. Since James Ivory shot *Room With a View* in Florence and the surrounding countryside in 1985, Tuscany has experiencexd something of a cinema renaissance, becoming a favourite setting for many Anglo-American productions with directors such as Kenneth Branagh (*Much Ado About Nothing*), Jane Campion (*The Portrait of a Lady*), Bernardo Bertolucci (*Stealing Beauty*) and more recently Franco Zeffirelli with his *Tea With Mussolini* and *Up At The Villa* directed by Philip Haas.

But Tuscany and cinema have a long history together that stretches back as far as 1910, when the Futurists shot their unusual *Vita Futurista* of which only photo documents now exist. Various episodes, including one which was censored and another of a fist fight, were shot at the Cascine and in Piazzale Michelangiolo.

In the 1930s, Italian film makers found ideal settings for their historical stories in perfectly intact medieval and Renaissance towns. A Florence devastated by war was used by Roberto Rossellini in 1946 to shoot *Paisà* and Tarkovsky shot *Nostalghia* in the hot springs of Bagni Vignoni.

In 1934, Giovacchino Forzano convinced Eduardo Agnelli and Mussolini to allow him to imitate California by building American-style film studios at Tirrenia, between Pisa and Livorno, called Pisorno. After initial success (130 films were shot here in ten years) and a few films made here after the war (including an American film by Joseph Losey, *Stranger in the Prow*) the studios declined and were almost completely abandoned, until 1986 when Paolo and Vittorio Taviani rebuilt an imaginary Hollywood here for their film *Good Morning Babylonia*. While hoping to be reawakened by Tuscan cinema's good fortune, for the time being the studios offer one of the best golf courses in Europe.

Daniel Day Lewis ignores the view.

Most Italians associate Tuscany with down-market comedy, a tradition begun with Mario Monicelli's *Amici Miei* (1975), which opened the way for such box-office sensations as Leonardo Pieraccioni's *Il Ciclone*, a romantic comedy about the arrival of a troupe of flamenco dancers in a sleepy Tuscan town, and Roberto Benigni's Oscar-winning *La Vita è Bella* (Life is Beautiful). Benigni is a hero in Tuscany – he was born in the small town of Misericordia in Arezzo and grew up in Vergaio in the province of Prato – where he is famous for his comical exploits in live one-man shows, in cinema and on TV.

MOVIEGOING IN FLORENCE

Italians appear to have an aversion to subtitling. Dubbing is big business in Italy, shooting to fame the actors who dub the voices of Hollywood stars such as Tom Cruise and Robert De Niro. However, *versione originale* (VO) films are slowly gaining popularity and more Florentine cinemas are showing foreign films with their original soundtracks. Another option for English speakers are the cineclubs, which offer more varied programmes.

If you speak Italian you can take advantage of the cheaper matinee shows (before 6.30pm) at many first-run cinemas on weekdays, or for the entire day on Wednesdays (L8,000 as opposed to the standard price of L12,000/L13,000).

You should be prepared for long queues on Friday and Saturday nights. If you don't arrive at least 40 minutes before the start of the film, don't be surprised if you end up sitting on the floor or standing at the back. When the *posto in piedi* light is on, the tickets being sold are standing-room only, though, irritatingly, they cost the same as regular tickets.

For screening times check the listings in *La Nazione*, *L'Unità* and *La Reppublica*. Most bars display *La Civetta,* an information sheet on what is showing in cinemas and theatres posted. For information on festivals and other special events, the monthly *Firenze Spettacolo* is a good source.

Ken and Em bandy words in the Tuscan hills in Much Ado about Nothing.

Cinemas

Ciak Atelier

Via Faenza 56r (055 212 178). **Shows** 4 or 5 per day, *last show* 10.45pm daily. **Tickets** L12,000. **No credit cards**.

On Mondays and Tuesdays it shows re-runs of classic films, but never in VO. For the rest of the week it operates as your average cinema.

Cinema Astro

Piazza di San Simone (no phone). **Open** *box office* 7pm, shows 7.30pm, 10pm Tue-Sun. **Tickets** L10,000; L8,000 Wed for students. **No credit cards**.

The only cinema in Florence which exclusively shows English-language films six days a week. Most films are recent releases, making the cinema something of a cultural lifeline for Anglophone ex-pats.

Goldoni

Via Serragli 109 (055 222 437). Bus 11, 12, 13, 36, 37 to Piazza della Porta Romana. **Open** *box office* 3.30pm, last show 10.45pm daily. **Tickets** L12,000/ L8,000. **Closed** June, July. **No credit cards**.

One of the first to show English-language films. Its regular VO night is Wednesday. Understandably popular with Florence's foreign students, you should go to an early show if you want to beat the crowds.

Odeon Original Sound

Via Sassetti 1 (055 214 068). **Open** *box office* times vary, acording to film. **Closed** late June-late Sept. **Tickets** L13,000. **No credit cards**.

English-language films are shown every Monday in this centrally located, comfortable cinema. Seeing the crowds on Monday nights, Sunday morning 11am matinees have been programmed.

Air-conditioning.

Teatro Verdi Atelier

Via Ghibellina 99 (055 212 320). Bus 14. **Open** occasional screenings at 9pm, Wed. **Tickets** L12,000. **No credit cards**.

This theatre occasionally transforms itself into a cinema to screen new films before they are actually released in the rest of Florence, although they are rarely shown in VO.

Cineclubs & bookshops

Film clubs in Florence offer avid moviegoers an alternative. They are relatively inexpensive to join, especially for students, and the first-run cinemas often offer discounts. Most film societies have discussions following screenings or presentations by local film makers.

CineCittà

Via Baccio da Montelupo 35 (055 732 1035). Bus 6A. **Shows** 8.30pm Wed-Sun. **Tickets** L7,000, plus L9,000 membership. **No credit cards**.

Run by the Casa del Popolo Fratelli Taddei (community centre). Films range from Hollywood action pictures to festivals of obscure Italian classics.

Istituto Francese

Piazza Ognissanti 2 (055 239 8902/fax 055 217 296). **Tickets** L8,000; L5,000 with a *tessera Istituto Francese* membership card. **No credit cards**.

Sponsored by the French government to promote French culture, the Istituto (unsurprisingly) shows a rich diet of mainly French films. It also sponsors France Cinema and other conferences and cultural events throughout the year – which can often include films by French, Italian, American and English directors.

Libreria del Cinema e dello Spectacolo
Via Guelfa 14r (055 216 416). **Open** 9.30am-1pm, 3.30-7.30pm, Mon-Sat. **Credit** MC, V.
This bookstore specialises in cinema, film memorabilia and rare books. It also organises conferences and exhibitions on film-related topics, and sponsors screenings. A great place to find out about upcoming film events in and around Florence.

Spazio Uno/Cineteca
Via del Sole 10 (055 215 634). **Open** 2 or 4 shows 5-9.15pm/10.30pm Tue-Fri, Sun; last screening 10.30pm; *bar* 8pm-2am daily. **Tickets** L5,000, plus membership L4,000. **No credit cards.**
This former left-wing recreational centre now operates as a film library with a bar and arthouse cinema open to all. Classics shown include Marx Brothers, Polanski and various seasons on important directors. On Sundays, football matches take precedence and screenings start at 6pm. Often in VO, not just in English.

Stensen Forum/LunediClub
Viale Don Minzoni 25a (055 576 551/fax 055 582 029). Bus 1, 7, 12. **Shows** 9.15pm Mon. **Tickets** L5,000, plus L2,000 membership. **No credit cards.**
Both Italian and foreign films are the staple of this film club. You must become a member of the group by purchasing an annual membership (*abbonamento*). Along with film screenings, the group sponsors lectures, debates and presentations by film makers.

The central **Odeon Original Sound.** *See p139.*

Festivals & summer programmes

Two major international film festivals occur annually in Florence and one in Fiesole. Films are usually screened in *versione originale*. The **Festival dei Popoli** takes place during the first two weeks of December, with films shown in various clubs and cinemas throughout Florence. The festival's theme changes each year but always centres around a social issue, showing both narrative and documentary films.

For information, contact Festival dei Popoli, Borgo Pinti 82r (055 244 778) or www.festivalpopoli.org. The **France Cinema** festival, usually held in November at the French Institute and at the Teatro della Compania, Via Cavour 50r (055 217 428), has been growing each year. It always has an impressive turnout of French directors and stars on the jury and for debates and discussions. The **Premio Fiesole ai Maestri del Cinema** is held in July in the open-air Roman theatre and homage is paid to a great film director with this award and a series of his or her films is shown.

Florence closes most of its cinemas during June, July and August. Instead of sitting inside during the warm evenings, Florentines go to watch films *all'aperto* (outside). The following three function every summer, but it is worth keeping an eye out for other *cinema all'aperto* starting up.

Arena di Marte
Palazzetto dello Sport di Firenze, Viale Paoli (055 678 841). Bus 10, 20, 34. **Dates** mid June-late Aug. **Shows** 9pm, 11pm, daily. **Tickets** L10,000. **No credit cards.**
The Cooperativa Atelier organises two outdoor cinema seasons in Florence: Arena di Marte and Raggio Verde. There are two screens at the Arena di Marte, both with two shows nightly.

Esterno Notte at the Poggetto
Via M Mercati 24b (055 481 285). Bus 4, 8, 14, 20, 28. **Dates** June-Sept. **Shows** 9.30pm daily. **Tickets** L10,000. **No credit cards.**
Films from the previous 12 months are screened outdoors, with the occasional special screening.

Chiardiluna
Via Monte Uliveto 1 (055 233 7042). Bus 12, 13. **Dates** June-Sept. **Shows** 9.30pm daily. **Tickets** L10,000. **No credit cards.**
Recent commercial releases, at a site off Viale Raffaele Sanzio, between Ponte Vittoria and Porta Romana.

Raggio Verde
Palacongressi Firenze, Viale Strozzi (055 260 2609). **Dates** late June-early Sept. **Shows** 9.30pm, 11pm daily. **Tickets** L10,000. **No credit cards.**
If you don't want to leave the city centre then the arena here is another option for filmwatching under the moonlight. Two different films are shown nightly. Located near Santa Maria Novella train station.

Gay & Lesbian

Liberal and liberated, Tuscany has always had pulling power.

In 1795, under Grand Duke Ferdinando III, Tuscany became one of the first states in Europe to repeal anti-homosexual laws. In fact, these laws had been largely ignored for centuries, apart from the imposition of paltry fines by the so-called *Uffiziali di Notte* (night-guardians); apparently, in the 1400s, about half of the city's youths were fined by the Uffiziali. The city was a tolerant place, home to gay artists of the calibre of Leonardo da Vinci, Botticelli, Benvenuto Cellini and Michelangelo Buonarroti, as well as the prominent Medicis. Not surprisingly, in the era of the Grand Tourists, Tuscany became extremely popular with homosexuals from all over Europe, especially Britain and Germany.

More recently, gay and lesbian groups have made great strides in gaining acceptance in Italian society – but there is still a long way to go. It is still difficult to live as an openly lesbian woman or gay man in most small towns of Tuscany, but Florence is one of the most gay-friendly cities in Italy.

The most useful port of call on arrival in Florence is **Azione Gay e Lesbica**. It's also worth scanning the Internet, particularly the excellent site www.gay.it/gigliofucsia.

Bars

Le Colonnine

Via dei Benci 6r (055 234 6417). **Open** 7am-1am Tue-Sun. **Credit** AmEx, DC, JCB, MC, V.

Near to Crisco is this café-bar/tobacconist; a favoured spot for planning the evening's entertainment.

Crisco

Via Sant'Egidio 43r (055 248 0580). **Open** 10pm-3am Mon, Wed, Thur, Sun; 10pm-5am Fri, Sat. **Credit** MC, V.

A strictly members-only club, open only to men (although free temporary membership is available on the door), Crisco (the name of an American vaseline brand) is bar plus dark room and video room. Occasional live shows on Saturdays. Worth a visit.

Piccolo Café

Borgo Santa Croce 23r (055 241 704). **Open** 5pm-1am daily. **No credit cards**.

This tiny art café has become popular with gays and lesbians of all ages. It's an excellent venue for artists of all kinds: every fortnight Antonio (the friendly lad who runs the place) hosts shows of photography, paintings and sculpture.

Clubs

Flamingo

Via Pandolfini 26r (055 243 356). Bus 14a, B, C. **Open** 10pm-5am Mon, Wed-Sun. Closed Aug. **Admission** free, but minimum drinks charge L12,000-L15,000. **Credit** AmEx, V.

Near Santa Croce, this gay disco has a cocktail bar plus a back room and a video room on the upper level (Tabascobar) and a disco on the lower. Women are admitted, but Flamingo isn't popular with lesbians. The music is a mix of international techno and retro hits. Live shows on Saturdays.

Tabasco

Piazza Santa Cecilia 3r (055 213 000). **Open** 10pm-3am Mon-Thur, Sun; 10pm-6am Fri, Sat. **Admission** *men only* L15,000 Mon-Thur; L25,000 Fri, Sat. **Credit** AmEx, V.

Opened in the 1970s, this was Italy's first gay bar and is arguably the best-known. It is run by the same lad, Marco, who owns Flamingo (*see above*) and Florence Baths (*see below*). Besides the disco and a bar there is a dark room and video room. It's usually filled with a young crowd (men only) at the weekends, although it's not always easy to get beyond the bouncers. The music is similar to Flamingo's. It can be hard to find – it's located at the far side of a tiny dead-end alley on Via Vacchereccia, just off Piazza della Signoria.

Cruising areas for gay men

Florence is generally a safe town, but walking at night in the parks can be dangerous. Night-time areas for cruising include: a downtown route from Piazza della Repubblica to Piazza Santa Croce through Via Calimala, Via Vacchereccia and Via dei Neri; the Viale P Paoli parking lot by Campo di Marte Stadium; and the amphitheatre in the Cascine. The Tuesday morning market in the Cascine is another meeting spot.

Gay & lesbian organisations

Azione Gay e Lesbica

Via San Zanobi 54r (tel/fax 055 476 557/counselling 055 488 288/gaylesbica.fi@agora.stm.it). **Open** 4-8pm Mon-Sat.

Previously part of the national gay and lesbian group Arcigay Arcilesbica, but in 1997 the national organisation was divided into two sections, Arcigay and Arcilesbica. The Florentine group refused to

accept this division and decided to become an autonomous, mixed gay-lesbian group. The centre is involved in social and political activities and demonstrations. It has a library and message board and offers free, confidential HIV testing and legal services. It also organises parties such as the renowned Timida Godzilla evenings. English, French and Spanish spoken.
Website: www.agora.stm.it/gaylesbica.fi

Ireos-Queer Community Service Center

Via del Ponte all'Asse 7 (on the terrace) (055 353 462). **Open** 4-7pm Mon-Fri.
A health and social centre offering information, counselling, courses and a message board.

L'Amando(r)la

Info: Antonella (0360 311 058). **Meetings** 9.30pm Wed, but call to confirm.
Radical lesbian association.

Hotels

Florence boasts a few gay-friendly hotels:
B&B *Borgo Pinti 31 (055 248 0056).* Women only.
Hotel Morandi alla Crocetta *Via Laura 50/52 (055 234 4747/fax 055 248 0594).*
Dei Mori *Via Dante Alighieri 12 (055 211 438).*
Hotel Porta Rossa *Via Porta Rossa 19 (055 287 551/2/3/fax 055 282 179).*
Hotel Pensione Medici *Via Dei Medici 6 (055 284 818/fax 055 216 202).*
PLP Guest-House *Via G Marconi 47 (tel/fax 055 572 005).*
Hotel Tina *Via San Gallo 31 (055 483 519/fax 055 483 593).*
Hotel Wanda *Via Ghibellina 51 (055 234 4484/fax 055 242 106).*

Restaurants

The following, although not exclusively gay, are gay-friendly. That said, as long as you are fairly discreet, you should have no problem in most restaurants. Also try **Momoyama**, *see chapter* **Restaurants** and **Rose's**, *see chapter* **Nightlife**.

Baby-Lone *Borgo la Croce 59r (055 240 799).* **Open** 8pm-1am daily. **Credit** MC, V.
Very new-age bar offering vegetarian food (with a Japanese slant) and live music.

Cantina Barbagianni *Via Sant'Egidio 13r (055 248 0508).* **Open** noon-2.30pm, 7.30-11pm, Mon-Sat. **Credit** AmEx, DC, JCB, MC, V.
Tuscan cuisine in elegant and intimate suroundings.

Mastro Ciliegia *Via M Palmieri 34r (055 293 372).* **Open** noon-3.30pm, 7pm-midnight, Tue-Sun. **Credit** MC, V.
Inexpensive pizza-pasta joint, often crowded.

La Vie en Rose *Borgo Allegri 68r (055 245 860).* **Open** *summer* 7.30pm-midnight Mon, Wed-Sun; *winter* noon-2.30pm, 7.30pm-midnight, Mon, Wed-Sun. **Credit** AmEx, DC, MC, V.
New Italian cuisine, busy at the weekends.

Saunas & gyms

The **Palestra Ricciardi** (*see chapter* **Sport**) is a favourite with gay men.

Florence Baths

Via Guelfa 93r (055 216 050). **Open** *winter* 2pm-1am daily; *summer* 3pm-1am daily. **Admission** L25,000; membership L10,000. **Credit** AmEx, MC, V.

Sex and the city

For many people the lure of Florence does not stop at (or even include) the artistic treasures of churches, museums and art galleries. The fabled city on the Arno has a deeper and darker side. When the museums close their doors and the trattorias close their kitchens, Florence's 'other' emerges. Like so many other cities Florence has its share of urban blight, prostitution, drugs and AIDS – but the sex for sale on its streets is both male and female, ambiguous, androgynous, atypical.

Just after 11pm, you will begin to notice the lovely 'women' materialising in certain sections of the city, particularly the areas by the station and the Parco delle Cascine. You might see a number of these *travestiti* and *transsessuali* clothed only in their *pellicce* (furs). There are two transvestites for every female prostitute on the streets of Florence.

While Florence is considered to be the quintessential Italian city, steeped in tradition, Florentine society has always been extremely open and nobody seems to feel that men who dress up like women are anything out of the ordinary. Florentines appear to respect and tolerate what many would describe as being 'unnatural', given the strong Catholic values of Italian society. Perhaps it's a form of rebellion against Catholicism that sends such a large number of men to seek sex on the streets. Or maybe it's the ambivalence that Italian men feel towards their often overbearing *mamma* that makes the extreme femininity of the transvestites so alluring, or the androgyny of the transsexuals so tempting. For whatever reason, both Italian men and foreigners continue to frequent the Florence underground.

Gone fishing? **La Lecciona**, *south of Viareggio.*

The only gay sauna in Florence is popular with tourists. It has a sauna, steam room, Jacuzzi, video-room, snack bars and relaxation rooms.

Tuscany

The biggest gay scene in Tuscany is in Florence. In summer, the heart of the scene transfers to the coast to Torre del Lago, close to Viareggio. You can pick up a copy of the gay and lesbian map of Tuscany from Azione Gay e Lesbica in Florence and the site www.gay.it/ gigliofucsia has lots of information on bars, clubs and preferred venues in the region; we have listed some of the main attractions.

Arcigay Pride! Group for Gay Action

Via San Lorenzo 38, Pisa (tel/fax 050 555 618). **Open** 4.30-7.30pm Mon-Fri.
This branch of Arcigay has a bar and cultural centre.

Bar/Discoteca Barrumba

Viale Kennedy 6, Torre del Lago, Viareggio (0584 351 717). **Open** *bar* 10pm-3am Mon, Wed, Thur; *club* 10pm-5am Fri, Sat. **Admission** *bar* L12,000; Fri L25,000; Sat L30,000 (incl 1st drink). **No credit cards.**
Café-bar and restaurant with garden and solarium. A beer costs L10,000.

Café-Bar Bistrot

Via del Rialto 4, Siena (0577 47243). **Open** 7.30pm-3am daily. **No credit cards.**
A mixed gay-straight café-bar.

Frau Marleen

Viale Europa, Torre del Lago, Viareggio (0584 342 282). **Open** 11pm-4am Thur-Sun; *winter* Fri, Sat only.
Gay and lesbian disco from Thursday to Sunday.

Gay-Friendly Farm Holidays Center

Agriturismo Priello, Caprese Michelangiolo, 15km west of Sansepolcro (0575 791 218). **Rates** *double* L125,000.
Bed and breakfast (with organic food) establishment.

Le Notti della Mantide

The Nights of the Mantis, Cave Club, Scali d'Azeglio 32, Livorno (0330 731 694). **Open** 10pm-3am Wed. **Closed** summer.
Predominantly gay event in a rock club.

Siesta Club

Via di Porta a Mare 27, Pisa (050 42075). **Open** *winter* 3pm-1am daily; *June* 5pm-1am daily; *July, Aug* 8pm-1am daily. **Admission** *1st visit* L30,000; *subsequent visits* L20,000. **No credit cards.**
Sauna, steam room, Jacuzzi, videos, relaxation rooms and snackbar. Gay men only, membership card required. Due to move in late 1999.

Beaches

There are plenty of beaches in Tuscany where nudists are tolerated. Nudity is not illegal in Italy but, depending on the whim of the local authorities, it is sometimes discouraged by the police. The rule of thumb is to keep away from beaches overcrowded with middle-class families. Try some of the following beaches; however, be careful in the *pinetas* (pine forests), where the cruising scene can get heavy.

Carbonifera North of Follónica, close to Pappasole Camping, this beach has a fine view of Elba. Popular with lesbians.

La Lecciona Long beach 3km south of Viareggio on Viale dei Tigli, about 500m past Bar La Lecciona. The nearby pineta is a daytime cruising zone.

Le Marze Beach 5km south of Castiglione della Pescáia, next to the campsite and Pineta del Tómbolo.

Le Piscine On the isle of Elba, between Seccheto and Fetováia is this mixed gay-straight, seawater pool in the granite cliffs.

Rimigliano South of San Vincenzo (Livorno), 6km of beach and daytime cruising in the pineta along the Strada della Principessa.

Sassoscritto Gay and lesbian beach with high cliffs, south of Livorno. If taking the bus, get off at Il Romito near the Restaurant Sassoscritto.

Media

All the news you can use.

Newspapers

The local news-stand, which once took up the space of a modest street corner, has become a sort of a media supermarket, submerged by newspapers and magazines that are packed with bulky 'gifts' such as perfumes, sunglasses, toys and tapes. All this effort to promote sales has, however, failed to check the decrease of newspaper sales in Italy – only one in ten Italians reads a daily newspaper.

Fuori Binario

Florence's *Big Issue,* is sold on the streets by the homeless, who also have a slot on Controradio (*see below,* **Radio**). Any contribution is accepted – but it tends to sell for the cost of a newspaper (L1,500).

International Herald Tribune

Publishes *Italy Daily*, a supplement produced in collaboration with *Corriere della Sera* that contains a digest of the main news and business stories.

Il Manifesto

This small left-wing paper produces some decent journalism, especially of a cultural bent. One page is always dedicated to Florence and Tuscany.

La Nazione

Selling some 160,000 copies daily, this is the most popular newspaper in Tuscany. Founded in the mid-nineteenth century by Bettino Ricasoli, *La Nazione* is also one of the oldest papers in Italy. It consists of three sections (national, sport and local) and each province has its own edition. Basically right-wing and gossipy, the level of journalism leaves much to be desired.

La Repubblica

The youngest of Italy's major papers is centre-left and its coverage of the Mafia and the Vatican is particularly strong. On the down side, it has a tendency to pad the news section out with waffle and gossip. It is one of the most widely read Italian newspapers. The Tuscan edition has about 20 pages dedicated to local and provincial news.

Il Tirreno

Livorno's newspaper focuses on life along the coast.

L'Unità

This former Communist Party organ became a shining beacon of independent Italian journalism in the mid-1990s when edited by Walter Vetroni, who was then whisked off to a high office in the government and the New Labourite PDS party. Since then this worthy but dull daily has lost its way – and many of its readers. On Mondays there is a media supplement. It normally carries four pages of Tuscan news.

Il Vernacoliere

A satirical monthly, published in Livorno, whose targets include TV stars, politicians and the Pisans.

Classified ads

La Pulce comes out every Monday, Wednesday and Friday, and *Portobello* every Friday. Here you can find ads for anything. Some ads are in English.

Foreign titles

Most news-stands in the centre of town hold foreign titles, but you'll find the widest range under the arcades in Piazza della Repubblica and at Santa Maria Novella train station.

Berlusconi even dominates the headlines.

Media moguls

Though the Cecchi Goris are the most prominent Florentine dynasty of modern times, they are not quite twentieth-century Medicis. Mario, the patriarch, founded the television-broadcasting empire in 1953, when he set up Massima film with Dino De Laurentiis. For the following 40 years, Cecchi Gori was the king of Italian low- to middlebrow comedy, producing classics of the genre (Dino Risi's *Il Sorpasso*, 1962) as well as frankly forgettable titles like *My Wife is a Witch* and *Seven Kilos in Seven Days*.

His son Vittorio (*pictured*) never had much of a career dilemma: he was 14 when he first started helping dad, and for the next 25 years combined cinematic duties with water-skiing and a series of flirtations that kept Italy's gossip press busy. Finally, in 1983, he met Yugoslav dental hygienist turned B-movie actress Rita Rusic on the set of *Attilla, Scourge Of God* – a film so bad it soon achieved cult status. They were married the same year.

Rita took over the film production side of the Cecchi Gori empire, with startling results – *Il Ciclone*, a romantic comedy set in rural Tuscany, broke all previous box-office records, grossing a massive $40 million. 'I've found an excellent producer but I've lost a wife,' said a prescient Vittorio; the couple recently split.

Rita now manages an estimated 70 per cent of Italian film production – she was the only Italian to appear in *Variety* magazine's list of 50

people that will have a decisive role in the future of cinema.

Vittorio looks after the TV side of things – he owns the two national Telemontecarlo channels. As well as holding down a seat in the Italian Senate he is standing in the European elections and following the fortunes of Fiorentina football club, of which he is chairman. The rest of his energies are spent duelling with his former partner and now arch-enemy, Silvio Berlusconi.

Rita and Vittorio separated in May 1999 and it was unclear how this would affect their empire as the guide went to press.

Magazines

Firenze Oggi/Florence Today

Most hotels have this freebie in their reception area. It is a useful, fairly accurate, but far from comprehensive listings mag in English and Italian.

Firenze Spettacolo

Patchy listings mag with an English-language insert called Florencescope.

Florence Concierge Information

There's no cover price for this handy little number found at tourist offices. It lists events, useful information, timetables and suchlike in English.

Vista

Glossy quarterly with the odd interesting feature.

Online

Bellosguardo

www.bellosguardo.it

Colourful site with information (in Italian) on public services such as bus timetables and 24-hour pharmacies. There's also information on shopping, restaurants and Florentine nightlife. Free pages for volunteer associations. Online shopping too.

Firenze.net

www.firenze.net

News, maps, chat, where to go, links and photos. It also has classified ad pages. In Italian and English.

The district of Florence

www.comune.firenze.it

Official site of the city. Timetables, events, services, links to museums. In Italian.

Fiorentina Football Club

www.fiorentina.it

Team news, online chat, photographic archives, listings for Viola clubs and pubs. In Italian.

Firenze Online

www.fionline.it

This colourful site specialises in arts and entertainment, with information on theatres, art galleries and museums. There's a section on how to go about finding a job in Italy. E-mail info@fionline.it for further information. In English and Italian.

In Italy Online

www.initaly.com

A monthly e-zine, *In Italy* contains useful info about where to stay, eat and enjoy yourself in Tuscany. It includes quirky details about museums and festivals, outdoor markets and destinations for walking and driving tours. E-mail: italy@initaly.com. Online hotel reservations available. In English.

Italian Internet Winery

www.ulysses.it

Travel, maps, lists of local wineries, how to order via e-mail. E-mail: info@ulysses.it. In English.

Museums online

www.museionline.it

Information on events and exhibitions and all the museums in Italy by region. In Italian.

Welcome to Italy

www.emmeti.it

Information in English, Italian, German and Japanese can be searched by venue, itinerary or location – the latter being the easiest. It lists more than 1,000 places to stay (online reservations available), restaurants, local events, shopping, plus articles on fashion, food and drink. E-mail queries to museum@graffiti2000.com.

Radio

Controradio *93.6 MHz*

The best music station in Florence. Dub, hip-hop, gangster rap, drum'n'bass and indie rock all feature heavily in its scheduling. Every evening a feature called City Lights is broadcast in which all the night's entertainments are listed.

Nova Radio *101.5 MHz*

No ads. Run by volunteers and committed to social issues, it broadcasts jazz, soul, blues, reggae, World music, hip hop and rap.

Radio Diffusione Firenze *102.7 MHz*

Mainstream pop music.

Radio Montebeni *108.5 MHz*

Classical music only.

Radio Montecarlo *101.5 MHz*

Mellow jazz and soul.

Television

Italy has six major networks (three owned by state broadcaster RAI, three by Silvio Berlusconi's Mediaset group), together with two channels operated across most of the country by Telemontecarlo.

Mediaset shows all the familiar American series (*Baywatch*, *X Files*, *The Simpsons*), Brazilian *telenovelas* and Japanese cartoons, but these and the best films are all riddled with ad breaks. RAI channels have better quality programming, but there is still a relentless stream of quiz shows and high-kicking, bikini-clad bimbettes. When these have bored you, there are numerous local stations featuring cleaning demonstrations, dial-a-fortune-tellers (surprisingly popular), prolonged adverts for slimming machines and late-night trashy soft porn.

Video Music, Italy's equivalent to MTV, is now based in Florence but, since being acquired by film mogul Cecchi Gori (*see* **Media Moguls**), and changing its name to TMC 2, it has adopted a policy of replacing back-to-back video clips with naff, self-produced programmes and old repeats.

RAI has launched a digital satellite channel, Rai News 24, available simultaneously on TV and the Internet, 24 hours a day (free of charge in Europe and the Mediterranean).

Sky and CNN broadcast news in English in the early hours of the morning on TVL (local TV) and TMC. The French channel Antenne 2 is also accessible in Tuscany.

Advertising's the same the world over.

Music: Classical & Opera

Opera may have been invented here, but when it comes to ringing the changes, the Florentines are having none of it.

While hardly innovative, Florence's musical scene is lively. There is always a lavish operatic production at the **Teatro Comunale** or an organ recital in an obscure church, but rarely anything cutting-edge. One reason for this is lack of funds: in Italy, state funds are generally ploughed into established institutions (in Florence's case, the Teatro Comunale). Regional funding is funnelled into local projects, but these tend to be the same every year, and little is left for more modest enterprises. Having said that, the standard attained by the main beneficiaries of public money is usually high, although whether that justifies the neglect of smaller, often more innovative initiatives is open to debate. It is almost impossible for emerging talents to attract investment; the money exists, but persuading potential benefactors to spend it on the arts is another matter. There is no tax relief in Italy for such donations, so why bother?

Hand-in-hand with this problem is the attitude of the Florentine opera- and concert-going public. They'll pack the theatre night after night for an ordinary *Turandot* or *Rigoletto*, but only a handful will turn up to hear anything new. The superb production of Alban Berg's *Wozzeck* in May 1998 by William Friedkin (director of *The Exorcist*), for example, was one of the most interesting shows in recent years, yet the theatre was only ever three-quarters full. A few years ago, a spectacular production of Silvano Bussotti's *L'Ispirazione* used up the whole year's opera budget to play to practically empty houses. Often, if a producer dares to break the mould with a traditional opera, they suffer a booing, whistling audience. Is it any wonder the safe standards win all the funding?

Opera-going here is an interactive experience – there is no shortage of feedback, good or bad. Shows can be held up for several minutes after an aria that has been particularly well (or badly) received, and the Teatro Comunale has an unofficial clique that attends everything and leads the audience vocals.

Smaller events are promoted on fly-posters around town and in local papers and listings mags (*see chapter* **Media**). From June to October, there is a proliferation of outdoor concerts at villas, gardens and museums, many of which are free (call 055 262 5971). These are not always well-advertised, but tourist offices usually have information, and the monthly magazine *Firenze Spettacolo* lists events in Tuscany.

TICKETS

For the main ticket agencies in Florence, *see chapter* **Shopping & Services**. Many hotels and travel agents book tickets for the main venues. Tickets for the Teatro Comunale can be hard to come by as a large proportion of seats are sold to season--ticket holders. However, individual tickets are put on sale and you can get lucky. Unless otherwise stated, box offices do not accept credit cards.

Principal institutions

Accademia Bartolomeo Cristofori

Via di Camaldoli 7r (055 221 646). Bus B. **Open** 4.30-7pm Mon, Wed, Thur.

Named after the eighteenth-century Florentine 'inventor' of the *pianoforte*, the academy is based in an unassuming street at the heart of San Frediano. It houses a fine collection of early keyboard instruments and runs a workshop for restoration and repair. Concerts and seminars are held in the small, beautiful concert hall next door.

Amici della Musica

Via Sirtori 49 (055 608 420/607 440).

This organisation programmes international level chamber music concerts, mostly presented at the **Teatro della Pergola** (*see below*).

Orchestra Regionale Toscana

Via Ghibellina 101 (055 281 792/e-mail www.dada.it/ort-ort@dada.it). **Open** *ticket office* see Teatro Verdi. **Season** Dec-May.

The ORT is a young 40-strong chamber orchestra founded in 1980. Its remit was to take classical music into Tuscany. In season it plays two or three times a month in Florence, and 35 to 40 concerts in other Tuscan towns. Since the 1993 Ufizzi bombing of Santo Stefano, most concerts are now in the Teatro Verdi (*see below*). International names appear among soloists and conductors, and the orchestra's repertoire covers everything from baroque to contemporary.

Floodlights and fresh(ish) air in Piazza Signoria at the **Maggio Musicale Fiorentina** *festival.*

Scuola Musica di Fiesole

Villa la Torraccia, San Domenico (055 597 851). Bus 7, then a ten-minute walk. **Open** 8.30am-8.30pm daily. **Tickets** L10,000; concessions for students, OAPs.

A sixteenth-century villa in extensive grounds is the setting for the Fiesole Music School. Piero Farulli, viola player of the legendary Quartetto Italiano, is the school's lifeblood and the influence behind the Concerti per gli Amici series, which takes place in the villa's 200-seat auditorium from September to June and is worth the trip to San Domenico.

Teatro Comunale

Corso Italia 16 (055 211 158/055 213 535/fax 277 9410/tickets@maggiofiorentino.com). Bus C. **Open** *box office* 10am-4.30pm Tue-Fri; 9am-1pm Sat; and one hour before performance. **Credit** AmEx, DC, MC, V.

Florence's municipal theatre devours a huge chunk of public funds, but presents a year-round programme of top quality. It is home to a full symphony orchestra (L'Orchestra del Maggio Musicale Fiorentino), chorus and ballet company (Maggio Danza). Constructed in 1882 and renovated in 1957, the building itself is architecturally unexciting. The best seats, in terms of acoustics, are in the second gallery and these, happily, are the cheapest. After a period of stability under Zubin Mehta (principal conductor since 1985), and an increase in the number of young orchestra and chorus members, the theatre is on good form. Regular guests include Semyon Bychkov, Seiji Ozawa, Andrew Davis, and Giuseppe Sinopoli (the new principal guest conductor). The operatic principal line-up may not be studded with stars, but emerging talents often get breaks here. On the production side, David Hockney, Derek Jarman, Franco Zeffirelli, Jonathan Miller, Ken Russell and Graham Vick have all worked here. The orchestra and chorus tour regularly and in 1998 spent a month in Beijing working on a production of Puccini's *Turandot* by Zhang Yimou of *Red Lantern* fame.

The theatre's performing year is divided into three parts. January to March is the **Concert Season**, when a new programme is offered each week. October to December is the **Opera and Ballet Season** with about four operatic productions, a couple of ballets and the odd concert. The highlight is the **Maggio Musicale Fiorentino** festival which runs from the end of April until July. Founded in 1933, it is the longest-running festival in Italy and, with Salzburg and Bayreuth, one of the oldest in Europe. It offers an interesting mix of opera, ballet, symphony concerts and recital programmes, which generally have a theme. The festival culminates with two free, open-air jamborees in Piazza Signoria: a concert and an evening of dance. The main venue is the Teatro Comunale, but the exquisite eighteenth-century Teatro della Pergola (*see below*) and, more recently, the tiny Teatro Goldoni are also used.

Teatro Goldoni

Via Santa Maria 15 (box office 055 210 804). **Open** *box office* 1 hour before performance.

This divine little theatre, dating from the early eighteenth century and seating only 400, is tucked away behind Piazza Santo Spirito. After years of internal squabbling, restoration was completed in 1998 and the theatre re-opened with a performance of Monteverdi's *Orfeo* to celebrate the 400th anniversary of the birth of opera. (It is generally accepted that opera was 'invented' in Florence in 1598.) It is used for sporadic performances of chamber music and small-scale operas and ballets (often under the auspices of Teatro Comunale or Amici della Musica, *see above*), which fit its intimate atmosphere perfectly.

Teatro della Pergola

Via della Pergola 12-32 (055 247 9651). **Open** *box office* 9.30am-1pm, 3.30-6.45pm, Tue-Sat; 10am-noon Sun. **Season** Oct-Apr.

Inaugurated in 1656, the Pergola is acknowledged to be the oldest theatre in Italy. Exquisite and intimate, it is ideally suited to chamber music and small-scale operas. The Amici della Musica (*see above*) season of chamber concerts, most of which are held here, offers world-class performances. Settembre Musica (in September) is a month of early music concerts. Some of the world's great string quartets (Borodin, Emerson, Tokyo, Alban Berg) and recitalists play at this seventeenth-century jewel. Concerts are usually on Saturday and Sunday at 4pm or 9pm. Be prepared for distractions from the rest of the audience: some are more interested in the social scene than the music.

Teatro Verdi

Via Ghibellina 99 (055 212 320). Bus 14, A. **Open** *box office* 10am-7pm Tue-Fri;10am-1pm Sat.

Teatro Verdi opened as an opera house in 1854, and while these days it looks a little shabby from outside, it hosts a huge variety of productions. From Bruce Springsteen to the Philadelphia Orchestra, from *The Rocky Horror Show* to *The Nutcracker*, from *The Merry Widow* to Lindsay Kemp; they've all appeared in the 1,500-seat, red and gold auditorium.

Minor musical associations

Agimus

Via della Piazzola 7r (055 580 996/fax 0555 80301).

An association of young musicians that organises events throughout the year. Most interesting is the Festival Estate in July and August in the courtyard of Palazzo Pitti (*see chapter* **Tuscany by Season**).

Chiesa Luterana

Lungarno Torrigiani 11 (tourist office 055 290 832).

Year-round organ recitals and other chamber music, often involving early repertoire, in Florence's Lutheran church. Concerts are usually free.

Florence Symphonietta

Via Santa Riparata 40 (no phone).

This young organisation promotes concerts in and around Florence.

L'Homme Armè

Via San Romano 56, Settignano (tel/fax 055 697 719).

A small, semi-professional chamber choir whose repertoire ranges from medieval to baroque. There are summer and autumn seasons of three concerts each.

Orchestra da Camera Fiorentina

(055 783 374).

This young Florentine chamber orchestra plays a season of mostly baroque and classical concerts from February to September, with a break in August.

Orchestra Storica di Firenze

(0348 602 6167).

Gimmicky but fun, the OSF performs Renaissance and baroque music in costume. There are more concerts in tourist season and around Christmas.

Teatro Comunale Garibaldi

Piazza Serristori, Figline Valdarno (055 915 5986)

A provincial theatre which hosts some interesting chamber and orchestral concerts.

Events

See also chapter **Tuscany by Season**.

Annual events in Florence

Christmas concerts (Dec/Jan) on Florence's antique organs *(055 262 5971).*

New Year Concert (1 Jan) by the Scuola di Musica di Fiesole *(055 597 851).*

Tavernelle Val di Pesa (from late May) Concerts at the superb monastery of Badia in Passignano *(tourist office 055 807 7832).*

Vaglia (June) Summer concerts in the grounds of Villa Demidoff *(tourist info 055 290 832).*

Vittorio Gui Conducting Competition (Oct) at the Teatro Comunale *(055 27791).*

Annual events in Tuscany

Rassegna Internazionale di Canto Corale (June) *(Impruneta tourist office 055 231 3729).*

Estate Fiesolana (July, Aug) A festival of music, dance and theatre at the Roman Amphitheatre in Fiesole. *See also chapter* **Theatre & Dance**. *Teatro Romano, Fiesole (055 597 8308).*

Puccini Opera Festival (July to mid-Aug) Puccini's villa on the shore of Lago di Massaciuccoli, provides an atmospheric setting for the staging of two or three of his operas. You are advised to take mosquito repellent. Tickets are sold all year from the ticket office, some travel agencies and the booking services. *Torre del Lago (0584 359 322/fax 0584 350 277). Train to Viareggio, then bus to Torre del Lago.* Ticket office open 9.30am-12.30pm Tue-Sat. Tickets L50,000-L155,000.

Barga Opera Festival (July to mid-Aug) Combines instrumental and vocal courses with a concert series involving both teachers and students. *Via Fornacetta 11, Barga (0583 723 250/operabarga@ mclink.it/ Barga tourist info 0583 723 499).* Ticket office open *July* 9am-1pm daily. Tickets L15,000-20,000. *Website http://www.essein.it/operabarga*

Estate Musicale Chigiana (July, Aug) *Accademia Chigiana, Via di Città 89, Siena (0577 46152).* Courses and concerts by this musical academy take place in venues such as the spectacular abbeys of San Galgano and Sant'Antimo. The Settimana Musicale Senese is the most important period.

Incontri in Terra di Siena (July, Aug) Chamber music festival featuring renowned artists and idyllic settings near Pienza and Montepulciano. Programmes are guaranteed to be interesting as one of the Festival's principal commitments is to the promotion of rarely performed chamber repertoire. *La Foce, Chianciano Terme (0578 69101).* Tickets L30,000.

Metastasio Classica (Dec-Apr) Chamber music and orchestral concerts at Prato's famous theatre. *Teatro Metastasio, Via B Cairoli 59, Prato (0574 608 501). Box office* 10am-noon, 4-7pm, Tue-Sat.

Music: Rock, Roots & Jazz

Florence's humdrum scene shows signs of life in the summer.

Even by Florence's perennially anorexic standards the last couple of years have been an impoverished period where nightlife and live music are concerned. No new venues have appeared to provide a re-kindling blast of seraphic light to the city's spreading neurasthenia, and the old haunts tend to stick to play-safe outmoded formulas or slump down into the general nocturnal apathy pervading the city centre.

Considering the city hosts an enormous university with thousands of students bristling with excess energies, it's difficult to explain why Florence is so bereft of fun spots. Many blame it on the conservative Florence council who are quick to deny planning permission to any midnight stomping ground where youth may congregate in numbers. Local musicians themselves all complain about the lack of venues to play in the city. **CPA Fi-Sud**, a year or two ago a thriving alternative venue to the bland city-centre clubs, has steadily declined due perhaps to an administrative lack of initiative and self-satire, utterly failing to emulate Bologna's vivacious and groundbreaking Link.

Florence's underground stronghold, the **CSA Indiano**, another of the illegally squatted sites, has its moments but can also be morbidly self-absorbed and too rough around the edges for the likes of many people. These *centri sociali*, like Florence as a whole, tend to be set in their ways. Also, many find them too politically abrasive.

Palasport (Viale Paoli, 055 678 841), a huge arena by the football stadium at the Campo di Marte, holds several thousand punters and is the stopping-off point for major artists if they decide to play Florence but mostly plays host to crooning Italian middle-of-the-road singers.

Only in the summer when there's the crackle and spill-off of unexpended sexual energies in the air does the possibility of being spoilt for choice fitfully arise. In fact there is a great contrast between winter-time Florence and the city in the summer. Midway through June the stages and strobes of the open-air venues are brought out of hibernation and all of a sudden there's more to Florence than its museums and pizzerias. The **Anfiteatro** in the Cascine park, **Le Murate** and various piazzas within the city play host to concerts in the evenings, Santo Spirito in particular. There are also the festivals, beginning with Arezzo Wave in the city's main piazza in June, a showcase for many of Italy's best up-and-coming bands. In mid July it's the turn of Pistoia Blues – three days of diehard blues and rock legends.

Florentine acts include Litfiba and Diaframma, both old rock stalwarts who have notched up considerable success in Italy while remaining unknown elsewhere. Two more recent additions to the Florentine music scene, Govinda and Masala have, on the other hand, made waves on the international market. Both share a heavy Indian influence, though no one can quite explain what the attraction of sitars and bamboo pipes are to the

The meditative Masala.

new wave of Florentine musicians unless it's the presence of the Hare Krishna centre just outside the city. Masala's latest CD, the excellent *Music for Meditation,* refers to their brand of sound waves as 'Ancient ragas, liquid grooves, electronic flow and modal jazz feeling'. There seems to be a nostalgia in Florence for all things psychedelic. Many of the new bands – such as Mirabilia, Neganeura, Interzone – profess a fondness for old 1960s and 1970s faves such as Syd Barrett's Pink Floyd, Love and Kraut Rockers Can and Neu. De Glaen, on the circuit since 1994, are another group making a name for themselves. A three-piece band specialising in experimental acoustical distortions they're signed to an independent Florence-based label, Cockney Music. Also worth a mention are C.S.I, Andrea Chimenti (who has collaborated with David Sylvian), Negrita and Emme.

Anfiteatro

Parco delle Cascine (no phone). Bus 29, 30, then 10-min walk. **Open** 9pm-late. **No credit cards.**

From mid-June to August this place opens for concerts. It often becomes something of a small festival site with thousands of people skinning up and chilling out on the surrounding parkland. Planning permission granted, which tends to be problematic every year with the fussy and punitive Florentine council, the Anfiteatro hosts concerts more or less every evening and provides a poignant open-air setting among the old Roman stones. Concerts are followed by a disco which kicks into the small hours. Bar prices are pretty average. The Anfiteatro is difficult to get to without your own transport – you can get a bus there, but they stop running at night, so it's not advisable to leave on your own.

Auditorium Flog

Via M Mercati 24b (055 490 437). Bus 8, 14, 20, 28. **Open** Thur-Sat. Call for details. **No credit cards.**

A largeish student venue outside the city centre, Flog hosts concerts every Thursday, Friday and Saturday night. Friday is often dedicated to reggae and ska. Admission prices vary depending on the goods on offer – L10,000 is about average. On a good night Flog, though acoustically not infallible, can be fun. Red Snapper and Jonathon Richmond are among the artists to have recently played there. In the summer its surrounding grounds double up as an outdoor cinema. Closed the rest of the week except for private functions.

Be Bop

Via dei Servi (no phone). **Open** 6pm-1am daily, but erratic. **No credit cards.**

Like many of the clubs in the city centre, Be Bop is a windowless underground cave. It's often packed to the rafters with students and Americans and it can be difficult to get to the bar or even move. There's no dance floor to speak of. The music varies though it's rarely original: you might encounter a band doing Beatles covers or old blues standards, or else a motley crew of Italian wannabe rastafarians muddling their way through a set of reggae classics. Drinks are pretty expensive, though there is no admission fee. Monday can be a good night when many other clubs are closed.

Caffè la Torre

Lungarno Cellini 65r (055 680 643). Bus 12, 13, 23, D. **Open** 8.30am-5am daily. **No credit cards.**

Concerts by some of Florence's best jazz musicians are the standard fare most nights in this small club along the river. *See also chapter* **Nightlife.**

Jazz Club

Via Nuova de'Caccini 3 (055 247 9700). **Open** 9.30pm-2am Tue-Fri; 9.30pm-2.30am Sat. **Admission** L10,000 annual membership. **No credit cards.**

Situated in a dark side street off the main drag, this is a sophisticated and slightly prim jazz club. It's a popular hangout for courting couples and a slightly older clientele who take their music very seriously. There's live jazz most nights: ranging from smoky fusion, modern experimental to good old traditional fare. On Tuesday nights there is a free jamming session where any musician is welcome to stand up and do his or her thing. Average price drinks: cocktails L10,000, beer L7,000.

Le Murate

Via Verdiana (no phone). **Open** 9pm-late. **Admission** free. **No credit cards.**

Another open-air venue which opens up in the summer months. Le Murate was once a female prison (you can walk around some of the old cells which have still got their original graffiti) and it provides an unusual setting for concerts, theatre, dance and events. Drinks are cheap. Last summer Masala were among the bands to have played there. Expect a hip and politically correct crowd of university and art students.

Parterre

Piazza della Libertà (No phone). Bus 1, 7, 8, 17. **Open** Jun-Sept 9pm-2am daily.

Open-air amphitheatre built during the Fascist regime and outstandingly ugly to behold. Open only during the summer months, beginning early in June, it can be popular with the smart set. Concerts are generally middle-of-the-road Italian schmaltz.

Pongo

Via Verdi 57r (055 234 7880). **Open** times vary. **Admission** varies. **No credit cards.**

Once a week, Thursdays, Pongo gives space to local underground bands like Mirabilia, Interzone and +VCC. *See also chapter* **Nightlife.**

Rock Café

Borgo degli Albizi 66r (055 244 662). **Open** 10pm-late Mon-Sat. **No credit cards.**

Snubbed by Florence's fashion and music snobs, Rock Café is a favourite haunt of provincial Italian university students. It has a labyrinthine crypt not for claustrophobics. Only occasionally are there live acts and these generally consist of university students ineptly thrashing their way through a set of covers.

Spazio Uno

Via del Sole 10 (055 215 634). **Open** *bar* 8pm-2am daily. **No credit cards**.

A small venue near Piazza Santa Maria Novella which plays host to various conglomerations of amateur jazz musicians. Hardly the venue if you're out for a showstopping night on the town. However, Spazio Uno deserves immense praise for its independent cinema upstairs. *See also chapter* **Film**.

Tenax

Via Pratese 46 (055 308 160/fax 055 307 101). Bus 29, 30. **Open** 10.30pm-4am Wed-Sun. **Admission** L15,000-L20,000. **No credit cards**.

Just about everything goes on at Tenax from Tricky to the participants in the San Remo Festival, Italy's answer to the European Song Contest. Bands touring Italy who are not big enough to fill the big concert arenas will often stop off here. Located just outside the centre, the spacious club boasts an enormous raised dance floor and antechambers gorged with computers, pool tables and bars. It can be painfully difficult to get a drink on a busy night as the ticket cashier is at only one end of the long bar – never mind, the drinks are overpriced and the beer is awful. Upstairs there are more bars, sofas and café-type seating areas with balconies to watch the go-go jive-jivers below. Tenax follows every gig with a disco.

Centri Sociali

The *centri sociali autogestiti* are a widespread and distinctive feature of contemporary Italy; no major city is without at least one. These mega-squats are usually located in abandoned buildings and run by rebel ex-university students. They act as unofficial social and arts centres, putting on gigs, exhibitions, films and sometimes offering courses and counselling. The atmosphere in these urban leisure centres is on the whole grubby and minimalistic; on a bad night all the males have long hair and all the females short hair and seem to be conducting a post-mortem among themselves.

Florence's three centri sociali have similar left wing political views – views which have undergone little or no refinement since the protesting heyday of the 1960s. Yet, for reasons best known to themselves, they shun any interaction or co-operation with each other. They also shun any idea of turning these venues into anything even faintly resembling a commercial venture, preferring to keep the operation within the 'family'.

Bologna's Link, which isn't afraid of making money, is far more successful – with a full and stimulating programme of concerts and happenings by artists from all over Europe and the world. **CPA Fi-Sud** and **CSA Indiano** are both worth a visit, especially if you happen to pick a good night, but as a ritualistic option will soon leave you tiring of the same old faces.

Other centri sociali in Tuscany include: Antinebbia in Arezzo; Macchia Nera in the San Michele district of Pisa; and the Godzilla on Via del Ulmo in Livorno. For more information (in Italian) on centri sociali try www.ecn.org.

CSA Indiano

Piazzale delle Cascine, Parco delle Cascine (no phone) Bus 29, 30. **No credit cards**.

The Indiano is the city's oldest centro sociale. Occupied for more than 12 years, it always had the reputation of being more downbeat and less politically mannered than the other centri. Bored by the limited options on offer in Florence its founders wanted to have a good time on their own terms and give exposure to top punk and hard-core bands (particularly from the US). After a couple of years the police closed it down and designated the building as the new HQ for the mounted carabinieri, who patrol the nearby Cascine park. However, the city administration abandoned the project and the building and the squatters moved back in. So, freshly painted and renamed, it started all over again. The Indiano organises concerts and raves, but also occasional political demonstrations in support of political prisoners around the world.

Every weekend the Indiano stages dance nights with local DJs running through selections of techno, dub, drum 'n' bass and jungle. Gigs by Italian and foreign bands provide entertainment on other nights. The dance nights, however, are usually far more engaging than the majority of the concerts. Entrance is cheap, usually L5,000, as are food, drinks and the smart drugs. The centro, located at the far end of the Cascine park, is easily accessible by car. By bus, take the number 30 from the train station then walk another 100 metres in the direction of Vivai Fiorentini.

CPA Fi-Sud (Centro Popolare Autogestito Firenze Sud)

Viale Giannotti 79 (no phone). Bus 23, 31, 32. **No credit cards**.

Located in the southern part of Florence, this ten-year-old centro is the biggest and most active of the three. Its 1,000-capacity concert hall, known as the 'spaceship', is the largest alternative concert venue in the city. Techno and dub usually provide the soundtrack on dance nights. The centro also runs a vast range of other activities including a small library, a gym, a small cinema, three rehearsal rooms for local bands, a theatre where the resident dance/theatre group Kinkaleri put together their performances, various theatre and film clubs and a photography group. You can get supper here for L6,000. The most interesting project here is the provision of shelter for homeless non-EC citizens. Every Wednesday a public assembly is held where all the centro's various groups meet. Concerts and parties are usually at weekends, but check out the flyers around the city for precise details. Again the prices

Hoary old rockers Litfiba have hit the heights in Italy, if not elsewhere.

are low: L5,000 entrance, L500 for a plastic cup of wine and not that much more for beer and spirits. In the surrounding grounds one can play basketball or volleyball or just sit and watch the innumerable stray dogs frolic about amid the rubble.

CPA, however, is in the midst of a political battle for survival. The site is owned by the CO-OP, a supermarket chain affiliated with the PDS political party – now known simply as the DS (Democratici Sinistri – or in other words the old Communist party. A similar predicament faced the CO-OP in Bologna where after shutting down a centro sociali the PDS suffered repercussions when many students withdrew their vote in protest.

Is the CPA worth saving? A couple of years ago the answer would have been in the affirmative. Having invested in a sound system, overhauled the large concert arena and arranged a three-day festival which attracted thousands of punters, things seemed to be looking up. However, since then the place has been going downhill with the stray dogs starting to outnumber paying punters. Through its inability to attract anyone bar the diehard disciples due to the fiercely anti-establishment, political idealism and an unenterprising, self-interested administration, the centre has become more of a protest site than a live music venue. The elaborate claims of its press releases – a multi-cultural outlet for the inhabitants of Florence – might be far-fetched but nevertheless on a good night CPA is worth a visit.

CSA Ex-Emerson

Via Niccolo' da Tolentino (no phone). Bus 14B. **No credit cards.**

Florence's third centro sociale is the most politically engaged – maintaining its connections with the *Autonomia Operaia*, the Italian protest movement of the 1970s. Its ideology, together with its style sense, is still stuck in a time warp: the world's troubles are down to conspiracies by the corporations and conservative governments. It was particularly active a few years ago but operates a more low-key operation now (it doesn't put up flyers). Every Monday is movie night (the films are free). Gigs are held every Friday and Saturday from about 9pm – usually by little-known Italian bands. Ex-Emerson is self-consciously scruffy and its inner sanctum of longhaired social outcasts sometimes appear so unimaginatively clichéd you begin to wonder when the punchline is going to arrive.

Nightlife

The hidden depths of Florence after dark.

Florentines rarely eat before 9pm, although they may sip a leisurely aperitif in a bar beforehand. Consequently, bars, pubs and clubs don't ever get going until around 11pm. The only Italians you are likely to find out drinking before this time are desperate carabinieri youths, who have an 11pm curfew. When the natives do finally flock in, don't be surprised if many of them make one drink last most of the night. Italians see booze more as a gentle social lubrication than the shortcut to oblivion favoured by northern Europeans. Many venues are laid out to ensure maximum pose factor for the clientele. Dancing is regarded by most Florentine club-goers as just another way to get noticed.

Clubs often have set nights for specific musical styles – keep a look out for flyers for the when and the where. Most clubs have a card system for paying that may seem confusing, but it is, in fact, fairly simple. If you're not asked for an entrance fee, you will be handed a small card, which must be given in at the counter when buying drinks and using the cloakroom. It will be stamped, returned to you and requested at the till when you leave. It can be a shock to the system having to pay for six pints and a couple of cocktails all at once, but the doormen are famously unrelenting when it comes to blagging your way out.

Many of Florence's central bars and clubs are underground and have no air-conditioning – lots of them shut down in summer as the scene moves out to the coast.

Opening times and closing days of bars and clubs are notoriously vague and erratic, and change without warning. Phones that are answered are the exception rather than the norm, so be prepared to take a chance.

Pubs & bars

Amadeus

Via dei Pescioni 5r (055 239 8229). **Open** 7am-3.30am Mon-Fri; 7pm-3.30am Sat, Sun. **No credit cards.**

A central bar, which doubles up as a café by day and attracts a crowd from the nearby language schools. The place has a clinical feel: the tables are in rigid rows against the walls and the staff are often charmless. The sound system is pretty good, though, and normally hums to retro hits and rap. Beers are L7,000; a gin and tonic is L8,000. There are discounts for students, but no happy hour. It can get rowdy.

Apollo

Via dell'Ariento 41r (0338 413 7303). **Open** 8pm-2am daily. **No credit cards.**

An easily missable bar by San Lorenzo market. Narrow and long, it has the bar down one side and wall seats line the other; in between there's just enough space to stand and chat. After 11.30pm the bar fills with a see-and-be-seen Italian crowd. The music can drown conversation, but when the DJ is spinning wicked tunes (as often happens), who cares?

L'Art Bar

Via del Moro 4r (055 287 661). **Open** 7pm-1am Mon-Sat. **No credit cards.**

A cosy bar doling out top cocktails. During happy hour (7-9pm) all drinks are L6,000 so you can get sloshed for little dosh. A beer normally costs L7,000; a gin and tonic L12,000. The place is small and gets packed early with sophisticated Florentines who barely start their drinks before leaving.

Blob

Via Vinegia 21r (055 211 209). **Open** 7pm-4am daily. **No credit cards.**

Blob can be difficult to find as it's hidden away on a side street behind an anonymous black door. There is a small bar on the ground floor, generally mobbed by Florence's art students. The mezzanine has tables and comfy chairs and serves as a viewing gallery over the small dance floor below. The crowd is friendly (English owner Donato included), the opening hours long, and the measures generous. Some nights have live music, buffets and early-evening videos. Known (together with Lochness, *see below*) to expats as 'the belly of the beast', where you enter a timeless dimension before being spat out into the streets to see the sun rise over the Arno. Beer is L7,000, a gin and tonic is L8,000; during happy hour (7-10pm) beer is L5,000; G&T L7,000.

Cabiria

Piazza Santo Spirito 4r (055 215 732). **Open** 8am-1am Mon, Wed-Thur; 8am-2am Fri-Sun; *summer* also open Tue. **No credit cards.**

This trendy dive doubles up as a café during the day, and maintains a cosy, exclusive air whether it's 2am or 2pm. The main congregating area is unfortunately in the micro corridor alongside the bar, where long hair will be dipped in drink after drink as wellfollicled felons struggle towards the toilet. The loo is a work of art in itself, plastered in 'adult' cartoons of women with gravity-defying E-cups. The main seating area in the back room is beautiful yet functional with stunning chandeliers, nailed-

down chairs and tables and a huge 'bar at the Folie Bergères' mirror. The DJs start up around 9pm and play an eclectic selection of sounds, including trip hop, reggae and jazz. Beer costs L6,000; a gin and tonic L8,000. There's seating outside.

Caracol

Via Ginori 10r (055 211 427). **Open** 5.30pm-1.30am Tue-Sun. **Credit** AmEx, DC, JCB, MC, V.

A good location to hit after an afternoon's bargain hunting in San Lorenzo market, Caracol is modelled on the archetypal Mexican watering hole, with every type of tequila imaginable. Happy hour is 5.30-7pm when the place will be jam-packed for half-price drinks. Salty tortilla chips and spicy salsa make perfect partners for the brain-blowing Margaritas. There are high stools along the huge wooden bar, otherwise it's standing room only.

Chequers

Via della Scala 7/9r (055 287 588). **Open** 6.30pm-1.30am Sun-Thur; 6.30pm-2.30am Fri, Sat. **Credit** AmEx, DC, MC, V.

A huge watering-hole off Piazza Santa Maria Novella – you can create your micro-climate in a far corner. It's popular with uniformed military cadets, who do their year of national service round the corner and have two things on their minds: pulling a foreign woman and making sure their hats don't get squashed. Music is the in-yer-face indie-rock variety. There's a happy hour (6.30-8pm) when drinks are half price; otherwise a beer is L7,000 and a G&T L10,000. Chequers comes into its own during major football matches when its big screen draws the crowds. During Manchester United's victorious Champions League final, several military cadets' hats suffered minor damage.

Dolce Vita

Piazza del Carmine (055 284 595). **Open** *bar* 11am-2am Mon-Sat; 5pm-2am Sun; *restaurant* 12.30-2.30pm, 7.30-11.30pm, Mon-Sat. **Average** L30,000. **Credit** AmEx, DC, JCB, MC, V.

The wannabe 'it bar' of the city's nocturnal scene, but the atmosphere can be sterile and cold. There is seating outside and at the back, including an area with armchairs and beautiful Peppino Campanella crystal light fittings. The bar area is standing-room only and the crowd often spills out on to the street. Standing, a beer costs L4,000, a G&T L8,000; seated it's L7,000 and L12,000 respectively.

Fiddler's Elbow

Piazza Santa Maria Novella 7r (055 215 056). **Open** 3pm-1am daily. **No credit cards**.

Crammed with a mix of young foreign students searching for adventure, and a bouncy crowd of hungry local and military youths. this is not one of the best bars in Florence but, thanks to its central location, almost certainly one of the busiest. It's open all day, has satellite television and shows sporting encounters on request. A beer costs L7,500, a gin and tonic is L7,000. There is no happy hour.

Gap Café

Via dei Pucci 5A (055 282 093). **Open** 7am-1am daily; Aug closed Sun. **No credit cards**.

The allure of cheap drink, central location and late-night opening draws crowds of revellers to Gap Café on a budget oblivion-seeking tip. The décor is bare yet stylish. If you want sophistication and long drinks steer clear. Beer (normally L7,000) is L5,000 and spirits (normally L8,000) are L6,000 at happy hour (5-8pm).

Genesi

Piazza del Duomo 20r (055 287 247). **Open** 9pm-2am Tue-Sun. **No credit cards**.
Lurking in the shadow of the Duomo, Genesi is patronised by the more discerning sinner. An immense ceramic snake greets you as you enter, it winds off to frame the bar and looks onto an airy brasserie-style room with comfy wall sofas. Smooth jazz chords drift from a band in the corner most nights. Prices are what you might expect for a central bar: L12,000 for long drinks and cocktails brought to your table. The ground floor doesn't get full until midnight, but if you want a seat in the eccentric Wild West bar in the basement get there by 11pm or reserve a table.

James Joyce

Lungarno B. Cellini 1r (055 658 0856). **Open** 5pm-1am Mon-Thur; 5pm-2am Fri, Sat; 3pm-1am Sun. **No credit cards**.
Situated on the Arno, James Joyce is the best of Florence's pubs in spring and summer, thanks to its large, enclosed garden and long wooden tables; the mood is always high-spirited and sunny side up. Before 9.30pm drink prices are reasonable (L6,000 for a beer; L7,000 for G&T) and accompanied by free nibbles; after 9.30pm prices go up. The homage to the myopic Irish writer consists of a small book shop where you can browse a selection of paperbacks, some of which are in English.

Joshua Tree

Via della Scala 37r (no phone). **Open** 5pm-1am daily. **No credit cards**.
Pokey dive near the station with good intentions and a U2 obsession. Techno heads sometimes gather here before catching the bus to some rave beyond the city walls. A collage of photos of regular punters on the wall will let you know what kind of company to expect if you're planning on digging in for the evening. Happy hour until 9pm.

Lion's Fountain

Borgo degli Albizi 34r (055 234 4412). **Open** 6pm-2am daily. **No credit cards**.
One of Florence's many Irish pubs, but the atmosphere and homey décor make this cut above the rest. Two TVs show sporting events for the beer-swillers. They pull a fair pint of Guinness and the atmosphere is friendly. It tends to fill up quite early – chiefly with young American students. Snacks are served. A beer costs L8,000; a G&T L10,000.

Lochness

Via dei Benci 19r (055 241 464). **Open** 8pm-late daily; closed summer. **Admission** *tessera* L15,000; L10,000 students. **No credit cards**.
Get messy with Nessie. Behind a little green door on Via dei Benci is Lochness, a late-night hole for the flotsam and jetsam of the night. Its budget interior is decorated with ridiculous cartoons of its namesake. It has no windows and is often packed with drunken revellers. A pool table and football table provide some entertainment. The predominantly male customers are there to keep their systems overflowing with alcohol and scour for any females still standing.

Loonees

Via Porta Rossa 15r (055 212 249). **Open** 8pm-3am daily. **No credit cards**.
Another underground nocturnal sanctuary in the heart of the city, Loonees is anything but loony. An easy, relaxed atmosphere pervades the place where drinkers from all over the globe co-exist on more or less the same wavelength. The large, vaulted room has such high stools that getting on them can be something of a co-ordination dilemma towards the end of an evening, especially if you take advantage of the free shot with every pint. Loonies is principally a bar live music, which starts around 11pm but it's nothing to get too excited about (rock five nights a week, salsa and blues the other two). The music is so loud you can barely hear yourself think. Admission is free. Beer is L8,000, a G&T L9,000.

Montecarla

Via dei Bardi 2 (055 234 0259). **Open** 10pm-4am daily. **Admission** free. **No credit cards**.
No bar in Florence has quite such a reputation as Montecarla. It's one built on Chinese whispers, the two chief rumours being that it was a brothel (it wasn't, but its décor of low-slung leopardskin couches, dimly lit, hidden recesses and oriental drapery encourages the idea). Nor is the proprietor Italy's most famous transsexual, though the bar's clientele could happily restage the *Rocky Horror Picture Show* of an evening. Soft background music plays and there's a friendly, relaxed waiting service. The drinks, predominantly cocktails, come in monster measures The house special, Montecarla (gin, rum, Cointreau and orange) will slip down as easily as you will off the sofa. Non-alcoholic drinks are L10,000; others are L12,000.

Old Stove

Via Pellicceria 2/4r (055 284 640). **Open** noon-2.30am Mon-Thur; 3pm-3am Fri, Sat. **No credit cards**.
This cramped den is all tables, chairs and a tiny bar, with full table service. Prepare to be singed by gesticulating cigarette smokers, ignored by overworked waitresses and to break a leg slipping on the floor of the toilet after 9pm on a Saturday. Outside seating in summer. A beer costs L8,000, a G&T L10,000.

Public House

Via Palazzuolo 27r (055 290 530). **Open** 8am-2am daily. **Credit** AmEx, DC, JCB, MC, V.
You could be forgiven for thinking you'd just walked into a junk shop when you step into this small pub, which is crammed with weird artefacts. It's more suited to in-depth conversation than threshold-breaking adventure. The Sicilian barman

Sottosopra *has its ups and downs. See p159.*

Gianluca is a salt-of-the-earth character and enjoys flexing his English. Low volume trip hop means you don't have to shout to make yourself heard. A good place to get to know recent acquaintances better. A beer costs L7,000, a G&T L6,000.

Rex Caffè

Via Fiesolana 25r (055 248 0331). **Open** 5pm-1.30am Mon-Thur, Sun; 5pm-2.30am Fri, Sat. **Credit** MC, V.

Gaudí-esque mosaics decorate the central bar, art nouveau wrought-iron lamps shed a soft light and a luscious red antechamber creates a secluded space for intimate gatherings. Friendly staff serve tapas during happy hour (5-9.30pm), when the bar can get lively. Sounds vary from blues to trip hop. The place is rammed at weekends. Rex is primarily a cocktail bar; most are about L10,000; wine is about L5,000 a glass. You can sling your gins until 2am.

Rose's

Via del Parione 26r (055 287 090). **Open** 8am-1am Mon-Sat; 7pm-1am Sun. **No credit cards.**

Tucked away on a side street off Via Tornabuoni, Rose's has a sophisticated, minimalist feel in orange, with interesting modern art and black-clad clientele that have Zoe (*see below*) written all over their nightlife past. The ambience is amiable and relaxed and it's rarely crowded. Speed of service is not the bar's best feature. A gin and tonic costs L8,000, wine or beer is L5,000, L7,000 after 9pm. There's also a sushi bar (7-11pm, except Monday).

Caffè la Torre

Lungarno Cellini 65r (055 680 643). **Open** 8.30am-4am daily. **Credit** MC, V.

For drinks, food and cigarettes in the wee hours, La Torre is virtually the only place in Florence to go. Situated in the San Niccolò district, and easily identified by the medieval tower next to it, it's a great place to go after a club session. Decent fare is on offer: pasta, crostini and tapas. Beer is L6,000 before 6.30pm. Live bands play some nights.

Sant'Ambrogio

Piazza Sant'Ambrogio 7 (055 241 035). **Open** 8pm-1.30am Mon-Fri; 8pm-2am Sat, Sun. **Credit** MC, V.

To escape the tourist masses try Sant'Ambrogio, its crowd is predominantly Italian and the bar has a fine selection of malt whiskies and wines. There are cocktails too, but avoid the sweet, synthetic Pink Floyd. The sound system trundles along on a diet of 1980s hits. A beer costs L7,000, a G&T is L10,000. All drinks are L6,000 during happy hour (6.30-9.30pm), and there's excellent nibbles.

The William Pub

Via Magliabechi 7-11r (055 263 8357). **Open** 6pm-1am Mon-Thur, Sun; 6pm-2am Fri-Sat. **Credit** AmEx, DC, JCB, MC, V.

For a taste of British pub culture, a diverse crowd from butch bikers to caressing couples flock by the busload to the William. The downstairs bar is generally packed, while the second floor and the back room have enough space for you to sip your pint and munch on a ploughman's or panini. Throughout, the walls are adorned with photos and paintings of sporting heroes or village scenes, all overlooked by two ceiling frescoes by an unknown Florentine. It's one of the few places in the city where you'll find Newcastle Brown Ale, but while the bottled beer is good, the quality of the draft is not. There is friendly table service throughout the night though it's not exactly fast, especially the delivery of your change. A beer costs L8,000; a gin and tonic L10,000.

Zoe

Via Dei Renai 13r (055 243 111). **Open** 8am-1am Mon-Thur; 8am-2am Fri, Sat; 6pm-1am Sun. **Credit** AmEx, MC, V.

Friendly staff are a feature of this elegant bar. During happy hour (5-10pm) they ensure the bar and tables are provided with crisps, popcorn and Tuscan treats. Try the Zoe cocktail: a lethal mix of vodka, gin and Cointreau, blended with fresh strawberries, sugar and crushed ice. The place is always throbbing with a loud crowd of cocktail gluggers . By midnight, the crowd spills onto the street, where there are seats in summer. Beer is L7,000; a G&T L9,000.

Clubs

Central Park

Via Fosso Macinante 2 (055 353 505). **Open** *summer* 11pm-late daily; *winter* 11pm-late Thur-Sat. **Admission** L15,000 before 4am Mon-Thur, Sun;

L20,000 before 5.30am Fri, Sat (includes 1st drink). **No credit cards**.

Central Park is an ideal location in the summer when the vast outdoor area, with bamboo and palm trees, comes into its own. Logic, on Thursday nights features some of the best drum'n'bass in Italy. DJ Fabio X mans the decks on Friday nights and spins some decent tunes. Saturday nights, on the other hand, are cheesy, with the obligatory cat-and-mouse charade played out by finger-lickin' Italian romeos and sanitary, blonde American backpackers. There's a great sound system downstairs with a big, fat, dirty bass. There are bars everywhere. Drinks cost L15,000. The card system can be excruciating when you want to leave and have to face the hordes bearing down on the coat desk and cash till.

Full-Up

Via della Vigna Vecchia 25r (055 293 006). **Open** 11pm-4am Tue-Sat; closed June-Sept. **Admission** free; L15,000 after midnight (includes 1st drink). **Credit** AmEx, MC, V.

Cutting breakbeat and jungle? Crazy happenings? You'll be lucky. Though Full-Up may help you to see local clubs back home in a better light. It has a tiny dance floor with a column slapped bang in the middle, where the Don Giovannis indulge their hips to the pretty lame music. Babes seeking a Mediterranean orgasm will have a field day. There's a piano bar and a roulette table. Drinks average out at L12,000.

Gallery

Via Villani 5a (fax 055 233 6896). **Open** 10.30-late Tue-Sun. **Admission** varies. **No credit cards**.

A pernicious card system operates here: once inside you have little idea how much you'll be hit for when you leave. Tales of bad experiences are rife and it's difficult to establish just how much anything costs. Entrance might be L20,000, or it might be free. Drinks tend to be L15,000, as does leaving an item in the cloakroom. Two dance floors throb to a midsummer mixture of cheesy house and Eurotrash. To each their own…

Lido

Lungarno Pecori Giraldi 1r (055 234 2726). Bus 23. **Open** 1pm-2am Tue-Sun; 1pm-2.30am Fri, Sat; *lunch served* 1-3.30pm; closed Jan, Feb. **Admission** free. **No credit cards**.

One of the prettiest bars in Florence, by virtue of its Arno view. Inside, Lido's interior doesn't appear to be very large, primarily because the dance floor doubles up as the queue for the bar. Music varies from R&B to more avant-garde sounds. Large glass doors open to a garden that extends down to the riverbank. Admission is free and drinks are reasonable: L7,000 for beer, L10,000 for a long drink. Look out for DJ Pise, who organises events, makes collectable flyers and specialises in Incredibly Strange Music. Enjoy the ambience but slap on plenty of mosquito cream. From 1-7pm you can hire a boat (L15,000/hour). Sunday brunch costs L20,000.

Maracana Casa di Samba

Via Faenza 4 (055 210 298). **Open** *restaurant* 8.30-11.30pm; *club* midnight-4am Tue-Sun. **Average** L65,000. **Admission** L20,000. **Credit** (restaurant only) AmEx, DC, JCB, MC, V.

This latino club is Club-Med classy. Don't expect to see the 'suits' downing jugs of sangria and loosening their ties, though, they're too busy watching the dancers. A superficial level of decorum is maintained until about 3am, but then the expensive, watery beer kicks in, the meat market opens up and the people pair off. The club's central dance floor is surrounded by poser platforms; balconies assure views of cleavages and bald patches. Bottled beers costs L12,000, draught L10,000, and spirits L12,000. The music is a mix of 1970s disco, samba and salsa. Beware the video cameras which zoom in on women and freeze frame a shot of them on the huge screen.

Maramao

Via dei Macci 79r (055 244 341). **Open** 11pm-3am Tue-Sat; closed May-Sept. **Admission** L20,000 (includes 1st drink). **Credit** AmEx, DC, MC, V.

Sleek and back-combed with an electric blue sheen, Maramao is perhaps the most Italian of the city's clubs. It attracts the smart set and the music spun out by a DJ imprisoned in a self-contained attic 12 feet above the minimal dance floor has an emphasis on silver-streaked Latin rhythms. There's soft acid house on Tuesdays when DJ Matteo is at the controls; happy house on Wednesdays courtesy of DJ Dr Rose. Drinks average out at around L10,000.

Meccanò

Viale degli Olmi 1 (055 331 371). Bus 1, 9, 12, 17, 26, 27, C. **Open** *restaurant* 9.30-midnight Tue-Sat; *club* 11pm-6am. **Average** L35,000. **Admission** L20,000 (incl 1st drink). **Credit** AmEx, DC, MC, V.

As a belated concession to feminism, Meccanò has done away with the naked female dancers who used to perform in its cages, but these measures have done little to stop the eager hedonists, who flock here. Huge and labyrinthine, Florence's most famous disco is fiercely commercial in its vision and has no qualms about catering to the masses. The music is shopworn commercial stuff. Smart threads are a prerequisite – it's popular with the showcase-your-shopping-spoils set. In summer, the outside forum opens up. It isn't cheap, drinks are L10,000 a pop.

The Mood 1

Corso Tintori 4 (no phone). **Open** 11pm-5am Thur-Sat. **Admission** L15,000 including first drink. **No credit cards**.

Like several other clubs in Florence, Mood 1 is situated underground. It's divided into three distinct zones: the dance floor where DJ Pise sometimes spins classic house anthems; the chill-out lounge, where a cocktail will set you back L15,000 and a beer L10,000, and the open courtyard lit by torches, where one can dissolve into the cool night shadows. Saturday is gay night, when Florence's drag queens and trannies cross-pollinate on the dance floor to the dulcet strains of 'lounge cocktail and freaky disco' (sic).

'Ere we go, 'ere we go, 'ere we go... But is it Butlins or **Space Electronic***?*

Pongo

Via Verdi 59r (055 234 7880). **Open** 10pm-3am Mon-Sat; closed Sun, June-Sept. **Admission** L10,000-L20,000 (incl 1st drink). **No credit cards**.

Pongo prides itself on being unfashionable. There's no dress code and no slogans; Pongo is happy to provide a temporary home for all those who can't be bothered with mirrors or fashion mores. There's live music most nights; Thursdays showcase up-and-coming Florentine bands. The musical fodder is essentially rock-orientated; the subsequent disco shies away from digital distortions and cutting edges. The card system is usually fair.

Soulciety Club

Via San Zanobi 114b (055 830 3513). **Open** 11.30pm-4am Tue-Sun; closed June-Sept. **Admission** *tessera* L10,000, then free. **No credit cards**.

Away from the madding crowds of the centre, Soulciety is one of Florence nightlife's better-kept secrets. During the week it's not normally busy, giving you the chance to appreciate the phat-rococo décor. Weekends, however, see all forms of *firenze* life squeeze into this club, yet the atmosphere is akin to a private party. Slabs of funk, hip-hop and soul are served up to the dance floor at the back. The squalid solitary toilet sometimes forces the desperate onto the streets to relieve themselves. Probably the best funk in Florence. Beer is L6,000; G&T L10,000.

SottoSopra

Via dei Serragli 48r (055 282 340). **Open** 8pm-2am daily; closed June-Sept. **No credit cards**.

'Tonight you'll be *sotto*, tomorrow you'll be *sopra*.' This club, close to Santo Spirito, has a bar upstairs and dance floor in the basement. The atmosphere is relaxed and the music generally strikes the right party notes. Despite free entry, it's never really full.

Space Electronic

Via Palazzuolo 37 (055 293 082). **Open** 10pm-2am daily; *winter* closed Mon. **Admission** L25,000 **Credit** AmEx, MC, V.

Much maligned, ever popular. Music and fashion snobs beware: Space is 1970s kitsch and 'ere-we-go, Brit abroad territory. The owners are Brit-friendly and promise reduced entry to anyone carrying this guide. There's karaoke downstairs, in a far corner there's a miniature replica of a pub and in another corner there's a TV with Sky Sports. The upstairs dance floor has a great sound system and an expansive dance floor, though it's a good idea to get trolleyed first to put your critical faculties into abeyance where the tunes are concerned. Entire coach parties are welcomed with open arms, so you could find yourself face to face with a pack of lurching vikings. Insistent lecherous Italian males are bounced. Space Electronic could be transplanted to a British holiday camp without any modification. Drinks cost between L5,000 and L10,000.

Yab

Via Sassetti 5r (055 215 160). **Open** 9pm-4am Mon, Wed-Sun; closed June-Sept. **Admission** free, L30,000 min drinks charge Fri, Sat. **Credit** AmEx, DC, V.

Most of this huge place is taken up by a dance floor, surrounded by wall-to-wall bars on raised platforms. The management leave a lot to be desired: beware of the card system (and bouncers) employed here. Yab isn't all bad, however; the music is often good, particularly hip hop night on Mondays with DJ Master Freeze.

Zoom Novantenove

Via delle Oche 19r (055 286 131/0339 469 5402). **Open** 11am-6am daily; closed June-Aug. **Admission** free Mon-Thur; L10,000-L15,000 Fri-Sun (incl 1st drink). **No credit cards**.

This new and centrally located club has drum'n'bass and hip-hop nights at the weekend. Though not huge, it has three different rooms. While techno thuds out on the ground floor, there'll be tripped-out trance down in the sweaty bowels of the club. The space can get too hot and crowded for comfort on busy nights.

Theatre & Dance

Money's tight, but the shows must go on.

Italian theatre is one of the most evolved in Europe, with a long and distinguished history. In the past, every town in Tuscany had its theatre and there are still around 300 in the region, many dating back to the fifteenth and sixteenth centuries. Some of the most interesting are in Montalcino, San Casciano, Santa Croce sul'Arno, Siena, Lucca and Pisa. Florence has two historic theatres: Teatro della Pergola and Teatro Goldoni (*see chapter* **Music: Classical & Opera**). The old **Teatro Verdi** looks a little neglected these days, but hosts a varied programme of productions. The Metastasio in Prato also attracts big-name directors such as Luca Ronconi and Massimo Castri.

Of course, most theatre productions in Tuscany are in Italian, but there is plenty of non-verbal theatre. Jean Claude Penchenat's ballroom-dancing show, *E ballando... ballando,* and Roberto de Simone's Neapolitan rollick *Gatta Cenerentola* were both recent hits. Otherwise you can see anything from Pirandello, Goldoni and foreign classics (in Italian) to mainstream contemporary and, occasionally, a radical fringe show. Critically acclaimed productions in the 1998-99 season included Lithuanian director Eimuntas Nekrosius' *Three Sisters* (following the success of his *Hamlet* in 1997) and a controversial version of Pasolini's *Orgia*.

The main problem with theatre in Florence is the lack of public curiosity; people want to see safe, middle-of-the road productions. Since these are the shows that put bums on seats, theatres are inevitably less willing to stage higher-risk, avant-garde shows. Hand in hand with this predicament is the fact that public theatres in Italy are controlled and partially funded by the state-run Ente Teatrale Italiano (ETI) and the biggest share of the pie goes to mainstream institutions. Despite the chronic lack of cash for smaller initiatives, individual enthusiasm and hard graft continue to produce many interesting projects.

If Italian theatre suffers from lack of funding, Italian dance has an even tougher time of it, in part because there is no state law to protect it as there is for theatre and music. The meagre funding provided by the governing institutions has not allowed for any stable, long-term investment. Nevertheless dance artists and organisers continue to generate a great deal of energy.

Full-length classical and contemporary productions by **Maggio Danza** are performed at the **Teatro Comunale**; modern work comes from the likes of regional company **Balletto di Toscana**, and other experimental companies, who perform throughout the year. The summer season offers a panorama of events in beautiful venues such as the **Boboli Gardens** or **Piazzale Michelangiolo**. Outside Florence, dance companies visit Fiesole's ancient **Teatro Romano**, **La Versiliana** in Marina di Pietrasanta and the **Armunia Festival della Riviera** in Castiglioncello.

ToscanaDanza was formed recently with the idea of promoting new performances by a handful of selected regional dance companies and co-ordinating events throughout Tuscany.

For listings information try *Firenze Spettacolo*.

Venues

The Tuscan theatre season is short, running approximately from September to April. For **Teatro Comunale**, **Teatro della Pergola**, **Teatro Goldoni** and **Teatro Verdi**, *see chapter* **Music: Classical & Opera**.

Il Fabbricone

Via Targetti 10, Prato (0574 690 962). **Open** *box office* 10am-noon, 4-7pm, Tue-Sat. **No credit cards**.

It was in the 1970s that this fabric factory was first used as a theatre, and it's since gained a reputation for good quality experimental repertoire.

Teatro della Limonaia

Via Gramsci 426, Sesto Fiorentino (055 440 852). Bus 28A, 28C. **Open** for telephone bookings only 10am-6.30pm Mon-Fri. **No credit cards**.

A tiny, delightful space which could be in New York rather than staid Florence. Shows are mainly alternative. Look out for the Intercity Festival (*see below*).

Teatro Le Laudi

Via Leonardo da Vinci 2r (055 572 831). Bus 1, 17. **Open** half an hour before performances. **No credit cards**.

Venue for works by Molière, Pirandello and Goldoni,

Curtain call at the **Teatro Comunale**, *Florence's municipal theatre.*

contemporary Italian writers such as Pier Paolo Palladino and Elsa Aglbato, chamber music concerts (usually Monday evenings), kids' theatre and cinema.

Teatro Manzoni

Corso Gramsci 127, Pistoia (0573 99161). **Open** *box office* 10.30am-noon, 4-7pm, Tue-Sat. **Credit** MC, V.
An important venue on the Tuscan theatre circuit. Many productions are shared with the Pergola and Metastasio (*see below*).

Teatro Metastasio

Via Cairoli 59, Prato (0574 608 501). **Open** *box office* 10am-noon, 4-7pm, Tue-Sat. **No credit cards**.
This sixteenth- to seventeenth-century Teatro Al'Italiano, with layers of boxes, pink and gold décor and 680 seats, is one of the best theatre venues in Tuscany; indeed in Italy. Its season runs from October to May, and big Italian names, both actors and directors (Luca Ronconi, Massimo Castri, Eduardo De Filippo and Vittorio Gassman) have worked here.

Teatro Puccini

Piazza Puccini (055 362 067). Bus 17, 22, 30, 35. **Open** *box office* 4-7.30pm Mon-Fri. **No credit cards**.
Light opera, musicals and one-man variety shows fill the bill at this large, Fascist-style building.

Teatro di Rifredi

Via Vittorio Emanuele 303 (055 422 0361). Bus 4, 14, 28. **Open** *Sept-Apr* 4-7pm Mon-Fri, half an hour before performance. **No credit cards**.
Resident company, Pupi & Fresedde, has moved to the Teatro Manzoni (*see above*), and the future of this theatre hangs in the balance while confirmation of funding comes through. The programme is varied, offering productions from classical Pirandello and Shakespeare to contemporary and fringe shows.

Dance companies

Balletto di Toscana

Via Monteverdi 3A (055 351 530). Bus 22.
This small company has become the leading expression of modern dance in Tuscany. Founded in 1986 by ballerina Cristina Bozzolini, the company has grown through work with choreographers such as Mauro Bigonzetti, Fabrizio Monteverde and Angelin Prejocaj and had successful tours in America and Europe.

Compagnia Virgilio Sieni Danza

Via San Romano 13 (055 655 7435).
Dancer and choreographer Virgilio Sieni directs one of the few local avant-garde dance companies to have achieved international fame. Performances are often creative collaborations with musicians and designers, including the Balanescu Quartet and Miuccia Prada.

Florence Dance Centre

Borgo della Stella 23r (055 289 276).
Directed by Marga Nativo and American choreographer Keith Ferrone, this eclectic centre offers advanced dance classes. Also each month Etoile Toy, a programme dedicated to the visual arts, presents exhibitions coupled with chamber performances of music and dance in the centre's spacious studios. It has produced several groups, including FloDance Corps, Baldanza, and Opus Ballet. The centre also organises the Florence Dance Festival.

La Follia

Via Vacciano 24, Grassina (055 645 146). Bus 31.
La Follia ('madness'), directed by Flavia Sparapani, stages only Renaissance pieces. Beyond the regular activity of presenting work in a theatrical context, La Follia is popular for offbeat performances in museums and fairs. The lavish costumes, music and choreography are well researched. It also organises workshops in Renaissance dance.

Maggio Danza

Corso Italia 16 (055 211 158/055 213 535).
Under new direction by choreographer Davide Bombana, Maggio Danza, Teatro Comunale's resident company offers a broad range, from *Giselle* and *La Sylphide* to contemporary works by visiting choreographers. It also performs at the Teatro della Pergola and the Maggio Musicale Fiorentino (*see chapter* **Tuscany by Season**) from May to June. In summer performances are held in the Boboli Gardens.

ToscanaDanza

Teatro Manzoni, Corso Gramsci 127, Pistoia.
This centre for the development of dance in Tuscany represents a handful of select companies including Balletto di Toscana, Compagnia Virgilio Sieni Danza, L'Ensemble di Micha Van Hoeke, Kinkaleri and Compagnia Roberto Castello.

Fringe theatre companies

L'Arca Azzura

Borgo degli Albizi 15 (no telephone).
Founded in 1983 by playwright and director Ugo Chiti, this company identifies strongly with Tuscany, its traditions and language. It is the driving force behind the **Teatro delle Regioni** festival (*see below,* **Festivals**).

Compania di Krypton

Piazza Santa Croce 19 (055 234 5443).
Founded by Giancarlo and Fulvio Cauteruccio in 1982, when their lighting, stage and sound techniques were very avant-garde, this company experiments with video, projections, lasers, microphones and other effects. 1998/99 productions included reworkings and improvisations on classic authors; *WWW Shakespeare* and *I pensieri di Mariana Fiore* (after James Joyce).

Il Teatro delle Donne

Piazza Santa Croce 19 (055 234 7572). **Open** office hours 10am-4pm Mon-Fri.
This company, directed by Maria Christina Ghelli, promotes works by women playwrights.

Pupi e Fressedde

Teatro di Rifredi, Via Vittorio Emanuele 303 (055 422 0361).
A young company that does a lot of work with schools and has an eclectic repertoire.

Teatro del' Carretto

Piazza del Giglio 13, Lucca (0583 48684).
It's well worth a detour to see this dynamic company. Founded in 1983 and based in Lucca, their work is full of surprises – music, machines and visual effects – and has a dream-like quality.

Festivals

Armunia Festival della Riviera

Piazza della Vittoria, Castiglioncello, Livorno (0586 754 202). **Date** July.
Armunia takes place in Castello Pasquini. Dance troupes such as Compagnia Virgilio Sieni and l'Ensemble di Micha Van Hoecke are regular visitors.

Estate Fiesolana

Teatro Romano, Vai Portigiani 1, Fiesole (055 219 853). Bus 7.
Dance plays an important part in this festival of all forms of music, from pop, classical to contemporary and gospel. It takes place in one of Italy's most ancient Roman amphitheatres.

Fabbrica Europa

Borgo Albizi 15 (055 248 0515). **Date** May.
The former Stazione Leopolda provides a wonderful performance space for the innovative programme of dance, music, theatre, circus and multimedia events presented by Fabbrica Europa. The stagings and installations of the 1999 season included a reworking of Kafka's *The Trial.*

Florence Dance Festival

Borgo della Stella 23r (055 289 276).
The festival, now in its tenth year, brings the great names of contemporary, traditional and classical dance to Florence. Brainchild of Marga Nativo, Keith Ferrone and the Florence Dance Centre, the festival presents 12 performances by acclaimed companies, while also dedicating evenings to upcoming choreographers. There is a choreography competition, seminars and art exhibitions.

Intercity Festival

Teatro della Limonaia, Via Gramsci 426, Sesto Fiorentino (055 440 852). **Date** Sept, Oct.
This festival provides a rare (in Florence) opportunity to see contemporary theatre in its mother tongue. Each year, a city is chosen (Madrid, Lisbon, Budapest and London have featured) and playwrights, actors and theatre companies from the country concerned are invited to participate. London warranted two years in 1996 and 1997. In 1999 it's Intercity Paris II and for the millennium the chosen city is likely to be Berlin.

Teatro delle Regioni

(055 219 851/055 234 0429). **Date** 4 days in May.
A short festival with plays in regional dialect.

La Versiliana

Viale Morin 16, Marina di Pietrasanta (0584 23938).
Summer season of music, operetta, prose and dance based in Marina di Pietrasanta. The main venue is the open-air Teatro della Versiliana.

Sport & Fitness

Your sporting chances.

Canoeing

If you want to canoe on the Arno, you'll need to join one of the clubs below.

Società Canottieri Comunali dal 1935

Lungarno Ferrucci 6 (055 681 2151/055 681 2649). **Open** 8.30am-9pm Mon-Fri; 8.30am-7pm Sat; 8am-1pm Sun; *office* 3-8pm Mon, Thur. **Membership** *annual fee* L180,000 registration plus L510,000; *three-month fee* L250,000.
Free lessons and training are given to new members. There's also a gym. Bring two photos to the office to apply for membership.

Societa Canottieri Firenze

Lungarno Luisa de' Medici (055 238 1010/055 211 093). **Open** 8am-8pm Mon; 8am-9.45pm Tue-Sat; 8am-12.45pm Sun. **Membership** *registration* L800,000; *3-month fee* L200,000; *1-month* L120,000.
This rowing society enjoys a prime location on the bank of the Arno under the Uffizi. There are also gym facilities, a tank and showers.

Car & motorbike racing

Autodromo del Mugello

Near Scarperia (055 849 9111). **Date** Mar-Nov. **Admission** Formula 1 trials L10,000.
Top-notch racing includes Formula 3 and motorcycle world championship competitions.

Climbing

Guide Alpine Agai

Via Torre degli Agli 65 (055 431 974/055 407 409).
This rock climbing company organises courses for all levels, such as a five-day beginners (L350,000), with the first day on a climbing wall in Montecatini. It also runs personalised treks or expeditions in Tuscany and around Italy.

Football

Florentines are football fanatics. And the *Viola* (Fiorentina fans) had something to cheer about in the 1998/99 season as their team led Serie A for much of the way (only to fade at the last) and reached the final of the Coppa Italia, only to lose to Parma over the two legs.

Star striker Gabriel 'Batigol' Batistuta has become a folk hero. The loyal Argentinian has consistently topped the goalscoring charts of Serie A and he was badly missed in the latter stages of the 1998/99 season when he was out through injury. Fiorentina did manage third place behind AC Milan and Lazio, which secured them a crack at the Champions League.

Fiorentina's recent forays into Europe have been marred by crowd trouble. They were banned from staging European ties after Barcelona's English coach Bobby Robson was hit by a bottle in a Cup Winners Cup tie in 1997. And in 1998, a firework thrown at one of the match officals in a match in Salerno against Grasshoppers caused them to be thrown out of the UEFA Cup – although the Viola still claim their innocence.

Fiorentina play at the **Stadio Artemio Franchi** (055 507 2245), which has a capacity of 45,000. The season runs from August to May. Games are generally played on Sundays and begin at 2.30/3pm. Tickets range from around L30,000 (for seats on 'le curve', where the rowdier fans sit) to L200,000, depending on the opposition.

Golf

Circulo Golf Ugolino

Via Chiantigiana 3, Grassina (055 230 1009). **Open** 9am-7pm daily. **Rates** *18 holes* L90,000 Sat, Sun. *9 holes* L70,000 Mon-Fri; L80,000 Sat, Sun. **Credit** AmEx, DC, JCB, MC, V.
This course in Impruneta, south of Florence, is the nearest to the city. Tournaments are often played on the weekends, at which time the course is not open to the public. Phone for reservations.

Gyms

Indoor Club

Via Bardazzi 15 (055 430 275/055 430 703). **Open** 10.30am-11pm Mon-Thur; 10.30am-10pm Fri; 10.30am-8pm Sat. **Membership** *annual fee* L100,000 plus *2-month* L470,000; *1-day* L30,000. **No credit cards**.
Sauna, indoor pool, weights and classes.

Palestra Gymnasium

Via Palazzuolo 49r (055 293 308). **Open** 10am-10pm Mon-Fri; 10am-6pm, Sat. **Membership** *registration* L50,000 (L30,000 if you quote *Time Out*); *1-year* L780,000; *3-month* L290,000; *1-month* L120,000; *1-day* L20,000. **Credit** MC, V.
Equipped with free weights, machines and sauna (costs extra). There are also body-building, step and aerobics classes.

Hot to *trotto*

Tuscans are 'the architects of sports betting', according to Graham Wood of snai (sindicato nazionale agenzie ippiche), the organisation based in Tuscany which oversees Italian betting.

The region is littered with racecourses and the racing calendar is choc-a-bloc. In Tuscany's *ippodromi* (racecourses), there are two main types of racing. The most popular is *Il trotto* (trotting) where the driver sits in a carriage behind the horse; if the horse gallops, discomfort and disqualification ensue. Trotting takes place all year round. The *galoppo* (gallop) is flat racing and a spring and summer sport.

At the tracks you'll usually find a relaxed and amiable atmosphere, with spectators ranging from immaculately dressed teenage girls accompanied by their daddies to scruffy, smoking regulars. If you can't get to the track, however, try an Agenzia Ippica (bookmakers) – they're generally full of earthy collections of barbours, baldies and bellies. These agencies are privately run and offer betting opportunities on horse racing, football, including totocalcio (Italy's version of the pools), cycling and basketball. Betting on sports other than horseracing only became legal in Italy in June 1998.

Betting defies the usual norms of Italian bureaucracy – there are no forms to fill in, just go to the counter and place your *scommessa* (bet). Specify the city in which the race is taking place, the name of the course, the number of the race and the horse. This information will be posted on walls of the betting office or can be found in Italy's racing newspaper, *Sport e Scommessse*. Look out for leading Tuscan jockeys such as Muzzi in the galoppo or Enrico Bellei, Italy's best trotto driver.

There are all manner of bets that you can make but the most basic are: *Il vincente* for the winner; *accoppiata* for first and second place (irrespective of order); and *il trio a girare*, for the first three horses over the line. The odds are calculated on a *totalizzatore* (tote) system.

Tuscany's main racing events include the Premio Pisa at San Rossore, Pisa in March and the Premio Duomo at Le Mulina, Florence in June – the Sienese Palio is not officially a betting event.

Agenzia Ippica in Florence: *Via Il Prato 6r (055 219 877); Via Villa Demidoff 3-7 (055 352 557); Via Giuseppi Verdi 55r (055 214 810); Via G delle Bande Nere 13 (055 681 0410); Via Cairoli 8r (055 572 216); Via Ginori 36r (055 294 708).*

THE MAIN TUSCAN RACECOURSES

Trotting (*Il Trotto*)

Florence *Ippodromo Le Mulina, Viale del Pegaso (055 422 6076).* **Admission** L7,000.

Montecatini *Ippodromo Sesana, Via Cadorna 16 (0572 78262).* **Admission** L9,000.

Flat racing (*Il Galoppo*)

Florence *Ippodromo il Visarno, Via delle Cascine (055 353 394).* **Admission** L7,000.

Pisa *Ippodromo San Rossore, Tenuta di San Rossore 153 (050 530 011).* **Admission** L6,000.

Siena *Ippodromo Pian delle Fornaci, Strada Statale 73, Ponente (0577 394 347).* **Admission** L5,000.

Grossetto *Ippodromo Casalone, Via Aurelia Antica 35 (0564 24241).* **Admission** L5,000.

Livorno *Ippodromo Federico Caprilli, Ardenza, Via dei Pensieri 46 (0586 814 481).* **Admission** L6,000.

Palestra Porta Romana

Via G Silvani 5 (055 232 1799). Bus 11, 12, 36, 37. **Open** 9.30am-10pm Mon, Tue, Thur, Fri; 12.30-10pm Wed; 10am-12.30pm Sat. **Cost** *registration* L30,000; *6-month* L420,000; *3-month* L240,000; *1-month* L100,000; *1-day* L15,000. **No credit cards.**
Weights' room plus aerobics and step classes, karate and boxing.

Palestra Ricciardi

Borgo Pinti 75 (055 247 8462). **Open** 9am-10pm Mon-Fri; 9.30am-6pm Sat. **Membership** *1-year* L740,000; *6-month* L440,000; *3-month* L250,000; *1-month* L120,000; *1-day* L740,000. **No credit cards.**
The largest, most central and modern of Florence's gyms; it is also the most expensive.

Palestra Women Club

Via Corelli 83 (055 430 202). **Open** 10am-10pm Mon-Fri. **Membership** *1-month* L110,000. **No credit cards.**
Women-only private gym.

Top Club

Via Masaccio 101 (055 574 786). **Open** 10am-10pm Mon-Fri; 10am-5pm Sat. **Membership** *3-month* L220,000; *1-month* L100,000; *1-day* L15,000; *30 visits* L300,000; *10 visits* L120,000. **No credit cards.**
Small but has character. Mainly free weights and some bikes. Closes at 3pm on Saturdays in summer.

Horse riding

Maneggio Marinella

Via Di Macia 21, Travalli Calenzano (055 887 8066). **Open** 9am-1pm, 3-7pm, Mon-Fri. **No credit cards.**
Rides are normally organised daily and cost L20,000 per person per hour. You should phone during the week to reserve a spot. They can also arrange lessons and special/group trips on request.

Pool

Gambrinus

Via Vecchietti 16r (055 287 201). **Open** 1.30pm-1am daily. **Cost** tables L12,000 per hour.
The only pool hall in central Florence. There are nine pool tables and eight tables without pockets, where you can literally try your hand at *boccette* or *cinque birilli* (on the same table but with a cue). The clientele is predominantly male, who are serious but not hostile.

Running

Most joggers head for the **Giardino dei Semplici**, **Bobolino** or **Forte Belvedere** (*see chapter* **Sightseeing**). If you are interested in taking part in organised events, or running with groups, contact the following:

Organizzazione Firenze Marathon

Casella Postale 597, 50100 Firenze (055 572 885).
Contact for details of Florence's marathon, which is usually on the last Sunday of November.

Associazione Atletica Leggera

Viale Matteotti 15 (055 571 401/fax 055 576 616). **Open** 9am-1pm, 3.30-6.30pm, Mon-Fri.
Well-informed and helpful organisation which can supply information on running clubs and races.

Skating

There are no ice-skating rinks in Florence, but in Piazza Santa Croce in December a temporary rink is set up which stays until mid-January. You pay by the session (there are three or four a day); the last finishes at around eleven in the evening.

Le Pavoniere

Viale degli Olmi Cascine (055 367 506). **Open** 3-7.30pm Mon-Fri; 10am-8pm Sat, Sun. **Cost** L8,000/hr.
Rollerskate hire for concrete cruisers.

Pista Patinaggio

Via di Soffiano 11 (055 702 591). **Open** hours vary Mon, Wed, Fri, Sat (call in advance to book). **Cost** approx L5,000 each depending on size of group.
This roller skating rink in the Oltrarno charges a monthly fee of L70,000, for unlimited access.

Sport clubs/unions

Centro Universitario Sportivo (CUS)

Via delle Rovere 40 (055 450 0224). **Open** 9am-1pm; 3-8pm Mon-Fri. **Membership** *annual* L10,000.
Membership of this students-only sports complex is

Local legend Gabriel 'Batigol' Batistuta.

a bargain (you'll need a medical certificate). Facilities and equipment offered include basketball courts, football tennis and weight-training.

Complesso Affrico

Viale Fanti 20 (055 610 681). **Open** 8am-7pm Mon-Fri. **Membership** *annual* L140,000; *tennis courts* L16,000-L18,000 per hour.
This public sports facility has tennis courts, basketball courts and football fields. The complex has tennis coaches and runs basketball and football teams.

Sports shops

Casa dello Sport

Via Tosinghi 8/10r (055 210 867). **Open** 3-7.30pm Mon; 9.30am-7.30pm Tue-Sat. **Credit** AmEx, DC, JCB, MC, V.
Stocks a decent range of clothes and boots.

Galleria dello Sport

Via Ricasoli 25-33r (055 211 486). **Open** 9am-7.30pm Mon-Sat. **Credit** AmEx, DC, JCB, MC, V.
Of the centrally located sports stores, the Galleria offers the widest selection of gym attire and trainers.
Branch: Via Venezia 18/20 (055 580 611).

Nadine

Lungarno degli Acciaiuolo 22-28r (055 283 666). **Open** 9.30am-7.30pm daily. **Credit** AmEx, DC, JCB, MC, V.
Make your sweat designer with clothing from this Versace, Armani and Dolce & Gabbana outlet.

Universosport

Piazza Duomo 6r (055 284 412). **Open** 10.30am-1.30pm, 2.30-7.30pm, Mon, Sun; 9.30am-1.30pm, 2.30-7.30pm, Wed-Sat. **Credit** AmEx, DC, JCB, MC, V.
A chic shop with the latest Oakley's, Nike's and other fashionable brand names.

Swimming pools

Amici del Nuoto

Via del Romito 38b (055 483 951). Bus to Santa Maria Novella station, then 5-min walk. **Open** *pool* 11am-4pm Mon, Tue, Thur-Sat; 6-10pm Wed. **Membership** *registration* L50,000; *1-month* L90,000. **No credit cards**.
Members can use the pool twice a week.

Fiorentina Nuoto

Via di Ripoli 72 (055 687 758). **Open** 9am-8pm Mon-Fri; 9.30am-12.30pm Sat.
Has extensive information on swimming teams, competitions and lessons.
Its main pools are:
Piscina Bellariva *Lungarno Aldo Mono 6 (055 677 541). Bus 14.* **Open** *summer* 10am-6pm daily & 8.30-11pm Mon-Fri; *winter* 8.30-11pm Tue, Thur; 9.30am-12.30pm Sat, Sun **Admission** L10,000; members L9,000.
Piscina San Marcellino *Via Chiantigiana 28 (055 653 0000). Bus 31, 32.* **Open** 10am-9pm Mon-Sat; 9.30am-12.30pm Sun. **Membership** L85,000 per month (unlimited access).

Yoga

Yoga Centro

Via Bardi 5 (055 234 2703). **Open** 8am-9.30pm Mon-Fri. **Cost** L10,000 per lesson.
Claims to be one of the most important yoga centres in Italy. It runs four, hour-long classes a day in various disciplines.

Calcio

One of the most spectacular, colourful and violent events of the Florentine year is the celebrated **Calcio in costume** or **Calcio storico**. Strapping representatives of the city's four ancient quarters – Santa Croce, Santa Maria Novella, Santo Spirito and San Giovanni, clad respectively in blue, red, white and green costumes, parade through the city before settling ancient rivalries in Piazza Santa Croce. The game is a no-holds-barred version of football, the origins of which may be as old as the city itself. Calcio was certainly going strong in the fifteenth century and, although the tradition fell into disuse at the end of the eighteenth century, it was revived in 1930. The game is played over one hour by two teams of 27 men, with the only rule being that you have to get the ball over your opponent's end line to score. It is, unsurprisingly, a pretty violent affair. Four matches are played annually, usually in June, with the final on 24 June (*see also chapter* **Tuscany by Season**).

Tuscany

Tuscany

The heart of Italy.

A well-heeled local bus driver who had travelled around the region for decades put it perfectly: not only is Tuscany located at the heart of Italy, it is the heart of Italy. While Milan may be its brain and legs, Rome its soul, and Naples its creativity and imagination, Tuscany pulsates with Italy's history and is a microcosm of its geography like no other region in the country.

Fuelled by the endless infighting between its *comuni*, which climaxed between the thirteenth and fifteenth centuries, Tuscany continued to gather commercial strength, muster military respectability and, most significantly, outpace its neighbours artistically and culturally. Eventually it imposed its language on the rest of the country and produced an unmatched plethora of everything from poets and scientists to explorers and architects. Tuscany's rulers also had the foresight to amass the largest amount of artistic wealth anywhere in Europe. To this day, the region has the highest concentration of art anywhere in the country and – by extension – in the world, as Italy

by most accounts holds over half of the planet's artistic treasures. Tuscany's geography also went a long way towards ensuring its overall unity amid constant internal squabbling. Over 90 per cent of its territory is mountainous or hilly, which leaves only small slivers of level ground around the rivers and along the coast.

Tuscany's inescapable and reductive popular image is that of picture-perfect, sunset-drenched and cypress-lined rolling hills known across the world simply as 'the Chianti'. Needless to say, there is much more. The rugged Alpi Apuane in the north and the Apennine peaks to the east set the region apart and provide ski resorts, high-altitude trekking and cave exploration. From these, self-contained, forested valleys such as the Garfagnana and Lunigiana, which stretch north from Lucca, and the Valtiberina, which branches east from Arezzo, have always provided both the basic ingredients for Tuscany's culinary tradition and the backdrop for many of its paintings. The area around Siena is striking for its lunar-like rock formations known as the Crete.

Grosseto is the unassuming provincial capital of the Maremma, a large expanse of scarcely populated and previously malaria-infested swampland which was once the region's poorest part, but is today a coastal playground for Italy's rich and famous. At the north end of the coast is the port of Livorno, Tuscany's historical melting pot, and the Versilia, with its proliferation of beach umbrellas and swinging night spots.

The region's identity and that of its inhabitants is multifaceted, but it is permeated by a profound sense of belonging known as *campanilismo* – visceral attachment to one's city, town or village, or to whatever cluster of buildings is grouped around the inevitably oversized campanile, tower or steeple, nearby.

Having foregone the habit of assaulting each other's walled enclaves, today's Tuscans re-enact their historical enmities mostly verbally, and often colourfully and musically, from the stands of football stadia.

Florence is generally despised, though the intolerance is more towards the domineering regional capital on account of its historical arrogance and to Florentines as a group than towards individual *Fiorentini*. Each city and province displays characteristics that resiliently resist the test of time, and each seizes any chance it has of getting its own back on its neighbours.

Florence's two largest challengers for regional supremacy have historically been Pisa and Siena. While Pisans are also universally disliked, it is the Sienese, fully conscious of being frozen in their medieval glory, who epitomise the sense of belonging and of identification with place and history. A citizen of Siena is first a *contradaiolo*, or member of his neighbourhood *contrada* (*see p212* **Le contrade**), and then a Sienese. Being an Italian or a European is a minor concern.

Tuscany's other large cities have found their own ways to make room for themselves. Prato is a wealthy city of elbowing entrepreneurs who demand the respect that goes with economic weight and have carved themselves a province to go with it. Squeezed by Florence and Lucca, Pistoia was quick to steal Lucca's territorial jewels such as Montecatini Terme when Mussolini made it a provincial capital. Lucca's proverbial prudence and commercial inclination have enabled it to pay off putative conquerors and salvage its communal liberty.

Bourgeois Arezzo has also maintained a high standard of living while being incorporated under Florentine dominion, while working-class Livorno was founded as a penal colony and has always been an open-minded city with loud-mouthed inhabitants and a pioneering spirit. Each seems to suffer from a lingering superiority complex and a pervasive, underlying vindictive spirit towards the Tuscan next door.

Of course, not everything can be reduced to communal rivalries. Tuscany personifies the greater Italian struggle between tradition and innovation. The region illustrates a clear case of political innovation versus cultural traditionalism. Tuscany's position along the so-called *linea gotica,* which divided the Nazi-occupied north from the liberated south in World War II, made it a hotbed of predominantly communist partisan groups, which subsequently ensured that the region and all of its main cities, bar Lucca, were governed by the political left. This led to a strong accent on social justice issues and generally effective city government, but was coupled with an equally

strong conservative approach to safeguarding landscape and city architecture down to the last stone. This combination of factors, by and large, continues still holds true, though left-leaning political majorities have shown signs of shifting, and pressures are mounting for further construction and for a loosening up of the highly regulated building laws.

Tuscans are not only aware of their formerly glorious place in world history, but have developed a sane scepticism (some would say cynicism) to go along with it. They are a particularly contentious and polemical race. A no-holds-barred verbal debate will bring out their pungent prose and cutting sarcasm, which they usually reserve more for each other than they do for other Italians. Those in the limelight have a knack for making enemies. Dante punctiliously ensured that all those who had crossed him were appropriately denigrated, and turned the result into one of the world's greatest literary pieces (*see also p14* **The people's poet**).

Today, Italy's most famous journalist, the sanguine Indro Montanelli, speaks his mind against virtually everyone and is much revered for doing so. The Tuscans' quarrelsome nature has its practical side. The concept of *bischerate* (mean-spirited treatment) comes from the Florentine Bischeri family who were brutally expelled after refusing to leave the lands allotted to Florence's Duomo.

On the lighter side, Tuscany has a tradition of *burle* (practical jokes) and a long line of nationally renowned comedians to go with it. The most famous of these is Oscar-winning Roberto Benigni, who has a habit of lifting up and kissing Italy's most prominent and staid political leaders on the mouth.

Allow yourself time to soak all this up – Tuscany and the *Toscani* will have plenty of time for you.

Tuscan wines

Classic Classicos, super Super Tuscans and noble Nobile.

Over the last two decades Tuscany has moved away from being a complacent supplier of flask Chianti to become Italy's most creative and innovative producer of premium wines.

Much of the progress has been with the classic red wines – Brunello de Montalcino, Vino Nobilo de Montepulciano and Chianti and, more recently, the Super Tuscans. A new breed of white wine – Chardonnays that are Burgundian in style such as that produced by **Isole e Olena** – has also emerged.

Italian wine classifications

The following classifications are a brief guide to help when purchasing wine:
VdT (*Vino de Tavola*): Basic table wine.
IGT (*Indicazione Geographica Tipica*): Simple table wine, from a distinct geographic origin.
DOC (*Denominazione di Origine Controllata*): Wine from a specified, defined and controlled locality. Conforming to certain rules regarding grape varieties, yields, alcoholic content and ageing.
DOCG (*Denominazione di Origine Controllata e Garentita*): the same as DOC wines but for better quality wines which have to conform to more stringent controls.

Red wine

Super Tuscans

Super Tuscans is the name given to the new style of wines that have emerged out of Tuscany over the last fifteen years. The Antinori family were the first to produce such a wine. Initially made with a large percentage of Cabernet Sauvignon, and aged in *barrique*, these wines are now an established product. Now Merlot and Syrah are also being planted to blend with the indigenous Sangiovese as this movement continues to innovate.

Because they are so different from traditional wines, these wines are graded at IGT level, but command very high prices.

Super Tuscans worth looking out for are: Querciagrande (**Podere Capaccia**); Ceparello (**Isole e Olena**); Olmaia (Val d'Orcia); Fontalloro (**Felsina**); Flaccianello (**Fontodi**); Ghiaie della Furba (**Capezzana**); and Sassicaia, Ornellaia and Tignanello from the Antinori.

Chianti

Chianti, the region that lies between Florence and Siena, is the dominant force in Tuscan viticulture. Chianti's countryside is almost entirely made up of vineyards and olive groves, dotted with castles and medieval villages. Only the wine produced in the Chianti heartland can be called Chianti Classico – it can be light and quaffable, or elaborate and complex with an austere edge.

In the late thirteenth century Chianti was highly regarded for its white wine, today the region is irrevocably a red wine producer. In terms of wines, the region is split into seven subzones, namely Classico, Montalbano, Colli Fiorentini, Rúfina, Colli Senesi, Colline Pisane, and Colli Aretini. Apart from **Classico** and **Rúfina**, most use the generic title Chianti.

Classico

The heartland of Chianti is defined by the townships of Radda, Gaiole, Castellina, and Greve (including Panzano). With the elevation to DOCG status in 1984, the amount of production declined and a marked improvement in quality followed. For the first time producers were entitled to use up to 100 per cent Sangiovese in their wines, something many had practised covertly for years. This change in regulations also permitted up to ten per cent of a non-traditional grape – Cabernet Sauvignon, Merlot or Syrah.

Badia a Coltibuono

Gaiole in Chianti (0577 749 498). **Open** *gardens* 2.30-4pm Mon-Sat; *shop* 9.30am-1pm, 2-7pm, daily. **Admission** *gardens* L5,000. **Credit** MC, V.
The winery is on the site of a 700-year-old abbey and wine has been made here for hundreds of years. The abbey is now owned by the Stucchi Prinetti family, which runs the winery, a restaurant and a well-known cookery school. They also produce Sangioveto, a good VdT which is 100 per cent Sangiovese. You can taste wine and other estate products, such as honey and olive oil, at the abbey's restaurant, Ristorante di Badia a Coltibuono (0577 749 031, open 12.30-2.30pm, 7.30-9.30pm, daily; bistro 2.30-6pm).

Isole e Olena

Località Isole, 50021 Barberino Val D'Elsa (055 807 2283). **Open** 9am-noon, 2.30-5pm, Mon-Fri. **Credit** MC, V.
The De Marchi family bought the estate in the 1950s. Paolo de Marchi has been a wine maker since 1976

A vineyard in spring, overlooked by the former Sienese garrison town of Monteriggioni.

and has made a name for himself both in Italy and internationally. Few producers in Chianti can match Isole for quality and value. As well as Chianti Classico, Isole produces Ceparello, the 100 per cent Sangiovese Super Tuscan named after the Borro Ceparello, a small stream that runs through the estate. Great emphasis is placed on use of Cabernet Sauvignon and Syrah. Also in 1989, a new vineyard was planted with five different clones of Chardonnay from Burgundy which came into full production with the 1994 harvest. Isole e Olena's Vin Santo is also highly regarded.

Felsina

SS Chiantigiana 484 (nr Castelnuovo Berardenga) (0577 355 117). **Open** 8.30am-7pm Mon-Sat. **Credit** MC, V.

This winery on Chianti Classico's southernmost border produces some of the region's best. The site has been inhabited since Etruscan times and was bought by the Poggiali family in 1966, with the aim of making great wines from the Sangiovese grape. The winery is run by Giuseppe Mazzocolin with the help of consultant Franco Bernabei. Since 1983 the story has been one of uninterrupted success and the estate is widely regarded as a trendsetter. As well as making great Chianti Classico, and single vineyard Vigneto Rancia, they produce a range of acclaimed VdTs: Fontalloro (100 per cent Sangiovese), I Sistri, Chardonnay and Maestro Raro (from Cabernet).

Fontodi

Azienda Agricola, Panzano in Chianti (055 852 005). **Open** 8am-noon, 1.30-5.30pm, Mon-Fri. **Credit** MC, V.

The Manettis have been producing wine since 1969. The 51-hectare estate's wines have grown steadily in stature since consultant Franco Bernabei was hired in 1980. This area of Chianti is known as the *Concha d'Oro* (golden shell) because of how ripe the grapes get. The vineyards are all south-facing, 300-400 metres in altitude and grown on Galestro Scistous clay soil which produces the best Sangiovese. The Chianti Classico is 100 per cent Sangiovese and aged in various sizes of barrel for about a year before bottling. The resulting wine is velvety in texture and shows great finesse. The highly lauded VdT Flaccianello, Syrah and Pinot Nero also come from the house of Fontodi.

Podere Capaccia

Località Capaccia, Radda in Chianti (0577 738 385/ capaccia@chianticlassico.com). **Open** 9am-noon, 2-5pm, Mon-Fri; 9am-noon, 2-7pm, Sat, Sun. **Credit** MC, V.

Podere Capaccia was once a small medieval settlement in the heart of the Chianti Classico region. The land was acquired by the Pacini family in 1975. Current proprietor, the charming Giampaolo Pacini, has undertaken the renewal of the estate. His thoroughly modern cellar has stainless steel vats, Slovakian oak *botti* for the Chianti, and three types of barriques for the Super Tuscan Querciagrande. Output is only 30,000 bottles per year – not much, but quality is king at Capaccia, from the picking of the grapes (by family friends) to bottling and labelling. Tutored tastings are available by appointment. Other produce of interest are a dessert wine, Spera di Sole, and a delicious extra virgin olive oil.

The quest for *tipicita*

The Chianti of today is very different from that of the 1970s and no doubt the Chianti of tomorrow will be distinct from the present. But the question of *tipicita* remains. The closest direct translation of tipicita is authenticity; it expresses the idea that a wine should accentuate those characteristics particular to the grapes it is made from.

Modern Chianti is made in a vinomatic vat with a short fermentation time, sometimes only three days. The blend will include up to ten per cent Cabernet Sauvignon – the thinking being that its synergistic marriage with Sangiovese brings greater complexity to the wine. A short maturing period of three to six months in new French oak precedes bottling as early as regulations allow, to hit the markets in as short a time as possible. The resulting wine will have a *tipicita* score of zero.

A more traditional method of producing Chianti would be to follow the original recipe set down in 1872 by Baron Bettino Ricasoli, whose emphasis is on the Sangiovese, the core, making up between 70 and 90 per cent of the blend. For colouring, five to ten per cent of the Canaiola grape will be added. The final seasoning is Malvasia in minuscule quantities to build fragrance and soften the palate. Fermentation is of medium length, one to seven weeks, to extract maximum colour and tannin from the grapes. Maturation takes place in old Slovenian oak *botti* for up to two years (or anything up to nine years for *riserva*). The end result is a wine of great longevity, well balanced and complex in nature and requiring extended bottle ageing to be seen at its best.

Market forces will ultimately decide the direction Chianti takes, but hopefully it will never become a boring homogenous wine. Wiser heads are sticking with the core, Sangiovese variety, whose character is determined by the unique combination of soil, climate and variety, impossible to duplicate elsewhere in the world. Victory to the new wave, or 'I told you so' from the traditionalists? Decide for yourself in the enotecas, restaurants and wine estates of Tuscany.

Riecine

Gaiole in Chianti (0577 749 098/fax 0577 744 935). **Open** 9am-6pm daily. **Credit** AmEx, MC, V.

This small estate is owned by American Carl Bauman, who bought it from John Dunkley, an Englishman who had come to be counted as one of the best small producers in Chianti. The 1980s and early 1990s saw steady improvement with the arrival of barrique and a young winemaker, Sean O'Callaghan. The Chianti Classico is elegant and intense and the Super Tuscan, La Gioia is 100 per cent Sangiovese. Tastings by appointment.

Rúfina

Situated in the north-eastern zone of Chianti, Rúfina, was one of the four production zones identified for its superior wines in 1716 by Cosimo III de'Medici in his *decrete motu proprio,* the world's first wine-quality control law.

This area has always enjoyed an excellent reputation, much of which is due to location – vineyards are protected by a series of low mountains to the north forming a warm, dry microclimate. The soils are similar to the clay and limestone marls surrounding Panzano in Classico. The quantity of production has remained low and many *ceppe storichi*, or old vines are used. Despite these advantages, Rúfina has endured a certain obscurity, bringing with it low prices even for estates with international reputations.

Fattoria Selvapiana

Via Selvapiana 43, Rúfina (055 836 9848). **Open** 9am-1pm, 3-7pm Mon-Fri. **Credit** AmEx, MC, V.

Current owner Francesco Giuntini, is a descendant of the estate's original proprietor Michele Giuntini, who bought it in 1827. Today Francesco's adopted son Federico is in charge of the winemaking, with the aid of consultant Franco Bernabei.

Montalcino

This hilltop town lies 40km south of Siena along the old Via Cassia and occupies a panoramic position overlooking the Val d'Asso and the Val d'Orcia. Wine has been produced in the area since Etruscan times, but only recently has the business been taken seriously. In the middle of the nineteenth century enthusiastic growers started to experiment with the Sangiovese. The result was the development of the Brunello grape, a Sangiovese clone, Sangiovese Grosso. It has been used, unblended, to create the wine on which Montalcino's reputation rests, **Brunello di Montalcino** (DOCG). Brunello was virtually unknown outside the region until the mid 1960s, but today it has an international reputation and is considered one of Italy's top wines. Its production is strictly controlled by the local consortium, a regulatory body to which most growers belong, which determines factors such as grape variety, length of ageing and maximum yields per acre. All wine is tasted and examined before being labelled

Brunello and, as a result, quality is high. Brunello is 100 per cent Sangiovese grape and is aged for at least four years minimum, three of these in wood. The wine is full-bodied, slightly tannic and well balanced with great ageing potential. The nose is fruity; blackberry, raspberry and violets predominate, but there are subtle overtones of oak and vanilla. Brunello ages well and can be kept for between ten and 30 years depending on the producer and the vintage.

Rosso di Montalcino (DOC) is made from the same grape as Brunello but is aged for only a year, resulting in a lively, fresh fruity wine. It is considerably less expensive than its classy relation and is a wine for drinking young. The third wine produced in the area is **Moscadello di Montalcino** (DOC), a sweet dessert wine which was drunk at the English court in the seventeenth century. It is made from the Moscato Bianco grape, producing a fruity, fragrant, fresh dessert wine. It is made in three styles: still, sparkling (*frizzante*) and late harvest (*passito*).

Villa Banfi

Castello di Poggio alle Mura, Località Sant'Angelo Scalo (0577 840 111). **Open** *summer* 10am-7pm daily; *winter* 10am-6pm daily. **Credit** AmEx, MC, V.

This American-owned concern is one of the largest producers in the area, with more than 800 hectares of vines and producing over five million bottles a year. It boasts one of Italy's largest, most modern wineries and it is extraordinary to note that it has all been constructed in the last 20 years, under the direction of Ezio Rivella. Banfi produces a classic Brunello, an exceptional Riserva, Poggio all'Oro, and a highly drinkable Rosso di Montalcino, Centine. Wine makers are also experimenting with Chardonnay, Pinot Noir, Syrah and Cabernet. The restored castle that houses the tasting rooms is also home to the Museo dei Vetri, which has a large collection of Roman glassware.

Il Poggione

Sant'Angelo in Colle (0577 844 029). **Open** 8am-1pm, 3-6pm, Mon-Fri; 8am-noon Sat. **No credit cards.**

Located in the village of Sant'Angelo in Colle, this estate has a long tradition of making top Brunello. Their wines had a considerable reputation in the 1920s and 1930s; by the 1960s their Brunello was thought to be one of the best in the region. The vineyards enjoy one of the warmest microclimates in the region. Until recently, winemaking was in the hands of Pierluigi Talenti, a man utterly passionate about his work, but he has now retired to run his own winery across the road, Pian di Conte. Talenti continues to collaborate with the Franceschi, who now own Il Poggione. The wines are powerful and long-lived, in the classic style. If you are here at lunchtime, Il Pozzo in the village centre serves great Tuscan food and has an excellent selection of local wines.

Montepulciano

This graceful, dignified town is surrounded by vineyards and olive groves. Wine has been made here since the sixth century at least; poet Francesco Redi hailed the wine of this region as 'the king of wines'.

The town is best known for Vino Nobile di Montepulciano (DOCG), the first Italian wine to gain this status. It is made from a mixture of grapes: Sangiovese, known in these parts as Prugnolo Gentile because of its plummy taste, Canaiolo and Mammolo. It is aged for a minimum of two years in oak barrels, three for *riserva*. Vino Nobile has a pronounced smell of violets and a strangely attractive, bitter aftertaste. In the past, high-quality wines were the prerogative of aristocratic families, hence the name Nobile. The wines are fuller and stronger than those of Chianti, say, due to the local climate.

The second-string wine is Rosso di Montepulciano, which occupies a similar niche to Rosso di Montepulciano, a young, fruity wine which does not require cellaring. It is made from Prugnolo Gentile and Canaiolo grapes and is considerably less expensive (and less alcoholic) than Vino Nobile.

Avignonesi

Via di Gracciano nel Corso 91, Montepulciano (0578 757 872). **Open** 9am-1.30pm, 2.30-8pm, daily. **Credit** AmEx, DC, MC, V.

This 175-hectare estate was established by the Falvo family in 1974. The Falvos are one of the main players on the Montepulciano wine scene and are largely responsible for improving the image and quality of the product. They have three vineyard sites; Le Cappezzine, I Poggetti and La Selva. The latter is outside the Vino Nobile production zone and grows mostly for their VdTs, which include Grifi (a blend of Sangiovese and Cabernet) and Marzocco – a barrique-aged Chardonnay. The Vino Nobile and the Riserva are full-bodied wines that take years to reach their potential. They also produce a highly acclaimed Vin Santo called Occhio di Pernice, which is aged for ten years in 13-gallon barrels. The people of Montepulciano call this a meditative wine; it should be drunk on its own, in small quantities, from large, wide glasses. You can taste some of the wines and visit the cellars, which date back to the sixteenth century, on the Corso in the centre of Montepulciano.

Fattoria del Cerro

Via Grazianella 5, Montepulciano (0578 767 722). **Open** 9am-noon, 2.30-6pm, Mon-Thur; 9am-noon, 2.30-5pm, Fri. **Credit** AmEx, MC, V.

This is one of the largest estates in the region, with over 140 hectares of vines. The vineyards are spread out over the hills of Argiano, one of the best areas for Vino Nobile. Del Cerro is at the cutting edge of viticulture, setting up experimental projects to select the most valid biotypes in terms of ageing. You can visit and take a tour of the hi-tech wine-making cellar or visit the tasting rooms in Montepulciano's Piazza Grande. The wines include Vino Nobile, Vino Nobile Riserva and two very good VdTs: Cerro Rosso (100 per cent Cabernet) and a Chardonnay, Cerro Bianco.

Poliziano

Via Fontago 11, Montepulciano (0578 738 171). **Open** 8.30am-noon, 2.30-6pm, Mon-Fri. **Credit** MC, V.
With 80 hectares of vineyards on three sites, the company was established in 1962 and has been run by Federico Carletti since 1984. It produces three different Vino Nobiles, two of which are single-vineyard wines. The two VdTs are Le Stanze, mainly Cabernet Sauvignon with a small addition of Cabernet Franc, and Elegia which is 100 per cent Sangiovese. The Rosso di Montepulciano is fresh and fruity.

Carmignano

'Carmignano is softer than Rúfina, not as well built as Classico, but suave and round,' according to a Florentine inscription of 1907 attributed to Giacomo Tachic, describing the wines found in this ancient, but recently reborn production zone. Carmignano was one of the four DOC areas mentioned in Cosimo III de'Medici's grand ducal edict of 1716. During the Renaissance the Medici exported this wine to England.

Carmignano was the first DOC (now DOCG) permitted to use up to 20 per cent Cabernet Sauvignon blended in with Sangiovese. The key to Carmignano's wines is the region's peculiar climate: grapes here ripen one or two weeks earlier than elsewhere in Tuscany. Throughout the summer ripening season days are hot, evenings are cool, due to the elevation, 200m above sea level. North winds from the Tuscan Emilian Appenine and regular, staggered rainfall reinforce the cooling effect and the land is some of the stoniest in Tuscany. This individual microclimate gives wines lower acidity and firmer tannins than those of Chianti Classico. Its greatest exponent in Tuscany is:

Capezzana

Via Capezzana 100, Seano (055 870 6005). **Open** 8.30am-12.30pm, 2.30-6.30pm, Mon-Fri. **Credit** MC, V.
The name derives from 'Captium' one of Caesar's veterans, to whom he gave the land between the Arno and Ombrone Pistoiese. Today the ancient farm estate is owned by the Contini-Buonacossi family. Winemaker is Benedetta Contini-Buonacossi, who with the help of consultant Stefano Chioccioli produces Capezzana's portfolio: Carmignano, Carmignano Riserva, Barco Reale, Ghiaie della Furba, Vin Ruspo (rosé), Vin Santo, Grappa and a fantastic extra virgin olive oil. The same family owns the Trefiano estate, also in Carmignano, where Vittorio Contini-Buonacossi has implemented some very innovative vinification techniques, making him one of the rising stars. *See also chapter* **Around Florence**.

While in the area another estate worth visiting is:

Immobiliare Castelvecchio

Via delle Mannelle 19, 59015 Carmignano (055 870 5451). **Open** 9am-1pm, 3-6.30pm, Mon-Fri; 9am-12.30pm Sat. **No credit cards**.

White wine

Tuscany is a predominantly red wine region although some good white wines are produced and, with the change in the DOC laws, this situation will probably improve. The traditional Tuscan white grape is Trebbiano, which is used in Galestro and Bianco della Toscana.

Winemakers are starting to experiment with non-traditional grape varieties such as Chardonnay and Sauvignon, and also to use surplus Malvasia (no longer used in Chianti) so it is probable that there'll be rapid developments in the next few years.

Vernaccia

Vernaccia di San Gimignano (DOCG) has been made since at least the thirteenth century and was thought to be Michelangelo's favourite wine. A lot of ordinary wine has been sold under this label but the quality has improved recently with the revival of interest in white wine production. Success is no doubt due to the fact that other Tuscan whites made from Malvasia and Trebbiano are bland by comparison. The wine is made from the Vernaccia grape in two distinct styles: a heavier style which is gold in colour and rich in flavour, and a lighter which is pale, fresh and dry. Good producers are Teruzzi e Puthod, who also experiment with other grape varieties; Panizzi, one of the area's up-and-coming wineries, making Vernaccia Riserva and Chianti Colli Senesi; Falchini who make good traditional wines and Vin Santo, and also lead the way with innovative VdTs.

To taste in San Gimignano try Bar Enoteca Chianti Classico in Via San Matteo which has a range of Vernaccia as well as other Tuscan wines available by the glass.

Vin Santo

Vin Santo is a sweet dessert wine which has been produced all over Tuscany for centuries. The name Vin Santo possibly derives from the Greek word Xantos which means yellow and is the name of a Greek island which produces a similar wine. Malvasia and Trebbiano grapes are dried on straw mats after harvest and crushed between late November and the end of March. They are then fermented in *caratelli*, brandy casks containing the remains of the previous year's wines, known as *madre*. The barrels are sealed and the wine is left to age for a minimum of three years, but often longer. Quality varies and there is a bewildering array of styles from ultra sweet to bone dry. The wine is a deep gold colour and usually served with *cantucci*, or almond biscuits. Notable producers include **Avignonesi**, **Tenuta di Capezzana**, **Poliziano**, **Fattoria Selvapiana** and **Isole e Olena**.

Food in Tuscany

Raw ingredients, simple pleasures.

Meat...

...and more than two veg.

It makes more sense to talk about food in Tuscany than about Tuscan cuisine, because cuisine implies cooking, whereas much of what is tastiest in this region involves little or no cooking at all. The three staples of the Tuscan diet are bread, olive oil and wine; add to these locally cured meats and salamis, subtle sheep's milk cheeses, and local vegetables preserved in oil and you have the ingredients for a delicious picnic or a feast of *antipasti*.

Summer, autumn, winter and spring are clearly differentiated in this region, and each brings with it particular foods that the Tuscans will have looked forward to for several weeks. The very first pressing of olive oil will be mopped up on cubes of bread; the first broad beans of the season will be eaten with olive oil and pieces of week-old Pecorino cheese; the first porcini mushrooms will be grilled over wood and served with nothing but bread and olive oil; and even chestnuts – so common in Tuscany – will be eaten as a delicacy the first time they appear.

L'ANTIPASTO

Meals generally start with the *antipasto*, literally, 'before the meal'. In Tuscany, the most common *antipasto* is *crostini*, chicken liver pâté on bread or toast. Cured meats are a regional speciality – usually pork and wild boar, which are butchered or hunted during the cold winter months. *Prosciutto crudo* comes from a pig haunch that has been buried under salt for three weeks, then swabbed with spicy vinegar, covered with black pepper and hung to dry for a further five months. *Capocollo* is a neck cut cured the same way for three days, then covered with pepper and fennel seed and rolled round in yellow butcher's paper and tied up with string so that it looks sausage-shaped. It's ready for eating a few months later. The most typical Tuscan salami is *finocchiona*, made of pork and flavoured with fennel seed and whole pepper corns. *Salamini di cinghiale*, or small wild boar salamis, include plenty of chilli pepper and a little fatty pork to keep them from going too hard (wild boar is a very lean meat). Look out as well for *milza*, a delicious pungent pâté, made from spleen, herbs, spices and wine.

IL PRIMO

The *primo*, or first course, is carbohydrate-based. In most parts of Italy the carbohydrate will be pasta or rice. Here in Tuscany it's as likely to be a bread-based salad or soup. Old bread is never thrown away, but is mixed with what could be called the second tier of Tuscan staples – tomatoes, garlic, cabbage and *fagioli* (Tuscan white beans). These form such dishes as *panzanella* (stale bread that is soaked in water, squeezed out, mixed with raw onion, fresh tomato, basil, the odd salad leaf, and dressed with oil, salt and pepper), *ribollita* (rich bean and cabbage soup with bread), *acqua cotta* (toasted bread rubbed with garlic and covered with crinkly dark green cabbage and the water it was cooked in – topped with premium olive oil, sometimes with an egg broken into it), *pappa al pomodoro* (an exquisite porridge-like mush of a soup made with onion, garlic, plenty of tomatoes, basil, a touch of chilli pepper and dressed with a swirl of olive oil). To say nothing of the ultimate winter ritual: *bruschetta* – toasted

Green gold

Thick, green and syrupy: olive oil is a pressing matter in Italy. There are festivals every November to celebrate the olive harvest, reams of medical literature are generated to promote oil's healthy qualities, and trade fairs sponsor competitions to single out the best oil. In fact, in Italy olive oil receives as much attention and scrutiny as wine and producers proudly refer to their product as 'green gold'.

The consensus is that the best oil comes from groves located slightly inland away from the varying temperatures and high moisture levels of the coast. But pin-pointing the best oil regions is almost impossible: each area of Tuscany is fiercely proud of its oil and claims to have the region's best. Tuscany claims to have Italy's best olive oil, but don't tell that to the growers in Puglia or Umbria.

Olive trees must be at least 50 years old for a quality crop and the fruit must be hand-picked to avoid bruising that causes a bitter taste. The olives should also be pressed within a few hours of the harvest and only the first squeeze produces extra virgin oil – darker and richer in minerals than the subsequent presses.

Olive oil producers all over Tuscany invite visitors to tour their groves and taste their product. Some of the best places for tastings are: **Oliveto Fonte di Foiano** (0565 766 043) near Castagneto Carducci; **Azienda Agricola Giovani** (0565 845 135) near Suvereto; and **Antico Frantoio Ravagni** (0575 789 244) near Anghiari.

bread rubbed with garlic and soaked in freshly pressed olive oil with a sprinkle of salt on top.

Fresh pasta in Tuscany usually takes the form of *tagliatelle* (flat ribbons made with flour, water and egg), *ravioli* (envelopes of the same mixture containing ricotta and spinach); *tordelli* (from around Lucca, stuffed with chard, meat and ricotta); in the south you'll find *pici* (just flour and water extruded into fattish strings) and in the Mugello *tortelli* (a double carbohydrate whammy stuffed with potato and bacon). *Ravioli* are best eaten with a topping of *burro e salvia* (butter and sage) or with a sprinkling of Parmesan or Pecorino. Flat ribbony pastas (like *papardelle*) go well with gamey sauces such as *lepre* (hare) and *cinghiale* (wild boar), and also *anatra* (duck), as well as the ubiquitous *ragù* (made with tomato and minced beef or, occasionally, lamb) and *salsa di pomodoro* (tomato sauce, usually spiced up with chilli pepper).

IL SECONDO

Cacciagione (game), *salsicce* (sausages) and *bistecca* (beef steak) are the main meats eaten in the region, though there is good lamb in some areas (look out for *agnellino nostrali*, with means young, locally raised lamb). Also common are *coniglio* (rabbit, usually roasted, sometimes with pine nuts, sometimes rolled around a filling such as egg and bacon) and *pollo* (chicken: look out for *ruspante*, free-range). During the winter you'll find plenty of slowly stewed and highly spiced *cinghiale* (wild boar). This is a species that was cross-bred with the domestic pig about 20 years ago, producing a largely herbivorous creature so prolific that it has become a threat to crops and has to be culled. Other common game includes *lepre* (hare) and *fagiano* (pheasant). The famous *bistecca fiorentina* is a vast T-bone steak that tends to be served very rare and is quite enough for two or even three people. Though a *fiorentina*, grilled over a herby wood fire, might now seem synonymous with Tuscany, the habit of eating huge beef steaks was in fact, introduced last century by English aristocrats homesick for roast beef. Have no qualms: the *Chianina* breed of cattle found locally are a salubrious lot.

IL CONTORNO

To accompany your meat course you're normally offered a side plate of vegetables or a salad. *Bietole* (Swiss chard) is available almost throughout the year. It is scalded in salted water and then tossed in the pan with olive oil, garlic and chilli pepper. *Fagiolini* (string beans) are more likely to be boiled and then dressed with oil and lemon or vinegar. The ubiquitous and sublime white Tuscan *fagioli* are served lukewarm with a swirl of good olive oil and a sprinkle of black pepper on top. *Patatine fritte* (French fries) are available almost everywhere, though boiled potatoes dressed with oil, pepper and a few capers are often much tastier.

It's a dog's life

Tuscan canines have fallen on hard times: they are dropping dead, and not from natural causes. Unsuspecting pooches wandering in the woodland have been wolfing down strychnine-garnished meatballs. Veterinarian Luigi Bigi saved more than 25 dogs rushed to his clinic in Città di Castello in 1997. In 1998 in Tuscany more than 59 dogs suffered from poisoning; 42 died. But where is the deadly bait coming from?

Many suspect the truffle hunters (*trifolai*) who use dogs to sniff out their precious prey and jealously guard their territory. The white autumnal truffle (*tuber magnatum pico*) is a valuable commodity. From £400 per pound in 1997, its prices rocketed to £800 in 1998, owing to a drought during the ten-week growing season. The black winter truffle, which grows from February to March, can fetch from £56 to £81 per ounce.

Part-time truffle hunters can stretch their income by as much as £4,000 a year with weekend searches. Simple mutts are trained from an early age to find the truffles, but not indulge; pedigree dogs are rarely used. Although unregistered and without papers, these specialised canines can cost up to £2,500. It could be that the *trifolai* are leaving the poisoned meat to kill off the competition.

But the dirty business of mutt murder may not be down to truffle wars. 'It is a drummed-up theory,' huffs one local, 'the poisoning coincides with the game-hunting season'. English author Muriel Spark, who lives in Chianti and has heartbreakingly lost every pup she has adopted over the last decade, agrees. The police also insist that the poisoning is by hunters trying to protect their territory from dogs that disturb their prey.

Whatever the motive, the peril is real. Dogs in Tuscany have certainly seen better days.

Pomodori (tomatoes) and *cipolle* (onions) that are sliced, spiced and baked *al forno* (in the oven) are highly recommended. To those accustomed to watery lettuce, radicchio salads may at first seem bitter: an acquired taste that will soon lead you to an appreciation of the many wild salad varieties. In early summer artichokes are often eaten raw, stripped of their tough outer leaves and dipped into olive oil and salt.

IL FORMAGGIO

The one true Tuscan cheese is Pecorino, made with ewe's milk. In fact the sheep you see grazing on the hillsides are not often there for mutton, lamb or wool, but for their milk. Thirty years ago each small farm would have raised enough sheep to provide the household with sufficient rounds of Pecorino, which can be eaten *fresco* (up to a month old), *semi-stagionato* after about a month of ripening, or up to six months later when the cheese is fully *stagionato*, and thus drier, sharper and tastier. Nowadays sheep farming, milk collecting and cheese-making are mostly the province of Sardinians, who came over to work the land abandoned by the Tuscans drawn to towns and factory employment.

Fresh *ricotta*, which is made from whey and is thus not strictly speaking a cheese, is soft, mild and wet and should be eaten with a sprinkling of black pepper and a few drops of olive oil on top.

LA FRUTTA

Cherries, then apricots and peaches, are readily available in the summer, grapes in the late summer, and apples and pears in the early autumn. Although citrus fruits imported from the south now take pride of place in the winter months, the indigenous fruits are quinces (*mele cotogne*, excellent baked, stewed or turned into a sort of jelly) and persimmons (*cachi*) – each sloppy sweet spoonful of which helps keep out the winter cold. However, for visitors to Tuscany fruit is perhaps at its most interesting in sweet/savoury combinations: *il cacio con le pere* (cheese with pears), *i fichi con il salame* (figs with salami), *melone* (or *popone*) *con prosciutto* (melon and cured ham).

IL DOLCE

Although the Tuscans are not great purveyors of desserts, they do like to conclude festive meals with a glass of a dry raisin wine called *Vin Santo* into which they dunk *cantucci*, little dry biscuits packed with almonds. Vin Santo is made with a special white grape variety which is dried out in bunches for a month, then crushed to obtain a sweet juice which is aged for at least five years. All this is highly uneconomical (you could get five bottles of wine out of the grapes you need for one bottle of Vin Santo), so that to offer a glass of Vin Santo is to honour a guest with the essence of hospitality.

IL CAFFÈ

An *espresso* may help you digest so much gastronomic indulgence. If the caffè seems too dark and strong, ask for *un po' di latte da parte*, a little milk with which to temper the bitter brew, or a *macchiato*, an espresso with a little frothy milk.

Around Florence

The Arno valley and beyond.

Most towns around Tuscany's capital have something to offer, without the push and shove of the Uffizi gang or *David* devotees. Prato's textile industry and shrewd business acumen has made it a place that Florentines hop to for shopping. Pistoia's immaculately preserved historical centre has been the setting for TV shows and films, and a zero-tolerance mayor has all but obliterated the town's age-old fame for trouble. The circular zone around the 'City of Flowers' (Firenze) is well-known for just that: an abundance of greenhouses and nurseries. Historic points of interest, from the birthplace of Leonardo da Vinci (the town of Vinci) to numerous Medici villas, all make pleasant day-trips from Florence.

The maze of roads in the Arno valley is not always clearly signposted so a diversion or two is inevitable. A relaxing drive through sometimes banal, sometimes breathtaking countryside is best taken without time constraints and with a detailed map to hand.

Carmignano

Carmignano appears to be untouched by the proximity of Florence's hubbub. The doors of the thirteenth-century church of San Michele and San Francesco on the main street of Carmignano remain unlocked, even though one of Pontormo's most famous works, *Visitation* (1530), and paintings by Andrea di Giusto grace the interior.

Bar Ristorante Roberto in the main square (Piazza Vittorio Emanuele, 055 871 2375. Open bar 7am-3pm, 5-9pm, daily; restaurant 11am-3pm daily. No credit cards) has become a local legend. In the modest dining-room the indomitable Fedora will ply you with delicious homely food (pasta with lamb ragù; salted cod cooked with wild leeks, onions, fresh tomatoes and Swiss chard), wine and a coffee for only L20,000.

For a taste of the blended wine that has brought the town its fame, **Il Poggiolo** (Via Pistoiese 90, 055 871 1242. Open 8am-noon, 2-6pm Mon-Fri; 8am-noon Sat. Credit AmEx, DC, JCB, MC, V) or **Castelvecchio** (Via delle Mannelle Carmignano, 055 870 5451. Open 9am-1pm, 3-6.30pm, Mon-Fri; 9am-12.30pm Sat. No credit cards) carry their own elegant, balanced reds. These wines marry Sangiovese, Cabernet and Canaiolo grapes with the Cabernet. *See also chapter* **Tuscan wine**. Nearby villa-farms that offer tastings of Carmignano wines are **Capezzana** (Via Capezzana 100, Seano, 055 870 6005. Open 8.30am-12.30pm, 2.30-6.30pm, Mon-Fri, free tours by appointment. Credit MC, V), and **Bacchereto** (055 871 7191. Open shop 4-6pm Tue, Thur; tours by arrangement. Rates L50,000-L75,000 per person. No credit cards). The latter also has a restaurant and rooms to rent.

On the road between Carmignano and Florence is **Da Delfina** (Via della Chiesa 1, Località Artimino, 055 871 8074. Open 12.30-2.30pm, 8-10pm Tue-Sat. Average L60,000. No credit cards), an elegant restaurant that overlooks the multi-chimneyed Medici villa of Artimino. Try the *sfomato di ortiche* (a pale green mousse of wild leaves served with a purée of pumpkin) or the *gnocchi alla parietaria* (featherlight gnocchi with butter and fresh herbs). **Biagio Pignatta** (Viale Papa Giovanni XXIII 1, 055 871 8086. Open 12.30-3pm Mon, Tue, Fri-Sun; 7.30-10pm daily; winter closed Wed. Average L60,000. Credit AmEx, DC, JCB, MC, V) earned its name serving fantastic stuffed rabbit and such dishes as pecorino cheese ravioli with scallions and truffles. **Fattoria di Artimino** (Viale Papa Giovanni XXIII, 055 879 2051. Open 8.30am-12.30pm, 2-6pm, daily. No credit cards) produces DOC and DOCG wines on 740 hectares of beautiful land. Open for tours with tastings (by arrangement 8am-noon, 1-5pm, Mon-Sat). They also produce extra virgin olive oil and grappa.

Certaldo Alto

This settlement's main claim to fame is that Giovanni Boccaccio (1313-75, author of *The Decameron*) was born and died here. Its historical centre monopolises a stunning view over the Val d'Elsa, looking over to Volterra. During the first week in August the town is bathed in candlelight for the Mercantia – a festival aimed at recreating the atmosphere of the town as it was before electricity. The **Palazzo del Vicario** (Piazzetta del Vicario, 0571 661 219. Open summer 10am-1pm, 2.30-7.30pm, daily; winter 10am-12.30pm, 3-6pm, daily. Admission L5,000. No credit cards) is worth a visit for its beautiful frescoed rooms.

There are two hotels and three restaurants in the upper town. The **Osteria del Vicario** (Via Rivellino 3, tel/fax 0571 668 228. Open 12.30-2.30pm, 7.30-10pm Mon, Tue, Thur-Sun. Rates double L110,000-L130,000. No credit cards) has five double rooms, a small dining-room and a wis-

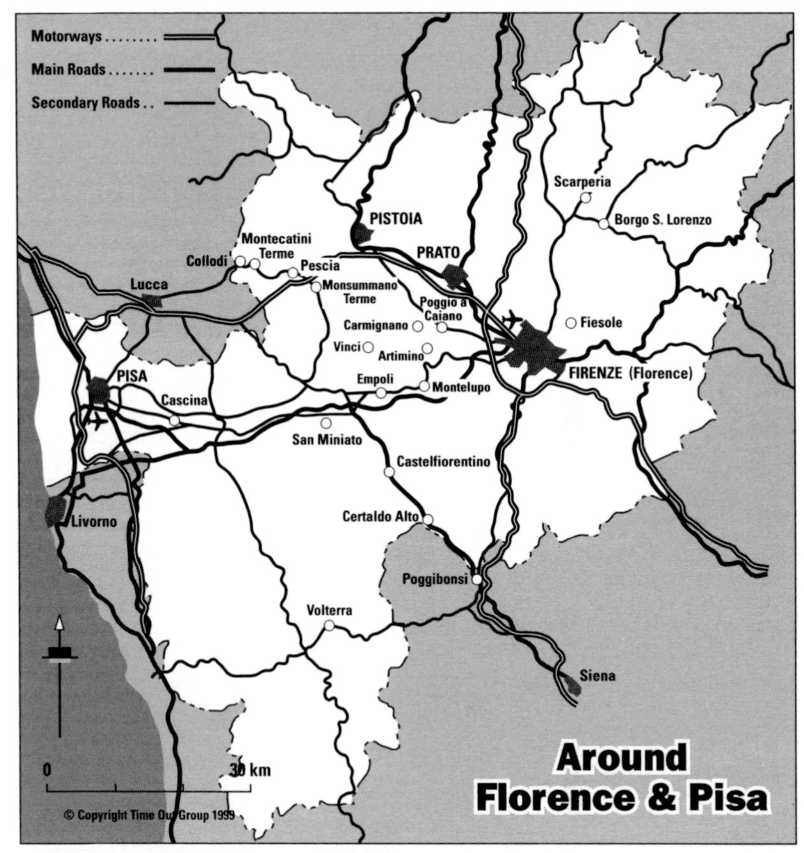

teria-clad portico, where gourmets will enjoy the inventive dishes devised by Enzo Pette, who takes his culinary calling very seriously. **Il Castello** hotel and restaurant (Via G della Rena 6, tel/fax 0571 668 250. Open 12.30-2.30pm, 7.30-10.30pm, Mon-Thur, Sat, Sun. Average L40,000. Credit AmEx, DC, JCB, MC, V) has a funicular which can carry up to 30 passengers (tickets L2,500) up to the terrace, where candlelit tables surround a seventeenth-century fountain. The roasted meats rubbed with rosemary are exceptional. Antique Russian samovars and Tuscan shields and swords sustain the heavy, medieval atmosphere inside.

Fiesole

Many Florentines dream of living in Fiesole to escape the madness of the city, but little Fiesole can get as packed as Florence. Fortunately the masses that invade small Faesulae (as it was known to the Etruscans) come mainly in high summer.

Without Fiesole, there would have been no Florence. For this stubborn Etruscan hill-town proved so difficult for the Romans to subdue, that they ended up setting up camp in the river valley below. When the Romans eventually took Fiesole, it became one of the most important towns in Etruria; it remained independent until the twelfth-century, when Florence finally vanquished it in battle.

Fiesole soon found a new role as a refined suburb where aristocrats could escape the heat and *hoi polloi* of Florence. In the fourteenth century, it was to the villas of Fiesole that Boccaccio sent his courtly raconteurs to escape the plague and tell the stories of *The Decameron*; and half a millennium later, it was to Fiesole that EM Forster had his corsetted Edwardians picnic and Lucy have her first kiss in *Room With A View*.

The main square, Piazza Mino, named after the artist Mino da Fiesole, is lined with cafés and restaurants and dominated by the immense honey-stone campanile of the eleventh-century Duomo. Inside, the columns are topped with capitals dating from Fiesole's period under Roman occupation. There are more relics of Roman Fiesole down the hill: a theatre which is still used for plays in summer, and the **Musei di Fiesole** (Via Portigiani 1, 055 59416. Open summer 9.30am-7pm daily; winter 9.30am-4.30pm; closed 1st Tue of month. Admission L10,000, L6,000 concessions. Credit MC, V), which combines a museum and a replica Roman temple with archaeological finds from Bronze Age, Etruscan and Roman Fiesole. A complex of partially restored Roman baths and remains of Etruscan walls is nearby.

Head up Via San Francesco to see the church of Sant'Alessandro, founded in the fifth or sixth century on the site of Roman and Etruscan temples. There are fabulous views from its terrace, and vibrant onion marble columns within. San Franceso, further up, has a collection of souvenirs from China brought back by missionaries.

There are some lovely walks around Fiesole, but the best is down the steep, twisting Via Vecchia Fiesolana to the monastery of San Domenico, where painter Fra Angelico was a monk. The church still retains a delicate *Madonna and Angels* (1420) by him. At the hamlet of Maiano, three kilometres away, past the Villa San Michele hotel, **Le Cave di Maiano** (Via delle Cave 16, 055 599 504. Open 7.30pm-midnight Mon; 12.30-3pm, 7.30pm-midnight Tue-Sun. Average L60,000. Credit AmEx, DC, JCB, MC, V), is a pleasant place for a meal on the terrace. Its speciality is the deliciously crisp and light *fritto misto* (deep-fried mixed vegetables and flowers). Also try the *riso allo spazzocamino* (literally, chimney-sweep's risotto), a dish of beans and rice; the rice is cooked with red cabbage, so it goes black. For dessert, cross the road for one of the best ice-creams in the vicinity of Florence at **Gelateria Maiano**, open until late.

See chapter **Accommodation** for places to stay in Fiesole, including the **Camping di Fiesole**, the brainchild of proprietor Gino, who started with a permit for a doghouse that, over the years, he has developed into a series of terracotta-floored bungalows perched on a fabulous lookout in the midst of rolling hills. Five minutes drive up the road, **Disco Petit Bois** (Via Ferrucci 51, 055 59578. Open piano bar 9.30pm-2.30am Tue, Thur, Sun; club 10.30pm-3.30am Wed, Fri, Sat. Admission L15,000-L20,000, incl 1st drink) is strictly for the over-25s. For fresh air and a snack, head up the hill to **Trattoria Le 4 Strade** (Via Faentina 335, Località Olmo, 055 548 920. Closed Mon. Average 40,000. No credit cards). Try the *crostini di polenta* (fried polenta) with *funghi porcini* but skip the house wine.

Montecatini Terme

Montecatini has a restrained elegance that has always attracted petit bourgeois from around Europe. Times are changing, however: the town's sleeping places are often filled by younger tourists who can't find a bed in Florence. A request was filed by the city some years ago for a permit to open a casino. Though it has been turned down until now, overriding opinion has it that by the year 2001, permission will be granted.

With all the glitz and flashy exteriors, it's tough deciding where to eat. **Gourmet Restaurant** (Via Amendola 6, 0572 771 012. Open 12.30-2pm, 7.30-10.30pm, Mon, Wed-Sun. Average L80,000. Credit AmEx, DC, JCB, MC, V) is good for fresh seafood and does a sublime crème caramel. **Egisto**'s (Piazza Cesare Battisti 13, 0572 78413. Open 12.30-2pm, 7.30pm-1am Mon, Wed-Sun. Average L40,000. Credit AmEx, DC, JCB, MC, V) slick design and non-traditional pastas, alongside Tuscan classics has made it popular with the more adventurous locals. **San Francisco** (Corso Roma 112, 0572 79632. Open 7.30pm-5am. Mon-Wed, Fri-

The flashy exteriors of **Montecatini Terme**.

Sun. Average L60,000, pizza L25,000. Credit AmEx, DC, JCB, MC, V) gets the louder crowd in from Florence. Its saving grace is wood-oven pizza until 4am. For sampling Tuscan wines, **Il Chicco d'Uva Vineria** (Viale Verdi 35, 0572 910 300. Open 10am-1pm, 5pm-midnight Tue-Sun. Average L30,000. Credit AmEx, DC, JCB, MC, V) provides laid-back expertise. Stand at the bar for wine by the glass and home-made snacks, or lounge in the back room where there are cushioned booths.

Recently refurbished **Hotel Savoia and Campana** (Viale Cavallotti 10, 0572 772 670/fax 0572 901 366. Rates single L70,000, double L100,000. Credit AmEx, DC, JCB, MC, V) is housed in one of Montecatini's oldest buildings, though most of the original character was been wallpapered over. The owners also have **Hotel Verena** (Viale Cavallotti 35, 0572 72809. Rates single L35,000; double 70,000. Credit AmEx, DC, JCB, MC, V), a gem of a pensione on the same street with 12 rooms. You could also try the **Minerva Palace Hotel** (Via Cavour 14, 0572 92811/fax 0572 78629. Rates single L100,000; double L160,000).

Tourist Office (Viale Verdi 66, 0572 772 244. Open 9am-12.30pm, 3-6pm, Mon-Sat; 9am-noon Sun).

Monsummano Terme

Monsummano is a pleasant, if unthrilling, town with two major spa hotels. If you can take the time (and have the money), go for the four-star treatment at **Grotta Giusti Hotel**, which has its own spa (Via Grotta Giusti 171, 0572 51165/fax 0572 51269/ spa 0572 51008). Open 1 Mar-30 Nov; spa 24 Mar-1 Nov. Rates single L150,000-L190,000; double L250,000-L290,000. Credit AmEx, DC, JCB, MC, V). It is located in a well-appointed villa in a park. From there you can take an invigorating 3km hike up to Monsummano Alto where you get a view of the surrounding Valdinievole (Valley of the Clouds).

Montelupo

The people of Montelupo have been making glazed pottery since the Middle Ages. In 1973 an old public laundry in the Castello district was dismantled to reveal a 2m-wide well that had been filled over the centuries with ceramic rejects and shards, many of which are now in the **Museo della Ceramica** (Via Sinibaldi 34, 0571 51352. Open 9am-noon, 2.30-7pm Tue-Sun. Admission L5,000; L3,500 concessions. No credit cards).

The locals have never forsaken their vocation and, every third Sunday of the month, their products are displayed for sale in the old cinema and surrounding stalls . The town also hosts a flower festival the first Sunday in April, an antiques market in May and a Festa Internazionale della Ceramica during the last week of June.

Pistoia

If Prato is Florence's sparky little sister, Pistoia is its maiden aunt; an old-fashioned place, where the pace is slow and life is still in tune with the countryside. Encircled by walls dating back to the fourteenth century, the quiet, historic centre has a number of fine Romanesque and Gothic buildings, leading in towards its elegant colonnaded cathedral.

Local goodies include the savoury *biroldo*, a sort of spicy boiled sausage, the *migliaccio,* a pancake made with pig's blood, pine-nuts, raisins and sugar, and *confetti*, small, spiky white sweetmeats. You can find the latter at Corsini in Piazza San Francesco and Bertinotti in Viale Ardua. You should also try the excellent bread baked in traditional wood-burning ovens at the Forno della Paura in Via N Sauro. In 1864, when foundations were being laid for the construction of **Valiani Caffè Pasticceria** (Via Cavour 55, 0573 23034. Open 7am-1.30pm, 3-8pm, Mon, Wed-Sun. No credit cards) on the site of a former oratory, frescoed walls from the school of Giotto were uncovered. Upon completion, the café's regulars included the likes of Verdi, Rossini, Bellini, Leoncavallo, Giordano and Puccini. It also houses a private art gallery.

Things to see

The **Duomo** has a simple Romanesque interior and a campanile with exotic tiger-striped arcades on top. Opposite is the octagonal, fourteenth-century, green-and-white-striped Baptistery. The **Museo Civico** (0573 371 296. Open 10am-7pm Tue-Sat; 9am-12.30pm Sun. Admission L6,000; free Sat pm, under-18s, over-60s. No credit cards) behind the Duomo has fine fourteenth-century paintings displayed on the ground floor and some fairly dreadful late Mannerist works two floors above. In the middle is a section on Giovanni Michelucci (1891-1990), one of Pistoia's foremost scions and architect of Florence's Santa Maria Novella station. **Palazzo Tau** (Corso Silvano Fede 30, 0573 30285. Open 9am-1pm, 3-7pm, Tue-Sun; 9am-12.30pm public hols. Admission L6,000; free Sat pm, under-18s, over-60s. No credit cards) houses the Centro di Documentazione e Fondazione (0573 30285) devoted to the other Pistoian of renown, sculptor Marino Marini (1901-80). **Ospedale del Ceppo** is famous for its splendid Della Robbia ceramic frieze (1526-29). The parish church of **Sant'Andrea** features a magnificent carved stone pulpit (1298-1301) by Giovanni Pisano.

Where to stay

Hotel Leon Bianco *Via Panciatichi 2 (tel 0573 26675/fax 0573 26676)*. **Rates** *single* L105,000; *double* L155,000. **Credit** AmEx, DC, MC, V. Centrally located, pleasant hotel.

Hotel Piccolo Ritz *Via A Vannucci 67 (0573 26775/fax 0573 27798)*. **Rates** *single* L90,000;

The quiet loggias of **Pistoia**.

double L130,000. **Credit** AmEx, MC, V. Convenient for the station, but an unremarkable hotel.
Villa Vannini *Villa di Piteccio (0573 42351).* **Rates** *single* L70,000; *double* L140,000. **Credit** MC, V. You'll find a country-house atmosphere and great food at the comfortable, slightly eccentric Vannini.

Where to eat

Lo Storno *Via del Lastrone 8 (0573 26193).* **Open** noon-3pm Mon-Wed; noon-3pm, 7-10pm, Thur-Sat. **Average** L30,000. **No credit cards**. A traditional osteria serving dishes such as tripe, spelt and bean soup and salted cod with leeks. For pudding try *cantuccini* di Pistoia washed down with Vin Santo.
La BotteGaia *Via del Lastrone 4 (no phone).* **Open** 10.30am-2.30pm, 5.30pm-1am, Tue-Sat. **Average** L10,000. **No credit cards**. No more than a cellar with a few tables but the wines, home-made flans and local cheeses are very good.
Tarabaralla *Via del Lastrone 13 (0573 976 891).* **Open** 12.30-9.30pm Mon; 7am-3pm, 4.30-9.30pm, Tue-Sat. **No credit cards**. Superb pizza from L7,000.

Events

Arts & Crafts show and market of local products held in the ex-Breda coach factory (May/June); **Pistoia Blues** music festival (July); **Giostra dell'Orso** procession and jousting tournament in traditional costume (25 July).

Prato

Poor old Prato suffers badly from the little sister syndrome: Florence is so much more famous and beautiful that few visitors pay any attention to her industrial sibling with a population devoted to the manufacture of worsted cloths. Unassuming Prato has a lot to say for herself. Hurry through her unprepossessing outskirts and make for the walled city centre and the pale swallow-tailed Ghibelline bastions of the thirteenth-century Emperor's Castle, built by Frederick II to protect his pro-Imperial representative from the locals.

Like her big sister, Prato was a dynamic trading centre back in the Middle Ages. Accountancy was virtually invented here in the fourteenth century by one Francesco di Marco Datini, whose meticulous accounts and sheafs of private letters eventually gave Iris Origo enough material to write *The Merchant of Prato*.

Things to see

The **Duomo** is an amazing Romanesque-Gothic building in pinkish brick with a half-finished green-and-white striped marble façade. On one corner, canopied by what looks like a Chinese parasol, is a fifteenth-century pulpit designed by Michelozzo and carved with reliefs of dancing children and cherubs by Donatello (now replaced by casts). Inside there are frescoes by Paolo Uccello and Filippo Lippi: the latter was responsible for the *Lives of Saints John the Baptist and Stephen* in the choir, and apparently used his nun-lover Lucrezia Buti as a model for *Salome at Herod's Banquet*. The **Museo dell' Opera del Duomo** (Piazza Duomo 48, 0574 29339. Open 9.30am-12.30pm, 3-6.30pm Mon, Wed-Sat; 9.30am-12.30pm public hols. Admission L8,000) is located in the Palazzo Vescovile to the left of the Duomo. Exhibits include Donatello's bas-reliefs of dancing putti, a fresco attributed to Paolo Uccello and works by both Filippo and Filippino Lippi. It is closed until 2000, but some of the most important works from its collection can be seen in **Museo di San Domenico** (Piazza San Domenico, 0574 440 501. Open 10am-1pm, 3.30-7pm, Mon, Wed-Sat; 10am-1pm Sun. Admission combined ticket L8,000). San Domenico, sometimes called Museo di Pittura Murale, also houses major works from the **Galleria Comunale** (0574 616 302. Open 9.30am-12.30pm, 3-6.30pm, Mon, Wed-Fri; public hol 9.30am-12.30pm), normally housed in the Palazzo Pretorio, but under restoration until 2001. Galleria Comunale's collection includes some Della Robbia terracottas, a Filippino Lippi tabernacle and Filippo Lippi's *Madonna del Ceppo* (1453) with its realistic portrayal of the Prato merchant Datini (1330-1410). **Palazzo Datini** his pre-Renaissance residence. The church of **Santa Maria delle Carceri**, opposite the tourist information office, is a masterpiece of early Renaissance architecture designed by Giuliano da Sangallo. The city's singular religious icon, *Sacro Cingolo* (Mary's girdle), which has its own chapel, is paraded through the Duomo during the **Ostensione della Sacra Cintola** from its Donatello pulpit to the main altar every Easter, 1 May, 15 August and 25 December.

Museo d'Arte Contemporaneo Luigi Pecci (Viale della Repubblica 277, 0574 5317. Open 10am-7pm Wed-Mon. Admission free; exhibitions L10,000-L12,000. No credit cards) on the outskirts of town, near the autostrada exit Prato Est. Since its opening in 1988, this museum has quickly established itself as Italy's leading centre of contemporary art. The complex was designed by Italo Gamberini, whose thesis on Tuscan rationalism in architecture formed the basis for the design of Santa Maria Novella station in Florence. Initially the museum only held temporary exhibitions, however a permanent collection of contemporary works was added in 1998. Although the exhibits displayed in the collection rotate, there are works by Italian artists Carlo Guaita, Daniela De Lorenzo and Fabrizio Plessi along with a significant contingent of international artists including Sol LeWitt and the French born Anne and Patrick Poirier, whose *Exegi monumentum aere perennius* dominates the sculpture garden.

Prato hosts the **Annual National Comic Book Conference** in February. **Prato Estate** (July/Aug) is when the city hosts a series of concerts, films, open-air shows all over the city; **Musica d'Autunno** (Oct/Nov) is a series of classical and traditional music concerts. The two largest and most prestigious theatres of Prato, Metastasio and Fabbricone Theatre, kick off their season in November. Grab a copy of the free listings mag *Pratomese* to get an idea of what else goes on.

Where to eat

Prato has one of the largest Chinese communities in Tuscany, and hence some of the best Chinese food.

Dal Moro *Via Negri 25 (0574 462 602).* **Open** 11.30am-3pm, 7.30pm-midnight daily. **Average** L35,000. **Credit** AmEx, DC, JCB, MC, V. Try the deer ham (*prosciutto di cervo*), goose salami (*salame d'oca*), and anything with fresh mushrooms.

Enoteca Barni *Via Ferucci 22 (0574 607 845).* **Open** noon-3pm, 7.30-10.30pm, Mon-Fri; 7.30-10.30pm Sat. **Average** L60,000. **Credit** AmEx, DC, JCB, MC, V. Family-owned spin-off from the 40-year-old deli next door. The *lasagnette con porri, cipollotti e tartufo nero* (lasagne with leek, onion and black truffle) or *cervo in salsa di vino rosso* (deer in red-wine sauce) are recommended.

Hua Li Du *Via Marini 4 (0574 24163).* **Open** noon-3pm, 6.30pm-midnight, Mon, Wed-Sun; 6.30pm-midnight Tue. **Average** L25,000. **Credit** AmEx, DC, JCB, MC, V. One of the best Chinese restaurants in the Florence area.

Il Baghino *Via Accademia 9 (0574 27920).* **Open** 7.30-11.30pm Mon; 12.30-3pm, 7.30-11.30pm, Tue-Sat & *winter* 12.30-3pm Sun. Average L45,000. **Credit** AmEx, DC, MC, V. Tuscan cuisine with local specialities such as stuffed celery.

La Cucina di Paola *Via Banchelli 14 (0574 24 353).* **Open** 9am-2.30pm, 7-11pm, Tue-Sun. **Average** L55,000. **Credit** AmEx, DC, JCB, MC, V. Top-notch local fare, including a breakfast buffet for L10,000.

Where to stay

Art Hotel Museo *Viale della Repubblica 289 (0574 5787/fax 578 880).* **Rates** *single* L200,000; *double* L250,000. **Credit** AmEx, DC, MC, V. Stylish hotel and restaurant, out near the Luigi Pecci Museum.

Hotel Flora *Via Cairoli 31 (0574 33521/fax 0574 40289).* **Rates** *single* L100,000-L160,000; *double* L140,000-L230,000. **Credit** AmEx, DC, MC, V. Central hotel with a vegetarian restaurant (average L40,000) serving imaginative food at lunchtime.

Hotel Giardino *Via Magnolfi 4 (0574 26189/fax 606 591).* **Rates** *single* L120,000-L140,000; *double* L160,000-L200,000. **Credit** AmEx, DC, MC, V. Agreeable establishment just behind the Duomo.

Villa Rucellai *Via di Canneto 16 (tel/fax 0574 460 392).* **Rates** *double* from L130,000. **No credit cards**. Wonderful villa with a medieval tower that has been home to the Rucellai family for generations. Simple, but full of character and, with its hillside setting, a great getaway from industrial Prato.

Tourist Office (Via Santa Maria delle Carceri 15, 0574 24112. Open summer 9am-6.30pm Mon-Sat; winter 9am-1pm, 3-6pm Mon-Sat).

Museo d'Arte Contemporaneo Luigi Pecci.

San Miniato

Snaking along the crest of a lofty hill, with views to Fiesole and to the coast, this town was able to dominate both the Pisa-Florence road and the Via Francigena (*see p199* **Corridor of Power**), which brought pilgrims from the north to Rome. In the twelfth and thirteenth centuries it was fortified and became one of Tuscany's foremost Imperial centres, but succumbed to Florence in the mid-1300s. Unfortunately the interiors of both the thirteenth-century **Duomo** and the slightly later church of **San Domenico** were subjected to some heavy-handed baroque 'improvements'. The spacious loggiati di San Domenico are used for an antiques and collectibles fair on the first Sunday of each month, an organic foods market on the second, and an arts and crafts market on the third. The surrounding area is rich in truffles and November weekends are devoted to tasting them.

Tourist Office (Piazza del Popolo, 0571 42745. Open summer 9.30am-1pm, 3.30-7.30pm daily; winter 9am-1pm, 3-6.30pm daily).

Where to eat

Good food and wine are to be had at the family-run **L'Antro di Bacco** (Via IV Novembre 13, 0571 43319. Open noon-2pm, 8-10.30pm, Mon, Tue, Thur-Sat; noon-2pm Sun. Average L40,000. Credit AmEx, DC, JCB, MC, V). Likewise, just outside town at **Il Convio** (Via San Maiano 2, 0571 408 114. Open 10am-3pm, 6-11pm, Thur-Tue. Average L50,000. Credit AmEx, DC, JCB, MC, V), run by Luciano Ciulli. **Caffè Centrale** (Via IV Novembre 19, 0571 43037. Open 6.30am-1am Tue-Thur; 6.30am-2am Fri-Sun. Average L15,000. No credit cards) serves a delicious beetroot pasta, among other light lunch dishes, and has music at night.

Scarperia in the Mugello

The Mugello covers the area north to north-east of Florence, towards the border with Emilia-Romagna. It is divided into the Sieve Valley, Mugello and Upper Mugello. Space-loving Medicis adored its gentle hills and valleys, and its potential for building villas and estates. In fact, the origins of the six balls on the Medici coat of arms are attributed to the legend that a Carolingian knight named Averardo (one of the first Medicis) clashed with a giant, whom he defeated, not far from Scarperia. In battle, the knight suffered six, bone-jarring blows, each represented by a ball (*see also p60* **A load of balls**).

Scarperia is a pleasant little town in the rolling Mugello countryside. Founded in 1306 as northernmost military outpost of the Florentine Republic, because of its strategic location, it enjoyed considerable prosperity until the eighteenth century, when the main road over the Apennines to Bologna opened further west. The town is most famous for its knife grinding. The traditional bone-handled pocket knives that older folk in Italy sometimes use for their husbandry and at the table have a particular prestige. Each is considered an individual masterpiece that waits until its true owner claims it. The **Conaz** factory (Via G Giordani 2, 055 846 197. Open 8.30am-noon, 2-5pm, Mon-Sat. Tours free), outside the walled nucleus of the town, holds demonstrations of knifemaking, but the true artesans are a dying breed. Scarperia hosts an international knife exhibition during the first half of September.

In the spacious central square is the **Palazzo dei Vicari**, built in the thirteenth century on designs by Arnolfo di Cambio. Distinctly reminiscent of the Palazzo Vecchio in Florence, it was the residence of the Republican governors, whose coats of arms decorate the façade. Inside are frescoes dating back to the fourteenth to sixteenth centuries, including a *Madonna and Child with Saints* by the school of Ghirlandaio.

For Mugello cuisine, try **Il Torrione** (Via Roma 78-80, 055 843 0263. Open noon-2.30pm, 7-11pm, daily; winter closed Mon. Average L35,000. Credit MC, V), or **Fattoria il Palagio** (Viale Dante, 055 846 376. Open 12.30-2.30pm, 7.30-9.30pm, Tue-Sun. Average L50,000. Credit AmEx, DC, JCB, MC, V) just outside the walls. Locals swear by a restaurant right beside the A1 exit for Barberino di Mugello: **Cosimo de' Medici** (055 842 0370. Open noon-2.30pm, 7-10.30pm Tue-Sun. Average L60,000. Credit AmEx, DC, JCB, MC, V), where the cuisine makes up for the unprepossessing location. Another great place much favoured by locals is **Il Paiolo** (Via Cornocchio 1, Barberino di Mugello, 055 842 0733. Open noon-3pm, 7.30-11.30pm, Mon, Wed-Sun. Average L60,000. Credit AmEx, DC, JCB, MC, V), which specialises in grilled meat.

The **Uffizio Promozione Turistico** is near Scarperia in Borgo San Lorenzo (Via P Togliatti 45, 055 849 5346. Open 8.15am-1.30pm Mon, Wed, Fri; 8.15am-1.30pm, 2.30-6pm, Tue, Thur). **Promo Mugello** (Piazza Martin Luther King 5/6, 055 845 8742 or toll-free in Italy 167 405 891) has a free hotel-booking service and also assists with bed and breakfast (agriturismo) and camping.

Medici villas are dotted all over the Mugello. One of the most fascinating is in the **Parco Demidoff** (055 409 427. Open 10am-8.30pm Thur-Sun; closed Nov-Mar. Admission L5,000. No credit cards), before the town of Pratolino on the SS65 from Florence. Francesco I had Buontalenti design this fantasy-world playground for his beloved Bianca Cappello. In 1872, Russian prince Demidoff took over and restored the 30 hectares of park grounds with fountains, a pool and stunning statues – most impressive is the Giambologna sculpture, *Apennine*, a massive, Goliath-like figure.

Vinci

As the birthplace of Leonardo (*see p26,* **Pure genius**), this little town attracts a constant stream of visitors. The **Museo Leonardiano** (Via la Torre 2, 0571 56055. Open winter 9.30am-6pm daily; summer 9.30am-7pm daily. Admission L7,000. No credit cards) features models of machines and instruments devised by the Renaissance polymath.

To refuel flagging energy, try **La Torretta** (Via della Torre 19, 0571 56100. Open 12.30-2pm, 8-10pm Tue-Sat; 12.30-2pm Sun. Average L40,000. Credit MC, V) or **Leonardo** (Via Montalbano Nord 16, 0571 567 916. Open noon-3pm, 7pm-1am Thur-Tue. Average L35,000. Credit AmEx, DC, JCB, MC, V)

Pisa & Livorno

Neighbours – but not good friends.

When planning a Tuscan holiday, neither Pisa nor Livorno stand out as priorities. Pisa is used to getting the cold shoulder. After the Leaning Tower tour and a quick sandwich, most visitors head back to Florence or on to other points of interest. Bless low-key Livorno; it has a hard time distinguishing tourists from locals. The two towns sit almost on top of each other – only 20 kilometres apart – but their life-long rivalry makes them as compatible as cacti and balloons.

Pisa

Pisa has not one, but three leaning towers. It also claims two New Years per year. When the rest of Europe opted for the Gregorian calendar (introduced in Tuscany in 1749 by ducal decree) that starts on 1 January, Pisa stuck to 25 March, the zodiacal new year, when the Sun passes into Aries, and the generally accepted date of the Annunciation (when the angel delivered the results of Mary's unsolicited pregnancy test).

This means Pisans reached a new millennium before everyone else in the world. Unfortunately, NATO began bombing Serbia the week before revelries commenced, and Pisans, not wanting to give the impression of celebrating the start of the war, cut the fireworks. The rest of the party rocked on until dawn after a medieval-style meal sponsored by the city.

Though Pisa's days of glory are gone, the attitude isn't. Ask 'How could Pisa have been a maritime republic if it isn't on the coast?' and it drives any Pisan insane. But at least now it's likely to elicit a decent response, since in January 1998 the original harbour was discovered only 500 metres from the Leaning Tower. In April 1999, ten perfectly preserved, 2,000-year-old ships were uncovered in such good shape that the Italian Minister of Fine Arts and Culture called it the marine equivalent of Pompeii. A museum is being planned to display the findings and Pisans are predicting that it will give interest in its history a shot in the arm.

The city of Pisa straddles the river Arno, enclosed within the remains of its medieval walls. Between Piazza della Stazione and the Arno, the Mezzogiorno (south) part of the city contains few sights. The main focus for visitors is north of the river in Tramontana, especially around the Campo dei Miracoli.

Every year, on the eve of San Raniero, the patron saint of Pisa (16 June), the **Luminaria** takes place, when Pisa is bathed in candlelight; candles outline the roofs along the Arno, as well as the porticoes of the Leaning Tower. The following day Pisa hosts a **Regatta** to celebrate the city's former maritime glories with a parade and boat displays by representatives from the ancient quarters of the city.

Pisa is one of the four maritime republics of Italy that take it in turns to host another Regatta, usually on the first Sunday in June. This is a boat race in which the maritime republics, Amalfi, Venice, Genova and Pisa, battle it out against each other. The next time Pisa hosts it will be 2002. More information on festivals in Pisa is available on the website www.turismo.toscana.it.

Campo dei Miracoli

It's a miracle that the 'Site of Miracles' is still in evidence at all. Between the eleventh and thirteenth centuries, stark white structures were planted on this field, reclaimed from the marshes, but not one building on this expanse of grass and stone could pass a builder's test today, since they all tilt in different directions. The layout of the Duomo, Baptistery, Leaning Tower and Camposanto seems haphazard, to say the least. Perhaps realising that future generations would not understand the complex layout, thirteenth-century court astrologer Guido Bonatti detailed the cosmological symbolism of the *Archiepiscopatus Pisanorum*, attributing it to the theme of Aries.

Information

050 560 547. Bus 1 from train station to Piazza del Duomo or 20-min walk through Pisa's medieval quarters. **Open** *Apr-Sept* Duomo 10am-1pm, 3-7.40pm, Mon-Sat; 1-7.20pm Sun; all other monuments 8am-7.20pm daily. *Mar, Oct* Duomo 10am-1pm, 3-5.40pm, Mon-Sat; 1-5.40pm Sun; all other monuments 9am-5.40pm daily. *Jan, Feb, Nov, Dec* Duomo 10am-12.45pm daily; Baptistery, Campo Santo, Museo delle Sinopie & Museo del Duomo Museo dell'Opera del Duomo 9am-4.20pm daily. To see the church on Sunday mornings, do the pious thing and go to mass. **Ticket offices** are in the south-east corner of the Piazza, sharing a room with the entrance to the Museo dell'Opera del Duomo, a shop and tourist information office. **Admission** L18,000 (all sights); L15,000 (any four sights); L10,000 (any two sights); L3,000 (Duomo).

Duomo

Pisa's cathedral is one of the earliest and finest examples of Pisan Romanesque architecture. Begun in 1063 by Buscheto, the blindingly white marble and delicate four-tiered façade incorporates Moorish mosaics and glass within the arcades (examples can be more closely inspected in the Museo dell'Opera del Duomo, *see below*). Buscheto's tomb is set in the wall on the left side of the façade. The brass doors (touch the lizard for good luck) by the school of Giambologna were added in 1602 to replace the originals, destroyed in a fire in 1595. The main entrance facing the Leaning Tower is called the Portale di San Ranieri and features bronze doors by Bonanno da Pisa (1180), which survived the fire. After the fire, the Medici family came to the rescue and immediately began restorations, but at the time nothing could be done for Giovanni Pisano's superb Gothic pulpit (1302-11), which was all but incinerated and lay dismembered in crates until the 1920s. Legend has it that the censer suspended near the now-restored pulpit triggered Galileo's discovery of the principles of pendular motion, but, in fact, it was cast in 1587 – six years after his discovery. Crane your neck to admire the Moorish dome, decorated by a vibrant fresco of the *Assumption* by Orazio and Giralomo Riminaldi (1631). Behind the altar is a mosaic by Cimabué of *Saint John* (1302).

Baptistery

The marble Baptistery was designed by Diotisalvi (meaning 'God save you') in 1153, but not completed until 1395. Originally capped with a 12-sided pyramid, the building was not declared complete until a more harmonious, onion-shaped dome was placed over the original. Most of the Baptistery's precious artwork has been shuffled off to the Museo dell'Opera del Duomo for safekeeping. Nicola Pisano's pulpit of 1260 was the first of the commissions, setting the style for the rest. Before you leave, tip one of the guards and he will sing – the echoes turn the voice of a soloist into what sounds like an ethereal chorus of angels.

Leaning Tower

Located in the south-east corner of the Campo dei Miracoli, the tower has a seven-tiered campanile (though its bells haven't been rung since 1993) begun in 1173; the commemorative plaque says 1174, owing to the off-beat Pisan new year. It started to lean almost as soon as it was erected. The top level, housing the seven bells, was added in 1350. In 1989, the last year the tower was open to the public, more than a million visitors scrambled up its 293 steps. The best views of the campanile are from the courtyard of the Museo dell'Opera del Duomo, and by night when lit by spotlights. According to Pisan superstition, seeing the tower before an exam will bring disastrous results. *See p189* **That way inclined**.

Campo Santo

The Campo Santo (Holy Field) centres on a patch of dirt that, according to legend, was carried from the Holy Land to Pisa by the Crusaders. Lining the Gothic cloisters around the edge of the field are the gravestones of Pisans special enough to be buried in holy soil. On the west wall hang two massive lengths of chain that were once strung across the entrance to the Pisan port to keep out enemy ships. Stolen by Genoa, and passed to Florence, one bit of chain was only returned to Pisa in 1848 by Florence, and the other returned by Genoa in 1860. In 1944, an Allied bomb landed on the Campo, destroying frescoes and sculptures, including a reportedly fabulous cycle by Benozzo Gozzoli. A few did survive, however, including *Triumph of Death*, *Last Judgement* and *Hell*, hammering home the transitory state of worldly pleasures.

Museo dell'Opera del Duomo

This museum, in the shadow of the Tower, contains works from the Baptistery, the Campo Santo and the Duomo itself. Highlights include a lanky, wooden *Christ on the Cross* by Borgognone, vibrant, concentric mosaics from the Duomo parapet and a clutch of works by Giovanni Pisano, notably his ivory *Madonna and Crucifix* and *Madonna and Child*. Go to the tranquil courtyard for a crowd-free view of the Leaning Tower. There's a mixed bag of paintings, *intarsia* (mosaic woodwork), costumes and assorted relics on the first floor. The sixteenth-century intarsia show painstaking attention to perspective and geometrical design. The ticket office, tourist information and bookshop for the Campo dei Miracoli are in the lobby.

Museo delle Sinopie

The 1944 bombings and subsequent restorations uncovered *sinopie* (the reddish-brown preliminary sketches) from beneath the frescoes in the Campo Santo. Such designs were meant to be hidden for ever after the artist covered over the original *arriccio* (dry plaster on which the sketches were made) with a lime-rich plaster called *grassello*. The museum has two floors of fourteenth- and fifteenth-century sinopie by Buffalmacco, Traini (a Pisan), Gaddi, Antonio Veneziano and Spinello Aretino. On the first floor is an enormous *Christ Holding the Circle of Creation*, with nine layers of angels, the zodiac, stars, moon, fire and air, surrounding the centre of the world, divided into Asia, Europe and Africa.

Other sights

Piazza dei Cavalieri

Pisa's second most important piazza is home to the Palazzo dei Cavalieri, seat of one of Italy's most esteemed universities, the Scuola Normale Superiore established by Napoleon Bonaparte in 1810 (his mum was of Pisan descent, *see p254* **Exile in Elba**). The piazza has long been a focal point of the city. The Romans used it as their forum, and Cosimo I based his religious/military order, the Cavalieri of Santo Stefano, here in the sixteenth century. Vasari designed most of the piazza's buildings, as well as decorating the façade of the university. He com-

Diotsalvi's **Baptistery** *took 242 years to complete – and needs constant restoration.*

menced work on the Chiesa dei Cavalieri in 1565, and left the façade for Don Giovanni de' Medici to finish. The church's campanile, also by Vasari, was erected in 1570-72.

Facing the church is the Palazzo della Conventuale, erected as home to the Cavalieri of Santo Stefano. This and the neighbouring Palazzo del Consiglio dell'Ordine and Palazzo Gherardescha are all Vasari creations. The Palazzo Gherardescha occupies the site of a medieval prison: in 1288 Count Ugolino della Gherardesca and three of his male heirs were condemned to starve to death there for engaging in covert negotiations with the Florentines. It took Ugolino nine months to die (during which time he allegedly snacked on his own kids). Dante, horrified by his plight (and cannibalism), seized another chance to get at the Pisans and depicted the Count gnawing on someone's head for eternity in Hell (*Canto XXXIII, Inferno*).

You will see the Maltese Cross everywhere in this piazza but nowhere else in Pisa; Cosimo wanted to hammer home the parallel between his new Cavalieri of Santo Stefano and the crusading Knights of Malta. Elsewhere you are likely to spot the Pisan cross, with two balls resting on each point. When the Medici moved in, they emblazoned their *palle* (*see p60* **A load of balls**) everywhere to show Pisans who was boss.

Santa Maria della Spina

Lungarno Gambacorti.

This gorgeous, tiny Gothic church on the bank of the Arno is still (after five years) closed for restoration and swaddled in a chrysalis of scaffolding. Originally an oratory, the church took its present form in 1323. It gets its name from the fact that it used to own what was claimed to be a thorn from Christ's crown, brought back by Crusaders.

San Nicola

Via Santa Maria 2 (050 24677). **Open** 8-11.30am, 5-6.30pm, Mon-Sat; 9am-noon, 5.30-6.30pm, Sun.

Dating from 1150, this church is dedicated to one of Pisa's patron saints, San Nicola da Tolentino. In one of its chapels is a painting showing the saint protecting Pisa from the plague, some time around 1400. The campanile, built on unstable Pisan ground, consequently leans. An arcade joins the church to Palazzo Reale. It was from the tower of this palazzo, called the Verga d'Oro (the rod of gold) that Galileo Galilei let Grand Duke Cosimo II look through his telescope to see the satellites of Jupiter.

Museo Nazionale di San Matteo

Piazza San Matteo in Soarta, Lungarno Mediceo (050 541 865). **Open** 9am-7pm Tue-Sat; 9am-1pm Sun, public holidays. **Admission** L8,000.

The twelfth- to thirteenth-century building once housed the convent of the Sisters of San Matteo. It now contains a collection of Pisan and Islamic medieval ceramics and paintings by Masaccio and Fra Angelico, a *Madonna and Child with Saints* by Domenico Ghirlandaio and a bust by Donatello. There's authentic Gioco del Ponte gear here too; the garb worn by medieval Pisans when they locked heads on the Ponte di Mezzo.

Museo Nazionale di Palazzo Reale

Lungarno Pacinotti 46 (050 926 539). **Open** 9am-2pm daily, closed holidays; times vary depending on exhibitions. **Admission** free.

Housed in a Medici palace dating from 1583, many of the museum's works have been donated by private collectors of Medici and Savoy pieces. Portrait paintings represent members of various European dynasties depicted as Madonna-like figures, angels, kings and with some striking Pisan backdrops. A vast assortment was donated by Dr Antonio Ceci, a noted Italian surgeon, who, on his death in 1921, left half his collection to the city of Pisa.

Orto Botanico

Via L Ghini 5 (050 560 045/fax 050 551 345). **Open** 8am-1pm Mon-Fri. **Admission** free.

Step out of Campo dei Miracoli into an oasis. Founded by Luca Ghini in 1543, then replanted in different parts of the city, the oldest university botanical garden in Europe found its permanent home on this site in 1595. It was originally used to study the medicinal values of plants. Look out for the 200-year-old myrtle bush the size of a tree, and a clump of papyrus reeds in the arboretum. Groups of ten or more must have an appointment.

Accommodation

Reserve during high season, and well in advance for the Luminaria, Regatta and Gioco del Ponte (*see page 8, chapter* **Tuscany by Season**).

Consorzio Turistico Pisa È (Booking Centre) *Via Carlo Cammeo 2 or PO Box 215, Pisa 56125 (050 830 253/fax 050 830 243/pisa.turismo@traveleurope.it).* **Open** 9.30am-1pm, 2-6.30pm, Mon-Sat.

This tourist agency and booking centre offers a free room-booking service.

Website: www.traveleurope.it/pisa.htm

Hotel Amalfitana

Via Roma 44 (050 290 000/fax 050 25218). **Rates** *double* L110,000. **Credit** AmEx, MC, V.

The rooms are clean, modern and equipped with air-conditioning and TV. Book ahead.

Albergo Bologna

Via Mazzini 57 (050 502 120/fax 050 43070). **Rates** *single* L75,000; *double* L110,000; *triple* L140,000; *quad* L170,000. **Credit** AmEx, DC, MC, V.

No air-conditioning, but rooms are spacious and there's a private car park in this central hotel. The bar lounge is a great place to stretch out.

Albergo Galileo

Via Santa Maria 12 (tel/fax 050 40621). **Rates** *single* L60,000; *double* L80,000. **No credit cards.**

It's illegal to use Galileo Galilei's full name for commercial purposes in Pisa, so this pensione gets away with half of it. Five of the nine rooms are capped with vibrant seventeenth-century frescoes. Ask for room nine or ten.

Albergo Gronchi

Piazza Arcivescovado 1 (050 561 823). **Rates** *single without bath* L32,000; *double* L56,000; *triple* L75,000. **No credit cards.**

Pleasant and clean, and ideal if you have dreamed of spending the night under the tower. There's a midnight curfew.

Campeggio Torre Pendente

Viale delle Cascine 86 (tel/fax 050 561 704). Bus 5. **Rates** *caravan room* L40,000 (1-2 people); *bungalow* L50,000-L150,000 (up to 5); *tent* L8,000 plus L9,500 per person. **Open** Apr-Oct. **No credit cards.**

If taking the bus, ask for the *campeggio*, or take the 15-minute walk from Piazza Manin. Midnight curfew.

Camping Internazionale

Via Litoranea in Marina di Pisa 7 (050 36553). **Rates** L8,000-L11,000; *children* L6,000-L8,000; *tent* L10,000-L17,000; *camper van* L12,000-L17,000. **Open** May-Sept. **Credit** MC, V.

With a private beach, bar and pizzeria, campers never need to leave this upbeat campsite. No reservations are taken, but staff claim there's always a pitch. Take ACIT bus from Piazza della Stazione to Marina di Pisa/Tirrenia and ask for *campeggio*.

Casa della Giovane

Via F Corridoni 29 (050 43061). **Rates** *double/triple* L30,000 per person. **No credit cards.**

As this boarding house caters mostly to students, the place is usually packed in term-time. Curfew is 10pm but it is close to the station.

Centro Turistico Madonna dell'Acqua

Via Pietrasantina 15 (050 890 622). Bus 3. **Open** office 6-11pm. **Rates** *double* L30,000 per person; *triples or bigger* L20,000 per person. **No credit cards.**
The only youth hostel in Pisa. If you're feeling penitent you can attend Sunday mass in the little church of the Madonna dell'Acqua nearby.

Grand Hotel Duomo

Via Santa Maria 94 (050 561 894/fax 050 560 418). **Rates** *single* L200,000; *double* L280,000; *suite* L330,000. **Credit** AmEx, DC, MC, V.
The bubble-lettered sign above the entrance should hint at what's in store. Inside you'll find plush

That way inclined

The Pisan campanile started leaning almost as soon as it was constructed (1173). In 1989, tourists were stopped from climbing its 293 steps as it was deemed too dangerous. In 1992, a monitoring system was installed to measure its movement which, in May 1993, recorded its maximum discrepancy from the vertical of 4.47m, at which point the most earnest correction project in the tower's history commenced.

The project, which has cost the Italian government L30 billion and will see a L150 million contribution from the EU during 1999, is headed by Michele Jamiolkowsh, the professor of engineering at Turin University. But straightening the tower is considered impossible. According to the plans of Pisan architect and sculptor, Bonanno Pisano, responsible for the royal doors to the Duomo, the tower was already leaning (northward) by the time the third storey of the tower had been completed, because the sand and clay beneath the tower was unable to support its weight. Work was postponed in 1178 to allow the ground to 'settle'. By the time work recommenced in 1272, the tower had actually shifted, using the little firm soil that existed beneath it as its fulcrum, and had begun to lean in its present direction, southwards. To create the illusion that the tower was upright, loggias were built around it at an angle. This phase in the tower's construction means that if engineers today succeeded in bringing the tower to an upright, the result would be a campanile that appeared to lean northwards.

The aim of the latest project, therefore, is to stabilise the building and eliminate future risk of its collapse. This means reducing the angle of the lean by a fraction of a degree – not enough to notice visibly. To allow time to think up a feasible plan, several short-term precautions have been taken to stop the tower collapsing, including the placement of 830 tonnes of lead on the foundations of its north side and the installation of a 'support belt' to strengthen the weak south wall. Another belt higher up is attached to a pair of cables that run over the Campo dei Miracoli to individual 150-tonne counterweights to help hold the tower in place.

The long-term solution involves extracting soil from under the north side of the tower to reduce the difference in depth between the north and south side. This recorded its first success on 7 March 1999 when the lean was seen to have decreased. Jamiolkowsh said at the time that, 'once the project is completed we will have guaranteed the stability and safety of the Tower of Pisa for at least the next 300 years'. The tower is still structurally weak, however, and stands on marsh; problems which have yet to be fully addressed. It's early days for the tower's rescue operation; the positive results witnessed so far may not continue – but tourists should still be inclined to come and see it.

Useful information

Tourist information

Azienda Promozione Turistica (APT) *Via Benedetto Croce 26 (administration 050 40096/050 40202/fax 050 40903).* **Open** 9am-1pm Mon-Fri.
Branches *Piazza della Stazione 11 (050 42291).* **Open** 8am-5pm Mon, Thur; 8am-2pm Tue, Wed, Fri. *Via Cameo (050 560 464).* **Open** 9am-8pm daily.

Transport

Airport Galileo Galilei airport *(050 0707).* **Open** 11am-5pm Mon-Sat; 11am-2pm Sun. For full details, *see* **Directory**.
Railway station Pisa Centrale *Piazza della Stazione (050 28117; train info 1478 88 088).* Ticket office **open** 24hrs daily. From the main train station board a train for Rome (L27,000, 3 hours Intercity, 4 hours otherwise), Genoa (L15,000, 2 hours) Lucca (L3,400, 25 minutes), Livorno (L2,000, 15 minutes), or one of the frequent trains for Florence via Empoli (L7,200, one hour). Some trains also stop at Pisa Aeroporto and San Rossore (the latter is closer to the Campo dei Miracoli).

Taxis
Radio Taxi *(050 541 600).* There are taxi ranks at Piazza Stazione, Piazza Duomo and Piazza Garibaldi.

Emergency services

Ambulance *Via San Frediano 6 (050 581 111), Via Bargagna (050 941 511), Via Pietrasanta 161A (050 835 544).*

Carabinieri (112).
Via Guido da Pisa 1 (050 542 541).

Police (113).
Questura *Via Mario Lalli 1 (050 583 511).*
Polizia Stradale (Road Police) *Via M Canevari (050 580 588).*
Vigili Urbani (Local Police) *Via del Moro 1 (050 501 444 or 050 502 626).*

Post Office *Piazza Vittorio Emmanuele II 8 (050 24297).* **Open** 8.15am-7pm Mon-Fri; 8.15am-noon Sat, public holidays.

Hospital Santa Chiara *Via Roma 67 (050 992 111).*

green carpets, a business atmosphere and a huge complex. Ask in advance if you want to use the garage, for which a service charge of eight per cent is added.

Royal Victoria

Lungarno Pacinotti 12 (050 940 111/fax 050 940 180). **Rates** *single* L135,000; *double* L165,000. **Credit** AmEx, DC, MC, V.
This elegant hotel has been run by the Piegaja family since 1839. The building, parts of which are more than 1,000 years old, has been carefully preserved. Many rooms face the Arno; river breezes make up for the lack of air-conditioning. Book in advance.

Bars, cafés & gelaterie

Bar Duomo

Via Santa Maria 114 (050 561 918). **Open** 8am-7pm Mon-Wed, Fri-Sun. **No credit cards**.
Join the crowd at one of Pisa's busiest bars if you feel like sipping a prosecco at a table facing the Campo dei Miracoli.

Brasserie La Loggia

Piazza Vittorio Emmanuele II 11 (050 46326). **Open** 7am-2am Tue-Sun. Closed 1st week Jan. **Credit** AmEx, DC, MC, V.
Art deco-ish hangout near the station. Sit out in warm weather and nibble on crêpes, gelati or hot dishes and snacks.

Pasticceria Salza

Borgo Stretto 46 (050 580 144). **Open** 7.45am-8.30pm Tue-Sun. **No credit cards**.
The most distinguished café in Pisa, anyone who is someone tends to congregate here to sip their aperitif or cappuccino.

Pizzicheria Gastronomia a Cesqui

Piazze delle Vettovaglie 31 (no phone). **Open** 7am-1.30pm, 4-8pm, Mon, Tue, Thur-Sat; 7am-1.30pm Wed. **No credit cards**.
Part the beaded curtains and stock up on cheeses, pastas, wines and take-away hot snacks.

Restaurants

Cèe alla Pisana (eels) has been one of Pisa's culinary assets for centuries (*cèe* comes from *ciechi*, blind ones). Unfortunately, the poor little creatures have been fished close to extinction and few venues still serve the costly dish. It is a winter delicacy prepared before the end of February, when the eels develop a hard fin that makes them difficult to swallow. In season they are fished out of the Arno and tossed immediately in warm oil, garlic and sage, then sautéed and served seconds after they cease wriggling.

Bruno

Via Luigi Bianchi 12 (050 560 818). **Open** noon-2.30pm Mon; noon-2.30pm, 7.30-11.45pm, Wed-Sun. **Average** L60,000. **Credit** AmEx, DC, MC, V.
For locals, there was one distinct reason to go to Bruno: *cèe*. The squirming speciality was served under the table to anyone willing to pay L100,000 a plate. Concentrating on other Tuscan specialties, try the *ribolita*, supposedly the best this side of the Arno, and the *baccalà alla Pisana*.

Cagliostro

Via del Castelletto 26-30 (050 575 413/fax 050 973 256/cagliostro@csinfo.it). **Open** 12.45-2.30pm, 7.30pm-1am, Mon, Wed, Thur, Sun; 12.45-2.30pm, 7.30pm-2am, Fri, Sat. **Average** L25,000 (lunch); L45,000 (dinner). **Credit** AmEx, DC, MC, V.
This intriguing enoteca and restaurant, located off Via Ulisse Dini near Piazza dei Cavalieri, is named after a Sicilian Count who masqueraded as an alchemist in France and Italy during the eighteenth century. An extensive wine list complements the eclectic menu which draws on recipes from all over Italy.

La Mescita

Via Cavalca 2 (050 544 294). **Open** 8-10.30pm Tue, Wed; 1-2.15pm, 8-10.30pm, Thur-Sun. Closed Aug. **Average** L35,000. **No credit cards**.
Run by Elisabetta and Stefano Banti, La Mescita is a pretty, tranquil restaurant at the heart of the Vettovaglie market; you'll find it on the right after leaving the loggia. The wine list is huge and the *sformati* of cheese and vegetables delicious.

La Nando Pizzeria

Corso Italia 103 (050 27242). **Open** 10.30am-2.30pm, 4-10pm, Mon-Sat. **Average** L11,000. **No credit cards**.
You can't help but be enticed by the smells. Pizzas are around L7,000 (L2,000 a slice). There's no table service. Sit in the back, or perch on a stool at the bar and people-watch.

Numero Undici

Via Cavalca 11, Market Vettovaglie (no phone). **Open** noon-3pm, 6-10pm, Mon-Fri; 6-10pm Sat. **Average** L7,000. **No credit cards**.
A tiny place in the heart of the market, serving wine and snacks. Sit at one of the four fruit-coloured tables inside or under a huge parasol amid the market's fruit carts. The focaccia sandwiches are excellent. Focaccina cost L3,000-L7,000, or a hot dish of the day is around L5,000. No table service.

Osteria del Tinti

Vicolo del Tinti 26 (050 580 240). **Open** noon-3pm, 7pm-midnight, Mon, Tue, Thur-Sun. **Average** L20,000. **Credit** MC, V.
Crossing Ponte di Mezzo in the direction of Piazza del Duomo, take the second right off Via Guglielmo Oberdan and turn down the alley beneath the neon sign of a woman bearing pizza. There are 18 types of pizza (up to L12,000) and a three-course menu. It is pretty touristy, but the food is good enough to compensate. The *menu turistico* is L12,000.

Pizzeria Trattoria Toscana

Via Santa Maria 163 (050 561 876). **Open** 11am-11pm Mon, Tue, Thur-Sun. **Average** L20,000. **Credit** AmEx, DC, MC, V.
Located not far from Campo dei Miracoli amid the restaurant agglomeration of tents and neon signs. The food here is fine, if as generic as its name suggest. Pizzas cost from L6,000; the *menu turistico* from L18,000.

Il Ristoro del Vecchio Macelli

Via Volturno 49 (050 20424). **Open** 1-3 pm, 8-10pm, Mon, Tue, Thur-Sat; 8-10pm Sun; closed 10-24 Aug. **Average** L50,000. **Credit** AmEx, DC, MC, V.
Loved by Pisan sophisticates, this place is known for the quality of its ingredients and standard of presentation. The Vanni family make a meal around your choice: *di terra* (meat) or *di mare* (seafood). You may not want to dwell on the fact that the building is a restored fifteenth-century slaughterhouse. Booking advised.

Il Turista

Piazza dell'Archivescovado 17 (050 560 932). Open noon-3pm Mon, Tue, Thur-Sun. **Average** L20,000. **Credit** AmEx, DC, JCB, MC, V.
Though the name is off-putting, you can get a decent *pappardelle alla Pisana* (pasta with goose liver, porcini, wine and tomatoes) or a *bordatino* (bean soup with cabbage) and a drink for about L20,000.

Il Vecchio Dado

Lungarno Pacinotti 21/22, nr Ponte di Mezzo (050 580 900). **Open** 12.30-3pm, 7.30pm-12.30am, Mon, Tue, Fri-Sun; 7.30pm-12.30am Thur. **Average** L35,000. **Credit** AmEx, DC, MC, V.
A warm atmosphere and a river view are two of the pluses of this Tuscan pizzeria next to the Royal Victoria Hotel. There's a huge range of pizzas, pastas, *contorni,* meat and seafood. Reservation is advisable or you may find yourself standing.

Nightlife

It's worth stopping in Pisa to get away from the manic crowds of Florence without giving up the Arno, the sparkling lights and charm.

Borderline

Via Vernaccini 7 (050 580 577). **Open** 9pm-1am Mon-Sat. **Admission** free; *tessera* L10,000; *concerts* L5,000-L12,000. **No credit cards**.
Good for late drinks or taking in the occasional live gig. A beer costs L5,000, as does a gin and tonic.

Happy Drinker Pub

Via Del Poschi 7 (050 578 555). **Open** 7pm-1am Wed-Mon. **Admission** free. **No credit cards**.
A jolly drinking joint just off Borgo Stretto. Beer costs L7,000 a pint, and there's also bottled Guinness, sandwiches and snacks. Upbeat British music keeps the Anglophile Italian crowd happy.

Dottorjazz

Via Vespucci 10 (050 985 233). **Open** 9pm-2am Tue-Sat; closed June-Sept. **Admission** free; *tessera* L15,000; *concerts* L10,000-L20,000. **No credit cards**.
Small candlelit tables guarded by pictures of jazz greats on the walls. This jazz venue attracts folk from in and out of town, bonded by a love of turtlenecks and black-rimmed glasses.

Lo Sfizio

Borgo Stretto 54 (050 580 281). **Open** 7.30am-1am Mon-Sat; *June* daily. **Credit** AmEx, DC, MC, V.

This sizable café offers cocktails and *gelati*. The name means 'little vice', but it's actually a thoroughly wholesome place. The price of drinks more than doubles when you take a seat.

Lo Spaventapasseri

Via La Nunziatina 10 (050 44067). **Open** *summer* 11.30am-1am Tue-Fri; 6pm-1am Sat, Sun; *winter* 11am-1am Tue-Fri; 4pm-1am Sat, Sun. **No credit cards.**
Look for the sign with a scarecrow. Two rooms in back have table space and blaring music.

Teatro Verdi

Via Palestro 40 (050 941 111/fax 050 941 158). **Open** *ticket office* 9am-noon Tue, Thur, Sat, Sun; 9am-noon, 5.30-7.30pm, Mon, Wed, Fri. **Credit** MC, V.
Come here to enjoy an evening of dance, drama or music, but be punctual when attending events: latecomers are not allowed to enter.

Shopping

Most pricier shops and strongholds of Pisan shopping are on Corso Italia. Stop in **Mellani** (44) to ogle amazing crystal, silver and porcelain. Across the Ponte di Mezzo is a funkier shopping zone starting at the Loggia of Borgo Stretto. Where Borgo Stretto meets the Ponte di Mezzo you'll find the **Mercatino Antiquario**, the second weekend of every month. The **Mercato Vettovaglie** is the fruit and vegetable market, open every morning.

Outside Pisa

Marina di Pisa

About five kilometres out of Pisa towards the beach you will come across the eleventh-century church of San Pier in Grado. This area used to sit on Pisa's river estuary, but the Arno altered its course and left the church of Saint Peter out on a limb. Built on the spot where Saint Peter is said to have first set foot off the boat from Antioch, there is now a conspicuous lack of water. Vibrant fourteenth-century frescoes depict the lives of Peter and Paul, and sit above 24 columns of different orders. An excavation to the rear of the church revealed a pillar from the first century, attesting to the church's age.

Right on the coast, you can have a meal looking out to the island of Gorgona (used as a prison) at the **Cliff** (Via Repubblica Pisana 4, Lungomare, Marina di Pisa, 050 36830. Open noon-3pm, 6pm-midnight, daily; winter closed Mon. Average L35,000). This restaurant has an attractive, covered outdoor area and the bar attracts a drinking-only crowd at weekends, when the place stays open later than usual.

Tirrenia

Still on the coast, south of Marina di Pisa, toward Livorno is Tirrenia, where you will find a number of private beaches, a US military base, a zoo and the flashy **Grand Hotel Continental**, which sits directly on the beach (Largo Belveder 26, 050 37031/fax 050 37283. Rates single L140,000-L190,000; double L220,000-L300,000). It boasts 200 luxury rooms, an Olympic-size pool, tennis courts, beach access and parking. Book well in advance in summer.

The huge **San Rossare** park (Via Aurelia Nord 4, 050 525 500. Open *information* 8am-2pm Mon-Fri), offers nature lovers guided walks, bike tours, horse treks and jaunts in horse-driven carriages.

Casciana Terme

Tucked in the Pisan hills, this spa town – Castrum ad Aquas to the Romans – was destroyed during the World War II and rebuilt in the 1960s. With a modern pool and drinking fountains, **Terme di Casciana** (Piazza Garibaldi 9, 0587 64461/fax 0587 644 629. Open 7-11.30am, 3-6.30pm, Mon-Sat; 9.30-12.30pm, 4-7pm, Sun) is less popular, and less crowded, than Tuscan cousins such as Montecatini and Saturnia. Check out the lovely **La Speranza** hotel (Via Cavour 44, 0587 646 215/fax 0587 646 000. Rates single L95,000, double L120,000) down the street from the thermal waters or the greener **Villa Margherita** (Via Marconi 20, 0587 646 113/fax 0587 646 153/margherita@tdnet.it. Rates single L90,000, double 110,000) with garden and a bar where you can get a mean Martini.

One kilometre east of Calci, **Certosa di Pisa** (Open summer 9am-6pm Tue-Fri; 10am-10pm Sat, Sun; winter 9am-6pm Tue-Sun. Admission L6,000 Tue-Sat; L8,000 Sun) is a vast complex that was originally a monastery (1366). It was used on and off until being definitively abandoned by the Carthusian monks in 1969. The interior includes a fourteenth-century church, various cloisters, gardens and a view of the Campo dei Miracoli to the west. The **Natural History Museum** (050 937 751. Open 10am-1pm, 3-11pm, Mon, Wed, Fri, Sun; 5-11pm Tue, Thur. Phone for a tour) belongs to the University of Pisa and was founded in 1591 by the Grand Duke Ferdinando I; it is considered one of the top three natural history museums in Italy.

Livorno

Livornese like to quip that they are like their local dish, *cacciuco*. That is not to say they are a steamy dish of sea-beast parts cooked in wine, but they are a *mélange* of inhabitants from everywhere who, together, form an embracingly vibrant whole. A look in the local directory is telling: letters usually passed by in Italian (j, h, k, w) are more in abundance here than in any other region in the country.

The 1997 film success *Ovosodo* (hard-boiled egg) by Livornese director Paolo Virzì, portrays local character with a tragicomic resignation. The Livornese are among the most left-wing Italians – traditionally hard-working fishermen or factory employees. Native flavours are strong, but fresh and warming; *il torpedino* is a short coffee with a chilli

Teepee or not teepee? The souvenir stalls in Piazza del Campo.

and locally produced rum. Wild boarhead, drained of its blood for three days, emptied, spiced, then restuffed and stitched up is another speciality.

Livorno happened when Pisa was in a pinch. The Arno silted up and the maritime republic of Pisa found itself without any sea, so Cosimo I pounced on this tiny fishing village in 1571. A far-sighted constitution (1593) allowed foreigners to reside in the city regardless of nationality and religion, instantly endowing Livorno with a cosmopolitan mentality.

The Porto Mediceo, with the red-brick bastion of the Fortezza Vecchia designed by Sangallo the Younger in 1521, quickly became the focus of city life. From here the canals of Venezia Nuova (or I Fossi) extend, tracing the pentagonal perimeter of Francesco I's late sixteenth-century plan for an ideal city.

Blanket bombing during World War II did away with most of Livorno's historic monuments, and post-war reconstruction finished the job: Buontalenti's Piazza Grande was cut in two and all that remains of the sixteenth-century Duomo is Inigo Jones's fine portico.

Osteria da Carlo (Viale Caprera 43/45, 0586 897 050. Open 12.30-2.30pm, 7.30-10.30pm, Mon-Sat. Average L30,000) is run by Carlo himself, who, apart from helping run Livorno's rugby team, has been serving traditional dishes since 1963. Try the *cacciucco*, which supposedly originates from a Turkish recipe (*kuzuk* meaning small in Turkish, in this case small pieces of sea food); a medley of fish and crustaceans cooked with wine and chillis, is served with garlic bread. Otherwise, try **Gennarino** (Via San Fortunata 11, 0586 888 093. Open lunch & dinner Mon, Tue,Thur-Sun. Average L45,000) or the excellent **La Chiave**, across the moat from Fortezza Nuova (Scali delle Cantine 52, 0586 888 609. Open dinner Mon, Tue, Thur-Sun. Average L50,000). Other great spots to sample typical Livornese dishes are **L'Antica Venezia** (Via dei Bagnetti 1, 0586 887 353. Open lunch & dinner Tue-Sat. Average L40,000) and **Il Sottomarino** (Via de'Terrazzini 48, 0586 887 025. Open lunch & dinner Mon-Wed, Fri, Sat; lunch Sun. Average L55,000), where portions are generous.

Disco-pubs are flourishing on Livorno's canals. **The Barge** (Scali delle Anchore 6, 0586 888 320. Open 8am-1.30am Tue-Sun), built in the bow of an old mast ship, has live music on Saturdays and Livornese tapas. Round the corner, **Mediterraneo** (Scali del Ponte di Marmo 14, 0586 829 799. Open 8pm-3am Mon, Wed-Sun. Tessera L5,000) is lower-key but slots into the Livornese pub crawl. A good place for vino and snacks is **Enoteca DOC** (Via Goldoni 40-44, 0586 887 583. Open shop 9am-1pm Tue-Sun; food 5pm-3am Tue-Sun. Average L30,000). A hopping, dance-on-the-table restaurant/bar is **Sotto Costa** outside of Livorno at Quercianella. **Pappafico** in Marina di Pisa is a true discopub where Pisans and Livornese actually get along.

Tourist Information

Piazza Cavour 6 (0586 898 111/info@livorno.turismo.toscana.it). **Open** 9am-1pm Mon, Wed, Fri, Sat; 9am-1pm, 3-5pm, Tue, Thur.

Chianti & Siena Province

Land of the lone cypress tree.

This part of Tuscany casts a spell on almost everyone that passes through it. Its magic is a perfect blend of elements: stunning unspoiled countryside, excellent food and wine, a rich cultural heritage and proximity to Florence. But its most inebriating effect is an unshakeable desire to just settle down and live there. Many do just that, Italians and foreigners alike, by buying and restoring crumbling fifteenth-century farmhouses. But many more leave Chianti reluctantly, haunted by the confirmation that they've seen their personal paradise.

Chianti

The ultimate Tuscan dreamscape, Chianti serves up a knockout twofold punch: breathtaking natural beauty and plenty of wine. Vine trellises outline the sensual curves of the land and restored stone farmhouses pop out from the most picturesque perches. To fully appreciate the land you'll need a car, as public transport is sporadic and Chianti is best experienced at leisure, over a lazy weekend, without bus timetables and ticket counters. A car will also allow you to explore La Chiantigiana, or the SS222 that wiggles its way south of Florence to Siena through hilltop towns such as Greve and Castellina. This section is organised along the North to South route of the SS222.

Around San Casciano in Val di Pesa

Only 17 kilometres south of the Florence Certosa motorway junction (where the main roads to Siena and Rome begin), this tiny little agricultural centre would be gobbled up by sprawling cement suburbs if it existed in another part of the world. Despite its proximity to the Tuscan capital, San Casciano is nestled safely in full-blown Chianti countryside. Inside the stone village is the fourteenth-century Gothic Santa Maria del Prato church with a painted crucifix allegedly by Simone Martini.

Seven kilometres north is the tiny hamlet of Sant'Andrea in Percussina where Machiavelli lived while writing his despot's handbook *The Prince*, in between furious card games with the local gravedigger. His house is now the Antica Fattoria Machiavelli, a private winery.

South of here near Montefiridolfi is the **Fattoria La Loggia** (Via Casciano 40, 055 824 4288/fax 055 824 4283. Rates double L200,000. No credit cards) an agricultural estate (not 'hotel' please) consisting of restored medieval apartments and small private houses.

One of Tuscany's most highly rated restaurants is located northwest of San Casciano in the village of Cerbaia. **La Tenda Rossa** (Piazza del

San Gimignano's **Collegiata**. *See p197.*

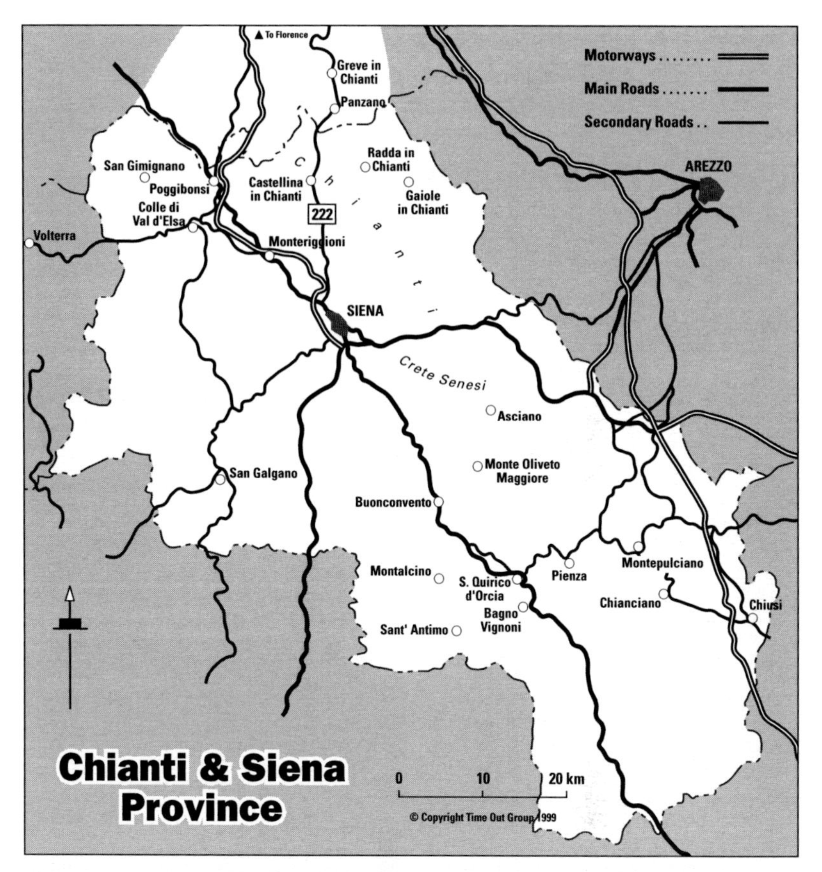

Monumento 9/14, 055 826 132. Open 12.30-2pm, 8-10pm, Tue-Sat; 8-10pm Sun. Average L130,000. Credit AmEx, DC, MC, V) serves up local delicacies such as wild boar, but its authentic country tastes are slightly tainted by a stuffy atmosphere.

Greve in Chianti

Greve makes an excellent base from which to explore the surrounding area. Not only does it have a lovely main square, Piazza Matteotti, with wine bars, well-stocked food stores and a bookshop, but it also has the area's largest **Tourist Office** (055 854 5243. Open 9am-1pm, 2.30-5pm, Mon-Fri; 9am-1pm Sat). Ask about Greve's September wine festival, one of Chianti's biggest events.

Cream-coloured buildings with green shutters line the triangle-shaped Piazza Matteotti where grandmothers walk arm in arm under the piazza's arcaded perimeter, gossiping and window-shopping. One of the places they flock to is the exceptional butcher, **Macelleria Falorni** (Piazza Matteotti 69/71, 055 853 029. Open 8am-1pm, 3.30-8pm, daily).

Off the main square is a handy Co-op supermarket (locals emerged from the nearby towns to celebrate its grand opening in 1999), good for stocking up on supplies for extended stays.

Giovanni da Verrazzano hailed from these parts before discovering the New York harbour in 1524, as the statue in Greve's main square testifies. Oddly enough, another pioneer, Amerigo Vespucci, the sixteenth-century explorer who gave his name to America, was born in the nearby fortified village of Montefioralle. A tiny road of hairpin turns leads to the village from Greve's northern side. The road is so narrow that, in places, only a single car can squeeze through at a time.

If you're looking for a room in Greve, the best option is probably the **Albergo Giovanni da**

Verrazzano (055 853 189/fax 055 853 648. Rates single L120,000; double L140,000. Credit AmEx, DC, JCB, MC, V), located on the main square with an attractive restaurant on its geranium-lined second-floor terrace.

Panzano in Chianti

Another seven kilometres to the south (either along the SS222 or the road from Montefioralle) is the fortified village of Panzano, with its stunning views of the Conca d'Oro Valley.

To the right of the church, the little **Enoteca Il Vinaio** (055 852 603. Open 10.30am-11pm Mon, Wed-Sun; 10.30am-5pm Tue. Average L20,000. Credit AmEx, DC, JCB, MC, V) run by Paolo Gaeta and his wife, serves up hearty *pappa al pomodoro* and *ribollita* accompanied by a vast selection of local wines on a vine-covered terrace.

For restaurant fare, try the nearby **Il Vescovino** restaurant (055 852 464. Open 12.30-2.30pm, 7.30-10pm, daily. Average L45,000. Credit AmEx, DC, JCB, MC, V) which does an excellent roast duck in orange juice and has a large terrace with a wonderful view.

Located on an eroded dirt road about eight kilometres north-west of the town, the Badia a Passignano was once a centre of the wealthy Vallombrosan order. The eleventh-century abbey is now in private hands, but the adjacent church can be visited.

On the road to the Badia is another dirt road turn-off for **La Cantinetta di Rignana**. Set among ancient farmhouses, this is the quintessential Tuscan restaurant that fantasies are made of (055 852 601. Open 12.30-2.30pm, 7.30-10.30pm, Mon, Wed-Sun. Average L45,000. Credit AmEx, DC, JCB, MC, V). In season, meals start off with sensational steamed artichokes, followed by classic primi such as papardelle with rabbit sauce, and end with choice cuts of succulent grilled meats. La Cantinetta is one of Chianti's best-kept secrets, possibly because it's so hard to get to.

Castellina in Chianti

A sudden bend in the SS222, and the hilltop town of Castellina comes into postcard-perfect view. The surrounding hills marked the battlefront between the warring armies of Siena and Florence, hence Castellina's heavy fortification. The town's main square, Piazza del Comune, lies under the shadow of the imposing Torre (now the local town hall) and a covered walkway gives Castellina a chilly fourteenth-century feel.

If you're staying, the **Colle Etrusco Salivolpi** (Via Fiorentina 89, 0577 740 484/fax 0577 740 998. Rates double L150,000. Credit AmEx, MC, V) is a restored farmhouse-turned-country club with a flower-filled garden and outdoor pool. About 200 metres away is the **Ristorante Albergaccio** (Via Fiorentina 63, 0577 741 042. Open 12.30-2pm, 7.30-9.30pm, Mon, Fri, Sat; 7.30-9.30pm Tue-Thur. Average L70,000. No credit cards) where young chef Francesco Cacciatori offers a fixed menu of *sapori toscani* (taste of Tuscany).

Just north of town on the Chiantigiana is the terraced **Bar-Ristorante Pietra Fitta** (0577 741 123. Open restaurant 7pm-3am Mon, Tue, Thur-Sun; bar 11am-7pm. Average L40,000. Credit AmEx, DC, JCB, MC, V) that looks almost like a truck stop but is a fantastic spot to lunch. Try the *chitarrucci al cavolo nero* (black cabbage) but watch out for midget doggy Arturo, whose muscular legs easily propel him to table level.

Around Radda in Chianti

About one kilometre before Castellina, a fork in the road indicates the direction (N429) for Radda, yet another Chianti jewel. Radda was the capital of the medieval League of Chianti, a chain of Florentine defensive outposts against Siena that included Castellina and Gaiole. The Etruscan tomb-rich area around Volpaia, seven kilometres to the north, is also worth exploring.

An enchanting option for accommodation is the **Podere Terreno** pensione (Via della Volpaia, 0577 738 312/fax 0577 738 400/podereterreno@chianti.net.it. Rates L155,000 per person. Credit AmEx, MC, V). Located outside of Volpaia, this stone farmhouse sits in the middle of 120 acres of oak groves and chestnut trees. In Radda, **Giovannino** (Via Roma 8, tel/fax 0577 738 056. Rates double L80,000. No credit cards) is one of the only choices for budget travellers.

Around Gaiole in Chianti

On the steep eastern edge of Chianti and surrounded by the Monti dei Chianti, the area around Gaiole is wild and rustic, but well explored. The **Badia a Coltibuono**, four kilometres north of Gaiole, is a Vallombrosan abbey set amid cedar forests and is a great starting point for hikers. After walking off yesterday's meal, head back to the abbey's restaurant (0577 749 031. Open 12.30-2.30pm, 7.30-9.30pm, daily. Average L45,000. Credit MC, V) that specialises in local game.

South of Gaiole is one of Chianti's best-known castles, and one of the few that are visitable: the **Castello di Brolio**. What you see is largely a nineteenth-century reading of what a castle should look like – the original was wrecked by Spanish troops in 1478 and destroyed by the Sienese 50 years later. It was rebuilt in 1860 by Baron Bettino Ricasoli, the entrepreneur responsible for pushing Chianti's wine industry into the major league. You can visit the Baron's apartments (0577 749 411; phone for an appointment).

West of Siena

The Poggibonsi exit of the Si-Fi (Siena-Florence) motorway quickly gives access to western Siena Province and the Etruscan town of Volterra in Pisa Province. Although Poggibonsi itself is an ugly commercial centre with eyesore cement buildings and factory-dotted suburbs, the nearby town of Colle di Val d'Elsa makes an excellent base from which to explore San Gimignano, Monteriggioni and the Elsa Valley. The birthplace of Arnolfo di Cambio (the architect responsible for both Florence's **Duomo** and the **Palazzo Vecchio**), Colle's medieval core is worth exploring even if its outer ring of modern housing developments might put you off at first.

San Gimignano

For Italy's best skyline, head to San Gimignano – nicknamed Tuscany's Medieval Manhattan because of the city's 13 stone towers that look like a clump of oversized cypress trees from far away. At its political and financial peak in the twelfth and thirteenth centuries, it had 72 towers. San Gimignano's good fortune and wealth came from its strategic position on the Via Francigena trade route (*see p199* **Corridor of power**), which passes through this perfectly preserved Medieval city.

Today, tourism has brought it more wealth – and masses of day trippers. Its narrow streets are often congested with sightseers that bottleneck between the city's two main squares, and many of the locals work in servicing this invasion. See it in the early morning when *la città delle torri* is at its most magical or in the off season, otherwise San Gimignano is like Manhattan at rush hour.

What to see

It makes sense to buy a combined museum ticket (L18,000; L14,000 per person for families; L10,000 per person for groups of 15 or more) that includes the city's main sights: the Collegiata, the Museo Civico, the Torre Grossa, the Museo Ornitologico and the Museo d'Arte Sacra/Museo Etrusco. The first three are must-sees, but you can afford to skip the latter two's motley collections. Also ignore the exploitative Museo della Tortura on the Via del Castello that, at L15,000 per ticket, would make you a masochist in more ways than one.

There are two main entrances to the town: through the Porta San Matteo to the north that leads up the Via San Matteo, or through the Porta San Giovanni and up the Via San Giovanni that climbs up from the south. Whichever way you enter, both roads lead up a steep incline to the heart of the Medieval city: the Piazza della Cisterna and the adjacent Piazza del Duomo. The Piazza della Cisterna has a functioning thirteenth-century well in its centre and the Torre del Diavolo looms overhead. The 'Devil's Tower' earned its name when its owner convinced his neighbours that it had grown taller on its own. The Piazza del Duomo is the town's cultural and political hub. Facing the so-called Duomo (technically it is the Collegiata), the Palazzo del Popolo (home to the town hall, the Museo Civico and the Torre Grossa) stands to your left, and the Palazzo del Podestà is behind you.

The plain Romanesque façade of the **Collegiata**, or cathedral (0577 940 316. Open Apr-Oct 9.30am-7.30pm Mon-Fri; 9.30am-5.30pm Sat; 1-5pm Sun; Nov-Mar 9.30am-5pm Mon-Sat; 1-5pm Sun. Admission L6,000. No credit cards) stands in stark contrast to the glorious interior. Almost every inch of wall space is frescoed, animating the Bible in two separate cycles. On the left wall is the Old Testament fresco cycle by Bartolo di Fredi, flanked by the expressive New Testament cycle (1333), allegedly by Lippo Memmi, on the right wall. Before the altar is the waxy body of Santa Fina, and to the right is the Cappella di Santa Fina. Santa Fina is the patron saint of San Gimignano who spent most of her short life after age ten lying on wooden planks in a dark rat-infested room, after her mother scolded her for accepting an apple from a boy who had fallen in love with her. These details are depicted in the chapel's frescoes.

The **Museo Civico** (Piazza del Duomo, 0577 940 340. Open Mar-Oct 9.30am-7pm daily; Nov-Feb 9.30am-1.30pm, 2.30-4.30pm, Tue-Sun. Admission tower L8,000; museum L7,000; both L12,000. No credit cards) houses Lippo Memmi's masterpiece, the *Maestà* (1317) and Taddeo di Bartolo's *Scenes from the Life of St Gimignano* (1393), which shows the saint holding the whole city in his lap against a golden background. Access to the **Torre Grossa** – at 164m the tallest tower in town and the only one you can climb – is through a courtyard in the museum. Sweating it to the top is worth the effort for the fantastic aerial views, but should not be underestimated (the climb ends with a near vertical ladder).

Where to stay

There is not a wide selection of hotels within the city walls, but there's a sprawling network of *agriturismi* both in the city and the surrounding countryside. For more information on these, go to the friendly **Tourist Office** (Piazza del Duomo 1, 0577 940 008. Open 9am-1pm, 3-7pm, daily).

L'Antico Pozzo *Via San Matteo 87 (tel/fax 0577 942 014).* **Rates** *single* L155,000; *double* L210,000. **Credit** AmEx, MC, V. Complete with its own well and frescoed rooms, this is one of San Gimignano's classiest joints.

La Cisterna *Piazza della Cisterna 24 (0577 940 328/0577 942 080).* **Rates** *single* L118,000; *double* L155,000-L195,000. **Credit** AmEx, DC, JCB, MC, V. Located on one of the two main squares, this ivy-covered fourteenth-century palazzo is the best bet for some peace and quiet.

Where to eat

Gelateria di Piazza Piazza della Cisterna (0577 942 244). Open 9am-midnight daily; closed Nov-Feb. No credit cards. Claims it serves the world's best

Monteriggioni – *one of Tuscany's earliest examples of military architecture.*

ice-cream – and they are very good. Owner Sergio Dondoli sent a tray of his emerald green pistachio blend to a vacationing Tony Blair in 1998, a few days before the signing of the peace agreement with Northern Ireland.

Dorandó *Vicolo dell'Oro 2 (0577 941 862).* **Open** *summer* 12.30-2.30pm, 7.30-9.30pm, daily; closed Feb. **Average** L80,000. **Credit** AmEx, DC, MC, V. One of San Gimignano's more elegant places that serves food based on Etruscan, Medieval and Renaissance recipes. Try the *pici* with mint pesto washed down with the local white, Vernaccia di San Gimignano.

Osteria delle Catene *Via Mainardi 18 (0577 941 966).* **Open** 12.30-2pm, 7.30-9.30pm, Thur-Tue. **Average** L45,000. **Credit** AmEx, DC, MC, V. Located on the northern side of town, this osteria offers regional cooking, with an alternative slant. Try the rabbit cooked in local Vernaccia wine.

Festivals

The Carnival procession in February is the best time to visit in the off season, as is 12 March, the day of patron Saint Fina, when the museums are free of charge. In July, a series of daily concerts billed as the Festival Internazionale include classic piano recitals and opera.

Volterra

Volterra stands proud on a 531-metre peak between the Cecina and Era Valleys in Pisa Province. Traces from the Neolithic period were discovered here, but it wasn't until the fifth century BC that Etruscan culture flourished and Volterra's population grew 25,000 strong – it became one of 12 states in the Etruscan nation. Velathri (the city's Etruscan name) put up a hearty resistance to the expansionist Romans and was the last Etruscan city to fall to the Empire in 260 BC, when it was renamed Volaterrae. The town as it appears today was built in the twelfth and thirteenth centuries and virtually all traces of the Etruscans in the city have been erased except for patches of the fortified walls that reveal Etruscan foundations. Etruscan buffs should not miss the Museo Etrusco that houses one of the world's most complete collections of artefacts from this mysterious ancient population – including the celebrated 'evening shadow' statuette seen in cheap reproductions countless times over in souvenir shops throughout Tuscany. The thin, elongated statue was found by a local farmer and used as a firestoker until someone recognised its importance.

Since Etruscan times, Volterra's most important industry has been making alabaster artefacts. The area around the city contains one of Italy's largest deposits of the stone. Once used to adorn abbeys and palaces, today alabaster is turned into everything from thimbles to life-sized horse heads – anything that can be carted away in a tour bus.

Monteriggioni

Whichever way you approach it on the Si-Fi motorway, Monteriggioni stands out as one of Tuscany's most surreal visions. Fourteen stone towers built on thick walls that encircle a tiny medieval hamlet make Monteriggioni look like a crown resting on top of a grassy hill. Dante, on the other hand, saw it as an enormous well filled with horrible giants and described it as such in the *Divine Comedy*. Interpretations aside, it is one of Tuscany's earliest examples of military architecture and remains a perfectly preserved walled city. The walls – that form a perimeter of 570 metres – were built by Siena (1213-19) and reinforced half a century later to protect Siena's northern territories from Florence's invading armies.

But there's not much inside besides a bar, a few homes, and the Romanesque-Gothic Pieve di Santa Maria. It takes less than five minutes to get a good sense of the town and walk its length. If you decide to stay longer, two good restaurants and a four-star hotel are also squeezed in. **Il Piccolo Castello** (Via I Maggio 2, 0577 304 370. Open noon-2.30pm, 7-10.30pm, daily. Average L45,000. Credit AmEx, MC, V) has an attractive garden. The slightly more expensive **Il Pozzo** (Piazza Roma, 0577 304 127. Open 12.15-2.40pm, 7.45-10pm, Tue-Sat; 12.15-2.40pm Sun. Average L70,000. No credit cards) serves up delicious Tuscan staples. The **Hotel Monteriggioni** (Via I Maggio 4, 0577 305 009. Rates single L200,00; double L340,000. Credit AmEx, DC, V) has 12 rooms.

If you're looking for a meal accompanied by a good ghost story, head to the nearby Benedictine monastery of **Abbadia Isola**. Founded in 1001 when the area was swampland, this was the last outpost for food before Siena for pilgrims travelling along the Via Francigena. According to legend, two drunk monks stumbled across the abbey at night looking for booze. Instead, they got locked up and a nasty spell was cast on them inhibiting them from enjoying wine. If you come here the night of 11 July (Benedict's Saint Day), listen for the hiccuping and slurred speech of two inebriated spirits still locked up within the walls. Even better, book a table at the **Antica Osteria La Leggenda dei Frati** (Piazza Garfonda 7, 0577 301 222. Open 12.30-2.30pm, 7.30-10.30pm, Tue-Sun. Average

Corridor of power

All roads may lead to Rome, but one of the most important pilgrim and trade routes, heavily trafficked throughout the Middle Ages, spanned the entire length of Tuscany and carved a corridor of commerce and communication that forever enriched the region. The Via Francigena (or Via Romea or Via Francesca) draws a line across Europe connecting London and Northern Europe south through France, the Swiss Alps and down the Italian peninsula to the seat of Christianity. Thousands of pilgrims, merchants and clergymen walked this route, travelling no more than 20 kilometres per day with the south-shining sun relentlessly in their eyes, to make the holy journey to the Apostles' tomb in Rome and receive indulgences from the Pope. Even Sigerico, the Archbishop of Canterbury, made the journey in 990, keeping a detailed journal of his travels that describes treacherous terrain, dangerous road bandits and a booming local economy generated by the route. Only about 20 per cent of the Via Francigena exists today and this has become a popular hiking trail – also events are being planned along the route to celebrate 2,000 years of Christianity.

The ancient route's Tuscan segment started at Pontrémoli where locals commanded hefty ferry fees from pilgrims seeking to cross the Magra River at the Cisa pass. It led south to Massa & Carrara's seaport where pilgrims who could afford it, opted to travel more comfortably by boat down to Rome. Those who continued by foot passed through shabby trading villages like Lucca and San Gimignano, sleeping in hospices (*spedali*), in exchange for the goods they carried with them. The towns located on the road's path quickly grew rich, investing their money in architecture and artistic patrimony. One of the most spectacular examples of pilgrims' cash injection is San Gimignano where locals, at a loss on how to spend their newfound wealth, invested in a tower-building frenzy. The route continued to the Abbey of Sant'Antimo, Monteriggioni, and on to Siena. Siena was one of the most important stations along the Via Francigena and its artistic wealth today is a direct consequence of the road. The city's Spedale di Santa Maria della Scale, a hospital catering to fatigued and sick pilgrims, became the era's most modern medical facility because of the constant flow of patients and doctors. But not only Tuscany's economy benefited from the pilgrims. Merchants and traders carried spices and ingredients with them that are now incorporated in the local cuisine – chocolate, for example, commonly used with meat in medieval Tuscan dishes – was a new and exotic taste. It also opened the region to communication with northern Europe. The English word 'route' comes from 'rupte,' a word used to describe unmarked segments of the Via Francigena. The end of the road was Rome, and the pilgrims who survived the journey were consoled with the knowledge that they had earned their ticket to paradise.

L60,000. Credit AmEx, DC, JCB, MC, V) – just go easy on the house wine.

Abbazia di San Galgano

This abandoned abbey is worth a detour even if you're reaching overdose point on Tuscany's abundance of churches. Located in the Valdimerse midway between Siena and Roccastrada on SS73, **San Galgano** is something out of a fairy tale – or a nightmare. Built between 1218 and 1288, the abbey was a Cistercian powerhouse up until the fourteenth century. Its monks devised sophisticated irrigation systems, and sold their services as doctors, lawyers and architects (helping to build Siena's cathedral). But the abbey was sacked one time too many and eventually abandoned.

It went from being one of the greatest Gothic buildings in Italy, to a monument to nature's destructive forces. The roof and bell tower collapsed during a mass in 1786, and by the beginning of the nineteenth century it had become a barn for local herders. Nonetheless, the ruins retain an atmosphere of eerie spirituality.

Saint Galgano Guidotti himself lived in a hut on a hilltop adjacent to the abbey where the **Cappella di Montesiepi** now stands. He was a knight from a local noble family who renounced his warlike ways to become a Cistercian hermit. When fellow knights persuaded him to return to his old self in 1180, he defiantly stabbed a stone with his sword and it miraculously slid in. The (alleged) sword in the stone is now on display in the centre of the curious circular Romanesque chapel, which also has fading frescoes by Ambrogio Lorenzetti.

The much-visited **Monte Oliveto Maggiore**.

South-east of Siena

No sooner does the red Sienese skyline disappear behind you as you travel south on the Via Cassia (SS2, which traces an ancient trade route used by the Romans), than the landscape dramatically changes. The wooded hills of Chianti give way to rolling hills of open fields, whose machine-perfect rows of budding crops are only disturbed by that quintessentially Tuscan lone cypress tree.

The secondary southern route (N438) to **Asciano** is less trafficked and passes through the rippled core of the Crete Senesi, an area of white clay hills and deep gullies that look like a stylised quattrocento drapery. Asciano is a pleasant town in the heart of the Crete Senesi, where the main action is around card tables in a smoke-filled back room of the Bar Hervé on the central Piazza Garibaldi. About three kilometres north of here is the riotous **La Pievina** (Via Lauretana 9, La Pievina, 0577 718 368. Open 8-10pm Wed-Sat; 1-3pm Sun. Average L80,000. No credit cards), where three flirtatious older ladies will entertain you and stuff you with home-cooked goodies.

If you enter Siena Province by train from Rome, chances are you will change trains at the hub of **Chiusi** (lines for Siena, Montepulciano, and Pienza start here). To fill in time between trains, don't miss the **Museo Archeologico Nazionale** (Via Porsenna 93, 0578 20177. Open summer 9am-8pm Mon-Sat; 9am-1pm Sun; winter 9am-1pm Mon-Sat; 9am-1pm Sun. Admission L8,000; free under-18s, over-60s), which houses an excellent selection of Etruscan artefacts.

Monte Oliveto Maggiore

The red roof of Italy's most visited Benedictine monastery (0577 707 611. Open summer 9.15am-6pm daily; winter 9.15am-5pm daily) screams out in technicolor brilliance against the white gullies of the Crete Senesi and surrounding pine forests. Once on the grounds, however, that loud first impression soon fades into quite spiritual meditation. A signpost welcomes you 'to silence and prayers in this sacred place'. Founded in 1313 by Bernardo Tolomei, a scion of one of Siena's richest families, the monastery began as a solitary hermitage in an area so arid it was referred to as a

Bagno Vignoni's *thermal pool is off limits, but there's other soaking spots nearby.*

deserto. But Bernardo soon drew a large following and the Olivetan order was recognised by the Pope in 1344. Expanded territory brought wealth that was channelled into embellishing the buildings and creating a library. (Unfortunately, the library has been closed to the public since someone ran off with an armful of priceless volumes, but you can peek through the exquisite carved wooden doors.) But the biggest project was the Saint Benedict fresco cycle. Ghost-like, white-robed monks greet you as you enter the arcaded cloister and, once inside, that technicolor brilliance starts up again. The panels were painted by Giovanni Antonio Bazzi, better known as Il Sodoma, and Luca Signorelli. The frescoes are fascinating for what you can read in between the brush strokes. Sodoma was a colourful character with a taste for exotic pets and young boys (if Vasari and his nickname are to be believed), who let his inner soul flow freely in the often bizarre scenes from the saint's life: notice the backside views of the Saint's younger helpers and other renditions of human anatomy. Outside the cloister is a Benedictine gift shop that sells home-brewed *amaro* drinks and herbal medicines.

Montalcino

Montalcino's claim to fame is as a producer of one of Italy's premier wines. The robust Brunello di Montalcino's consistent quality has earned it Italy's highest wine honour: the DOCG (super DOC) seal. Brunello ages in oak for five years to acquire its body and aroma. Look out for the 1995 vintage and the highly anticipated 1997 vintage that will be ready in 2002. If you want younger and less solemn, try the year-old Rosso di Montalcino.

The existence of a hilltop town here can be traced to 814 when it was ceded to the nearby Abbey of Sant'Antimo. Under Siena's rule in the thirteenth century, four families dominated the town's political identity and are represented today in Montalcino's four *contrade*. Montalcino's proudest moment came in 1555 when it became the temporary seat of power of the Sienese Republic (a group of exiled Sienese nobles held out here when Siena fell to Cosimo I de' Medici). Soon after, the town fell on hard times and plague and, until the late 1950s, it was one of Tuscany's poorest corners. Today tourism, olive oil and the mighty Brunello have turned Montalcino's luck.

What to see

All roads in Montalcino lead to Piazza del Popolo, this peculiar triangle marks the heart of the town and nearby is the **Tourist Office** (0577 849 331. Open 10am-1pm, 2-6pm, Tue-Sun). On the piazza is the shield-studded **Palazzo Comunale** (with the tall tower) modelled after Siena's Palazzo Pubblico in 1292. Around the corner, annexed to the Sant'Agostino church, is the **Museo Civico** (Via Ricasoli 31, 0577 846 014. Open Jan-Mar 10am-1pm,

2-5pm, Tue-Sun; Apr-Oct 10am-6pm Tue-Sun; Nov-Dec 10am-1pm, 2-6pm, Tue-Sun. Admission L8,000; L10,000 combined with Rocca (*see below*). No credit cards). Opened in 1997, the museum's collection includes Sano di Pietro's *Madonna dell'Umiltà,* in which, curiously, the Virgin is shown kneeling. The Gothic-Romanesque Sant'Agostino church (1360) has superb frescoes by Bartolo di Fredi and, for a change of pace, head to the downright neoclassic **Duomo** (1818-32) built on the site of an older church.

Montalcino's most rewarding attraction is the **Rocca**. Built in 1361 on Sienese orders, the fortress remains one of Tuscany's best examples of military architecture. A climb up the ramparts will reveal stunning views that extend all the way to Siena on a clear day. Tickets are purchased in the Enoteca inside the fortress walls (0577 849 211. Open summer 10am-8pm Tue-Sun; winter 10am-1pm, 2-6pm, Tue-Sun. Admission L3,500; L10,000 combined with Museo Civico. No credit cards) that offers a extensive selection of Brunellos at slightly marked-up prices.

Where to stay

Albergo Il Giglio *Via S Saloni 5 (tel/fax 0577 848 167).* Rates *single* L80,000; *double* L120,000). Credit MC, V. A family-run place with 12 frescoed rooms in its main building and an additional 5 (no bath) in an adjacent building. The restaurant is worth a visit.

Residence Montalcino *Via S Saloni 31 (tel/fax 0577 847 188).* Rates double L120,000-L150,000. Credit AmEx, DC, JCB, MC, V. Clean and comfortable apartments, each with their own little kitchen.

Where to eat

Montalcino is where *pici* (stringy pasta made without eggs) originates. Also try *ossi di morto*: flat almond cookies that crumble just like brittle bones.

Fiaschetteria Italiana *Piazza del Popolo 6 (0577 849 043).* Open 7.30am-midnight Mon-Wed, Fri-Sun. Credit AmEx, DC, JCB, MC, V. A local institution for people-watching and Brunello-sampling.
Bacchus *Via G Matteotti 15 (0577 847 054).* Open 8am-10pm Mon, Wed-Sun. Average L20,000. Credit AmEx, DC, MC, V. This enoteca is a great lunch spot for *cinghiale* and goose salami washed down with plenty of Brunello.
Trattoria Sciame *Via Ricasoli 9 (0577 848 017).* **Open** 12.30-2.30pm, 7.15-9.30pm, Mon, Wed-Sun. Average L40,000. Credit AmEx, DC, JCB, MC, V. Renowned for its *zuppa di fagioli* (bean soup with slivers of red onion and parmegiano cheese on top).

Abbazia di Sant'Antimo

One of three roads that radiates south of Montalcino's Rocca indicates the direction for Sant'Antimo. This sensational country road snakes through ten kilometres of unspoiled landscape and is best appreciated if you have three hours to walk it. The road leads to an isolated green valley and the Abbey of Sant'Antimo, built in creamy travertine with translucent alabaster highlights. This Benedictine abbey stood empty for 500 years before a handful of French Premonstratensian monks – a Cistercian branch – moved here in 1979. Its founding is attributed to Charlemagne in 781 and it is said to be the first of more than 20 abbeys established by the emperor. In 1118, funds were granted to construct the present church and additional monastic buildings that have since fallen to rubble. This grant was so important that it was literally written in stone – engraved in the steps of the altar. For three centuries Sant'Antimo grew into a regional powerhouse thanks to the Via Francigena trade route. By the thirteenth century financial mismanagement led to the abbey's demise. Siena divided up its territory and in 1462 Pope Pio II evicted the remaining monks, citing moral degeneration.

Inside are carvings in onyx and alabaster. Don't miss Daniel in the Lion's Den (second column from the right of the nave) by a mysterious Spanish carver. If you time it right you can relax to the ethereal resonance of the Gregorian chants that echo off the ancient walls when mass is celebrated. If you miss the real thing, CDs are on sale.

Bagno Vignoni

Bagno Vignoni, just south of San Quirico d'Orcia, has to be seen to be believed. Piazza delle Sorgenti – Bagno Vignoni's main square – has a large pool of thermal water at its centre flanked by a ragged collection of houses and a low Renaissance loggia. The pool, featured in a memorable scene in Tarkovsky's *Nostalgia*, has been off limits since 1979 because the crowds grew too big. But there is a little stream of thermal run-off about 200 metres south of there (a bit tepid at this stage) that is perfect for soaking tired feet in.

Bagno Vignoni also boasts an outstanding restaurant. The **Osteria del Leone** (Piazza del Moretto, 0577 887 300. Open 7.30-9.30pm Tue; 12.30-2.30pm, 7.30-9.30pm, Wed-Sun. Average L45,000. Credit AmEx, DC, JCB, MC, V) has a cosy rustic feel with chunky wooden tables, friendly staff and a different menu every day, sometimes including an excellent suckling pig cooked with fennel flowers. It's difficult to get a table, so either come early or be prepared to wait.

The village also has two hotels: the rather run-down but comfortable **Le Terme** (0577 887 150/fax 0577 887 497. Rates single L78,000; double L130,000. Credit AmEx, DC, JCB, MC, V) located on the main square and the modern **Hotel Posta Marcucci** (0577 887 112/fax 0577 887 119. Rates single L88,000-L105,000; double L176,000-L210,000. Credit AmEx, DC, JCB, MC, V. Website www.hotelposta.marcucci.it) that has an open-air thermal swimming pool. Access to the pool for non-guests is L12,000 for a half day. You'll struggle to find a more memorable experience in Tuscany than gazing dreamily across the valley while bathing in the pool at sunset.

Pienza

It was built as an 'ideal humanist city' and in many ways it still is. Aeneas Silvius Piccolomini, the Renaissance humanist elected Pope Pius II in 1458, probably had something more imposing in mind when he gave architect Bernardo Rossellino *carte blanche* to build an ideal city here in 1449. Pius II, born in backward Corsignano, apparently nurtured an inferiority complex because of his insignificant home town. He set to work on realising his dream of transforming it into a utopia of Renaissance principles and even renamed it 'Pienza' after himself. But he died a few years following its completion and today this sleepy place of under 1,500 inhabitants has the haunting feeling of an abandoned movie set.

Pienza's focal point is the Piazza Pio II. Stand in the centre and gyrate slowly: everything you see was either put up or reconstructed between 1459 and 1462 – the Duomo, the Palazzo Vescovile, the Palazzo Comunale and the Palazzo Piccolomini. The travertine Duomo contains works by Vecchietta and Sano di Pietro in the side chapels, and a marble altar by Rossellino. Sadly, in order to please Pius II's wish of a luminous south-facing church, the Duomo was built on unstable sandstone and is still dangerously tilted on the far end. The **Palazzo Piccolomini** (0578 748 503. Open Sept-June 10am-12.30pm, 3-6pm, daily; July-Aug 10am-12.30pm, 4-7pm, Tue-Sun. Admission L5,000) was reserved for the Pope and modelled after Alberti's Palazzo Rucellai in Florence. Strictly martialled guided tours take you through Pius II's lavishly furnished private apartments.

In 1998, Pienza moved its art collection to the new **Museo Diocesano** (0578 749 905. Open 10am-1pm, 2-6.30pm, Mon, Wed-Sun. Admission L8,000). Inside, the highlights are a golden *Madonna and Child* altarpiece by Pietro Lorenzetti and a collection of Flemish tapestries.

The **Tourist Office** (Corso Il Rossellino 59, 0578 749 071. Open 9.30am-1pm, 3-6.30pm, daily) rents outs 50-minute taped tours of the city for L10,000 and can help with accommodation options. But if you hit Pienza at lunchtime, head to the far east end of town to the **Trattoria Latte di Luna** (0578 748 606. Open lunch & dinner Mon, Wed-Sun. Average L35,000. No credit cards). Typical Tuscan nourishment and refreshments (of both the red and white variety) enjoyed on the trattoria's outdoor terrace help to make Pienza very human indeed.

Montepulciano

It's hard to imagine anyone voluntarily pushing heavy oak wine barrels up a two kilometres precipitous cobblestone road in August. But that's exactly what Montepulciano's proudest do each year in the highly anticipated Bravio delle Botti competition. Eight rival contrade battle it out for the honour of being the first to painstakingly roll their barrel to the town's highest point: the best easily complete the task in under ten minutes. The winner gets doused in the local wine, appropriately named Vino Nobile di Montepulciano, and brings glory to his contrade. Montepulciano oozes the philosophy: 'no sweat, no glory,' something worth keeping in mind during the unrelenting uphill climb (in more like 30 minutes) to the town's core. The prize is a cool drink on the Piazza Grande, where most of the buildings on display are the legacy of the town's boom years following 1511, when Montepulciano finally declared its allegiance to Florence after waffling between it and Siena for over a century. Eminent architects of the time such as Antonio da Sangallo the Elder and Vignola were brought in to rework the town's medieval fabric and the town put up some lasting Renaissance monuments. Sangallo was especially active, rebuilding many of the buildings on the central square before excelling himself down at San Biagio.

Things to see

The best way to see the town is by huffing it up the steep Via del Corso that starts at Montalcino's northern entrance, Porta al Prato. The Roman and Etruscan marble plaques cemented into the base of the Palazzo Bucelli (No.73) are worth a look. A bit further up you'll notice (it's hard not to) a clock tower topped by a mechanical clown that strikes the hour. This Bavarian touch was apparently the warped artistic vision of an exiled Neapolitan noble with a lot of time on his hands. Further up, the Piazza Grande is the town's highest point and its most beautiful. The spacious piazza carpeted with chunky stones is reminiscent of Pienza's 'ideal city' layout. Don't let the unfinished rough brick façade of the **Duomo** put you off. Inside is a treasure trove: there is a fine Gothic *Assumption* by Taddeo di Bartolo over the altar (1401) and towards the top of the left of the nave, a *Madonna and Child* by Sano di Pietro. Note the *Ciborium*, a rare marble sculpture work to the right by fresco artist Vecchietta. But the highlight is the delicately carved tomb of humanist Aragazzi (1428) by Michelozzo.

Also in the square are Sangallo's Palazzo Tarugi, with loggia; the thirteenth-century Palazzo Comunale, which deliberately echoes the Palazzo Vecchio in Florence, and the Palazzo Contucci across the square. Whatever else you see, the pilgrimage church of San Biagio, a 20-minute walk from Porta al Prato, is a must. Designed by Sangallo and built between 1518 and 1545, this Bramante-influenced study in proportion is a jewel of the High Renaissance.

Where to stay

The friendly **Tourist Office** on Via del Corso 59A (0578 757 341. Open 10am-noon, 4-6pm, Mon-Sat) has hotel options in and around town.

Il Marzocco *Piazza Savonarola 18 (0578 757 262/fax 0578 757 530).* Rates single L90,000, double L120,000. Credit AmEx, DC, MC, V. Just inside the Porta al Prato in a sixteenth-century palazzo, Il Marzocco has spacious rooms, some with terraces.

La Terrazza *Via Pié al Sasso 16 (tel/fax 0578 757 440).* Rates single/double L85,000-L95,000; 4-bed apartment L170,000. Credit DC, MC, V. Centrally located on a quite street, this is Montepulciano's best value for travellers minding their wallets.

Where to eat

For drinks or light midday snacks, don't miss the Antico Caffè Poliziano midway up the Via del Corso. This local, decadently art deco institution is also a great place to sample Montepulciano's Vino Nobile.

L'Angolo *Via Galilei 20, Località Acquaviva, Montepulciano (0578 767 216).* **Open** noon-2.30pm, 7.30pm-12.30am, Tue-Sun. **Average** L35,000. **Credit** AmEx, DC, MC, V. It looks like the sort of place you'd come to get your bike repaired – but that's before you get a whiff from the kitchen. Try the light crispy pizza that comes with an entire truffle to shave on top.

La Grotta San Biagio *Località San Biagio 15 (0578 757 607).* **Open** 12.30-2.15pm, 7.30-10pm Mon, Tue, Thur-Sun. **Average** L60,000. **Credit** AmEx, DC, MC, V. This decidedly upmarket joint occupies the room where Sangallo lived while working on the church. It offers vaguely francophile readings of local specialities, including *pollo al Vino Nobile*. Tables outside in summer.

Festivals

In August the town hosts the **Cantiere Internazionale d'Arte**, a modern music/festival workshop with poetry readings and amateur opera night. The last Sunday in August is the day for barrel pushing at the **Bravio delle Botti**.

Siena

A city of animal magic.

It's the little things that count when it comes to understanding Siena. A fountain adorned with marble goose heads, a giraffe poster, or a tiny ceramic caterpillar plaque on a wall reveal a world of proud and competitive tradition that has riveted this city for more than seven centuries. These zoological road signals map out just three of the city's 17 contrade (*see box*) and represent the fiercely independent identities of their citizens. New babies are baptised in the fountain of their contrade, and the dead are buried with their contrade flag.

The well-preserved medieval city of Siena perches on three hills surrounded by two fertile valleys. Its red-brick skyline stands out against a backdrop of grape vines, olive trees and fields. The historic centre is divided into three districts: Terzo di Città includes the Piazza del Campo and the Duomo; Terzo di Camollia, to the north, is the religious heart of the city, with churches and basilicas built by the Dominicans and the Franciscans; to the south-east is the Terzo di San Martino, Siena's most unspoiled neighbourhood.

The beautiful **Piazza del Campo**. *See p206.*

SOME HISTORY

Siena's history begins in mystery: who founded this ancient outpost and where does its name originate? Traces of primitive fortifications dating from the Bronze Age suggest the city's geographic vantage point has always been envied and highly contested. The Etruscans settled here, creating an important trading colony with Volterra, and one theory is that the city was named after the prominent Etruscan Saina family. The city was refounded as a Roman colony, Saena Julia, by Emperor Augustus and only 1,000 years later did it become an independent republic.

What really put Siena on the map was Via Francigena (*see p199* **Corridor of power**). Siena became an important station along this pilgrim's route and thus acquired political weight and assertiveness. By 1125, the young city had amassed enough self-confidence to pick fights with its neighbours. Siena embarked on a plan to expand its territory, but this did not go unnoticed by Florence.

The hatred between Tuscany's sister cities over the following 100 years was one of history's more malevolent rivalries. Things came to an explosive climax on 4 September 1260, when Siena won the bloody Battle of Montaperti. A 15,000-strong Sienese army killed 10,000 Florentine soldiers and captured 15,000. The jubilant Sienese danced on the bodies of the fallen Florentines with nails in their shoes to hammer home the victory.

It was short-lived. Nine years later the two cities clashed again in Colle di Val d'Elsa and Florence came out on top. This 1269 defeat marks a profound shift in Siena's social and political identity that paradoxically forged the way for its prosperous Golden Age.

With their minds taken off expansion, the Sienese channelled their creative juices into commerce. Gradually, successful merchants and bankers gave rise to a wealthy middle class. Trade with France and England brought in cash and nourished a flourishing wool industry. Siena's civic side strengthened and in 1287 its governing body, the Council of Nine, was established in friendship with Florence. The city's most important public works occurred under the Council of Nine. The Gothic **Palazzo Pubblico**, much of the

Duomo, the Torre del Mangia and the Piazza del Campo (divided into nine brick sections to represent the Council) were constructed.

Siena's Golden Age came to an abrupt halt in 1348, when the Black Death struck. Siena's population dwindled from 100,000 to 30,000 in less than a year. Siena never fully recovered from this blow; internal fighting ensued and brought down the Council of Nine in 1355. Forty four years later the city fell under the control of Gian Galeazzo Visconti, Grand Duke of Milan, until his death in 1402. He was eventually followed by the tyrannical, exiled nobleman, Pandolfo Petrucci.

In 1552 the Spanish king, Charles V, besieged the city, but only three years later, a popular insurrection against the Spanish left the city open to Cosimo I de' Medici. Reduced to a mere 8,000 inhabitants, Siena could not defend itself. A group of Sienese nobles tried to keep their republic alive in exile for a few years in nearby Montalcino, but the effort proved fruitless. The definitive end of the Sienese Republic came in 1559.

Once again, Siena poured its energies into banking and sports competitions, building on surviving achievements. One of the world's oldest banks, the Monte dei Paschi di Siena, founded in 1472 as a protectionist measure against Florence's heavy taxes, slowly matured into an economic powerhouse. But one of the most spectacular institutions to be born from the 1600s is Siena's **Palio**.

In 1859, Siena became the first major Tuscan city to join a united Italy. Two years later, the city was plugged into the nation's budding railway system, allowing for faster communication and commerce with the rest of the country. More importantly, it marked the beginning of a lucrative tourist trade.

Sights

Piazza del Campo

One of Italy's most beautiful squares, built on the site of an ancient Roman forum, the shell-shaped piazza lies at the base of Siena's three hills and curves downward on the southern side to the **Palazzo Pubblico** and **Torre del Mangia**. The Campo was paved in 1347 and its nine sections pay homage to the city's governing Council.

The Fonte Gaia designed by Jacopo della Quercia (built 1408-1419) sits on the north side of the piazza. In 1868, the eroded marble panels of the basin were replaced by copies and what's left of the originals can be seen in the loggia of the Palazzo Pubblico. The fountain's basin serves as a terminus for the elaborate network of underground wells and aqueducts (totalling 25km throughout the province) developed by Siena. According to legend, before Fonte Gaia was built, a construction team uncovered a perfectly preserved antique marble statue of Venus. The statue was erected where the fountain is today. When the Black Death struck, the Sienese blamed their newly unearthed treasure. Convinced the statue had brought a curse, it was smashed to pieces and the fragments were buried in Florence's territory.

Palazzo Pubblico

This elegant example of Gothic architecture was built between 1288 and 1342. The brick and stone building housing the town hall and the **Museo Civico** (*see below,* **Museums**) is a symbol of medieval Siena's mercantile wealth and its façade – with its she-wolf and Medici balls – reads like a history book of the city.

Torre del Mangia

Piazza del Campo. **Open** *summer* 10am-7.30pm, *winter* 10am-3.30pm, daily. **Admission** L5,000.

Architects Minuccio and Francesco di Rinaldo were instructed to build their tower as tall as possible, and what they completed in 1348 is, in fact, medieval Italy's tallest tower (102 metres) with views that extend over much of Siena province. The tower is named after one of its first bell-ringers, a pot-bellied fellow nicknamed *Mangiaguadagni* (eats profits), who bulked up at the local trattoria but never burnt off excess fat despite a daily climb up the tower's 503 steps. At the foot of the tower is the Gothic Cappella di Piazza finished in 1352 to commemorate the end of the plague.

Churches

The tourist office offers a L12,000 combined ticket (also available at the Duomo) that includes admission to the Libreria Piccolomini, **Battistero**, Museo dell' Opera Metropolitana and the **Oratorio di San Bernardino**.

Basilica di San Domenico

Piazza San Domenico (0577 280 893). **Open** 7am-1pm, 3-6.30pm, daily. **Admission** free.

This soaring brick edifice was one of the earliest Dominican monasteries in Tuscany. Begun in 1226 and completed in 1465, it has not been treated kindly by history. Fires, military occupations and earthquakes have all wreaked havoc, and what you see today is largely the fruit of mid twentieth-century restoration. A few things of interest have survived intact; at the end of the nave, for example, is a *Madonna Enthroned* attributed to Pietro Lorenzetti. Halfway down the nave on the right is the restored chapel of Siena's patron saint: St Catherine. The frescoes are by Sodoma (1526) and inside the chapel is a container with Catherine's head. Her body was chopped up by heretics after her death and various Italian cities made off with pieces, but Siena, her birthplace, got the grand prize.

Basilica di San Francesco

Piazza San Francesco (0577 289 081). **Open** 8.30am-12.30pm, 3-6pm daily. **Admission** free.

The Franciscans built this grand, somewhat severe church of Gothic origins in 1326 with a spacious interior. Little of its original artwork survived a devastating fire in 1655 – the mock Gothic façade is a

– Torre del Mangia.

twentieth-century addition. One work that does remain is Pietro Lorenzetti's *Crucifixion* (1331) in the first chapel of the transept. In the third chapel are two frescoes by his brother Ambrogio Lorenzetti, a *St Louis of Anjou before Boniface VIII* and *Martyrdom of the Franciscans* (1331).

Battistero

Piazza San Giovanni (no telephone). **Open** *winter* 7.30am-1pm, 2.30-5pm daily; *summer* 7.30am-7.30pm Mon-Sat. **Closed** for Mass 9am and 10am. **Admission** L3,000.

Squeezed under the Duomo's apse is the oddly rectangular Baptistery (most are octagonal). Its unfinished Gothic façade includes three arches adorned with human and animal busts. On the inside, colourful frescoes by various artists, mainly Vecchietta, fill the room (1447-60). The focal point is the central font (1417-34) designed by Jacopo della Quercia and considered one of the masterpieces of early Renaissance Tuscany. It features a gilded bronze bas-relief by Jacopo, Donatello and Lorenzo Ghiberti.

Duomo

Piazza del Duomo (0577 47321). **Open** *winter* 7.30am-1pm, 2.30-5pm daily; *summer* 7.30am-7.30pm Mon-Sat. **Closed** for Mass 9am and 10am. **Admission** free.

The Siena Duomo is one of Italy's first Gothic cathedrals. Construction started in 1150 on the site of an earlier church, but plans for what was to have been a massive cathedral had to be abandoned owing to the Black Death of 1348 and technical problems resulting from an unlevelled foundation. The result is Gothic in style, but Romanesque in spirit.

Even in its more modest state, the Duomo is an impressive achievement. The black and white marble façade was started in 1226, and 30 years later work began on the dome, one of the oldest in Italy. The lower portion of the façade and the statues in the centre of the three arches were designed by Giovanni Pisano (built 1284-96). Inside, the cathedral's polychrome floors are its most immediate attraction – if you can see them. Worked on by more than 40 artists between 1369 and 1547, the intricately decorated inlaid boxes are often covered with protective planks. They are visible only from 15 August to 15 September. The most impressive are those beneath the dome by Domenico Beccafumi (designed 1517-1547), who single-handedly created 35 of the 56 scenes. In the apse there is a splendid carved wooden choir (fourteenth-sixteenth centuries) and above this is a stained-glass rose window (7m across), one of Italy's earliest, made by Duccio di Buoninsegna in 1288. It depicts the life of the Virgin in nine sections. The tabernacle has Bernini's *Maddalena* and *San Girolamo* statues.

Another highlight is the pulpit carved in about 1266 by Nicola Pisano with the help of his son Giovanni and a young pupil, Arnolfo di Cambio. The Piccolomini altar includes four statues of saints by a young Michelangelo (carved 1501-1504) and above that there is a *Madonna* attributed to Jacopo della

Quercia. At the far end of the left aisle a door leads to the **Libreria Piccolomini** (admission L2,000), built in 1495 to house the library of a Sienese nobleman, Aeneas Silvius Piccolomini, the Renaissance humanist who became Pope Pius II. This vaulted chamber was constructed at the behest of his nephew (who became Pope Pius III for a brief 28 days), and frescoed between 1502 and 1509 by Pinturicchio (his last work), who was reportedly assisted by a young Raphael. The vibrant frescoes depict ten scenes from Pius II's life, including a scene in which he meets James II of Scotland.

Oratorio di San Bernardino

Piazza San Francesco (0577 42020). **Open** *mid-Mar-Nov* 10am-1pm, 2.30-5.30pm, daily; *winter* closed. **Admission** L2,000.

To the right of San Francesco, this oratory was built in the fifteenth century on the site where St Bernard used to pray. On the first floor is a magnificent fresco cycle painted between 1496 and 1518 by Beccafumi and Sodoma, along with their lesser contemporary, Girolamo del Pacchia.

Museums

Museo Civico

Palazzo Pubblico, Piazza del Campo (council cultural office 0577 292 230/ticket office 0577 292 263). **Open** *summer* 10am-7pm Mon-Sat; 9.30am-1pm Sun; *winter* 9am-1.30pm daily. **Admission** L8,000.

Access to the museum is through the courtyard of Palazzo Pubblico and up an iron staircase. The first four rooms of the museum house work by artists from the sixteenth to nineteenth centuries. The Sala del Risorgimento pays homage to the fact that Siena was one of the first cities of the region to embrace a united Italy. In the Sala del Concistorio, there are frescoed vaults by Domenico Beccafumi (painted 1529-35), on a judicial theme, and a marble portal sculpted in 1448 by Bernardo Rossellino.

In the anticappella you can admire Taddeo di Bartoli's (1362-1422) frescoes that reflect his fascination with Greek and Roman antiquity and mythological heroes and a *Madonna and Child with Saints* by Sodoma at the altar of the Cappella del Consiglio. The Sala del Mappamondo was decorated by Ambrogio Lorenzetti around 1320-30; its barely visible cosmological frescoes depict the universe and celestial spheres. This room also houses one of Siena's most cherished jewels: the *Maestà* fresco painted by Simone Martini in 1315, thought to be one of his earliest works. It is also considered one of the first examples of 'political painting', because the devotion to the Virgin Mary depicted is said to represent devotion to the Republic's princes. The faces of the main figures are repaints, as Martini got a second inspiration following a visit to Giotto's masterpiece in Assisi. The equestrian *Il Guidoriccio da Fogliano* (1328) is also attributed to Martini and celebrates a victorious battle in Montemassi.

Museo dell'Opera Metropolitana

Piazza del Duomo 8 (0577 283 048). **Open** *Nov-Mar* 9am-1.30pm daily; *Apr-Sept* 9am-7.30pm daily; *Oct* 9am-6m daily. **Admission** L6,000.

The museum occupies the planned, never completed, nave of the Duomo, and displays works taken from the cathedral. On the ground floor is a large hall divided into two by an incredibly beautiful fifteenth-century wrought-iron gate. Along the walls you can enjoy a better view of Giovanni Pisano's 12 magnificent marble statues (carved 1285-97) that once adorned the façade of the Duomo. In the centre of the room is the bas-relief of the *Madonna and Child with St Anthony* by Jacopo della Quercia, commissioned in 1437 and probably not quite completed when the artist died in 1438.

On the first floor is the *Pala della Maestà* (1308-1311) by Duccio di Buoninsegna, painted on both sides and used as the high altar of the Duomo until 1506. The front has a *Madonna with Saints* and the back depicts 26 religious scenes; all in dazzling colours on a gold background. A climb upstairs to the Facciatone (the unfinished nave) affords a beautiful view of the city.

In Sala delle Pace, also known as the Sala dei Nove and the meeting place for the Council of Nine, there is another stupendous fresco cycle: Ambrogio Lorenzetti's *Effects of Good Government and Bad Government* (1338-40).

Sweet treats from the Nanninis.

Useful information

Tourist information

Centro Servizi Informazioni Turistiche Siena (APT) *Piazza del Campo 56 (0577 280 551/270 676).* **Open** *summer* 8.30am-7.30pm Mon-Sat; *winter* 8.30am-1pm, 3-7pm Mon-Sat.

Transport

Railway Station
Piazza Fratelli Rosselli (0577 280 115).
The station is at the bottom of the hill on the east side of the city. Siena is on a branch line in the Italian railway system, meaning you will need to change trains at the Chiusi station if you are heading south to Rome. A direct train to Florence takes under an hour. For Pisa, change in Empoli.

Buses
Piazza San Domenico (0577 204 245).
Regional buses leave from the piazza. Bus 1 connects to the train station. Buses to Florence are faster than the train.

Bicycle & Moped Hire
DF Bike *Via Massetana Romana (0577 271 905).*
Automotocicli Perozzi *Via del Romitorio 5 (0577 223 157).*

Car Hire
AVIS *Via Simone Martini 36 (0577 270 305).*
Hertz *Viale Sardegna 37 (0577 45085).*

Taxi *Radio Taxi (0577 49222).*

Markets

Siena's fantastic **general market** (Wed morn, 8am-1pm) covers an area from Piazza La Lizza to the Fortezza. Get there early for the best goods. Every two years an **Antiques Show & Market** is held between February and March in the Magazzini del Sale at Palazzo Pubblico.

Festivals

The **Palio** (*see box*) takes place on 2 July and 16 Aug.
Siena Jazz (0577 271 401) is a major summer event with international musicians (end July, early August).
The **Settimana dei Vini**, a showcase of upcoming wines from the region, takes place in the Fortezza Santa Barbara (Medicea) during the first half of June.
The music conservatory **Accademia Chigiana** (0577 46152) organises an outdoor concert cycle in June and puts on a classical concert season (Oct-Mar).
Teatro dei Rinnovati (0577 292 265) runs a lively theatre season (Nov-late Mar).

Emergency services

Ambulance Misericordia (0577 222 199); night-time and holiday emergency service (0577 280 110).
Hospital *(0577 586 466/586 111).*
Carabinieri *(112).*
Municipal Police *(0577 292 558).*
Police Headquarters *(0577 201 111).*

L'Ospedale di Santa Maria della Scala

Piazza del Duomo 2 (0577 224 811). **Open** *winter* 10.30am-4.30pm daily; *summer* 10am-6.30pm daily. **Admission** L8,000.

This is a former hospital and a museum in progress. Siena was an important stop-over point for pilgrims on the Via Francigena (*see p199* **Corridor of power**) and this hospital, founded in the ninth century, was considered the finest of its time. Named after the Duomo's marble staircase and funded by donations from local noble families, it was one of the first to ensure disinfected medical equipment and bug-free cots.

From 1440 to 1443, the Pellegrinaio (pilgrim's room), which was an emergency care unit, was embellished with frescoes by Domenico di Bartolo, among others, that depict the history of the hospital. Although the hospital is currently being restored to house a major arts centre, progress – would you believe it – is slow. The **Museo Archeologico** (Open 9am-2pm Mon-Sat; 9am-1pm 1st and 3rd Sun of month. Admission L4,000) is housed here and has several rooms devoted to Etruscan and Roman artefacts.

Pinacoteca Nazionale

Palazzo Buonsignori, Via San Pietro 29 (0577 281 161). **Open** *July-Sept* 8.30am-7pm Mon-Sat; 8am-1pm Sun; *Oct-June* 8.30am-1.30pm Mon-Sat; *group visits* 2.30pm, 4pm, 5.30pm, Mon-Sat; 8am-1pm Sun. **Admission** L8,000.

the Pinacoteca Nazionale is one of Italy's foremost and most wonderful art collections, holding more than 1,500 works of art, housed in the lovely fifteenth-century Palazzo Buonsignori. It is renowned for its Sienese *fondi d'oro* (paintings with gilded backgrounds). The second floor is devoted to Sienese masters from the twelfth to fifteenth centuries, including Guido da Siena, Duccio di Buoninsegna, Simone Martini and the Lorenzettis. Don't miss Lorenzetti's cubist-in-feel *A City by the Sea*, one of the first examples of landscape painting.

The first floor features works by the Sienese Mannerist school of the early 1500s, including Sodoma and Beccafumi. The large room on the third floor is devoted to the Spannocchi Collection: works by northern Italian and European artists of the sixteenth and seventeenth centuries.

Monuments

Fonte Branda

Via di Fontebranda.

It's a steep walk down from Via di Città to this monumental twelfth-century spring. Housed in a red brick structure with three arches, the fountain is fed by the miles of underground aqueducts across Tuscany. In its day it supplied half the city with water and provided the necessary power for numerous flour mills. Today, it is inhabited by large fish.

Fortezza Medicea

Viale C Maccari.

This huge red-brick fortress slightly outside the city to the north-west, is a sore reminder of Siena's troubled past. In fact, Charles V of Spain forced the Sienese to build a fortress here in 1552, but as soon as his reign ended, the Sienese celebrated by demolishing it. Then only a few years later Cosimo I de' Medici annexed the city and demanded the fortress be rebuilt. When Florentine rule finally came to an end, Siena named the square within the fortress walls Piazza della Libertà. The fortress also houses the **Enoteca Italiana** (*see below*).

Piazza Salimbeni

This beautiful square is flanked by three of Siena's most glorious palaces: the Palazzi Tantucci, Spannocchi and Salimbeni. The Palazzo Salimbeni serves as the headquarters of one of the world's oldest banks: the Monte dei Paschi di Siena. Founded in 1472, the bank was born of a need by shrewd Sienese to protect themselves and their savings from hefty levies and taxes imposed on them by Florence.

Restaurants

When the Sienese taste a winning combination, they stick with it. Many of the recipes used today have survived since medieval times, such as *pici* (noodle-like pasta with bread crumbs) and *panzanella* (dried bread soaked in water, then blended with basil, onion, and tomato). Unique Sienese desserts include: *panforte* (a dense slice of nuts, candied fruits and honey), or *ricciarelli* (almond biscuits topped with powdered sugar).

Expensive

Al Marsili

Via del Castoro 3 (0577 47154). **Open** 12.30-2pm, 7.30-10.15pm, Tue-Sun. **Average** L65,000. **Credit** AmEx, DC, MC, V.

The place to go to get dressed up and splurge. The food is classic Tuscan from crostini to *faraona alla Medici* (fowl cooked with pine nuts, almonds and plums). Next door, the Enoteca Marsili is filled with sumptuous wines stashed in a cave carved out of stone that dates back to the Etruscans.

Cane e Gatto

Via Pagliaresi 6 (0577 287 545/fax 0577 270 227). **Open** *lunch* by appointment; *dinner* 8-11pm Mon-Wed, Fri-Sun. **Average** L60,000; *menu degustazione* L90,000. **Credit** AmEx, DC, MC, V.

A family-run restaurant that offers a *menu degustazione* that will teach you everything you ever wanted to know about Sienese cooking.

Moderate

Antica Osteria da Divo

Via Franciosa 25-29 (0577 284 381). **Open** noon-2.30pm, 7-10pm, daily. **Average** L45,000. **Credit** AmEx, DC, JCB, MC, V.

Subterranean cellars, vaulted ceilings and niches carved in tufa stone give this osteria a distinctly archaeological feel. Dishes to try include: *acqua cotta alla senese* (vegetable soup with mushrooms), rabbit leg stuffed with vegetables or beef with chestnuts.

Osteria Castelvecchio

Via Castelvecchio 65 (0577 49586). **Open** 12.30-2pm, 7.30-9.30pm, Mon, Wed-Sun. **Average** L40,000. **Credit** AmEx, DC, MC, V.

Located just a few steps away from the Duomo and built in former horse stables, Castelvecchio shines out against the array of anonymous eateries in Siena's centre. The *fusilli verdi al limone* (green corkscrew pasta with lemon) makes an excellent first course. Mauro and Simone offer vegetarian dishes at least twice a week.

La Taverna del Capitano

Via del Capitano 6/8 (0577 288 094). **Open** 12-3pm, 7-10pm, Wed-Mon. **Average** L50,000. **Credit** AmEx, MC, V.

This place oozes Siena: from vaulted brick ceilings to dark wood furnishing. On Fridays you can try *baccalà* (cod), a Sienese specialty. The house wine is excellent.

Cheap

Hosteria il Carroccio

Via del Casato di Sotto 32 (0577 41165). **Open** noon-2.30pm, 7.30-10pm, Mon, Tue, Thur-Sun. **Average** L35,000. **Credit** MC, V.

In 1991, Renata Toppi opened this small restaurant that she runs with her children. Try the *tegamate di maiale*, pork cooked in a ceramic bowl, based on an old Sienese recipe that is virtually extinct today.

Nuovo Ristorante Tullio ai Tre Cristi

Vicolo di Provenzano 1 (0577 280 608). **Open** 10.30am-2.30pm, 7.30-10pm Mon, Wed-Sun. **Average** L35,000. **Credit** MC, V.

Founded in 1830, this is the traditional eaterie of the giraffe *contrade*; witness the banners and symbols on every available bit of wall space. There's a lively neighbourhood atmosphere and Tullio cooks up specialities such as potato *gnocchetti* with asparagus, or luke-warm steak marinated with spices.

The Palio

The Palio is not just a horse race: it is the explosive culmination of centuries-long neighbourhood rivalries and is the moment in which the social, cultural and political fabric of urban Siena is defined each year.

There is a single objective of the Palio: to win. How you win doesn't matter and the concept of 'fair play' is brushed off as trivial. Cheating, biting, putting large dosages of laxatives in a horse's food the night before the race (a recent phenomenon) is all admissible. In fact, getting a jockey over the finish line isn't the point and many of the bareback riders fall off their horses anyway before the end of the race. The jockeys are dismissed as mere mercenaries and are rarely Siena natives. Many come from Sardegna and others are rented horsemen or 'cowboys' from the 'wild west' of southern Tuscany, the Maremma. The winning horse brings year-long glory to the *contrade* (*see box*) it represents. The horse, unlike the jockey, is adored by the contrade receiving is own special rites and banquets to motivate it for the race.

The Palio takes place in the Piazza del Campo. Twice a year, commemorating the feast of the Virgin Mary and the Assumption (2 July and 16 August) the square is carpeted with dirt and tall protective walls padded with mattresses are erected. On the Piazza's perimeter balconies and stands are set up for those spectators (usually wealthy tourists) willing to shell out L500,000 to watch the race in comfort. The majority of the Sienese, as many as 30,000 of them, opt to stand under the blazing sun in the jam-packed centre of the square where the real action is. The square is divided in sections representing each contrade and their supporters stick together wearing contrade colours, waving banners and singing in a frenzy of excitement. The Palio starts in the late afternoon with a parade of drummers and flag carriers all dressed in medieval costumes. Of Siena's 17 contrade only 8 are selected by lottery to participate in the race. The horses charge three times around the square and the first one over the line wins the Palio – earning a banner of the Virgin Mary as a trophy. The race is over in less than 90 seconds.

The reactions of the Sienese, depending on their allegiance, rages from weeping and tearing out of the hair, to rapturous kissing and embracing. Banquets and festivities sponsored by the winning contrade last well into September and hatred between the first and second placed teams lasts until the following year.

L'Osteria

Via de' Rossi 79/81 (0577 287 592). **Open** 12.30-2.30pm, 7.30-10.30pm, Mon-Sat. **Average** L35,000. **Credit** AmEx, DC, MC, V.
An informal haunt of students where you eat simple, well-cooked Tuscan food at wooden tables.

Osteria la Chiacchera

Costa di Sant'Antonio 4 (0577 280 631). **Open** noon-3pm, 7pm-midnight. **Average** L25,000. **Credit** MC, V.
Charming spot for traditional Sienese recipes. Friendly service and decent house wine.

Bars, enoteche & gelaterie

Bar Gelateria in Monte

Piazza Salimbeni 95/99 (0577 281 094). **Open** 7.30am-8.30pm daily. **Credit** MC, V.
A small haven for Italian ice-cream fanatics. Also a good location for an afternoon aperitif.

Bar Pasticceria Conca d'Oro

Via Banchi di Sopra 24 (0577 41591). **Open** 8am-8.30pm Mon, Sun; 7.30am-11.30pm Tue-Sun. **Credit** MC, V.
A classic, lively bar with a 1950s feel. One of the best places to buy Siena's famous Nannini pastries – try the *ricciarelli* (almond biscuits). A cappuccino costs L1,800 at the bar; L4,000 at a table.

La Costarella

Via di Città 33 (0577 288 076). **Open** 8.30am-midnight Mon, Wed-Sun. **No credit cards.**
If you've hoofed it up the steep hill from the Fonte Branda, consider the excellent ice-cream and home-made *cornetti* (like a croissant) your prize.

Enoteca Italiana

Fortezza Medicea (0577 288 497). **Open** noon-8pm Mon; noon-1am Tue-Sat. **Credit** AmEx, MC, V.
A refreshing surprise for those who thought anything run by the fumbling Italian government can't amount to much. Located in the massive vaulted viscera of the fortress is Italy's only national wine cellar. The enoteca stocks more than 900 wines from all over the country, 400 from Tuscany alone. Groups can indulge in organised tastings, and night owls can enjoy the concerts sometimes held here.

Enoteca i Terzi

Via dei Termini 7 (0577 44329). **Open** 11am-4.30pm, 6.30pm-1am, Mon-Sat. **Credit** AmEx, DC, MC, V.
Michele and Marcello set up this wine cellar in December 1995. Also serves light snacks.

Le contrade

The *contrade* are districts of the city that trace their roots back to the twelfth century and vaguely represent the military groups that once protected the city from its enemies. At the head of each was a mayor and a central governor (*Podestà*) flanked by councillors. Originally the city was divided into 42 contrade, but the numbers shrank to the current 17 in 1729. If you walk through the city's streets you will see little plaques on street corners marking the territories of the contrade that are symbolised by animals or objects: Tartuca (tortoise), Onda (wave), Lupa (she-wolf), Oca (goose), Nicchio (shell), Istrice (porcupine), Drago (dragon), Civetta (owl), Chiocciola (snail), Pantera (panther), Aquila (eagle), Bruco (caterpillar), Leocorno (unicorn), Montone (ram), Giraffa (giraffe), Selva (forest), and Torre (tower). Each contrade has its own church and its own museum. But the biggest task of the contrade is gearing up to win the Palio (*see box*).

Nightlife

Siena is a sleepy town that does not offer much in the way of nocturnal activity.

Incontro

Via Giovanni Dupré 64 (0577 42650). **Open** 7pm-3am daily. **No credit cards.**
Five kinds of beer on tap and a mixed crowd of visiting foreigners and Siena University students.

L'Officina

Piazza del Sale 3 (0577 286 301). **Open** 5pm-3am daily. **No credit cards.**
This club is a venue for local bands and has an impressive selection of bottled beers. It's a bit hard to find at the north end of the Terzo di Camollia section of town.

Tea Room

Via Porta Giustizia 11 (0577 222 753). **Open** 9pm-3am Tue-Thur; 5pm-3am Fri-Sun. **No credit cards.**
Ilario Bondani, who set up the Tea Room in 1991, organises live music (mostly jazz) two evenings a week in summer and concerts most Saturdays. It has 50 different teas and infusions.

Accommodation

Siena has a number of hotels to choose from, but never enough to meet demand – book in advance. Also consider trying nearby towns with connecting bus services, such as Poggibonsi, Colle di Val d'Elsa or Asciano.

Expensive

Certosa di Maggiano

Strada di Certosa 82 (0577 288 180/fax 0577 288 189). **Rates** *double* L600,000-L1,000,000. **Credit** AmEx, DC, MC, V.
Raised from the ruins of a thirteenth-century monastery and Siena's most luxurious hotel. Located just south of the city, it offers a stunning garden, tennis court, swimming pool and even a heliport.

Villa Scacciapensieri

Via di Scacciapensieri 10 (0577 41441/fax 0577 270 854). **Rates** *single* L215,000; *double* L370,000. **Credit** AmEx, DC, JCB, MC, V.
Like the name ('squish your thoughts') suggests, you can leave your worries behind once you're here. It's 3km north of the city – follow the signs up a private tree-lined drive to the crest of the hill. The family-run hotel has an excellent restaurant, a tennis court and swimming pool.

Moderate

Antica Torre

Via di Fieravecchia 7 (tel/fax 0577 222 255). **Rates** *single* L140,000; *double* L170,000. **Credit** AmEx, DC, JCB, MC, V.
Hop, skip, jump – do whatever you can to get a reservation at Siena's most eclectic hotel. Rooms in this restored sixteenth-century tower get booked up weeks in advance with just two rooms per floor around a central staircase.

Chiusarelli

Viale Curtatone 15 (0577 280 562/fax 0577 271 177). **Rates** (incl breakfast) *single* L112,000; *double* L165,000. **Credit** AmEx, DC, JCB, MC, V.
Well priced for a three-star hotel on the edge of the historic centre. Rooms are unexceptional but offer all the necessities. Ask for a quiet room in the back.

Duomo

Via Stalloreggi 38 (0577 289 088/fax 0577 43043). **Rates** *single* L150,000; *double* L220,000. **Credit** AmEx, DC, JCB, MC, V.
A stone's throw away from the Duomo, this hotel's location can't be beat… but the sterile, sober rooms can. Ask for one of the two rooms with a small balcony that overlook the Duomo and Siena's characteristic red roofs. Service is informal and friendly.

Pensione Palazzo Ravizza

Pian dei Mantellini 34 (0577 280 462/fax 0577 221 597). **Rates** (incl breakfast) *single* L200,000; *double with bath* L240,000. **Credit** AmEx, DC, JCB, MC, V.
Owned by the same family for more than 200 years, this 1800s palazzo still has its original furnishings. Many of the 38 rooms overlook a charming, well-kept garden, others have a view of the city.

Cheap

Centrale

Via Cecco Angiolieri 26 (0577 280 379/fax 0577 42152). **Rates** *double* L115,000-L120,000. **Credit** MC, V.
One block north of Piazza del Campo on a quiet street. It has seven large, comfortable rooms.

Piccolo Hotel Etruria

Via delle Donzelle 3 (0577 288 088/fax 0577 288 461). **Rates** *single* L70,000; *double* L110,000. **Credit** AmEx, DC, JCB, MC, V.
Located just off Siena's commercial artery, Banchi di Sotto. It has 13 rooms.

Tre Donzelle

Via delle Donzelle 5 (0577 280 358/fax 0577 223 933). **Rates** *single* L45,000; *double* L75,000-L95,000. **Credit** MC, V.
With 27 spacious rooms, the Tre Donzelle is a handy alternative if the Piccolo Hotel Etruria next door is full. One drawback is the midnight curfew.

Camping

Colleverde

Strada Scacciapensieri 47 (0577 280 044). **Open** Mar-Nov. **Rates** L12,000-L15,000; children L6,000-L7,500. **No credit cards.**
The closest campsite to the city and one of southern Tuscany's most attractive.

Shopping

The main shopping street is the Via di Città, which branches into two above the Campo: Banchi di Sotto heads down, and Banchi di Sopra climbs up to Piazza della Posta. Just before sunset, the locals emerge to take the *passeggiata*, or stroll through town.

Consorzio Agrario

Via Pianigiani 5 (0577 2301). **Open** *shop* 8am-8pm Mon-Sat. **Credit** MC, V.
A local co-operative where farmers sell their goods in the big city, so quality and freshness can't be beat.

Dolci Trame

Via del Moro 4 (0577 46168). **Open** 3-8pm Mon; 9.30am-1pm, 3-8pm, Tue-Sat. **Credit** AmEx, DC, JCB, MC, V.
Hip women's clothing at the back of Piazza Tolomei.

Enoteca San Domenico

Via del Paradiso 56 (0577 271 181). **Open** 9am-8pm daily. **Credit** AmEx, DC, MC, V.
Owner Francesco Bonfio sells some fine wines, grappas and local specialty sauces and jams.

Libreria Senese

Via di Città 62-66 (0577 280 845). **Open** 9am-8pm Mon-Sat. **Credit** AmEx, DC, MC, V.
A family-run bookshop with plenty on local art and history, including publications in English.

Morbidi

Via Banchi di Sopra 73 (0577 280 268) or Via Banchi di Sotto 27 (0577 280 541). **Open** 8.15am-1.15pm, 5-8pm, Mon-Fri; 8.15am-1.15pm Sat. **Credit** AmEx, DC, JCB, MC, V.
A long room full of savoury Tuscany treats.

La Nuova Pasticceria di Iasevoli

Via Giovanni Dupré 37 (0577 40577). **Open** 8am-12.30pm, 5-7.30pm, Tue-Sat; 8am-12.30pm Sun. **No credit cards**
Choose from the fine selection of Sienese baked confectionery such as *cantuccini*, *pan dei santi* (bread with raisins and walnuts made for All Saint's day), *cavallucci* (dry bread buns spiced with aniseed), *panforte* and *ricciarelli* (almond biscuits).

Massa-Carrara & Lucca Provinces

Marble, mountains and megaclubs.

The provinces of Massa & Carrara and Lucca couldn't be further apart in spirit, despite the fact they lie side by side, with only the Alpi Apuane mountain range between them. One of Tuscany's most travelled areas, Massa & Carrara is an endless stretch of all-night discos, bikini-clad bodies, bumper-to-bumper traffic and industry. Ancient trade routes like the Via Aurelia have been on the map since Roman times, and today much of the Italian peninsula's north-south traffic passes through here. Lucca, on the other hand, is an Alpine wonderland with snow-capped peaks and chestnut-covered valleys. It is also one of Italy's least explored regions.

The Versilia Riviera

Versilia is an unbroken belt of sand, bathing establishments and traffic, extending from the Ligurian border (north) to Viareggio (south). The main road that runs its length is the Via Aurelia, which becomes a solid mass of bumper-to-bumper cars in summer. Don't count on pretty views to salvage a gridlocked trip either; the area is heavily industrialised and littered with huge blocks of unfinished marble from Carrara waiting for export.

Viareggio

Viareggio's main attraction is the beach. Its palm tree-lined promenade is flanked by art deco villas and outdoor cafés. Summer nights in Viareggio pulsate to the sound of techno, and party-goers crowd the city's megaclubs; Florence's club scene virtually transplants itself here in the hot summer months. By day, the *stabilimenti balneare* (bathing establishments) are full of sun-worshippers. One of Europe's first *stabilimenti* was founded here in 1827: the Balena is currently being modernised to include a bigger pool, massage rooms and an underground sports centre.

Viareggio's 130-year-old carnevale is one of Italy's wildest. Oversized floats poking fun at local celebrities flood the streets on four consecutive Sundays (three before and one after Mardi Gras, *see chapter* **By Season**).

Six kilometres south of town is the reed-fringed Lago di Massaciuccoli. On its shore is Torre del Lago Puccini, where the composer spent his summers. His villa is open to visitors (0584 341 445. Open 10am-12.30pm, 3-6pm, Tue-Sun. Groups by appointment. Admission L7,000), but it contains little of interest. During the first week of August the town hosts an outdoor Puccini festival (*see chapter* **Tuscany By Season**).

What to see

Hangar-Carnevale *top (inland) end of Via Marco Polo*. **Open** 9am-8pm daily. **Admission** free. In a cluster of graffiti-covered aircraft hangers, you can peek at last year's carnival floats or watch artists assembling next year's papier-mâché masterpieces.

Where to stay

Viareggio has more than 100 hotels, but rooms are still difficult to find in high season. Try Via Vespucci, Via Leonardo da Vinci and Via IV Novembre, which run down to the sea from the station.

Hotel Garden *Via Ugo Foscolo 70 (0584 44025/ fax 0584 45445)*. **Rates** *single* L100,000-L135,000. *double* L160,00-L200,000. **Credit** AmEx, DC, MC, V. A glorious Liberty-style building with 40 rooms.

Hotel Plaza et de Russie *Piazza d'Azeglio 1 (0584 44449/fax 0584 44031)*. **Rates** *single* L200,000-L250,000; *double* L240,000-L380,000. **Credit** AmEx, DC, MC, V. *Fin de siècle* luxury in this refurbished nineteenth-century historic building complete with glass chandeliers and a roof garden.

Where to eat

La Darsena *Via Virgilio 150 (0584 392 785)*. **Open** noon-2.30pm, 7.30-10.45pm, Mon-Sat. **Average** L50,000. **Credit** AmEx, DC, JCB, MC, V. This fish restaurant attracts dockworkers and locals for its huge portions and economic prices.

Osteria N.1 *Via Pisano 140 (0584 388 967)*. **Open** noon-3pm, 8-10.30pm, Mon, Tue, Thur-Sun. **Average** L35,000. **No credit cards**. A fantastic fish joint located on a quiet back street. Dishes include the unique *seppie stufate con le bietole* (squid stuffed with a sour, spinach-like vegetable) and giant grilled shrimps.

Gelateria Mario *Via Petrolini 1 (0584 961 349)*. **Open** *summer* 11am-midnight daily; *winter* 11am-midnight Sat, Sun. **No credit cards**. A popular spot with the best ice-cream in town and superb fruit-based sorbets.

Pescia – *the 'capital of flowers'. See p216.*

Going out

La Capannina *Viale Franceschi, Forte dei Marmi (0584 80169).* **Open** *summer* 9pm-6am daily; *winter* special occasions only. **Admission** L30,000-L50,000 including 1st drink. **No credit cards**. This revered dancing institution attracts clubbers of all ages. Next to the sea (but without access to the beach), Versilia's oldest and most resilient nightspot keeps the crowds coming and its two dance floors are packed all summer long, despite the extraordinary entrance fee.
La Canniccia *Via Unità d'Italia 1, Marina di Pietrasanta (close to the Versilia exit on the A12 motorway) (0584 745 685).* **Open** 10.30pm-4am Thur-Sun. **Admission** L30,000 (includes 1st drink). **Credit** AmEx, MC, V. An outdoor club with a garden the size of a meadow, tree-lined walkways, a fish-filled lake and a dance floor under a vine-covered garden gazebo. The abundance of green, open space makes this place hard to fill. There are three bars and a late-night restaurant.
Seven Apple *Viale Roma, Marina di Pietrasanta (0584 20458).* **Open** 11pm-4.30am Fri-Sun. **Admission** L30,000 (including one drink). **No credit cards**. Versilia's trendiest club. Located on the beach, there is an outdoor bar with tables straddling a swimming pool, and two floors of dancing. L15,000 a drink.
Il Giardino *Via IV Novembre, Forte dei Marmi (0584 81462).* **Open** 7am-2am Wed-Mon. **No credit cards**. Good meeting spot for drinks before heading to the clubs. It's popular with 20-something *figli di papa* (rich kids who cruise around in Daddy's car), but its garden makes it worth putting up with them. Beer at the bar L4,000; seated L6,000. Gin and tonic is L10,000 at the bar; L12,000 seated.

Pietrasanta

Carrara is home to the raw material, but Pietrasanta (holy stone) is where intellect and muse transform marble into creative expression. This beach town and artistic community is full of studios where sculptors work with bronze, clay and marble. In summer, the town's Piazza Duomo becomes an open-air exhibition space for artists to display work against the splendid backdrop of the thirteenth-century cathedral and the Rocca Arrighina (the citadel up the hill from the square). Wandering through Pietrasanta's back streets you can see modern-day Michelangelos with folded newspaper hats (preferred by marble carvers over cloth hats because they absorb sweat, but filter the fine marble dust). For refreshment, try the local speciality, a *Bersagliere* (white wine with a drop of red Campari).

Massa & Carrara

Locked between the sea and the Apuane Alps, these twin cities are barely distinguishable from the general mesh of industry and traffic that congest the area. Massa is of little interest, but Carrara is a marble mecca for sculpture enthusiasts (*see p218* **Set in stone**). Carrara's Piazza Alberica is lined with pastel-coloured buildings with a lion fountain in the middle. Off the north-east end of the square, Via Ghibellina opens up to a seductive view of the eleventh-century Duomo, with a Pisan façade and a fourteenth-century rose window carved from a single slab of marble. Three kilometres out of town, the **Museo Civico del Marmo** (Località Stadio, Viale XX Settembre, 0585 845 746. Open June-Sept 10am-8pm Mon-Sat; Nov-Apr 8.30am-1.30pm; May, Oct 8am-5pm. Admission L6,000) is a good place to learn about marble history and methods of production.

For the quarries, take the scenic route, marked *strada panoramica per le cave*, in the direction of Colonnata. This road snakes its way up steep ravines of open quarries, where pure white marble is cut out of the mountains.

East of Lucca

Heading west of Florence towards Lucca either on the A11 motorway or the congested SS435 takes you past Prato, Pistoia and Montecatini Terme. A few kilometres before the Lucca Province border, this industrialised area has two towns worth visiting.

Collodi

Collodi is the birthplace of the author of Italy's most cherished fairy-tale character: Pinocchio (*see p218* **No strings attached**). Pinocchio fuels a micro economy, supporting this otherwise minor Tuscan town. The surrounding area is plastered with adverts for **Pinocchio Park** (0572 429 342. Open 8.30am-sunset daily. Admission L12,000; L7,000 under-14s), which boasts fun for all the family, but, in truth, is of little interest to anyone over the age of five. The theme park was opened in 1956 and features a walk-through maze and Pinocchio statues, including one by Emilio Greco, a colourful mosaic-lined courtyard by Venturino Venturi and a restaurant designed by Giovanni Michelucci. The nearby **Giardino Garzoni** (Piazza della Vittoria 1, 0572 429 590. Open summer 9am-8pm daily; winter 9am-noon, 2-5pm, daily. Admission L10,000) has attractive baroque gardens that took more than 170 years to complete after the construction of the Garzoni residence in 1633. Designed by the marquis Romano di Alessandro Garzoni, the gardens are a masterpiece of perspective and symmetry.

Pescia

In a protective valley, straddling the humid banks of the Pescia River, Pescia profits from a soothing microclimate. Describing itself as the capital of flowers, it is the hub of Italy's budding flower industry. Everything from chrysanthemums to Bonsai olive trees are cultivated here, auctioned and exported to other markets. The surrounding hills are dotted with greenhouses and flower merchants gather here for Pescia's international fairs. Smell the results for yourself at the 40,000 square-metre Centro di Commercializzazione dei Fiori, just south of the railroad station. Or pop into Pescia's historic centre on a Saturday morning, when stalls of flowers and fruit line Piazza Mazzini. The nearby **Pizzeria Pucci** (Via L Andreotti 6, 0572 476 176. Open lunch & dinner Fri-Wed. Average L30,000) serves excellent first courses, but ask for a table in the back room as it tends to get noisy up front.

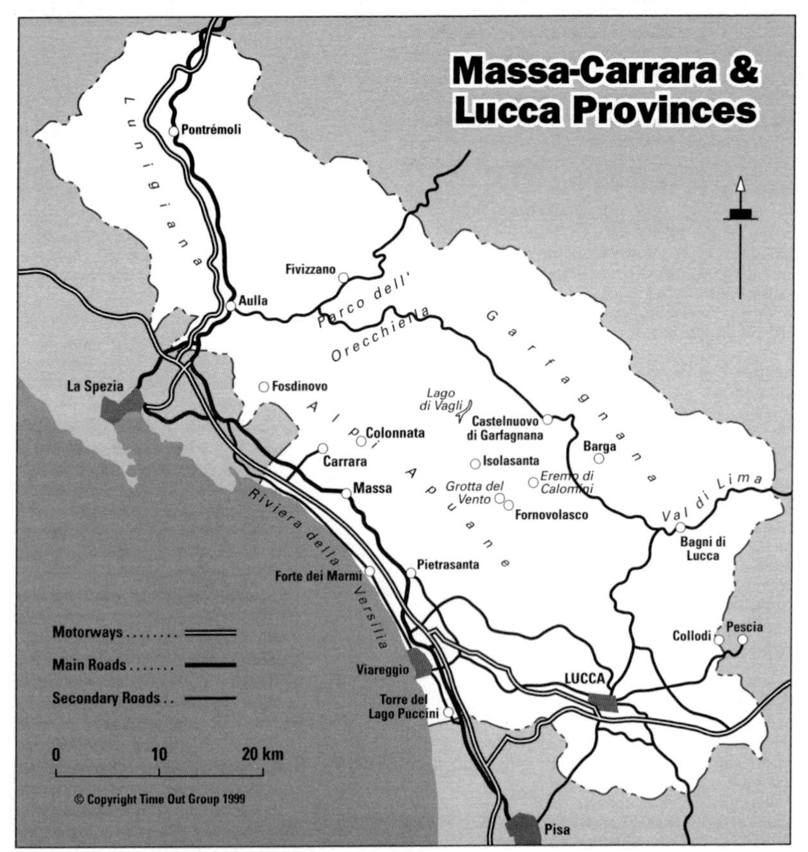

No strings attached

The Adventures of Pinocchio has been published in so many different languages and in so many different editions, that only the Bible and the Koran beat it. At least, that's what the official Pinocchio fan club in the town of Collodi tell you.

Carlo Lorenzini, the author of the fairy tale, selected Carlo Collodi as his *nom de plume* because Collodi was his beloved mother's birthplace. Lorenzini himself was born in Florence in 1826 and gained fame as a journalist and writer of educational children's books for his prose, colourful writing and love of music. In fact, he was able to incorporate music in his writing, often inventing sing-song names for his character such as Gianettino and Pinocchio.

Soon after Lorenzini witnessed the Unification of Italy, he began writing for one of Italy's first children's magazines, *Il Giornale per i Bambini*. His main contributions were instalments of the story of Pinocchio, which soon attracted a steady base of young followers. Just as the story's final episode was published in the magazine, *The Adventures of Pinocchio* was published as a complete book and soon translated into English for sale in Britain and the United States. Lorenzini died in 1890 and is buried in the San Miniato al Monte cemetery, Florence, but Pinocchio's incarnation as a Walt Disney animated feature in 1940 secured his immortality.

The Garfagnana

Heading north through the Lower Serchio Valley from Lucca, the cultivated flat land that radiates from Lucca's circular walls soon piles up into the mighty Alpi Apuane mountains. Within an hour's drive, snowy peaks and verdant river valleys lined with chestnuts and wild flowers make this Tuscany's mountain paradise.

Abetone

If you don't want to fork out the hefty fees charged by northern ski resorts, but are willing to try gentler slopes, head towards Abetone. Just 53 miles from Florence, it is easy enough to get to for the weekend or even a day trip. Wide runs make Abetone ideal for beginners and intermediate skiers, but unlike other, lesser-known slopes in Italy, this stretch of 30 miles is connected by 27 ski lifts. One-star hotel **Noemi** (Via Brennero 244, 0573 60168/fax 0573 606 705. Rates single L40,000-L50,000; double L70,000-L80,000. No credit cards) has 26 rooms, seven of which have a bath (place your request when making reservations).

For tourist information, call 0573 60231. Ski boot hire costs L20,000 per day; ski passes are L42,000 per day Monday to Friday, L49,000 at the weekend. Before departing, ring Telefono Blue Inverno, a service that gives slope conditions 05 144 0055.

Bagni di Lucca

It's hard to believe this tiny spa village buried in the narrow reaches of the Lima Valley once attracted hordes of the intellectual elite. Puccini, Heine, Shelley and Byron all visited for its saline and sulphurous thermal waters. Elisa Bonaparte Baciocchi (the Grand Duchess of Tuscany and Napoleon's sister) had a summer home here (now the Hotel Roma). Once Napoleon had fallen, his sister's place was taken by Grand Duke Carlo Ludovico, under whose reign Europe's first licensed casino opened in 1837. Today, the casino's entrance is carpeted with weeds and the building is in dire need of a fresh lick of paint. Bagni's lustre is long gone and so is much of its population: many emigrated to America after World War II. The local economy is largely fuelled by artisans who hand-assemble Christmas figures for nativity scenes, which Italians traditionally prefer over trees.

To soak in spa waters try the **Terme di Bagni di Lucca** (Località Bagni Caldi, 0583 87221. Open 7am-noon Mon-Sat; also 8am-noon Sun in summer. Admission L21,000), which offers a range of services including mud treatments and hydro massage. For an overnight stay, the **Hotel Roma** (Via Umberto I 110, 0583 87278. Rates single L55,000; double L75,000) is marvellously old-fashioned and decorated in old-world decadence. Otherwise try **Locanda Maiola**, if only for the privilege of eating at its restaurant (Località Maiola di Sotto, 0583 86296. Rates double L90,000. Average L40,000). Owner Enrico Franceschi travels the region seeking out the best cheeses and cold meats to serve with other specialities such as baby river trout.

Eight kilometres south of Bagni, on the SS12, is the Ponte della Maddalena, nicknamed the Devil's Bridge. It spans the Serchio River with an asymmetric series of five arches. It was built in the eleventh century by (according to legend) Beelzebub himself in return for the soul of the first person who crossed it. The locals sent a dog.

Barga

This perfectly preserved medieval city is majestically framed against a mountainous landscape and

Set in stone

Throughout the year, the steep ridges of the Alpi Apuane flanking Carrara glow brilliant white with the world's largest concentration of pure marble. The ancient Romans mined here and built most of their Imperial City with it. Today, Carrara marble lines the lobby of the World Trade Center in New York. Michelangelo considered Carrara's marble the purest and whitest in the world. Its greatest asset, according to artists, is that it has a translucent quality that reflects light off its thinnest outer layer, giving the stone a wax-like lustre.

The mountains contain a seemingly unlimited quantity of the stone – 1.5 million tonnes are mined each year – but new economic factors have thrown the local industry into crisis. Changing architectural trends and increased competition have hit hard. Carrara is mining less marble, gaining fewer contracts to work it, and exporting less. As you drive along Via Aurelia, you'll see blocks of unfinished marble waiting to be exported, as well as mass-produced *Venus* and *David* reproductions. Unemployment in this area is the highest in northern Italy and many miners are hoping for a large construction contract to turn Carrara's struggling marble industry around.

Carrara's natural resource comes in six types: the legendary bianco coveted by Bernini and Michelangelo; rare and precious Saturio, admired for fine veins which criss-cross the stone; the roughly veined Arabescato and Venato; the ivory Calacata Crema; and the more common Bardiglio, a grey stone used for lesser commissions.

Once hammer and chisel were used to split large pieces of the marble and transporting such pieces was often impossible, so many works were commissioned on site. Even recently, miners have uncovered exquisitely carved columns and statues abandoned in the quarries since ancient times. Now diamond-studded wires slice easily through the rock, creating movable blocks. The blocks are cut into thinner slices, polished downhill in Massa and Carrara, and then shipped off as finished wall panels or ornaments. Carrara's marble industry remains in place, but the rock itself may have lost some of its lustre.

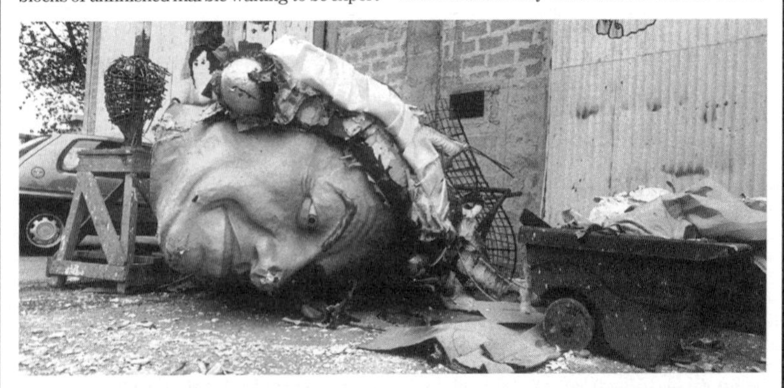

the lush Serchio River valley. Its red roofs climb up to the town's highest point, dominated by a grassy square and the brilliant sunlit façade of Barga's eleventh-century Duomo. Built in a pale local stone called Albarese di Barga, the cathedral's most striking feature is its pulpit, carved by Como sculptor Guido Bigarelli in the thirteenth century. It is supported by carved lions and dwarves, the latter a symbol of crushed paganism. A fleamarket is held every second Sunday of the month. If you come when there's a market, be sure to visit **Vecchia Enoteca Puccini** (Via di Mezzo 46, no phone. Open only with the fleamarket), for its extensive collection of ancient wine bottles covered in dust, with labels faded by years of humidity. The cantina houses the beloved collection of a local wine connoisseur, who died in 1984. His widow Eda Puccini opens this magical place to any adventurer patient enough to dust off the bottles in a treasure hunt of a priceless vintage. In summer, Barga hosts a slew of cultural activities, the most worthwhile being the jazz festival held in the middle week of August. For a late afternoon aperitif, head to the central **Caffè Capretz** (Piazza Salvo Salvi, 0583 723 001). Founded in 1870, this antique café has outdoor tables beneath a wood-beam loggia that used to host the town's vegetable market. Barga's trendy **Osteria Angelio** (Piazza Angelio 13/14, 0583 724 547. Open lunch & dinner Tue-Sun. Average L30,000. No credit cards) serves Tuscan fare to classical background music.

L'Eremo di Calomini

The monastery of L'Eremo di Calomini is on the other side of the Serchio river valley from Barga. Built into a vertical cliff, it looks suspended in mid-air. It has an outdoor restaurant, the **Antica Trattoria dell'Eremita** (0583 767 020. Open Mar-Oct lunch Mon; lunch & dinner Tue-Sun. Average L35,000), where grilled trout fresh from the Serchio River is served and the chef makes a fine trout sauce with spaghetti. Enjoy the fish on a shady, sycamore-lined terrace with great views. There are a rooms to rent in the monastery (ask in the restaurant) and a little shop run by monks sells herb syrups and extracts of medicinal plants.

Grotta del Vento

Seven kilometres of hairpin bends and steep ridges from L'Eremo di Calomini lead to the semi-abandoned town of Fornovolasco and the entrance to Tuscany's geological wonder: the Grotta del Vento (wind cave), packed with stalactites, stalagmites and underground lakes. Cold air that blows from the cave's entrance gave it its name and a practical purpose: it was used as a refrigerator until the seventeenth century. It wasn't until 1898, when local bullies forced a four-year-old girl to go in through its narrow entrance and she re-emerged telling of a gigantic underworld, that scientific experts first heard of it. There are one-, two- or three-hour tours of the cave (0583 722 024. Open Apr-Sept in daylight hours daily. Admission L18,000-L25,000).

Vagli di Sotto

Another valley pass into the Apuane Alps leads to the artificial lake of Vagli, fed by the Edron River. Under millions of tonnes of water lies Tuscany's own Atlantis. When the lake was formed, the authorities forced the abandonment of the tiny stone town of Fabbriche di Careggine. Every ten years the lake is emptied for maintenance and the ruins of the ghost town come back into view. Vagli's next emptying is scheduled for 2004, but local authorities plan a sneak preview in 2000. If you don't make the date, Careggine's church tower is always visible above the water.

Castelnuovo di Garfagnana

Castelnuovo is Garfagnana's capital and makes an excellent base from which to explore the area. Encased by ancient walls and dominated by a thirteenth-century castle, the historic centre is a pleasant place to refuel and pick up supplies despite the nasty traffic junction at its centre. If you want to explore the surrounding park, visit the region's biggest **Tourist Office** (Piazza delle Erbe 1, 0583 65169. Open summer 9am-1pm, 3.30-7.30pm, daily; winter 3.30-5.30pm Mon; 9am-1pm, 3.30-5.30pm, Tue-Sun). For snacks, **Il Vecchio Mulino** (Via Vittorio Emanuele 12, 0583 62192. Open 7.30am-8pm Mon-Sat. Average L30,000. No credit cards), run by brother and sister Andrea and Cinzia Bertucci, is a wine bar with top-notch salamis and cheeses. For stop-overs try the **Hotel-Ristorante Ludovico Ariosto** (Via Azzi 28, 0583 62369. Rates single L60,000; double L100,000. No credit cards).

Parco Orecchiella

Orecchiella park is perhaps the most beautiful portion of the Alpi Apuane. Hiking and biking paths of varying length and difficulty criss-cross its 5,000 hectares. Late spring or early autumn are the best times to visit. Abundant rain gives this part of Tuscany a rich texture of lush forests and meadows. Wildlife includes deer, wild boars, wild goats, the predatory Apennine wolf; there are more than 130 bird species including the eagles that are the park's symbol. Consult the **Visitors Centre** (0583 619 098/0583 65169. Open June, Sept 10am-5pm Sat, Sun; July, Aug 9am-7pm daily; spring & Oct 10am-5pm Sun; winter by arrangement. Admission free; museum area L2,000).

The Lunigiana

Named after the Luni, the area's aboriginal population, the Lunigiana is Tuscany's least explored region. The Cisa pass (where the A15 motorway runs) and the area surrounding Pontrémoli and Aulla (the hub for buses and transport to the rest of the area) are way off standard tourist itineraries. The people of the Lunigiana are a category apart, as they don't identify with either Tuscany or nearby Liguria or Emilia Romagnia. They are a curious blend of all three and this is reflected in the dialect and cuisine.

Fosdinovo

Lunigiana hasn't always been Tuscany's most isolated corner. From prehistory and the Romans to the heyday of the traffic-heavy Via Francigena trade route (*see p199* **Corridor of power**), this region was considered of utmost geographic significance for more than ten centuries. The river valleys that slice into the imposing Apuane Alps form important passageways between the northern and central sections of the Italian peninsula. With prime location comes fortification and other evidence of military might, intended to control the passage of people and goods. This mountainous area is consequently dotted with more than 100 castles and towers. The castle of **Fosdinovo** (0187 68891. Tours summer 10am, 11am, noon, 4pm, 5pm, 6pm, Mon, Wed-Sun; winter 9am, 10am, 11am, 4pm, 5pm, 6pm, Mon, Wed-Sun. Admission L6,000) is one of Lunigiana's best examples of a feudal residence (and one of the few actually open to visitors) with impressive, strategic views of both mountains and sea. Built by local warlords, the Malaspinas, the castle miraculously remains in Malaspina hands after 800 years and some heirs still live here.

Fivizzano

Lunigiana's effervescent-sounding town, Fivizzano is actually a tranquil place, quite isolated from the rest of the world. On the main square, the regional branches of two Italian political parties (the DC and the PCI) that folded shortly after the fall of the Berlin Wall are still a gathering place for wrinkled old men. The polished party insignias are still on display and hint at the fact that Fivizzano could have slept through the last decade. Also on Piazza Medicea (sometimes called Piazza V Emmanuele) is a fountain with four white marble dolphins – a gift from Cosimo III in 1683 when the town served as the Medici government's Lunigiana capital. Behind the fountain is the church of San Jacopo and San Antonio, built on the site of a thirteenth-century church. For a seated view, the **Caffè Elvetico** (Piazza Medicea, 0585 926 657. Closed Thur in winter) has tables that spill into the square. If you want to spend the night, the elegant **Hotel Il Giardinetto** (Via Roma 151, 0585 92060. Open lunch & dinner Tue-Sun; daily July-Sept. Average 35,000. Rates single L35,000; double L60,000. No credit cards) attracts a clientele that looks like it comes from a different era. North-east of Fivizzano on SS63 is the Castello della Verrucola, also built by the Malaspinas, who controlled the whole area from here to Carrara.

Pontrémoli

Located at the junction of the Magra and Verde rivers, Pontrémoli is the biggest town of the Lunigiana, though it has only 11,000 inhabitants. The town's wealth grew from its position as an important station on the Via Francigena trade route and the Cisa pass. It boasts the fourteenth-century Torre del Campanone, built by Castruccio Castracani, and quaint, narrow, arched streets. Beyond the historic centre, Pontrémoli is not a welcoming place: the tourist office has closed and the **Hotel Napoleon** (the better of Pontrémoli's two hotels) can best be described as bland and overpriced (Piazza Italia 2, 0187 830 544. Rates single L80,000; double L120,000); on the plus side, however, the staff are friendly and you can eat well. The **Trattoria del Giardino di Bacciottini** (Via Ricci Armani 4, 0187 830 120. Open summer lunch & dinner daily; winter closed Mon, Sun dinner. Average L45,000) serves an excellent version of local speciality *testaroli* with pesto or try the *torte di erbe*, a savoury quiche made with herbs.

The main reason to visit is to see the mysterious 19 prehistoric stele statues in the **Museo del Comune** (0187 831 439/460 111. Open 9am-noon, 3-6pm, Tue-Sun. Admission L5,000), housed in the Castello di Piagnaro. All the statues were found in the Pontrémoli area. Dating from the third millennium BC (the end of the Neolithic period and beginning of the Bronze Age), each statue is different but can be categorised into one of three groups. The first group dating from 3000-2000 BC are simple rectangular blocks with domed heads, barely distinguishable arms and unstylised facial expressions. Distinguishing marks demonstrate that some are female (with protruding breasts) and some male (a triangle). The second group (2000-800 BC) have spade-shaped heads, not connected to the main body, but with more realistic facial expressions. The last group (800-200 BC) have still more detail and most hold weapons in each hand. The statues are fascinating for their sophistication and simplicity – qualities not lost on Henry Moore, who was apparently transfixed by them. Although it is known they were made by the ancient Ligurian-Apuani tribes, the statues' purpose remains a mystery.

Lucca

A city with a turbulent past and a somnolent present.

As you approach Lucca, you won't see it. Completely sunken and sheltered behind its magnificently preserved sixteenth- to seventeenth-century walls, the city remains a mystery right up until the moment you walk through one of its six gates. More than for any other Tuscan city, Lucca's walls and ramparts are an intrinsic part of its identity, constantly reminding us of its past glory and reinforcing the lingering mental insulation and traditionalism of the Lucchesi. Healthy neutrality, commercial vigour and careful parsimony have all kept the city in a kind of time warp.

Lucca is a city for the serendipitous. It doesn't require careful planning, strict itineraries or long lines. There are no exorbitant prices charged for fast meals here. It isn't even really on Tuscany's often clogged tourist trail, and doesn't particularly want to be.

A tranquil stroll through the pedestrianised streets – the centre is virtually devoid of cars as the Lucchesi prefer bicycles – is very rewarding. Turn a corner and you're in for a surprise. The ornate white façades of its Romanesque churches – overplayed **San Michele in Foro**, the glistening mosaic of **San Frediano**, the asymmetrical **Duomo di San Martino** – all appear unexpectedly. The unique oval shape of the Piazza dell'Anfiteatro, which has retained the shape of the ancient Roman amphitheatre, opens up through a gate. The tree-lined ramparts and oak-topped **Torre Guinigi** afford splendid views of the cityscape. Lucca's flatness and relatively simple grid plan make everything easily accessible. Nothing here seems to require a great deal of effort.

SOME HISTORY

Possibly the site of a Ligurian and then an Etruscan settlement, Lucca acquired political significance as a Roman municipium in 89 BC and hosted the signature of the first triumvirate between Pompey, Caesar and Crassus in 56BC. Lucca was crucially positioned at the crossroads of the empire's communications with its northern reaches, and controlled the Apennine passes along the Serchio valley.

Despite Rome's fall the city continued to maintain its supremacy in Tuscany, first as capital of Tuscia under Lombard rule and then as the seat of the Frankish Margravate beginning in 774AD. By the turn of the millennium Lucca had grown into Tuscany's largest city and consolidated itself as a commercial powerhouse thanks to the wool and silk trades and to its command of a strategic juncture of the Via Francigena (*see p199* **Corridor of power**). Wealth engendered commercial rivalry with its upstart neighbours, which soon turned into open military clashes with Pisa and a gradual loss of political dominance to Florence during the drawn out Guelph/Ghibelline conflict. The fourteenth century was tumultuous for Lucca. A short-lived heyday as the capital of a mini-empire in western Tuscany under the helm of the condottiere Castruccio Castracani (1320-28) soon gave way to a series of setbacks leading to domination by Pisa starting in 1342. But in 1369 Lucca was granted its autonomy and independence by Emperor Charles IV of Bohemia. This was to last, unbroken, until 1799.

Having given up claims to regional leadership, Lucca moved into relative obscurity and turned in on itself. An oligarchy of ruling families, foremost among them the Guinigi, tightly controlled all public offices and private wealth and set about enlarging the medieval urban nucleus. In 1805 Lucca passed under the direct rule of Elisa Baciocchi, Napoleon's sister, and then in 1817 to the infanta Maria Luisa di Borbone of Spain. Both did much to recast the city architecturally and patronised a brief but intense period of artistic ferment. In 1847 Lucca was ceded to the Grand Duchy of Tuscany and then joined a united Italy in 1860.

The city's almost uninterrupted history as a consistently opulent, free comune has left it largely unadulterated architecturally and unfased psychologically by outside developments. Indeed, by very literally minding their own business the Lucchesi have stayed both safe and prosperous: in their own, telling, words 'a minuscule and fragile republic entirely dedicated to commerce and defenseless against the uproar of war'.

All quiet in Piazza San Michele.

Sights

Churches

Duomo di San Martino

Piazza San Martino (0583 957 068). **Open** *summer* 7am-7pm daily; *winter* 7am-5pm daily. Sacristy with Tomb of Ilaria del Carretto 10am-5.45pm Mon-Fri; 9.30am-7pm Sat; 9-10am 1-5pm Sun Admission L3,000). **No credit cards**.

At a first glance, Lucca's Romanesque cathedral seems somewhat out of kilter and unbalanced. A closer look reveals why: the oddly asymmetrical façade has the arch and the first two series of logge on the right literally squeezed and flattened by the campanile. Nobody is really to blame (or commend) for this, as the Lombard bell tower was erected before the rest of the church in the years around 1100 and completed only 200 years later. It predates the Duomo, on which work began in earnest only in the twelfth century. The asymmetry of the façade, designed by Guidetto da Como, only adds to the overall effect of exuberance and eccentricity provided by the carvings of beasts, dragons and wild animals in the capitals and in the multi-chrome columns. In the atrium, the array of bas reliefs portray everything from scenes in the life of St Martin above the central portal to, on the right, allegorical renditions of the months and on the left an Annunciation, Nativity Scene and Deposition by Apulian sculptor Nicola Pisano.

San Martino's dimly lit interior is broken up midway up the left nave by Matteo Civitali's octagonal marble *Tempietto* (1484), home to a dolorous wooden crucifix known as the *Volto Santo* (Holy Visage) perpetually surrounded by candle-holding worshippers in rapturous devotion. The effigy (what we see is a copy) was supposedly begun by Nicodemus and finished by an angel, set on a pilotless ship from the Orient in the eighth century and, following a landing nearby, brought into Lucca on a cart drawn by steer. This miraculous arrival quickly spawned a cult following and it soon became an object of pilgrimage throughout Europe. Nowadays the relic is draped in silk and gold garments and ornaments and marched through Lucca's streets in nighttime processions on 13 September.

The Duomo's Sacristy contains the other top attraction: the Tomb of Ilaria del Carretto (1408), a delicate sarcophagus sculpted by Sienese master Jacopo della Quercia representing the young bride of Paolo Guinigi, Lucca's strongman at the time. The Sacristy also houses a natural altarpiece by Domenico Ghirlandaio, the *Madonna Enthroned with Saints*. On the way out, Giambologna's *Altar of Liberty* crowned by a rising Christ and Tintoretto's raucous *Last Supper* in the right nave are worth a glimpse.

San Francesco

Via della Quarquonia (no telephone). **Open** 7.30am-noon, 3-6pm daily; 9am-1pm, 3-6pm public hols. **Admission** free. **No credit cards**.

The eerie grey interior of this fourteenth-century, barn-shaped church is only slightly lit by the light streaming in from the rose window in the façade. San Francesco houses the tombstone (but according to the parish priest not the body) of one of Lucca's greatest sons, the fourteenth-century adventurer Castruccio Castracani, who gave the city its brief

The façade of **San Michele in Foro** *– Lucca's take on the Pisan-Romanesque style.*

Useful information

Tourist information

Azienda di Promozione Turistica (APT) *Vecchia Porta San Donato, Piazzale Giuseppe Verdi (tel/fax 0583 419 689).* **Open** 8am-7pm daily. *Piazza Guidiccioni 2 (0583 491 205/6).* **Open** 8am-2pm Mon-Sat.

Transport

Airport *Tassignano (0583 936 062).*

Bicycle Hire
Barbetti *Via Anfiteatro 23 (0583 954 444).*
Poli Antonio *Piazza Santa Maria 42 (0583 493 787).* The largest concentration of bike hire shops is in Piazza Santa Maria. Standard hire rate is L4,000 per hour, L20,000 per day.

Bus station *Piazzale Guiseppe Verdi.*
CLAP buses to towns in Lucca province (0583 587 897).
LAZZI buses to Florence, Pistoia, Pisa, Prato, Abetone, Bagni di Lucca, Montecatini and Viareggio (0583 584 876).
At least one bus an hour leaves Florence for Lucca (first 5.58am; last 8.15pm) and from Lucca to Florence (first 6.25am; last 7.45pm). Journey takes from an hour and three quarters to two and a quarter hours.

Car Hire: **Pittore** (Eurodollar), *Piazza Santa Maria 34 (0583 467 960).*

Parking within the city walls is expensive and free only for hotel customers; there is spacious, free car park just outside the walls past Porta San Donato.

Railway Station
Piazza Ricasoli (0583 467 013).
The station is two minutes' walk from the southern gate, Porta San Pietro. Trains from Florence to Viareggio stop at Lucca (as well as Prato and Pistoia). The 78-km (50-mile) journey takes about an hour and 15 minutes, with trains leaving almost every hour from 7.40am to 10.10pm, usually at around 20 minutes to the hour.

Taxis: **Piazza Napoleone** (0583 492 691); **Railway station** (0583 494 989).

What's on

The English-language monthly *Grapevine* has news and info on what's happening in the Lucca area

Markets

General market (Wed & Sat Via dei Bacchettoni by the eastern wall) selling clothes, food, flowers and household goods; **antiques market** (third weekend of each month Piazza San Martino and surrounding streets); **craft market**, arti e mestieri, (last weekend of the month in Piazza San Giusto).

Festivals

Stagione Teatrale at Teatro del Giglio (Jan-Mar).
Santa Zita Flower Show and Market (four days end Apr) in Piazza Anfiteatro and Piazza San Frediano.
Villas in Bloom Festival (last ten days of May) garden festival at Villas Mansi, Torrigiani, Bruguier, Reale, Grabau and Oliva.
Summer Music Festival in Piazza Anfiteatro (July) – big names schedule but don't always confirm, check with APT.
Luminara di San Paolino (11 July) torchlit commemoration of Lucca's patron saint.
Luminara di Santa Croce (13 Sept) procession of the Volto Santo.
Settembre Lucchese (Sept, Oct) cultural, religious and sporting events.
Stagione Lirica at Teatro del Giglio (Sept, Oct).
Natale Anfiteatro (Dec) – market of regional products and specialties.

Emergency services

Ambulance (0583 49233/0583 494 902).
Carabinieri (112).
Police (113).
Fire Brigade (115).
Campo di Marte Hospital, Via dell'Ospedale (0583 9701).

glorious age of conquest in the early 1300s. There is also a plaque to Giacomo Puccini (*see p227* **Music maestro**). Its rather dusty and not exactly understated inscription reads 'artistic great and genius whose exquisitely human art moved and will forever move the entire world'.

San Frediano

Piazza San Frediano (no telephone). **Open** 7.30am-noon, 3-6pm daily; 9am-1pm, 3-6pm public hols. **Admission** free. **No credit cards.**

San Frediano's strikingly resplendent Byzantine-like mosaic façade is unique in Tuscany, rivalled only by that above the choir of San Miniato al Monte in Florence. On this site, a church was founded by Fredian, an Irish monk who settled in Lucca in the sixth century and converted the ruling Lombards by allegedly diverting the river Serchio and saving the city from flooding. This miracle put the finishing touches on Christianity's hold on Lucca and earned him a quick promotion to bishop which led to eventual canonisation. A few centuries later, in the 1100s, Fredian then had this singular church built for him. Apart from the mosaic, the façade of San Frediano – attributed to the school of Belinghiero Berlinghieri –

is in the Pisan-Romanesque style of many of Lucca's other churches and was the first to face east, reflecting a change in urban growth. The façade's mosaic is an Ascension in which a monumental Jesus is lifted by two angels over the heads of his jumbled apostles. Inside, immediately on the right is a small gem: the *fonte lustrale*, or baptismal font, carved by unknown Lombard and Tuscan artists who surrounded the fountain with scenes from the old and new testaments. Behind it is a glazed terracotta Ascension by Andrea della Robbia. In the chapel next to it is another of Lucca's revered relics, the miraculously conserved though somewhat shriveled body of Saint Zita, a humble servant who was canonised in the thirteenth century and whose mummy is brought out for a close up view and a touch by devotees on 27 April. The marble polyptych of the *Madonna and Child* (1422) in the Cappella Trenta is by Jacopo della Quercia.

San Giovanni e Reparata

Via del Duomo (0583 490 530). **Open** *June-Sept* 10am-6pm Tue-Sun; *Oct-May* 10am-5pm, Mon-Fri; 10am-6pm Sat-Sun. **Admission** L2,000 or L7,000 (with Museo della Cattedrale); L2,000 for excavations. **No credit cards**.

Originally Lucca's cathedral, the twelfth-century basilica of San Giovanni, now part of the Duomo, is on the sight of a pagan temple and according to some also rests on Roman thermal baths. The church's main draw is the stratification of architectural remains uncovered by excavations in the 1970s, ranging from a mosaic dating back to Imperial Rome to a fifth-century, early Christian basilica.

Santa Maria Corteorlandini

Piazza Giovanni Leonardi (no telephone). **Open** 7.30am-noon, 3-6pm daily; 9am-1pm, 3-6pm public hols. **Admission** free. **No credit cards**.

This overwhelming late Baroque church is Lucca's odd man out. Its trompe l'œil frescoed roofs, an abundance of coloured marble, and the gilded and ornamented tabernacle by local artist Giovanni Vambre' (1673) provide a break from the stark and grey interiors of the city's other churches.

Santa Maria Forisportam

Piazza Santa Maria Forisportam (no telephone). **Open** 7.30am-noon, 3-6pm daily; 9am-1pm, 3-6pm public hols. **Admission** free. **No credit cards**.

Located on the square known to Lucchesi as *piazza della colonna mozza* (referring to the truncated column at its centre), Santa Maria takes its name from its location just outside Lucca's older set of walls. The unfinished marble façade dates mostly from the twelfth and thirteenth centuries and is a slightly toned down version of the Pisan-Romanesque style present throughout the city, with lively carvings in the lunettes and architraves above the portals. The shadowy interior has an awkward mix of objects, including a nativity scene, an early Christian sarcophagus turned into a baptismal font and a bronze eighteenth-century Baroque tabernacle.

San Michele in Foro

Piazza San Michele (no telephone). Open 7.30am-12.30pm, 3-6pm daily. **Admission** free. **No credit cards**.

San Michele's façade is a feast on the eyes. Set on the site of the ancient Roman forum, Lucca's consummate take on the Pisan-Romanesque style is one of the city 's most memorable sights. Each element lightly plays off against the other: the knotted, twisted and carved columns with their psychedelic geometric designs, the fantastical animals and fruit and floral motifs in the capitals. The façade culminates in a winged and stiff Saint Michael precariously perched while vanquishing the dragon. San Michele's sombre interior contrasts sharply with its façade. On the right as you enter, is a *Madonna and Child* by Matteo Civitali – a copy of the original is on the church's right hand outside corner. Further on is Filippino Lippi's *Saints Jerome, Sebastian, Rocco and Helena*, all of whom helped the Madonna deliver Lucca from the plague in 1480.

San Paolino

Via San Paolino (no telephone). **Open** 7.30am-noon, 3-6pm daily; 9am-1pm, 3-6pm public hols. **Admission** free. **No credit cards**.

Giacomo Puccini received his baptism of fire here in 1881, with his first public performance of the Mass for Four Voices. San Paolino had, in fact, always been the Puccini family's second home, with five generations of them serving as its organists. Built from 1522 to 1536 for Lucca's patron St Paulinus, who allegedly came over from Antioch in AD65 and became the city 's first bishop and whose remains are buried in a sarcophagus behind the altar, this church is Lucca's only example of late Renaissance architecture. In the left chapel a fifteenth-century Florentine *Coronation of the Virgin* is set against a backdrop which may be Lucca, with across from it a peculiar *Burial of St Paulinus* attributed to Angelo Puccinelli.

Museums

Casa Natale di Giacomo Puccini

Corte San Lorenzo 9, off Via di Poggio (0583 584 028). **Open** *2 Jan-28 Feb* 10am-1pm Tue-Fri, 10am-1pm, 3-6pm, Sat-Sun; *1 Mar-31 May & 1 Oct-31 Dec* 10am-1pm, 3-6pm, daily; *1 June-30 Sep* 10am-6pm Tue-Sun. **Admission** L5,000; L3,000 under-14s and groups of ten and over. **No credit cards**.

The birthplace of Lucca's most famous son has been turned into a charming museum which offers some interesting insights into his sheltered youth, turbulent private life and artistic genius (*see p227* **Music maestro**). The rooms include such memorabilia as the original librettos of his earlier operas *Mass for Four Voices* and *Symphonie Caprice*, his private letters on subjects both musical and sentimental, the piano on which he composed the *Turandot* and the gem-encrusted costume used in the opera's American debut in 1926.

Museo della Cattedrale

Via Arcivescovado (0583 490 530). **Open** *May-Oct* 10am-6pm daily; *Nov-Apr* 10am-5pm Mon-Fri; 10am-

6pm Sat, Sun. **Admission** L5,000 or L7,000 (including San Giovanni). **No credit cards**.
Many of the treasures from the **Duomo di San Martino** and from nearby **San Giovanni** (*see above*) have been transferred and arranged in strict chronological order in this recently opened, well curated museum. It displays everything from the cathedral's furnishings, its gold and its silverware to its sculptures – some of these, including Jacopo della Quercia's splendid *Apostle*, were removed from the church to save them from eventual decay. A model of the Duomo itself and a number of the Volto Santo's slightly gaudy ornaments are also on view.

Museo Nazionale di Palazzo Mansi

Via Galli Tassi 43 (0583 55570). **Open** 9am-7pm Tue-Sat; 9am-2pm Sun, public hols. **Admission** L8,000; free for EC citizens under 18 and over 60. **No credit cards**.
The sixteen- to seventeenth-century palazzo which hosts this collection of mostly Tuscan art is Lucca's most remarkable example of Baroque exaggeration. While the frescoed Salone della Musica and the neo-classical Salone degli Specchi are still light on the eye, the overindulgence then climaxes in the Camera della Sposa, an over-the-top bridal chamber with a *baldacchino* bed. The artwork is largely uninspiring, and includes samples from the Venetian school with lesser known works by Tintoretto and Tiziano and some Flemish tapestries. Perhaps Palazzo Manzi's best draw is Pontormo's Manneristic portrait of his nasty patron, Alessandro de' Medici.

Museo Nazionale di Villa Guinigi

Via della Quarquonia (0583 496 033). **Open** 9am-7pm Tue-Sat; 9am-2pm Sun. **Admission** L4,000; free to EC citizens over 60 or under 18. **No credit cards**.
This porticoed, pink brick villa (1403-20) surrounded by greenery was erected at the height of rule by Lucca's 'enlightened despot' Paolo Guinigi. After various vicissitudes it was finally turned into a museum focused almost exclusively on art from Lucca and its region. The first floor has a recently expanded selection of Roman and Etruscan finds and some thirteenth- and fourteenth-century capitals and columns by Guidetto da Como taken from the façade of **San Michele in Foro** (*see above*). The rooms upstairs start with thirteenth-century painted crucifixes and wooden tabernacles. The highlights though are Matteo Civitali's *Annunciation*, impressive altar pieces by Amico Aspertini and Fra Bartolomeo and the intarsia panels by Ambrogio and Nicolao Pucci.

Monuments

Ramparts

Lucca's defining landmark, *le nostre mura* – as the Lucchesi adoringly call them – are among Italy's best preserved and most impressive city fortifications. Built in the sixteenth and seventeenth centuries, they measure 12 metres in height, 30 across, and just over 4km in circumference and are punctuated by 11 sturdy bastions, meant to ward off the most heavily armed of invaders. A proper siege, though, has never occurred, and the only real use they ever got was in 1812 when they allowed the city to hermetically close itself off to floodwaters. Soon after, Maria Luisa di Borbone turned them into a public park and promenade, dotting them with plane, holm-oak, chestnut and lime trees. Today, Lucchesi flock there to picnic, cuddle or simply stroll and take in the wonderful views of the city from above. A view inside one of the bastions can be had by phoning ahead to the **Centro Internazionale per lo Studio delle Cerchia Urbane** (CISCU) (0583 496 257).

Torre Guinigi

Via Sant'Andrea 42 (0583 48524). **Open** *Nov-Feb* 10am-4.30pm daily; *Mar-Sept* 9am-7.30pm daily; *Oct* 10am-6pm daily. **Admission** L5,000; L3,000 concessions. **No credit cards**.
The fourteenth-century, 44 metre Torre Guinigi offers spectacular, 360-degree views over Lucca's rooftops and on to the countryside past the walls.

Parks & gardens

Giardino Botanico

Via del Giardino Botanico 14 (0583 442 160). **Open** summer 9.30am-12.30pm Mon-Fri; 9.30am-12.30pm 3.30-6.30pm Sat, Sun; winter 9.30am-12.30pm Mon-Fri. **Admission** L5,000; L3,500 children, over-60s; free under-6s. **No credit cards**.
These gardens are set up against the walls. The greenhouse and arboretum are planted with a wide range of Tuscan flora and provide Lucca's greenest and most exotic spot for a stroll.

Palazzo Pfanner

Via degli Asili 33 (0583 48524). **Open** *1 Mar-31 Oct* 10am-6pm daily; *Nov-28 Feb* by appointment. **Admission** L3,000; under-8s free.
The statues in this palazzo's interior courtyard are a well-known Luccan landmark, as is the open-air marble staircase. Both can also be viewed from the walls above. The eighteenth-century palazzo itself, though, is perennially under restoration.

Restaurants

The nearby Garfagnana valley contributes many prime ingredients, including chestnut flour, river trout, olive oil and above all *farro,* the spelt grain made into soup, which pops up on every menu. The signature sweet is *buccellato*, a doughnut-shaped sweet bread flavoured with aniseed and raisins and topped with sugar syrup.

Osteria Baralla

Via Anfiteatro 5-9 (0583 440 240). **Open** 12.30-2.30pm, 7.30-10.30pm Mon-Sat and third Sun of month. **Average** L30,000-L35,000. **Credit** AmEx, DC, MC, V.
Recently reopened, Osteria Baralla is a hit with the locals and offers lighter fare such as an antipasto of *spuntini Toscani* or a *minestra frantoiana* (with mixed

vegetables and herbs) and excellent grilled meats. To finish off there's a crumbling dark chocolate *crostata*.

Locanda Buatino

Borgo Giannotti 508, nr Piazzale Martiri della Libertà (0583 343 207). **Open** 11am-3.30pm, 6pm-midnight Mon-Sat. **Average** L25,000. **Credit** MC, V.

If all you have time for is one meal, step outside Lucca's walls into this *locanda*, the city's most memorable inn and eaterie. Il Buatino originally fed the farmers from the Garfagnana in town for the local agricultural market. Today, owner Giuseppe Ferrua serves up high quality and inventive Tuscan food at exceptional value for money: L23,000 for a three course meal with wine and coffee. There's even the odd ethnic food night. Unbeatable.

La Buca di Sant'Antonio

Via della Cervia 3 (0583 55881). **Open** 12.30am-2.30, 7.30-11pm Tue-Sat; 11am-3pm Sun. **Average** L50,000-60,000. **Credit** AmEx, DC, MC, V.

A Lucca fixture, La Buca is located in a restored nineteenth-century hostelry steps away from San Michele and has traditional offerings which occasionally dip into innovation. Soups include a Lucca classic *minestra di farro alla Garfagnana*, and among the primi, *tordelli lucchesi* (oversize tortelloni). The *capretto allo spiedo* (spit roasted kid) makes for a handsome *secondo*.

Da Giulio in Pelleria

Via della Conce 45 (0583 55 948). **Open** noon-3pm, 7-10.30pm Tue-Sat & third Sun of month. **Average** L30,000. **Credit** AmEx, DC, MC, V.

One of Lucca's best known haunts, Da Giulio is a vast trattoria with a huge following, though not the most courteous of places. Typical Tuscan dishes at good value for money include an age-old Lucchese dish such as *la concia* (essentially chitterlings) and more mainstream primi such as *gnocchetti al pomodoro* and a *rustic pollo al mattone* (chicken roasted against fiery brick).

Da Guido

Via Cesare Battisti 28 (0583 467 219). **Open** noon-2.30pm, 7.30-10pm, Mon-Sat. **Average** L20,000. **Credit** AmEx, MC, V.

Prezzi modicissimi (unbeatable prices) is Da Guido's motto. But this wood-paneled trattoria is a Lucca favourite more for its reliably good food and the warm welcome guaranteed by the friendly Barsotti brothers. *Zuppa di farro*, home rolled *tortelli al ragú* and *coniglio alla cacciatora* (roasted rabbit) fill the stomach without emptying the wallet. For dessert, try the Lucchese *torta di verdure* (sweet spinach cake).

Da Leo

Via Tegrimi 1 (0583 492 236). **Open** noon-2.30pm, 7.30-10.30pm Mon-Sat. **Average** L30,000. **No credit cards**.

The din of Da Leo echoes onto the street. The regulars squeezed into its main room are well served by an alternating menu with *primi* such as a *farinata Garfagnana* (similar to a *ribollita* with corn flour) and, for *secondo*, a *rosticciana in umido* (small chunks of stewed pork and olives in a tomato sauce). Don't worry if while you're devouring the delicious fruit tiramisu you feel a strange paw on your lap. It's Da Leo's mascot Nerina, a sprightly black dog which comes around at dessert time.

Gli Orti di Via Elisa

Via Elisa 17 (0583 491 241). **Open** 12.30-2.30pm, 7.30-10.30pm Mon, Tue, Fri-Sun; 7.30-10.30pm Thur. **Average** L25,000. **Credit** AmEx, MC, V.

A good lunch place if you're in Lucca's eastern end, with a self-service salad bar, straightforward but filling pastas and pizzas and even the odd grilled meat for seconds. The pizzeria stays open until 11.30pm.

La Mora

Località Ponte a Moriano, Via Sesto di Moriano 1748, Sesto di Moriano (0583 406 402). **Open** noon-2.30pm, 7.30-10pm Thur-Tue. **Average** L65,000. **Credit** AmEx, DC, MC, V.

Culinary heavyweight Sauro Brunicardi has turned this old post-house just north of Lucca into a regionally renowned upmarket osteria and a marvellous outdoor eating experience. Two dishes stand out – the *gran farro* is true to its name and the *piccione ai pinoli e uvetta* (pigeon with pine nuts and raisins) is mouth-wateringly eccentric.

Ristorante Puccini

Corte San Lorenzo 1/2, off Piazza Cittadella (0583 316 116). **Open** *summer* noon-3pm, 7-10.30pm Mon, Thur-Sun; 7-10.30pm Tue, Wed; *winter* closed Tue. **Average** L65,000. **Credit** AmEx, DC, MC, V.

The Lucchesi like their bikes.

Music maestro

Though much has been done recently to play up and publicise Puccini's ties to Lucca, he has not always been seen in a favourable light by his fellow citizens. Puccini was born in nearby Celle in 1858 and grew up in Lucca, but his restless nature kept him elsewhere for most of his career, and his non-conformist attitude, artistic unpredictability and unrepentant womanising made him enemies among Lucca's staid upper echelons.

Giacomo was the last in a long family line of organists and composers and led a secluded, petit-bourgeois lifestyle, which dramatically turned into a bohemian, penniless existence following his move to study in Milan's conservatoire in 1880. A recalcitrant student, he had previously been won over to study composing through days spent with his music teacher and surrogate father Carlo Angeloni, though their conversations tended to revolve more around wildlife hunting (Puccini's other great passion).

Following some flops, his big break came in 1893 when he committed to music the heart-wrenching tragedy of *Manon Lescaut*. The success put him on his feet financially and he was able to move to his own, private hunting Eden at Torre del Lago on Lake Massaciuccioli, where he remained for most of the rest of his life. Surrounded by serenity, the box office hits began to flow from his fingertips – *La Bohème, La Fanciulla del West* (The Golden Girl of the West), *Tosca* and *Madama Butterfly*. He wrote librettos right up until his death in Brussels in 1924, when he was still working on the unfinished *Turandot*.

Privately, his life was an emotional roller-coaster: he fathered a son with a married woman, Elvira Bonturi, whom he continued to depend upon, despite countless other escapades. The love affair most murmured about was that with flashy German Baroness, Josephine von Stangel, consummated in the pine forests of his beloved Torre del Lago. In the eyes of the careful and most proper Lucchesi, Puccini's was a life of transgression. To the rest of the world, his operatic genius ranks him along with Verdi as one of Italy's greatest composers.

Set in the city's 'Puccini corner', this is a classy restaurant with outdoor seating. It's also Lucca's best bet for fish. Specialties include the *ravioli di mare in salsa di scampi* (fish stuffing and a tasty shrimp sauce) and the *coda di rospo in funghi porcini e pomodoro* (angler in a porcini and tomato sauce).

Pizza

Tuscany is not known for its pizza, but Lucca's tradition of immigrants from the south has spawned two pizza places worthy of mention. **Da Felice** (Via Buia 12. 0583 494 986. Open 11am-2.30pm, 4-8pm, Mon; 9.30am-2.30pm, 4-8pm, Tue-Sat. No credit cards), close to San Michele, is great for snatching a crispy slice on the run. **La Sbragia** (Via Fillungo 144/146, 0583 492 641. Open noon-2pm, 6pm-1am, Tue-Sat; 6pm-1am Sun. Average L15,000. No credit cards) at the upper end of Lucca's main shopping artery has both sit down and takeaway pizza and swarms of customers.

Bars, cafés & gelaterie

If you're in Lucca for nightlife you're going to be disappointed. The big night spots are out towards the Versilia coast, the closest is the **Riva Marina** (c/o Bar Casina Rossa, Via Sarzanese 1978, 4km towards Viareggio, 058 439 5264) an expansive 1960s disco with eaterie and swimming pool which has recently reacquired its past fame.

Antico Caffè della Mura

Piazzale Vittorio Emanuele 2 (0583 467 962). **Open** 6pm-midnight Mon, Wed-Sun. Average L70,000. **Credit** AmEx, JCB, MC, V.

Overlooks Lucca from its ramparts. Slightly stuffy atmosphere but wonderful outdoor tables and open late in summer.

Bar San Michele

Piazza San Michele 1 (0583 55387). **Open** *summer* 7.30am-8pm daily; *winter* closed Sun. **No credit cards**.

Strategically placed facing San Michele and the morning sun. Great for people watching.

Caffè di Simo

Via Fillungo 58 (0583 496 234). **Open** 7.30am-8pm Tue-Sun; *restaurant* noon-3pm. Average L30,000. **Credit** DC, MC, V.

Lucca's ultimate belle époque café-pasticceria, whose early twentieth-century habitués included poet Pascoli and composers Mascagni and Puccini. Di Simo's has a clubby feel and excellent pastries. Worth the expense.

Mirror, mirror on the wall

One proverb sums up the communal rivalries that are the backbone of Tuscan history and identity better than any other: *'meglio un morto in casa che un Pisano all'uscio'* – better a death in the family than a Pisan on your doorstep. This macabre expression was coined in Lucca, though it has been happily adopted in Livorno, Florence and elsewhere. Its origins are unclear, but there is a historical anecdote that would seem to justify it.

In 1288, following decades of taunts and threats, Lucca lashed out in an uncharacteristic fit of aggression and conquered the Pisan fort of Asciano. To add insult to injury, the Lucchesi proceeded to erect four massive mirrors on its walls so that the Pisans could reflect on their defeat, so to speak. Pisa got its own back in 1313 when the Ghibelline leader Uguccione della Faggiuola besieged Lucca and called a truce before invading so that he could set up two huge mirrors of his own on Lucca's walls to the same ends.

Lucca's Guelph leadership was relieved to have avoided an invasion and swallowed the humiliation, but the squabbles didn't stop there. The terms of the truce required Lucca to embrace all its Ghibelline outcasts. Among these was Castruccio Castracani, a long-exiled, canny adventurer in search of a power base. His rise to power required ridding Lucca of its Guelph dominion, so he struck a Trojan horse-style secret deal with Uguccione and opened up Lucca's gates one night.

What followed was a week of rampaging and bloodshed in which Lucca's Guelphs were all but eliminated. Setting aside any Ghibelline loyalties, Castracani then went on to subdue Uguccione and most of western Tuscany. Never again did a Pisan pass through Lucca's gates unnoticed.

Casali

Piazza San Michele 40 (0583 492 687). **Open** *summer* 7am-11pm daily; *winter* 7am-8.30pm Thur-Tue. **Credit** MC, V.

Perfect for a pre-dinner aperitivo outdoors in the early evening with a view across Piazza San Michele.

Gelateria Veneta

Chiasso Barletti 22 (0583 493 727). **Open** 11am-midnight Mon, Wed-Sun. **Closed** 6 Jan-1 Mar. **No credit cards.**

This venerated gelateria has set Lucca's ice-cream standards for 150 years.

Branch Via Vittorio Veneto 74 (0583 467 037).

Accommodation

You can count Lucca's hotels located within its walls on the fingers of one hand, and there are no signs this is going to change any time soon. Lucchesi like it that way, and have no intention of turning their precious city into an appendage of the overcrowded Versilia coast.

Diana

Via del Molinetto 11 (0583 467 795/fax 0583 47 795). **Rates** *single* L55,000; *double* L105,000. **Credit** AmEx, DC, MC, V.

Small but conveniently located between the cathedral of San Martino and the railway station. A good option if you're looking for something within easy walking distance of the sights.

Locanda Buatino

Borgo Giannotti 508 (0583 343 207/fax 0583 343 298). **Rates** *single* L30,000-L45,000; *double* L50,000-75,000. **Credit** MC, V.

Even in a land as tradition-bound as Tuscany and in a city as set in its ways as Lucca the *locande*, or hostelries which used to provide well-deserved rest and food for farmers from the surrounding countryside have gradually disappeared. The Buatino is the only one remaining. Just a few minutes outside the walls to the north, its five rooms are as welcoming as they come, and there's the added bonus of a terrific restaurant downstairs (*see above*). For breakfast try the luscious pastries at L'Angolo Dolce (closed Mon) just across the street.

Locanda L'Elisa

Via Nuova per Pisa (0583 379 737/fax 0583 379 019/locanda.elisa@lunet.it). **Rates** *single* L250,000-L330,000; *double* L420,000-L480,000. **Credit** AmEx, DC, MC, V.

Out in its own league in more ways than one, this elegant five-star hotel is quite simply one of the region's best. The villa's current appearance dates back to 1805 when Napoleon's sister and Lucca's ruler Elisa Baciocchi had the interiors and gardens refashioned. Highlights include a restaurant modelled after an English conservatory, eighteenth-century furnishings throughout, recently revamped gardens and a large swimming pool.

La Luna

Corte Compagni 12 (0583 493 634/fax 0583 490 021). **Rates** *single* L100,000; *double* L140,000; *suite* L200,000. **Credit** AmEx, DC, MC, V.

Easily the best bargain in this price range, with a great location at the upper end of busy Via Fillungo. Set in two seventeenth-century palazzi facing each other across a courtyard, with 30 welcoming rooms.

Piccolo Hotel Puccini

Via di Poggio 9 (0583 55421/fax 0583 53487). **Rates** *single* L90,000; *double* L125,000. **Credit** AmEx, DC, MC, V.

Paces away from Puccini's boyhood home, this is a wonderfully cosy *pensione* with helpful English-speaking staff, great views from most rooms and, of course, Puccini memorabilia. Book ahead.

Rex

Piazza Ricasoli 19 (955 443/fax 954 348). **Rates** *single* L120,000; *double* L160,000. **Credit** AmEx, DC, MC, V.

Just outside the walls by the railway station, this modern hotel has air-conditioned rooms, fridge-bars, cable and satellite TV and unfriendly staff.

Il Serchio Youth Hostel

Via del Brennero 673, Salicchi, 2km north of Lucca (0583 341 811). Bus 6. **Open** 10 Mar-4 June, 1 Sept-10 Oct. From 1 Jan-29 Feb and 5 June-31 July only for groups who have pre-booked. **Rates** L19,000; family room L21,000 per person. **No credit cards**.

This youth hostel with 62 beds in 12 rooms can be reached by taking the number 6 bus from Piazzale Verdi or the railway station or by driving north up Via Civitali which turns into Via del Brennero. A small garden in the back can be used for camping. Phone ahead as space is very limited.

Universo

Piazza del Giglio 1 (0583 493 678/fax 0583 954 854). **Rates** *single* L120,000-195,000; *double* L184,000-260,000. **Credit** MC, V.

The choice in Lucca for a long time, the Universo feels like it belongs in an Eastern European capital. Crumbling fixtures and confusioned staff don't, however, detract from its passé charm.

Shopping

Lucca's main shopping artery is Via Fillungo, the city's winding showcase of art nouveau façades.

La Bottega di Mamma Rò

Piazza Anfiteatro 4 (0583 492 607). **Open** 3.30-8pm Mon; 9am-8pm Tue-Sat & 3rd Sun of month. **Credit** AmEx, DC, JCB, MC, V.

Hand-painted ceramics, hand-dipped candles and bright country cotton fabrics.

Cacioteca

Via Fillungo 242 (0583 496 346). **Open** 7am-1.30pm, 3-8.30pm Mon, Tue, Thur-Sat; 7am-1.30pm Wed. **Credit** MC, V.

An intense waft of seasoned cheese emanates from this inconspicuous but well-known specialist at the northern end of Via Fillungo. Typical products from the Garfagnana include the pecorino *in grotta* (in a cave) and *in barile* (in a barrel).

DelicaTezze di Roberto Isola

Via San Giorgio 5 (0583 492 633). **Open** 7am-1pm, 3.30-7.30pm Mon, Tue, Thur-Sat; 8am-1pm Wed. **Credit** AmEx, DC, MC, V.

This excellent deli has a great selection of home-made ravioli and tortelli, olive oils, farro, porcini and cheeses. There's also a constant choice of wine, cheese and cold cuts ready for tasting.

La Grotta

Piazza Anfiteatro 2 (0583 467 595). **Open** 8am-2pm, 4-8pm Mon, Tue, Thur-Sat; 8am-2pm Wed. **Credit** AmEx, MC, V.

Among Lucca's oldest *insaccatori* (literally, sausage baggers), La Grotta is located in what used to be caves for salt storage. Peppered Tuscan prosciutti are lined up alongside a Lucchese peculiarity known as *biroldo* – salami made of pig's blood with raisins.

Panificio Amedeo Giusti

Via Santa Lucia 18/20 (0583 496 285). **Open** 8am-1pm, 4-7.30pm Mon, Tue, Thur-Sat; 8am-1pm Wed. **No credit cards**.

The city's best bakery is an institution, where customers elbow for both the savoury and sweet.

Vini Liquori Vanni

Piazza del Salvatore 7 (0583 491 902). **Open** 4-8pm Mon; 9am-1pm, 4.30-8pm Tue-Sat. **Credit** AmEx, DC, EC, MC, V.

This enoteca's seemingly endless cellar is a treasure for those seeking out Lucca's better vintages. Call ahead and book a wine lesson and *degustazione*, and a mini tour of this thirteenth-century cantina. Local wines from the Colline Lucchesi and Montecarlo regions up for sampling include Maiolina, Tenuta da Valgiano, Michi and Fattoria Colleverde.

The tranquil side streets of Lucca.

Arezzo Province

The best of eastern Tuscany.

The four valleys that make up Tuscany's eastern province branch out like spokes in a wheel along the Arno, Tiber and Chiana rivers from the city of Arezzo at its centre. Each fiercely defends its own identity forged by the Appenine peaks, crucial waterways and dense forests that divide them, but none can really outdo the others. Whether it's for a monastery or a memorable eating experience, they all offer something to make a visit worthwhile.

Encased between the imposing Pratomagno Appenine range to the north and the gentler Chianti hills to the south lies **the Valdarno**, a largely industrial and manufacturing region connecting Florence to Arezzo. North of the Arno, the Setteponti, or seven bridges, route along the Pratomagno foothills crosses the river's tributaries amid olive and chestnut groves and is an amenable way of making the trip between the two cities.

The gateway to **Castelfranco di Sopra**.

The Casentino is abruptly closed off to the north by some of the Appenine's highest peaks. It has always been a peaceful area, with one blatant exception: the bloody Battle of Campaldino in 1289, which saw Arezzo's capitulation to Florence. Today, serenity emanates over the valley from the monastery of Camáldoli and the sanctuary of La Verna.

The Valtiberina is Tuscany's easternmost fringe and takes its name from the Tiber as it gathers momentum, flowing down from the Appenine peaks. As its inhabitants unabashedly remind visitors, this valley significantly marks the border between a land that has produced the likes of Michelangelo, Piero della Francesca and the, well, rather less sophisticated Umbri and Marchegiani next door, to the south.

Etruscan heartland and modern-day agricultural flatland, over the centuries **the Valdichiana** whetted the appetites of Arezzo, Siena and Florence, with the Medici eventually appropriating or buying control of virtually all of it by the late fifteenth century. Its name today is synonymous with Chianina beef, an even leaner, more tender and flavoursome variety of its northern cousin, la Fiorentina. The valley west of the Chiana river is dotted with self-contained outposts such as Monte San Savino and Lucignano, but it is to the east of the river where Arezzo province shows off its very best: in splendid, sandstone **Cortona**.

This chapter is divided into: the Valdarno (West of Arezzo); the Casentino (North of Arezzo); the Valtiberina (East of Arezzo); and the Valdichiana (South of Arezzo).

The Valdarno

Castelfranco di Sopra

The first worthwhile stop along the Setteponti route is Castelfranco di Sopra, founded as a Florentine military outpost in the late thirteenth century. Just outside it is the **Badia di San Salvatore a Soffena**, a twelfth-century abbey repeatedly restored since the first half of the 1400s. Its bright interior sports an *Annunciation* on the

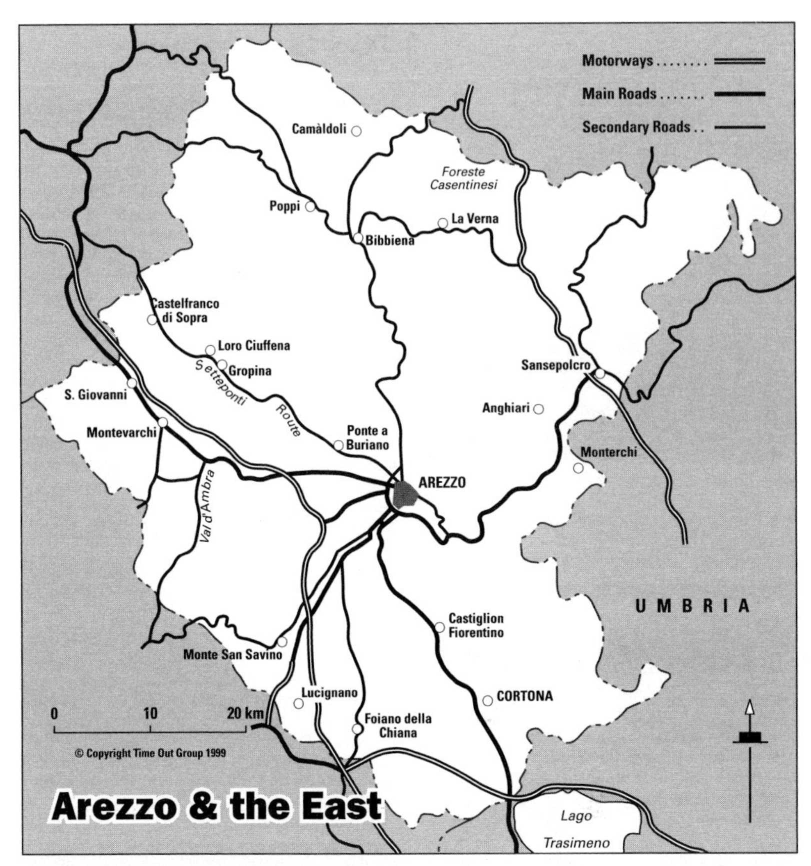

right and other pastel-coloured frescoes. It's worth stepping into the cloister built around a well to the right of the abbey and, if you insist, the non-communicative caretaker may let you steal a peek into a room containing his secret boxes of bones yielded by recent excavations.

Loro Ciuffenna & Gropina

Precariously set on the edge of a gorge over the roaring Ciuffenna torrent, Loro has grown up around its ancient *borgo*, or quarter, known as Il Fondaccio, a small maze of winding alleys pushed up against the stream's gully. The town has its own Ponte Vecchio and a working flour mill.

In Piazza del Municipio, the Venturino Venturi Museum of Contemporary Art displays abstract sculptures and drawings. Tucked away round the corner is **Osteria da Pippo** (Via Nannini, 055 917 2770. Open lunch & dinner Mon, Tue, Thur-Sun. Average L45,000) offering traditional Tuscan fare. Nearby is Loro Ciuffenna's odd and exotic corner: Anarkali Bazar, with its selection of Eastern craft products. The **Locanda la Torre** (Via Dante 20, 055 917 2032. Open lunch & dinner Mon, Wed-Sun. Average L45,000) located further upstream serves tasty *ravioli ai funghi gratinati* (with slightly breaded mushrooms) and has some rooms should you want to stay overnight.

Only a couple of kilometres outside Loro on the Arezzo road, a twisting dirt path breaks off towards the stark and simple church of San Pietro a Gropina, a Romanesque parish church which dates back to the ninth century. The carved detail on the capitals and knotted columns on the pulpit, with stylised human figures, grapes, knights and hunting eagles, represent a pre-Christian, pagan rendition of the circle and knot of life.

San Pietro a Gropina. See p231.

The Setteponti's last attraction before reaching Arezzo is Ponte a Buriano, a harmonious thirteenth-century bridge, which is the Arno's oldest and pre-dates the Ponte Vecchio in Florence by almost 100 years.

The Val d'Ambra

The Val d'Ambra is technically Chianti's easternmost reach and it offers a sense of timelessness and removal from Tuscany's well-beaten tracks. It is nestled up against the Monti del Chianti, past the Valdarno's two main cities, San Giovanni Valdarno and Montevarchi, both significant manufacturing and leather centres. Hidden away are places like Cennina, where a crumbling castle is sentinel to the sprawling Valdarno below, and Civitella in Val di Chiana, a perfectly preserved medieval village.

One of the highlights of Val d'Ambra is off the road between Montevarchi and Mercatale Valdarno. The well-signposted **Osteria di Rendola** (Via di Rendola 78, 055 970 7490. Closed Wed and Thur lunch. Average L65,000) is at the helm of Tuscany's gastronomic avant-garde. Alberto Fusini and young owner and chef Francesco Berardinelli have created a welcoming space with cubist artwork and jazz *sottofondo* while maintaining the feeling of a roadside osteria. And their innovative dishes strike a delicate balance with their Tuscan roots. Among the first courses are a sublime *tortelli di cernia in salsa di granchio,* fish-filled tortellini in a tangy crab sauce. The secondi include a delicious *piccione in salsa ristretta* (roast pigeon in its own condensed sauce) and the desserts deserve 'to-die-for' clichés.

The Casentino

Poppi & Camáldoli

Poppi slopes down through arcaded streets from the thirteenth-century **Castello dei Conti Guidi** (0575 529 964. Open 9.30am-12.30pm, 3-6pm daily. Admission L5,000). This bears a close resemblance to Florence's Palazzo Vecchio and offers a staggering view of the Casentino from its top. Visible are the Foreste Casentinesi National Park, which surrounds the monastery and the *eremo*, or hermitage, of Camáldoli.

Romualdo, an itinerant Benedictine monk, set up the Camaldolite congregation within the larger Benedictine order in 1012 to take monastic life one step further. Romualdo's followers still meditate in the splendid isolation of the holy retreat amid the fir trees of Tuscany's stunning woodland, with their individual cells visible only through a gate. Romualdo's original cell, with its wooden panelling and cot, is open to view, as is the overwhelmingly baroque church standing in stark contrast to the ascetic exterior.

Three kilometres downhill, the monastery is the Camaldolites' link to the outside world. Its church contains some early Vasaris, including a *Madonna and Child* and *Nativity*. The young artist took refuge here from 1537 to 1539, following the murder of his patron Alessandro de' Medici.

The dark wood *farmacia* around the corner has an interesting selection of monk-made soaps and liqueurs. **Il Rustichello** (Via del Corniolo 14, 0360 514 111/fax 0575 556 046. Rates single L70,000-L80,000; double L100,000-L110,000) is the best accommodation in this neck of the woods.

La Verna

In 1214 St Francis' vagabondage brought him to La Verna, an isolated peak at 1,129 metres, where he and some followers were inspired to build some cells for themselves. Ten years later, Italy's most famous saint received the stigmata here and since then this evocative spot has been a must-see on the Franciscan trail. The Basilica contains a reliquary chapel with the saint's personal effects and, in the walkway towards the stigmata chapel, a door leads to the place St Francis used to rest, a humid cavern, whose rocks miraculously split apart at the moment of Christ's death. The sanctuary also contains what must be the highest concentration of Andrea della Robbia glazed terracottas anywhere. This impressive religious compound of interconnected chapels, churches, corridors and cloisters inevitably attracts large numbers of visitors, but, on a quiet weekday, the stunning sight of a sunset over the Casentino can still stimulate meditative silence.

The Valtiberina

Sansepolcro

The Valtiberina's largest town and only centre with any sizeable population, Sansepolcro's name and origin are linked to the relics of the Holy Sepulchre brought here in medieval times. First a free community, it passed under Papal rule until 1441, when the Medici incorporated it in their fold. Today, Sansepolcro sits at an important crossroads between Tuscany, Umbria and the Marche, and its healthy commercial pace relies less on local artisans producing lace or goldsmithery than on the market for its food, especially pasta. In fact, before you reach the rectangular, walled centre, the sprawling Buitoni pasta factory founded more than 150 years ago leaps into view.

Once through the Porta Fiorentina, Via XX Settembre, the town's pleasant and pedestrianised main thoroughfare, gently breaks up the grid streetplan by curving its way among Renaissance and Mannerist palazzi interspersed by the odd medieval tower.

Sansepolcro is best known as the birthplace of the early Renaissance maestro of perspective and proportion, **Piero della Francesca** (c1420-1492) (*see p235* **All in the detail**), whose works are prominently displayed in the recently reorganised **Museo Civico** (Via Aggiunti 65, 0575 732 218. Open summer 9.30am-1.30pm, 2.30-7.30pm, daily; winter 9.30am-1pm, 2.30-6pm, daily. Admission L10,000). The *Madonna della Misericordia*, commissioned in 1445 by the local confraternity of the Misericordia, demanded that della Francesca overturn the laws of proportion by depicting an all-encompassing, monumental Madonna dwarfing the faithful and protecting them with her mantle, which takes on the shape of a church's apse. The silence and fatalism in her expression and stance closely resemble those of the *Madonna del Parto*, in Monterchi (*see below*), painted around the same time. Della Francesca can't resist placing himself among the Virgin's followers, facing us, to her left.

Loro Ciuffenna *has its own Ponte Vecchio.*

There is an even more apparent self-portrait in *The Resurrection* (c1460), in which an all-powerful, muscular Christ steps from his own tomb, carrying with him a renewal of life, both within the Valtiberina naturalistic backdrop, which transforms from winter deadness to spring fertility, and in the imminent reawakening of somnolent soldiers at his feet. It's easy to recognise della Francesca among them, again facing us, to the left of Christ. The Casa di Piero della Francesca, the painter's home and base for most of his life, and which today houses the artist's foundation, is nearby but not open to the public.

The fourteenth-century Romanesque Duomo contains on its left altar an imposing wooden crucifix known as the Volto Santo, probably brought to Sansepolcro from the Orient, and strikingly similar to its better known and more revered equivalent in Lucca's Cattedrale di San Martino. Less apparent is an Ascension by the school of Perugino on the left wall.

Local events include a torchlit Easter procession on Good Friday and Sansepolcro's traditional crossbow tournament known as the Palio della Balestra, held the second Sunday in September.

Sansepolcro offers central, albeit somewhat sterile, accommodation at the **Albergo Fiorentino** (Via L Pacioli 60, 0575 740 350/fax 0575 740 370. Rates single L65,000, double L95,000) on the corner of Via XX Settembre. The friendly owners also run a restaurant on the hotel's first floor, **Ristorante Fiorentino** (open lunch and dinner, closed Fri), where fresh tagliatelle and *pappardelle* and roasted meats are served at reasonable prices.

Ristorante da Ventura (Via Aggiunti 30, 0575 742 560. Open lunch and dinner Mon-Fri, Sun. Average L70,000), probably provides Sansepolcro's best meal, though at a price. This busy place also serves pasta with wild mushrooms (mostly ceps) or truffles, along with excellent grilled meats.

Ristorante Al Coccio (Via Aggiunti 83, 0575 741 468. Open lunch & dinner Mon, Tue, Thur-Sun. Average L35,000) has recently changed ownership and its attempt at moving upmarket hasn't really come off – though the *ravioli al fumo*, with smoked fish, are worth a try.

You can top off, or warm up to, a meal at the **Enoteca Guidi** (Via L Pacioli 44, 0575 741 086. Open summer 9am-10pm, winter 9am-8pm, Mon, Tue, Thur-Sun. Average L25,000) and sample the local red or white Terra di Piero della Francesca or the home-made vin santo.

Monterchi

No Tuscan town craves to be as associated with a single piece of art as this cluster of hilltop homes on the road between Arezzo and Sansepolcro does with Piero della Francesca's delicate œuvre *Madonna del Parto*.

Monterchi, whose name stems from its earliest beginnings, Mons Ercules, a centre for the cult worship of the pagan figure of Hercules, has indeed made herculean efforts to create a multimedia centre in the local school for the study of Sansepolcro's famous son. The **Museo Madonna del Parto** (Via Reglia 1, Monterchi 0575 70713. Open 9am-1pm, 2-7pm, daily. Admission L5,000) is a veritable trove for aficionados. Centre stage, of course, is the rotund Madonna, her hand protectively and proudly rested on the slit in her dress revealing her pregnant state, and circled symmetrically by angels lightly drawing back a canopy.

Off the tourist trail in **Montevarchi**. *See p232.*

This is Piero's sublime rendition of a sacred yet rustic maternal figure, the only one of its kind in Renaissance art. The exhibit also contains a detailed and fascinating display of the work involved in the restoration of a number of Piero's pieces, including his masterpiece *The Legend of the True Cross*, displayed in the church of San Francesco (*see chapter* **Arezzo**).

Anghiari

Perched on a hill overlooking the Valtiberina and Sansepolcro from the south, Anghiari's dominant position and impressive walls made it an impregnable stronghold, from which Florence controlled Tuscany's far east, following its victory over the Milanese Visconti family in the Battle of Anghiari in 1440. Leonardo consigned the event to posterity in his (unfinished) rendition on display in the Palazzo Vecchio in Florence. Today, thanks to its maze of vaulted alleys, it is easier just to wander through Anghiari than to follow the earnest attempts at signposting. Squeezed in just behind the central Piazza del Popolo, seat of the Palazzo Pretorio, is the curiously asymmetrical, thirteenth-century Chiesa della Badia.

Today, Anghiari is renowned for its traditions of wood crafting and antique furniture restoration. It hosts the annual Valtiberina crafts market in late April and an antique fair on the third Sunday of every other month. The **Museo Statale di Palazzo Taglieschi** (Piazza Mameli 16, 0575 788 001. Open 3-7pm Tue-Fri; 9am-1pm, 3-7pm Sat, Sun; Tue, Thur 9am-1pm by appointment. Admission L4,000) is essentially a crafts museum containing numerous local artefacts, a polychrome terracotta by Della Robbia, and a striking wooden sculpture of the Madonna by Jacopo della Quercia.

Across from the museum is the Istituto Statale d'Arte, a training school for the restoration of furniture and wooden antiques. The products of this technique can be seen in the workshop of Mastro Santi (Via Nova 8), who specialises in carving and marquetry.

Anghiari's other significant traditional and commercial draw is the proud workmanship of its woven and naturally dyed textiles, exemplified by the **Busatti** store-cum-factory (Via Mazzini 14, 0575 788 013. Open 4-8pm Mon; 9am-1pm, 4-8pm Tue-Sat). The deafening shuttle looms in its workroom, some of them almost a century old, produce everything from wedding lace to curtain fabrics, using only natural fibres.

The popular **Locanda Castello di Sorci** (0575 789 066/fax 0575 788 022. Open lunch & dinner, closed Mon. Average L30,000) is situated on the estate of a fifteenth-century castle just off the main Arezzo-Sansepolcro route. Owners Primetto and Gabriella want to serve 'the masses tired of fast foods the taste of natural products and fresh air'.

All in the detail

In 1992, on the 500th anniversary of Piero della Francesca's death, British television aired a fascinating documentary on the life and work of a painter previously unknown to a wider public. The 1990s have, in fact, seen an enormous and justifiable swell in interest in Piero's art, both in Italy and abroad. Born in around 1420, what little is known of the artist's early and private life is sketchy at best. He shied away from the limelight and the big city, going to Florence in 1439 for training but soon returning to his native Sansepolcro. Piero's preference lay with more peripheral noble courts such as the Este in Ferrara and the Montefeltro in Urbino and, of course, Arezzo.

He is perhaps best known for the precision and the quasi-maniacal obsession with detail in every aspect of his compositions. Perspective, proportion, light and shade, colour and shape: according to Piero, all needed to be portrayed following strict and unchanging mathematical and geometric laws. These in turn derived – as he would theorise in two treatises written in his later life – from a superior rational order that regulates a universal cosmic harmony.

Though his approach was highly humanist and rationalist, his subject matter remained almost exclusively sacred, with only the odd commissioned portrait of a patron. He was strongly influenced by Flemish and Northern European art, as well as by classicism in architectural design and, in turn, had a profound influence on twentieth-century cubist and metaphysical painters like Cézanne, Seurat and De Chirico.

His reclusive, low-key lifestyle was refreshing, during a period crammed with exhibitionists and polemicists. Piero's legacy is one of lasting innovation. His quiet death in Sansepolcro on 12 October 1492 coincided with another event taking place across the ocean: the discovery of the New World.

WHERE TO SEE HIS WORK

Arezzo *Legend of the True Cross* (1455-56), church of San Francesco; *Santa Maria Maddalena* (1460), Duomo. *See page 239.*
Sansepolcro *Madonna della Misericordia* (1445-60) and *Resurrection* (1460), both in Museo Civico.
Monterchi *Madonna del Parto* (1455-60), Museo Madonna del Parto.
Florence *Portraits of Battista Sforza and Federico da Montefeltro* (1465-72) and *Triumphs of Federico da Montefeltro and Battista Sforza* (1465-75), Uffizi.
Urbino *Flagellation of Christ* (1455-60), and *Madonna di Senigallia* (c1470), Galleria Nazionale delle Marche.
Rimini *San Sigismondo and Sigismondo Pandolfo Malatesta* (1451), Tempio Malatestiano.
Milan *Madonna with Child and Six Saints* (1472-74), Pinacoteca di Brera.
Venice *St Jerome* (1450), Gallerie dell'Accademia.
Paris *Portrait of Sigismondo Pandolfo Malatesta*, (1451), Louvre.
London *Baptism of Christ* (1445-50), National Gallery.

The L30,000 menu changes daily and features a rota of Tuscan classics such as *tagliolini con fagioli* (thin tagliatelle with beans), *ribollita* or *farro* with polenta. The quality of the cooking is good, as are the views, and it's a refreshing place for a break if you're in the area.

The Valdichiana

Monte San Savino

Typically round and enclosed, Monte San Savino is a prominent town provincially, though its Renaissance heyday was brief, and coincided with the commercial patronage and religious power exercised by the Di Monte family in the late 1400s and 1500s. The town's two main architectural attractions, which bear the family's imprint, face each other along the climbing Corso Sangallo.

The quintessentially Renaissance Palazzo Di Monte, today Palazzo Comunale, designed in 1515-17 by Antonio Sangallo the Elder, contains an arcaded courtyard in its interior, through which you reach hanging gardens and an open-air theatre overlooking a cypress-dotted landscape. Across from it is the Vasari-like Loggia dei Mercanti, attributed to architect and sculptor Andrea Sansovino (1460-1529), Monte San Savino's most eminent son. Sansovino's hand also retouched the nearby Piazza di Monte and helped embellish the Church of Santa Chiara with two terracottas – the Madonna and Saints Lawrence, Sebastian and Rocco.

A summer sequence of events, known as the Estate Savinese, includes open-air concerts and films in July, the Festival Musicale in the first half of August and the Sagra della Porchetta all-you-can-eat roast suckling pig celebration in mid-September.

The town is traditionally known for its engraved pottery, designed in delicate floral motifs on display at the **Ceramiche Artistiche Lapucci**

Cortona

Both refined Tuscan and rustic Umbrian in feel, architecture and dialect, Cortona belongs in a league of its own. Its jumble of irregular, angular buildings, its windswept city walls, its layered urban development and its strategic position dominating the Valdichiana distinguish it among central Italy's historic cities.

Most probably founded as an Umbrian fortress, Cortona grew into an important Etruscan outpost around the eighth century BC and then passed under Roman rule. Following its depredation by the Goths, Cortona thrived as a free community from the eleventh century on and, though sacked by Arezzo in 1258, it bounced back and was taken over and quickly sold by the King of Naples to Florence in 1411. Since then, it has prospered safely behind its walls.

Today Cortona is a quintessential *città d'arte*, which carefully balances tradition and innovation. The local authorites have healthily channelled Cortona's constant foreign presence and even inserted events by foreign study groups into its cultural calendar. If on the one hand it hosts qualified art exhibitions and nationally known antiques and handicraft fairs, it also provides a spectacular venue for the final days of the Umbria Jazz Festival and for the sizzling Sagra della Bistecca, a Chianina beef feast.

Things to see

Cortona is best absorbed while sitting on the staircase leading up to the crenellated clock tower of the heavy-set Palazzo Comunale, and looking out over uneven Piazza della Repubblica where town life inevitably centres.

Adjacent is Piazza Signorelli, containing the arcaded Teatro Signorelli, both dutifuly honouring Cortona's foremost offspring – High Renaissance artist Luca Signorelli (c1445-1523). On the piazza is the small but eccentric **Museo dell'Accademia Etrusca** (0575 630 415. Open 1 Apr-30 Sept 10am-7pm, 1 Oct-30 Mar 9am-1pm, 3-5pm, Tue-Sun. Admission L8,000) located in the Palazzo Casali. It includes local Etruscan findings, such as a bronze lamp decorated with sirens and satyrs, and spans from ancient Egyptian remnants to visionary Futurist pieces by Gino Severini (1883-1966), another of Cortona's natives.

A few steps on is the Piazza del Duomo which opens onto a picturebook view of the valley. Facing the rather bland Duomo is the **Museo Diocesano** (0575 62830. Open Apr-Sept 9.30am-1pm, 3.30-7pm Tue-Sun; Oct 10am-1pm, 3.30-6pm; Nov-Mar 10am-1pm, 3-5pm Tue-Sun. Admission L8,000), home to Beato Angelico's glorious *Annunciation*, and representative works by Signorelli and Pietro Lorenzetti.

More of Cortona's rewarding sights are found scaling Via Berrettini towards the Fortezza Medicea. Among these is the fifteenth-century church of San Nicolò with its delicate courtyard and baroque-roofed interior, containing a Signorelli altarpiece.

(Corso Sangallo 8/10, 0575 844 375. Open daily; ring doorbell for admission).

The medieval **Castello di Gargonza** (0575 847 021/fax 0575 847 054/gargonza@teta.it), has been renovated and turned into group of furnished mini-apartments, with some singles (L145,000-L165,000) and doubles (L175,000-L195,000).

Lucignano

Tiny Lucignano is as classically Tuscan as Tuscan towns come. A stroll along its concentric alleys set in a remarkable elliptical urban plan inevitably leads up to the crumbling staircase of the church of the Collegiata di San Michele. Behind it is the thirteenth-century church of San Francesco, in its barn-like, striped simplicity.

The **Museo Civico** (0575 838 001. Open summer 10.30am-12.30pm, 4-7pm daily; winter 10.30am-12.30pm, 3.30-6.30pm daily, or on request. Admission L5,000) next door is inside the Palazzo Comunale and exhibits Lucignano's symbol, the Albero di San Francesco, a large late-Gothic golden reliquary representing a cross, along with wooden panels by Signorelli and a triptych by Bartolo di Fredi.

Within a few metres is **Albergo e Osteria Da Totó**, a delightful family-run hotel with competitive prices (Piazza del Tribunale 6, 0575 836 763/fax 0575 836 988. Rates single L80,000; double L100,000) set in a converted monastery containing a small swimming pool. Owner and chef Lorenzo Totó takes pride in his herb-based cooking. Three multi-course menus at L25,000, L35,000, and L45,000 start with *primi* such as *ravioli con ricotta e borragine* (with borage) or *gnocchi alle erbe*. Save some energy to investigate his impressive range of 54 fruit-, flower- and root-based grappe.

Foiano della Chiana

Foiano's buildings and steeples are distinguished by the warm, reddish tones of their *cotto* bricks. Its oval shape centres on Piazza Cavour, dominated by the Palazzo delle Logge, formerly a Medici

Cortona's only flat surface is lively Via Nazionale, dotted with antique and wood-crafting stores. Among these, at number 54, Giulio Lucarini's laboratory showcases traditional terracottas in typical yellow-red sunflower patterns. Aromas emanate from the *pasticceria* at number 64, which makes sublime pastries.

Where to stay

Albergo Athens *Via Sant'Antonio 12 (0575 630 508/ fax 604 547).* **Rates** *single* L40,000; *double* L60,000. **No credit cards.**
The only budget option within Cortona's walls offers barren dorm-like rooms at unbeatable prices.
Hotel Italia *Via Ghibellina 7 (0575 630 254/fax 0575 630 564).* **Rates** *single* L90,000; *double* L130,000. **Credit** AmEx, MC, V.
Recently renovated with rooftop views from top-floor rooms and terrace.
Hotel Sabrina *Via Roma 37 (0575 630 397/fax 0575 604 627).* **Rates** *single* L75,000-L85,000; *double* L105,000-L120,000. **Credit** AmEx, MC, V.
Small but tastefully decorated rooms. Same family-run operation as Hotel Italia (*see above*).
Hotel San Luca *Piazza Garibaldi 1 (0575 630 460/fax 630 105).* **Rates** *single* L95,000; *double* L145,000. **Credit** AmEx, DC, MC, V.
Generic and modernish, but spectacularly placed overlooking valley.
Hotel San Michele *Via Guelfa 15 (0575 604 348/ fax 630 147).* **Rates** *single* L120,000; *double* L220,000. **Credit** AmEx, DC, MC, V.
Classy and central: unique 1700s ceiling in breakfast room.

Where to eat

Osteria del Teatro *Via Maffei 5 (0575 630 556).* **Open** noon-2.30pm, 7-9.30pm, Mon, Tue, Thur-Sun. **Average** L40,000. **Credit** AmEx, DC, JCB, MC, V.
The place for a memorable dining experience in a locale with an operatic theme. Pastas are rolled daily, the *antipasto misto* of Tuscan *crostoni* is a winner and the *straccetti* (delicately shredded beef) al Chianti are superb. The honey-nut *semifreddo della casa* rounds a meal off superbly.
Preludio *Via Guelfa 11 (0575 630 104).* **Open** June-Oct 12.30-3.30pm, 7.30pm-midnight, Tue-Sun; Nov-May 7.30pm-midnight Tue-Sun. **Average** L50,000. **Credit** AmEx, MC, V.
Offers an interesting variety of options. The gnocchi with chestnuts or funghi porcini are worth trying.
Tonino *Piazza Garibaldi 1 (0575 630 500).* **Open** lunch & dinner daily. **Average** L50,000. **Credit** AmEx, DC, MC, V.
Good for Tuscan *antipastissimo* and lovely views over the valley.
Trattoria Dardano *Via Dardano 24 (0575 601 944).* **Open** lunch & dinner Mon, Tue, Thur-Sun. **Average** L30,000. **No credit cards.**
Locals' haunt with home cooking and reasonable prices.

Events

Copperware fair (late April to early May); **Giostra dell'Archidado**, crossbow competition (late May); **Umbria Jazz** (late Jul); **Antiques Fair** (late Aug-early Sep); **Sagra della Bistecchа** (mid Aug).

hunting lodge. Today, it houses the Fototeca Furio del Furia, an engrossing display of early twentieth-century snapshots of rural life in Italy, recently expanded and now even available on a CD-ROM developed by state broadcaster RAI.

Just outside the walls is Foiano's other main draw, the neoclassical Collegiata di San Martino. It houses a vintage Andrea della Robbia glazed terracotta, the Madonna of the Girdle, and Signorelli's last work, *Coronation of the Virgin* (1523), in which della Francesca's influence shines through in the cloaked Madonna protecting a huddle of followers. Foiano's workshops compete for best allegorical figure in its carnival on the three Sundays leading to Lent.

Castiglion Fiorentino

Castiglion Fiorentino (formerly Castiglion Aretino and, briefly, Castiglion Perugino) is a bustling mid-sized town set against the lower Appenines and overlooked by its impressive Cassero tower – situated in a quiet corner at the town's highest point.

Its Etruscan origins were reaffirmed by recent excavation of walls and the discovery of artefacts dating to the fifth century BC, now on display in the crypt of the Chiesa di San Angelo al Cassero. Above this is the **Pinacoteca Comunale** (Via del Cassero, 0575 657 466. Open summer 10am-12.30pm, 4-6pm; winter 10am-12.30pm, 3.30-6pm; closed Mon. Admission L5,000), which has paintings by Giotto's godson and follower Taddeo Gaddi and fifteenth-century artist Bartolomeo della Gatta along with some gold and bronze relics.

Castiglion Fiorentino's most pleasant spot is the Loggiato Vasariano in the Piazza del Municipio. Just past the Loggiato is the minuscule **Panificio Melloni** (Via San Michele 48), with its alluring bakery products piled up behind a tiny wooden door. At the lower end of town, near the Porta Fiorentina and next to the thirteenth-century church of San Francesco Da Muzzicone, **Piazza San Francesco 7** (0575 658 403. Open lunch & dinner Mon, Wed-Sun. Average L42,000) is your best bet for refuelling.

Arezzo

There's more to Tuscany's golden city than meets the eye.

Arezzo has never appeared quite as glamorous as its Tuscan neighbours to the north and west. In the past its military prowess and artistic achievements have been underestimated and an ungracious Dante even went so far as to call the Aretini people *botoli ringhiosi* (growling and waspish) – this despite the fact that the city sheltered him in exile. However, Arezzo has never succumbed easily in battle and prides itself on rebelling six times while under Florentine domination. The city has prospered economically, produced and hosted eminent artists and even had its share of savvy political leaders, without being driven by an uncontrollable desire to become a regional powerhouse.

Today, the city has a welcoming simplicity; there is nothing exalted about its buildings, but **Piazza Grande** is one of Italy's most eclectic squares. While it is not overrun with visitors, those that come find no sense of grandiosity; more a feeling that the Aretini know how they want their city and have worked hard to keep it the way it is.

The city has embarked on an ambitious programme to restore a number of its palazzi and its main artistic attraction: Piero della Francesca's fresco cycle. Arezzo isn't really a *citta' d'arte* as are Florence and Siena – it lives primarily on income from its industrial and commercial activities. Arezzo is known in Italy more for its goldsmiths, jewellers and its antiques market than for Piero's masterpieces.

DARK DAYS & DECADENT GLORY

Strategically built at the intersection of four fertile valleys – the Casentino, Valdarno, Valtiberina and Valdichiana – Arezzo has seen much external conquest with only a brief period of city-state independence. In the seventh century BC, the settlement of Arretium was a significant member of the

Useful information

Tourist information

Azienda di Promozione Turistica (APT)
Piazza della Repubblica 22 (0575 377 678/fax 20839/info@arezzo.turismo.toscana.it). **Open** *Oct-Mar* 9am-1pm, 3-6.30pm, Mon-Sat; 9am-1pm 1st Sun of month; *Apr-Sept* 9am-1pm, 3-7pm, Mon-Sat; 9am-1pm Sun.

Transport

Bicycle Hire: **City Bike** *Via de' Cenci 16 (0575 24541).*
Buses: *Piazza della Repubblica.*
There are lines heading out to rural areas from the terminal opposite the station. For info and tickets call ATAM Point in the same square (0575 382651).
Car Hire: **Avis** *Piazza della Repubblica (0575 354 232)*; **Hertz** *Via Gobetti 35 (0575 27577).*
Railway Station: *Piazza della Repubblica (0575 27353).* The InterCity and InterRegionale trains take 40 minutes to reach Florence; local trains make more stops and the journey takes an hour (IC trains require a supplement).

Markets

Every Saturday there's a general market selling clothes, food, flowers and household goods. On the first Sunday of each month and the previous Saturday the city centre is completely taken over by the Antiques Fair. The APT has a handy Italian-English glossary of terms and a map with individual salespoint listings useful to get around the maze of stores and stands.

Festivals

Stagione teatrale at Teatro Petrarca *(0575 23975)* (Nov-Mar).
Stagione teatrale at Piccolo Teatro *(0575 27721)* An annual festival of one-act plays (Oct-Dec).
Arezzo Wave *(0575 911005).* A vibrant festival of indie music in the stadium in early July.
Giostra del Saracino Arezzo's heated jousting tournament (June, Sept, *see chapter* **Tuscany By Season**).
Concorso Polifonico Internazionale Guido d'Arezzo International choral competition (Aug).

Emergency services

Ambulance Croce Bianca *(0575 22660)*; Misericordia *(0575 24242).*
Carabinieri *(112).*
Police *(113).*
Health Services San Donato Hospital *(0575 305 747)*; USL (Unita Sanitaria Locale – local health office) *(0575 3051).*

Piero della Francesca's Mary Magdalene, *in the* **Duomo**. *See p240 & p235* **All in the detail**.

Etruscan federation. It soon caught the eye of upstart Romans moving north. Arezzo was among the first to switch allegiances to become a Roman military stronghold and the town flourished as an Imperial economic outpost. By 89 BC its people were granted honorary Roman citizenship, which brought with it an amphitheatre, baths and fortified walls. With the glory came decadence. Arezzo's trade routes were supplanted and its territory overrun by waves of barbarians, who successfully undermined its development by dismembering and depopulating it. The darkest days came under the Lombards in the sixth century, but gradually a feudal economic system centred on the secular control of the clergy and, to a lesser extent, of the landed nobility, pulled the city from its slump and paved the way for Arezzo's 'golden age' in the 1200s.

The turning point came in 1100, when the emerging merchant class started to question its subservience to Arezzo's clerical-feudal overlords. Secular power began to shift to the budding bourgeoisie and in 1192 the Commune was established. There was extensive building and Arezzo began to take on its current urban contours. However, once again a foreign power, this time Florence, set its sights on the city. The two clashed in the Battle of Campaldino in 1289, which left Arezzo still independent, but from which it never fully recovered. Political prestige and military assertiveness returned briefly under the rule of Bishop Tarlati (1312-27), under whom Arezzo had another spurt of cultural activity. Following Tarlati's death, internal strife brought Arezzo's sale to Florence in 1384.

Political submission did not, however, equal artistic or cultural paralysis, it meant that Arezzo's natives went elsewhere to achieve success. Among these, most notable were Giorgio Vasari (1511-74), the Medicis' official architect and historiographer (*see p241* **The life of the artist**), and Pietro Aretino (1492-1556), a court poet and satirist (*see p243* **Fine lines**). Henceforth, in fact, the city's artistic and cultural achievements were carried out under the Medici and then the Lorraines. Foreign domination meant Arezzo's population turned in on itself, growing rural and conservative. The city only regained a strong sense of identity in the twentieth century, when it reasserted itself as a manufacturing and gold-producing centre.

Sights

Churches

Duomo

Piazza Duomo (0575 23991). **Open** 7am-12.30pm, 3-6.30pm, daily.

More than 250 years in the making, Arezzo's Gothic Duomo was started in 1277 on a site previously occupied by an early Christian church. Work was pushed along considerably by Arezzo's two real power brokers at the time: bishops Guglielmo degli Ubertini (1278-89) and Guido Tarlati (1312-27), but the finishing touches were made only in the early 1500s. Most of the work on the interior was undone and recast during the course of the next 300 years. The Duomo's campanile was erected in the mid 1800s and its façade was completed in 1914.

The effect of the Duomo's size and the vertical thrust of its ogival vaulted ceilings is inspiring, though there's barely enough light to appreciate it. The little light there is comes through the exquisite stained-glass windows (c1515-20) by Guillaume di Marcillat. The Duomo's real attractions are along the left aisle. Screened off from the rest of the church, the Cappella della Madonna del Conforto guards a terracotta Madonna. It is kept good company by a number of less emotionally charged Della Robbia school terracottas. Just beyond is Vasari's grandiose choir stall, Bishop Tarlati's monumental funerary urn and next to that, almost hidden, another of Piero della Francesca's precious creations: *Mary Magdalene* (c1465), holding the ointment for Christ's feet.

San Francesco

Piazza San Francesco (0575 20630). **Open** 8.30am-noon, 2-6.30pm, daily.

No visit to Arezzo is complete without stepping into San Francesco to take in what's visible of Piero della Francesca's magnum opus: *The Legend of the True Cross* (c1453-64). This unassuming church has had a convoluted history: begun by Franciscan friars in the 1200s, its interior was adorned with frescoes, chapels and shrines throughout the 1500s thanks to the largesse of Arezzo's merchant class. Following a fire in 1556, the church was overhauled, its chapels destroyed and its walls whitewashed, though most of the art was left unharmed. By the nineteenth century San Francesco had been deconsecrated and was being used as a military barracks.

In the 1980s, state-of-the-art restoration techniques were employed on the *Legend of the True Cross* (there is a fascinating exhibition about this in **Monterchi**, *see* **Arrezo Province**) and now the authorities promise that the painstaking work will soon reveal Piero's fresco in its entirety – presumably in 2000. The left wall of the three-part series was unveiled in 1998 and can be visited with a tour (mandatory advance booking on 0575 355 668/fax 299 973 or at the Basilica office, open 9.30-11.30am, 3-5pm, Wed-Fri; 9-11.30am, 2.30-5pm, Sat; 2-5pm Sun). Visits are every half-hour and in Italian and cost L10,000). The fresco cycle was begun in 1453, the same year that Constantinople fell to the Ottoman Turks, and interprets the collective fear felt throughout the Christian world. The artist's focus is on visual effect and metaphor more than on narrative.

Pieve di Santa Maria

Corso Italia (0575 22629). **Open** 8am-12.30pm, 3-6.30pm, daily.

A striking example of Romanesque architecture erected mostly in the twelfth and thirteenth centuries. The

The life of the artist

There are few Tuscan towns that do not somehow bear the imprint of Giorgio Vasari (born Arezzo, 1511; died Florence, 1574). His skills included painting, architecture and biographical writing. Vasari spent most of his life in Florence as the official Medici architect, but had free reign to travel and take care of his interests in Tuscany and beyond. In his youth he swore there was nothing he would not attempt to draw, wherever it was and, true to his word, Vasari's output was prodigious. His canvases are admittedly soon forgotten, but he spawned a school of followers who replicated his technique. His trademark *logge* are striking, and seem to be everywhere; the best are the Palazzo delle Logge in Arezzo's Piazza Grande and the panoramic loggia in Castiglion Fiorentino. He also designed the **Uffizi**, Michelangelo's tomb in **Santa Croce** and the Palazzo dei Cavalieri in Pisa.

Vasari's vocation, however, was writing. For most of his later life he worked on one of the most influential biographies of Renaissance artists and architects ever published: *Le Vite de' più Eccellenti Pittori, Scultori e Architettori* (*Lives of the Artists*, 1550, revised 1568). Its anecdotal detail and insight into the changing cultural attitudes and artistic trends of the day remains an invaluable source of information and, of course, the last of the eminent *Lives* he writes about is that of 'Giorgio Vasari, painter and architect from Arezzo'.

façade is built in chalky sandstone and the weather has taken its toll: the loggias look about to crumble. These are ordered in three increasingly busy layers set above five arcades. The ornate columns that hold up the loggias, all 68 with an eccentric motif, reach a climax in the bell tower, known as *delle cento buche* (of the 100 holes). The stark simplicity of the interior is pervaded by a grey light, which just illuminates a gold-framed polyptych by Sienese painter Piero Lorenzetti, the *Madonna with Child and Saints* (c1320). Beneath it in the crypt is a bust of San Donato (1346) by an ancestor of Arezzo's living goldsmiths.

San Domenico

Piazza San Domenico (0575 22906). **Open** 7am-1pm, 3.30-6pm, Mon-Sat; 8am-1pm, 3.30-6pm, Sun, public hols.

San Domenico was started by Dominicans in 1275, around the same time as their Franciscan brothers were getting underway with San Francesco. It faces a simple, open square and has an attractive quaintness about it, accentuated by its uneven Gothic campanile with two fourteenth-century bells. At the end of the long nave is a *Crucifix* by a young Cimabue (c1260).

Santissima Annunziata

Via Garibaldi (0575 26774). **Open** 8am-12.30pm, 3.30-7pm, daily.

A miracle in which a statue of the Madonna began to weep before a passing pilgrim apparently occured on this site in 1460, in what was then an oratory belonging to the company of Santissima Annunziata. The owners lost no time in capitalising on the event and began building a church the same year, entrusting the job to Bartolomeo della Gatta. Inspired by Bramante's work in Rome, he designed the classical atrium seen upon entering the church, whose right wall is broken up by a precious Guillaume di Marcillat stained-glass window, the *Virgin's Wedding*.

Santa Maria delle Grazie

Via Santa Maria (0575 20620). **Open** 8am-noon, 4-7pm, daily.

On the site of an ancient sacred fount known as the Fonte Tecta to Arezzo's south, the religious complex built around Santa Maria delle Grazie is known for having the Renaissance's first porticoed courtyard. Started in 1428, the series of religious buildings were imposed by San Bernardino of Siena on the recalcitrant Aretini. In a well-publicised gesture San Bernardino marched over from San Francesco, brandishing a wooden cross and proceeded to destroy the fount and replace it with a *Madonna della Misericordia* by local artist Parri di Spinello. Fortunately, the enlightened vision of Antonio da Maiano, who created the loggia and was one of the Renaissance's foremost architects, managed to reconcile the church's late-Gothic, essentially medieval design (partly by covering it up) with the then emergent, classical style. Hence what resulted from San Bernardino's inquisitorial tactics has coexisted harmoniously with the thinking of the humanist artist who succeeded him and carried out his fervent wish.

Museums

Casa Vasari

Via XX Settembre 55 (0575 409 040). **Open** 9am-7pm Mon, Wed-Sat; 9am-1pm Sun. **Admission** free.

Arezzo's own multitalented Medici insider, Giorgio Vasari thought well to buy, furnish and paint himself a house shortly before entering Florence's big league in 1564. Today it houses the Archivio e Museo Vasariano, with a number of contemporary paintings by the master's school, some scattered artefacts and a garden at the back. The star attraction though is the *piano nobile*, with its richly decorated Sala del Trionfo della Virtù (Room of the Triumph of Virtue).

Just down Via XX Settembre from Vasari's house, at number 37, you'll be forgiven for missing an inconspicuous building, which is said to be the poet Pietro Aretino's childhood home (*see p243* **Fine lines**), before he set out to court the powerful, make enemies and confirm that the pen is mightier than the sword.

Museo Statale d'Arte Mediovale e Moderna

Via San Lorentino 8 (0575 409 050). **Open** 9am-7pm Tue-Sat; 9am-1pm Sun. **Admission** L8,000; free under-18s, over-60s.

Arezzo's main art museum doesn't really live up to its name, offering little medieval and nothing modern. The Palazzo Bruni-Ciocchi that houses it is built around a courtyard attributed to humanist architect Bernardo Rossellino (*see chapter* **Chianti & Siena province**), and has a Gothic-era first floor and Renaissance upper levels. Used as a customs house in the early nineteenth century, the palazzo was completed by the influential Ciocchi family from Monte San Savino. Its collection amounts to a smattering of representative, though in no way memorable, paintings, frescoes, metalwork and sculptures by Aretines. The ground floor has an assemblage of Romanesque capitols, stone carvings and fragments of sculptures found in the area. The baroque vestibule on the first floor is dominated by Vasari's *Wedding Feast of Ahasuerus and Esther* (1548). Just past it is a series of rooms with thirteenth- to seventeenth-century glazed ceramics, some terracottas from the Della Robbia school and a rare Medicean porcelain. The only reason to venture one more flight up would be to get a taste of Mannerism with Rosso Fiorentino's *Madonna and Child.*

Museo Archeologico Mecenate

Via Margaritone 10 (0575 20882). **Open** 9am-2pm Mon-Sat; 9am-1pm Sun, public hols. **Admission** L8,000; free under-18s, over-60s.

A feeling of dusty abandonment pervades this assortment of artefacts, mostly Roman and Etruscan. The museum is named for Maecenas, an Arezzo native, ancient Roman patron of poets such as Virgil and Horace and counsellor to Emperor Augustus. Its two floors follow the curve of the amphitheatre in what used to be an Olivetan monastery. The Etruscan collection comprises votive figurines, vases and funerary urns in terracotta, alabaster and travertine, as well as a unique coin collection. More noteworthy are the ceramics, which include a number of ancient Roman vases dating back to the first century BC and known as coralline thanks to their deep red painted hues.

Monuments

Piazza Grande

On first impact, Arezzo's sloping Piazza Grande is a visual feast of architectural irregularity. A second glance reveals an odd harmony to the square's (or rather trapezoid's) steep gradient and jumble of styles; the end result is extremely easy on the eye. It is the product of the piazza's growth from peripheral food market to the city's political heart. The architectural styles begin with the arcaded, rounded back of the Romanesque Pieve di Santa Maria visible in

How many steps to Heaven? Arezzo's **Piazza Grande** *has an odd harmony.*

the square's lowest point next to the Fontana Pubblica erected in the sixteenth century. The eye moves over to the baroque Palazzo del Tribunale, and next to it the Palazzo della Fraternità dei Laici designed mostly by Bernardo Rossellino. Unsurprisingly, Vasari had a hand in Piazza Grande as well. His is the typically arcaded Palazzo delle Logge, which presides over the assortment of medieval homes around the rest of the square.

Like Siena, Arezzo holds its own historic event in its main square. The **Giostra del Saracino** (June, Sept) is one of Italy's more famous jousting tournaments. It claims to be rooted in raids carried out by and against the Saracens during the Crusades in the 1200s, although the first Giostra historically took place in 1535 (*see chapter* **Tuscany by Season**).

Anfiteatro Romano

Located on the city's south east side and currently visible only through a gate, it takes some imagination to picture what the Roman amphitheatre must have looked like packed with up to 10,000 people in the second century. Its travertine and sandstone blocks were overrun by Germanic tribes in the fifth century and plundered by Medici Grand Duke Cosimo I for the **Fortezza Medicea** (*see below*) following the Florentines' decision to strengthen their hold on Arezzo in 1531. Today, its elliptical shape and the stage can be made out, along with parts of what must have been the stands.

Fortezza Medicea

When the Medici finally decided to turn Arezzo into a duchy in 1531, they set about improving the city's defences. The introduction of cannons prompted the Florentine family to embark on another (the eighth) stint of wall-building. The final perimeter is visible in sections around the city and dominated by the architecturally revolutionary Fortezza Medicea (1538-1560). The fortress's pentagonal form, punctuated by four doors and seven mighty bastions, was designed by Antonio da Sangallo the Elder and required the razing of towers, alleys and medieval palazzi in the surrounding hill of San Donato. The result is eminently rationalistic and highly pragmatic.

Parks & Gardens

Il Prato

City authorities have gone to great lengths to clean up Arezzo's only park, which lies between the Duomo and the Fortezza Medicea with views overlooking the town. During the daytime it offers respite to those determined to get to the town's top, while on summer nights it hosts the frenzied outdoor activity of the **Casina del Prato** (*see below*).

Restaurants

Arezzo's culinary specialities draw heavily on the products of the four rich valleys which encircle it. First courses almost always include pasta variations with *funghi porcini* (ceps) or *tartufo nero* (black truffle). For seconds, no self-respecting *osteria* in Arezzo is without a local Chianina steak on its menu, and oddities such as *grifi* (stewed cheek of veal) and *zampucci* (pig leg) occasionally feature.

Antica Osteria L'Agania

Via Mazzini 10 (0575 295 381). **Open** noon-2.30pm, 7-10.30pm, Tue-Sun. **Average** L32,000. **Credit** AmEx, DC, MC, V.

This cosy two-level hideaway exudes warmth in its traditional décor and no-frills service. The primi, such as the *tagliatelle al tartufo* or *funghi porcini* are more mainstream than the secondi – *grifi con polenta*.

Fine lines

Born in Arezzo in 1492 into a family of cobblers, but claiming to be the illegitimate son of a noble, Pietro Aretino was a controversial court poet and satirist, whose biting verses were feared, but whose company was coveted by popes and princes alike. He left Arezzo at the age of 12, never to return, and wandered the country working as a waiter, a singer and a dishwasher, with numerous run-ins with the law.

His early, irreverent writings drew the attention of Pope Leo X, who in 1512 brought him to Rome as the papal poet. Aretino was quick to settle in and surround himself with sycophants and servants. His double-edged, caustic writings and his penchant for blackmail and *imbroglio* earned him the respect, but also the hatred, of the powerful, to the point where a failed attempt on his life convinced him to leave Rome. In 1527 he moved to Venice, Europe's most cosmopolitan and degenerate city at the time, and soon became a literary superstar.

His *Ragionamenti* (Discussions) are a denigratory attack against his previous patrons, delivered through apparently innocuous conversations between commoners. Aretino's finest hour came with his *Letters* – a slew of custom-made missives, ranging from the seductive to the insulting, written on demand and fuelled by his insatiable desire for fame and fortune. Aretino's life was spent riding that fine line between adulation and blackmail, ostracism and idolatry. He embodied the very vices he saw in others and wrote about so fervently. When the conformist and hypocritical age known as the Counter-Reformation set in, Aretino's fortunes turned. He died in 1556 a poor man, not before reconciling himself with the papacy and confessing himself clean with his parish priest.

Buca di San Francesco

Via San Francesco 1 (0575 23271). **Open** noon-2.30pm Mon; noon-2.30pm, 7-9.30pm, Wed-Sun. **Average** L50-60,000. **Credit** AmEx, DC, MC, V.
Upmarket and touristy, La Buca offers variations on the classics, like roast chicken stuffed with herbs (from the Valdarno) and *zuppa di farro* (spelt soup).

Il Cantuccio

Via Madonna del Prato 76 (0575 26830). **Open** 12.30-2.30pm, 7-10.30pm, Mon, Tue, Thur-Sun. **Average** L35,000-L40,000. **Credit** AmEx, DC, MC, V.
Il Cantuccio's vaulted cellar is the city's most rustic. Home-made pasta offerings include *tortelloni alla Casentinese* (with potato filling) and *taglioloni in passato di fagiolini* (bean-based sauce).

Cecco

Corso Italia 215 (0575 20986). **Open** 12.30-2.30pm, 7.30-9.30pm, Tue-Sun. **Average** L25,000. **Credit** AmEx, DC, MC, V.
Conveniently located at the lower end of Corso Italia, Cecco's main pull is price. At L18,000 for the 'tourist menu', you can fill up on a standard pasta course, a meat and vegetable and even a fruit for dessert.

Sbarbacipolle

Via Garibaldi 120 (0575 299 154). **Open** 7am-8pm Mon-Sat. **Average** L15,000. **No credit cards.**
A colourful corner deli with a good selection of panini and cold dishes. Great for a quick bite and immensely popular with the locals.

Life is beautiful at **Caffè dei Costanti**.

Trattoria Il Saraceno

Via Mazzini 6A (0575 27644). **Open** 12.30-3pm, 7-11pm Mon, Tue, Thur-Sun. **Average** L40,000. **Credit** AmEx, DC, MC, V
Covered with photos of turn-of-the-century Arezzo, Il Saraceno offers fine food, including a funghi porcini soup, the *pici al cinghiale* (egg pasta in wild boar sauce with pine nuts and juniper) and the *fagioli cannellini all'uccelletto* (white beans in red sauce).

Il Torrino

Località Il Torrino 1 (0575 360 264). **Open** noon-3pm, 7-10pm, Tue-Sun. **Average** L40,000-45,000. **Credit** AmEx, DC, MC, V.
Up a windy road off the Arezzo-Sansepolcro route, Il Torrino is a vast, bright dining hall, unnervingly reminiscent of the hotel hall in *The Shining*. The food is anything but creepy. Try the *tagliolini al tartufo bianco* (with white truffles) and the *cappelli d'alpino* (large ravioli stuffed with ricotta, spinach and herbs in cream sauce), and for secondo, a *filetto alla ghiotta* (steak on a bed of porcini mushrooms).

Bars, enoteche & gelaterie

The wines produced in Arezzo's hinterland have always been held in lower esteem than their famous counterparts from Chianti and Siena. But things are changing, with affirmation of the Colli Aretini vintages and a consequent growth in the number and quality of Arezzo's wine bars.

Caffè dei Costanti

Piazza San Francesco 19-20 (0575 21660). **Open** *Oct-May* 7am-9pm Tue-Sun; *June-Sept* 7am-midnight Tue-Sun; closed 4-18 Aug. **Credit** AmEx, DC, JCB, MC, V.
The oldest café in Arezzo and a popular meeting place. The Costanti appeared in Benigni's *La Vita è Bella* and has since named a *gelato* after the movie and covered the barfront with Benigni memorabilia. Movie-mania aside, this is a wonderful, spacious tearoom that will outlive its current fame.

La Casina del Prato

Via Palagi 1, in the Prato (0575 299 757). **Open** 10am-2am Mon, Wed-Sun. **No credit cards.**
Set in the city's only green patch, this is an open-air summer hot spot overflowing with the hipper Aretini crowd. Some snacks are available.

Enoteca La Torre di Gnicche

Piaggia San Martino 8 (0575 352 035). **Open** noon-3pm, 6pm-1am, Mon, Tue, Thur-Sun. **Credit** DC, MC, V.
A tastefully decorated bar with a superb selection of local wines, including its standard-bearers Bricco di Gnicche, Bigattiera di Val d'Ambra and a number of Gratena reds. Warm food such as a superlative *zuppa di cipolle infornata* (onion soup), *pappa al pomodoro* and local *grifi* are also served here.

Enoteca VinoDivino

Via Cesalpino 19 (0575 299 598). **Open** 10am-10.30pm Mon-Sat. **Credit** AmEx, DC, MC, V.

VinoDivino's interior is covered in tastefully restored frescoes. A rotating 15-wine *degustazione* (tasting) includes some smooth Galatrona and Gratena reds.

Fiaschetteria de'Redi

Via de' Redi 10 (0575 355 012). **Open** noon-3.30pm, 7pm-midnight, Tue-Sat & 1st Sun of month; 7pm-midnight Sun. **Credit** DC, MC, V.
A bustling wine bar just off Corso Italia. Welcoming dark wood, relaxing tan walls and a good selection to boot. Also serves osteria-style food for about L25,000.

Il Gelato

Via dei Cenci 24 (0575 300 069). **Open** *summer* 11am-midnight Mon, Tue, Thur-Sun; *winter* 11am-1pm, 2.30-8pm, Mon, Tue, Thur-Sun. **No credit cards.**
An unassuming and always busy ice-cream parlour. The *pinolata* (with pine nuts) and *arancello al liquore* (liqueur orange) are worth a try.

St Anton Pub

Via Garibaldi 150 (0575 352 676). **Open** 7pm-1am Mon, Tue, Thur-Sun. **Credit** MC, V.
A sound choice for a drink with a young crowd.

Accommodation

Arezzo's accommodation is disappointing, with mostly middle-of-the-range, congress venue-type places. There's better choice outside the city walls.

Hotel Continentale

Piazza Guido Monaco 7 (0575 20251/fax 350 485). **Rates** *single* L100,000; *double* L160,000; *breakfast* L15,000. **Credit** AmEx, DC, MC, V.
Earnest attempts at refashioning the interior with artificial-looking wood and wall-to-wall carpeting have rendered the Continentale acceptable.

Hotel Milano

Via Madonna del Prato 83 (0575 26836/fax 21925). **Rates** *single* L140,000; *double* L200,000. **Credit** AmEx, DC, MC, V.
An overhaul and a name change to Cavalieri Palace Hotel are in the offing to make this place more luxurious. For now, beyond the cramped lobby, the rooms are probably the best choice within Arezzo's walls.

Val di Colle Residenza di Campagna

Località Bagnoro (tel/fax 0575 365 167). **Rates** *double* L230,000-L310,000. **Credit** AmEx, DC, MC, V.
The urge to splurge may bring you to this refined, recently refurbished fourteenth-century country residence 4km from the town (beyond the stadium on the south side). The hotel's eight rooms are a delight.

Villa Burali

Località Policiano SS71, 154 (0575 979 045/fax 979 296). **Rates** *for two* L150,000-L180,000; *for four* L240,000-L270,000. **No credit cards.**
Though not exactly a bargain, this is a great option if there's a group of you. This seventeenth-century villa has been divided into 11 apartments and is well situated on the road to Cortona, about 7km from Arezzo. Its swimming pool is another draw.

Villa Severi Youth Hostel

Via dei Cappucini, or if coming by bus: Via Redi 13 (0575 299 047). **Rates** *double* L40,000-L60,000; *breakfast* L3,000. **No credit cards.**
Good value for money and relaxed atmosphere with rooms sleeping between two and 10 people. Take Bus 4 from outside the station towards the Ospedale Vecchio and get out at the Ostello della Gioventù.

Shopping

As you climb Corso Italia, mainstream stores peter out to make way for a proliferation of antique stores around Piazza Grande. Stray off the beaten Corso to find there's more to Arezzo than just antiques.

L'Artigiano

Via XXV Aprile 22 (0575 351 278). **Open** 8.30am-1pm, 3-8pm, daily (ring bell). **No credit cards.**
One of Arezzo's last goldsmiths to carry on the tradition of the *mosaico fiorentino* – intricate pendants and picture frames inlaid with mosaics.

Casa della Renna

Piazza San Michele 15 (0575 356 774). **Open** 8am-1pm, 4-7.30pm, Mon-Sat. **No credit cards.**
Custom-made buckskin and calf leather jackets, natural and treated, are this store's trademarks.

Libreria Einaudi

Via Oberdan 31 (0575 353 085). **Open** 4-8pm Mon; 9.30am-1pm, 4-8pm, Tue-Fri; 9.30am-1pm Sat. **No credit cards.**
Arezzo's outlet for Italy's best known publishing house and a space for exhibitions and events.

Macelleria-Gastronomia Aligi Barelli

Viale della Chimera 20 (0575 357 754). **Open** 8am-1pm, 4.30-8pm, Mon, Tue, Thur, Fri; 8am-1pm Wed, Sat. **No credit cards.**
Justly renowned *macelleria* with mouth-watering salamis from the Casentino and a range of ready-made meat-based dishes.

Mondo Antico I Coloniali

Via Cavour 24/26 (0575 21801). **Open** 3.30-7.30pm Mon; 9.30am-1pm, 3.30-7.30pm Tue-Sat. **Credit** AmEx, DC, MC, V.
An exotic and colourful Indonesian furniture store with perfumed textiles, woven bamboo recliners and lampshades made from banana and corn leaves.

Pane e Salute

Corso Italia 11 (0575 20657). **Open** 7am-1pm, 4.30-8pm, Mon-Sat. **No credit cards.**
Traditional Tuscan breads including *schiacciate* (flattened bread peppered with rosemary) and oven-baked sweets.

Pasticceria de'Cenci

Via de' Cenci 17 (0575 23102). **Open** 8am-1pm, 4-8pm Tue-Sat; 8am-1pm Sun. **No credit cards.**
Chock full of elegant delights such as *bigne' al limone* (lemon cream puff).

Grosseto & South Tuscany

Seaside scenery and the ancient Etruscan heartland.

It seems odd that this area is so backward in coming forward about what it has to offer. The 1980s development boom in Italy that helped increase tourist earnings in most of Tuscany barely touched the sliver of land known as the Maremma. With the exception of the most popular resorts, such as **Orbetello**, which are as crowded as the French Riviera in August, or yachting crowd favourites such as **Porto Ercole** and **Porto Santo Stefano**, this area is relatively unexplored.

Visit with a purpose, be it to hike through the woods, wonder at the 2,500-year-old Etruscan necropolises, trek through one of the huge WWF nature reserves, which shelter wildlife that is disappearing from other parts of Tuscany, or sail to one of the islands.

Grosseto

The largest Tuscan town south of Siena, Grosseto is the capital of the province of Southern Tuscany. During the Middle Ages, Grosseto represented civilisation for inhabitants of the malaria-ridden, south-Tuscan swamplands. Bombing during World War II destroyed almost everything in the city centre, but left the sixteenth-century walls intact.

The SS223 from Siena to Grosseto is poorly marked in and around Siena, but it is one of the most inspiring routes in Tuscany. Its twisting miles lead through rugged hills and craggy olive groves that gasp into chasms and valleys, then over the 891-metre high viaduct before you reach Grosseto. Further along, on the SS223 near Civitella

Palazzo del Comune in ***Grosetto*** *– a town that makes for a leisurely day out.*

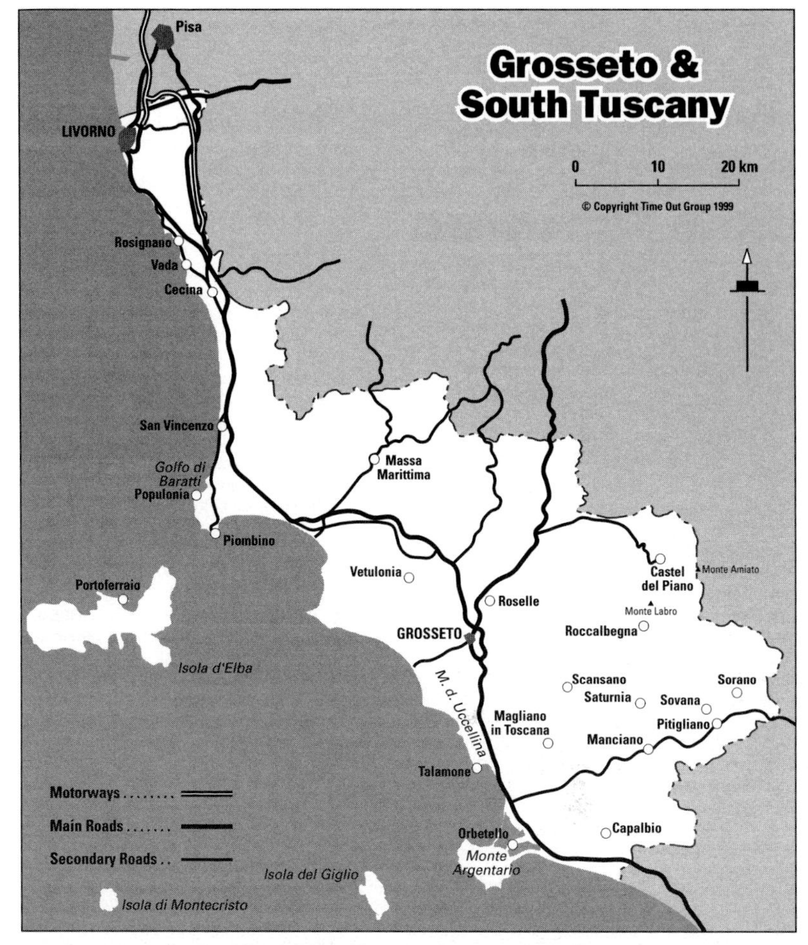

Marittima, **Le Milandre** (0564 900 683. Open 7am-midnight Mon, Tue, Thur-Sun. Average dinner L35,000) is a real gem and perfectly located for an en-route lunchstop. The main room sports reproductions of photos of Maremma cowboys, who are often pointed out by the customers as uncles or grandpas. Outside, tables are set up overlooking the family's olive grove. Fresh fish arrives on Thursdays and whoever happens to be in the bar is recruited to unload the flopping victims.

Grosseto itself makes for a leisurely day. Grand Duke Ferdinando I erected hexagonal defensive walls in 1593 that were rarely called to service, most of the invasions by marauding Aldobranescas and Sienese happened before they were built. The city traces its roots back to the fifth century BC, when it was an Etruscan settlement. That history can be seen in the **Museo Archeologico e d'Arte della Maremma** & **Museo d'Arte Sacra del Diocesi di Grosseto** (Piazza Baccarini 3, 0564 417 629. Open 10am-1pm, 5-8pm daily. Admission free).

Down an inconspicuous side street **Trattoria Fucini** (Via Fucini 15, 0564 28673. Open lunch by appointment; 6pm-midnight Mon-Sat. Average L28,000) is cosy and has a roof terrace with a pergola. It boasts of Maremma cooking, but since seafood is quite prevalent on the menu, it's actually more typically Grossetan, with small wild beans and grilled fish. The elegant but relaxed **Buca San Lorenzo** (Viale Manetti 1, 0564 25142. Open lunch & dinner Tue-Sun. Average L50,000) attracts the diamonds-and-pearls set of Grosseto as well as sailors on a spending spree.

The **Tourist Office** (Viale Monterosa 206, 0564 414 303. Open 8am-3pm Mon-Sat) will suggest hotels. There's also an information booth on Via Fucini 43c (0564 414 303).

About eight miles north-east of Grosseto, just off the SS223 Siena road is Roselle, the excavated ruins of an Etruscan city, which was conquered by Rome in the third century.

The Etruscan Riviera

The stretch of coastline between Livorno and Piombino has been dubbed the Etruscan Riviera. Apart from the pricey, parasol-stabbed beaches chaotic with holiday-makers, there are a number of discreet, sandy coves encompassed by dunes and pine groves if you explore and are willing to walk. A little further inland, between the coast and the Colline Metallifere to the east is the northern section of the Maremma; stretching between Cecina and Follonica this is known as the Pisan Maremma.

Cecina

For a pleasant seaside picnic stop in Cecina at the **Rosticceria** at Viale Galliano 5, open only during peak season (from April to October). You can pick up whole, roasted chickens, bread and wine. Once you've stocked up with picnic supplies, head for Marina di Cecina; the beaches are free and tend not to be too crowded, but you'll need your own parasol.

South of Cecina is Italy's first World Wildlife Fund (WWF) nature reserve, the Oasi di Bolgheri, a nesting haven for rare ducks, geese and storks.

Tourist Office (Piazza S Andrea, Cecina Mare, 0586 620 678. Open 9am-noon, 3-6pm, Sat, Sun).

San Vincenzo

Roughly half way between Livorno and Grosseto on the Via Aurelia, is this former watchtower base, where a Pisan tower from 1304 still stands.

Many visitors come to San Vincenzo to eat at the **Gambero Rosso** (Piazza della Vittoria 13, 0565 701 021. Open lunch & dinner Wed-Sun. Average L120,000). Eating here is as much about status as appeasing your appetite and the atmosphere can be a little stuffy, but the food is very good. If you're not in the mood for snobbery, pop next door to **Il Bucaniere** (0565 705 555. Open June-Sept noon-2.30pm, 7.30-10.30pm, Tue-Sun. Average L60,000), which serves simpler fare.

About 20 kilometres north of San Vincenzo, there is a left turning off the Via Aurelia leading up to Bolgheri, where the Romantic poet Giosuè Carducci (1835-1907) grew up and where the stunning, medieval Gherardesca castle still stands. This minor road, lined by tall, slim Cypress trees, was described by Carducci in his poems.

Piombino

Though not the first stop on anyone's itinerary, Piombino is the place to catch a ferry to a number of destinations on Corsica, Elba, and Pianosa. However, this rather run-down little town deserves more than a little respect. Once an island, from 1399 to 1815 it was the capital of a small, independent state. Now evidence of its steel and iron-mining industries dominate the town.

The stretch of coastline north of Piombino up to the ruins of Etruscan Populonia is sandy and rocky by turns. This area is replete with mystifying rock formations, necropoli and unspoiled waters. The easiest beach to get to is Cala Moresca. Leave the car in Piombino's main car park and follow signs for the beach, which will take you along a series of tiny trails that follow the coastline to the Golfo di Baratti.

Populonia, with its Etruscan necropolis, is the tiny fishing port of Baratti. Official guides can be contacted through the Piombino tourist office (Via del Popolo 3, 0565 63269. Open summer 9am-3pm, 5-11pm); an on-the-spot guide (agree the price first) might be more colourful, though perhaps less informed.

If you opt for the coastal road south from Piombino to Grosseto, Castiglione della Pescaia is an attractive place to stop for food or to stretch your legs. It combines the no-nonsense bustle of a fishing port with a good selection of hotels and restaurants. Alternatively, make an inland diversion for Massa Marittima, an unexpected enclave of art, history and civic pride.

Massa Marittima

Massa's position, together with its mineral wealth and fresh water supply, helped it survive as an independent city state for 110 years before being taken over by Siena in 1335. Massa dominates the high southern ranges of the Colline Metallifere, a rich source of the iron copper and other minerals, that were one of the economic driving forces behind the early Renaissance. When the mines were closed in 1396, Massa's boom years were followed by half a millennium of neglect, until a small-scale return to mining and the draining of the surrounding marshes turned the tide in the middle of the nineteenth century. As a result, the town has preserved one of the most uniform examples of thirteenth-century town planning anywhere in Tuscany.

Recent restorations have put a new polish on the Pisan-style Duomo, Le Fonti dell'Abbondanza and Museo Civico Archeologico. The Duomo harmoniously blends Romanesque and Gothic details, despite the time lapse between its foundation in the early thirteenth century and the addition of the campanile in 1400. The bare stone interior is a treasure-house with a Baptistery famous for thirteenth-century bas-reliefs by Giroldo da Como, and the Arca di San Cerbone behind the altar.

In the second half of the thirteenth century *la fonte nova* was the hub of town life, and the saviour of the community when surrounding social chaos forced the townsfolk to hold up for extended periods. Named **le Fonti dell'Abbondanza** (the fountains of abundance), the basins ceased to be used and suffered neglect for several centuries. Restoration work has opened up the original source, so waters flow from the fount once again.

In the thirteenth-century Palazzo del Podestà on Piazza Garibaldi is the **Museo Civico Archeologico** (0566 902 289. Open Apr-Oct 10am-12.30pm, 3.30-7pm, Tue-Sun; Nov-Mar 10am-12.30pm, 3-5pm. Admission L5,000), with an expanded Etruscan collection and a marvellous 1330 *Maestà* by Ambrogio Lorenzetti. Up Via Moncini is the Città Nuova, or 'new town' (the fourteenth century bit rather than the twelfth-thirteenth century bit) with a fine Sienese arch.

Another Massa draw is the festival of **Balestro del Girifalco** on the first Sunday after 22 May, the feast day of San Bernardino of Siena, who was born here. The locals take this pageant seriously: the Renaissance costumes are dazzling, the *sbandieratori* (flag-throwers) faultless, and the final contest – when teams from the town's three *terzieri* attempt to shoot down a mechanical falcon with their crossbows – is a sight worth seeing.

If you fancy staying overnight, opt for the three-star **Sole** (Corso Libertà 43, 0566 901 971/fax 0566 901 959. Rates single L80,000; double L120,000. Credit AmEx, MC, V), which is housed in an old palazzo. As for dining, **Da Tronca** (Vicolo Porte 5, 0566 901 991. Open dinner Tue, Thur-Sun. Average L35,000. Credit MC, V) is a cheap osteria in the town centre serving creative regional fare. Also try **Enoteca Grassini** (Via della Libertà 1, 0566 940 149. Open 9am-3pm, 5-10pm, Mon-Sat. Credit MC, V) for a plate of local food, such as the town's famous lentil and pheasant soup, or put together a picnic at the counter.

South-east Tuscany

Saturnia

Were it not for its proximity to the small tributary of Albenga, there would be little reason to come so far off the beaten track to Saturnia. Once you become accustomed to the steamy stench of sulphur, relaxing in the hot waters of the Albenga is sheer bliss. You can either pay for a luxurious experience at **Hotel Terme** (*see below*) or travel further down the road to Montemerano and bathe (for free) in the pretty Cascate del Gorello falls and pools, where the rocks are stained copper green. On a warm, clear night, it is magical. According to legend, Saturn, to punish those who thought only of war, sent down a thunderbolt which split the earth open, from which poured forth steamy water. In this liquid the disobedient earthlings found rejuvenation and became calm again.

For overnight stays, the **Saturnia Country Club** (Località Pomonte Scansano, 0564 599

Saturnia's fabulous Cascate del Gorello falls and pools are popular all year round.

The massive walls of **Manciano** *– the administrative centre of the Maremma.*

188/fax 0564 599 214. Rates L120,000 per person. Restaurant open lunch & dinner Mon, Wed-Sun. Average L45,000) offers everything from horseback excursions, guided tours and free access to the thermal pools at **Hotel Terme** (0564 601 061/fax 0564 601 266. Rates single L295,000; double L510,000). Hotel Terme also offers mud treatments, fitness classes and massage therapy.

The closest restaurants to Saturnia are in Montemerano, six kilometres south. **Da Caino** (Via Canonica 3, 0564 602 817. Open lunch & dinner Mon, Tue, Thur-Sun; low-season closed Thur lunch. Average L100,000) serves local pheasants with seasonal side dishes. **Osteria Passaparola** (Via del Bivio 16, 0564 602 827. Open lunch & dinner Mon-Wed, Fri-Sun. Average L40,000. Rates double L70,000) is a cheaper option.

The **Tourist Office** (Piazza Vittorio Veneto 8, 0564 601 280. Open summer 9.30am-12.30pm, 4-7.40pm, Mon-Sat; winter 10am-4.40pm Mon-Sat. Website: www.laltramaremma.it) is the central point for information on the Maremma.

Manciano

The massive, grey walls of Manciano loom up defensively out of the landscape, but its coat of arms bears an outstretched hand in a gesture of friendship. This is the administrative centre of the Maremma, with a hospital, clinic, vet and post office and connecting buses between Grosseto and the surrounding Etruscan sights. Outdoor cafés are plentiful, should you have to wait a while here and there's also a **Museum of Prehistory and Protohistory** (Via Corsini, 0564 629 222. Open 9am-3.30pm Tue-Sat; 9.30am-1pm Sun. Admission L3,000). **Il Poderino** (SS Maremmana km30,650, 0564 625 031. Rates double with hydromassage bath L80,000 per person; agriturismo rooms L55,000-L100,000 Fri-Sun; L45,000-L95,000 Mon-Thur) is a country inn ten minutes' drive from Saturnia and 20 from the Giannella and Feniglia beaches at Argentario.

Pitigliano

At dusk, with its lights twinkling golden against the reddish tufa limestone, Pitigliano looks like something out of an Arthurian tale. It sits on a high plateau surrounded by steep cliffs and was dubbed the Eagle's Nest by the Etruscans. The dramatic drop into the valley below is accentuated by an immense aqueduct, built in 1545, that connects the lower and upper parts of town. The tower of the church of Madonna delle Grazie (1527) provides a great vantage point of the surrounding countryside.

The Orsinis built up the town's grandeur in the fourteenth century. They were preceded by the Aldobrancescas, who ruled over Maremma for about 500 years. Both families' coats of arms are displayed in the Orsini-family palace courtyard.

The Jewish community that was attracted here by increasing Medici tolerance in the sixteenth century either left, or was forced out during World War II. All that is left of the diaspora today is a small Museum of Jewish History, housed in the former synagogue in Via Zuccarelli, and a pasticceria around the corner, that still makes a local Jewish pastry called *sfratti* (the evicted).

The **Museo Civico Archeologico** (Piazza Orsini, for info call council 0564 616 322. Open

9am-noon, 3-7pm, Tue-Sun. Admission L5,000) has a small, but well-presented collection of Etruscan and Roman artifacts from the area.

Osteria Tufo Allegro (Vicolo della Costituzione 2, 0564 616 192. Open lunch & dinner Mon, Wed-Sun; Average L40,000) with its rough, stone interior is homely. It serves one of Tuscany's best white wines, Bianco di Pitigliano, under a variety of labels. **Trattoria dell'Orso** (Piazza San Gregorio VII 14/15, 0564 614 273. Open summer lunch & dinner daily, winter closed Thur. Average L35,000) has an almost exclusively local clientele, but provides a hyper-friendly service and, in season, wonderful artichokes.

Sovana

North-west of Pitigliano, four miles by road, lies Sovana. Although it is semi-abandoned now, this was once an important Etruscan town. Between the ninth and the twelfth centuries it became a thriving bishopric under the dominion of the wealthy Aldobrandini family. One of the clan's most famous scions, the great reforming pope Gregory VII (after whom the calendar is named) was born here in around 1020. There is a small museum of local history in the thirteenth-century Palazzo Pretorio, next door to the arched Loggetta del Capitano. At the other end of town is the Duomo, a Lombard Romanesque structure with a luminous interior and a fine carved portal on the left side.

The walls of the medieval Santa Maria church were whitewashed at the end of the last century, its fifteenth-century Siena school frescoes smeared with chalky paint. Thankfully, they have since been restored. The church – one of the most beautiful in Tuscany – is a blend of Romanesque and Gothic with a unique ciborium from the eighth or ninth century.

Pitigliano – *a town built on tufa.*

Sovana has two of the best places in the area to dine: **La Taverna Etrusca** (Piazza del Pretorio 16, 0564 616 183. Restaurant open lunch & dinner; closed Mon. Average L40,000) where the pasta and the *agnelli con capperi* (lamb with capers) are consistently good and the ricotta-based desserts outstanding, and the **Scilla** (Via Rodolfo Sidiero 1/3, 0564 616 531. Restaurant open lunch & dinner; closed Tue. Average L35,000).

In a valley below the town to the west is one of the most completely preserved Etruscan necropoli, a series of tombs cut into the tufa walls of the Fosso Calesina. Among the tombs is the second-century BC Tomba Ildebranda, complete with pedestal and sculpted columns. It is free to wander around; for information on the more obscure tombs, ask in the Taverna Etrusca.

Sorano

Heading north-east from Sovana, towards the Umbrian border, this village of dark, greyish tufo is a dizzying sight perched precariously high above the Lente river. Under the Orsini empire, Sorano was a defence post, but at times itself more dangerous than rampaging enemies. A series of landslides encouraged a slow but steady exodus of people. Masso Leopoldino, a terraced, giant tufo cliff peers down on the town.

An archaeological park covering the three Etruscan strongholds of Sorano, Sovana and Vitozza has been opened in preparation for 2000.

La Città del Tufo (Tufo City)

(0564 633 671). **Cost** *Italian guide* L150,000; *English-speaking guide* L250,000 for groups of up to 40.
A tour that encompasses newly opened and restored sites from the Bronze age, Etruscan, medieval and Renaissance periods. Guided tours leave from San Quirico, Sovana, Sorano and San Rocco.

The Maremma

The town of Grosseto marks the most northerly point of the southern stretch of the Maremma (as opposed to the Pisan Maremma, *see above* **The Etruscan Riviera**). The Maremmans have seen centuries of ruthless overlords and dynasties. 'Mangiavamo pane con la nostra miseria' (we ate bread with our misery) is a renowned local expression. Now, the area's past struggles lend it a distinct character and cuisine that has little to do with the gentle, privileged image of the rest of Tuscany.

Most of the Maremma's southern hilltop towns have a view of the sea, but no seaside culture. Only recently, with a slight increase in tourism, has

Tomb raiders explore Etruscan Tuscany.

seafood been introduced to the inland towns, such as **Capalbio**. Some may call it underdevelopment, others respect for the environment, but the end result is that the air feels fresher, the sun warmer and the sky hangs a touch bluer over so much unspoiled terrain.

Monti dell'Uccellina

This WWF-protected nature reserve has some incredible hikes. Birds, both migratory and resident, thrive in abundance in this 7,750-hectare reserve. Ospreys, falcons, kingfishers, herons and the rare Knight of Italy can all be spotted. The terrain ranges from the mudflats and umbrella pines of the estuary to the untouched woodland of the hills, taking in gorse, wild rosemary, dwarf pines and cork oaks.

Cars are not allowed inside the park – leave it in the car park in the square near the reserve headquarters at Alberese, where the main entrance is located. There is a train service from Grosseto to Marina di Alberese; from the station, take a bus or a four-kilometre walk to the entrance. The L7,500 entrance fee includes a trail map and the bus ride to Pratini. The main attraction is undoubtedly the beach, which can also be reached from Marina di Alberese (*see below*), but takes more time and effort.

To the north of the park, Marina di Alberese beach 'resort' and the salt marshes are open every day from 9am until one hour before sunset. Not as pristine as the bay in the park itself, the waters are still strikingly clean.

At the southern edge of the Monti dell'Uccellina reserve is the quiet, unspoiled port town of Talamone, which offers the only accommodation for miles. **Hotel Capo d'Uomo** (Via Cala di Forno, 0564 887 077/fax 0564 887 298. Open Apr-Oct. Rates single L100,000-L150,000; double L150,000-L190,000) is a three-star hotel. More expensive is **Telamonio** (Via Garibaldi 4, 0564 887 008. Rates single L140,000-L180,000; double L220,000). **La Buca di Nonno Ghigo** (Via Porta Garibaldi 1, 0564 887 067. Open lunch & dinner daily; winter closed Mon. Average L35,000) serves up steamy plates of *cozze* (mussels with garlic and olive oil) which can be washed down with a lightly sparkling local white.

Orbetello

In the middle of the central of the three isthmuses that connect Monte Argentario to the mainland, Orbetello has remnants of Spanish fortifications dating from the sixteenth and seventeenth centuries, when this was the capital of the Stato dei Presidi, a Spanish enclave on the Tuscan coast. There is a small antiquarium with some uninspiring Etruscan and Roman exhibits, and the cathedral has a Gothic façade, but Orbetello is really more about atmosphere than sightseeing. Join the evening *struscio* (the promenade up the Corso Italia) before dining on a plate of eels (fished from the lagoon) at one of the town's simple trattorias like **Il Nocchino** (Via dei Mille 64, 0564 860 329. Open lunch & dinner; closed Wed. Average L40,000). Of the town's three cheaper hotels, the **Piccolo Parigi** (Corso Italia 169, 0564 867 233. Rates single L50,000; double L100,000), is the nicest option.

Ansedonia

This is the Beverly Hills of the Etruscan Riviera, not much is left that reflects its ancient history. Roman ruins from 170 BC overlook the villas with flower-draped walls, and the nearby Museo di Cosa displays artefacts from the area. Daily trains from Grosseto stop at Capalbio station, from where you can either walk three kilometres down to the beach alongside the Lago di Burano lagoon (now a WWF reserve). If you time it right you will be able to eat in the **Stazione Bar** (Piazza Aldo Moro, Stazione de Capalbio. Open lunch & dinner Mon, Wed-Sun. Average L40,000), an unassuming station bar with an excellent trattoria.

The coastline that stretches south from Ansedonia offers 18 kilometres of beach with heavenly clear water to paddle in. There are a number of camp sites to choose from; try **Campeggio Chiarone** at Chiarone (0564 890 101. Open May-Sept. Rates L10,000-L18,000 per tent; L10,000-L16,000 per person).

Monte Argentario

A mountain rising abruptly from the sea, Monte Argentario is the Tuscan coast at its most rugged.

It looks as though it should be an island, and it was until the eighteenth century, when the two long outer sand-spits created by the action of the tides finally reached the mainland. It has two port towns:

Porto Ercole

On the south-east corner of Argentario lies the exclusive Porto Ercole, where the painter Caravaggio died drunk on the beach in 1610. As with Orbetello and Santo Stefano, Easter and August holidays see this small bay full to the gills. **La Conchiglia** (Via della Marina, 0564 833 134. Rates single L70,000; double L90,000-L100,000) and the two-star **Hotel Marina** (Lungomare Andrea Doria 30, 0564 833 055. Rates single L115,000; double L170,000) both overbook and often send clients away, even with reservations, so confirm the day before arrival. If you can afford it, splash out on the secluded **Il Pellicano** (Località Sbarcatello, 0564 833 801. Open May-Oct. Rates double L600,000-L1,070,000), some three kilometres out of town, with its own private, rocky beach and hotel disco.

Porto Santo Stefano

The place to get a ferry for the island of Giglio in summer (five ferries a day in summer operated by **Toremar** (0564 810 803) (*see below*, **The Islands**). At the lower end of the price scale for local restaurants, **Trattoria/Pizzeria Il Moletto di Amato & Figli** (Via del Molo, 0564 813 636. Open lunch & dinner Mon, Tue, Thur-Sun. Average L50,000) serves pizza and seafood and has views out over the bay. The prawn and pine nut risotto is recommended, as is the *tonnarelli*. One of the nicest places to eat in Porto Santo Stefano is **Dal Greco** (Via del Molo 1/2, 0564 814 885. Open lunch & dinner; closed Tue. Average L80,000), a seafood restaurant with a terrace overlooking the quay.

The seafront is lined with bars. One of the hipper ones is **Il Bucco** (Lungomare dei Navigatori 2, 0564 818 243. Open 7am-2am Mon, Wed-Sun), where the well-dressed and tanned have their Camparis and Martinis. If you feel like dancing the night away **Le Streghe** on Via Panoramica strikes a happy balance between high-school dance and sophisticated night on the town.

Tourist Office (Corso Umberto 55a, 0564 814 208. Open summer 9am-1pm, 4-6pm; winter 8am-2pm).

Capalbio

Close to the Lazio border, Capalbio has been developing into something of an HQ for Rome's poets, musicians and politicians over the last 20 years. What brings most people here is its proximity to the long beach that stretches all the way from Chiarone to Ansedonia (*see above*).

Trattoria la Torre da Carla (Via Vittorio Emanuele 33, 0564 896 070/896 617. Open lunch & dinner Mon-Wed, Fri-Sun. Average L45,000) serves robust Tuscan cuisine. Its terrace looks over the forest where your *cinghiale* (wild boar) was probably shot. Before he was strung up in 1896, the renegade bandit Tiburzi ate here. His photo, along with that of several of his contemporaries, adorns one of the restaurant's walls. **Hotel Valle del Buttero** (Via Silone 21, 0564 896 097/fax 0564 896 518; Rates single L85,000, double L130,000, apartments L45,000-L100,000 per person, discounts for longer stays, L15,000 less off-season), is a three-star hotel on the first turn up the hill to Capalbio. The **Trattoria da Maria** (Via Comunale 3, 0564 896 014; Open restaurant lunch & dinner Mon, Wed-Sun; Average L50,000. Rates double L80,000), also rents rooms, but call in advance. **Agriturismo Ghiaccio Bosco** (Via della Sgrilla 4, 0564 896 539; Rates L70,000-L100,000 per person), just outside of Capalbio, is a country home with ten rooms to let.

Il Giardino dei Tarocchi

Località Garavicchio Capalbio (0564 895 122). **Open** 2.30-7.30pm Mon-Sat. **Admission** L20,000, L12,000 concessions; free under-7s.

This is an amazing walled garden to the south-east of Capalbio. It was founded in 1976 by Anglo-American artist Niki de Saint Phalle. She has created over 20 massive sculptures of splinters of mirror, coloured tiles and sculpted stone to represent the main characters from the tarot deck: the *High Priest* and *Priestess*, the *Moon*, *Sun* and so on. Some of the sculptures house four-storey buildings, which you can enter. The artist herself made her home in the immense *Empress* for a while: she slept in the right breast and ate in the left.

The Islands

Isola del Giglio

A torturously winding road connects the island's three villages – Giglio Porto, where the ferry docks, Campese on the other side, Giglio Castello on the ridge between the two, with its medieval walls and steep narrow lanes.

Overlooking Giglio Porto, the three-star **Castello Monticello** (Via Provinciale, 0564 809 252. Rates single L85,000-L110,000; double L130,000-L220,000) occupies a crenellated folly. For the ultimate sun and sea experience, try **Pardini's Hermitage** (Cala degli Alberi, 0564 809 034/fax 0564 809 177. Rates full board L160,000-L280,000), in a secluded cove only accessible on foot or by boat (the staff will fetch you). **Tony's** (0564 806 452. Open Mar-end Oct 7.30am-1am daily), on the north end of the beach in Giglio Campese below the tower, can be relied on for everything 'from a cappuccino to a lobster'. Pizzas start at L8,000. Tanned yachters and kids frequent **I Lombi Disco** at Giglio Castello (0564 806 001. Open 11pm-5am Sat; July, Aug 11pm-5am daily. Admission L15,000), which also has a piano bar open from 9.30pm.

Exile on Elba

When the French Emperor Napoleon Bonaparte (1769-1821) was exiled in 1814, he must have felt salt was being rubbed into his wounds. The great conqueror's dreams of a vast world empire had been reduced to the reality of a tiny chunk of Tuscany: the island of Elba. In fact, he had been exiled to his origins.

Looking west on a clear evening, he could have seen his birthplace, Corsica, looming up out of the sea in front of the setting sun. Looking east, only some ten kilometres from the main town of Portoferraio, he would have seen mainland Tuscany, the land of his father's ancestors. The Buonaparte family were already established in San Miniato al Tedesco in the twelfth century when the town was an important administrative centre for the Holy Roman Empire. As Florence became the dominant power in northern Tuscany, the Buonaparte family naturally became Florentine nobles and these honours descended to Napoleon himself. There are still Buonaparte tombs in the cathedral at San Miniato, as well as a Piazza Buonaparte in the town, and relics there, which once belonged to Napoleon's family.

With the decline of the Florentine economy in the sixteenth century, the family moved to Corsica. Just before Napoleon's birth, Genoa, then the island's owner, sold it to France. This made the Corsicans technically French, though many, including Napoleon's parents, who were leaders of a resistance, objected.

Being French meant that Corsican children of wealthy families could be sent to French military schools – as Napoleon was. So Napoleon, really half-Tuscan, half-Corsican, eventually became a French officer; First Consul in 1799, and Emperor.

Italians, who have a particularly dry sense of humour towards the French, tell the following story, which may well be true:

After Napoleon made himself Emperor in 1804 and placed the Iron Crown upon his own head he turned to his Italian aide and complained, 'Tutti gli italiano sono ladri' (All Italians are thieves). The aide, who probably lost his head later on in the day replied, 'Non tutti, Imperatore…' (Not all, Emperor…), '…solamente la buona parte' (…only most of them).

Tourist Office (Via Umberto 1, Pro Loco Isole di Giglio, 0564 809 400. Open summer 8.30am-1pm, 4-7.30pm, daily; winter 9am-12.30pm, 3.30-6.30pm, daily).

Elba

Part of the Tuscan Archipelago, Elba is Italy's third largest island with 142 kilometres of coastline. In August its resident population of 30,000 is swollen to almost a million.

Portoferraio is the island's capital and main ferry terminal. It's also the focus of Napoleonic interest (*see above* **Exile on Elba**): the man's town residence, the Palazzo dei Mulini, is worth a visit for its views and Empire-style furnishings, incongruous to this Mediterranean setting. His summer retreat, the neoclassical Villa Napoleonica di San Martino (six kilometres south-west of town, off the road for Marciana), is strictly for pilgrims.

Choosing between Elba's many seaside village resorts can be a problem. One unusual option for accommodation is just out of town. The agriturismo at the **Monte Fabbrello** winery (Località Schiopparella 30, 0565 933 324. Rates 4-person apartments L80,000-L180,000 per night) gives clients discounts on their wines. Heading west from Portoferraio, passing through Sorgente and Punta Aquaviva, Capo d'Enfola juts out into the waters and between there and Biòdola are the best options for accommodation, food and clean beach packages.

Pretty Marciana Marina in the west has **Rendez-Vous**, on the buzzing Piazza della Vittoria (0565 99251. Open dinner & lunch daily, closed Wed in winter. Average L60,000), which prepares Elban specialties – try the potatoes stuffed with seafood salad. **Casa Lupi** right outside Marciana Marina (Località Ontanelli, 0565 99143. Rates single L50,000-L70,000; double L75,000-L110,000) is a modest one-star hotel. Marciana itself has fine medieval and Renaissance quarters. Start here for the ascent of Monte Capanne.

In Marmi di Procchio is Smania, the biggest Elban producer of *Limoncino*, which – like its cousin *Limoncello,* produced on the Amalfi coast – is a yellow liqueur made from lemon peels and a perfect digestifo on a hot day.

On the east side of Elba, the area from Porto Azzuro to Capoliveri is the main wine production area of the island. **La Laterna** (Via Vitaliani 5, Porto Azzuro, 0565 958 394. Open lunch & dinner Tue-Sun; closed Nov. Average L40,000) offers a decent choice of the local wines and a mean *torta bria'a*, a dessert that uses Aleatico wine as one of its principal ingredients.

Tourist Office (Calata Italia 26, Portoferraio, 0565 914 671. Open summer 8am-8pm daily; winter 8am-1pm, 3-6pm, Mon-Sat).

Directory

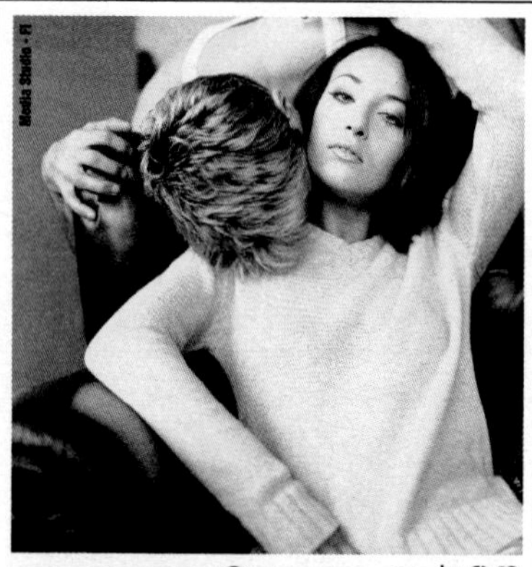

informer
Understanding Italy

Directory

Getting Around

Arriving in Florence

By Air

If you are arriving by air, you will most likely land at either Pisa's **Galilei Airport,** Bologna's **Marconi Airport** or the tiny-but-busy **Vespucci Airport** to the west of Florence at Peretola. All three have easy access to and from Florence.

Vespucci, Florence

Vespucci Airport (055 373 498/24hr flight information 055 306 1702). **Open** 7.30am-10pm daily.

This small airport, known locally as Peretola, handles over 70 scheduled flights a day. Situated about 5km west of central Florence, the airport is linked to the city by two bus lines. SITA coaches stop outside the arrivals building, and run to the SITA bus station in Via Santa Caterina da Siena, adjacent to Santa Maria Novella station. They run about every 45mins from 9.45am to 10.35pm and tickets (L6,000) can be bought on board. ATAF city bus 62 stops outside the main gate (a bit of a trek with luggage) and runs every 20 minutes from 6.30am to 10.45pm. Tickets cost L1,500. A taxi from the airport to the centre of Florence costs about L25,000, plus extras for luggage and surcharges for nights and public holidays. Journey time into Florence is about 25 minutes. The Vespucci Airport branch of the Tuscan Tourist Board (APT) is open 8.30am-10.30pm daily.

Galilei, Pisa

Galilei Airport (Flight information 050 500 707). **Open** *airport* 5am-midnight daily; *information* 6.30am-8.30pm daily).

Galilei airport is south of Pisa, 80km west of Florence. It handles national and international (but not intercontinental) flights, both scheduled and charter. The Galilei airport branch of the Tuscan Tourist Board (APT) is open 10.30am-4.30pm Mon-Sat. The journey into Florence by car is along the Firenze-Pisa-Livorno dual carriageway, which runs into the west of the city. There is a direct train service to Florence's Santa Maria Novella station which takes just over an hour, stopping at Pisa Centrale and Pontederra on the way. Tickets (L7,400) can be purchased at the information desk in the main airport concourse (open 7am-9pm daily, but varies). Service times are not designed to coincide with flights; trains run roughly every hour from 10.27am to 5.44pm. There is another, less direct, service into Florence from Pisa Airport via Lucca, but trains are less frequent and the journey time is nearly two hours; it is worth looking into train departures from Pisa Centrale; the information desk has a timetable and a taxi into Pisa will cost about L12,000. CPT bus 5 leaves for the city centre and train station every 15 minutes. Tickets are available at the information desk.

The first train to Pisa from Florence is 6.47am from Santa Maria Novella station, and trains run almost every hour between 11.05am and 5.05pm.

There is a check-in facility on platform five. Minimum check-in time is 15 minutes before your train to Galilei airport is due to leave, or five minutes with only hand baggage. Tickets to the airport cost L2,000 more than the normal fare if bought here. A flight information service is also provided (055 216 073).

Marconi, Bologna

Marconi Airport (051 647 9615). **Open** 5am-midnight daily.

Bologna's Marconi airport lies 10km north-west of the city. Extensive work has been carried out in recent years (the runway is being extended to allow for 747s), and it handles many more flights than Pisa. It has two terminals – A and B. Charter flights and British Airways leave from B. Since it's in Emilia Romagna, there is no Tuscan tourist information.

An airport bus stops outside terminal A (arrivals); this departs for Bologna train station every 15 minutes and costs L7,000. Tickets are available from the machine in the terminal building or on board; the journey time is about 20 minutes. A taxi to the station will cost about L25,000. From Bologna Centrale station, trains to Florence are frequent and take anything from 50 to 90 minutes; ticket prices also vary considerably. The fastest (and most expensive) trains are the Eurostars, swish and speedy with first- and second-class seats. These carry a supplement; make sure you tell the vendor at the ticket window which train you want to catch. They run regularly between 6.30am and 9.45pm. Back to Bologna from Florence, they run from 7.15am to 10.20pm. A single second-class ticket costs L25,000. The Intercities are less expensive (L16,600) and reasonably fast. If you hire a car, the journey time into Florence is about one and a half hours south on the A1.

Major airlines

Alitalia *Lungarno Acciaiuoli 10/12r (24-hour international flight information 1478 65643). Bus to Ponte Vecchio.* **Open** 9am-4.30pm Mon-Fri. **Credit** AmEx, DC, MC, V.

British Airways *Galilei Airport, Pisa (050 40866/flight information 167 215 215).* **Open** *office* 8am-8pm Mon-Fri; 9am-5pm Sat; *information* 8am-8pm Mon-Fri; 9am-5pm Sat.

GO *(Freephone 147 887 766).* **Open** 7am-11pm daily. Information and telephone sales only.

Ryannair *Galilei Airport, Pisa (050 503 770).* **Open** 8.30am-9pm daily.

Meridiana *Lungarno Vespucci 28r (055 230 2314). Bus B.* **Open** 9am-1pm, 2-5pm, Mon-Fri.

By bus

If you come to Florence by coach, you will arrive at the SITA or LAZZI bus station, both near Santa Maria Novella station. *See also* **Transport in Tuscany**, *below*.

SITA

Via Santa Caterina da Siena 15 (information 055 483 651). **Open** 8.30am-12.30pm, 2.30-5.30pm Mon-Sat; 8.30am-1pm Sun.

LAZZI

Piazza Stazione 47r (information 055 351 061). **Open** 9am-12.30pm, 3-5.30pm daily.

By train

Train tickets can be bought from the ticket desk or cash-only vending machines in the station, or from travel agents displaying the FS (Ferrovie dello Stato – state railways) logo. When boarding a train in any Italian city, stamp your ticket and any supplements (*convalidare*) in the small, yellow machines at the head of the platforms. Failure to do this may result in a fine. Left luggage facilities are available at Santa Maria Novella station (Firenze SMN), where virtually all long-distance trains arrive in Florence. Taxis service the station on a 24-hour basis, and many city buses stop here. If you are travelling light, it is only a ten-minute walk into the centre of Florence. If you arrive late, head for the taxi rank or for one of the night buses (67, 68, 70 or 71) that stop here (*see below* **Night buses**). Many trains arriving during the night also stop at Campo di Marte station to the north-west of the city, where buses 67 and 70 also stop. Some Eurostars stop at Rifredi station as well as SMN.

Campo di Marte

Via Mannelli (055 235 4130). Bus 12, 70.

This is the principal station in Florence when Santa Maria Novella is closed during the night. Many long-distance trains stop here. The ticket office is always open.

Rifredi

Via dello Steccuto 1 (055 235 2224). Bus 14, 28, 67.

Local trains and some Eurostars stop here.

Santa Maria Novella

Piazza Stazione (055 235 2061). **Open** 4.15am-1.30am daily; *information office* 7am-9pm daily; *ticket office* 5.45am-10pm daily.

Train information

(1478 88088). **Open** 7am-9pm daily. This is the centralised information service of the state railways (FS-Ferrovie dello Stato) and provides information on national and international routes, and some English is spoken. Calls are answered in a queuing system.

Disabled train enquiries

(055 235 2275). **Open** 7am-9pm daily. English is spoken.

Ufficio assistenza disabili (055 235 2533). Platform 5, Santa Maria Novella station. **Open** 7am-9pm.

Public transport

Buses

Florence is a small city and its only internal public transport is the bus network, run by the ATAF bus company, which is comprehensive and reasonably efficient. The most useful routes are outlined below.

ATAF

Information: Piazza Stazione (055 565 0222). **Open** 7.30am-8pm daily. The main ATAF information desk has English-speaking staff, but if you make your enquiry by phone, you may not be so lucky. Here you can buy a variety of bus tickets (*see below* **Tickets**), and get a booklet with details of all routes and the different tickets. Basic information on prices is also available in English.

Daytime services

Most ATAF routes run 5.30am-9pm with a frequency of between 10 and 30 minutes depending on the route. After 9pm, there are four night services (*see below* **Night Buses**). Buses usually leave their departure point on time, but heavy traffic can cause delays en route. The orange-and-white *fermata* (bus stops) list the stops along the route, and each stop has its name indicated at the top. You must have a ticket before boarding as they are not available on the bus (except for the 70, *see below,* **Night buses**), and it must be stamped in the machine near the door. If you are using a ticket for two consecutive journeys, stamp it on the first bus.

Useful routes

7 from Santa Maria Novella station, via Piazza San Marco to Fiesole;
10 to and from Settignano;
13 a circular route via Santa Maria Novella station, Piazza della Libertà, across the river, Viale Michelangiolo, Piazzale Michelangiolo and San Miniato;
62 to and from Vespucci Airport (*see* **Arriving in Florence**, *above*).

ATAF has recently introduced some environmentally-friendly electric buses, which run four routes: **A**, **B**, **D** and the Sunday and holiday service, **P**. Their diminutive size means they can cope with narrower streets (impossible for their larger counterparts), and these routes make wonderful unofficial sightseeing tours, taking in most of the important sights, north and south of the river. They also have a special monthly season ticket for only L23,000; the routes are detailed in ATAF's booklet.

Night buses

Three bus routes operate until 12.30am/1am (the 67, 68 and 71), but only one, the 70, runs all night and leaves Santa Maria Novella every hour. It passes through the centre of town, goes north, calls at Campo di Marte station (useful for night-time train departures and arrivals), and returns to Santa Maria Novella via a long, circular route. Tickets are available on board, but cost double what they would during the day.

Tickets

All ATAF bus tickets must be bought in advance. They are available from the ATAF office in Piazza Stazione (open 7am-8pm daily) and (except for monthly season tickets) automatic machines (in Piazza Stazione, Piazza San Marco and Piazza Unità, as well as Piazza Mino, Fiesole), tabacchi, newsstands and some bars, all of which display an orange ATAF sticker. When you board the bus, stamp the ticket in one of the machines, usually placed by the front and rear doors. Plain-clothes inspectors circulate frequently and anyone without a ticket is fined L75,000 on the spot.

60-minute ticket (*biglietto 60 minuti*) L1,500; valid for an hour of travel on all buses. You can use as many different routes as you want within this time.
Multiple ticket (*biglietto multiplo*) L5,800; four tickets, each valid for 60 minutes, and must be stamped.
3-hour ticket (*biglietto 3 ore*) L2,500; valid for three hours.
24-hour ticket (*biglietto 24 ore*) L6,000; great-value one-day pass which must be stamped at the beginning of the first journey.
Monthly pass (*abbonamento ordinario*) L53,000; A passport-sized photo is required for this season ticket. It can be bought from the ATAF office at Santa Maria Novella station, or from any of the normal outlets displaying an *Abbonamenti ATAF* sign.

Disabled travellers

Disabled facilities in Florence are not as they should be, but people are usually willing to help. New buses (grey and green) share routes 3, 7*, 9, 12, 13*, 16, 23*, 27, 28, 30, 31, 34, 36 with the old (all orange), and these are fully wheelchair accessible with an electric platform at the rear door and space for a wheelchair on board; an asterix denotes the routes with the most new buses. The small electric bus route D, which goes through the centre of town, is also fully equipped. Trains that allow space for wheelchairs in the carriages and have disabled loos have a wheelchair logo on the outside, but there is no wheelchair access up the steep steps. Call the information office (055 235 2275, English spoken) for assistance. Taxis take wheelchairs, but warn them when you book. There are free disabled parking places throughout Florence, and disabled drivers displaying the sticker have access to pedestrian areas of the city. There are toilets for the disabled at Florence and Pisa airports and Santa Maria Novella train station, as well as in many of Florence's main sights. Many museums are fully wheelchair accessible with lifts, ramps on steps and disabled toilets.

The Provincia di Florence produces a booklet (also in English) with descriptions (how many steps on each floor, wide doorways and so on), of venues throughout the province (not all of Tuscany) and what sort of disabled facilities are provided in each place. This is available from all tourist offices.

Transport in Tuscany

As long as you have time and patience, it is quite possible to see a good deal of Tuscany on public transport. There are little local trains (*diretto* or *locale*), which stop the old-fashioned stations of tiny villages; to plan your routes you will need to buy a comprehensive train timetable, available at most large stations.

The Tuscan bus network is pretty comprehensive, although in most remote villages, buses are timed to coincide with the school day, leaving early in the morning and returning at lunchtime, which means you either have to limit yourself to a morning in a certain place, or commit yourself to staying overnight. It is not difficult to hitch in the countryside, as long as you are reasonably neatly dressed (no self-respecting Italian would want to be associated with a scruffy passenger). There is no national bus network in Italy.

Within Tuscany there are several bus companies; the main ones are:

CAP *Via Nazionale 13, Florence (055 214 627). Information & tickets Largo Fratelli Alinari 10 (055 214 537).* Northern Tuscany.

LAZZI *Piazza Stazione 47r, Florence (055 351 061).*

RAMA *Via Topazo 12, Grosseto (0564 454 169).* Grosseto and the Maremma.

SITA *Via Santa Caterina da Siena 15, Florence (055 483 651).*

TRA-IN *Piazza San Domenico, Siena (0577 204 111).* Siena Province.

Taxis

Licensed taxis are white with yellow graphics and have a meter. Each one has a code name of a city or country plus a number on the door by way of identification; for example, *Londra 6*. If you have any problems, take note of this code. It can be difficult to flag one down in the street.

Fares & Surcharges

Taxis are expensive in Florence, but fares are standard for all the legitimate companies working in the city. When you get in, the meter will read at least L4,400; this is the minimum charge. The fare increases at a rate of L1,440 per kilometre. There is an overall minimum fare of L7,100. From 10pm-6am, there is a L5,100 night supplement; on Sundays and public holidays, there is a L3,100 supplement from 6am-10pm and then the night supplement resumes. Each item of luggage in the boot costs extra, and destinations beyond the official city limits (Fiesole, for example) cost considerably more.

Taxi ranks

Ranks are indicated by a blue sign with 'TAXI' written in white, but this is no guarantee any cars will be waiting. There are ranks in Piazza della Repubblica, Piazza della Stazione, Piazza di Santa Maria Novella, Piazza del Duomo, Piazza San Marco, Piazza Santa Croce and Piazza di Santa Trinità.

Phone cabs

You can phone for a taxi from any of the numbers listed below. When your call is answered, give the address where you want to be picked up, remembering to specify if the street number is *nero* or *rosso* (see **About the Guide**). You will be given the taxi's code and a time; for example, '*Londra 6 in tre minuti*' (Londra 6 in three minutes). The meter is running from the moment your call is answered, so do not be surprised if there is a hefty sum on the clock when you get in.

Taxi numbers: 055 4390; 055 4798; 055 4242; 055 4386.

Driving in Florence

Florence's streets are so jammed with traffic, and the air quality is so poor, that the municipal council has recently started taking steps to improve the situation. When pollution levels reach a certain limit, cars that use diesel or leaded fuel are banned altogether from within a large radius of the city (eco-friendly cars have special window stickers). Digital notices above the main roads into town give notice of these bans. An extraordinarily stone-age warning system, somewhat akin to smoke signals is also in place: street lights go on for 15 minutes at noon, 2pm and 4pm of the day prior to a ban. If the citizens of Florence see the lights on all three times (all three, mind), they know to use the bus the next day. On ban days, if you do not have an appropriate vehicle, you cannot drive between 8am and 6pm. Hire cars and vehicles with foreign number plates are excluded from the ban.

In addition there are the permanent Traffic Free Zones (ZTL). These areas (lettered A-E), include the *centro storico* (historic centre) and are gradually expanding outwards. Only residents or permit-holders can enter from 7.30am to 6.30pm, Monday to Saturday. This is extended in the summer to exclude cars from the centre in the evenings (times vary year to year) from Friday to Sunday. Access to hotels on arrival and departure is permitted, and foreign-plated cars are again excluded from the ban.

Parking is a major problem and is severely restricted in the centre of town. You are advised to use a car park rather than risk a fine or being towed. For details of car parks, *see below* **Parking**.

The best and quickest way to get around Florence is on foot. In pedestrian areas, beware of bicycles and mopeds; do not be surprised if you meet two-wheeled vehicles coming the wrong way up a one-way street. In a move to counteract pollution electric scooters are being introduced (*see p49,* **Viva la Vespa!**). Don't expect cars to stop instantly for a traffic light, and do expect them to ignore red lights when making right turns from side streets. If you really want to take your life in your hands, hire a bicycle or scooter.

Breakdown services

It is advisable to join a national motoring organisation, like the AA or RAC in Britain, or the AAA in the US, before taking a car to Italy. They have reciprocal arrangements with the **Automobile Club d'Italia (ACI)**, who will tell you what to do in case of a breakdown, and provide useful general information on driving in Europe. Even for non-members, the ACI is the best number to call if you have any kind of breakdown.

If you require extensive repairs and wish to go to a manufacturer's official dealer, these are listed in the Yellow Pages under *auto*. Specialist repairers are listed under categories such as *gommista* (tyres), *marmitte* (*exhaust*), and *carrozzerie* (bodywork and windscreens). The *English Yellow Pages* has a list of English-speaking mechanics.

Automobile Club d'Italia (ACI)

Viale Amendola 36 (055 24861/24hr information in English 064477/24hr emergency line 116). Bus 8, 14, 31. **Open** 8.30am-1pm, 3-5.30pm Mon-Fri. The ACI has English-speaking staff, and while no longer providing free service for foreign drivers, prices are reasonable. Members of associated organisations are entitled to basic repairs free, and to other services at preferential rates. Membership is not needed to use the phone lines, but non-members will be charged for services. Phone 44 77 for information on ACI services, driving regulations and customs formalities in Italy and for traffic and weather information.

Parking

In unrestricted areas, parking is free in most side streets, while most main streets are strictly no-parking zones. No parking is allowed where you see *Passo Carrabile* (access at all times) and *Sosta Vietata* (no parking) signs. Disabled parking spaces, are marked by yellow stripes on the road. Blue lines on the road indicate a paid-parking area, where an attendant will issue you with a ticket. A *Zona Rimozione* (tow-away area) sign at the end of a street is valid for the entire length of the street. Most streets in town are washed regularly, usually in the early hours of the morning. All vehicles have to be removed from the area or they will be towed away. It is easy to get caught out by this, but permanent street signs tell you when cleaning takes place, and notices are distributed two days in advance.

The safest place to leave a car in Florence is in one of the underground car parks, but it's pricey. The two listed here have surveillance cameras, and are open 24 hours a day.

Parcheggio Parterre *Via Madonna delle Tosse 9 (055 500 1994). Bus to Piazza della Libertà.* **Open** 24 hours daily. **Rates** L2,000 per hour; L25,000 per 24 hours; L70,000 per week. If you are staying in a Florentine hotel and produce a receipt, you can park here at a special rate of L15,000 per day. You will also be given the free loan of a bike while the car is parked.

Parcheggio Piazza Stazione *Via Alamanni 14/Piazza Stazione 12/13 (055 230 2655).* **Open** 24 hours daily. **Rates** L3,000 per hour; L2,500 per hour 9pm-7am Mon-Thur; L140,000 for five days.

Prices at these smaller, central car parks depend on the car size.

Garage Lungarno *Borgo San Jacopo 10 (055 282 542).* **Open** 7am-midnight. **Rates** L10,000 first two hours; L38,000 24 hours.

International Garage *Via Palazzuolo 29 (055 282 386).* **Open** 7am-midnight Mon-Sat; 7am-noon, 6pm-midnight Sun. **Rates** L8,000 first two hours; L35,000 for 24 hours.

Garage Europa *Borgo Ognissanti 96 (055 292 222).* **Open** 6am-2am daily. **Rates** L10,000 first two hours; L35,000 per day; L165,000 per week.

Car pounds

If your car is not where you left it, it has probably been towed. Phone the municipal police (*vigili urbani*) on 055 32831, or the central car pound (*Depositeria Comunale*) on 055 308 249 to find out which pound it has been taken to, quoting your registration number.

You will have to pay a towing charge, which depends on whether it was towed away during the day or at night. Rates are L90,000 and L104,000 respectively for the first 24 hours, and L12,000 per day after that. Payment can be made by cheque or cash. On top of these charges, you will also be liable for a parking fine. The three car pounds in Florence are:

Via del Olmatello *Bus 62.* **Open** 24 hours daily.

Via Arcovata 6 *Bus 23, 33 to Viale Corsica.* **Open** 7am-7pm Mon-Sat.

Parcheggio Parterre *Via Madonna delle Tosse 9. Bus to Piazza Libertà.* **Open** 7am-1am daily.

Petrol

Most petrol stations sell unleaded petrol (*senza piombo*) and regular (*super*). Diesel fuel is *gasolio*. All offer full service on weekdays; many offer a discount for self-service. Pump attendants do not expect tips. At night and on Sundays most stations have automatic self-service pumps that accept L10,000 or L50,000 notes, in good condition.

There are petrol stations on most of main roads out of town, and their normal opening hours are 7.30am-12.30pm, 3-7pm, Monday to Saturday. There are no permanently staffed 24-hour petrol stations in Florence; the nearest are on the motorways. The following AGIP stations have 24-hour self-service machines: Via Bolognese, Via Aretina, Viale Europa, Via Senese, Via Baraca.

Roads

There are three roads in Tuscany which you have to pay a toll in order to use. They are the *autostrade*: A1 (Rome-Florence-Bologna); A11 (the coast-Lucca-Florence); and A12 (Livorno, along the coast to the north). All *autostrade* are indicated by green road signs. As you drive on to one, you pick up a ticket from one of the toll booths and you hand this into another booth as you leave the road. The ticket indicates how many miles of roads you used. To give you some idea of the price, it costs L35,000 to drive the 270km from Rome to Florence. You can pay in cash or with a Viacard, a magnetic swipecard available from newsagents and the ACI. If you're not in a hurry, the smaller roads can be a real pleasure to use, but be warned that some are not surfaced and it's almost impossible to overtake if you get stuck behind a slow-moving truck.

Vehicle hire

Car hire

Branches of the major car hire companies are conveniently near the station around Borgo Ognissanti (Bus B or a short walk from Santa Maria Novella station). It is worth shopping around for the best rates; prices given below are an indication of what you should expect to pay, but they vary according to season. Opening times also change with the seasons.

Avis

Borgo Ognissanti 128r (055 213 629). Bus B. **Open** 8am-7pm Mon-Fri; 8am-1pm, 3-6pm, Sat. **Credit** AmEx, DC, MC, V.
The cheapest grade B car costs around L290,000 for a (three-day) weekend and L590,000 for the week. **Branches**: Peretola Airport (055 315 588); Pisa Airport (050 42028).

Europcar

Borgo Ognissanti 53/55 (055 290 438/290 437). Bus B. **Open** 8am-1pm, 2.30-7pm Mon-Fri; 8am-1pm Sat; *summer* also 8.30am-12.30pm Sun. **Credit** AmEx, DC, MC, V.
A Fiat Punto costs about L180,000 for a weekend and L595,000 for a week. **Branches**: Peretola Airport (055 318 609); Pisa Airport (050 41017).

Moped & bike hire

To hire a scooter or moped (*motorino*) you need a credit card, ID and a cash deposit. Helmets are required on bikes up to 50cc for under-18s. Cycle shops normally ask you to leave ID rather than a deposit.

Alinari

Via Guelfa 85r (055 280 500). **Open** 9.30am-1pm, 3-7pm, Mon-Sat. **Credit** MC, V.
Rental of motorino (for use of one person only) L45,000 per day.

Motorent

Via San Zanobi 9r (055 490 113). **Open** 9am-noon, 2.30-7pm daily. **Credit** AmEx, MC, V.
Bike hire costs L3,500 per hour, L20,000 per day, L100,000 per week. Moped hire prices are from L10,000 per hour, L50,000 per day and L250,000 for a week. VAT at 20% should be added on to these prices; they include a full tank of petrol.

(Almost) Free Bikes

Santa Maria Novella station (information 055 500 0453). **Open** 8am-8pm Mon-Sat.
The city council provides bikes at various pick-up points, the most central of which are Piazza Cestello, Porta Romana, Piazza Strozzi, Santa Maria Novella station, Piazza San Marco and the central market. These bikes are so cheap as to be almost free; L1,000 per day or L20,000 per year, although you have to return them at night. You will be asked for a photocopy of an ID document.

Essential Information

Visas

For EU citizens, a passport or national identity card valid for travel abroad is sufficient, but all non-EU citizens must have full passports. Unrestricted access is granted to all EU nationals. Citizens of the USA, Canada, Australia and New Zealand do not need visas for stays of up to three months. In theory, all visitors to Italy must declare their presence to the local police within eight days of arrival. If you are staying in a hotel, this will be done for you. If not, contact the *Questura Centrale*, the main police station, for advice. Foreigners staying for longer than three months (or eight days if non-EU), or intending to work or study in Italy, need to register and then to procure additional documents. For further details about these, *see below*, **Living & Working**.

Customs

EU nationals do not have to declare goods imported into or exported from Italy for their personal use, as long as they arrive from another EU country. Random checks are made for drugs.

For non-EU citizens the following limits apply:

- 400 cigarettes or 200 small cigars or 100 cigars or 500 grams (17.64 ounces) of tobacco
- 1 litre of spirits (over 22 per cent alcohol) or 2 litres of fortified wine (under 22 per cent alcohol)
- 50 grams (1.76 ounces) of perfume.

There are no restrictions on the import of cameras, watches or electrical goods. Visitors are also allowed to carry up to L20 million in cash.

Insurance

EU nationals are entitled to reciprocal medical care in Italy on production of an E111 form. This covers emergencies, but it will mean you have to deal with the intricacies of the Italian state health system, which can be overwhelmingly frustrating. The E111 will only cover partial costs of medicines.

Non-EU citizens should take out private medical insurance for all eventualities before their visit. For further details on health *see below,* **Health**.

Tourist information

Florence's provincial tourist board, the *Azienda Promozionale Turistica*, or **APT**, and the municipally run **Ufficio Informazione Turistiche** have helpful multilingual staff who do their best to supply up-to-date and reliable information. This is not easy as museums and galleries have a habit of changing their opening hours without keeping the tourist offices informed. There is no central information service for other cities and sights in Tuscany; you have to contact the APT in each district. The local English-language press is a useful source of information (*see chapter* **Media**) and the Italian listings monthly *Firenze Spettacolo* has an English section. The *English Yellow Pages* lists English-speaking services and useful numbers; it is available from all main bookshops (*see chapter* **Shopping**).

A good street map is available free from APT offices. The ATAF bus service publishes a free booklet that outlines all bus routes and fare information. It is available at the Santa Maria Novella station ATAF information office and some bars and hotels. Telecom Italia supplies subscribers with a free, detailed street atlas, *TuttoCittà*; most bars and hotels have one for perusal.

APT Firenze

Via Manzoni 16 (055 23320). Bus 6. **Open** 9am-1pm Mon-Sat.
This is the APT headquarters and has an information office open to the public. The most central office, however, is in Via Cavour. There are also offices in Florence and Pisa airports. The APT provides information and brochures on events in Florence and the surrounding province (NB, not all Tuscany, but the Provincia di Firenze). As well as free maps, it also publishes a brochure, *Firenze per i Giovani,* aimed at young people, with listings for language courses, Internet services, clubs, bike hire, hostels and so on. APT provides hotel lists but not a booking service.
Branches: Via Cavour 1r (055 290 832); Piazza Mino 37, Fiesole (055 598 720). Bus 7.

Consorzio Informazioni Turistiche Alberghiere (ITA)

Stazione di Santa Maria Novella (055 282 893). **Open** *summer* 9am-9pm daily; *winter* 9am-8pm daily.
Personal callers only are assisted at this hotel-booking service. It provides a list of accommodation, and charges between L3,000 and L10,000 according to the category of hotel. It is obligatory to pay for the first night when booking.
Branches: AGIP service station at Peretola (055 421 1800) on the A11 Firenze-Mare motorway; Chianti Est service station (055 621 349) on the A1 Autostrada del Sole motorway; Vespucci airport (055 315 874). No booking service.

Ufficio Informazione Turistiche

Borgo Santa Croce 29r (055 234 0444). **Open** *winter* 9am-1.45pm Mon-Sat; *summer* 9am-7pm Mon-Sat; 9am-1.45pm Sun.
Run by the city of Florence, these offices provide tourist information, free maps, restaurant and hotel lists.
Branch: Piazza Stazione (055 212 245).

Tourist Help

Open *Easter-end-Sept* 8am-7pm daily.
This useful service is run by the *vigili urbani* from two vans, one in Piazza della Repubblica and one just south of the Ponte Vecchio in Via Guicciardini. APT personnel and the municipal police provide practical help and information. This is also where to register complaints about abusive restaurant or hotel charges.

Consulates

There are no embassies in Florence; there are some consular offices, which offer limited services. The nearest consulates for Australia and New Zealand are in Rome.

British Consulate

Lungarno Corsini 2 (055 284 133/ fax 055 219 112). **Open** 9.30am-12.30pm, 2.30-4.30pm, Mon-Fri. Telephone enquiries 9am-1pm, 2-5pm, Mon-Fri.
Outside these hours, a message on the number above will tell you what to do.

South African Consulate

Piazza dei Salarelli 1 (055 281 863). No office; call to make an appointment.

United States Consulate

Lungarno A Vespucci 38 (055 239 8276/fax 055 284 088). **Open** 9am-12.30pm, 2-3.30pm, Mon-Fri.
In case of emergency call the above number and a message will refer you to the current emergency number.

Crime

Serious street crime is not a hazard in Florence, and it remains a relatively safe city to walk in, even late at night. Drug problems are on the increase, however, and in certain areas (some streets around Piazza Santo Spirito, for example) you may come across pushers blatantly trading their wares and looking rather intimidating. Streets in the centre are well-lit and, especially in summer, there are usually plenty of people around. As in most cities, shady characters tend to gravitate toward the train station at night, so avoid that area. It is said that crime in general is increasing, but as a tourist, you are unlikely to come up against any serious problems. Your biggest hassle will probably be pickpockets, often in the form of gypsies (*zingari*) with their kids who hang around the main tourist spots waiting to prey on unwary visitors. The kids are sent in to create a distraction (they may try flapping papers or card) and, before you know it, deft hands have slipped into bags or pocket. These gangs can be insistent. If you are approached, keep walking, keep calm, and hang on to your valuables. You can even try shouting loudly at them; they will soon scuttle off.

For details of what to do if you are a victim of crime, *see below* **Police & security**. You will find that a few basic precautions will greatly reduce a street thief's chances:

Useful numbers

Emergencies (ambulance, fire service police)	113
Medical emergencies	118
Car breakdown (ACI)	116/064477
Police (Florence central police station)	055 49771
IAMAT (multilingual doctors)	055 475 411
Anna Meyers Children's Hospital	055 56621

Electricity

The world of plugs and sockets in Italy is varied and complex, but there is only one electrical current, 220V, which works with British and US-bought products. Buy two-pin travel plugs before leaving, as they will be hard to find in Italy. Adapters for different Italian plugs can be bought at any electrical shop (look for *Casalinghi* or *Elettricità*).

Health

Emergency healthcare is available for all travellers through the Italian national health system. EU citizens are entitled to most forms of treatment for free, though many specialised medicines, analyses and tests will be charged for. To get treatment you need an E111 form (*see* **Insurance**, *above*). For hospital treatment, you have to go to one of the casualty departments listed below. If you want to see a GP, take your E111 to the state health centre (USL) for the district where you are staying. USL are listed in the local phone book and are usually open 9am to 1pm and 2pm to 7pm, Monday to Friday.

Using the state system inevitably means dealing with a whole series of bureaucratic hurdles, and short-term visitors are recommended not to rely on the E111 form but to use private travel insurance. Embassies provide lists of English-speaking doctors and clinics, and they are also listed in the *English Yellow Pages*.

Non-EU citizens with private medical insurance can make use of state facilities on a paying basis, but for anything other than emergencies, it will be more convenient to go directly to private medicine.

Complementary medicine

Most conventional pharmacies also sell some alternative medicines which are quite commonly used in Italy. These medicines are, however, expensive; bring supplies from home if you use them regularly.

Antica Farmacia Sodini

Via dei Banchi 18/20r (055 211 159). **Open** 9am-1pm, 4pm-8pm, Mon-Sat. **No credit cards.**
The English-speaking staff at this homeopathic pharmacy are very helpful. They carry a huge range of medicines and make up prescriptions as well as giving advice.

Ambulatorio Santa Maria Novella

Piazza Santa Maria Novella 24 (055 280 143). **Open** 3-7.30pm Mon, 9am-1pm, 3-7.30pm, Tue-Fri. **No credit cards.**
This is a large group practice where several homeopathic doctors have consulting rooms and offer a range of alternative health services. A full check-up will cost from about L100,000, and some English is spoken. Call to make an appointment first.

Contraception & abortion

Condoms and other forms of contraception are widely available in pharmacies and some supermarkets. If you are in need of further assistance, the Consultorio Familiare at your local USL state health centre (*see above*) will provide advice and information free of charge, though for an examination or prescription you will need an E111 form or private insurance. An alternative is to go to a private clinic like those run by the AIED.

AIED

Via Ricasoli 10 (055 215 237). **Open** 3-6.30pm Mon-Fri.
The clinics run by this private family-planning organisation provide help and information on contraception and related matters and medical care at low cost. Treatment is of a high standard and service is often faster than in state clinics. An examination will usually cost around L60,000 plus L20,000 compulsory membership, payable on the first visit and valid for a year.

Dentists

The following dentists speak English. Call for an appointment.

Dr Derek Murphy

Via Maffei 39 (055 577 545). Bus 1. **Open** 9am-noon, 3.30-7pm, Mon, Wed; 9am-noon Thur.

Dr Maria Peltonen Portman

Via Teatina 2 (055 218 594). **Open** 9.30am-6.30pm Mon-Fri.

Emergencies/hospitals

If you need urgent medical care, it is best to go to the *Pronto Soccorso* (casualty) department of one of the hospitals listed; they are open 24 hours daily. Otherwise call *Soccorso pubblico di emergenza* (general emergency service) on 113; or the medical emergency service on 118 for an ambulance (*ambulanza*). You can also call 118 to find a doctor on call in your area (emergencies only). The most central hospital for emergencies is **Santa Maria Nuova**. One of the obvious anxieties involved with falling ill abroad is the language problem. If you need a translator to help out at the hospital, *see below*, **AVO**.

AVO (Association of Hospital Volunteers)

(055 425 0126/055 234 4567). **Open** 4-6pm Mon, Wed, Fri; 10am-noon Tue, Thur.
If you are hospitalised while staying in Florence and do not speak Italian, there is a group of volunteer interpreters who will come to your rescue by helping out with explanations to doctors and hospital staff. They also provide support and advice on what to do in this situation. They speak 22 languages. The opening times are office hours. At other times call the first listed number.

IAMAT (Associated Medical Studio)

Via Lorenzo il Magnifico 59 (24hr phone service 055 475 411). Bus 8, 13. **Open** *clinic* 11am-noon, 5-6pm, Mon-Fri; 11am-noon Sat.
IAMAT is a private medical service which organises home visits by doctors. Catering particularly for foreigners, they will send a GP or specialist to your hotel or temporary residence within an hour and a half. English and French are spoken fluently by the medical staff. A home visit will cost between L120,000 and L150,000. IAMAT also runs a clinic where a consultation will cost L60,000 (or L50,000 for students).

English-speaking GP

Dr Stephen Kerr, Via Porta Rossa 1 (055 288 055/0335 836 1682). **Surgery** *by appointment* 9am-1pm Mon-Fri; *drop-in clinic* 3-5pm Mon-Fri. **Credit** AmEx, MC, V.
Dr Kerr practises privately in Florence and makes house calls. His charges are fairly reasonable for Florence; L80,000 for a consultation in his surgery (L50,000 for students enrolled in a school in Florence), L130,000 for a house call.

Ospedale Istituto Ortopedico Toscano (Orthopedics)

Viale Michelangiolo 41 (055 565 771). Bus 12, 13.

Ospedale Meyer (Children)

Via Luca Giordano 13 (055 56621). Bus 11, 17.

Ospedale Torregalli

Via Torregalli 3 (055 719 2447). Bus 83.

Policlinico di Careggi

Viale Morgagni 85 (055 427 711). Bus 8, 14c.

Santa Maria Nuova

Piazza Santa Maria Nuova 1 (055 27581). Bus 11, 14, 17, 23.
This is the most centrally located hospital in Florence. There is also a 24-hour pharmacy directly outside it.

Helplines & agencies

Alcoholics Anonymous

English-speaking group: St James' Church, Via Rucellai 9 (055 353 6254). Bus to Santa Maria Novella station.
The English-speaking branch of AA in Florence is attached to the American Church. Meetings are held on Tuesdays and Thursdays at 1.30pm, and on Saturdays at 5pm. These are also open to anyone with drug-related problems.

Drogatel

(167 016 600). **Open** 9am-9pm daily. A national freephone number with English speakers who can refer you to the correct number to call in Florence if you should need help. They also give advice on alcohol-related problems.

Linea Verde Aids

(freephone 1678 61061). The national help and information line dedicated to HIV-related problems. Some English may be spoken.

Consultorio per la Salute Omosessuale

Via San Zanobi 54r (055 47 6557). Bus 11, 17. Run by the ARCI Gay organisation, this centre provides various services relating to AIDS and HIV. English is spoken. Telephone counselling is offered 4-8pm Monday to Friday, and counsellors are also available in person. AIDS tests are carried out on Wednesdays 4-5.30pm. Staffed by volunteers, all these services are free.

Pharmacies

Pharmacies (*farmacia*, identified by a red or green cross) function semi-officially as mini-clinics, with their staff giving informal medical advice and suggesting medicines as well as making up prescriptions from your doctor. Normal opening hours are from 8.30am to 1pm and from 4pm to 8pm, Monday to Saturday. At other times, a duty rota system is in operation.

A list by the door of any pharmacy indicates the nearest one that is open outside normal hours. The daily rota is also published in all the local papers, and there are phone lines for information on which chemists are open in each district (call 182; operators do not usually speak English). At duty pharmacies there is a surcharge of L5,000 per client (though not per item) when only the special duty counter is open, which, in most cases, is between midnight and 8.30am. The following pharmacies all provide a 24-hour service, and there is no supplement for night service:

Farmacia Comunale

N13 Interno Stazione Santa Maria Novella (055 216 761/055 289 435). **Open** 24 hours daily. **No credit cards**.

Farmacia Molteni

Via Calzaiuoli 7r (055 215 472/055 289 490). **Open** 24 hours daily. **Credit** AmEx, MC, V. English spoken.

Farmacia all'Insegna del Moro

Piazza San Giovanni 20r (055 211 343). **Open** 24 hours daily. **Credit** V. Some English spoken.

Lost property

Anything mislaid on public transport, or stolen, then discarded, may turn up at one of the lost property offices (*ufficio oggetti rinvenuti*).

For numbers to call if you lose a credit card or travellers' cheques, *see below* **Money**.

ATAF

Via Circondaria 17B (055 328 3942). Bus 23, 33. **Open** 9am-noon Mon-Sat.
Anything found on an ATAF bus should end up at this municipal office.

FS/Santa Maria Novella (SMN) Station

Interno Stazione Santa Maria Novella (055 235 2190). **Open** 8am-noon, 2-6pm, daily.
Articles found on state railways in the Florence area are sent to this office on platform 16, next to the left luggage deposit. Staff speak minimal English.

Money

The Italian currency is the lira (plural *lire*), usually written as L, less often as £ or Lit. Coins are confusing: there are L50, L100, L200, L500 and L1,000 coins, but three different sizes of L50 and L100 are in circulation. Bank notes start with the multicoloured L1,000 and go through L2,000, L5,000, L10,000, L50,000, L100,000 up to the L500,000 note. It's unlikely you will see the latter, and even more unlikely that anyone will change it for you.

Prices are rounded up to the nearest L50 and, by law, after any transaction you must be given a receipt (*scontrino fiscale*). Most places insist you take it, (they risk prosecution otherwise) but others may try to avoid giving you a receipt for tax reasons, in which case it is your right to ask for one.

Banks

Most banks are open from 8.20am to 1.20pm and 2.35pm to 3.35pm Monday to Friday, although these times may vary slightly from bank to bank. All banks are closed on public holidays and staff work reduced hours the day before a holiday, usually closing at around 11am. Florence branches of most banks are found around Piazza della Repubblica. *See also* **Business**, *below*.

Foreign exchange

Banks usually have better exchange rates than private bureaux de change (*cambio*). To change travellers' cheques you need a passport or other ID. Beware of 'no commission' claims, as the rate of exchange will generally be terrible.

Major credit and debit cards can be used in most cash machines and there are several automatic exchange machines in the city centre, which accept most currencies, but only in notes in good condition. The best method to have money sent to you is through **American Express**, **Thomas Cook** or **Western Union**.

As well as the places listed here, the main post offices (*see below*, **Post**) change money. Commission on cash transactions is L1,000; on travellers' cheques up to a value of L100,000, commission is L2,000 and L5,000 above that.

If you lose a card, phone one of the emergency numbers listed below. All lines are freephone (1678) numbers, have English-speaking staff and are open 24 hours daily.

American Express (card emergencies 1678 64046/travellers' cheques 1678 720 00).
Diners Club (1678 64064).
Mastercard/Access/Carta Sí/ Eurocard (1678 68086).
Mastercard (1678 70 866).
Visa (1678 77232).

Agency Prime Link

Via Panicale 18 (055 291 275). **Open** 9.30am-1.30pm, 3-7pm, daily.
The quickest, but not the cheapest way to send money across the world.

American Express

Via Dante Alighieri 22r (055 50981). Bus 23. **Open** 9am-5.30pm Mon-Fri; 9am-12.30pm Sat.
This office also has a travel agency.

Change Underground

Piazza Stazione 14, interno 37 (055 291 312). **Open** 9am-7.30pm Mon-Sat; 9am-1.30pm Sun. In the underground shopping mall under Santa Maria Novella train station.

Deutsche Bank

Via Strozzi 16r (055 27061). **Open** 8.20am-1.20pm, 2.40-4pm, Mon-Fri.
Cash and travellers' cheques can be changed for a standard fee of L10,000.
Branch: Via Porta Santa Maria 50 (055 283 832).

Frama

Via Calzaiuoli 79r (055 214 003). **Open** 10am-7pm Mon-Sat; 10am-6.30pm Sun. A hefty 9.6 per cent is charged on larger transactions, or a minimum of L4,000.
Branch: Via Martelli 9r (055 288 246).

Thomas Cook

Lungarno Acciaiuoli 6/12 (055 289 781). **Open** 9am-7pm Mon-Sat; 9.30am-5pm Sun. One of the few exchange offices open on a Sunday. No commission charged for cash withdrawal via Mastercard, Eurocard or Visa.

Western Union

(Toll-free number 1670 16840). Agenzia STS Via Zanetti 18 (055 284 183). **Open** 9.30am-1pm, 3.30-7pm, Mon-Fri.

Tax-free shopping

By law, all non-EU residents in Italy are entitled to a VAT (IVA) refund on purchases of L300,000 and over. Ask for a *fattura* (invoice) or a tax-free cheque when shopping. Goods bought must be declared at customs on leaving the EU and a customs stamp obtained no later than three months after the date of purchase. Return the stamped invoice to the store within four months of the date of purchase and they will return a reimbursement of the VAT amount.

Police & security

Italian police forces are divided into four colour-coded units. The *vigili urbani* (municipal police) wear navy blue. They are unarmed and deal with all traffic matters within the city. The two forces responsible for dealing with crime are the *polizia statale* (state police), who also wear blue but have paler trousers, and the normally black-clad *carabinieri*, part of the army. Their roles overlap. The *guardia di finanza* (financial police) wear grey and deal with financial and customs irregularities. They have little to do with tourists.

In an emergency go to the nearest carabinieri post (*commissariato*) or police station (*questura*), and say you want to report a *furto*. A *denuncia* (statement) of the incident will be made. You need the *denuncia* to make an insurance claim. A lost or stolen passport should be reported to your embassy or consulate. The best place to report a crime in Florence is at the **Questura Centrale**.

Commando Regione Carabinieri

Borgo Ognissanti 48 (055 24811). Bus 12. **Open** 24 hrs daily. A carabineri post near the town centre.

Questura Centrale

Via Zara 2 (055 49771). **Open** 24hrs daily; *Ufficio Denuncio* 8.30am-8pm daily. To report a crime, go to the Ufficio Denuncie, where you will be asked to fill in a form.

Post

The Italian postal system is notoriously unreliable. Some letters do, of course, arrive in reasonable time, but unpredictability is the key word, so expect delays. If a letter or parcel needs to arrive at its destination on time, use a courier service (*see* **Business**, *below*).

Stamps can be bought at *tabacchi* or post offices. A letter or postcard to any EU destination costs L800; to the US both cost L1,300 air mail. Post boxes are red and have two slots, *Per la Città* (for Florence) and *Tutte le altre Destinazioni* (everywhere else). A letter takes about five days to reach the UK, and eight to the US. To speed things up, mail can be sent *raccomandata* (registered, L4,000 extra) or *assicurata* (insured, L6,400 extra). These services are only available from post offices. Don't fall for the L3,600 *espresso* supplement; the express bit applies only in the country of destination and will be no quicker leaving Italy, where any delay usually happens.

Heavier mail is charged according to weight. A 1kg parcel to the UK costs L30,700 (air mail); L33,300 to the US. Italian postal charges are notoriously complicated depending whether you are sending a letter, an open parcel, a sealed parcel and so on, so be prepared for variations.

Postal information

(160). **Open** 8am-7pm Mon-Fri; 8am-1pm Sat.
Based at the main post office, this phone line (some English spoken) will answer queries on the postal system. A call costs L600.

CAI Post courier service

Via Alamanni 20r (055 216 349/ 055 238 1065). **Open** 8.15am-7pm, Mon-Fri; 8.15am-12.30pm Sat.
This express letter and parcel service is run by the Poste Italiane. Within Europe, delivery is guaranteed between one and three days and costs L30,000 up to 500g to the UK; the same takes between two and four days to the US and costs L46,000. Within Italy the service is called Post Accelere Interno and costs L12,000.
Branch Via Pellicceria 3 (in main post office) (055 216 122).

Post offices

Local post offices (*ufficio postale*) in each district open from 8.15am to 1.30pm Monday to Friday, and from 8.15am to 12.30pm on Saturday. They close an hour earlier than usual on the last day of the month. The main post office has longer opening hours and a range of additional services.

Posta Centrale

Via Pellicceria 3 (information 160). **Open** 8.15am-6pm Mon-Sat.
This vast building on two floors is always busy and offers a full range of postal and telegraph services. There is a CAI Post courier office here (*see above*), and Telecom Italia run a mobile phone centre in the building. Letters sent Poste Restante (in Italian, *Fermo Posta*) should be sent here and addressed to Fermo Posta Centrale, Firenze. You need a passport to collect mail and you may have to pay a small charge.

Other central post offices:
Via Pietrapiana 53. Bus B. **Open** 8.15am-6pm Mon-Fri; 8.15am-12.30pm Sat.
Via Cavour 71r. **Open** 8.15am-1.30pm Mon-Fri; 8.15am-12.30pm Sat.
Via Barbadori 40r. **Open** 8.15am-1.30pm Mon-Fri; 8.15am-12.30pm Sat.

Public holidays

On public holidays (*giorni festivi*), virtually all shops, banks and businesses are shut, though most bars and restaurants stay open.
The public holidays are:
New Year's Day (*Capo d'anno*) 1 January; Epiphany (*La Befana*) 6 January; Easter Monday (*Lunedì Pasqua*); Liberation Day (*Venticinque Aprile*) 25 April; May Day (*Primo Maggio*) 1 May; Saints' Day (*San Giovanni*) 24 June; Feast of the Assumption (*Ferragosto*) 15 August; All Saints' (*Tutti Santi*) 1 November; Immaculate Conception (*Festa dell'Immacolata*) 8 December; Christmas Day (*Natale*) 25 December; Boxing Day (*Santo Stefano*) 26 December.

There is limited public transport on 1 May and Christmas afternoon. Holidays falling on a Saturday or Sunday are not celebrated the following Monday, but if a holiday falls on a Thursday or Tuesday many people make a long weekend of it, and take the intervening day off as well. Such a weekend is called a *ponte* (bridge). Many people also disappear for a large chunk of August, when *chiuso per ferie* (closed for holidays) signs appear in shops and restaurants, with the dates of closure. This, however, is organised on a rota system by the city council, so there should be something open in each area at any given time. For a calendar of Tuscany's traditional and modern festivals, *see chapter* **Tuscany by Season**.

Public lavatories

Florence is not well equipped with public loos, and it's usually easiest to go to a bar (they are obliged by law to let you use their facilities).

Public toilets can be found in Santa Maria Novella station, Palazzo Vecchio, the Palazzo Pitti and the coach park to the west of Fortezza da Basso.

Telephones

For many years, Telecom Italia has operated one of the most expensive systems in Europe, particularly for international calls. Recently, however, prices have dropped to fall in line with those in the rest of Europe. From a public call box, the minimum charge for a local call is L200; the day-time rate to the UK is L1,070 for the first minute, L535 per minute thereafter. Off-peak (10pm-8am Mon-Sat, all day Sunday), this falls to L1,016 and L469 respectively. Calling from a telephone centre costs the same as from a public phone box, but is more convenient for long-distance calls as you avoid the need for large amounts of change or several phone cards. Services are listed in the local phone book, the Elenco Telefonico.

Operator services

All these services operate 24 hours.
Operator & Italian Directory Enquiries (12).
International Operator (Europe) (170).
International Operator (rest of world) (170).
International Directory Enquiries (Europe) (176).
Intercontinental Directory Enquiries (rest of the world) (176).
Problems on local calls (182).
Problems on international Calls (17 23535).
Alarm calls (114). An automatic message will ask you to dial in the time you want your call (with four figures, using the 24-hour clock) followed by your phone number.
Tourist Information (110).

Phone numbers

All numbers beginning with 167 or 1678 are freephone lines. At the end of 1998, the Italian dialling system changed, and you must now include a dialling code with every number dialled, even when you're in the same area. If you are in Florence and wish to dial a Florence number, you have to dial 055 followed by a 5-, 6-or 7-digit number.

International Calls

To make an international call from Florence, dial 00, then the country-code, followed by the area code and individual number. To phone Florence from abroad, dial the international code, then 39 for Italy, 055 for Florence, followed by the number. To make a reverse charge (collect) call, dial 172, then the country code (hence 172 00 44 for the UK; 172 00 1 for the US) and you'll be connected directly to an operator in that country. In a phone box you need to insert L200, which will be refunded after your call.

Public phone boxes

Many public phones accept phone cards (*carte telefoniche*) or Telecom Italia credit cards only. The former cost L5,000, L10,000 or L15,000 and are available from tabacchi and some newsstands. When you use a new card, break off one corner as marked and insert the card into the slot in the phone. You need L100, L200 or L500 pieces to use public coin phones. The minimum for a local call is L200.

Phone centres

Via Cavour 21r. **Open** 8am-9.45pm daily.
At this Telecom Italia office, you are allocated a booth and can either use a phonecard or pay cash at the desk after you have finished making all your calls. They also have phone directories for all over Europe, information on telephone charges and phone cards.

Religion

There are Catholic churches all over the city, but even if you are not a practising Catholic, it is worth attending mass for the atmosphere. A few churches still sing mass, and if you want to hear some Gregorian Chant, go to **San Miniato al Monte** (Bus 12 or 13). Catholic mass is held in English at Santa Maria del Fiore on Saturdays at 5pm and at the Chiesa dell' Ospedale San Giovanni di Dio (Borgo Ognissanti 20) on Sundays and holidays at 10am. Other religions represented in Florence are listed below.

American Episcopal Church

St James, Via Rucellai 9 (055 29 44 17). Bus 1, 17 or Santa Maria Novella station. **Services** (in English) 9am, 11am Sun.

Anglican

St Mark's, Via Maggio 16 (055 294 764). **Services** 9am (Low Mass), 10.30am (Sung Mass) Sun; 6pm (Low Mass) Thur; 8pm (Low Mass) Fri.

Jewish

Comunita Ebraica, Via Farina 4 (055 245 252/055 245 253). Bus 6. **Services** 8.30/8.45am Sat. For Fri and Sat evening services, call for details as times vary.

Methodist

Chiesa Metodista, Via dei Benci 9. Bus 23, B. **Services** 11am Sun.

Time & weather

Florence is one hour ahead of Greenwich Mean Time, and clocks change at the beginning and end of summer on the same date as in the UK. The surrounding hills mean it can be cold and humid in winter and hot and humid in summer with temperatures soaring to 40+°. Spring and autumn are often warm and pleasant, but not without the risk of rain.

Business

Accountants

Arthur Anderson SpA
Viale Matteotti 25 (055 582 743/fax 055 574 439). **Open** 9am-1pm, 2-7pm Mon-Thur; 9am-1pm, 2-5pm Fri.

Coopers & Lybrand
Viale Milton 65 (055 462 7100/fax 055 476 872). **Open** 9am-1pm, 2-6.30pm, Mon-Fri.

Deloitte & Touche
Via Cavour 64 (055 267 1011/fax 055 282 147). **Open** 9am-1pm, 2-6pm Mon-Fri.

KPMG SpA
Corso Italia 2 (055 213 391/fax 055 215 824). **Open** 9am-1pm, 2-6pm, Mon-Fri.

Price Waterhouse SpA
Viale Milton 65 (055 471 747/fax 055 470 779). **Open** 8.30am-1pm, 2-6.30pm, Mon-Fri.

Banks

Most banks are open from 8.30am-1.20pm, 2.30-3.30pm, Mon-Fri; closed on Sat, public holidays. Banks close early (around 11am) on days preceding national holidays. *See also* **Money**, *above*.

Banca Commerciale Italiana
Via Tornabuoni 16 (055 27851/fax 055 219 976).

Banca Popolare di Lodi
Piazza Davanzati 3 (055 27651/fax 055 276 5207).

Banca Toscana
Via del Corso 6 (055 43911/fax 055 439 1618).

Cassa di Risparmio di Firenze
Via Bufalini 4/6 (055 26121/fax 055 261 2907).

Monte dei Paschi di Siena
Via de Pecori 6/8 (055 27341/fax 055 273 4239).

Chamber of commerce

Camera di Commercio, Industria, Artigianato e Agricoltura
Piazza Giudici 3 (055 27951/fax 055 279 5259).

Conference centres

Castello di Vincigliata
Via di Vincigliata 19, Fiesole (055 599 556).
This historic castle in the hills near Fiesole is used primarily for social receptions. It has beautiful gardens and commanding views of the area. Up to 150 people can be accommodated, and there are full catering and translation services available. Call for a quote.

Centro di Affari Firenze
Via Cennini 5 (055 27731/fax 055 277 3433).
This complex organises local and international business meetings and conferences. It can accommodate up to 1,800 and offers catering and translation services.

Convivium
Viale Europa 4/6 (055 681 1757/fax 681 1766).
Convivium owns a variety of *locales* – mostly villas – in Tuscany which it rents out for conventions and banquets. The buildings, surroundings and services are top quality; and the prices match. Depending on the occasion and services required, villa rental typically costs several million lire per day.

Firenze Expo
Piazza Adua 1 (055 26025/fax 055 211 830).
This centre includes Palazzo dei Congressi in the Fortezza da Basso. It specialises in international meetings; it can accommodate parties from five to 1,000.

Palazzo Budini Gattai
Piazza SS Annunziata 1 (055 210 832/fax 055 212 080).
This fifteenth-century palazzo is now used to hold business meetings and conferences for up to 120 people. Catering and translation services can also be arranged. Call for a quote.

Communications

Rates for Internet access vary between L6,000 and L10,000 per hour. Look out for special offers and preferential rates.

E-mail & the Internet

Cyber Office
Via San Gallo 4r (055 211 103). **Open** 10.30am-7.30pm Mon-Fri; noon-7.30pm Sat. **Credit** MC, V.
Near the university, this well-equipped email and PC centre offers all the usual services (Internet, e-mail, printing, scanning) plus special rates for students. The staff are friendly and a good range of software is on sale.

EDPU
Via Fabroni 76a (055 483 186). **Open** 9am-1.30pm, 3-6.30pm Mon-Fri. **No credit cards**.
This friendly establishment is the best place for Apple problems.

Internet B@r
Via De'Macci 8 (055 247 9465). **Open** *summer* 9am-2am Mon-Sat; *winter* 7.30am-10pm Mon-Sat.
The only Internet bar in Florence. It has four computers were you can surf and hold an e-mail mailbox.

Internet Train
Via dell'Oriuolo 25A (055 263 8968/oriolo@fionline.it). **Open** 10am-10.30pm Mon-Thur; 10am-8pm Fri, Sat; 3pm-7pm Sun. **Credit** MC, V.
This, the first Internet shop in Italy started off with four PCs. It is manned by friendly English-speaking staff. A new branch is due to open across the road at No.40 complete with air-conditioning and 25 computers.
Branches: Via Guelfa 24A (055 214 794/guelfa@fionline.it); Borgo San Jacopo 30r (055 265 7935/ pontevecchio@fionline.it).

Mondial Net Firenze
Via de'Ginori 59/r (055 265 7584/ mondialnet@interbusiness.it). **Open** 10am-9pm Mon-Sat; noon-4pm Sun.
Twelve computers, print and fax services.

Netgate
Via Sant' Egidio 10r (055 234 7967/fax 055 226 1035/firenze @thenetgate.it). **Open** *summer* 10.30am-10.30pm Mon-Sat; *winter* 10:40am-9pm daily.
A spacious work centre with 35 computers. It has another branch in Rome.

Netik
Via dell'Agnolo 65r (055 242 645/ fax 055 226 4493). **Open** 10am-8pm Mon-Sat. **Credit** AmEx, MC, V.
Tempting hourly rates for using the 15 computers (L6,000 per hour; 13 hours for L60,000). Its Net2Phone system offers cheap calls (L270/min to UK, Europe, US and Australia). Scanning and printing also available.

Il Varco
Via Ricasoli 47 (tel/fax 055 265 7806/ilvarco@iname.com). **Open** 9am-4pm Tue-Fri; 8.30pm-midnight Mon-Fri.

Set up by students as a non-profit-making scheme to provide everyone with Internet access. Events (concerts, dance classes) are also organised and are open to anyone.

Village
Via degli Alfani 11/13r (055 247 9398). **Open** 10am-midnight Mon-Sat; 2-8pm Sun. **No credit cards.**
Sixteen computers, a phone centre with low national and international rates, a fax service, scanner and colour printer. Offers various start-up deals and sells software.

Faxing & photocopying

Centro AZ
Via degli Alfani 20r (055 247 7855). Bus 31, 32. **Open** 9am-1pm, 3-7pm, Mon-Fri; 9am-12.30pm Sat. **No credit cards.**
Faxes carry a standard charge of L2,000 plus the cost of the call.

Copisteria Elletra
Via San Gallo 68r (055 473 809). Bus 11, 17. **Open** 8.30am-1pm, 3-7pm, Mon-Fri; 9am-12.30pm Sat.
Faxes cost L7,000 per page (EU countries) and L9,500 per page (US).

Couriers

Bartolini
Via Majorana 23, Osmannoro (055 30950/fax 055 375 578). **Open** 8.30am-noon, 2-6pm Mon-Fri. **No credit cards.**
Bartolini offers an express service in Italy and to the rest of Europe (excluding Scandinavia). To send a 5kg package to Rome costs L55,000; to the UK is L70,000 and takes three days. Prices include pick-up.

DHL
Toll-free 1678 345 345. **Open** 24 hours daily. **No credit cards.**
Letters (up to 150g) cost L59,000 to the UK; L57,000 to the US (guaranteed delivery within 48 hours). A 5kg package is L186,000 to the UK; L211,000 to the US (guaranteed delivery within 2-3 days). Free same-day pick-up is offered if you phone before 3pm.

Federal Express
Toll-free 1678 33040. **Open** 8am-7pm Mon-Fri. **No credit cards.**
Letters (up to 500g) cost L75,000 (plus VAT) to the UK; L49,600 to the US. A 5kg package is L157,500 (plus VAT) to the UK; L182,000 to the US. Next-day service is guaranteed for all deliveries placed before 10am (except on Friday). Free pick-up.

Menicalli
Via della Fonderia 79 int (055 229 480/fax 055 229 585). **Open** 8.30am-8pm Mon-Fri. **No credit cards.**
Europe-wide courier service with delivery promised within 24 hours. Standard letters within Italy cost L30,000 (plus VAT).

Pony Express
Via Corelli 27 (055 4387). **Open** 8.30am-7.30pm Mon-Fri. **No credit cards.**
Pony Express promise delivery in Florence within one hour and within 24 hours for other destinations in Italy and the rest of the Europe. A letter within Florence costs L15,000, and L39,000 to elsewhere in Italy. Packages up to 1kg cost L70,000 for delivery within 24 hours to the UK, and L110,000 within 48 hours to the US. Free pick-up is offered until 4pm.

UPS
Toll-free 1678 22 055. Open 8am-6.30pm Mon-Fri; 8.30am-1pm Sat. **Credit** MC, V.
Letters are L64,800 to the UK, L60,000 to the US (guaranteed delivery by 10.30am the next day). A 5kg package costs L193,200 to the UK, L218,500 to the US (guaranteed delivery within two days). Free same-day pick-up is offered if you phone before 1pm.

Translation services

Business Language Services
Via dei Fossi 15 (tel/fax 055 291 484). **Open** 8am-8pm Mon-Sat.
Offers an express translation service and can provide interpreters.

Centro Comit
Viale Lavagnini 54 (055 496 567/fax 055 499 496). **Open** 9am-1pm, 3-6pm Mon-Fri.

Emynet
Lungarno Soderini 5/7/9r (055 219 228/fax 055 218 992/emynet@emynet.com). **Open** 9.30am-1.30pm, 3-7pm Mon-Fri.
Emyservice claims to offer full written and spoken translations in 'all' languages. Prices vary depending on the service requested; phone for further details.

Interpreti di Conferenza
Via Faenza 109 (055 239 8748/fax 055 293 204). **Open** 9am-1pm Mon-Fri.
Specialises in interpreters for business meetings.

Packing & removals

Oli-Ca
Borgo SS Apostoli 27r (055 239 6917). **Open** 9am-1pm, 3.30-7.30pm, Mon-Fri; 9am-1pm Sat.
For full preparation (all materials and labour included) of a 70x40x25cm box, the cost is L15,000. It does not have a mailing service; the main post office is two blocks away.

Living & working

Anyone intending to stay in Italy for longer than three months has to acquire a bewildering array of papers to get a *permesso di soggiorno* (permit to stay).

The most important documents listed below are obtained from the *Questura Centrale* (main police station, *see above* **Police & Security**). Officially, all non-EU citizens and EU nationals who are working in Italy should register with the police within eight days of arrival and apply for a permit to stay. There is a useful computer at the Questura that prints out lists (in various languages) of the documents you need for every type of *permesso*. It is possible to get information over the phone, but, since the line is almost permanently engaged, it's usually easier to go along in person. EU citizens usually receive their permits the same day, but anyone else might face a longer wait.

Questura Centrale
Via Zara 2 (055 49771). **Open** 24hrs daily; *Ufficio Stranieri* 8.30am-12.30pm Mon-Fri.
To apply for your documents, go to the Ufficio Stranieri (Foreigners' section) early in the day (there are often long queues) where English-speaking staff are usually available. There is a number system (take a ticket from the dispenser when you arrive) and applications are dealt with at one of eight desks.

Accommodation

Listings for accommodation can be found in *Casa Dove?*, which is published on Wednesdays or the tri-weekly newspaper *La Pulce* (published Mondays, Wednesdays and Fridays, but can be bought the night before at the station) – also try the website, www.lapulce.co.it.
Look out for *posto letto* notices (room shares) or *camera singola* (single room). Alternatively place an ad asking for a room to rent (*Cerco una camera singola/un posto letto*). There are good bulletin boards in some bars, bookshops and Internet centres.

A one-bedroom flat in the *centro storico* should cost around L300,000; a single room will range from L550,000 to L700,000. Sharing a room will cost between L400,000-450,000 per month.

Before signing a contract check if the landlord will be living in the flat as this may affect your rights; there may be a phone or washing machine, but not for tenants' use. Ask if bills are included (*le spese sono incluse*) and it's wise to get a reference before coming to Italy in case the landlord asks for one.

Residenza (Residency)

Necessary if you want to buy a car or get customs clearance on goods brought into Italy, and obtained from the municipal office for the district (*circoscrizione*) where you are living. They are listed in the *TuttoCittà* street atlas. To apply you will need photocopies of your permesso di soggiorno (which must be valid for at least a year) and passport. The municipal police will then come round, without an appointment, to check that you live where you say you do.

Agencies

Agenzia Immobiliare Rag Alessio Vaccarino

Via dell Oriuolo 28r (055 234 7863/ 0338 957 0714/fax 055 243 991/ vaccarin@dada.it). **Open** 9am-1pm, 3-7pm Mon-Fri.

Italian Real Estate

Lungarno Cellini 25/cr (055 658 5515/fax 055 680 0175/ serviziimmobiliari@dada.it). **Open** 9am-1pm, 3-7pm Mon-Fri.
Website: www.italianrealestate.it

Lodging in Tuscany

Via Garibaldi 5r (tel/fax055 265 4061). **Open** 9am-7.30pm Mon-Fri.
Website: www.lodgingintuscany.com

Universo Immobiliare

Via Il Prato 19r (055 217 426/0339 319 6028/universo@dada.it). **Open** 9am-7.30pm Mon-Fri.
Website: www.lodginggeoide.com

Your Agency in Florence (YAIF)

Via Ghibellina 72r (055 282 899/ yaifflr@iol.it). **Open** 10am-6pm Mon-Fri.
Branch: *Piazza Santo Spirito 2r (055 282 899).*

Working in Florence

The classified ads paper *La Pulce* has job listings, and it's worth looking in the local English-language press. Some English-language bookshops have noticeboards where ads can be placed. For a serious job, look in the 'Firenze' section of *La Repubblica*, or in the local *La Nazione*. You will require a number of documents:

Codice Fiscale (Employment Number)

Essential if you are working legally, this can be obtained with relatively little hassle from the tax office, the Ufficio Imposte Dirette in Via S Caterina d'Alessandra 23 (055 47 28 51). The office is on the third floor and is open from 9am to 1pm Monday to Saturday.

Partita IVA (VAT Number)

Anyone doing business in Italy may also need a VAT number. It is now obtainable free of charge, but if you want to avoid the bureaucracy involved, pay an accountant to obtain it for you.

Permesso di Soggiorno (Permit to Stay)

Anyone, including EU citizens, wishing to work legally, enrol on a course, open a bank account, rent a flat or do anything much in Italy other than be a tourist will need at least this document. To obtain one you will need a photocopy of your passport, three passport-style photographs and (for non-EU nationals) a *marca da bollo* (an official stamp) which costs L20,000 and is available from tabacchi.

Permesso di Soggiorno per Lavoro (Work Permit)

Despite the Single European Market this is still required by EU nationals working in Italy. The requirements are the same as for the Permit to Stay, plus a letter from your employer.

Students

With over 20 US university programmes, countless language schools and art courses, the city's student population rivals its residents at some times of the year – when English can be heard spoken in bars and restaurants almost as much as Italian.

Permesso di Soggiorno per Studio (Students' Permit)

The same requirements as the Permit to Stay (*see above*), plus a guarantee that your medical bills will be paid (an E111 form will do), evidence that you can support yourself (such as a photocopy of your credit card or a letter from your bank or parents) and a letter from the educational institution at which you will be studying in Italy.

Finding a course

For information about courses in Florence, visit your college's study-abroad office. In the US, the best source of information on study opportunities are the **Institute of International Education**, the **Italian Consulate**, and the **CIEE**.

Associazione Scuole di Italiano come Lingua Seconda (ASILS)
Via del Ginnasio 20, 98039 Taormina (0942 23441).

Council of International Education Exchange (CIEE)
205E 32nd Street, New York, NY 10017, USA (212 666 4177/fax 212 822 2699).

Institute of International Education *809 UN Plaza, New York, NY 10017-3580, USA (212 883 8200).*

Directory

Italian Consulate *(US) 690 Park Avenue, New York NY 10021, USA (212 737 9100).*

Dipartimento attività produttive turismo e commercio *Via di Novili 26 (055 438 2111/fax 055 438 3064).* **Open** 9am-1pm Mon-Fri. In one of Tuscany's bureaucratic control centres, this place offers information about courses in Florence and Tuscany.

Universities

To study alongside Florentine undergraduates, contact an Italian consulate to apply to do a *corso singolo*, or one year of study at the University of Florence. Register at the Ufficio per Studenti Stranieri at the beginning of November. The fees for a corso singolo (maximum five subjects and exams), is approximately L1,950,000. To complete a degree course, you must have completed studies up to university level. For details see website www.unifi.it. Exchange programmes also exist for students within the EU (Erasmus and Socrates courses).

Georgetown University *Villa Le Balze, Via Vecchia Fiesolana 26 (055 59208/fax 055 599 584).* Contact: Michelle Siemietowski, Director of programmes for Villa Le Balze, Poulton Hall (2nd Floor), 143737 St NW, Washington DC, 20057.
Website: www.georgetown.edu

Middlebury College *Via Verdi 12 (tel/fax 055 245 790).* Contact: Michael Katz, Middlebury College, Language Schools, Middlebury, Vermont 05753, USA (graduate programme 802 443 5510/ languages@middlebury.edu undergraduate programme 802 443 5745/schoolsabroad@middlebury.edu) *Website: www.middlebury.edu*

New York University *Villa La Pietra, Via Bolognese 120 (055 50071/fax 055 472 725).* Contact: Study Abroad Admissions, 7 East 12th Street, Room 608, New York, 10003 (212 998 4433/fax 212 995 4103). *Website site: www.nyu.edu*

Sarah Lawrence in Florence *Palazzo Spinelli, Borgo Santa Croce 10 (055 240 904/fax 055 248 0044).* Contact: Sarah Lawrence Office of International Programs, Westlands, Bronxville, NY 10708, USA (914 395 2305/fax 914 395 2666). Intensive year-long courses taught by bilingual Italian professors.

Smith College *Piazza della Signoria 4a (055 238 1397/fax 055 238 674).* For applications and information contact: Office of International Study, Clark Hall, Smith College, Massachusetts, 01063, USA (413 585 4905/fax 413 585 4906). The university runs a junior year abroad for third year Italian university students from American universities.
Website: www.smith.edu

Syracuse University *Villa Rossa, Piazza Savonarola 15 (055 571 376/fax 055 500 0531).* Contact: Syracuse University, DIPA, 119 Euclid Avenue, Syracuse, NY, 13244-4170, USA (315 443 3471).
The largest American undergraduate year-abroad programme in Florence.

Universita di Firenze: Centro di Cultura per I Stranieri *Via Vittorio Emanuele 64 (Villa Fabbricotti) (055 472 139/fax 055 371 620/cecustra@cesit1.unifi.it).* **Open** 9am-noon Mon-Fri. Offers language and cultural courses.
Website:www.unifi.it/ccs

Universitario Europeo *Via dei Roccettini 9, 500016 San Domenica di Fiesole (055 468 5373/fax 055 468 5444/applyres@datacomm.iue.it).*

Information

Student Point

Viale Gramsci 9a (055 234 2857/ fax 055 234 6212). Bus 8, 12, 13. **Open** 2-6pm Mon, Wed, Fri.
The tourist board has established this office to help foreign students with their orientation in Florence. The staff will provide advice on accommodation, getting a *permesso di soggiorno*, study courses, doctors and events.

Societies

GBU Gruppi Bibblici Universitari

CP 18256, 50129 Firenze (055 211 082/gbu-italia@iol.it).
Part of the international fellowship of evangelical students (IFES).

Language courses

There are no end of language and culture courses in Florence, including many intensive one- or two-month courses, which should provide an everyday grasp of the language. Prices given refer to a standard four-week course with four hours' tuition a day.

ABC Centro di Lingua e Cultura Italiana

Via dei Rustici 7 (055 212 001/fax 055 212 112/info@abcschool.com). **Price** L850,000.
Language teaching at six levels and special preparatory courses for the entrance exam to the University of Florence.
Website: www.abcschool.com

British Institute

Piazza Strozzi 2 (055 284 031/fax 055 287 071/info@britishinstitute.it). Library and Cultural Centre *Lungarno Guicciardini 9 (055 284 032/fax 055 289 557).* **Price** L1,260,000 (£475).
Short courses in Italian language, history of art, drawing and cooking.
Web-site: www.britishinstitute.it

Centro linguistico italiano Dante Alighieri

Via dei Bardi 12 (055 234 2984/ fax 055 234 2766); Piazza della Repubblica 5 (055 210 808/ fax 055 287 828). **Price** L1,050,000.
Eleven language levels; opera and literature courses.

Koine

Via Pandofini 27 (055 213 881/fax 055 216 949/koine@firenze.net). **Price** L890,000.
This language school has its own researched teaching method. There are five different levels and courses. Private tuition can also be arranged.
Website: www.koinecenter.com

Istituto Lorenzo de' Medici

Via Faenza 43 (055 287 143 /fax 055 239 8920/LDM@dada.it). **Price** L860,000.
Four different courses in Italian language as well as classes in cooking, Italian cinema and art history.
Website: www.dada.it

Scuola Leonardo da Vinci

Via Bufalini 3 (055 294 420/fax 055 294 820/scuolaleonardo@scuolaleonardo.com). **Price** L800,000 (+L110,000 enrolment).
Versatile languages courses for all levels. Classes in history of art, fashion, drawing, design, cooking and wine are also on offer.
Website: www.scuolaleonardo.com

Scuola Machiavelli

Piazza Santo Spirito 4 (055 239 6966/fax 055 280 800/machiavelli.firenze@agora.stm.it). **Price** L750,000.
One of the smaller language schools in the city. This co-operative offers Italian language teaching at all levels. Pottery, fresco, mosaic, trompe l'oeil and book-binding classes are also available.

Istituto di Lingua e Cultura Italiana Michelangelo

Via Ghibellina 88 (055 240 975/fax 055 240 997/michelangelo@dada.it). **Price** L890,000.
Seven levels of language study with cultural courses and outings.
Website: www.michelangelo.edu.it

Libraries

Biblioteca Nazionale

Piazza Cavallegeri 1 (055 249 191). **Open** 9am-7pm Mon-Fri; 9am-1pm Sat.
You'll need a reference to get membership here not to mention a lot of patience and a cool temper. Ordering a book can take hours if not days and you still may not be able to take it out of the library.

Biblioteca Riccardiana

Via dei Ginori 10 (055 212 586/fax 055 211 379). **Open** 8am-2pm Mon-Sat; 8am-5pm Thur.
There are in fact two libraries here; together they provide an antique and specific selection of books and documents on the history of Florence and the region. Membership requires a reference and a passport. The library sometimes also hosts exhibitions.

British Institute Library

Lungarno Guicciardini 9 (055 284 032/fax 055 289 557/info@britishinstitute.it). **Open** 9.45am-1pm, 3-6.30pm, Mon-Fri.
Requires a membership fee, but

Art for art's sake

A bastion of Florence's innate resistance to the onslaught of our breakbeat century resides in its predisposition for restoring what is old and making it serviceable again. The driving imperative of the city's art schools makes little exception to this rule. Florence trades in a nostalgia for the way things were; tradition rather than change is its touchstone. You'll be hard-pressed to find someone willing to teach you how to preserve dead sharks or assemble a collage of used sanitary towels. If, on the other hand you are interested in subscribing to more traditional forms of artistic investigation, there are a number of schools specialising in the tried and tested techniques.

Florence's art schools contribute much of the pigment to the British and American social scene in the city. Many of the city's watering holes benefit from the patronage of the essentially upper-crust posse of British art students in Florence.

In addition to the official schools, painting and sculpture studios take on apprentices. Also there are a number of mercenary American schools that offer eclectic courses, whose aim seems to be to persuade rich parents to part with a hefty ransom in exchange for offering their offspring a cursory shot of Italian culture. The British Institute and John Hall also offer History of Art courses.

Arte Sotto un Tetto *Via dei Pandolfini 46r (tel/fax 055 247 8867/arte1@arteurope.it).* Courses include jewellery making, Florentine bookbinding, painting and conservation and art history. A previous portfolio is required for a year-long course; month courses are open to everyone.
Website: www.arteuropa.org/

Il Bisonte *Via San Niccolo 24 (055 234 7215).* Located among the artisans' workshops in the former stables of Palazzo Serristori, the school has specialist courses and theoretical/practical seminars to prepare students in the techniques of etching and printing 'by hand'.

Charles H Cecil Studios *Borgo San Frediano 68, Firenze (tel/fax 055 285 102).* The Church of San Rafaello Arcangelo was converted into a studio complex in the early nineteenth century. It now houses one of the more charismatic of Florence's art schools, whic is heavily frequented by Brits. It gives a thorough training in the classical techniques of drawing and oil painting. Twice a week the school hosts life-drawing classes for the general public. For a bit of extra cash, models are always needed at the school either for portraits or as nude figure models.

Florence Academy of Art *Via delle Casine 21r (055 245 444).* This Academy, in the Santa Croce area, is run by Daniel Graves, a former associate of Charles Cecil (*see above*) and, though preaching a similar technique (the sight-size method) tends to be more academic in practice and more American in tone. Its founder insists on a return to discipline in art and the direct study of nature and the Old Masters as the foundation for great painting. The school offers summer classes and a life-drawing class twice a week to the general public.

L'Istituto per l'Arte e Il Restauro *Palazzo Spinelli, Borgo Santa Croce 10 (055 246 001/fax 055 234 3701).* Widely considered one of the best art restoration schools in Italy, Spinelli offers a multitude of courses in the restoration of frescoes, paintings, furniture, gilt objects, ceramics, stone, paper and glass. Courses last between one and three years; one-month courses are held from July to the September in the same disciplines.
Website: www.spinelli.it

Oro e Colore: Laboratorio Scuola, restauro di opere dorate e dipinte *Via della Chiesa 25 (tel/fax 055 229 040).* Month- to year-long courses in art restoration, gold leaf restoration and other techniques. No previous experience is needed, however places on courses are limited and are all taught in Italian.
Website: www.oroecolore.com

Studio Art Center International (SACI) *Via San Gallo 30 (055 486 164/fax 055 486 230/info@saci-florence.org).* SACI offers five specific credit programmes for graduates and undergraduates. These include both academic and practical courses in the arts, ranging from museology to batik design. There is an entry requirement for certain courses.

Universita Internazionale dell'Arte *Villa il Ventaglio, Via delle Forbici 24-26 (055 570 216/055 571 503/fax 055 570 508/uia@vps.it).* Courses cover restoration and preservation, museum and gallery management and art criticism.
Website: www.vps.it/propart/uia

offers a reading room that overlooks the Arno and an extensive collection of art history books and Italian literature. Staff are well informed.

Kunsthistorisches Institut in Florenz

Via G Giusti 44 (055 249 111/ fax 055 249 1155). **Open** 9am-6pm Mon, Wed, Fri; 9am-7pm Tue, Thur.

One of the largest collections of art history books in Florence is held by the German Institute. A reference photocopy of passport and photo gets you a *tessera* to borrow books.

Biblioteca Marucelliana

Via Cavour 43-45 (055 27221/fax 055 294 393/marucelliana@cesit1.unifi.it). **Open** 9am-7pm Mon-Fri; 9am-1pm Sat.

The library holds a diverse range of books including some in English. No letter of presentation is needed for membership, only ID.

Villa I Tatti, Harvard University Center for Italian Renaissance Studies

Via Vincigliata 26 (055 603 251/ fax 055 603 383/ vit@vit.iris.firenze.it).

Open 9am-6pm Mon-Fri.

Graduate students need a letter of presentation to gain access to the 110,000 books at Harvard's exclusive library.

Women

Tuscany, while not one of the worst places for women travellers, still has its hassles. Italian women are used to being ogled, visitors can be a little daunted. It's normally a question of all talk and no action; you can usually get rid of would-be Latin lovers by ignoring them or using a few sharp words and a withering glance. One sign that Florence is becoming more aware of the problems encountered by women at night is the bus company ATAF's proposal to start a women-only night bus service. Contact ATAF for information (055 565 0222).

Network

Contact: current president (055 331 596/brusca@cesitl.unifi.it

Network is a professional women's organisation geared principally (not exclusively) towards permanent native English-speaking residents in the Florence area. It aims to improve communication, exchange ideas and information among the English-speaking community. Meetings are generally held on the second Wednesday of the month, but check with Christine Bruscagli, the president (until November 2000) as times and venues vary.

Health

The pharmacy in Santa Maria Novella station is open 24 hours (055 216 761). Tampons (*assorbenti interni*) and condoms (*preservativi*) are sold in pharmacies and supermarkets. Abortion is legal in Italy and is performed in hospitals, but the private clinics listed below can give consultation and references.

Artemisia Centro Donne Contro La Violenza Catia Franci

Via del Mezzetta 1interno (helpline 055 602 311). **Open** 10am-6pm Mon-Fri.

This crisis centre can provide a medical examination as well as counselling for women who have been sexually assaulted; they also give legal advice. The helpline is staffed during office hours. English is spoken.

Progetto Donna – Assessorato Pubblica Istruzione

Clinica Ostetrica, Ospedale di Careggi, Viale Morgagni (055 427 7493). Bus 14. **Open** 24 hrs daily.

Female victims of sexual assault should come here for medical attention. Legal services and psychological counselling are available 9am-1pm, 3-5pm, Mon-Fri (055 284 752) at Viale Santa Maria Maggiore 1, Careggi.

Santa Chiara

Piazza Indipendenza 11 (055 496 312/055 475 239). Bus 10, 11, 25. **Open** 8am-7pm daily, by appointment.

This private clinic offers gynaecological exams and general physicals. Call for an appointment.

Further reading

Walter L Adamson *Avant-garde Florence: From Modernism to Fascism*
A high brow look at early twentieth-century Florentine literati.

James Beck with Michael Daley *Art Restoration – The culture, the business and the scandal*
A vital analysis of the successes and disasters of art restoration in Italy.

Luigi Barzini *The Italians*
Hilarious (dated) portrait of the Italians.

Michael Dibdin *A Rich Full Death*
Amusing thriller with insight into nineteenth-century Florence society.

EM Forster *A Room With a View; Where Angels Fear to Tread*
Superb social comedy by the esteemed English novelist.

Matt Frei *Italy, the Unfinished Revolution*
Account of Italian politics leading up to the 'Clean Hands' scandals.

Paul Ginsborg *A History of Contemporary Italy: Society and Politics 1943-1988*
Comprehensive history book on modern Italy.

Carlo Graziano *Italian Verbs and the Essentials of Grammar*
A clear guide to Italian grammar.

Frederick Hartt *The History of Italian Renaissance Art*
The definitive word on all that is the Renaissance.

Christopher Hibbert *The Rise and Fall of the House of Medici*
What it says and very readable.

Monica Larner and Travis Neighbor *Living, Studying and Working in Italy*
Everything you need to know to live in the *bel paese*.

Magdalena Nabb *The Monster of Florence*
Thriller based on the serial-killer who murdered 16 campers in the 1980s.

Iris Origo *The Merchant of Prato; War in the Val d'Orcia*
The fascinating life and times of Francesco di Marco Datini, fourteenth-century wool merchant; and World War II in a Tuscan valley.

Tommaso Paloscia *Accadde in Toscana (Vol III)*
A beautifully illustrated who's who of Tuscany's contemporary artists.

Vocabulary

Any attempt at speaking Italian will always be appreciated, and is often necessary; away from services like tourist offices, hotels and restaurants popular with foreigners, the level of English is not very high.

When entering a shop or restaurant it's the practice to announce your presence with '*buon giorno*' or '*buona sera*', and in the street, feel free to ask directions. People will often go out of their way to help.

Italian is spelt as it is pronounced, and vice versa. Stresses usually fall on the penultimate syllable and, if not, are indicated by accents. There are two forms of the second person, the formal **lei**, to be used with strangers, and the informal **tu**. Men and masculine nouns are accompanied by adjectives ending in 'o', women and female nouns by adjectives ending in 'a'.

PRONUNCIATION

Vowels

a – as in **a**sk
e – like **a** in **a**ge (closed e) or **e** in s**e**ll (open e)
i – like **ea** in **ea**st
o – as in h**o**tel (closed o) or in h**o**t (open o)
u – as in b**oo**t

Consonants

c before a, o or u is like the **c** in **c**at
c before an e or an i is like the **ch** in **ch**eck.
ch is like the **c** in **c**at
g before a, o or u is like the **g** in **g**et
g before an e or an i is like the **j** in **j**ig
gh is like the **g** in **g**et
gl followed by an i is like **lli** in mi**lli**on
gn is like **ny** in ca**ny**on
qu is as in **qu**ick
r is always rolled
s has two sounds, as in **s**oap or ro**s**e
sc is like the **sh** in **sh**ame
sch is like the **sc** in **sc**out
z has two sounds, like ts and dz
Double consonants are always sounded more emphatically.

USEFUL PHRASES

hello and **goodbye** (informal) – *ciao*
good morning, good day – *buon giorno*
good afternoon, good evening – *buona sera*
I don't understand – *Non capisco/non ho capito*
do you speak English? – *parla inglese?*
please – *per favore*
thank you – *grazie*
how much does it cost/is it? – *quanto costa?/quant'è?*
when does it open? – *quando apre?*
where is... ? – *dov'è...?*
excuse me – *scusi* (polite) *scusa* (informal)
open – *aperto*
closed – *chiuso*
exit – *uscita*
left – *sinistra;* **right** – *destra*
car – *macchina;* **bus** – *autobus;*
train – *treno*
bus stop – *fermata d'autobus*
ticket/s – *biglietto/i*
I would like a ticket to... – *Vorrei un biglietto per...*
postcard – *cartolina*
stamp – *francobollo*
glass – *bicchiere*
coffee – *caffè*
tea – *tè*
water – *acqua*
wine – *vino*
beer – *birra*
bedroom – *camera*
booking – *prenotazione*
Monday *lunedì;* **Tuesday** *martedì;* **Wednesday** *mercoledì;* **Thursday** *giovedì;* **Friday** *venerdì;* **Saturday** *sabato;* **Sunday** *domenica*
yesterday *ieri;* **today** *oggi;* **tomorrow** *domani*
morning *mattina;* **afternoon** *pomeriggio;* **evening** *sera;* **night** *notte*

THE COME-ON

Do you have a light? – *Hai da accendere?*
What's your name? – *Come ti chiami?*
Would you like a drink? – *Vuoi bere qualcosa?*
Where are you from? – *Di dove sei?*
What are you doing here? – *Che fai qui?*
Do you have a boy/girlfriend? – *Hai un ragazzo/una ragazza?*

THE BRUSH-OFF

I don't smoke – *Non fumo*
I'm married – *Sono sposato/a*
I'm tired – *Sono stanco/a*
I'm going home – *Vado a casa*
I have to meet a friend – *Devo andare a incontrare un amico/una amica*

INSULTS

shit – *merda*
idiot – *stronzo*
fuck off – *vaffanculo*
dickhead – *testa di cazzo*
What the hell are you doing? – *Che cazzo fai?*

NUMBERS & MONEY

0 *zero;* **1** *uno;* **2** *due;* **3** *tre;* **4** *quattro;* **5** *cinque;* **6** *sei;* **7** *sette;* **8** *otto;* **9** *nove;* **10** *dieci;* **11** *undici;* **12** *dodici;* **13** *tredici;* **14** *quattordici;* **15** *quindici;* **16** *sedici;* **17** *diciassette;* **18** *diciotto;* **19** *diciannove;* **20** *venti;* **21** *ventuno;* **22** *ventidue;* **30** *trenta;* **40** *quaranta;* **50** *cinquanta;* **60** *sessanta;* **70** *settanta;* **80** *ottanta;* **90** *novanta;* **100** *cento;* **1,000** *mille;* **2,000** *duemilla;* **100,000** *centomila;* **1,000,000** *un miliardo.*
How much does it cost/is it? – *Quanto costa?/quantè?*
Do you have any change? – *Ha spiccioli?*
Can you give me any discount? – *Si puó fare uno sconto?*
Do you accept credit cards? – *Si accettano le carte di credito?*
Can I pay in pounds/dollars? – *Posso pagare in sterline/dollari?*

Index

Figures in bold indicate sections containing key information. Italics indicate illustrations.

n

o

p

Advertisers' Index

Please refer to the relevant sections for addresses/telephone numbers

Maps

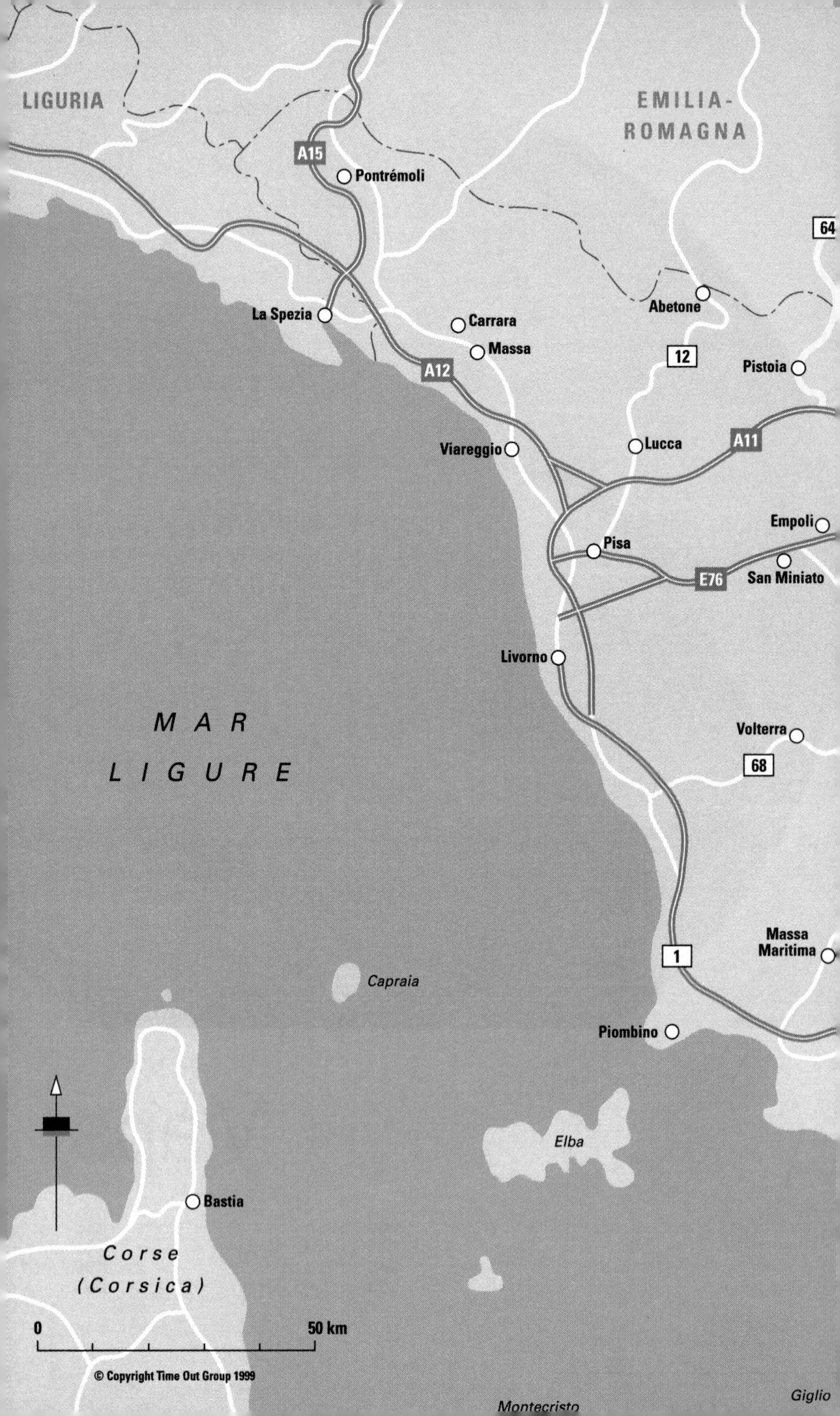

LIGURIA
EMILIA-ROMAGNA
A15
Pontrémoli
64
Abetone
La Spezia
Carrara
Massa
A12
12
Pistoia
Viareggio
Lucca
A11
Empoli
Pisa
E76
San Miniato
Livorno
MAR LIGURE
Volterra
68
Massa Maritima
1
Capraia
Piombino
Elba
Bastia
Corse (Corsica)
0
50 km
Giglio
Montecristo

Florence & Tuscany
MAR ADRIATICO
BOLOGNA
Ravenna
A14
A1
71
RIMINI
San Marino
Mugello
Borgo San Lorenzo
Prato
FIRENZE (Florence)
MARCHE
Greve in Chianti
429
Poggibonsi
222
Arezzo
71
Siena
326
TOSCANA
Montepulciano
PERUGIA
L. Trasimeno
3b
Montalcino
223
UMBRIA
2
Grosseto
Maremma
Terni
Lago di Bolsena
Viterbo
Orbetello
LAZIO
Monte Argentario

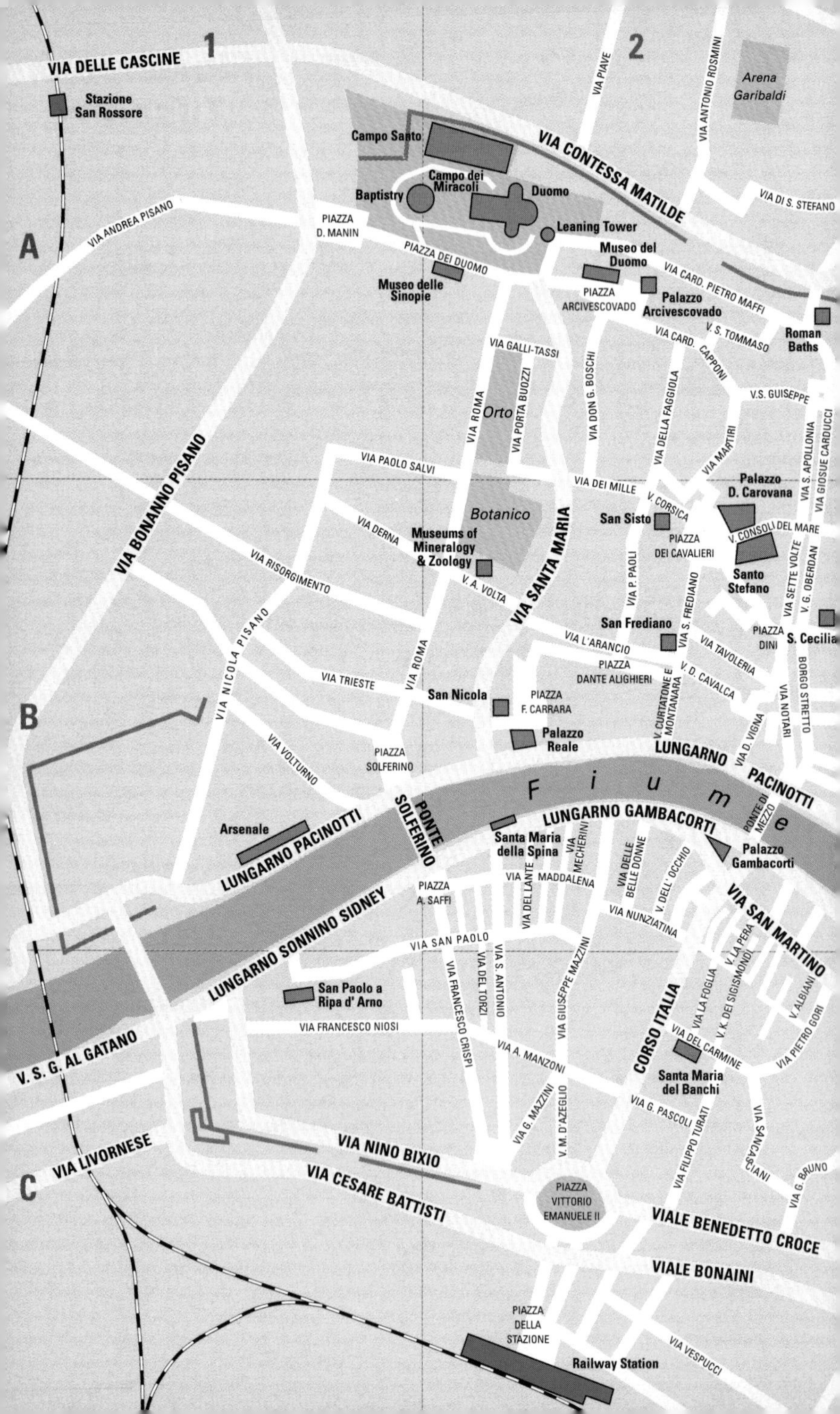
1
2
A
B
C
VIA DELLE CASCINE
Stazione San Rossore
Arena Garibaldi
VIA PIAVE
VIA ANTONIO ROSMINI
Campo Santo
VIA CONTESSA MATILDE
Campo dei Miracoli
Baptistry
Duomo
Leaning Tower
VIA DI S. STEFANO
VIA ANDREA PISANO
PIAZZA D. MANIN
PIAZZA DEI DUOMO
Museo del Duomo
Museo delle Sinopie
PIAZZA ARCIVESCOVADO
Palazzo Arcivescovado
VIA CARD. PIETRO MAFFI
V. S. TOMMASO
Roman Baths
VIA CARD. CAPPONI
VIA GALLI-TASSI
VIA DON G. BOSCHI
VIA DELLA FAGGIOLA
V.S. GUISEPPE
VIA ROMA
Orto
VIA PORTA BUOZZI
VIA MARTIRI
VIA S. APOLLONIA
VIA GIOSUE CARDUCCI
VIA PAOLO SALVI
VIA DEI MILLE
Palazzo D. Carovana
V. CORSICA
Botanico
San Sisto
V. CONSOLI DEL MARE
VIA BONANNO PISANO
VIA DERNA
Museums of Mineralogy & Zoology
PIAZZA DEI CAVALIERI
Santo Stefano
VIA RISORGIMENTO
V. A. VOLTA
VIA SANTA MARIA
VIA P. PAOLI
VIA S. FREDIANO
VIA SETTE VOLTE
V. G. OBERDAN
San Frediano
PIAZZA DINI
S. Cecilia
VIA NICOLA PISANO
VIA L'ARANCIO
VIA TAVOLERIA
PIAZZA DANTE ALIGHIERI
V. D. CAVALCA
BORGO STRETTO
VIA TRIESTE
VIA ROMA
San Nicola
PIAZZA F. CARRARA
V. CURTATONE E MONTANARA
VIA NOTARI
VIA D. VIGNA
Palazzo Reale
VIA VOLTURNO
PIAZZA SOLFERINO
LUNGARNO PACINOTTI
Fiume
PONTE DI MEZZO
PONTE SOLFERINO
Arsenale
LUNGARNO PACINOTTI
LUNGARNO GAMBACORTI
Santa Maria della Spina
VIA MECHERINI
VIA DELLE BELLE DONNE
V. DELL' OCCHIO
Palazzo Gambacorti
PIAZZA A. SAFFI
VIA MADDALENA
VIA DEL LANTE
VIA SAN MARTINO
LUNGARNO SONNINO SIDNEY
VIA NUNZIATINA
VIA SAN PAOLO
VIA DEL TORZI
VIA S. ANTONIO
VIA GIUSEPPE MAZZINI
V. LA PERA
V. K. DEI SIGISMONDI
VIA LA FOGLIA
San Paolo a Ripa d' Arno
VIA FRANCESCO CRISPI
CORSO ITALIA
V. ALBIANI
VIA FRANCESCO NIOSI
VIA DEL CARMINE
VIA PIETRO GORI
V. S. G. AL GATANO
VIA A. MANZONI
Santa Maria del Banchi
VIA G. PASCOLI
VIA G. MAZZINI
V. M. D'AZEGLIO
VIA SANCASCIANI
VIA FILIPPO TURATI
VIA G. BRUNO
VIA LIVORNESE
VIA NINO BIXIO
VIA CESARE BATTISTI
PIAZZA VITTORIO EMANUELE II
VIALE BENEDETTO CROCE
VIALE BONAINI
PIAZZA DELLA STAZIONE
Railway Station
VIA VESPUCCI

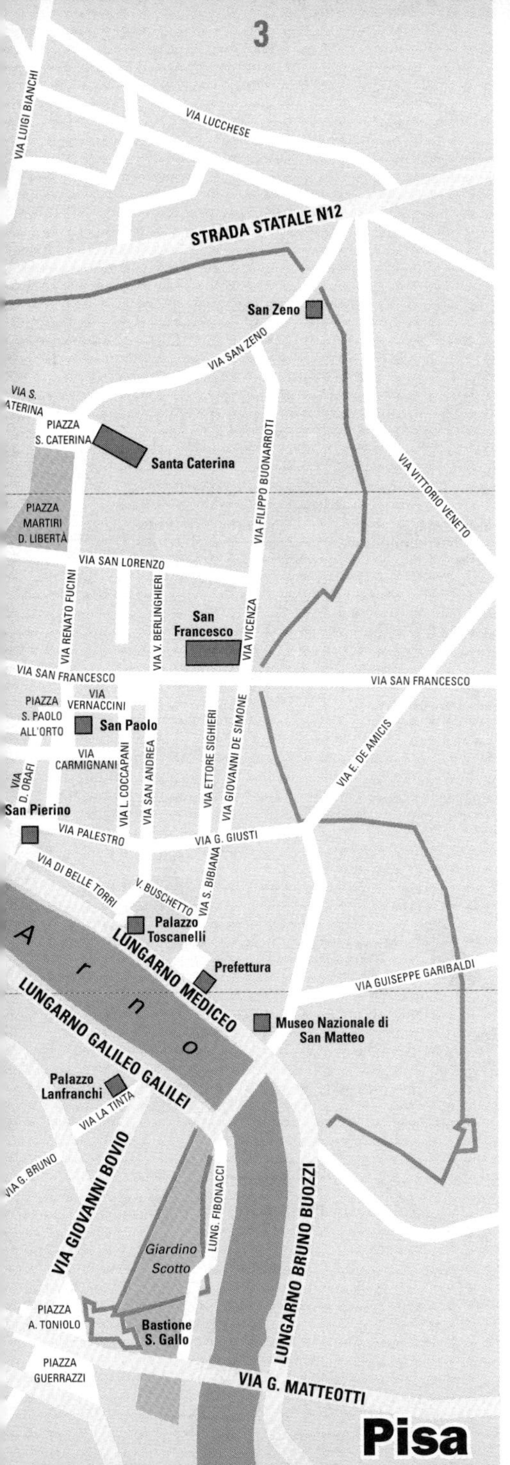

STREET INDEX

City Wall ....

Place of Interest and/or Entertainment ...

Parks ....

Railway Station ....

0 200 400 m

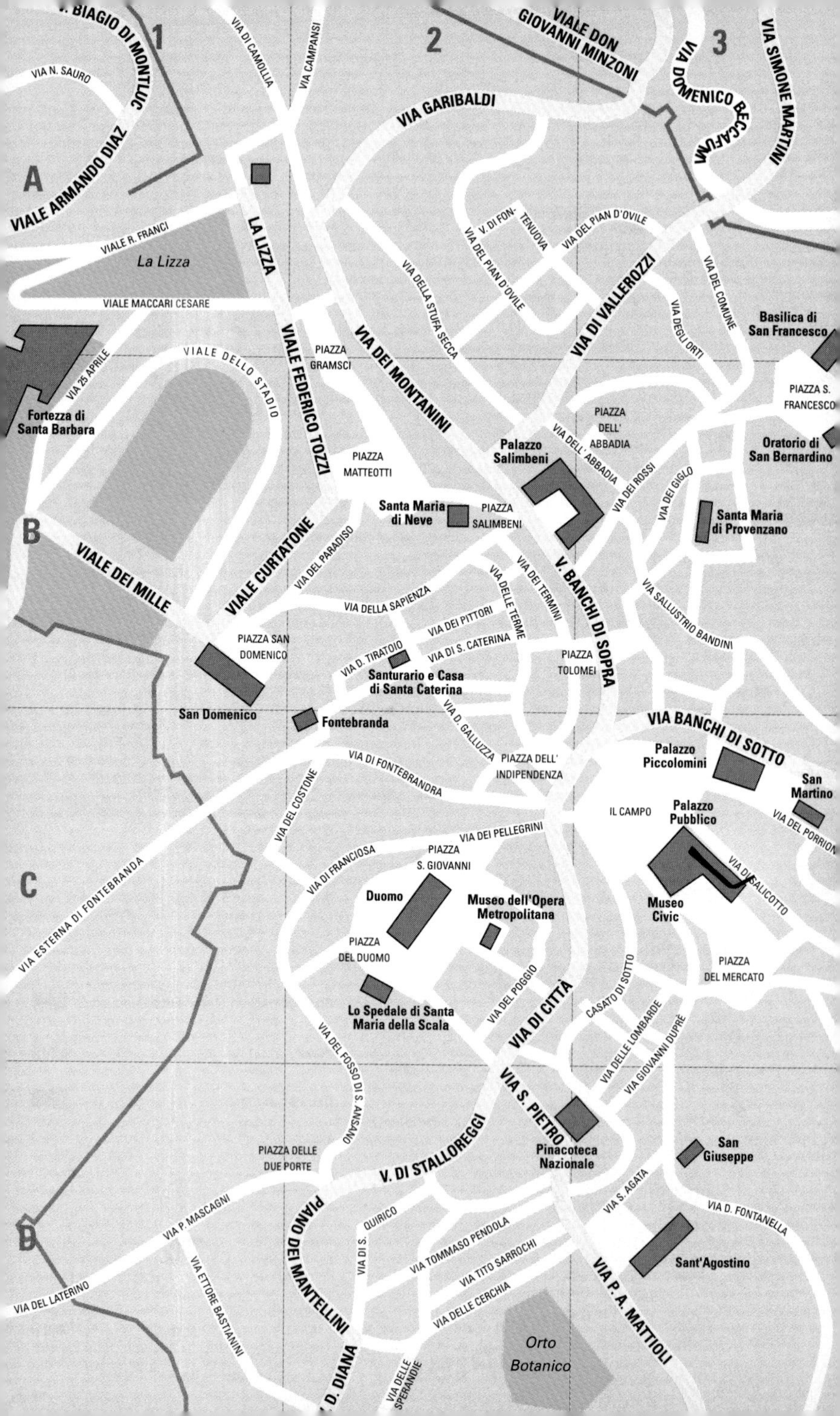

1
2
3
A
B
C
D
V. BIAGIO DI MONTLUC
VIA N. SAURO
VIALE ARMANDO DIAZ
VIA DI CAMOLLIA
VIA CAMPANSI
VIALE DON GIOVANNI MINZONI
VIA DOMENICO BECCAFUMI
VIA SIMONE MARTINI
VIA GARIBALDI
VIALE R. FRANCI
La Lizza
LA LIZZA
VIALE MACCARI CESARE
V. DI FONTENUOVA
VIA DEL PIAN D'OVILE
VIA DELLA STUFA SECCA
VIA DI VALLEROZZI
VIA DEL COMUNE
VIA DEGLI ORTI
Basilica di San Francesco
PIAZZA S. FRANCESCO
VIA 25 APRILE
VIALE DELLO STADIO
PIAZZA GRAMSCI
VIALE FEDERICO TOZZI
VIA DEI MONTANINI
Fortezza di Santa Barbara
PIAZZA DELL' ABBADIA
VIA DELL' ABBADIA
Palazzo Salimbeni
Oratorio di San Bernardino
PIAZZA MATTEOTTI
VIA DEI ROSSI
VIA DEI GIGLO
Santa Maria di Neve
PIAZZA SALIMBENI
Santa Maria di Provenzano
VIALE CURTATONE
VIA DEL PARADISO
VIALE DEI MILLE
VIA DELLE TERME
VIA DEI TERMINI
V. BANCHI DI SOPRA
VIA DELLA SAPIENZA
VIA SALLUSTRIO BANDINI
VIA DEI PITTORI
PIAZZA SAN DOMENICO
VIA DI S. CATERINA
VIA D. TIRATOIO
PIAZZA TOLOMEI
Santurario e Casa di Santa Caterina
San Domenico
Fontebranda
VIA D. GALLUZZA
VIA BANCHI DI SOTTO
VIA DI FONTEBRANDRA
PIAZZA DELL' INDIPENDENZA
Palazzo Piccolomini
San Martino
VIA DEL COSTONE
IL CAMPO
Palazzo Pubblico
VIA DEL PORRION
VIA DEI PELLEGRINI
PIAZZA S. GIOVANNI
VIA DI FRANCIOSA
VIA DI SALICOTTO
VIA ESTERNA DI FONTEBRANDA
Duomo
Museo dell'Opera Metropolitana
Museo Civic
PIAZZA DEL DUOMO
PIAZZA DEL MERCATO
VIA DEL POGGIO
CASATO DI SOTTO
Lo Spedale di Santa Maria della Scala
VIA DI CITTÀ
VIA DELLE LOMBARDE
VIA GIOVANNI DUPRÈ
VIA DEL FOSSO DI S. ANSANO
VIA S. PIETRO
V. DI STALLOREGGI
Pinacoteca Nazionale
San Giuseppe
PIAZZA DELLE DUE PORTE
VIA S. AGATA
VIA D. FONTANELLA
VIA P. MASCAGNI
VIA DI S. QUIRICO
VIA TOMMASO PENDOLA
PIANO DEI MANTELLINI
Sant'Agostino
VIA TITO SARROCHI
VIA P. A. MATTIOLI
VIA DEL LATERINO
VIA ETTORE BASTIANINI
VIA DELLE CERCHIA
Orto Botanico
V. D. DIANA
VIA DELLE SPERANDIE

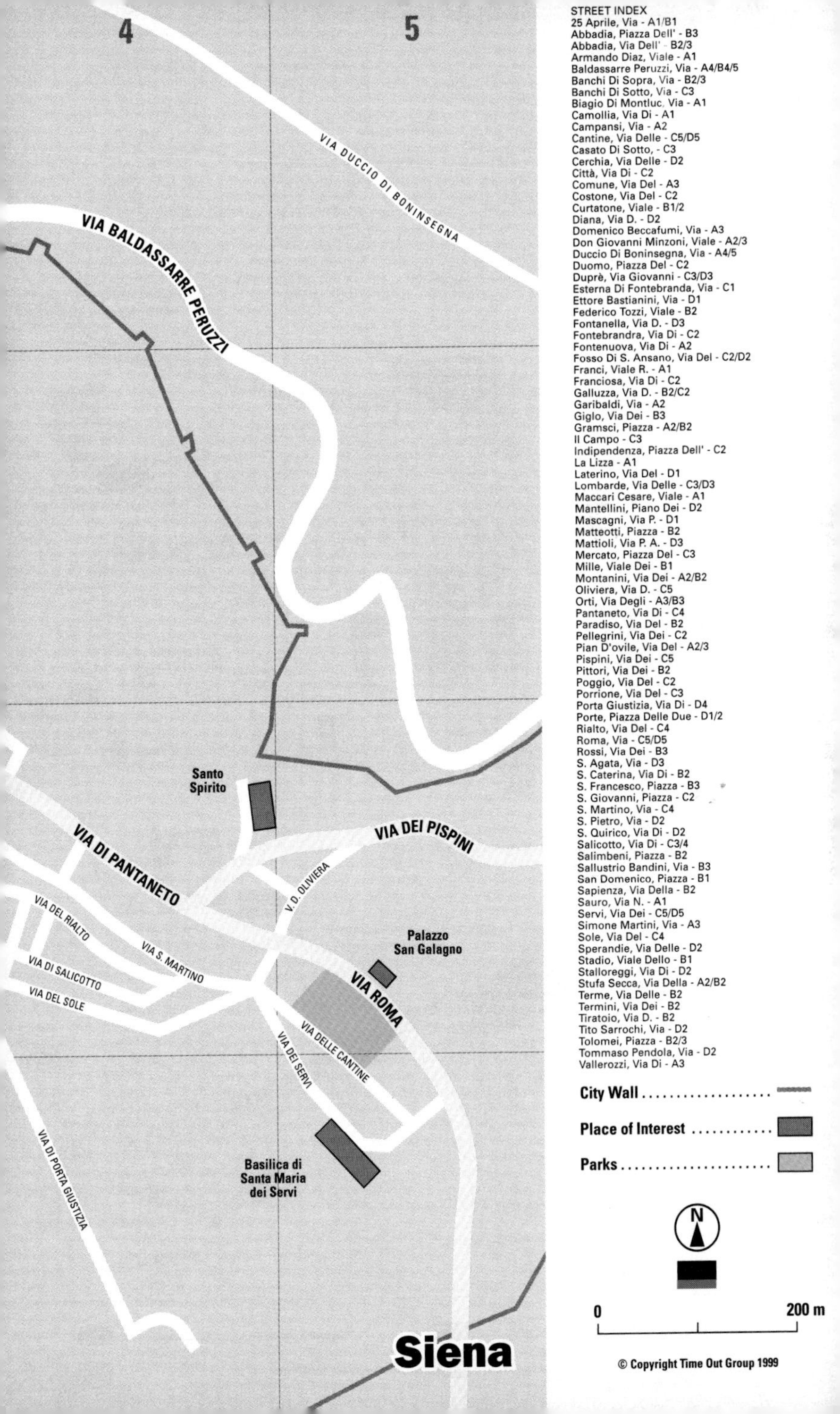
4
5
VIA DUCCIO DI BONINSEGNA
VIA BALDASSARRE PERUZZI
Santo Spirito
VIA DEI PISPINI
VIA DI PANTANETO
V. D. OLIVIERA
VIA DEL RIALTO
VIA S. MARTINO
VIA DI SALICOTTO
VIA DEL SOLE
Palazzo San Galagno
VIA ROMA
VIA DELLE CANTINE
VIA DEI SERVI
Basilica di Santa Maria dei Servi
VIA DI PORTA GIUSTIZIA
Siena
STREET INDEX
25 Aprile, Via - A1/B1
Abbadia, Piazza Dell' - B3
Abbadia, Via Dell' - B2/3
Armando Diaz, Viale - A1
Baldassarre Peruzzi, Via - A4/B4/5
Banchi Di Sopra, Via - B2/3
Banchi Di Sotto, Via - C3
Biagio Di Montluc, Via - A1
Camollia, Via Di - A1
Campansi, Via - A2
Cantine, Via Delle - C5/D5
Casato Di Sotto, - C3
Cerchia, Via Delle - D2
Città, Via Di - C2
Comune, Via Del - A3
Costone, Via Del - C2
Curtatone, Viale - B1/2
Diana, Via D. - D2
Domenico Beccafumi, Via - A3
Don Giovanni Minzoni, Viale - A2/3
Duccio Di Boninsegna, Via - A4/5
Duomo, Piazza Del - C2
Duprè, Via Giovanni - C3/D3
Esterna Di Fontebranda, Via - C1
Ettore Bastianini, Via - D1
Federico Tozzi, Viale - B2
Fontanella, Via D. - D3
Fontebrandra, Via Di - C2
Fontenuova, Via Di - A2
Fosso Di S. Ansano, Via Del - C2/D2
Franci, Viale R. - A1
Franciosa, Via Di - C2
Galluzza, Via D. - B2/C2
Garibaldi, Via - A2
Giglo, Via Dei - B3
Gramsci, Piazza - A2/B2
Il Campo - C3
Indipendenza, Piazza Dell' - C2
La Lizza - A1
Laterino, Via Del - D1
Lombarde, Via Delle - C3/D3
Maccari Cesare, Viale - A1
Mantellini, Piano Dei - D2
Mascagni, Via P. - D1
Matteotti, Piazza - B2
Mattioli, Via P. A. - D3
Mercato, Piazza Del - C3
Mille, Viale Dei - B1
Montanini, Via Dei - A2/B2
Oliviera, Via D. - C5
Orti, Via Degli - A3/B3
Pantaneto, Via Di - C4
Paradiso, Via Del - B2
Pellegrini, Via Dei - C2
Pian D'ovile, Via Del - A2/3
Pispini, Via Dei - C5
Pittori, Via Dei - B2
Poggio, Via Del - C2
Porrione, Via Del - C3
Porta Giustizia, Via Di - D4
Porte, Piazza Delle Due - D1/2
Rialto, Via Del - C4
Roma, Via - C5/D5
Rossi, Via Dei - B3
S. Agata, Via - D3
S. Caterina, Via Di - B2
S. Francesco, Piazza - B3
S. Giovanni, Piazza - C2
S. Martino, Via - C4
S. Pietro, Via - D2
S. Quirico, Via Di - D2
Salicotto, Via Di - C3/4
Salimbeni, Piazza - B2
Sallustrio Bandini, Via - B3
San Domenico, Piazza - B1
Sapienza, Via Della - B2
Sauro, Via N. - A1
Servi, Via Dei - C5/D5
Simone Martini, Via - A3
Sole, Via Del - C4
Sperandie, Via Delle - D2
Stadio, Viale Dello - B1
Stalloreggi, Via Di - D2
Stufa Secca, Via Della - A2/B2
Terme, Via Delle - B2
Termini, Via Dei - B2
Tiratoio, Via D. - B2
Tito Sarrochi, Via - D2
Tolomei, Piazza - B2/3
Tommaso Pendola, Via - D2
Vallerozzi, Via Di - A3
City Wall
Place of Interest
Parks
N
0
200 m
© Copyright Time Out Group 1999

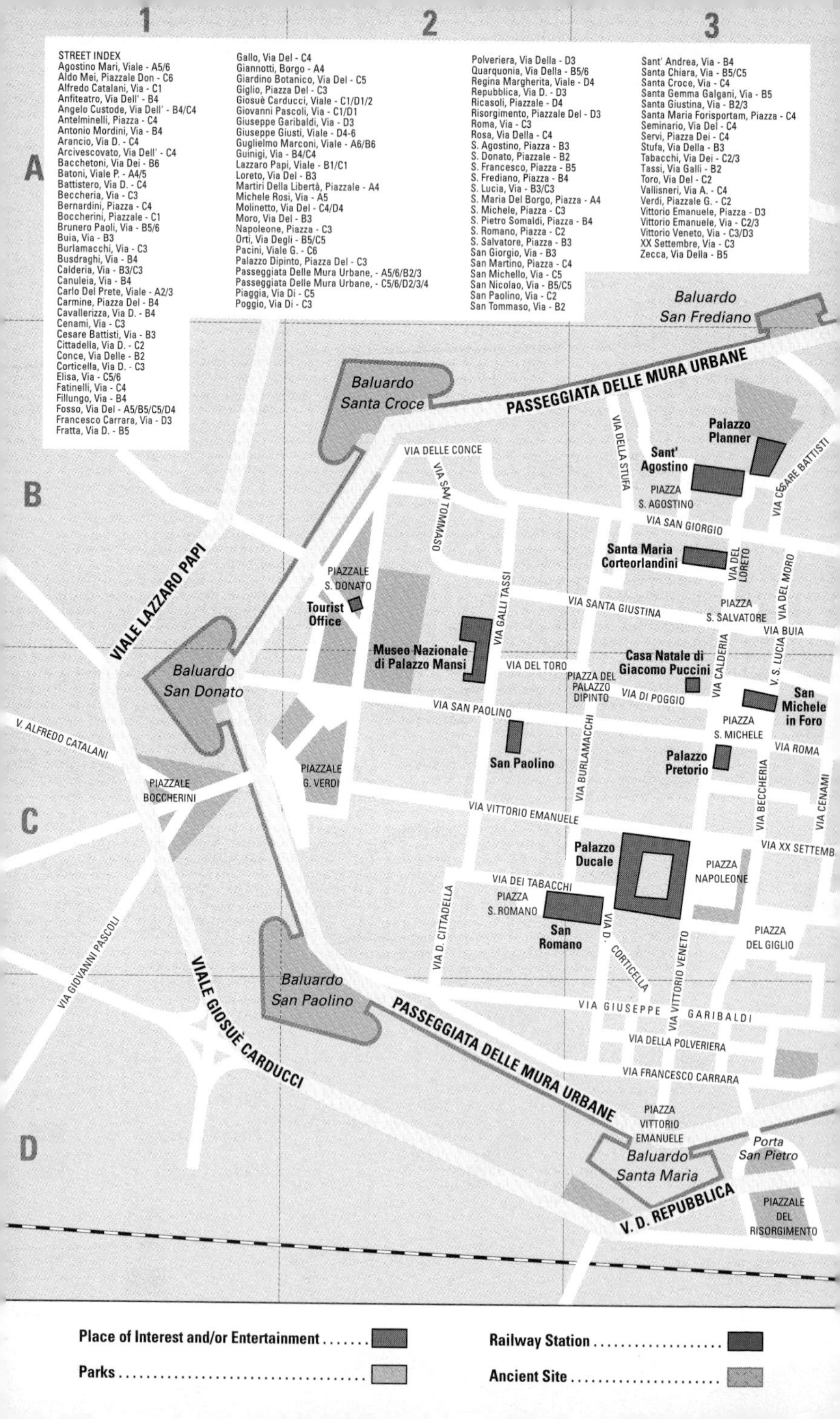
1
2
3
A
B
C
D
STREET INDEX
Agostino Mari, Viale - A5/6
Aldo Mei, Piazzale Don - C6
Alfredo Catalani, Via - C1
Anfiteatro, Via Dell' - B4
Angelo Custode, Via Dell' - B4/C4
Antelminelli, Piazza - C4
Antonio Mordini, Via - B4
Arancio, Via D. - C4
Arcivescovato, Via Dell' - C4
Bacchetoni, Via Dei - B6
Batoni, Viale P. - A4/5
Battistero, Via D. - C4
Beccheria, Via - C3
Bernardini, Piazza - C4
Boccherini, Piazzale - C1
Brunero Paoli, Via - B5/6
Buia, Via - B3
Burlamacchi, Via - C3
Busdraghi, Via - B4
Calderia, Via - B3/C3
Canuleia, Via - B4
Carlo Del Prete, Viale - A2/3
Carmine, Piazza Del - B4
Cavallerizza, Via D. - B4
Cenami, Via - C3
Cesare Battisti, Via - B3
Cittadella, Via D. - C2
Conce, Via Delle - B2
Corticella, Via D. - C3
Elisa, Via - C5/6
Fatinelli, Via - C4
Fillungo, Via - B4
Fosso, Via Del - A5/B5/C5/D4
Francesco Carrara, Via - D3
Fratta, Via D. - B5
Gallo, Via Del - C4
Giannotti, Borgo - A4
Giardino Botanico, Via Del - C5
Giglio, Piazza Del - C3
Giosuè Carducci, Viale - C1/D1/2
Giovanni Pascoli, Via - C1/D1
Giuseppe Garibaldi, Via - D3
Giuseppe Giusti, Viale - D4-6
Guglielmo Marconi, Viale - A6/B6
Guinigi, Via - B4/C4
Lazzaro Papi, Viale - B1/C1
Loreto, Via Del - B3
Martiri Della Libertà, Piazzale - A4
Michele Rosi, Via - A5
Molinetto, Via Del - C4/D4
Moro, Via Del - B3
Napoleone, Piazza - C3
Orti, Via Degli - B5/C5
Pacini, Viale G. - C6
Palazzo Dipinto, Piazza Del - C3
Passeggiata Delle Mura Urbane, - A5/6/B2/3
Passeggiata Delle Mura Urbane, - C5/6/D2/3/4
Piaggia, Via Di - C5
Poggio, Via Di - C3
Polveriera, Via Della - D3
Quarquonia, Via Della - B5/6
Regina Margherita, Viale - D4
Repubblica, Via D. - D3
Ricasoli, Piazzale - D4
Risorgimento, Piazzale Del - D3
Roma, Via - C3
Rosa, Via Della - C4
S. Agostino, Piazza - B3
S. Donato, Piazzale - B2
S. Francesco, Piazza - B5
S. Frediano, Piazza - B4
S. Lucia, Via - B3/C3
S. Maria Del Borgo, Piazza - A4
S. Michele, Piazza - C3
S. Pietro Somaldi, Piazza - B4
S. Romano, Piazza - C2
S. Salvatore, Piazza - B3
San Giorgio, Via - B3
San Martino, Piazza - C4
San Michello, Via - C5
San Nicolao, Via - B5/C5
San Paolino, Via - C2
San Tommaso, Via - B2
Sant' Andrea, Via - B4
Santa Chiara, Via - B5/C5
Santa Croce, Via - C4
Santa Gemma Galgani, Via - B5
Santa Giustina, Via - B2/3
Santa Maria Forisportam, Piazza - C4
Seminario, Via Del - C4
Servi, Piazza Dei - C4
Stufa, Via Della - B3
Tabacchi, Via Dei - C2/3
Tassi, Via Galli - B2
Toro, Via Del - C2
Vallisneri, Via A. - C4
Verdi, Piazzale G. - C2
Vittorio Emanuele, Piazza - D3
Vittorio Emanuele, Via - C2/3
Vittorio Veneto, Via - C3/D3
XX Settembre, Via - C3
Zecca, Via Della - B5
Baluardo San Frediano
Baluardo Santa Croce
PASSEGGIATA DELLE MURA URBANE
VIA DELLA STUFA
Palazzo Planner
Sant' Agostino
PIAZZA S. AGOSTINO
VIA CESARE BATTISTI
VIA DELLE CONCE
VIA SAN TOMMASO
VIA SAN GIORGIO
Santa Maria Corteorlandini
VIA DEL LORETO
VIA DEL MORO
PIAZZALE S. DONATO
Tourist Office
VIA GALLI TASSI
VIA SANTA GIUSTINA
PIAZZA S. SALVATORE
VIALE LAZZARO PAPI
Museo Nazionale di Palazzo Mansi
VIA BUIA
Casa Natale di Giacomo Puccini
VIA CALDERIA
V. S. LUCIA
Baluardo San Donato
VIA DEL TORO
PIAZZA DEL PALAZZO DIPINTO
VIA DI POGGIO
San Michele in Foro
VIA SAN PAOLINO
PIAZZA S. MICHELE
V. ALFREDO CATALANI
VIA ROMA
San Paolino
Palazzo Pretorio
PIAZZALE G. VERDI
VIA BURLAMACCHI
PIAZZALE BOCCHERINI
VIA BECCHERIA
VIA CENAMI
VIA VITTORIO EMANUELE
Palazzo Ducale
VIA XX SETTEMB
PIAZZA NAPOLEONE
VIA DEI TABACCHI
PIAZZA S. ROMANO
VIA D. CITTADELLA
San Romano
VIA D. CORTICELLA
PIAZZA DEL GIGLIO
VIA VITTORIO VENETO
VIA GIOVANNI PASCOLI
Baluardo San Paolino
VIA GIUSEPPE GARIBALDI
VIALE GIOSUÈ CARDUCCI
VIA DELLA POLVERIERA
PASSEGGIATA DELLE MURA URBANE
VIA FRANCESCO CARRARA
PIAZZA VITTORIO EMANUELE
Baluardo Santa Maria
Porta San Pietro
V. D. REPUBBLICA
PIAZZALE DEL RISORGIMENTO
Place of Interest and/or Entertainment
Parks
Railway Station
Ancient Site

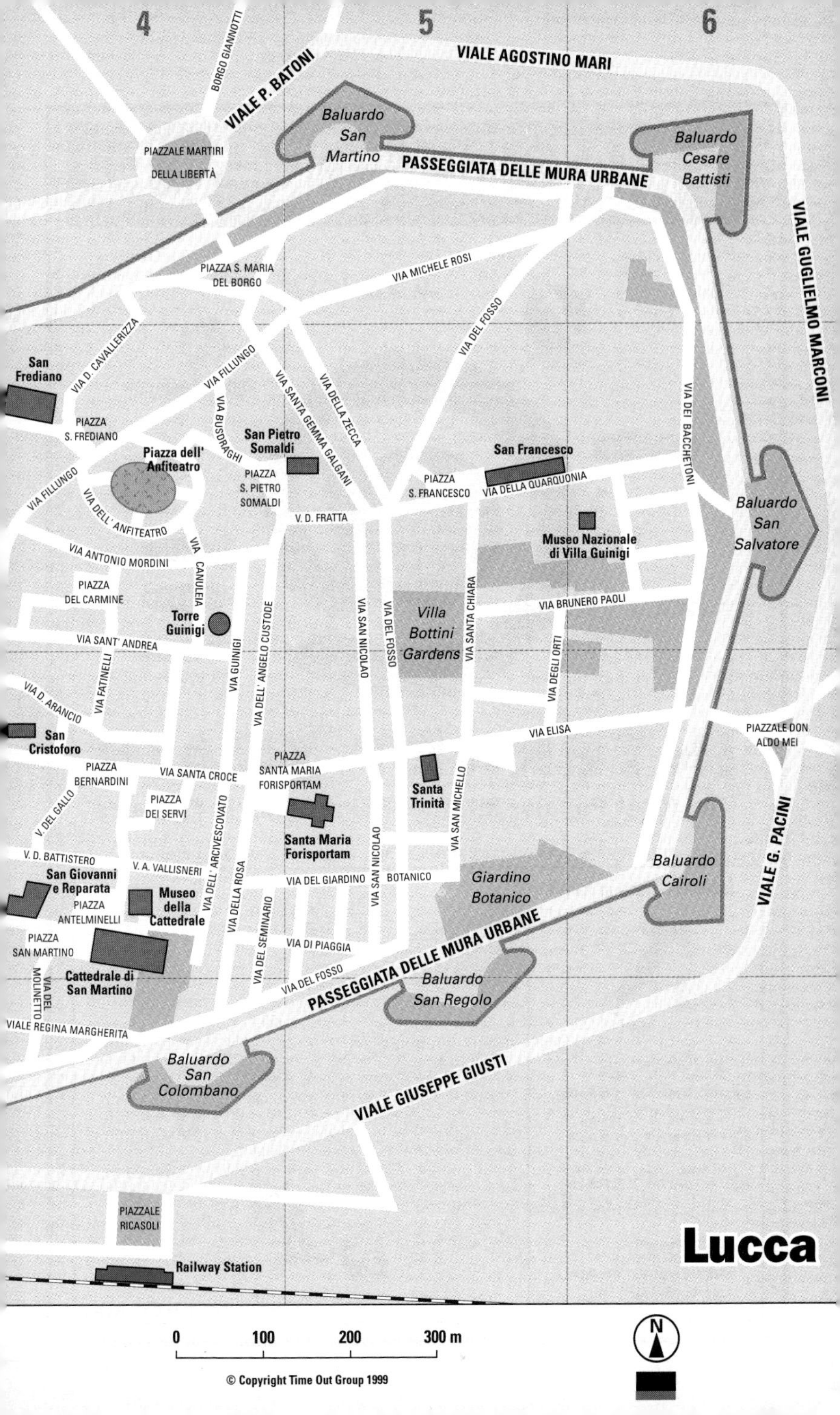

4
5
6
VIALE AGOSTINO MARI
BORGO GIANNOTTI
VIALE P. BATONI
Baluardo San Martino
PIAZZALE MARTIRI DELLA LIBERTÀ
PASSEGGIATA DELLE MURA URBANE
Baluardo Cesare Battisti
VIALE GUGLIELMO MARCONI
PIAZZA S. MARIA DEL BORGO
VIA MICHELE ROSI
VIA DEL FOSSO
VIA D. CAVALLERIZZA
San Frediano
VIA FILLUNGO
VIA SANTA GEMMA GALGANI
VIA DELLA ZECCA
VIA DEI BACCHETONI
PIAZZA S. FREDIANO
VIA BUSDRAGHI
San Pietro Somaldi
Piazza dell' Anfiteatro
San Francesco
PIAZZA S. PIETRO SOMALDI
PIAZZA S. FRANCESCO
VIA DELLA QUARQUONIA
Baluardo San Salvatore
VIA FILLUNGO
VIA DELL' ANFITEATRO
V. D. FRATTA
Museo Nazionale di Villa Guinigi
VIA ANTONIO MORDINI
VIA CANULEIA
PIAZZA DEL CARMINE
VIA SANTA CHIARA
VIA BRUNERO PAOLI
Torre Guinigi
VIA DELL' ANGELO CUSTODE
VIA SAN NICOLAO
VIA DEL FOSSO
Villa Bottini Gardens
VIA SANT' ANDREA
VIA GUINIGI
VIA DEGLI ORTI
VIA FATINELLI
VIA D. ARANCIO
VIA ELISA
PIAZZALE DON ALDO MEI
San Cristoforo
PIAZZA SANTA MARIA FORISPORTAM
PIAZZA BERNARDINI
VIA SANTA CROCE
Santa Trinità
VIA SAN MICHELLO
PIAZZA DEI SERVI
V. DEL GALLO
VIA DELL' ARCIVESCOVATO
Santa Maria Forisportam
VIA SAN NICOLAO
VIA DELLA ROSA
VIALE G. PACINI
V. D. BATTISTERO
V. A. VALLISNERI
Baluardo Cairoli
San Giovanni e Reparata
Museo della Cattedrale
VIA DEL GIARDINO
BOTANICO
Giardino Botanico
PIAZZA ANTELMINELLI
VIA DEL SEMINARIO
PIAZZA SAN MARTINO
VIA DI PIAGGIA
PASSEGGIATA DELLE MURA URBANE
VIA DEL MOLINETTO
Cattedrale di San Martino
VIA DEL FOSSO
Baluardo San Regolo
VIALE REGINA MARGHERITA
Baluardo San Colombano
VIALE GIUSEPPE GIUSTI
PIAZZALE RICASOLI
Lucca
Railway Station
0
100
200
300 m
N

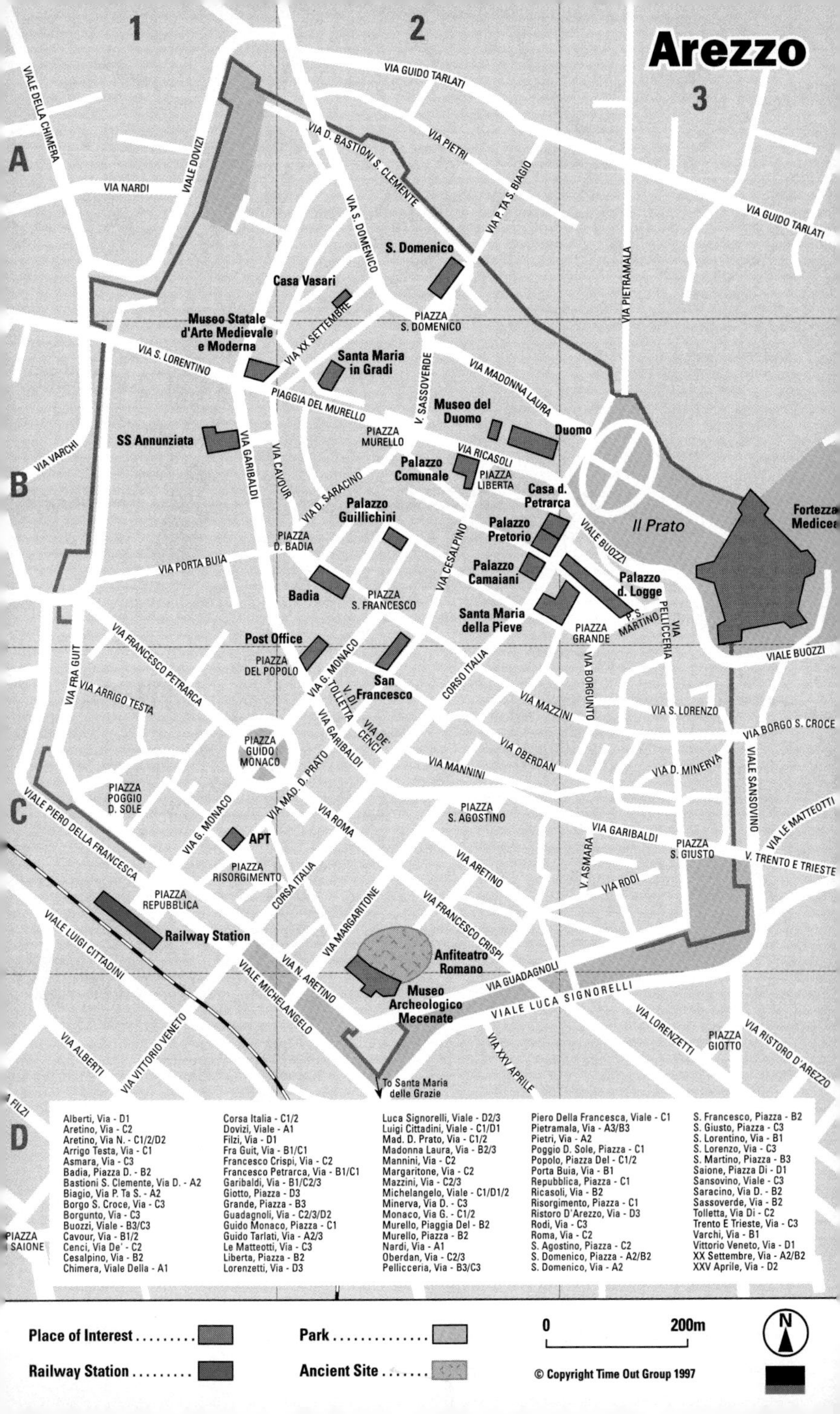
Arezzo
1
2
3
A
B
C
D
Viale della Chimera
Viale Dovizi
Via Nardi
Via Guido Tarlati
Via D. Bastioni S. Clemente
Via Pietri
Via P. Ta S. Biagio
Via S. Domenico
S. Domenico
Casa Vasari
Piazza S. Domenico
Via Pietramala
Museo Statale d'Arte Medievale e Moderna
Via XX Settembre
Santa Maria in Gradi
Via S. Lorentino
V. Sassoverde
Via Madonna Laura
Piaggia del Murello
Museo del Duomo
Duomo
Piazza Murello
SS Annunziata
Via Garibaldi
Via Ricasoli
Palazzo Comunale
Piazza Liberta
Via Varchi
Via Cavour
Via D. Saracino
Casa d. Petrarca
Palazzo Guillichini
Il Prato
Fortezza Medicea
Palazzo Pretorio
Viale Buozzi
Piazza D. Badia
Via Cesalpino
Via Porta Buia
Palazzo Camaiani
Palazzo d. Logge
Badia
Piazza S. Francesco
Santa Maria della Pieve
P. S. Martino
Via Pellicceria
Piazza Grande
Post Office
Via Francesco Petrarca
Via Fra Guit
Piazza del Popolo
Via G. Monaco
V. di Tolletta
San Francesco
Corso Italia
Via Borgunto
Viale Buozzi
Via Arrigo Testa
Via Mazzini
Via S. Lorenzo
Via Borgo S. Croce
Piazza Guido Monaco
Via de' Cenci
Via Garibaldi
Via Oberdan
Viale Sansovino
Via Mannini
Via D. Minerva
Via Mad. D. Prato
Piazza Poggio D. Sole
Viale Piero della Francesca
Via G. Monaco
Via Roma
Piazza S. Agostino
Via Le Matteotti
APT
Via Garibaldi
Piazza S. Giusto
V. Trento e Trieste
Piazza Risorgimento
Via Aretino
V. Asmara
Via Rodi
Piazza Repubblica
Corsa Italia
Via Francesco Crispi
Railway Station
Via Margaritone
Viale Luigi Cittadini
Anfiteatro Romano
Via N. Aretino
Via Guadagnoli
Viale Michelangelo
Museo Archeologico Mecenate
Viale Luca Signorelli
Via Lorenzetti
Piazza Giotto
Via Ristoro d'Arezzo
Via Alberti
Via Vittorio Veneto
Via XXV Aprile
To Santa Maria delle Grazie
Filzi
Piazza Saione
Alberti, Via - D1
Aretino, Via - C2
Aretino, Via N. - C1/2/D2
Arrigo Testa, Via - C1
Asmara, Via - C3
Badia, Piazza D. - B2
Bastioni S. Clemente, Via D. - A2
Biagio, Via P. Ta S. - A2
Borgo S. Croce, Via - C3
Borgunto, Via - C3
Buozzi, Viale - B3/C3
Cavour, Via - B1/2
Cenci, Via De' - C2
Cesalpino, Via - B2
Chimera, Viale Della - A1
Corsa Italia - C1/2
Dovizi, Viale - A1
Filzi, Via - D1
Fra Guit, Via - B1/C1
Francesco Crispi, Via - C2
Francesco Petrarca, Via - B1/C1
Garibaldi, Via - B1/C2/3
Giotto, Piazza - D3
Grande, Piazza - B3
Guadagnoli, Via - C2/3/D2
Guido Monaco, Piazza - C1
Guido Tarlati, Via - A2/3
Le Matteotti, Via - C3
Liberta, Piazza - B2
Lorenzetti, Via - D3
Luca Signorelli, Viale - D2/3
Luigi Cittadini, Viale - C1/D1
Mad. D. Prato, Via - C1/2
Madonna Laura, Via - B2/3
Mannini, Via - C2
Margaritone, Via - C2
Mazzini, Via - C2/3
Michelangelo, Viale - C1/D1/2
Minerva, Via D. - C3
Monaco, Via G. - C1/2
Murello, Piaggia Del - B2
Murello, Piazza - B2
Nardi, Via - A1
Oberdan, Via - C2/3
Pellicceria, Via - B3/C3
Piero Della Francesca, Viale - C1
Pietramala, Via - A3/B3
Pietri, Via - A2
Poggio D. Sole, Piazza - C1
Popolo, Piazza Del - C1/2
Porta Buia, Via - B1
Repubblica, Piazza - C1
Ricasoli, Via - B2
Risorgimento, Piazza - C1
Ristoro D'Arezzo, Via - D3
Rodi, Via - C3
Roma, Via - C2
S. Agostino, Piazza - C2
S. Domenico, Piazza - A2/B2
S. Domenico, Via - A2
S. Francesco, Piazza - B2
S. Giusto, Piazza - C3
S. Lorentino, Via - B1
S. Lorenzo, Via - C3
S. Martino, Piazza - B3
Saione, Piazza Di - D1
Sansovino, Viale - C3
Saracino, Via D. - B2
Sassoverde, Via - B2
Tolletta, Via Di - C2
Trento E Trieste, Via - C3
Varchi, Via - B1
Vittorio Veneto, Via - D1
XX Settembre, Via - A2/B2
XXV Aprile, Via - D2
Place of Interest
Railway Station
Park
Ancient Site
0
200m
N
© Copyright Time Out Group 1997

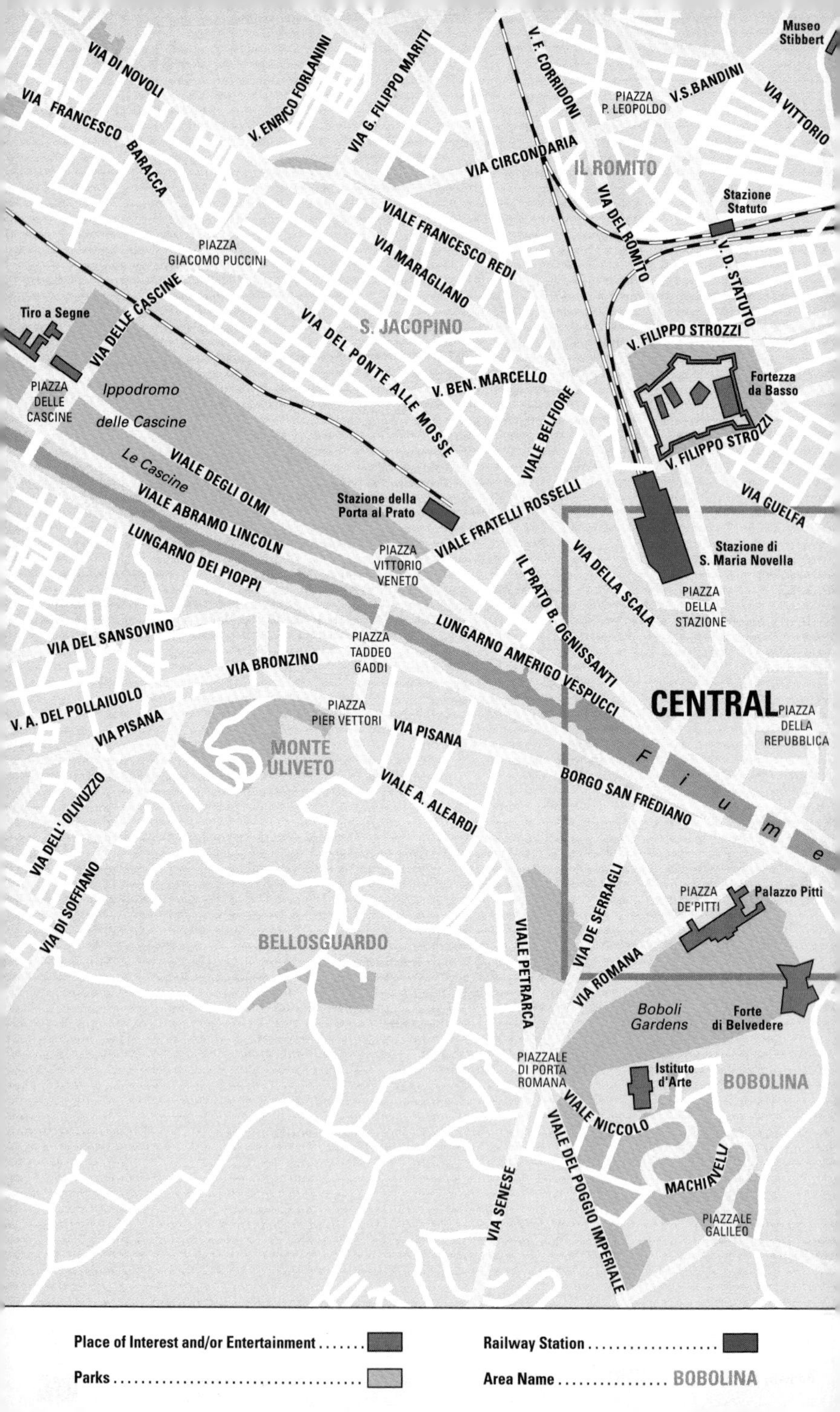
Museo Stibbert
VIA DI NOVOLI
VIA FRANCESCO BARACCA
V. ENRICO FORLANINI
VIA G. FILIPPO MARITI
V. F. CORRIDONI
PIAZZA P. LEOPOLDO
V.S.BANDINI
VIA VITTORIO
VIA CIRCONDARIA
IL ROMITO
VIA DEL ROMITO
Stazione Statuto
V. D. STATUTO
VIALE FRANCESCO REDI
VIA MARAGLIANO
PIAZZA GIACOMO PUCCINI
VIA DELLE CASCINE
Tiro a Segne
S. JACOPINO
VIA DEL PONTE ALLE MOSSE
V. FILIPPO STROZZI
Fortezza da Basso
PIAZZA DELLE CASCINE
Ippodromo delle Cascine
V. BEN. MARCELLO
VIALE BELFIORE
Le Cascine
VIALE DEGLI OLMI
Stazione della Porta al Prato
VIALE FRATELLI ROSSELLI
VIA GUELFA
VIALE ABRAMO LINCOLN
LUNGARNO DEI PIOPPI
PIAZZA VITTORIO VENETO
VIA DELLA SCALA
Stazione di S. Maria Novella
IL PRATO B. OGNISSANTI
PIAZZA DELLA STAZIONE
VIA DEL SANSOVINO
LUNGARNO AMERIGO VESPUCCI
PIAZZA TADDEO GADDI
VIA BRONZINO
V. A. DEL POLLAIUOLO
PIAZZA PIER VETTORI
VIA PISANA
CENTRAL
PIAZZA DELLA REPUBBLICA
MONTE ULIVETO
Fiume
BORGO SAN FREDIANO
VIALE A. ALEARDI
VIA DELL' OLIVUZZO
VIA DI SOFFIANO
PIAZZA DE'PITTI
Palazzo Pitti
VIA DE SERRAGLI
BELLOSGUARDO
VIALE PETRARCA
VIA ROMANA
Boboli Gardens
Forte di Belvedere
PIAZZALE DI PORTA ROMANA
Istituto d'Arte
BOBOLINA
VIALE NICCOLO
MACHIAVELLI
VIA SENESE
VIALE DEL POGGIO IMPERIALE
PIAZZALE GALILEO
Place of Interest and/or Entertainment
Railway Station
Parks
Area Name BOBOLINA

Florence Overview
FLORENCE
VIA BOLOGNESE
VIA FAENTINA
VIA FRANCESCO
VIA SAN DOMENICO
PIAZZA DELLE CURE
VIA XX SETTEMBRE
V. DON G. MINZONI
VIALE ALESSANDRO VOLTA
V. AUGUSTO RIGHI
PIAZZA DELLA LIBERTÀ
VIALE DEI MILLE
V. CALATAFIMI
PIAZZA V. FARDELLA DI TORREARSA
V. GIACOMO MATTEOTTI
V. MANFREDO FANTI
VIA D. ARTISTI
Stadio Comunale
VIA CAMILLO CAVOUR
VIA MASACCIO
V. PASQUALE PAOLI
VIALE EDMONDO DE AMICIS
FILAROCC
Giardino della Gherardesca
PIAZZA DONATELLO
VIALE MALTA
VIA GABRIELE D'ANNUNZIO
VIA DEGLI ALFANI
Ospedale Psichiatrico
PIAZZA C. BECCARIA
VIA VINCENZO GIOBERTI
PIAZZA L.B. ALBERTI
VIA ARETINA
VIA PIAGENTINA
V. G. LANZA
MADONNONE
V. QUINTINO SELLA
LUNG. ALDO MORO
LUNG. D. ZECCA VECCHIA
L. DEL TEMPIO
LUNGARNO C. COLOMBO
Arno
LUNGARNO B. CELLINI
LUNG. FRANCESCO FERRUCCI
PIAZZA RAVENNA
VIA DI VILLAMAGNA
PIAZZA F. FERRUCCI
PIAZZALE MICHELANGIOLO
V. COLUCCIO SALUTATI
VIALE DONATO GIANNOTTI
RICORBOLI
VIA DI RIPOLI
VIALE GALILEO
San Miniato al Monte
VIALE MICHELANGIOLO
V. TRAVERSARI
VIA ERBOSA
VIALE EUROPA
0
200
400 m
N
© Copyright Time Out Group 1997

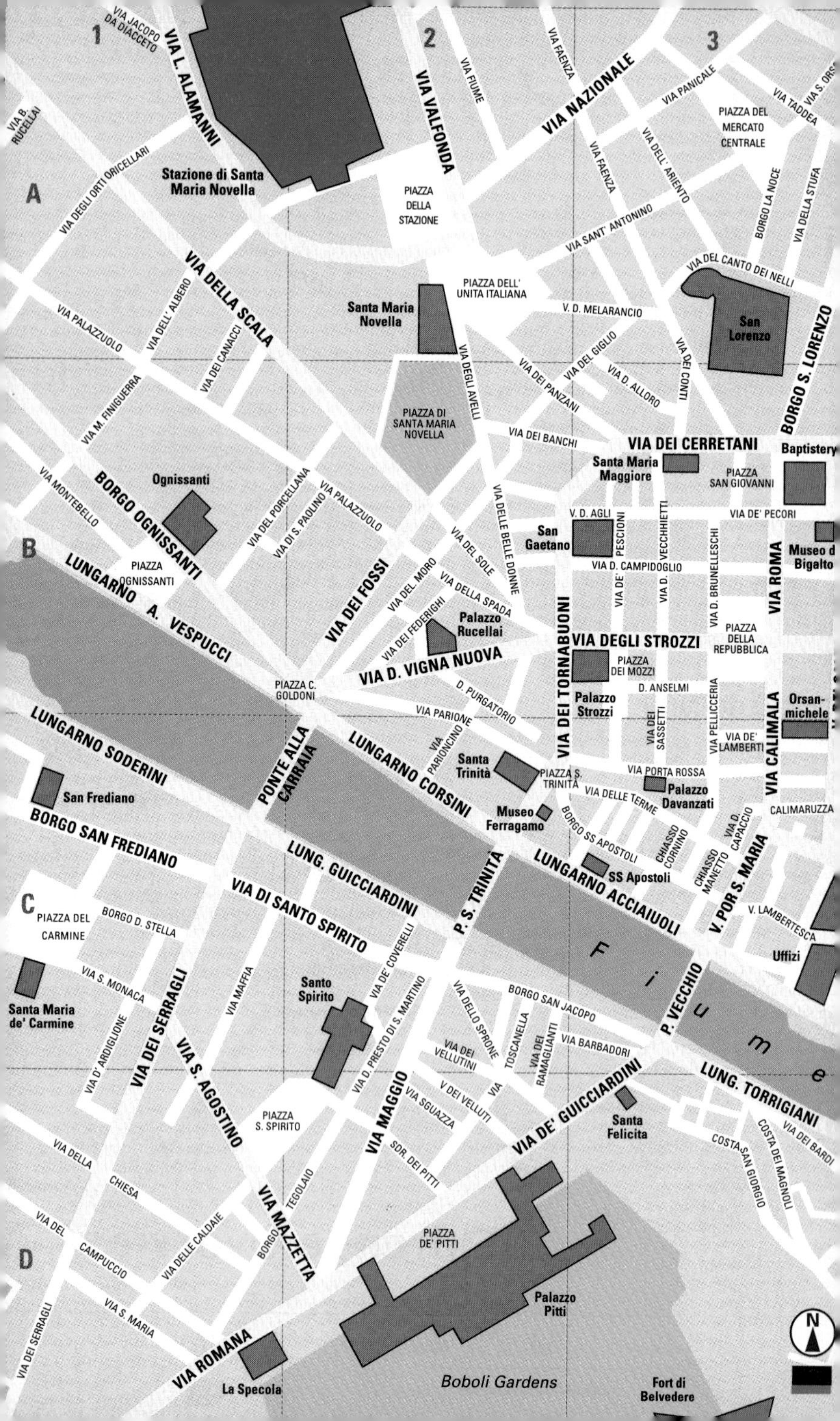

Stazione di Santa Maria Novella
Santa Maria Novella
Ognissanti
San Lorenzo
Baptistery
Santa Maria Maggiore
San Gaetano
Palazzo Rucellai
Palazzo Strozzi
Santa Trinità
Museo Ferragamo
Palazzo Davanzati
Orsanmichele
SS Apostoli
Uffizi
San Frediano
Santa Maria de' Carmine
Santo Spirito
Santa Felicita
Palazzo Pitti
La Specola
Boboli Gardens
Fort di Belvedere
Fiume
PIAZZA DELLA STAZIONE
PIAZZA DELL' UNITA ITALIANA
PIAZZA DEL MERCATO CENTRALE
PIAZZA DI SANTA MARIA NOVELLA
PIAZZA SAN GIOVANNI
PIAZZA DELLA REPUBBLICA
PIAZZA OGNISSANTI
PIAZZA C. GOLDONI
PIAZZA DEI MOZZI
PIAZZA S. TRINITÀ
PIAZZA DEL CARMINE
PIAZZA S. SPIRITO
PIAZZA DE' PITTI
VIA L. ALAMANNI
VIA VALFONDA
VIA NAZIONALE
VIA DELLA SCALA
BORGO OGNISSANTI
LUNGARNO A. VESPUCCI
VIA DEI FOSSI
VIA D. VIGNA NUOVA
VIA DEI TORNABUONI
VIA DEGLI STROZZI
VIA DEI CERRETANI
BORGO S. LORENZO
VIA ROMA
VIA CALIMALA
LUNGARNO SODERINI
PONTE ALLA CARRAIA
LUNGARNO CORSINI
BORGO SAN FREDIANO
LUNG. GUICCIARDINI
VIA DI SANTO SPIRITO
P. S. TRINITÀ
LUNGARNO ACCIAIUOLI
V. POR S. MARIA
P. VECCHIO
LUNG. TORRIGIANI
VIA DE' GUICCIARDINI
VIA MAGGIO
VIA DEI SERRAGLI
VIA S. AGOSTINO
VIA MAZZETTA
VIA ROMANA

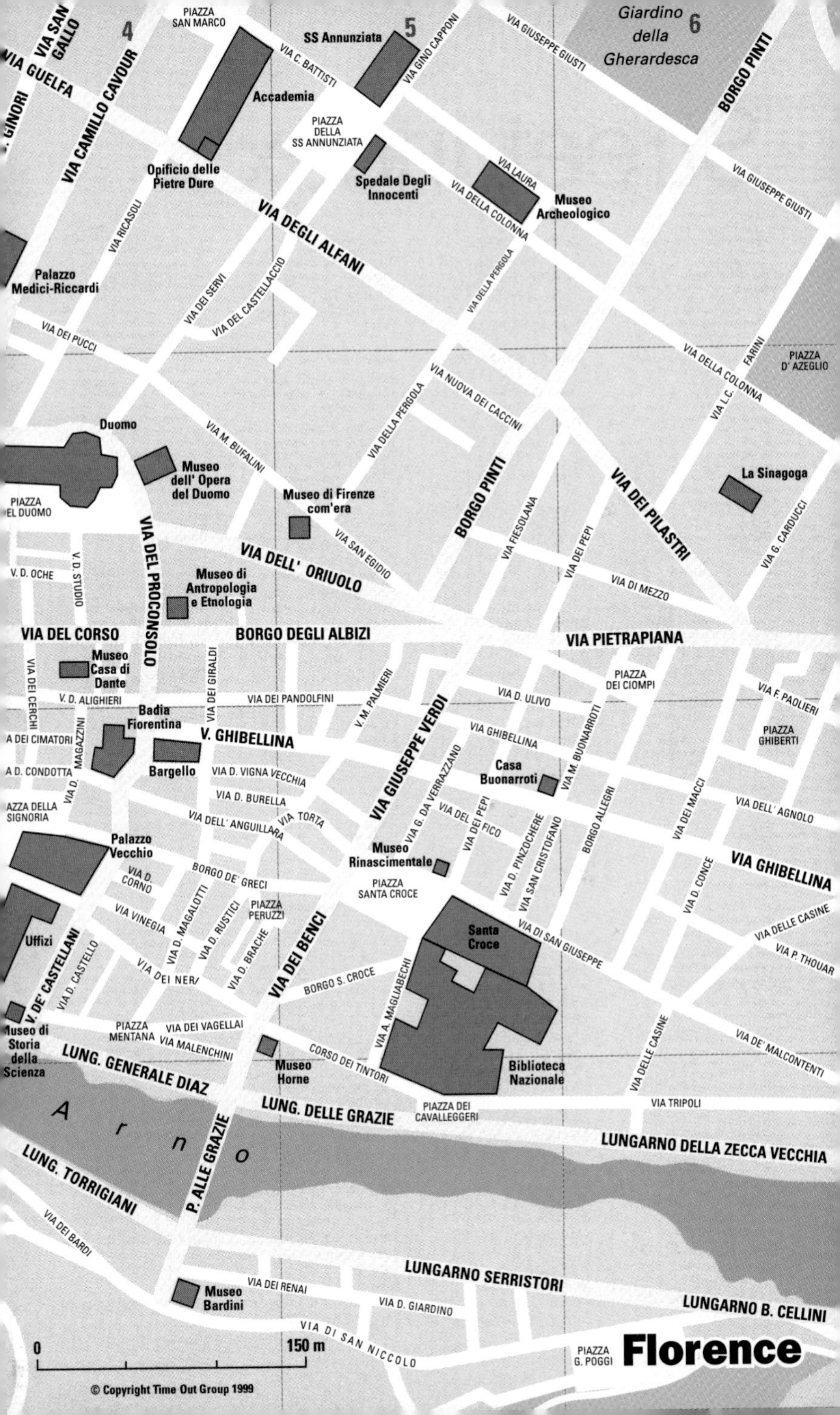
Florence
Giardino della Gherardesca
Piazza San Marco
SS Annunziata
Accademia
Piazza della SS Annunziata
Opificio delle Pietre Dure
Spedale Degli Innocenti
Museo Archeologico
Palazzo Medici-Riccardi
Piazza D' Azeglio
Duomo
Museo dell' Opera del Duomo
Piazza del Duomo
Museo di Firenze com'era
La Sinagoga
Museo di Antropologia e Etnologia
Museo Casa di Dante
Badia Fiorentina
Bargello
Piazza dei Ciompi
Piazza Ghiberti
Casa Buonarroti
Palazzo Vecchio
Museo Rinascimentale
Piazza Santa Croce
Piazza Peruzzi
Uffizi
Santa Croce
Museo di Storia della Scienza
Piazza Mentana
Museo Horne
Biblioteca Nazionale
Piazza dei Cavalleggeri
Arno
Museo Bardini
Piazza G. Poggi
Via San Gallo
Via Guelfa
Via Ginori
Via Camillo Cavour
Via C. Battisti
Via Gino Capponi
Via Giuseppe Giusti
Borgo Pinti
Via Laura
Via della Colonna
Via degli Alfani
Via Ricasoli
Via dei Servi
Via del Castellaccio
Via della Pergola
Via dei Pucci
Via L.C. Farini
Via Nuova dei Caccini
Via M. Bufalini
Via dei Pilastri
Via San Egidio
Via Fiesolana
Via dei Pepi
Via G. Carducci
Via dell' Oriuolo
Via di Mezzo
V. D. Oche
V. D. Studio
Via del Proconsolo
Via del Corso
Borgo degli Albizi
Via Pietrapiana
Via dei Cerchi
Via dei Giraldi
V. M. Palmieri
Via Giuseppe Verdi
Via D. Ulivo
Via F. Paolieri
V. D. Alighieri
Via dei Pandolfini
Via Ghibellina
V. Ghibellina
Via M. Buonarroti
Via dei Cimatori
Via D. Condotta
Via D. Magazzini
Via D. Vigna Vecchia
Via G. da Verrazzano
Borgo Allegri
Via dei Macci
Via D. Burella
Via del Fico
Via dell' Agnolo
Piazza della Signoria
Via dell' Anguillara
Via Torta
Via D. Pinzochere
Via San Cristofano
Via D. Conce
Via D. Corno
Borgo de' Greci
Via Vinegia
Via D. Magalotti
Via D. Rustici
Via dei Benci
Via di San Giuseppe
Via delle Casine
Via D. Castello
V. de' Castellani
Via D. Brache
Via dei Neri
Borgo S. Croce
Via A. Magliabechi
Via P. Thouar
Via dei Vagellai
Via Malenchini
Corso dei Tintori
Via de' Malcontenti
Lung. Generale Diaz
Lung. delle Grazie
Via Tripoli
Lungarno della Zecca Vecchia
P. alle Grazie
Lung. Torrigiani
Via dei Bardi
Lungarno Serristori
Via dei Renai
Via D. Giardino
Lungarno B. Cellini
Via di San Niccolo
0
150 m
4
5
6

Street Index